REBECCA SHAW
Three Great Novels:
The Barleybridge Novels

We hope you enjoy this book.
Please return or renew it by the due date.
You can renew it at **www.norfolk.gov.uk/libraries**
or by using our free library app. Otherwise you can
phone **0344 800 8020** - please have your library
card and pin ready.
You can sign up for email reminders too.

4/4/18
19/4/18

Rebecca Shaw

Three Great Novels: The Barleybridge Novels

A Country Affair
Country Wives
Country Lovers

ORION

2 4 6 8 10 9 7 5 3 1

This omnibus edition first published in Great Britain in 2005 by Orion,
an imprint of the Orion Publishing Group Ltd.

A CIP catalogue record for this book is
available from the British Library.

ISBN 0 75286 906 X

Typeset by Deltatype Ltd, Birkenhead, Merseyside

Set in Minion

Printed and bound in Great Britain by
Clays Ltd, St Ives plc

The Orion Publishing Group Ltd
Orion House
5 Upper Saint Martin's Lane
London, WC2H 9EA

Contents

A Country Affair

List of Characters at Barleybridge Veterinary Hospital

Mungo Price	Orthopaedic Surgeon and Senior Partner
Colin Walker	Partner – large and small animal
Zoe Savage	Partner – large animal
Graham Murgatroyd	Small-animal vet
Valentine Dedic	Small-animal vet
Rhodri Hughes	Small-animal vet
Scott Spencer	Large-animal vet

NURSING STAFF
Sarah Cockroft (Sarah One)
Sarah MacMillan (Sarah Two)
Bunty Page

RECEPTIONISTS
Joy Bastable (Practice Manager)
Lynne Seymour
Stephie Budge
Kate Howard

Miriam Price	Mungo's wife
Duncan Bastable	Joy's husband
Gerry Howard	Kate's father
Mia Howard	Kate's stepmother
Adam Pentecost	Kate's boyfriend

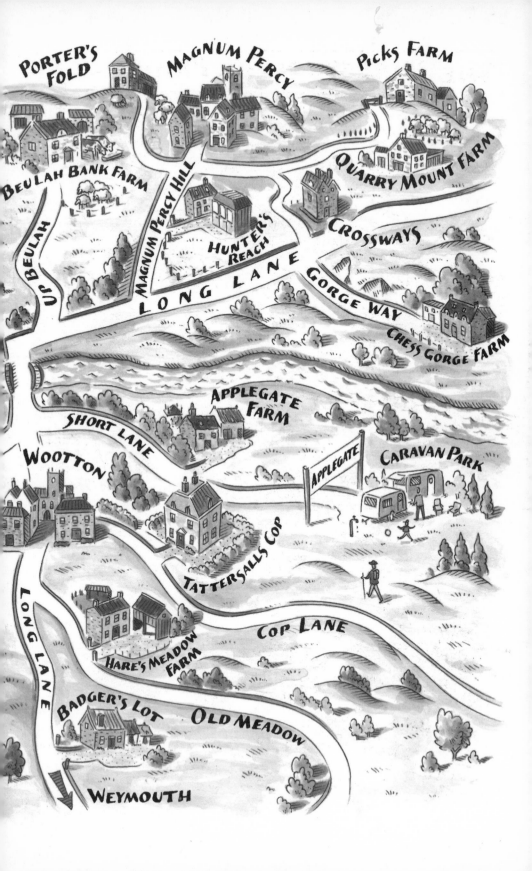

1

In the circumstances it would have been ridiculous to have arrived wearing a suit. So Kate had plumped for her smart – well, smarter – pair of black trousers, knee-length black cardigan and the pink shirt Mia had given her, which just managed to stay fastened without too much gaping between the buttons. That was one thing Kate envied about Mia, her ability to stay slim. She squeezed herself out of the car and looked around. It was certainly a beautiful setting. The hills rose almost immediately from the edge of the car park and if she shielded her eyes she could just make out Beulah Bank Top, one of the highest of the surrounding hills. Dotted all over the slopes were sheep, grazing in twos and threes. They looked to her to be Dorset Horns, lovely woolly sheep, grazing on land they'd grazed for hundreds of years making, Kate thought, an idyllic scene. Turning round she could see the town, which had now crept up the foothills making the hospital the last bit of civilisation before the hills.

Two Land Rovers, their wheels thick with dried mud, were parked in two of the spaces marked staff, along with several other cars, some large and opulent, others small and scruffy. Her hand trembled as she locked the car door and shook as she walked round to the front entrance. This was worse than starting at a new school. At least in school she'd been one of many new girls; here she was the only new girl and very green at that.

Kate remembered the weight of the imposing double doors from her interview and knew nothing less than a huge heave would open one. Then the inner glass door and she was in. Oh, God! That smell! She breathed it in, savouring the gloriously satisfying odour of disinfectant, of anaesthetic, of . . . well, of everything she had ever dreamt of. At five minutes to eight the clients hadn't yet arrived, so she was alone. In front of her was the reception desk, strikingly new, very twenty-first century, white and clinical. To her right stretched the waiting room, well supplied with spanking-new, springy, bendy chrome chairs, a huge cheese plant reaching the ceiling, every windowsill filled with jaunty pots all bursting with plants still with the full flush of the garden centre upon them. Four doors went off from the waiting area, each with the words 'Consulting Room' in bold, bright-blue, up-to-the-minute lettering.

The first sign of life was the sound of two people arguing somewhere at the back behind the reception desk. She could hear the anger but not the words. Female voices, one belligerent, one patient. They must have moved closer to her for now she could hear: 'I know you've taken her on to replace me; I'm not stupid.'

'I've told you twenty times, she is not replacing you. Kate is here to work on reception as and when, but mainly to do the accounts.'

'So ... What have I been doing these last three months? The accounts!'

'Only because there was no one else and you volunteered. You're small-animal reception, Stephie, as well you know. You hate the accounts anyway, so I don't know what you're grumbling about. You should be relieved.'

'Well, I'm not.'

'I've too much on this morning to be bothered with your sulks, so you'll have to get on with it, and make jolly sure you hand everything over in a systematic manner and with good grace, or you'll hear further from me.'

Kate heard a derisive snort and then: 'You might be in charge here, Joy, but there's no need to take that tone with me.'

An answer snapped back at Stephie almost before she'd finished speaking. 'Oh, I am in charge. There's no doubt about that and don't you forget it. Now get out on the desk and check today's appointments, there's a good girl.'

A young woman about her own age came through from the back, a dowdy-looking girl with a sallow skin, brown, lifeless hair tied back in a ponytail, dark, sulky eyes and a long, hollow-cheeked face. She managed a tight-lipped question: 'Yes?'

Kate, determining to be cheerful in adversity, said, 'I'm Kate Howard, the new receptionist.' She held out her hand to this Stephie, hoping flesh on flesh might make for peace between them.

Grudgingly Stephie shook hands. 'I'm Stephie Budge. You'd better report to Joy, she's in the back.' The phone rang and Stephie quickly picked it up, answering it brightly with none of her bad temper evident in her voice: 'Good morning! Barleybridge Veterinary Hospital. Stephie speaking. How may I help?' As she listened she kicked out behind her with her foot and pushed open the door, nodding her head in the direction of the back office.

Kate walked round the reception desk, and into the blessed warmth and comfort of Joy's own office. Warm and comfortable not because Joy had the heating on, for it was still warm, although the start of September, but because of Joy herself. She must have been fifty, which when you're only nineteen seems ancient, but Joy's fifty was different from other people's fifty. Her smooth, unlined face glowed with an inner light, which enveloped you and made you smile despite yourself. She must have looked like this at twenty and would still at eighty. Her blonde hair waved and curled about her face, her blue eyes twinkled at you with scarcely concealed mirth. Her office echoed her personality, soft yellow walls, flowers, brightly coloured files lined neatly on a shelf behind her head, a fish tank on top of the royal-blue filing cabinet, with fishes flashing around it among lush waving plants; even her state-of-the-art computer echoed the blue of her eyes.

Joy took to her new receptionist immediately. She'd liked her at interview and had decided straight away to employ her if she'd come. She liked the forthrightness of her eyes and the open expression on her face. Apparently far too intelligent for the job but if this was what she wanted then so be it. She'd liked the modest confidence behind the pleasant manner. She saw now that Kate was almost pretty, no that wasn't right, more classically good-looking perhaps, with a hint of good breeding. Most especially Joy had loved her happy outlook on life and, what was more, Kate reminded her of someone from the past whom she'd liked but couldn't quite put a name to. Joy stood up to greet her.

'Kate! How lovely! You are about to save my life. A nurse and a receptionist have called in ill this morning, and with Open Afternoon on Saturday that's all we need, so you're about to have a baptism of fire. But we'll cope, we always do! So you're on reception today, the accounts will have to wait. Welcome to Barleybridge!'

Kate drew confidence from her firm grasp and felt empowered. 'Thank you, I don't mind turning my hand to anything at all . . .'

'Can't find time to sort out a uniform for you at the moment, but you look very efficient and that's the impression we always try to give: efficiency larded with compassion. Twenty minutes to lift-off. I'll give you a quick tour.'

Joy came out from behind her desk and shot out of the door at the speed of light. Kate dashed after her, trying desperately to take in the operating rooms, the drugs store, the cages in the recovery room, the animals' waiting room with its row of steel hooks for hitching dogs' leashes up to, the staff room, Mr Price's office, the washing machine, the drier, the shower room, the staff wash rooms: endless space all so new, so ready for action.

'The consulting rooms are down that side with doors into the clients' waiting room and into the back here, of course. Golden rule, no clients beyond the consulting rooms. We've no secrets to hide but nevertheless ... This is where you'll be doing accounts when you get a chance. The farm-animal vets are devils where keeping records is concerned and these new laptops they take with them now are a real challenge for them. Keeps them on their toes, you see, but they're happier doing the job than keeping records but, as I tell them, if they don't make notes about all they do we can't invoice the farmers and then there'll be no money to pay their salaries, so it's up to them.' Joy grinned at her. 'Lovely people, though. Here's one of them now.' Joy was looking beyond Kate and giving one of her dazzling smiles.

Kate turned round and saw a lean, well-muscled man of at least six feet propped against the door frame. He wore one of those stiff-brimmed hats one imagines all Australian men always wear when going walkabout, a pair of very creased khaki shorts, a bush shirt and a grin that almost split his face.

'G'day! You must be this new Kate they're all talking about. I'm Errol Spencer.'

'How do you do.'

Joy interrupted with: 'He's Errol really but we all call him Scott.'

'Have you got Scottish parents, then?'

He burst out laughing. 'Guess not. They're always getting Aussies passing through this practice and the first one was called Scott and it's stuck. Saves a lot of trouble remembering names.'

'How do you do, Scott, then.' He was still holding her hand and she couldn't release it without making it obvious.

Joy raised an eyebrow. 'Put her down, Scott, give her a chance to get in through the door.' Kate blushed, Scott winked, Joy said, 'Your morning visits await you at reception. Get cracking, you've a lot to get through.'

'Slave driver, she is, beneath that charming exterior. Watch out for her, she keeps a whip in her top drawer and isn't afraid to use it.' He bunched his fingers, kissed them and departed.

Kate was laughing; she really couldn't help herself. He was such *fun*; if all the vets were like him she was in for a good time. Until now she'd thought of the veterinary world as a serious business, where saving lives and relieving pain were paramount, but apparently you could have an uproarious time, too, and that was just what she needed.

Joy looked up at her. 'Take him with a pinch of salt, my dear, he's broken more hearts than I can count and he's only been here three months. Farmers' wives, farmers' daughters, farmers' mothers even, you name 'em; there's girls carrying torches all over the county for that young man. Still, he does add spice to life, doesn't he?'

When Kate got back to reception she couldn't believe the change that had taken place in the ten minutes she'd been on her conducted tour. Stephie was at the desk, apparently answering three phones at once, as well as tapping furiously on the computer. The waiting room was filling up and that early-morning clinical aroma was being submerged by animal smells. Animals of all shapes and sizes had arrived, big ones, little ones, furry ones, feathered ones, brown and black, white and grey, some cowering, some bold and barking, some cats peering suspiciously from their carrying cages, other cats spitting at the dog taking too much interest in them and a massive Rottweiler sitting propped against his owner's legs, aloof and slavering.

As soon as Joy saw him she said quietly to Kate, 'I'd forgotten it was the first Monday of the month. Go and get the old fire bucket from the laundry room, fill it full of cold water and bring it here.'

It seemed the oddest thing to be doing but she filled it, carried it through, surprised at how heavy an old iron bucket filled to the brim with water proved to be, and asked Stephie where she should put it. Stephie pointed to the floor under the desk. 'Down there. Thanks. Can you answer that? It's the farm vets' phone.'

'Good morning. Barleybridge Veterinary Hospital. How may I help?'

The lilting Welsh voice, with its strong musical undertones, threw Kate for a moment but when she had adjusted her mind to the accent she realised the woman was wanting to speak to a Rhodri Hughes. 'Hold the line a moment, please.' Placing her hand over the mouthpiece, she asked Stephie what she should do. 'Tell her he's out on a call, take her number and we'll get him to ring her back.'

During a brief lull Stephie brought Kate up to speed on the telephone system. 'It's all so clever now you wouldn't believe. Talk about state of the art. All the farm vets have mobiles in their cars so if they're out on a call and a request for a visit comes in we ring the vet nearest to the farm wanting the visit and it saves them miles of driving. There's usually at least three vets out on call. Small-animal vets hardly go out on visits at all, most of them can come in, you see. This map on the wall here behind us, see, it's got a flag pinned on for every farm client we have, so you look on there, check today's lists and you know where they all are. Let's have a look at that number for Rhodri, see if I can recognise it.' She studied Kate's writing for a moment, then said in a fierce whisper, 'Welsh, was she?'

Kate nodded. 'Very definitely.'

'Look, I know her. That's Megan Jones. She fancies him something rotten, keeps ringing him up. He's not interested and he's desperate to avoid her. Next time say day off, or on holiday, or at a conference, or off ill, or something, anything to put her off. If he speaks to her by mistake he'll blow his top and that's not a pretty sight.'

'How long has this been going on?'

'Weeks and weeks, every single day. She must be mad.'

'Is he a good catch, then?'

Stephie looked sceptically at her. 'If you fancy short, thick-set Welshmen with a penchant for singing tenor in a male-voice choir and a liking for ferrets and total independence for the principality of Wales, then yes. I don't really understand what she sees in him; he's not my type at all.'

'What is your type, then?'

The phone rang again so Kate never got her answer. Then she spoke to an old lady, who was so small she could only just see over the top of the reception desk, about her nine o'clock appointment and whether that nice Mr Murgatroyd was running late or had she time to go to the toilet, or should she delay going until after her appointment because she didn't want to be in the toilet when her name was called because her cat was so very ill she really mustn't delay her appointment and was she new she hadn't seen her before and what was her name she was such a pretty girl. Kate was about to advise her to go to the toilet first, though she hadn't a clue if it was the right answer or not, when a terrible snarling sound began, which became louder and louder and louder. The fearsome noise turned out to be an Airedale terrier, which hurtled through from the back and, just missing knocking down the old lady, went like an arrow for the Rottweiler. But he was ready. The moment they'd all heard the first snarling sound the Rottweiler had been on red alert, his fur bristling, his fangs showing, on his feet ready for the inevitable skirmish. But it wasn't a skirmish, it was a full-scale fight. The owner was screaming, 'Adolf! Oh, God! Adolf! Get that bloody dog off him, get him off!' Every client clutched their pets to themselves and watched, frozen with horror. The two dogs took no notice whatsoever of Adolf's owner, swirling round, round and round, lunging and snarling open-mouthed, each trying as hard as the other to sink its fangs into its opponent's neck or indeed anywhere it could get a hold.

Stephie, as was to be expected at moments of crisis, was answering the phone. She clapped her hand over the receiver and shouted, 'The water! Throw it on them!'

Kate, too stunned to react for a moment, suddenly galvanised herself, grabbed the bucket and emptied the entire contents over the two dogs. The Airedale leapt back, shook itself free of the water, looked up at Kate and . . . well, he laughed at her. There was no other way to describe his expression: his tongue was lolling out of his open mouth, his eyes were bright with pleasure, his tail wagged furiously. She'd never seen a dog grin before and it gave her the distinct impression he found the whole incident very amusing indeed.

Outraged, she said in a loud voice, 'Who owns this dog? Because you're not keeping it under control. Please do so immediately.' She glared round the waiting room, in her panic and anger not noticing the deathly hush that had descended.

The old man with the two cats volunteered, 'It's not none of ours. It's Perkins, Mr Price's dog. Adolf and 'im are mates.' This brought a chuckle from the regulars.

'Mr Price?'

'Your Mr Price.'

Kate blushed, Stephie came off the phone, took Perkins by the collar and led him down through the back, muttering threats as she went. Joy emerged with a bucket and mop. 'Mop up, there's a dear, we don't want anyone slipping on that water. Sorry about that, everybody. You all right, Mr Featherstonehough?'

Adolf's owner exploded. 'How many times have I asked you to keep that blasted dog under control? You know I bring Adolf every first Monday for his injection and this happens every single time. You even have the water ready, so you do know what day it is. I shall be complaining to the Royal College of Veterinary Surgeons about this and don't think I won't because I shall. I've threatened before but this time I mean it. I know my rights. I shall sue your Mr Price for every damned penny he's got if my Adolf gets hurt. This is just once too often, this is.'

'Mr Featherstonehough, I can't understand how Perkins knows you're here. He was upstairs in Mr Price's flat, safely shut away, and then somehow he realised you were here. And you know it does take two to make a fight and Adolf does his share . . .'

A consulting-room door opened and a gruff Northern voice called out, 'Mr Featherstonehough, please? Good morning, Adolf. Been knocking hell out of Perkins again, have you? Do come through.'

Kate mopped up the water and went into the laundry to empty the mop bucket down the sink. Joy came through with a tray of mugs in her hands. 'Thanks for that, coffee time, take the weight off your feet. Here you are.'

The coffee tasted wonderful, but as she drank it Kate's conscience surfaced. 'What about Stephie? Shall I go and relieve her?'

'We'll both go, you can't be by yourself, not yet. Take your mug but if Mr Price comes through hide it. He doesn't like us drinking on duty – looks unbusinesslike.'

Mr Price, senior partner and lord of all he surveyed, did come through reception on the way to taking his orthopaedic clinic, and he did see her drinking and reprimanded her for it, and made her feel knee-high to a teaspoon and she wished the floor would open up. But of course it didn't, and Stephie heard the tail end of the conversation and sniggered. 'Tut! Tut! How sad! On your first day, too.'

Kate ignored her uncharitable comment. 'That's the great Mungo Price, is it? I'll never learn to put all the names to faces.'

'You will. Given time. But he's the one to watch. Old Hawk-Eye, I call him. Isn't he gorgeous, though? So suave, so sophisticated. He can ask eighty pounds for an orthopaedic consultation. And that's just the consultation, never mind the operation, or the drugs, or X-rays, or the repeat visits. I can't even earn that in a day. Some people!'

'I expect he's worked hard for years to get where he is.'

Stephie shrugged her shoulders. 'Even so ... Talking of working hard, I saw your CV. With A levels like yours, what you doing working here?'

'Ah!' Kate thought quickly. 'Always wanted to work with animals. Bit mushy, I know, but there you are.'

Stephie put her head on one side and, looking quizzically at Kate, said, 'Seems a funny thing to me.'

'Well, why are you here? You must like animals just like I do.'

Stephie shrugged her shoulders. 'Suppose I must. It's the smells I can't stand and as for being a nurse! All that blood! God help us, not likely.'

'But that really is the sharp end, where it all happens.'

'You sound a bit wistful to me. Why don't you be a nurse? The pay's not brilliant so they're always crying out for them.' Stephie began shuffling her papers about, in preparation for leaving. 'Anyway, I'm off for lunch, back at four. I hate split shifts. Too far to go home, really, too long to spend wandering round the shops, it only makes me buy things. Still, it's better than where the practice was before, at the back of nowhere. At least you feel at the hub of things here. Not a bad town once you get to know it. I'll be glad when the new shopping mall's finished; they say all the big stores will be there. Your mum and dad coming Saturday?'

'For the opening? Possibly.'

'They'll like to see where you're working, won't they?'

'Have a nice afternoon.'

'Thanks. We'll go through the accounts tomorrow. Can't afford to let them slip, otherwise it's hell. See yer!'

Kate watched her disappear through the big double doors. Funny girl. Nice one minute, nasty the next. Unpleasantness was one thing she hated and the conversation she'd inadvertently overheard when she'd first arrived had been unpleasant to the nth degree. She hadn't asked Dad and Mia yet, and rather guessed they wouldn't want to come. Not after the fuss Dad had made when she'd taken the job. She'd ask when she got home, the moment she got in the door.

Dad's car was in the drive; he was home early. Kate glanced at her watch – half past four, that was definitely early for him. She pushed down the door handle, which was slack and didn't always work first go, and wished for the umpteenth time her dad would get around to mending it.

'It's me!' Kate flung her bag down on the hall chair and went into the kitchen. With her eyes shut she could have done a painting of that kitchen scene because it was so familiar. The kitchen table under the window with its blue-and-white checked cloth and its bowl of flowers. Dad lounging in his rocker by the side of the range, the stub of a cigarette in his mouth, his jacket lying on a kitchen chair. Lost in thought, his pale, fleshy slab of a face turned upwards as though seeking heavenly inspiration, light-blue eyes focused on nothing at all, his stockinged feet thrust against the bottom of the range snatching at the warmth it generated and, without looking up, his muttered 'You're back, then'.

Even more predictable was Mia: thin, almost to the point of emaciation, seated on the special wooden kitchen chair she used when she was working. Mia raised her eyes, glazed with concentration, to look at her. 'Kate! Sit down. I want to hear all.' Putting down the tiny brush she was using, she sat back to study her work. It was a miniature painted from a photograph of a pretty girl, a present for the girl's twenty-first. Kate, always genuinely full of admiration for Mia's delicate skills, said, 'Why, Mia! That's wonderful! She'll be delighted. So lively!'

'Kiss! Kiss! Please.' Mia hooked her arm round Kate's neck to make sure her kiss reached its target. 'Glad you like it, I think it's one of my best. There's such a glow about her, isn't there? Do you think I've captured it? I do. Such a zest for life and I've caught the colour of her hair just right. Tea's still hot. Pour me a cup too and we'll listen to your news, won't we, Gerry? How did it go?'

'Absolutely brilliantly! I don't think I have had a more fantastic day in all my life. So interesting!'

'The staff, what are they like? Nice girls?'

'There's two Sarahs, they're nurses, and a round, plump one called Bunty. Two receptionists, Stephie Budge and Lynne Seymour, besides me. The senior receptionist – well, practice manager, I suppose – is called Joy. She was the one who interviewed me and she's lovely but she does have a steely backbone when necessary, I think. I've met Mr Price and got told off ...'

'Trust you.' This from Gerry.

'Gerry! What a thing to say. Kate's not like that. Go on, love, take no notice.'

Accustomed to her father's diminishing remarks to her, Kate ignored him. 'He is so superior. He can charge eighty pounds a consultation. Just think!'

'That could be you.'

'Don't talk daft, Dad. He's Dr Price really, and he trained for years and years.'

'You could have. With your ability.'

'Give it a rest, Gerry.' Mia reached across, patted Kate's leg and gave her a wink.

'I met this Australian called Scott but his real name is Errol.'

Gerry grunted. 'Right wimp he sounds.'

'You should see him, Mia. Talk about drop-dead gorgeous!'

Mia giggled.

'He's a vet.'

'Just what you should have been.'

Both Kate and Mia disregarded Gerry's comments.

'I met Graham Murgatroyd, Rhodri Hughes and Zoe Savage. They're vets but there's others I haven't seen today. It's all so exciting, I can't believe how much I've enjoyed myself.'

'You'd have enjoyed yourself a lot more if you'd done like I said.'

'Look, Dad ...'

'Gerry! Will you give it a rest. It's Kate's life not yours.'

Gerry sat up, threw his cigarette stub on the range and said, 'Did I or did I not *beg* her to take that A level again and reapply? She's wanted to be a vet all her life and one stumble, just one little stumble' – he measured the stumble between his thumb and forefinger – 'and she throws in the towel.' Gerry launched himself out of his chair. 'If I had my way ...'

'Dad! I did warn you that the school wasn't geared for teaching to a standard that would get anyone three As even though it's easier now. I did say. So it's no good going on about it. If I'd stayed there ten years I still wouldn't have got them.'

Gerry wagged a finger at her. 'Ah! But you'll soon have that money your Granny Howard left you. You could go private and pay for tuition.'

In the past Kate's immediate reaction to her father's ideas for furthering her career was flatly to deny them any merit, so she opened her mouth to do exactly as she had always done and then shut it again.

'See! I knew it! You have to admit it's quite an idea.'

'No, it isn't. It's no better than all the rest of your ideas. I can't but help remember when I was working all hours studying you saying to me that nothing on earth was worth all that devotion. You've certainly changed your tune. Not only have I a full-time job but now you're expecting me to study too. Well, believe you me, I've had it up to here with studying and I'm not going to do any more, so that's that.'

'You're a fool! One bit more extra push and you're there. A lifetime's ambition fulfilled! I'd be so proud of you. To say nothing of your satisfaction.'

Mia stood up. 'Think about it, Kate. No good finding when you're thirty that your dad was right all along and it's all too late.'

'Oh, my word! My dear wife's agreeing with me! That's a first.' Gerry disappeared off upstairs calling, 'I need something to eat, if anyone can spare the time.'

Mia began to clear away her painting.

Kate studied the miniature Mia was about to put safely away to dry. 'It's lovely, Mia, really lovely.'

Mia smiled at her and reached out to place the palm of her hand softly on Kate's cheek, saying, 'Thank you, Kate. You're my very dear girl. I love you very much and I'm glad you enjoyed yourself today.'

Kate got up to get out the knives and forks from the kitchen table drawer. It wasn't possible, was it, that her dad could be giving good advice for once? 'You think he could be right, don't you?'

Mia nodded. 'Think about it. It means another year of waiting but think of the rewards if you . . .' She hesitated a moment to choose her words, not wishing to cause hurt. 'If you win through, it's worth a try. You've already been accepted, it is only a question of improving your grades. Then you'd be wearing the white coat.'

'I see what you mean. I will think about it, but only because you think it's a good idea. Perhaps I have given up too easily, too quickly. Do we need spoons?'

'Yes.' Mia busied herself with the casserole, which had been slowly cooking most of the afternoon. She gave it a stir, added some cream and put it back in the oven. 'Adam rang, by the way.'

Kate's heart sank.

'He rang at lunchtime and again about an hour ago. He says he's coming round to hear how you got on. I told him to wait until we'd eaten. I thought you might need your meal in peace.'

Gerry, reaching the bottom of the stairs as Mia told her about Adam, said, 'Nice boy, that. Solid; good, steady job; you could do worse.'

Kate snapped back at him, 'Make up your mind, Dad, I can't marry Adam and go to vet college, can I?'

'True, true, but . . .'

'No buts, I can't.' Kate contemplated marriage to Adam as she got the plates out of the warming oven and saw the years unfolding before her. The regulation two children, one boy one girl, the nice semi in the nice road, the routine, the mind-numbing routine of Adam's life. The discussion of how close to the main entrance his current car-parking space was, of his desk and the quality of the chair he'd been allocated. Next year, perhaps, when they refurbished the office he'd get a bigger, better one, then he'd know he was finally going somewhere. The ritual of the Sunday pub lunch; it's Tuesday so it's his ten-pin bowling night; no he couldn't go swimming, his sinuses were playing up: the terrible shattering monotony of a future like that.

Almost instantly a picture of Scott bunching his fingers and kissing them as he'd left her and Joy that morning came into her mind's eye. Catch Adam doing it. He'd dismiss a gesture like that as flamboyant continental nonsense. How had she ever come to be involved with him? Well, she knew, really, she didn't need to ask. Because he'd been convenient, because he had money and she had only the money she earned on Saturdays working in the office at Apex Costings plc and in the café in Weymouth in the summer holidays. Because she hadn't time for emotions when she was working so hard at school. Because he was comfortable, like an old glove, and didn't demand anything of her. Because he was there and he was loyal in a kind of dumb-animal sort of way. Kate sat at the table.

'Is that enough potato for you, Kate?'

'Oh, yes, thanks.'

She told them the story of Perkins and Adolf, of the old lady worrying about the toilet and how very ill her cat was and how she didn't know what she would do if she died. And if Adam came she wasn't in.

'Not in!' Gerry choked on a carrot. 'Not in!'

'I can't stand him tonight. Tell him I've gone to bed with a migraine.'

'You never get migraines.'

'Well, a bad head, then. I'm too tired to bother with him.'

Mia said gently, 'Don't be unkind to him, Kate, he genuinely is concerned; he's rung twice, after all.'

'All right, then. I'll see him but I'm going to bed early.'

'Well, he'll understand that.'

'So he should, he's always having to get a good night's sleep because he has a "big day" tomorrow.'

Her father chased the last of his peas around the plate and having secured it said, 'I don't understand why you have such a down on him. He's a grand chap and I like him. He's got some worthy principles, which I greatly admire. You'll always be safe with him.'

Kate placed her knife and fork together on her empty plate. 'Oh, very safe, but absolutely bored to tears. Is there a pudding?'

'Your favourite, my love, apple sponge.'

'With cinnamon?'

Mia nodded. Kate rubbed her hands together. 'Just what a woman needs when she's been at the coalface all day.' They all three heard the front door open and a voice call out, 'It's me, Adam, the man of the moment.'

Kate raised her eyebrows at Mia and they both giggled. Mia answered, 'I know what you're doing, Adam Pentecost, and I have said before there's no need to take your shoes off when you come here.'

His voice, muffled by his exertions, could just be heard: 'Mum would kill me if she ever found out I hadn't taken them off.'

Mia and Kate giggled again.

Gerry frowned at them and shouted, 'Come on in, son. You're just in time for some pudding.'

Adam stood in the doorway, glowing with self-satisfaction. Kate liked tall men and he was certainly that but so thin he gave the impression of having outgrown his strength like a runner bean or something. Suitably, given his name, his Adam's apple was bigger and bonier than most, and bobbed up and down when he spoke; his shoulders were narrow, his bottom non-existent no matter which trousers he wore. Having said all that there was something very appealing about him, a kind of vulnerability that made women feel he needed mothering. Kate could tell he was bursting for someone to ask him his news. 'You've got something exciting to tell us, haven't you?'

He tried to dismiss his news as trivial but then couldn't resist telling them. 'No, no, no, it's nothing, really. Well, it is. I've been shortlisted for that promotion.'

Mia congratulated him. 'Oh, I am pleased. Your mum will be delighted.'

Adam looked for a response from Kate. 'That's lovely,' she said.

'There's four of us, but I'm the most likely one to get it. Longest service and all that. Second interview on Friday.'

'You'll have to get that best suit out.' Kate put his pudding in front of him and gave him her spoon. 'What will it mean if you get it?'

'I shall be second assistant to the deputy. It means another three thousand a year and a move to a vastly superior office. There'll just be the two assistants sharing instead of ten of us in that terrible Portakabin. Another step up the ladder.' Adam spooned apple sponge into his mouth, his self-satisfaction reaching new heights now he had an admiring audience.

'This calls for a celebration, son! That red wine you bought, Mia, get a bottle out.'

When they'd all finished their pudding they moved from the kitchen into the sitting room and Mia fussed about sorting out their best, long-unused wineglasses from the 1930s glass-fronted cabinet, giving them a surreptitious wipe first on a corner of her cardigan.

Gerry opened up the wine and took time sniffing its bouquet and studying the clarity of it by holding up the bottle to the window. 'Try that, Adam, son, first-rate I think you'll find. Mia's a gem at hunting down good wine.' He flashed her one of his loving smiles, which Mia didn't notice.

They'd been sipping their wine and admiring it, and listening to Adam outlining the changes in his working practices if he got the promotion, when he suddenly interrupted himself and said, 'Kate! I'm sorry I'm so taken up with my promotion. I've forgotten to ask you about your day.'

'I've had an excellent day, the best day of my life to date.'

Adam patted her hand. 'That's good, I'm really pleased. Nice people to work with?'

'Absolutely!' For sheer devilment she overemphasised the merits of the male vets. 'Scott's Australian and he's such fun, Adam, you've no idea. As for Rhodri Hughes, well! He's Welsh, which is obvious from his name, and he's handsome and he sings! And the clients all adore him. Terribly good vet. And you should see Valentine Dedic! Eastern European and sort of Omar Sharif kind of, olive-skinned, and his smile! It's Open Afternoon on Saturday. I shall be busy but would you like to come? You'll come, won't you, Mia?' Mia nodded. 'Are you coming, Dad? Last chance to see the operating rooms and the like, and a free feed.'

Gerry grunted but it was difficult to know whether it was a yes or a no. Kate turned to Adam and waited for his answer.

'I think I should like that, I think that might be very interesting. Yes, I'll come. We could celebrate afterwards, couldn't we? Me getting the promotion and you getting a good job.'

Gerry interrupted Adam's fantasy with an emphatic 'No. Not good enough, Adam, for Kate. She can do better than that. I want her to try again for veterinary college. Don't we, Mia?'

'It's Kate's decision. What do you think, Adam?'

'Frankly I think she'd be happier doing what she's doing. Five years' hard work is a long time out of a life and what's the point when she'll get married, settle down, have a family? She doesn't need to do it. No, not at all. She's better off where she is. Definitely.'

'Who says I'll get married?'

Adam shuffled his feet in embarrassment. 'Well . . .' Rather lamely he ended with, 'There's someone not so very far away from you this very minute who would be delighted if you said yes to him.'

'You mean *you*?'

Mia nodded to Gerry and they both slipped out quietly, leaving Kate laughing fit to die.

'I don't think it's that funny. I've been courting you for two years now. It's not altogether unexpected, is it?'

'Courting me? Courting me? So that's what you call it, is it?'

'Isn't that what I've been doing? I thought I was.'

She stopped laughing because she realised she was being cruel and that wasn't fair. 'I'm sorry, sorry for laughing, but I don't think a girl could have had a more peculiar proposal ever. Marriage is the last thing on my mind. Heavens above, I'm nineteen, that's all, and I've things to do with my life before I start thinking about babies and mortgages. Because I'm a woman it doesn't mean I take a job just to fill in time before I get married. I'm after a career. You're like something out of the ark, you really are.'

Adam's dark-brown eyes looked searchingly into hers. She reached out sympathetically to touch his hair and found he'd put too much gel on it. 'You're all sticky.'

'Sorry.'

'Anyway, if you want to settle down, as you put it, right now, then find someone else because honestly, Adam, I am not ready for marriage just yet.'

'Even if you want to wait for us to get married there's still no need to try for college again, is there? I mean, is there?'

'No. Only if I want to.'

'I love you, you see. There's no one else for me and with this promotion it makes it possible for ...'

'Adam! You're tempting fate saying that. Stop it! Let's change the subject. Shall we go out for a drink?'

'Do you think we should? I'm wanting some early nights, you know, second interview Friday ...'

Kate sprang up off the sofa. 'Right then, you go get your early night. Be seeing you.' She left the sitting room, leaving him to follow as and when. It might be an idea to try for college, she thought, just to spite him, him with his boring old-fashioned views. At twenty-five his attitude to life was older than her dad's. Kate heard the quiet closing of the front door from the kitchen where she was getting herself a drink of water. Mia looked at her. 'Well?'

'There was no need to leave unless you were just too overcome with merriment to stay. Don't worry, I'm not marrying him now or ever. I'm going to bed. He is such a *bore.*' Kate went upstairs, after giving Mia a goodnight kiss.

Gerry waited until the door was firmly shut and then asked Mia, 'Did she say bore or did she say boor?'

'The former for sure. Which he is; she's too lively for him. He'd snuff all her spirit out of her inside a year. Please, Gerry, don't encourage him.'

'But he is a nice, reliable chap. He'd look after her, not half, and he and I get on really well.'

'And that just about sums him up.'

'Eh!'

In bed, Kate let her mind wander to Scott. She honestly could not imagine *him* wanting an early night because he had an interview on Friday. He'd be far more likely to be living it up somewhere; preferably, she speculated, with Kate Howard in tow. Then blotting out that enthralling idea came the memory of the warning that she'd had from Joy about taking him with a pinch of salt.

2

Saturday morning dawned, cloudy but dry, for which Joy heaved a sigh of relief. It was still only six o'clock so she lay down to snatch ten more minutes of peace before she got up. Her list of things to check was by the telephone downstairs and she resisted the idea of dashing down to take yet another look at it. Open Afternoons were no joke for the staff, at least not for her. The younger ones seemed to take them in their stride, but for her the smooth running of them entailed meticulous planning and, frankly, she had enough on her plate with the practice opening in a new building without the clients galloping about all over the place, though she knew she would enjoy it when it all started to happen. She turned over to find herself the only occupant of the bed. That particular discovery did not augur well for the rest of the day.

Joy sat up, drew up her knees, wrapped her arms round them and thought. Where could he have gone? So early, too. Please, Duncan, please. Not today. But he would if he wanted. Nothing could stop him, not pleas, nor cajoling, nor shouting, nor complaining, and certainly not begging. She smiled grimly when she thought what she did every day of her life, namely stand by her man. Would it be better if he didn't go to the Open Afternoon at all? No one would miss him, for Duncan was no conversationalist. Yes, she'd not remind him. Just go off as if it were an ordinary day and she was going to work. Which in part she was, as emergencies had to be dealt with by someone; one couldn't leave an animal in pain simply because they all wanted to have fun. Mungo and she would be on duty.

The very mention of his name could still melt her bones. They'd known each other for more than twenty years; she'd been his first receptionist when he set up for himself and had stayed with him through all the ups and downs of his life. The worst had been when his darling Janie had been killed in that ferry disaster. After that for almost two years he'd lived on automatic pilot, unapproachable, silent, detached, but she'd put up with all that and just when she thought her moment had come he'd arrived out of the blue one afternoon with his new bride in tow: Miriam. Joy's pain and shock were so great that she felt as though Miriam herself had taken dozens of knives and forced them straight through her heart. But she'd kept answering the phone, counting money, making out receipts, helping clients, making appointments, as though having one's heart torn asunder was an everyday occurrence and not to be permitted to hinder one's devotion to duty.

The devil of it was that this Miriam was the nicest, kindest, loveliest, gentlest being any man could hope to have as a wife, or any woman hope to have as a friend; and that was exactly what Miriam determined on, that she and Joy should be friends. Strange thing was, considering Joy's devastating disappointment, it wasn't difficult to be Mungo's wife's friend. After fifteen years Miriam still considered Joy her great friend, not suspecting for a moment how Joy felt about Mungo. She knew that even now Miriam would be up and about, getting the desserts and the savouries she'd made for the lunch buffet out of the freezer, checking her lists of things to do and all for Joy's sake, not for the sake of the practice.

Thinking about Miriam didn't solve the problem of Duncan. Where the blazes was he? It was always the same when he was in the midst of one of his computer problems: he became totally absorbed by his work, with time for nothing and no one until he'd got it resolved; then gradually he came alive again and reasonable to live with, and more like the Duncan he used to be. Joy got out of bed and went to stand at the window. She could see way down the valley, could watch the road winding away down into the town, the gulls swirling and swooping in the brilliant sky, the cows returning to the fields from the milking parlour – all this but no sign of Duncan wandering about. Maybe he was in the house all the time.

Joy showered, dressed, dried her hair and went downstairs. She found Duncan fast asleep in the armchair in his office. Dead to the world. His hands felt cold so she fetched a rug from the linen chest on the landing and covered him. Why could he never find peace?

Duncan woke just as she brewed the tea for her breakfast. 'Bring me a cup!'

'You lazy monkey! Come and get your own, and eat with me.'

Duncan ambled in and sat opposite her at the table.

'You know how much I hate unwashed people at breakfast.'

He yawned. 'Sorry! I'll go and wash.'

'No, that's all right, I'll let you off. Here, toast?'

'Please.'

'You don't eat enough.'

'I do.'

'Tea?'

'Please. Working?'

'Yes.' Joy felt deceitful and toyed with the idea of telling him about the lunch and the Open Afternoon, but she couldn't judge his mood. His heavy-lidded eyes in their deep sockets hid much from everyone including her; his high, domed forehead gave the impression of an excellent intellect and she could vouch for that, but spiritually she knew he craved peace of mind and it showed in the perpetual frown and the twitch by his right eye when things got too much for him.

'How are you today?'

Duncan was doing his Indian head massage to relieve his tension. When he'd finished he combed through his hair with his fingers to straighten it and said, 'Not bad, actually.'

'Fancy an afternoon out? Well, lunch really.'

'With you, you mean?'

'Me and about twenty others. It's the Open Afternoon. Lunch for staff and spouses et cetera at twelve, then open house till five.'

Duncan nodded. 'Yes, I'd like that. Yes, definitely.'

'That's a date, then.'

'I'll find my own way there.'

'Are you sure? I could always come back for you.'

'Not at all, you'll have enough to do.'

'Thanks, I will. I'll get ready and be off, we've clients till eleven.' Joy kissed him, glad he was feeling well enough to go.

The next time she saw him he was deep in conversation with Kate in the accounts office. The computer was on and he was explaining something to her. She was nodding, obviously deep in thought, and he was more animated than she had seen him for a while. 'OK, you two?'

They both looked up, said at the same time 'Yes, thanks', and went back to what they were saying.

'You're needed for lunch in the flat. Right now, or you'll be too late. Sorry.'

Duncan apologised. 'We're coming. We'll talk about that later, Kate. It's so easy.'

'For you maybe.'

'No, for you too.'

Kate laughed. 'I doubt it. My hold on computer technology is slight to say the least.'

'You do yourself an injustice. You've grasped the concept; having done that, you've nothing to fear.' Duncan stood back to allow Kate through the door first and they sauntered amicably up to the flat, followed by Joy. The cheerful noise of people enjoying themselves came down the stairs to greet them. Joy quaked with anxiety, wondering how Duncan would cope, but she'd forgotten how Miriam could always put him at his ease.

With arms wide stretched Miriam called out, 'Duncan! You've come.'

She embraced him with such open, genuine love that he succumbed to her warmth and found he could face the crowd with comparative enthusiasm.

'Joy! Hurry up or it will all be gone. Mungo! Drinks for Duncan and Joy, and for Kate – it must be Kate?' She kissed her too, briefly, on the cheek and Kate caught a drift of a flowery, old-fashioned perfume. 'What will you have, my dear?'

Kate asked for mineral water.

'*Mineral water* on such an auspicious day!'

'I'll have something stronger when the clients have gone. I don't want to make a fool of myself.'

'Wise girl. Come along, get some food, just pile up your plate. I don't want anything left over of this labour of love for Mungo and me to finish off.' She grinned at Kate who immediately felt drawn into her enchanted circle. She, Miriam, wasn't a beautiful person as such but somehow her *joie de vivre* made her so, and the large brown eyes and the well-rounded cheeks became beautiful without the aid of make-up. 'Mungo! Where's Kate's mineral water?' Mungo didn't respond so Miriam raised her voice. 'Dearest! Mineral water for Kate. You're deserting your post.'

Mungo came over with Kate's drink. 'Here we are, Kate.' He raised his own glass to her and said, 'Hope you're getting well settled in.'

'Thank you. I am. I have to say it's a pleasure to work here, everyone is so helpful and so kind to me.'

'I wouldn't have it otherwise. There's no point in working with animals if you don't like both them and people, and I'm not talking about some slushy kind of sentimental love, I'm talking about *liking* them. There's no place for selfish sentimentality in veterinary work, you know.'

'Indeed not.' Kate felt something brush against her leg. 'Oh! It's you. Hello, Perkins. You've forgiven me for throwing water over you, then?' Kate bent down to stroke him and he looked at her with a happy grin on his face, only his small front teeth showing between his parted lips. As she patted him Kate looked up and gave Mungo a wide smile. 'Isn't he

great? He's the only dog I know who looks as though he's laughing . . .'
Seeing the expression on Mungo's face, Kate stopped speaking. His
colour had drained away and his normally pleasant features had
become pinched and anguished. His glass was rattling against his
wedding ring and to Kate's eyes he appeared to have experienced a
tremendous shock. She was too inexperienced socially to know how to
cope with the situation and all she could think to say was, 'I'm so sorry
if I've offended you.'

Mungo visibly pulled himself together. He took a quick sip of his gin
and said in a curiously uptight voice, 'About the accounts. Do you feel
happy about them?'

'I will shortly. There's a lot to get my mind round but I shall get
there.'

'Where did you learn?'

'I've worked Saturdays at Apex Costings for what seems like a decade
and for some reason with what I'd learned at school I picked it up really
quickly.'

'Logical mind, that's what's needed. Must circulate.' Mungo gave her
an unhappy smile and wandered off to Miriam who appeared to sense
his desolation and, slipping an arm through his, offered him a plate of
food. 'Can't have you going out on a call the worse for drink, dearest.'
She handed him a fork and napkin, briefly kissed his cheek and dashed
into the kitchen on some pretext or other.

Joy had witnessed the whole incident and, at the same time as
Mungo had received his shock, she had seen what he had seen in Kate's
laughing face and knew Kate would be dumbfounded by his reaction to
her. So that was why Kate had so appealed to her at the interview.
'Kate, you're not getting anything to eat. Come along now. We can't
have you falling by the wayside halfway through the afternoon. Have
your mum and dad not come?'

'They felt too shy to come for lunch so they're coming later in the
afternoon. Have I said something I shouldn't? Like, been too familiar?
Mr Price looked really angry with me.'

Joy said, 'He's not angry with you, trust me. Probably indigestion,
lives on his nerves, you know. Now, what will you have? Miriam has
certainly done us proud, hasn't she?'

At two o'clock the cars began to arrive by the score. Graham
Murgatroyd had his work cut out organising the car park and Scott,
who had been given the job of welcoming everyone, as only he could, at
the main entrance and giving each visitor a map of the building, was in
need of support. Joy, who'd been rushing around since eight that

morning and was feeling distinctly jaded, rather than help Scott herself sent Kate to give him a hand and to get her out of Mungo's way. Joy went to supervise the girls in the reception area serving cups of tea and slices of Miriam's cakes to the clients on their way round the hospital. Duncan was comfortably seated in the reception area with a cup of tea, watching the world go by. At least he'd stayed, that was something.

'OK?'

'Fine, thanks. They've done a wonderful job, haven't they, building this place? The capital involved! It's so well done, so pleasant, it's worth every penny.'

'Glad you like it. It's taken a lot of planning.'

'I've been listening to the clients' comments. They're well impressed. The client list is bound to increase.'

'Do you think so?'

'I certainly do. When you think of those cramped premises the opposition have in the High Street, I reckon they'll be out of business in six months. I mean, there's nowhere to park for a start.'

'Out of business! Oh, I hope not. I wouldn't want that to happen.'

Duncan looked at her and said, 'Take a pew for five minutes. You deserve it.'

Joy flopped down on the chair next to him.

'Cup of tea?'

Joy nodded. Duncan walked across to the long table where Bunty and Sarah One were pouring the tea. She couldn't remember the last time he'd done anything for her in the way of looking after her. He was so totally absorbed by himself and his work that sometimes she could kick his computer to the bottom of the garden or better still into the sea at high tide. She enjoyed the idea for a moment of him being free of the damned thing, free as air, the frown gone, the twitch cast into oblivion. Oh, happy day!

As Duncan walked back towards her Mr Featherstonehough came in. 'Well, I've come. I said I wouldn't, but I have. If you're going to murder my Adolf on these premises I might as well see for myself what they're like.'

Joy jumped up. 'How lovely of you to come. I am pleased to see you!'

'You are? I'm amazed.'

She ignored his sarcastic tone and asked if he'd like tea and cakes first or to have a look around. No sooner were the words out of her mouth than Perkins hurtled into the reception area, braking the moment he realised that Adolf wasn't with his master. His tail began to wag and he greeted Mr Featherstonehough like an old friend. The old man couldn't resist his welcome and bent down to stroke him. 'Oh, I see. I'm OK when Adolf isn't with me.' Perkins wagged his tail even harder and trotted away through the back.

'I've written to the Royal Veterinary College, you know, telling them what goes on. It's not right.'

'Adolf does quite enjoy sparring with Perkins, you know, and he's well able to defend himself. If he were too small to fight back Perkins wouldn't bother with him.'

Mr Featherstonehough looked long and hard at Joy as though weighing up how much of what she said was genuine and how much a defence of Perkins. 'You could be right. Yes, you could be right, but it's bloody annoying. Anyway, I've written.'

'That's your prerogative. Now which is it to be, cake and tea or tour?'

'Tour.'

'Tour it is. I'll get one of the girls to show you around.'

'I just hope it's that pretty one.'

'We're all pretty here.'

He laughed. 'You're right. But it's that nurse that held Adolf for his injection last Monday, the one that's a bit too big for her uniform.'

'You mean Sarah Two. I shall tell her what you've said. Wait there and I'll find her for you.'

Joy got back to her cup of tea only when it was going cold, so Duncan kindly got her another one.

Long used to his silences, she was surprised when he took the initiative and said, 'The new girl, she's got a good head on her shoulders. You'll have no trouble with the accounts once she gets cracking.'

'Think so?'

'I do. She understands the principles, you see.'

'Of book-keeping? I should hope so, that's supposed to be the main object of her employment.'

'Of computers, I mean. Logical brain.'

'Very bright. Too bright for what she's doing.'

Duncan had lost interest and was staring into his empty cup.

'Going?'

He nodded, got up and walked out.

Joy sighed. People must think him really peculiar. Just for once she would have enjoyed him being around, talking, helping, just being *there*.

Kate asked Scott if he minded if she left him to do the meet and greet on his own while she took her parents around.

'Moment they come you leave me to it. There's not so many arriving now anyway. What you doing tonight?'

'Going out with my boyfriend.'

Scott pulled a face. 'Boyfriend? What does he do for a living?'

'Manager of the despatch department at that big computer warehouse out on the bypass.'

With a wry twitch of an eyebrow Scott asked, 'Important job, is it?'

Kate giggled. 'He imagines it is, but it's mainly moving paper about, especially in triplicate. Order this, order that, see it gets to this company and that company, quite boring really. He should be here, but he's late. I tried to ring him last night. He had a second interview for promotion yesterday and I thought he would ring but he didn't. Talk of the devil, there he is.'

Adam parked his little Toyota, locked it and began to walk between the cars towards the entrance.

Scott muttered out of the side of his mouth, 'I don't see any horns.' They both laughed.

Seeing the two of them standing there in the sun, Adam thought they looked like a gilded couple in an exclusive club to which he knew he would never belong. He felt bitterly excluded, but to save face he determined not to let it show. He raised his arm in greeting. 'Hello, there!' To indicate to whoever this Adonis was standing beside her that Kate was his, Adam put his arms round her and kissed her lips as though he hadn't seen her for a month.

Kate pushed him aside as discreetly as she could but saw the amusement on Scott's face and knew her action hadn't escaped his notice.

'I rang last night, but you weren't in. What happened?'

He chucked her under her chin. 'Ah! Ah! Surely you know the answer to that?'

'You got the job!'

'You said it!'

'I'm very glad, very glad indeed. So pleased. Aren't you clever? So where were you last night when I rang?'

Adam smirked. 'Out with the boys, actually.'

To Kate this seemed the oddest thing for him to do and for a moment she didn't believe him, but then she remembered he never lied so it must be true.

Scott said 'Congratulations' and held out his hand. Adam pretended to have just noticed him. Scott added, 'I'm Scott from Aussie land.'

'How do you do. I'm Adam Pentecost. Pleased to meet you.'

'You haven't seen Mia and Dad on your way, have you?'

'No. Should I have?'

'They said they were coming.' Kate scanned the car park as though by doing so the two of them would materialise and they did. Gerry's Beetle trundled steadily into the car park. Kate waved and darted between the cars to where Gerry was carefully parking his treasure.

'That's Kate's ma and pa, is it?'

Adam nodded. 'Her dad and his second wife. She's a bit odd. Not quite my cup of tea. Paints.'

'Oh, well then. Wonderful car.'

'He's besotted with it. Can't think why, it costs him a fortune in upkeep.'

'Here, have these, I'll go take a look.'

Adam watched Scott amble away and resented being left holding the maps for handing out to the clients. What a cheek! Leaving him to hold the fort while he pranced about like an idiot, admiring Gerry's car. He could see from her body language that Mia had taken an immediate liking to Scott and recalled the sneer in his voice when he'd said, 'Oh, well then.' Adam found he had taken an instant dislike to Scott. This should have been his day and it wasn't, it was being snatched from him by a fly-by-night, here-today-gone-tomorrow type of chap, with more dash and go than he would ever muster. Life simply wasn't fair. He sank further into the depths of gloom.

At the deepest moment of his despair Joy came out to tell Scott and Kate they might as well come in now, seeing as it was half past four and they couldn't expect any more clients.

'Good afternoon, I see you've been left in charge.'

Adam thrust the maps into her hands. 'Yes. I'm Kate's boyfriend.'

'How nice to meet you. Scott's commandeered her, I see. Is that Kate's mum and dad?'

Adam didn't proffer the full explanation. 'Yes.'

'I'm Joy, by the way. You're . . .'

'Adam.'

'We're just about to clear away the tea things. I'll go and put a halt to it.' Joy went back indoors, leaving Adam alone.

He joined Gerry and Mia, accompanied by Kate who energetically explained everything as she took them round the various departments and introduced them to all the staff, poured cups of tea for them and handed them cake, but he couldn't raise any enthusiasm. Stephie Budge made a fuss of him, which pleased him, but other than that all he could see was that the whole place, in which Kate appeared to be so comfortable, presented a threat to his plans for his life. In no circumstances must Kate be permitted to go to college because if she did he would lose her for evermore and that wasn't to be allowed.

Mia helped Kate and Joy with the clearing away so Adam and Gerry hung around in reception.

'I'll take Mia home if you like, there's no need for you to stay.'

Gerry shook his head. 'We're going to a friend's straight from here, thanks all the same. Thought you and Kate might like a bit of privacy tonight.' Gerry nudged his elbow.

Adam blushed.

'What do you think, then, to this place? It's certainly cost a packet.'

Adam nodded.

'Oh, yes! But I've said this several times and I shall say it again. My Kate should try again for veterinary college. You can feel the . . . well, is it aura or is it privilege or is it authority or self-confidence or what all these vets have? But whatever it is you can feel it and I want it for our Kate.'

A rage grew up in Adam's narrow chest; it grew so huge he thought his chest must have swollen to twice its size. Anger flushed his face, swelled the blood vessels at his temples and finally exploded into words. 'Not if I can help it. I love her and I want her to marry *me* and settle down with *me*. All this' – he made a vigorous dismissive gesture with his hand – 'is a nonsense.'

Gerry looked at him, amazed. It was the first time since he'd known him that Adam had displayed such powerful opinions . . . no, it wasn't opinions, it was emotions. 'Why, Adam, you're not jealous of her, are you? There's nothing for you to be jealous of. You're climbing that ladder you've talked so much about too, you know, with this promotion.'

Adam's reply was a snort. He stood up and said, 'I'll see her back at your house.'

Gerry called after him, 'You'll need the key, you can't get in . . .' but he was too late. Adam had gone.

So he was outside the house waiting in his car when Kate got home well over an hour later. Before she left, Kate and Joy and Stephie and the two Sarahs, with Bunty and several of the vets, had all gone up to Mungo's and Miriam's flat to eat some of the food left over from the lunch buffet.

'Otherwise Mungo and I will still be eating it this time next week, so you must. I insist.'

Joy said Miriam had provided far too much and Miriam's reply, spoken with her face alight with laughter, was that her generous nature was to blame.

Mungo, who'd been out on a call during the afternoon, was back, tucking into the food. Whatever it was Kate had done to upset him seemed to have been forgotten, and he appeared relaxed and amused them all by relating the funny side of the call he had just made. Before she left they'd all decided that after they'd indulged themselves with Miriam's food they didn't need to eat, so they'd all go out for a drink together. Only Kate had declined, saying she had arranged to go out with Adam.

'Bring him with you, go on,' said Stephie. 'We'd like to get to know him and it's a good chance for you to meet everyone too. Go on, give him a ring on his mobile.'

'He hasn't got one.'

Stephie thought round this and said, 'If he's at your house waiting for you, go home and tell him we're going to the Fox and Grapes. He'll jump at the chance, believe me.'

So she did just as Stephie said. She tapped on the car window. 'Hi!'

Adam wound it down and snapped, 'Where have you been? I've been waiting ages.'

'I'm sorry. Miriam asked us all up to the flat to finish off the food. It would have been discourteous not to have accepted her invitation. If you hadn't gone off in a huff you could have gone upstairs too. Anyway, I'm here now. Come in while I get changed and have a wash because we're all meeting up for a drink and you're invited.'

'I've not eaten yet.'

'You can eat at the pub. They do lovely food there.'

'I thought we were celebrating tonight, just the two of us.'

'Look, I'm the new girl and I want to belong and I don't yet, so going out with them all will help. It'll be such fun. So please, for my sake.'

Adam didn't reply, but stared straight ahead, ignoring her.

'Please, you'll like them all. I know you will, they're such a friendly lot. Go on, please. Come in and wait. I shan't be long.'

'I think you'd best go on your own. I'll be here tomorrow at twelve as usual.'

Incensed by his refusal to indulge her, Kate said, 'Don't bother, Adam, thank you.'

'Not go out for lunch? But it's Sunday!'

'I know what day of the week it is. If I didn't know better I'd think you were jealous.'

'Of what?'

'Heaven alone knows. Go on, then, spend Saturday night with your mother. I'm sure she'll enjoy your company, which is more than I would with you in this mood.'

Kate slammed into the house, absolutely furious with him. She went to the Fox and Grapes, fully intending to have a good night. Which she did and later, in bed, she decided that she'd enjoyed herself an awful lot more than she would have done if she'd gone out with Adam. Then she felt guilty, then decided she didn't care if he didn't come round ever again, changed her mind and wished she had gone out with him, and changed her mind again when she finally came to the conclusion that Scott and Graham and Rhodri were much more fun, to say nothing of the two Sarahs who were such an incredibly funny double act they'd had her in stitches. She was in so much turmoil that it was two o'clock before she got to sleep.

Around that time Duncan came home. Joy had gone back straight from the practice, expecting to find him waiting for his meal, but he hadn't been there. She made it for him anyway and kept it under a plate, ready for the microwave when he did finally decide to return. But two o'clock in the morning was excessively late even for Duncan.

Joy leapt out of bed when she heard his key in the door and went downstairs dreading what she would find. If it were possible he appeared wearier than ever, his dark stubble emphasising the exhaustion in his face. He was soaked to the skin.

'Duncan! Duncan! Where on earth have you been? Here, let me help.' Between them they stripped off his wet clothes. Joy got a huge well-warmed towel from the airing cupboard and wrapped him in it. 'What you need is a hot shower. Have you eaten?'

Duncan shook his head.

'Come on, then, upstairs you go for a shower and I'll get your food ready. Clean jimjams in your top drawer.'

When he'd finished eating and been warmed by the heat of the stove and the food in his stomach Joy said, 'We can't go on like this.'

Duncan huddled himself still further into his dressing gown until it seemed as though all there was in the armchair was a dressing gown and a head. He stared at the logs burning away. 'It would be so easy to seek peace in drink.'

'I know. I know.'

'While ever I've got you . . .'

'I know.' She knelt beside his chair, laid her head on his chest and hugged him.

Duncan stroked her hair. 'I don't deserve you.'

'No, you don't. You do nothing to deserve me.'

Duncan chuckled, 'You're supposed to say "what nonsense".'

'It was the truth.'

'Ah! The truth. Don't give me any more truth, thank you, I may not want to hear it.'

'Best not. Eh?'

Duncan nodded his agreement. 'Great day today. I envy all of you, your purpose in life.'

Joy sat back on her heels. 'It did go well, didn't it?'

'Excellent. Such a turnout of clients. I doubt there was anyone left in the shops in town; I think they all came to see the new place.' Duncan rubbed a hand on her back. 'All thanks to you.'

'Where have you been?'

'Mostly sitting up on Beulah Bank Top. Great place for thinking.'

'What about?'

'Me.'

'Ah! Very self-indulgent.'

'More harrowing, really.'

'Did you come to any conclusions?'

'That I'm trapped, in a cage, and they've thrown away the key.'

'Duncan!'

'I'm going to bed.'

And he went.

Joy cleared up, closed the doors of the stove and followed him up the stairs. He was already asleep, curled in a foetal position as always and on her side of the bed. She pulled the duvet around his shoulders and climbed in herself, and thought about her day.

If she rated it on a score of one to ten then taking everything into consideration it rated ten – well, perhaps nine and a half, having remembered Mungo's face when Kate had stroked Perkins and looked up at him smiling. Joy sighed. One day she'd explain to Kate. Dear Kate, she was going to be such an asset to the practice. Joy cuddled up to Duncan's back and, letting the warmth of his body seep into her, fell asleep, enriched by the satisfying pleasures of a successful day doing what she loved most.

3

Monday morning dawned wet and cold, a typical English autumn day. Heavy traffic in the town centre had delayed Kate so that it was already just after eight o'clock by the time she parked her car. The wind blew down from Beulah Bank Top, making the car park the very last place on earth that she wanted to linger. Nothing irritated her more than being held up in traffic with the wipers going hell for leather all the time and scarcely able to see where she was going. As she leapt out of the car the wind blowing down from the hills hit her full in the face. Not stopping to lock it and with the hood of her anorak pulled over her head, she made a run for the main entrance.

Stephie had already laid a long length of matting from the glass door to reception to save the floor and was on the computer checking through the appointments for the day, and as Kate wiped her feet on the mat, the farm practice phone began ringing, as well as one of the others.

'Take that, will you, Kate.'

Answering the phones before the fourth ring was practice policy so Kate, without removing even her anorak, drew a deep breath and picked up the receiver. 'Good morning, Barleybridge Farm Practice. How may I help? Rhodri Hughes? Hold the line a moment, please.' She went into the farm practice office to see if Rhodri had come in yet and found him sitting with his feet propped up on the desk opening his post. 'Phone call for you.'

'This early.' He picked up the receiver saying, 'Rhodri Hughes speaking.'

Kate went back to reception and replaced the receiver.

'Client?'

'Don't know. I'll be back, just get myself organised. My shoes are soaking wet.'

Using the mirror in the women staff's cloakroom, Kate combed

36

through her hair and wished for the thousandth time she had naturally curly hair that would bounce back to life immediately she'd removed her headgear. But she hadn't so she combed through it, pushed it about with her fingers a bit, found she'd buttoned her uniform up wrongly and thought to herself that that fact alone augured a bad day.

The moment she opened the cloakroom door she could hear Rhodri shouting. Stephie was shouting back at him: 'I didn't answer the phone. It was Kate.'

Joy came out from her office saying, 'This noise is quite unacceptable. Kindly refrain, the pair of you. I will not have my staff spoken to like this, Rhodri. Whatever is the matter?'

'That bloody Megan Jones. They put her through to me. They know, I've told them, I don't want to speak to her. How many times have I to say it?'

Joy grinned. 'We're not here to field your personal calls, you know. You should tell her the truth, that you're not interested.'

'I don't want to hurt her feelings.'

'Oh, poor dear boy. If you're so kind why not take her out?'

Rhodri shuddered. 'Not likely. She's not my type.'

Kate apologised. 'I'm so sorry, it didn't click that it was her. I'd just rushed in and . . .'

'That's no excuse. Her accent is recognisable, for God's sake, surely. Don't ever do it again.' His dark eyes were almost boiling with temper and he quite intimidated Kate.

'I am so very sorry. I promise, cross my heart, that I won't let it happen again, it was just that . . .'

Rhodri wagged his finger at her. 'Best not, because I can't answer for the consequences.'

Joy bristled at his threat. 'Mr Hughes! You will not threaten my staff, if you please. It is entirely your fault that this situation has arisen. Apologise immediately.'

Though startled by the level of anger in Joy's voice, Rhodri had to recognise the rightness of what she said: he'd caused his sweet-tempered, gentle Joy to become distinctly ungentle all in a moment.

'I beg your pardon, Joy and Kate, for losing my temper . . .'

Stephie pouted at him. 'And what about an apology for me? You shouted at me too.'

'Yes, and you too, apologies all round.'

Joy stood with her hands on her hips, head to one side. 'So, are you going to sort it or shall I?'

Rhodri pondered the way out she had offered him. 'No, thank you. I'd be less than a man if I allowed you to do it. It's something I must do, hurt feelings or not.' He grinned. 'I've taken her out three times and I've known from the start she wasn't right for me. Let's face it, she was revolted by Harry and how can a man go out with a girl who doesn't like Harry?'

Kate, wondering who on earth Harry was, asked, 'Harry? Who's Harry, for heaven's sake?'

'My ferret.'

Kate began laughing and found she couldn't stop. Rhodri looked at her and for a moment she thought he was going to be angry again but he wasn't. He caught the infection of her laughter and he too began to laugh, the rich, musical sound echoing around reception to the delight of the clients who were just beginning to arrive.

When finally he stopped and had wiped his streaming eyes, he said between gasps, 'I'll have to be cruel and do the dirty deed. Tell her straight from the shoulder that it's no go. I'll ring her tonight. Curse the woman.'

Joy suggested a stiff whisky prior to dialling her number.

'Maybe you should give up Harry,' said Kate.

Rhodri looked appalled. 'Give up Harry? Certainly not. Love me, love my ferret.' He turned on his heel and went back to opening his post.

Stephie put down the receiver, altered an appointment on her computer and turned to Kate. 'Can you imagine that? "Love me, love my ferret." I ask you. It's a rotten, smelly thing, I've seen it. I can't believe anyone could fancy him, never mind him *and* a ferret.'

Kate's eyes twinkled. 'Oh! I don't know, all that Celtic emotion. He's quite attractive once he gets worked up.'

'He might be laughing now but he won't forget what you've done. He's like that, bears a grudge, you know, for ages.'

'In that case I shall deflect his annoyance by showing an interest in his ferret.'

Stephie raised an eyebrow. 'Well, if you're that hard up ... Adam OK?' She looked slyly at Kate while she waited for her to answer the phone and then asked again, 'Adam OK?'

'He's fine, thanks. Yes, fine.'

'Did you go somewhere exciting yesterday?'

Kate, who was printing out the visiting lists for the farm vets, shook her head and asked casually, 'Did you?'

'Well, Sarah One and I went to this new leisure complex that's opened. Expensive but brilliant. You and Adam should try it. I expect he's a good swimmer with his build.'

But the morning had begun in earnest and the two of them got no futher opportunity to discuss the weekend, for which Kate was grateful.

She hadn't, in fact, seen Adam apart from when he had sat outside her house from twelve until one, waiting for her to come out to go for their regular Sunday pub lunch. Dad and Mia had gone to a factory outlet place first thing so they hadn't seen him and Kate had refused to go out to speak to him. She'd already told him she wasn't going and, being in a temper because of his refusal to join her and the others for a drink the previous night, had decided he could sit there till the cows came home if he wanted to; after all, it was a free country. He had a right to park his car where he chose so long as he wasn't on a double yellow line. She'd peeped through the net curtain several times and twice nearly gone to the door to speak to him but defiantly changed her mind.

In fact, trying for vet college again had become more of a distinct possibility each time she'd looked out. Adam's horizons were so limited, and how could anyone be such a fool as to sit outside all that time and not knock on the door. But then he never had knocked on the door on Sundays, he'd always simply parked and waited for her to come out ... something about not disturbing Mia and Dad on a Sunday. Other days he knocked and walked in. A creature of habit was Adam. How he'd cope with the new job she couldn't imagine. But she was glad he'd got it, even if his behaviour had become so odd. Going out with the boys for the evening! That was a joke, surely?

'Kate! Hello-o-o!'

Jerked back into the present, Kate looked up from her lists. 'Sorry, Scott, just printed out your list. Here you are.'

'How's my favourite girl this morning?'

'First, I am not your favourite girl, and second here's your list, and third it's a long one, and fourth this call here I've just added on sounds critical.'

Scott groaned. 'Oh, God! Not Applegate Farm. I swear there's a curse on me. Cross it off my list and give it to Zoe, please, I beg you.' Scott got down on one knee and put his hands together as though in prayer. 'Please. For your favourite Aussie?'

'You know that Zoe, being pregnant, can't go because it's an abortion, so you'll have to go.'

'Stephie! Tell her I can't go. Please.'

But Scott's mistake had been calling Kate his favourite girl. 'Kate is in charge and she's right. Zoe can't go.'

'Very well, but if something goes wrong I shan't be responsible for my actions. That farm is the filthiest ...'

Kate stopped him speaking by placing her finger on his mouth, which he swiftly took the opportunity to kiss as she said softly, 'Not in front of the clients, please.'

Looking suitably chastened, Scott ambled out. He closed the glass door behind him and turned to press his face, contorted into an alarming grimace, against the glass. Kate waved her hand at him and then ignored him. He came back in to make another remark but thought better of it and left when he saw Joy taking over the reception desk.

'Accounts, Kate. You'd better get on.'

'Right, I will. Scott didn't want to go to Applegate Farm.'

'He never does, but he must.'

'Why doesn't he like it?'

'Because,' Stephie said, 'he always makes mistakes there.'

'Mistakes!'

Joy denied this. 'For some reason things always go wrong for him there and he's got a thing about it now. But he can't pick and choose.'

So the clients couldn't hear, Stephie whispered, 'Nasty man is Mr Parsons. Very rude. You should hear him on the phone. Disgusting!'

'Only because Mr Parsons thinks Mungo is the one vet capable of attending to his animals.'

Stephie muttered, 'Some animals! Well, we'll see what he has to say when he gets back.'

'That won't be for ages. I've given him a list long enough to keep him busy all day.'

'So you should, Kate, he has to earn his money. He gets paid enough, believe me. Off you go and you too, Stephie, and take a break. Please.'

Scott flung himself into the Land Rover, opened the windows wide, turned on the radio, checked he had his laptop with him, swung into gear and charged out of the car park in despair. Sure, he'd played the fool in his attempt to avoid this call, but underneath it all he seriously – oh, so seriously – didn't want to go. Most especially on a wet day. If only there'd been a nurse free to go with him, that might have helped, but with Bunty still away . . . He had a suspicion that her absence would be down to him. How could she expect a young, virile man to resist her charms? She was round and cuddly and blonde and tanned, and had what his ma would have called come-hither eyes. It had all happened so quickly, she eager, he hungry, and those sexy legs and the swing of her slender hips as she walked across the farmyard to the Land Rover for his drugs box . . . well, what with the dark and everything what else could she expect, having spent the evening egging him on.

But he hadn't meant for this to happen . . . just the once, as Pa would say if he were here, it only needs once, just once and she's up the spout. He brushed aside the thought that a little Spencer had most assuredly had his life snuffed out this week, signalled left onto the Applegate Farm track and thought about the thick mud that always covered the yard, be it drought or flood, and planned his precautionary strategy. Scott took off his precious Timberland boots and changed into his wellingtons before he got out. As his feet touched the ground a voice shouted, 'Taken long enough. Come on, then. Be sharp. It's Zinnia.'

'Morning, Phil. Wet day.'

Phil Parsons was a short, stocky man with a rotund waistline and massive red swollen hands, and an over-large head. He was never without, summer or winter, a black balaclava, which entirely covered his face and head except for a slit where his mouth and nose were, and two holes through which his eyes could barely be seen, as the holes didn't quite match where his eyes came. Consequently one never quite saw both eyes at once, which was disconcerting and affected one's relationship with him. Added to which, if one got too close he smelt strongly of the all-pervading odour of someone whose programme of personal hygiene had been severely neglected.

From the back of the Land Rover Scott pulled out some equipment he thought he would need, and slid and slithered his way to the cow byre. It was windowless so the only light came from the open door and two hurricane lamps hanging from the cobwebby ceiling. In addition, today there was Blossom Parsons, Phil's young wife, holding a torch.

'Morning, Mr Spencer. Poor morning. You been on call all night?'

'For a change, no, I haven't, Mrs Parsons.'

Scott, from the first moment he had met her, had retained a certain formality when speaking to Blossom Parsons for he was intensely aware that she fancied him and she made it abundantly clear even in front of her husband. Scott's technique was to ignore her remarks as though concentration on the animal he'd come to see was taking up all his mind. He went to have a word with the cow. He stroked her head and spoke softly to her, looked at her eyes to judge her temper, checked her gums to see if she was in shock.

'Hold the torch for me, Phil, right here, please. Let's see what's come away.'

'No, no, I can do it.' Mrs Parsons laid a hand on his back as she leant forward to get the beam shining where he wanted it. Her fingers began very subtly massaging his spine.

'She's not got rid of it all and she's not well either. Got a temperature, I would think. What is she, about fifteen weeks?'

Phil scratched his head through his balaclava. 'Couldn't say for certain, but about that.'

'Look in your records.'

'Do me a favour. Natural farming I go in for. If they're in calf they're in calf and if they're not, they're not. Writing it down doesn't put them in the club and what's more it takes up my time.' Phil peered at the bloody mess surrounding the tiny, immature dead calf laid on the byre floor. 'My bull knows his business better than me. Don't need no pen an' paper, he don't.'

'I see.' By this time Scott had his hand in the cow's uterus and Mrs Parsons had stopped massaging him.

'I'll go put the kettle on, shall I?'

There were some farms where Scott could enjoy a mug of tea sitting at the kitchen table talking farming and there were some where he couldn't. Applegate Farm came into the latter category. When he'd been offered tea the first time after a long, cold wait for a calf to arrive, he'd accepted and eagerly gone inside to get warm, but after the shock of seeing their filthy kitchen and the indescribable chaos which reigned in there he had vowed he'd die of hypothermia before entering that kitchen again.

'No, thanks, Mrs Parsons. I've more calls this morning than I can cope with. I'll just take a couple of blood samples and give Zinnia an antibiotic, and then I'll be away.'

'I'm real disappointed you won't have a cuppa. I made cherry cake yesterday and there's a slice left. Let me put it in a bag and you can take it home; do to finish your lunch with. Won't be a minute.'

'She should be all right now, Phil. Any ideas why this happened?'

Phil shook his head. 'None. Just one of them things.'

'I've said this before and I've got to say it again, this place needs cleaning up. Milk produced here! God help us! No wonder Milkmarque say you don't reach their hygiene standards and refuse to collect.'

'There's plenty of people'll buy my milk. Don't need no nosy-parking, puffed-up officials, I don't.'

Scott held up his hand to silence him. 'Say no more, I don't want to know. Right. But it's a disgrace. A complete disgrace. If I mention it in the right quarter you'll be in deep trouble, so make sure when I come back the day after tomorrow to see Zinnia that you've made a start. No, more than a start, actually done it. The cow byre, the yard, everywhere. Right?'

'I heard.' Phil sniffed his disgust and turned on his heel back into the byre.

Hoping to escape before Mrs Parsons came out of the farmhouse with his cherry cake, Scott headed straight through the yard, out of the gate and across the farm track to where he'd left his vehicle. He had stored his equipment and stripped off his protective clothing when she bellowed from the farmhouse doorway, 'Scott! Your cake! Here!' Mrs Parsons held up a brown paper bag, making no attempt to walk across to him. There was nothing for it: politeness and good client relations demanded that he walk over to get it. Taking a moment to replace his wellingtons, Scott crossed the farm track and slurped his way over to the house. The route from the byre to the track he knew, but he'd never walked from the track to the farmhouse door before and he unwittingly dropped up to his chest into the slurry pit which, through years of practice, Phil and Mrs Parsons and Zinnia and the rest of the herd would have known to avoid. The farm smelt, always, but Scott disturbing the slurry, as he did with the speed of his fall, spread an extra layer of stench not only over himself but the whole yard.

They pulled him out between them without a word being exchanged. Phil got a bucket, filled it from the tap in the yard and threw it over him, then another and another.

'No, no, come into the house. You can stand in the bath and strip off in there. I'll lend you something of Phil's.'

Three buckets of water had made little impression on the stinking mess that was Scott. His spanking-clean chinos were now thick with cow dung, his checked shirt, bought in Sydney the day he left, was weighed down with the thick sludge, his boots were filled with it, his bare arms and hands oozing the stuff. He took a moment to be grateful that he hadn't had time to change into his Timberland boots before she'd called him. Bitter desperation filled him. Strip off in front of Mrs Parsons? Not likely! An outfit belonging to Phil? Even less likely!

'Thanks all the same. Do you have some newspaper for the car, Phil? I'll get back to the practice and shower there. I keep a spare set of clothing there in case.' He didn't, but in circumstances like these a lie was neither here nor there.

He lumbered across to the Land Rover with filth squelching in his boots at every step. Before he got in he smoothed his hands all over himself and squeezed away as much of the loose stuff as he could. The newspapers he spread all over the seat and the back of it, and gingerly climbed in. Scott opened every window, reversed and was about to stamp on the accelerator when Mrs Parsons appeared beside him.

'Your cake! Don't go without it.' She held the bag up to the window, and Scott reached out a stinking, filth-streaked hand and thanked her politely for it. The ludicrousness of the situation struck him and he began to laugh and was still laughing, but by then somewhat hysterically, when he arrived back at the practice.

Finding the back door locked and no amount of hammering bringing a response, he clumped round to the main door and went in.

When the smell which was Scott reached Joy, she looked up from the desk and saw him standing dripping on the doormat with pieces of the newspaper from the seat still stuck to his back. The astonishment on her face struck Scott as highly comical. But there was nothing funny about her reaction. 'Get out, you absolute nincompoop! Out! Go on! Out!'

The clients patiently waiting their turns protested loudly at the smell. Covering their noses with handkerchiefs, they shouted, 'Get out, Scott! What a smell.'

Slowly the sodden cow dung on his socks began sinking into the doormat. Scott looked down at the mess he was creating and muttered plaintively, 'I can't help it. No one answered the bloody door when I knocked.'

'Oh. Language!' someone said.

Joy endeavoured to retrieve the situation by telling him to go round the back and she'd send someone out to help. Which Scott did. A client got up and opened the windows to let out the smell, while Joy went to ask Kate to give a hand outside.

She stood him on a grate by the back door and hosed him down till he was shuddering with cold. 'I've got to take my clothes off.'

'I'll go in and start the shower, leave your clothes out here and I'll sort them out and please, dry yourself off a bit with this dog towel before you come in.'

'Dog towel! Oh, thanks! Good on you, mate!'

'Otherwise we'll have filthy water everywhere. Go on, do as I say.'

Showered and warmed and dressed in Mungo's gardening trousers and shirt, Scott sat in the accounts office drinking the scorching-hot coffee Kate had made for him, muttering threats about Applegate Farm. 'I shall report him. I said I wouldn't, but I shall.'

'For what?'

'For selling milk on the quiet when Milkmarque won't collect from his farm. For keeping animals in disgraceful conditions, though I have to admit they do seem happy and are not actually in any danger. He knows every one of them by name.'

'How did you come to be like this?'

Scott's eyes gleamed with amusement over the rim of his mug. 'I fell into the slurry pit.'

'You didn't! How could anyone do that? Weren't you looking where you were going?'

'Parsons's pit isn't fenced.'

'But what about the cows, don't they fall in it?'

'Oh, no! They know where it is and walk round it. Trouble is the yard is so thick with mud and mess you don't see where the mud finishes and the pit starts. Thank God they were there to pull me out.'

Kate knew she shouldn't laugh because Scott was so dejected, but she couldn't help it and it began to bubble up inside her. He caught her eye and they both laughed.

Kate pulled herself together and said, 'Look, there's the rest of the calls still to do. You've got to go.'

He stood up. 'You're getting as bad as Joy, you are, and you've only been here a week. To cheer a miserable Aussie up, will you come out with him tonight?' Seeing the doubt in her face he added, 'For a drink?'

Gravely Kate studied him and answered, 'All right. I will. Just for a drink.'

'But of course, sweet one, as you say, just for a drink. Fox and Grapes about eight?'

Mia, Gerry and Kate were finishing their evening meal when the front door opened and they heard Adam's 'It's only me'.

There he was in the kitchen in his ten-pin-bowling outfit.

Gerry covered Kate's and Mia's surprised silence by saying, 'Come in, Adam. There's still some tea in the pot. Like some?'

Mia got up to get the extra cup and Kate looked up at him. 'Yes?'

Adam didn't quite look her in the eye, but answered, 'Thought I'd just pop round.'

'I didn't think you would be coming for me tonight, after Sunday.'

'Here, son.' Gerry pulled out the chair next to Kate. 'Sit here.'

Mia passed him his cup of tea and pushed the sugar bowl across to him.

Gerry made pleasant remarks about the weather, trying to lighten the atmosphere, and wondered why things didn't seem right.

Adam ignored him and said to Kate, 'I waited outside on Sunday but you didn't come out.'

'I know I didn't.'

Gerry and Mia tried to disguise their surprise. Gerry asked feebly, 'Why didn't you?' but got no reply.

'Well?'

'I told you not to come. I said I wouldn't go out to lunch.'

'But we always do.'

Seeing as Adam was disinclined to look at her, Kate twisted round in her chair and glared at him. 'You are a chump, Adam. Who in their right mind would sit outside a house for a whole hour and then drive away?'

'But I never knock on Sundays.'

'Exactly. But just once perhaps you could break the habit of a lifetime and knock. Where are you expecting to go tonight?'

Adam looked down at his beige sweatshirt and trousers, which in the catalogue had been described, stylishly as he thought, as taupe, and his immaculate white socks and bowling shoes. He plucked at his sweatshirt and said, 'Isn't it obvious?'

'Perfectly. Unfortunately I've made other arrangements for tonight.'

He couldn't have looked more surprised if she'd said she was going skinny-dipping. 'Other arrangements? What do you mean? It's Tuesday.'

Mia gently interrupted this painful dialogue. 'Adam, just for once Kate wants a change. Don't you sometimes want to do things differently?'

'Well, no, I don't. I'll miss it if we don't go.'

'I shan't. You're not very good at it and I'm tired of making a fool of myself for your sake. I try not to win and I do, every time.'

Mia couldn't believe how hurtful Kate was being to Adam and neither could Gerry, who felt a conciliatory word was required. 'I think you should cancel this outing you've planned and go with Adam, Kate. It's only fair.'

Kate got up from her chair. 'I don't want to hurt your feelings . . .'

Adam looked angry now and his anger disturbed Kate more than she liked to admit. Usually he flushed when he was upset but this time he was white to the gills. Through gritted teeth he said, 'It's too late, you already have.'

'To be honest, I've arranged to have a drink with . . . someone from work.'

Adam got to his feet. 'Well, there's no point going on my own.' Pushing his chair under the table he asked her outright, 'Is it that Aussie?'

'Well, yes, it is. He's had a really bad day today and he needed cheering up, and I thought after Sunday you wouldn't be coming.'

'I knew you should never have gone to work there. I just knew it. How can you contemplate having an evening out with someone else when you're *my girl*? You always spend Tuesday night with me. Ring him up and cancel it like your father said.' Kate didn't make a move so Adam pounded his right fist into his left palm and added with an unwholesome attempt at authority in his voice to which all three took exception, 'Do as I say!'

Mia, unaccustomed forcefulness in her tone, said, 'Don't speak to my Kate like that, I won't tolerate it. She's a free agent, she can go out with whom she pleases and whoever she is going with it's all right by me because I know I can rely on her. You don't own her, Adam, and you'll do well to remember that.'

Gerry was about to add his own comment to Mia's statement and opened his mouth to do so, but Adam glared at each one in turn and left the kitchen without another word.

When the front door slammed Gerry sat back appalled. 'What the blazes is up with him?'

Mia, very troubled by Adam's reaction, said, 'He's turning into a bully, that's what. Speaking like that to Kate! Don't let it spoil your evening; that Scott is a nice boy.'

'Perhaps I should go after him . . .'

Gerry, who'd championed Adam through thick and thin these last two years, said, 'No, best let the dust settle. The prospect of that promotion has gone to his head, speaking like that to you in my house. I won't have it.' He took out his wallet and, picking out a ten-pound note, handed it to Kate. 'I know you're short till you get your first month's salary so here, take this. I want you to be able to stand your corner. Doesn't do to be beholden to anyone, not even that Scott, nice though he is.'

'There's no need, Dad, but thanks.'

When Kate went into the Fox and Grapes she found Scott already there. He was sitting at a corner table with an enormous plate of food in front of him. She saw him pick up his knife and fork and begin to eat, and judging by the enthusiasm with which he dived into his food she guessed he hadn't eaten all day, so she decided to spend a couple of minutes in the ladies to give him a little time to take the edge off his hunger.

Her reflection in the mirror in there quite pleased her. She'd taken the trouble to put on make-up, which she didn't do every day, and she admired her new eyeshadow, then looked a little closer at her forehead thinking she could see lines appearing already and no wonder. What on earth had got into Adam? He had never been an emotional person but now, since his promise of promotion, he'd gone distinctly highly charged in the most unpleasant way. Perhaps she was to blame for she hadn't been quite fair, but there wasn't any need to go quite as ballistic as he had done tonight. Even Mia had taken exception, and her dad. Anyway, she and Adam weren't engaged or anything, so if she decided not to see him again she wouldn't. An evening with Scott was a very interesting alternative to trying to lose at bowling. She winked at herself in the mirror and charged out to find Scott.

When he saw her crossing the bar he put down his knife and fork and stood up. 'Kate! You've come!' He kissed her cheek.

She kissed him back. 'I have.'

They both beamed idiotically, enjoying the sight of each other.

'Here, look, sit down, I'll move my coat. Will you excuse me if I finish my meal?'

'Of course. Can I get you a drink? What would you like?'

'A coffee first, please. Here let me . . .' He dug his hand in his pocket and brought out loose change.

Kate said, 'This is on me.'

The cappuccinos looked tempting, and Kate spooned some of the froth and the chocolatey bits into her mouth. Looking up, she found Scott watching her and caught a look in his eyes she'd never seen in Adam's. Kate blushed and, to pass off her embarrassment, picked up a sugar sachet, opened it and let the sugar cascade into her coffee. Then another.

'Hey!'

'I like my cappuccino sweet. It's one of my "things".'

'You're quite sweet enough.'

'That's a corny remark if ever there was one.'

'I meant it, though. Thanks for coming out this evening, I've had a rotten day.'

'I know. That's why I came.'

Scott finished his meal and eyed the menu. 'One of my "things" is ice-cream sundaes.'

'And mine.'

He ordered two strawberry ones and waited at the counter while the girl made them up. She was laughing so much at his comments that it was a wonder they got their order at all. Kate couldn't quite put her finger on why it was he had this effect on women, but he did. And on her. He was so light-hearted and such fun that one really couldn't take him seriously.

They chatted and laughed their way through their desserts, enjoying the thick, cloying strawberry sauce, the nutty bits sprinkled on the rich cream piled right to the very top of the glasses and the fresh strawberries they kept finding even right down at the bottom of the glass.

'I've never had such a delicious sundae in all my life.'

Scott winked. 'She knows me, you see, she knows what I like.'

'You come here a lot, then?'

'When I've worked a ten-hour day and I've a night on call to face,

48

believe me, I'm in no mood for cooking when I get home and a fella needs food if he's to function well.'

'I wonder the farmers take you seriously.'

'What do you mean?'

'You don't seem like a responsible person.'

'Where my work is concerned, I am. I know I play the fool and such but I do know my job.'

'You enjoy being a vet, then?'

'I wouldn't want to be anything else. Nothing else in the whole wide world.'

She sensed passion and conviction in his voice, loved the light in his eyes and asked him which parts he liked the best.

'A cold winter's morning with a brilliant, rosy-red dawn just breaking, a warm cowshed, a fight to get a calf born alive, the sight of it slithering out and the joy of it breathing, and the mother, all toil forgotten, bending to lick it.' Scott looked embarrassed. 'Sorry for going all poetic, but that's what I like. Then you wash under the tap in the yard, or if you're lucky someone brings a bucket of hot water into the cowshed, and when you're clean you go into the warm kitchen and have a coffee laced with rum and a comfortable chat about things that really matter, then you go home.' He looked somewhere beyond her shoulder, lost in thought. 'More often than not, though, it's pouring with rain, pitch-black and you're chilled to the marrow, and the wife's away so there's no coffee, but still I love it. And lambing, now, there's a job and a half. You put your hand in and find two lambs tangled together and the ewe can push neither of them out, and you straighten them up, move a leg here and a head there, and hey presto, two beauties and the mother as proud as punch. Brilliant!'

Wistfully Kate said, 'It must be great.' And before she could stop herself out poured all her terrible disappointment about missing vet college, something she'd promised herself she would never do.

Scott listened hard to every word she said. When she'd finished he took hold of her hand saying, 'Look here, if you feel as strongly as that, isn't it worth having another try? Why stand on the touchline of life? Get in there and on with the game, a bold strike straight for the goal. This isn't a practice game, you know, you only get the one chance. For someone with your passion for the job that's the only thing to do, otherwise there'll be a terrible vacuum in your life all your days. What's holding you back?'

'I don't know, really.'

He encouraged her to explore her problem. 'You must know.'

'Well, it's the thought of all that studying. I tried so hard to succeed and it all came to nothing. I don't know if I can face such a defeat all over again. And that's only the start of it; five solid years of slog ahead.'

'But you've only the one grade to improve, not three.'

Kate nodded. 'I know.'

'Your ma and pa, what do they want?'

'They're like you, they want me to try again.'

'Well, then, there you are.'

'Adam doesn't want me to; in fact, he doesn't want me to work at the practice even.'

'You need to ditch that medieval horror.'

Kate withdrew her hand from his and said indignantly, 'Ditch him?'

'He's smothering you.'

'He isn't.'

'He is. He's a nutter.'

'He isn't.'

'Believe me. He is.'

Kate stood up. 'I wish I'd never told you how I felt. I promised myself I wouldn't tell anyone and I've told you, and now look what's happened, you're organising my life for me.'

'So why have you lost your temper? Is it because you know I'm right?'

His mobile phone began to ring. 'Damn.' He listened, answered and switched off. 'Got to go. Sorry. Should have known not to invite you out when I'm on call. We'll do this again one night when I'm not.'

'We will?'

Scott took her hand in his and squeezed it. 'Don't be cross, not with me. Just think about what I've said. I'm right about trying again and very right about that damned Adam. Goodnight, sweet one.'

He hurtled out of the bar, blowing a quick kiss to the barmaid who'd made the sundaes for them and calling 'Goodnight' to everyone as he went.

Kate bought herself a vodka and tonic, and sat thinking about Scott. There was nothing more poisonous than living one's life with regret . . . thinking 'if only' all the time. She liked his analogy of the game of life. She'd give it serious thought, but she'd have to be quick or the opening would be gone. It would mean goodbye to Adam for he wouldn't tolerate her going to college for five years; in fact, she knew he would actively persuade her not to try. The expression 'wouldn't tolerate' hung about in her mind and she thought, *What am I saying here? 'Wouldn't tolerate', is that love?* No, it most certainly wasn't. If he loved her Adam would be encouraging her surely?

Someone opened the door into the other bar and briefly she caught a reflection in the mirror behind the bar of someone standing there and she thought it was Adam. God! Now he was haunting her. Swiftly Kate finished her vodka and left.

Next morning, as though to confirm to her that Scott's advice was sound, the letter came from the solicitor with the cheque for ten and a half thousand pounds promised her in Granny Howard's will.

4

'Have you a first-class stamp, Mia? I want to get this letter in the post on the way to work. Before I change my mind.'

Mia passed her the fresh pot of tea. 'You've definitely decided, then?'

'Yes, I have. The shock of not getting three As totally threw me and I realise now I was far too hasty in giving up all hope of being a vet and applying for this job.'

'I thought you liked the job. Don't you?'

Kate pondered Mia's question for a moment. 'I like this job so very much. I like the people, I like the place, I like the animals, I like keeping the accounts in good order *but* at the same time I know I need more fulfilment. I'm not using my brain like I should and I know I would regret all my life not giving it another go.'

Mia patted her hand across the breakfast table. 'I've been dying for you to do this, but I knew it had to be wholly your decision. Your dad will be thrilled. It's what he wants for you too.'

'I know. I'm ringing Miss Beaumont tonight, see if she'll tutor me.'

'I thought that thin little man, I forget his name, taught you chemistry.'

'He did and I never got on with him because he was lazy. That's why I didn't get an A. He was useless. Miss Beaumont is brill, we got on really well.'

Mia brushed a strand of loose hair away from Kate's face. 'I'm so proud of you.'

'Thanks, Mia. I'm not telling anyone what I've done. Not till I've got a grade A, then if I don't, they won't be any the wiser.'

'I think Adam should know.'

Kate put down her slice of toast and studied Mia's loving face. 'He'll do his best to stop me.'

'He can't, though, can he, actually stop you. You're a free agent.'

'He'll finish with me.'

'Haven't you already finished with him?' The questioning look on Mia's face made Kate stare at her.

'Do you know, I think I already have, like you say. He's so peculiar at the moment. I don't even like him.'

'I certainly didn't like him the other night.'

'Truth to tell, you never really have liked him, have you?'

Mia fiddled with the sugar basin, put two spoonfuls into her cup and then, without thinking what she was doing, added another. 'It's that obsession of needing to do the same things at the same time every week. It demonstrates a strange kind of insecurity. Or is he a power freak? He lacks spontaneity. It's odd in such a young man. I never noticed it at first, or has it got worse?'

'Worse.'

'You see, it's only fair to tell him, because if you do get in it means him waiting another five years and he should know, or if he wants to find someone else, he knows where he is ... with you.'

Kate stood up to go, having seen the clock. 'Sometimes one has moments of blinding insight when one sees so clearly it's almost frightening.' Mia nodded. 'You asking me if I hadn't already finished with him made me realise that yes, I have. Trouble is, will he finish with me?' Kate shuddered slightly.

'Well, you must be honest, tell him outright, but very kindly. You know.'

'I know. Thank you, Mia, I don't know where I'd be without you.'

Staring into the distance, Mia answered, 'Whatever you do you mustn't drift into marriage just because someone is there and there isn't anyone else on the horizon, and he's comfortable and suitable. You musn't fool yourself. You've got to marry for love.'

'Did you marry for love?'

Mia looked up at her, smiling. 'Oh, yes! I married for love.' She reached out and, taking Kate's hand in hers, pressed it to her cheek.

Kate's face lit up with amazement. 'Not of me?'

Mia nodded.

'I didn't know. Thank you.' She was silent for a moment, taking in the full implication of Mia's words and of how she'd taken Mia's love all these years without giving it a thought, then brought things back to normality with, 'See you tonight. I'm split shift today so I'll go shopping this afternoon and be home about seven-thirty with any luck. If you and Dad are going out, don't worry about me. OK?' Kate bent to kiss Mia's cheek. 'Bye! Let *me* tell Dad.'

Bearing in mind Gerry's warning not to fritter away her granny's money, Kate decided to spend some of it that very afternoon. She desperately needed new clothes and she also intended treating herself to a nice lunch in the Bite to Eat café in the shopping precinct to celebrate having taken the big decision.

Most of the dress shops in her spending bracket had autumn sales on so after a splendid lunch, which she thoroughly enjoyed, she set off to spend, spend, spend.

It was a day for swift decisions and she made them. A suit, a party dress, some lingerie and a jacket. She came out of Next, turning left to head for her car, intending to put all her bags in the boot and to return for a pleasant reviving cup of tea on the Food Gallery surrounding the main shopping square. Kate set off at a pace and had gone quite a way when she realised she'd left the jacket she'd just bought in the shop. Without stopping to inspect her carriers to make sure, she swung round to return to the shop and bumped headlong into Adam.

'Ooh! Sorry! Adam! What a surprise! What are you doing here?'

Adam appeared as surprised as she was and twice as flustered. Kate asked him if he was not working today. 'Having a late lunch.' He looked at her, long and deep, and put out a hand to take her carriers. 'If you're leaving I'll help you with those to the car.'

'I've just bought a jacket in Next and I've left it on the counter, so I'm going back to get it.'

'I'll come with you, then.'

Kate retrieved her jacket and went with Adam to the car park. On the way she debated whether or not to go straight back to the practice, thus avoiding a talk with Adam, but she decided there was no time like now and asked him if he had time for a cup of tea. He glanced at his watch and accepted. 'I've put in a lot of hours this week. They can't complain.'

His Adam's apple was bobbing up and down quite vigorously and she wondered about the stress he must be under with this promotion. 'Are you settling in?'

'Settling in?'

'In your new job?'

'Oh, yes! Day off, is it?'

She explained about the split shift.

'I see.' He gazed over the balustrade, watching the shoppers walking about below. 'Nice spot, this. Come here often?'

'No, just sometimes. I got Granny Howard's money this week so, as I needed new clothes, I came shopping.'

'Come in handy, that will. Take care of it.'

'Handy for what?'

'Our deposit on a house.'

A terrible feeling of suffocation came over Kate and she had to breathe deeply to rescue herself. Things were much worse than she had thought; he must be losing his marbles.

'There's some nice starter homes being built the other side of town. I thought we might go and look at them.'

'You might, but I'm not.'

Adam picked up his cup and toasted her with it. 'To us. We'll look somewhere else, then.'

'We won't. I'm not ready to get married yet. Not for a long long while.' Now was the time to tell him what she'd done this morning on her way to work, but something in his eyes held her back from spilling the beans.

He continued eagerly as if she'd never spoken, 'I've just had the most tremendous idea. Mother's house is not suitable for an up-and-coming man. How about if she sells up and we use the money and your granny's to buy a bigger house, and we all live together. That way, if I were working long hours, which one does if one is in a top executive position, you'd always have someone at home for company and to give you a hand with the children. What do you think, eh? Good idea, isn't it?'

The nightmarish turn his conversation had taken scared Kate to death. Live with his mother! That martinet! That nitpicking, overindulged, idle hypochondriac of a woman! He must be going mad, or else she was. Kate, overcome by her inability to deal with the situation, glanced at her watch. 'Look at the time! I'm going to be late.'

'You've half an hour yet. What's the rush?'

'Anyone would think you hadn't a job to go to. Well, I have and I can't be late.'

'Think about it, will you, Kate?' He looked pleadingly at her.

'Adam, I've told you. I'm not ready to get married yet.'

'But I love you.'

His vulnerability, which she'd successfully ignored these last two or three weeks, struck her anew. She patted his clenched fist, saying, 'I know you do and I appreciate how you feel, but I don't want marriage and babies right now.'

'We'll go out for a drink tonight and we'll talk some more. I'll come round about eight. You've no other plans, have you?'

Kate sighed within herself. 'All right, then.'

She left him sitting at the table finishing his cup of tea. Looking back at him as she left the café she paused for a moment, trying to see him as others did. With great clarity of mind she recognised him as a loser: head down, shoulders bowed, clenched fists laid on the table he seemed ... Suddenly he looked directly at her and a shiver of fear ran down her spine. It confirmed as nothing else had done that Adam was not for her.

The clinic that afternoon was busy; it seemed to her that every single animal both large and small on their books had decided they were dying on their feet. Kate always found the four-till-seven clinic busy but this was ridiculous.

At five past four, little Miss Chillingsworth came in with her cat. 'I know I haven't an appointment, Kate dear, but she really is very poorly today.'

'Vomiting again?'

Miss Chillingsworth nodded bleakly. 'She can't keep a thing down. I've casseroled some chicken for her but she can't even manage that.'

Privately Kate thought Miss Chillingsworth would be all the better for eating the casserole herself, for today she seemed smaller and thinner than ever. 'Take a seat, Miss Chillingsworth, and I'll see what I can do. I've no doubt Mr Murgatroyd will find a space for you.'

Miss Chillingsworth's face lit up. 'Oh, he will when he knows it's me. He loves my Cherub.' As if to emphasise the fact, Cherub Chillingsworth howled pathetically. 'You see, she is in pain.'

Kate broke off to answer the phone and squeezed in yet another client appointment for Valentine Dedic in room three. Catching Graham between clients, Kate asked him if he would fit in Cherub Chillingsworth.

Graham grimaced. 'Not again. I swear there's nothing wrong with Cherub but old age and too much coddling. However, I will see her. Wheel her in after this next client. It's only a booster, shouldn't take long.'

Graham weighed Cherub and found she had lost weight, not much but enough to make him think Miss Chillingsworth might be right. 'Now see here, Miss Chillingsworth, we've done blood tests, found nothing, we've kept a close watch and found nothing, and now Cherub has lost weight again.'

'I knew she had, I could tell.' Miss Chillingworth's eyes flooded with tears.

'I'd like to X-ray her, her stomach and such, but ...'

'Yes?'

Graham propped himself against the examination table. 'But I hesitate to suggest it because it will cost money, you see, and you've already spent a lot. How do you feel about it? She's very old.' He checked the computer screen. 'Yes, as I thought, seventeen. That is old to go through an X-ray because she'll have to have an anaesthetic, you see, which won't be good for her.'

Her bottom lip was trembling but Miss Chillingsworth did her best not to let her voice shake. Defiantly she said, 'She may be old but she's . . . lively and still has a good quality of life, you know, when she's well.'

'I know. Yes, of course.' Gently Graham suggested, 'You could always go to the RSPCA. They can do it for nothing.'

Miss Chillingsworth was shocked. 'I am not in need of charity, Mr Murgatroyd, no, certainly not, and whatever Cherub needs she will get. I'll find the money.'

'Very well, but even if she has an X-ray that's no guarantee we can sort out what ails her. At her age . . .' Graham gravely shook his head.

'I know what you're trying to tell me, but Cherub and I will go down fighting.'

'Bring her tomorrow. Eight a.m. Can you manage that?'

Miss Chillingsworth drew herself up to her full height. 'Of course I can.' Picking up Cherub, who looked up at her owner as though having understood every word, Miss Chillingsworth went out of the consulting room.

Kate saw her sadness immediately and managed to catch Miss Chillingsworth's eye. 'How's things with Cherub?'

Miss Chillingsworth put Cherub gently on the reception counter and while Kate stroked the old cat comfortingly she got her answer. 'Dear Mr Murgatroyd, he's going to X-ray her tomorrow morning. Now, my dear, I want him to know he can do his very best for her without any anxiety about money. So can I put her in her carrying cage and leave her here while I go to the cash point and get the money out? I shall feel happier if it's here waiting and then Mr Murgatroyd can go ahead with whatever he needs to do.'

'There's really no need. You can pay tomorrow when you come to collect her. It's quite in order to do that.'

'No, my dear, I want the money here on the premises and I want you to tell Mr Murgatroyd it is here waiting and that he won't have to hold back on anything he needs to do.'

'But . . .'

'No, I insist. I don't like the idea he might think I'm too poor to pay and will take short cuts because of it. I shall feel more comfortable if he knows the money's waiting.'

'But I don't know how much it will be.'

'I shall bring one hundred pounds and if it's not enough I shall bring the balance. If it's too much then I know you'll take good care of it for me and give me back what's left over.'

'I don't know if I'm supposed to do this.'

'Well, then, it's just between you, me and Mr Murgatroyd. Now here's Cherub. You keep her behind the desk, she doesn't like all the dogs, you see.' She handed the cage over to Kate who put it on the floor near her feet.

'Mind how you go, Miss Chillingsworth.'

'I will.'

Lynne Seymour was on duty with Kate that night but somehow she had managed to disappear at the crucial moment when all hell was let loose. Two dogs had a serious go at getting a cat out of its basket, someone taking a sympathetic peep at their budgerigar let it out by mistake and to cap it all someone's dog cocked a leg down the front of the reception desk.

'Lynne! Lynne! Can you come, please?' Kate shouted and eventually at a pace more suited to a summer's afternoon stroll Lynne appeared.

'What's up?'

'What's up?' Kate was on the brink of giving her a piece of her mind but just then Miss Chillingsworth came back clutching her bag. She waited until peace was restored and handed the money to Kate.

'I'll give you a receipt; just a moment.'

'Don't worry, my dear. Please. I want to get home. Cherub must be tired.'

'I'd much rather . . .'

'Not at all.'

'Well, I'm on first thing tomorrow so . . .'

'Goodnight, dear. And thank you. Tell Mr Murgatroyd.' Miss Chillingsworth trotted out with her cat, waving cheerily to Kate. 'I'm full of hope for tomorrow.'

Kate didn't have her confidence. She wrote 'Miss Chillingsworth' on the envelope and put the money in a drawer under some papers until she had a moment to open the safe, which had to be done when two of them were free to do so.

The evening dragged its feet and by the time the last client had gone Kate was exhausted. Home, a meal and bed was all she could think about and then she remembered Adam was collecting her. Blast. She heard Graham and Valentine talking about the meal Valentine's wife had planned for the two of them, and Lynne and the two Sarahs agreeing to go to the Fox and Grapes.

Seeing a way of avoiding a whole evening chewing over Adam's plan of marrying her and dumping his mother on her, Kate asked, 'Could I join you there? Would you mind?'

Sarah Two looked at her and smiled. 'Why not? The more the merrier.'

'The only thing is Adam will be with me, do you mind?'

'Not at all. Lynne's dragging her two brothers out with her so we'll make a night of it. It'll be fun.'

'Thanks.'

In fact, the evening which Kate had dreaded but had hoped to rescue by giving Adam no chance to talk about their future turned into a complete disaster. First, Adam hadn't wanted to join them all but Kate had insisted. Lynne's brothers teased Adam mercilessly but in a very subtle way so that they were part-way through the evening before even Kate realised what they were up to.

Finally she made a move to leave while the night was still young.

'Don't go, the party's just getting going,' Lynne protested.

'I don't intend to sit here to watch Adam on the receiving end of your brothers' sarcasm. He's been very patient so far, but that's it. I've had enough.'

Eyebrows raised in surprise, Lynne pretended innocence. 'I don't know what you mean.'

'If you don't, they do.' Kate turned to the two young men and said, 'I think your behaviour has been childish in the extreme. It's about time you grew up and learned good manners. Goodnight.'

She stormed out, followed by Adam who had not recognised what they were up to. Kate, now thoroughly upset because she could hear the two of them laughing as they left the bar, turned the wrong way in the car park and had to ask Adam where his car was.

'It's over there on the other side. I thought they were interested in what I did. They kept asking questions.'

'Oh, they did, they were just leading you on. Didn't you see that? They are absolutely so arrogant. They think your job's the biggest joke ever.'

'Joke? But it isn't, it's important. What do they do, then?'

'They both work in the City at something exotic, which means they earn thousands and thousands a year. They were both at Oxford and think themselves exceedingly superior. Which in my opinion they most certainly are not.'

Adam unlocked his Toyota. 'I see.'

'Drive me home.'

'But they kept asking me questions about what my job involved.'

Kate sighed. 'Honestly, Adam, you are dim sometimes. They were mocking you. Couldn't you tell?'

'No.' He crashed the gears, which made him wince. 'I don't understand why they wanted to do it to me.'

'Well, you wouldn't, would you.' She shut her lips tight for fear she might tell him why. They'd set out to humiliate him because his job in their opinion – and she had to admit sometimes in hers too – was so ridiculously trivial as to be ludicrous and he hadn't realised it. She should have felt sorry for him but instead she felt nothing but . . . Well, go on, then, Kate Howard, what do you feel? That Adam was a joke? That her own self-worth made her not want to be associated with someone so full of his own importance that he couldn't recognise their blatant mockery? Sorry for him? A bit. But most of all she wanted to laugh. For a little while she smothered her true feelings and then they burst out of her in loud laughter. With her head thrown back, she simply roared.

The more she laughed the more annoyed Adam became. His driving turned erratic and finally he pulled into a layby at the side of the road, switched off the engine and folded his arms.

Kate had to stop out of consideration for Adam. The first thing she did when finally she could speak was to apologise. 'I'm so sorry, Adam. I don't know why I laughed. I shouldn't have done but I did. Those two arrogant, pompous . . . Who do they think they are?'

'I did say you shouldn't go to work at that place. I think you should give in your notice. In fact, I insist.'

'You do?'

'Oh yes!'

'You're on thin ice telling me what to do.' It was too dark for Adam to see her face. If he could have done he would have noticed that her lips were pressed firmly together.

'But if we are to make a go of it we ought to make decisions together.'

'But you've just *told* me what to do and I won't be told.'

'It's for the best if they're people like that.'

'They don't work with me, they just happen to be Lynne's brothers. This is getting nowhere. Drive me home.'

'See here . . .'

'See here nothing. Drive me home. Please.'

'I think there's one thing that should be understood between us: I'm the man and . . .'

'You are?'

'You're in a very funny mood tonight.'

Kate turned to look at him. 'I think we'd better finish, you and I, don't you?' Kate caught sight of his face in the headlights of an approaching car and wished to God she hadn't said what she'd said. 'You know, we're just not on the same wavelength any more and I think if we cooled it . . . you know . . . for a while . . .'

Adam gripped her forearm hard and pushed his face so close to hers that she could see in minute detail the tiny hairs in his nostrils and the beads of sweat on his upper lip. Taken totally unawares, Kate hadn't a chance to escape. With his blazing eyes focused on her own she knew real fear for the first time in her life. 'What are you doing? Adam! Let me go.'

His grip on her arm tightened. 'When I'm good and ready. If anyone is going to say we're finished it'll be me. Not you. You're mine, my girl. Do you hear? Mine.'

'Let go!' Kate tried to force his fingers from her arm but didn't succeed. 'Please!'

'You were laughing at *me*, weren't you? Not at them. *Me!*'

'I don't know who I was laughing at. Honestly. Just let go.'

His breathing was getting faster and deeper, as though his anger was coming to boiling point. His racing heart was pressed against the arm he held and the pain in it was increasing as fast as the fear in her heart. His other hand grasped her knee and Kate realised her predicament was becoming extremely serious. One wrong move and he'd do something she'd have to live with for the rest of her life.

He squeezed her knee hard.

'Get off me, Adam! What do you think you're doing? You're hurting me. Stop it!'

Her anger was inciting him to intimidate her further and she knew she'd have to change her strategy.

'I shan't ask you to go out with them again. You're right, as always, we won't bother with them any more.' His grip relaxed slightly. 'They're not worth it.' He relaxed a little more. 'They're cheap little nobodies, that's what, and not even amusing. I should have listened to you. You've more wisdom in your little finger than . . .' She reached up as though to stroke his hair. Catching him off guard, she took her chance. The chill night air hit her as she leapt in one swift movement out of the car and without stopping ran up the impossibly steep embankment on to the level bit at the top, then pelted hell for leather towards the chain of lights that she knew was Sainsbury's car park. For one blind, panicking moment she thought she heard Adam's footsteps behind her, but she was wrong. It was only his voice calling demandingly, 'Kate! Kate! Kate! Come here!'

Mia always insisted she have a phone card on her and Kate thanked her lucky stars she did. 'Dad! Dad!'

'Kate?'

'Dad! I'm at Sainsbury's, you know, the twenty-four-hour one. Can you come to pick me up? I'll wait in the main entrance.'

'What the blazes are you doing there at this time of night? Have you broken down?'

'No. Just come. I'll explain.' Gerry caught the panic in her as she began to make a mewing sound, too frightened now to speak.

'All right. All right. Calm down. Stay in the entrance where there's lights and somebody about. Ten minutes. Right.'

She fell into Mia's comforting arms and wept. 'I'm being stupid, Mia, I know I am, but I'm so frightened. He's not himself at all.'

'There, there, love, you're all right now. Mia's got you. Let's go, Gerry. You can tell me all about it when we get home.'

'Been trying it on, has he?'

'Gerry!'

'Might as well be honest about it. Well, has he?'

'No.'

'That's all right then.'

'Sometimes, Gerry Howard, you need to engage your brain before you speak. There, love, calm down now. Here's another tissue, look.'

'I don't know him any more. He's gone mad.'

The brandy her dad poured for her when they got home calmed her fear and Kate explained to them both why she'd had to ring. 'He went completely berserk. I should never have laughed, but it struck me as so funny that anyone could sit there all that time and never realise those chaps were taking the mickey. He's so full of his own importance, the stupid man.'

'Let me see your arm.' Mia turned to Gerry. 'He's bruised her arm. Just look at that bruise!' Gerry caught Mia's eye and frowned. Not a word passed between them but each knew what the other was thinking.

'Listen to me, my girl.' Gerry leant forward and took Kate's hand in his. 'If he rings and wants you to meet him somewhere you agree so's not to anger him, but *don't go*. Come home and tell Mia or me, and we'll stay at home with you. You're not to go with him anywhere at all, and if he's waiting outside the practice when you finish work go back in and get that nice Mrs Bastable to help. First thing tomorrow when I'm on the road I'm getting you a mobile phone.'

'Dad! There's no need. When it came to it Adam wouldn't hurt me.'

'Oh, really? Well, I say there is. If there's much more trouble with him I shall go to the police.'

'No. No. Don't do that! There truly is no need. It's just me being daft.'

Gerry pushed back her jumper sleeve and pointed to the bruising. 'Being daft? You say he loves you? Huh! You've heard what I've said and I mean it. Now, bed, with a couple of Mia's herbal thingamajigs to help you sleep.'

5

In the cold light of day Kate decided she'd panicked unnecessarily and that she'd made a complete idiot of herself over Adam. Her dad gave her a kiss as he left that morning and told her to be on red alert when he got back because he'd have her new phone with him. 'There's no need, honestly, Dad.'

'Can't a dad buy his daughter a present now and again?'

'OK, then, and I shall be glad of it.'

Mia waved Gerry off to work and came back in to sit with Kate while she ate her breakfast. She poured Kate a fresh cup of tea and asked her if she wanted more toast.

'Yes, I will. Are you eating this morning?'

'Don't feel like it.'

'Mia, you must. You're not worrying about me, are you? I'm all right now. I've come to my senses this morning, got things in proportion, you know. Come on, have this other slice of mine, I only need one.'

'All right, then. I will.'

'I've got to hurry, I don't want to be late.'

'You enjoy it, don't you?'

'Yes. Miss Chillingsworth's bringing Cherub in this morning. She's such a dear old thing and so worried about her cat. When you haven't got a pet of your own you don't realise how much people care about them till you see them in tears.'

Mia patted her arm. 'Don't take it too much to heart, will you, or you'll spend all your veterinary career weeping.'

'What career?' Kate had to laugh. 'You're right, there's no room for tears, is there?'

'I bet that Scott gets upset over things.'

'I believe he does.'

'He's a nice chap.'

Kate giggled. 'He is; women eat out of his hand.'

'Given half a chance, so could I.' They both giggled with mouths full of toast.

'I'm off.'

Kate parked her car in her usual place, picked up her bag, got out and as she locked the car she glanced up at the hills and drew in a deep breath. This weekend she'd go walking – with weather like this who could resist. There was a slight mist at the peak of Beulah Bank Top. Other than that it was as clear as clear, looking out across the hills. The wind was slightly blustery but pleasant. Kate dropped her car key, bent down to retrieve it and, as she straightened up, caught sight of the mawkish purple of Adam's car, all by itself at the top of the car park where the staff never needed to park.

If she'd been electrocuted she couldn't have felt greater physical fear. Her scalp prickled and her hair felt as if it stood on end. She staggered to the safety of reception as best she could. Halfway there it occurred to her that he might already be inside, for she was certain he wasn't sitting in the car. Or was he? Should she look? She glanced briefly over her shoulder. He didn't appear to be, Joy! Joy was on duty this morning. Joy.

She pushed open the glass door and called out to her, 'Has anyone been asking for me?'

Joy looked up. 'No. Should they be?'

'No, not really. There's no one been, then?'

'No, definitely not. I'm the only one here. My dear, what's the matter?'

'To be honest, it's just me being ridiculous.' Nevertheless she went into the laundry room, which gave her a view of the car park, and Adam's car wasn't there. She was definitely going mad. How could she be so stupid? What on earth would he be doing at this side of town at this time in the morning when his office was seven miles out on the other side? Come to that, though, what was he doing in town yesterday, having what he called a late lunch? Being paranoid about time, he would never take the risk of driving so far and back and eating lunch all in an hour. She must have dreamt his car was there. It couldn't possibly have been.

As she put on her uniform and sorted out her mind for the day ahead she remembered Miss Chillingsworth and ... Miss Chillingsworth's money. Heavens above, she'd never put it in the safe.

Kate went straight to the drawer where she'd put it for safe keeping, pushed her hand under the papers and couldn't feel the envelope. The phone rang twice for farm calls before she could get back to searching again. She took all the papers out of the drawer and put them back in one by one. No, the envelope hadn't slipped between anything at all. It was missing. She stood, looking at the drawer. Had she got the right one? Yes, she had. Had she and Lynne put it in the safe and she'd forgotten? The moment Lynne came out of the loo she'd ask her.

'I don't know anything about any money. We certainly didn't put it in the safe. I would have remembered. Sorry.'

Joy, watering the plants on the windowsills, overheard and asked what money they were talking about.

Now very worried about the whole incident, Kate went across to Joy to explain what had happened.

'You shouldn't have accepted the money, you know, Kate.'

'I know that, I was only trying to help. She was worried that Graham wouldn't do all he could for fear of embarrassing her about the money. Which I don't think she has, really. I think she's short but can't bear the thought of losing Cherub. She only wanted us to know the money was *there*.'

Joy emptied the watering can on the last plant, tested the soil with her fingers and said after a moment, 'Well, now it isn't. We have a golden rule, you see. Any money taken during the day must be entered and accounted for *on that day*. Otherwise, with different people being on duty we'd get into no end of a mess. Lynne should have done the sheet last night before she left and that hundred pounds should have been on it.'

'I know, but we were so busy we could have done with three of us on. She did do the sheet, but of course the hundred pounds wasn't on.'

'You did it with the best of intentions, I know, but I shall have to report it. You've thoroughly searched the drawers?'

'I've searched the one I put it in, yes.'

'Had everything out?'

Kate nodded.

'Say nothing at all to Miss Chillingsworth. She's brought Cherub, has she?'

'No, which is surprising because she promised to be here at eight.'

'That's odd. Leave it with me. I'll tell Mungo in my own time, but it'll have to be today.'

Kate had to say the words she didn't want to have to say: 'I haven't stolen it, I promise you that.'

Joy looked her in the face, frankly and openly. 'You don't need to say that to me, my dear. I know that. You're as honest as the day is long.'

'Thank you. I'm so sorry about it and if it doesn't turn up I'll find the money, because it was my responsibility.'

'That's a very fair offer but I can't accept it. You haven't worked here a month yet so I know for a fact you haven't received a penny in salary.'

'Yes, but my Granny Howard left me some money in her will and I got it this week, so by coincidence it isn't a problem.'

Joy patted her arm. 'Leave it with me.'

One by one the two Sarahs and Lynne were called into Joy's office for a discussion about the missing money. Hidden away in the accounts office, Kate was in anguish fretting and fussing over it, thinking of all the possibilities of where it could have gone. When she heard Mungo's footsteps coming down the stairs from the flat her heart sank. It could mean her instant dismissal and she didn't want that.

Joy called out, 'Mungo! Have you a minute?' Joy's office door was briskly snapped to and Kate knew her fate hung in the balance.

'Good morning, Joy. What's up? Can't be long, my first appointment's in ten minutes and I've still got the notes to read up.'

'Sit down. Won't keep you two minutes.'

Mungo folded his long body into a chair and waited. Loving him hopelessly, as she had for twenty years, Joy still experienced an instant explosion of happiness when she saw him. Was it his lean, intelligent face, his perfectly beautiful large brown eyes under their heavy brows, his handsome head of thick, well-cut black hair, or simply his lovableness which enraptured her?

'Yes?'

'Sorry. We have a problem. One hundred pounds has disappeared.' He listened gravely while Joy told him the whole story.

'Kate was trying to help, you see.'

'Help? Surely she knew our rules.'

'Of course, but she thought about efficiency well larded with compassion and it was the compassion that won.'

'She should have had more sense, a girl with her intelligence.'

'We are short-handed at the moment, Mungo, as you well know. She's new and was doing her best to cope.'

'New or not she should have known better.'

'And hurt Miss Chillingsworth?'

'The very least she could have done was to put it in the safe.'

'Exactly. I know that. I've interviewed the others and they claim no knowledge of the incident. Lynne was there when Kate put it in the drawer, but it doesn't mean she saw her do it and it doesn't mean she didn't. As I say, they were very busy last night.'

'So what does Kate propose to do about it?'

'She's offered to pay back the money.'

'Hm.'

'Well?'

'She'll have to be dismissed. Today.'

An angry flush flooded Joy's cheeks and she exploded with temper. 'Oh, no, she won't. I won't have it. She's the best girl we've employed in years. Efficient, caring, quick to learn, enthusiastic, hard-working, I don't want to lose her. I know, positively know, she isn't the kind who would steal. In any case I have her word on that and I believe her. We're short enough as it is. Bunty isn't back until next week and we're still one receptionist short. If you're prepared to do the accounts ...'

'You'll cope.'

'I won't.'

'I can't spirit new staff out of the air.'

'I don't expect you to, that's my job. I've only informed you because I must. You've always left the staffing to me. Anyway, I wasn't asking for your advice, simply telling you what had happened.'

'So ... I still say she should be dismissed.'

Joy tried a different tactic. 'I've worked for you for twenty years and striven always to do my best through thick and thin, but if you insist on Kate's dismissal then you'll have to dismiss me too.'

Mungo looked at her, eyebrows raised in amazement. 'You too? What do you mean? We can't manage without you. You know everything there is to know about this practice.'

'I'm not a permanent fixture here, you know, I am free to go if I wish.'

'But you wouldn't leave me!'

'Wouldn't I just! Might be the best move I've made in years. Better for all concerned. Fresh start. Break the old ties. I'll go to the practice in the High Street. I understand they could do with some help since we've opened up here.'

Mungo was lost for words.

'I know why you're taking this stance. I saw what you saw when Kate looked up and smiled at you when she was stroking Perkins. She brings back too many memories for you, doesn't she? Dismissing her would be a good way of ridding yourself of the problem.'

'You're being bloody stupid, Joy, or more likely bloody-minded. Sometimes you lose your sense of proportion, you know, always have done at moments of crisis.' He stood up and turned away from her to look out of the window, aware he'd been more rude to her than he had ever been and knowing she was right about Kate: that look she had given him at the lunch had rocked the boat and no mistake.

'Well, there's been plenty of moments of crisis working for you, believe me.' As an afterthought and between clenched teeth she snapped, 'And don't you dare swear at me.'

Mungo recognised the fury in Joy's voice and knew he'd gone too far. He held up a placatory hand. 'I'm sorry, love. Truly sorry. I shouldn't have lost my temper and I shouldn't have sworn. I won't tolerate theft, though. We have to be seen to take steps. React in whatever way you think fit. I'll leave it to you. Must go.' He opened the door, then looked back at her and smiled as only Mungo could. 'I'm sorry. You know? Friends?'

Her anger at his attitude melted away at his smile and she said, 'Friends.'

She could hear him greeting his clients and their dog, using all his charm to ease their anxiety and succeeding, for the clients were eating out of his hand before they even reached the consulting room. Joy smiled a little grimly at the way all his clients worshipped the ground he walked on. No wonder, though, because he was immensely good at his job. However, he couldn't solve her present crisis, could he, for all his charm and talent.

At lunchtime Joy issued an ultimatum. If the missing money was back in the drawer by the time they closed the cash sheet for the night then nothing more would be said. She knew she was avoiding the main issue entirely and that, in fact, it solved nothing, but at the moment it was all she could come up with.

During the afternoon Miss Chillingsworth was discovered by Kate sitting quietly in the reception area, having made no one aware of her arrival. 'Why, Miss Chillingsworth, you've come. I'll tell Mr Murgatroyd.'

Her tear-stained face told Kate all. 'Oh, no! Oh, dear, I am sorry.'

'In the night.'

'What happened . . . you know?'

'I am sorry. In the night I woke up and had this dreadful feeling inside. I went downstairs to the kitchen and there she was. She'd struggled out of her basket by the Aga – she always sleeps there: it's warm all night, you see – and was lying on the floor, breathing all funny, and I picked her up and loved her, and she died as I held her.' Tears rolled down her face.

Kate took a clean tissue from her pocket and offered it to Miss Chillingsworth, but she was too overcome to notice, so Kate gently wiped away her tears for her. 'What a lovely way for her to go, though, in your arms. That must have been so comforting for her.'

'She looked up at me as if she knew, just knew it was all over.

Seventeen years we've been together, the two of us. I'm not going to be able to go back into the house and find her not there, but I had to let you know because you were expecting me.'

'Well, that was kind of you, to come to tell us. A cup of tea. How does that sound?'

'Thank you, dear. Yes, that would be nice.'

Kate told Graham and he came out of his consulting room to see her. 'Miss Chillingsworth, let's go in the back and you can tell me all about it.'

'Oh, Mr Murgatroyd! What am I going to do?'

'You're going to be thankful that Cherub found a lovely way to go. She didn't have to be anaesthetised for the X-ray and she didn't have to go through an operation. She just quietly slipped away as though she knew it was of no use whatever we did. Be glad for her.'

'Oh! Mr Murgatroyd, you expressed that quite beautifully. I should be glad, shouldn't I, that she didn't have to suffer anything at all but simply went to her Maker as gently as she could.'

'Exactly. And what's more she had you to comfort her, didn't she?'

'You're right and I did.'

He handed her the tea Kate had brought her and watched her drink it, while he searched for the right words to say. 'Sometimes I think animals are wiser than we humans realise. They seem to have an intuitive sense about when the end is in sight. It's almost as if they are resigned to what happens to them and it makes life easier for them finally. They don't fight what is happening to them, if you see what I mean.' He paused for a moment, and then asked, 'So if I might mention it, where is she now?'

There was a short silence, then Miss Chillingsworth said, 'I've buried her in my garden under a tree she liked to climb in her youth. I did the whole funeral service for her, every word. I just hope the good Lord didn't mind her being a cat.'

Graham patted her shoulder and looked away.

'I'll take my money, that is if you don't mind. You won't need it now.'

'Of course. TTFN, Miss Chillingsworth.'

She got to her feet. 'Tommy Handley! Fancy you knowing about him. I shall miss our little chats. You're a dear boy.' They shook hands and she left to collect her one hundred pounds and he to catch up with his client list.

Kate needn't have gone to the cash point in her lunch break to get out the money, for the envelope with 'Miss Chillingsworth' written on the front of it in Kate's own hand was in the drawer ready and waiting.

Kate watched Joy hand it over and she broke out in a sweat of relief – relief which couldn't be measured.

When Miss Chillingsworth had left Joy winked at her. 'You needn't have gone to the bank.'

'But who . . . ?'

'No idea. But in future you make very sure all money is registered and banked. For whatever reason do not promise to take care of money for clients. Ever. There's a powerful lesson to be learned from this.'

'I know. What I can't understand is who and why?'

Joy had her suspicions but had vowed to keep them to herself and to keep a closer watch in future. She replied, 'Can't answer that because I don't know.'

Scott came in at about four, just as Kate was leaving. 'Sweet one! Long time no see. Just finished? Great!'

'Why?'

'Why?' Scott clapped a hand to his forehead in mock despair. 'She asks why. Because I've had a rotten day and need your company.'

'I see.'

'You haven't a prior engagement. Have you?'

'Are you leaving right now?'

'Just got these samples to hand over to Joy for despatch and then I'm all yours.'

'I'll wait in my car.'

Out of the corner of her eye Kate saw Lynne watching her with a slightly malevolent expression on her face and it occurred to Kate that it might be Lynne who'd removed the envelope from the drawer. But of course she wouldn't have, not Lynne. Now had it been Stephie . . .

Scott slid into the seat next to her and grinned. 'So where shall we go?'

'Actually, I can't go anywhere tonight because . . .'

'You're not going out with that Adam fella, are you?'

'What if I am?'

'I've told you he's a nutter.'

Memories of running along the embankment towards Sainsbury's car park flooded back. She avoided the issue by saying, 'If I tell you where I'm going you're not to breathe a word. Right?'

'Cross my heart and hope to die.'

'This is my first night going for tutoring for chemistry.'

Scott turned a delighted face to her. 'You're not! You've decided, then.'

Kate nodded.

'Well, I am pleased. Really pleased. You've made the right decision.

Yes, definitely. My chemistry is rusty but if you need any help, shout for Scott.'

'She's a great teacher and thrilled to be helping me.'

'Good girl! This calls for a celebration.'

'I need to eat before I go.'

'Quite right. Won't Mia be expecting you?'

'She will. I'll go back in and give her a ring.'

Scott scuffed about in the cavernous pockets of his Barbour and proffered her his mobile. 'Here, use this.'

'I don't know how.'

He squeezed closer to her and showed her how to make a call.

Kate spoke to Mia and explained. 'Now, how do I switch it off?'

'I'm amazed you haven't got one of your own. Time you did.'

'I shall have, tonight, if Dad does what he says.'

'He thinks you should have one, does he?'

'He does. Your car or mine?'

'Mine, of course. The whole inside absolutely stinks so I'll put a cloth over the passenger seat. It still hasn't recovered from my episode with the slurry pit.'

Kate smiled. 'I keep having a laugh about that, I thought it was so funny.'

'Thanks! Trust a Pommy to find it amusing. Doesn't say much for your sense of humour.'

'Oh! Sorry. It's a sign of maturity, you know, to be able to laugh at oneself.'

'Is it, now?' He spread a clean cover over the seat and she climbed in.

'Where are we going?'

When he looked at her there was that same gleam in his eye that she'd seen before and she felt a blush creeping over her cheeks. His admiring gaze stayed on her face while he said, 'People who show dogs use the expression "it fills the eye", meaning it's a first-rate dog with that special something that they're keen to find. That's just what you're doing tonight, filling my eye.' He leant towards her and placed a gentle kiss on her lips. Nothing more. 'Not the Fox and Grapes, I think. No, this calls for the King's Arms.'

'I'm not dressed for the King's Arms.'

He assessed her suitability by examining her from head to foot. 'Like I said, you fill my eye, so there's no need to worry. I've a clothes brush in the back for emergencies like these and I'll brush my trousers before I go in, and then we'll both be suitable. What the hell, they won't be feeding us for nothing, you know, so they'll put up with us, believe me.'

'I expect you know them all.'

'I do.'

'Thought so.'

And he did. He was greeted like an old friend by waiters and bar staff alike.

'Is there anywhere that food is served that you haven't tried?'

'Not many.'

They all looked curiously at her and she guessed he'd been in there with other girls before her. She wouldn't ask. What she didn't know wouldn't hurt her, as Mia would say.

They both ordered steak with French fries and vegetables, and Scott asked for lager for himself and cider for Kate. While they waited they discussed work.

'What's this I hear about Mungo and Joy having a row about you? What have you been up to? Explain yourself.'

She rounded off her explanation by saying that she could hear the raised voices but not the words and that they both sounded furious with each other but not angry about her at all.

'Ah! Well, didn't you realise that Joy carries a torch for Mungo? Has for years, apparently.'

'But she's married.'

'So? People marry for all kinds of reasons.'

'But she wouldn't, not Joy.'

'Wouldn't what?'

'Love someone else when she was married.'

'Like I said, people marry for all kinds of reasons.'

'So in your opinion why did she marry that nice man Duncan?'

'I haven't the faintest idea.'

'You're no help at all. I'll ask Bunty when she comes back on Monday. She'll know. She knows everything about everybody.'

'Does she?' Scott took a long drink of his lager and asked casually, 'She's been away two weeks, is it?'

'She's left-handed, so she couldn't assist at operations with things all bandaged up, or whatever.'

'All bandaged up?'

'Her finger.'

'Explain.'

'She dislocated the little finger on her left hand in an accident playing netball at school and since then it's kept dislocating itself on the slightest excuse, and it's so painful when it happens and puts her out of action for a few days each time, so they've operated on it and hopefully this will cure it for good.'

Kate realised that Scott was paying very close attention to every word she spoke. 'OK? Is there anything else you'd like to know? Like her blood group, for instance?'

'Is this true?'

'Why would I lie? Of course it's true.'

Why Bunty's finger being operated on should silence Scott Kate had no idea, but it did. He cheered up a little when they ordered their ice-cream sundaes and was forcing himself to be chirpy by the time their bill arrived at the table.

'Mustn't be long.' He looked at his watch. 'Nearly time to go. The sundae wasn't as good as the Fox and Grapes.'

'You're right. Thank you, though, I have enjoyed it. I'll be off. I shall need a lift back to the practice to pick up my car, if you wouldn't mind.'

'Of course. Yes.'

He waited until she'd started her car and returned her wave as she drove out of the car park.

So the question was, was Bunty pregnant and remaining so or had she fooled him completely by making him think she was away from work having an abortion when all the time she was having her damned finger operated on and she wasn't pregnant at all? Or was the dislocated finger a blind to cover a trip to an abortion clinic? If she was pregnant and she intended keeping the baby, should he do the right thing? Not likely. Marriage wasn't for him and most definitely not for him and Bunty. Women! Why did he bother? Well, he knew why he bothered but why did he always bother with the wrong ones? Answer: because they were the most fun.

But Kate was the exception. She was delicious, in a quiet, innocent kind of way. Refreshing, untouched. That was what made her so fascinating. And a virgin, because that Adam wouldn't have the guts. Well, he'd better not have. That clumsy, blundering nutter would have as much subtlety when making love as a bull in a china shop. But if she got her chemistry A level then that would be the key to getting her away from that blasted Adam. What was it about that nutter that made an insensitive, unperceptive Aussie feel such concern? The question hung about at the back of his mind all weekend.

6

On the Monday morning, having decided to tackle Bunty first thing before he went on his calls, he found her in the laundry room sorting the operating linen from Sunday. 'You're better, then.'

Bunty's bright-blue eyes met his. They stared at one another for a moment and Scott asked her again if she was better.

She turned back to the washing machine. 'As well as can be expected in the circumstances.'

'What are the circumstances?' He'd shed his normal casual approach to everything outside his work and was standing, hands out of his pockets, waiting to pounce like a panther. Bunty might not have been looking at him but she was fully aware this was a different Scott from the one she had known that hot, passionate night they'd shared.

'Well?'

She still didn't answer, so he covered the space between them in a moment and took hold of her arm. 'Look me in the face and tell me straight out. Why have you been absent from work?'

'Worried?'

'No, I am not. Just asking on a need-to-know basis, that's all.'

Bunty dropped the last of the bloodied linen into the machine and faced him. Holding up her left hand still encased in a plastic glove she said, 'Operation on finger. OK?'

A huge sweat of relief came out on Scott's body, which just as quickly disappeared when he realised how she'd tried to trick him. 'You lied to me. That's nasty, that is, Bunty, downright evil to lie about something as important as that.'

'Disappointed there isn't going to be a little Scott Spencer for you to coo over?'

'I would have walked away quick-smart, believe me, nothing surer. You could bet your life on it.'

'That's nice, that is.'

'It isn't, but it's the truth.'

'Typical man.'

'Believe me, I don't feel good about what's happened, but it did take two of us and I most certainly didn't force you.'

Bunty peeled off the plastic gloves, flung them in the bin and stormed out. Scott shrugged his shoulders. He caught up with her as she began preparing the operating room for the day. Putting his head round the door he said, 'By the way, you've not switched the machine on.' He slammed the door shut before whatever it was she'd thrown at him reached its target.

As he retreated he bumped into Joy who was looking for him. 'Scott! There you are. Your list awaits you. What are you up to?'

Scott flung his arms round her and kissed her on both cheeks.

'You naughty boy! What brought that on?'

'My reprieve! I'm on my way. I reckon I'm the only one who does any work around here.'

'You're not, believe me.' Joy watched him disappear into reception and went to greet Bunty on her first day back.

'Hello, Bunty. Now, how are you, dear?'

'I'm fine, thanks, Joy. Quite glad to be back. Mum's been fussing over me all the time.'

'So she should. You be thankful she did.'

'Yes, I expect you're right.'

'You're still looking peaky, though. Are you sure you should be back?'

Bunty was laying out instruments on the trolley and, without turning round, she said, 'I'm fine, thanks. Fine.'

'Finger working OK? Let me look.'

Bunty waggled her finger in the air. 'They've done a good job. I'll need a morning off in two weeks for a check-up.'

'Tell me the date and I'll fix it on the roster.'

Bunty nodded. 'Thanks.'

Joy, glad that the nursing side of her responsibilities was fully manned, closed the door behind her and went out to reception. On the counter were the appointment lists for the small-animal vets and the lists of calls for the farm practice side. She briefly checked them through. Rhodri and Scott were out on call this morning with Zoe, and Colin, now he was back, would be starting work at one. Graham and Valentine would be consulting this morning. Mungo's list was crammed with appointments all morning and he had two operations in the afternoon. She studied the names of his clients. Some she knew, others ... The phone rang. The Welsh accent gave the caller away.

'I'm sorry but Rhodri is out on call all morning. I thought he'd asked you not to call him any more at work. I can't employ staff to field his personal calls and I've told him so, and he promised it would stop. I'm sorry.'

When she replaced the receiver Joy pulled a face at Kate. 'Honestly, that woman! You'd think she'd have more pride, wouldn't you?'

'You would.'

Clients always checked in at reception when they came, and a steady stream of them and lots of phone calls kept Joy and Kate busy for the next half-hour.

It was Kate who answered the next time Megan Jones rang. 'I'm so sorry but Rhodri is still out on call. He's attending a whelping and it could be all morning. After that he has a full list of appointments. Good morning.'

Kate put the receiver back and said, 'That's a new line. Now she's talking about a sheep needing looking at.'

Joy raised her eyebrows and laughed. 'Our Rhodri must have a lot more to him than we realise.'

'I think he's really nice.'

'He is. But he's a dyed-in-the-wool bachelor. Forty and set in his ways.'

'Pity, that, he'd make a nice dad.'

'You're right, I think he would. How's your Adam?'

Kate didn't answer straight away, having a client who'd made a mistake about his appointment time and was over an hour late.

'Please take a seat. I'll tell Mr Dedic you're here and he'll fit you in. Yes, you're right, it is difficult to read the time on your card. We'll have to make sure we write more clearly next time. I haven't seen Adam for over a week, we've had a fallout.'

Joy looked speculatively at her. 'You don't appear to be unduly worried.'

'I'm not. He's started getting possessive and ordering me about, and I won't have it. Also he's boring.' She looked at Joy and smiled a little bleakly.

'I see. It's none of my business but I'm quite glad, I didn't think he was the one for you.'

'You didn't? Neither does Mia.'

'She seems nice; in fact, very nice.'

'She is a love. She's been so good to me. We get on so well. Same sense of humour, you know.'

'How long has she been your stepmother?'

'Since I was eighteen months old. I've no recollection of my own mother at all.'

'Your mother died, did she?'

Kate found a client far more important than answering Joy's question and Joy took the hint. Obviously it was delicate ground and she'd better keep off it. If Kate hadn't seen Adam for more than a week why had Adam's nauseous purple car been parked down a side street on Friday, obviously waiting to catch Kate leaving work? A shudder went down Joy's spine and she wondered if she should say something. She'd ask Duncan what he thought.

At this moment Rhodri bounded in, back from his whelping. 'Nine! And they're all beauties. All alive and kicking, born without a hitch. The first one was crossways on, that was the problem, and hey presto, after I'd straightened him up they popped out like shelled peas.' He was exhilarated and completely wound up with excitement. He clutched Joy round the waist and twirled her round saying, 'Nine! All beauties worth five hundred pounds apiece. Mrs Kent is so grateful.' He released Joy.

She pulled her uniform back into place and wagged a finger at him. 'I need a word with you.' Taking his hand, she pulled him into her office.

'Aren't you glad for me? My reputation has rocketed sky high with that Mrs Kent. She's weeping with gratitude, having thought she was going to lose both the bitch and the puppies.'

'Of course I am, but . . . this morning we've had two calls from that Megan Jones. I thought you'd stopped her ringing.'

Rhodri groaned. 'Not again. I told her, I did, I really did. She doesn't ring me at home any more. Honest, Joy bach.'

'I believe you. But one more and . . .'

'What?'

'I shall have a word with her. She's even mentioning sheep now, saying she has one in need of veterinary attention. I mean! It's her in need of the veterinary attention not a sheep.'

Rhodri spread his arms wide. 'What can I do? Eh? Advise me.'

'Well, I think you should . . . What the blazes is going on?'

Even though Joy's office door was closed both of them could hear the commotion outside in reception and Rhodri was convinced he could hear a sheep bleating.

'My God! That sounds like a sheep.'

'Don't be ridiculous.'

'It is. It's a sheep.'

They both rushed out into the reception area to discover a woman standing there with a full-grown sheep on a lead. It wasn't enjoying its adventure and was tossing its head and stamping its feet, and bleating for all it was worth. The woman, well-dressed in a Barbour jacket, brown cords and smart brown leather boots, appeared unconcerned by the commotion she was causing.

Kate was saying, 'Please, we don't have sheep in here, this is for small animals only. Please take it out.'

'I have been endeavouring to get a vet to come to my farm and attend to this sheep, but each time I get an answer someone says that I can't speak to Rhodri Hughes as he's at a whelping. I don't want to speak to Rhodri Hughes, at a whelping or not. All I want is someone to look at my Myfanwy and tell me what's wrong with her.'

'You're . . .?' Kate asked.

'Megan Jones, Beulah Farm. We're new.'

It was Kate who found her voice first. Joy and, in particular, Rhodri were too struck dumb with surprise and embarrassment to answer. 'Ah! It's a case of mistaken identity. I'm so sorry. We've been having nuisance phone calls, you see, from someone called Megan Jones and we mistook your calls for hers. I am very sorry.'

'There must be hundreds of Megan Joneses all over the world, so I can understand your mistake.'

'Look, Mrs Jones . . .'

'Miss.'

'Sorry, Miss Jones, would you be so kind as to take Myfanwy outside and I'll get a vet to come to have a look at her. Or if you prefer you could take her back home and someone will visit.'

Miss Jones thought this over for a moment and decided she'd have someone look at her straight away. 'It is urgent, you see.'

Rhodri, poleaxed by his first impressions of this new Megan Jones, found his voice and said, 'Could I be of any assistance?'

Miss Jones studied him coolly.

He nodded vigorously to encourage her to agree to him examining Myfanwy.

She nodded. 'Are you experienced with sheep?'

Joy knew he wasn't, not since his college days, and waited with bated breath to hear what appalling fib he was going to use to ingratiate himself.

'Oh, yes! My favourite animal. Dorset Horn, isn't she?'

Inwardly Joy groaned.

Miss Jones nodded. 'Yes. Come on, then, boyo.' Myfanwy took some persuading to leave and it needed Rhodri, Miss Jones and Joy to get her out through the door. As she and Rhodri heaved and pushed from the rear, while Miss Jones pulled from the front, Joy muttered, 'For God's sake mind what you do. If in doubt, shout.'

Finally Myfanwy was forced into departing. Joy returned to the desk and Kate asked quietly, 'Does he know anything at all about sheep?'

'Not a damn thing, not since college, anyway. I've never known him do a thing like this before, he must have gone mad.'

'By the looks of Rhodri he believes he's met his soulmate.' Kate laughed.

If Joy hadn't been so anxious she would have laughed too. 'I'm going to wash my hands – I stink of sheep – then I'm taking a peep outside from the laundry window. You look after the shop.'

One of the regular clients called out, 'Kate! There's one thing about coming here: you do see life. It's the first Monday so Adolf will be here soon. I just hope Graham's running late with his appointments or I shall miss the fun.'

'Oh, drat! I'd forgotten.'

Kate raced off into the laundry room for the fire bucket but got tempted into joining Joy at the window. Rhodri and Megan were holding an earnest discussion.

'Joy, are we witnessing the meeting of true minds here?'

'I reckon we just might be. This could be a moment in history to be savoured.'

'I wish these windows weren't double glazed and we could hear what they're saying.'

'Kate, honestly!'

'I wonder if she likes ferrets.'

'Had we better warn her before things get too advanced? Oh, look! There's Mr Featherstonehough's old van.'

'Adolf!'

Kate grabbed the fire bucket, Joy fled to shut the door to Mungo's flat, and Rhodri and Megan were left to discuss the nitty-gritty of Myfanwy's symptoms unobserved.

Both Joy and Kate were intrigued to know what had happened between the two of them but Rhodri returned by the back door and went straight to his consulting room without entering reception. The first they heard of his return was him singing 'Land of my fathers' in his wonderful tenor voice with such enormous enthusiasm that one was made deeply aware of the passion therein, but whether or not the passion was for Wales or for Miss Megan Jones they could only guess. Kate and Joy raised their eyebrows at one another and laughed, but not for long.

Miriam came down from the flat, carrying a cake for the staff in honour of Mungo's birthday, and before they knew it Perkins was down the stairs and in reception, going like an arrow for Adolf.

Joy shouted, 'I don't believe it!' But she was too late. He'd passed her and Perkins and Adolf were in the throes of yet another major fight. She grabbed the bucket and emptied it over them but they were too quick for her and she missed them both. 'Oh, no!'

Kate grabbed the bucket again and fled to fill it up, returned, aimed again and this time scored a hit. The two dogs broke apart and both shook off the water right in front of Joy, and drenched her before she could leap back.

'You two naughty boys! What are we going to do with you? Look at me.' The only sympathy she got from them was Perkins grinning at her. Adolf completely ignored her and went to sit, propped against Mr Featherstonehough and wetting his trouser legs in the process.

'Dry-cleaning bills, that's what you'll be getting next.'

Miriam apologised. 'I'm so sorry, it was my fault, I left the door open to our flat. I just don't know how Perkins knows you're here.'

'Neither do I. I could always move and go to that place in the High Street.'

'Well, of course, the choice is yours but we'd hate to lose you.' Miriam smiled her most enchanting smile.

Mr Featherstonehough, a rare old womaniser in his time, couldn't resist her charms and melted before her eyes. He rubbed a wry hand over his bristly chin and said slyly, 'Of course I could be persuaded to stay. Like I say, your staff are all so pretty, especially that one who spills out of her uniform.'

Miriam pretended to be shocked. 'Well, really, I must say, so that's why you're a client of ours. It's our attractive staff, not the expertise.'

'And you too, Mrs Price. I could do with you holding Adolf for his injection. Very nicely I could.'

'You flirt, you!' Miriam patted his arm and left with Perkins amid muffled giggles from the other clients waiting their turns.

That night at Mungo's birthday dinner Joy related the episode with Mr Featherstonehough to Mungo and he found it hugely amusing. 'The old reprobate. Threatening to leave me, is he? Well, he won't. We go back a long way, him and me. He wouldn't possibly leave *me*.'

His words were an echo of the ones he'd used to Joy when she'd threatened to leave the practice and she raised an eyebrow at him but he avoided her eyes. 'Do you know, he was my first client, was old Mr F. He had a huge Rottweiler then called Fang, a massive creature, totally unpredictable. He clamped his teeth on my arm more than once, the nasty devil.' Mungo pushed back his shirt cuff and showed a scar. 'See! I begged him to have him put down, but he wouldn't and then the dog bit his wife, and I mean bit, cracked a couple of bones in her wrist, he did, and she issued him an ultimatum: either the dog went or she did. It took him a week to make up his mind, which wasn't very flattering to his wife, but eventually he came in one day heartbroken and declared that he wanted him put down. He wept. Left the surgery with tears streaming down his face. I met him in the street weeks afterwards and he told me that the damn thing had bitten him more than once and that I'd been quite right, he had been dangerous, and at bottom he was glad he'd had him put to sleep.'

Miriam said, 'After all that, he's been and bought another one.'

'Yes, but not until after Mrs F. had died. Adolf's a big soft beggar, wouldn't hurt a fly.'

Duncan said he found it difficult to understand why people needed animals to love.

Miriam was appalled. 'Oh, Duncan, how can you say that? They're wonderful. Look at our Perkins. He's such a love.' Perkins, banished from the dining room while they ate, was sitting outside the door, heard his name and whimpered loudly to remind them of their extreme cruelty to him.

'You've got Mungo to love. Why do you need a dog too?'

'Well, he's not my dog, is he? He's Mungo's.'

'Why have you got him, Mungo?'

'He's my third Airedale and I wouldn't be without one.'

'There must be a reason. Come on.'

Joy kicked his foot lightly under the table. 'Just because, darling.'

'Joy's just kicked me to tell me to shut up, but I honestly want to know. Why do you need a pet to love?'

Mungo shuffled uneasily in his chair and then answered, 'If you must know, my Janie bought me an Airedale puppy for a wedding present and I loved him from the first moment. Don't ask me why, because I can't tell you, but I did.'

The silence this comment brought about was uncomfortable for all of them except Duncan, who remained unmoved. Joy because she knew the pain it caused Mungo even to say 'Janie'. Miriam because she wondered if Mungo would ever love her as he had loved Janie and Mungo because of the searing pain memories of Janie could still inflict.

'You see, you have no rational explanation, have you? How a highly intelligent, well set-up man of the world like you can find himself muttering about loving a *dog* I do not know. A dog! God!'

Mungo, on the verge of losing his temper, said tightly, 'Let it be the end of the matter. I do. Right?'

'So you're irrational, then.'

'If love is irrational, yes. Perkins is all I have left of Janie, his bloodlines are related to the first one she gave me and that's enough for me. Brandy, Duncan?'

'No, thanks. I think I'll be off.' He stood up. 'It's the same with children. Why do people bother? God! You can't go anywhere, do anything, without them damn-well trailing after you making a noise and embarrassing you with their supposedly innocent questions. Their continuous demands on your time, your money, your nerves! Who'd have children?'

Joy gasped in astonishment at his thoughtlessness.

'I would, Duncan, any day.' Miriam looked up at him, her eyes full of tears.

Duncan, brought up short by the sadness in her voice, remembered too late. 'I'm so very sorry, Miriam. Please forgive me. I'd forgotten.'

'That's all right. I can't expect other people to keep our tragedy in their hearts for ever like I do. They'd have been fourteen and twelve now if they'd lived.'

'Damn bad luck, that. Both of them. How careless of me and how inconsiderate. Forgive me. I've got the black dog on me tonight. I'd better leave. See you at home, Joy.'

The three of them listened as Duncan clattered down the stairs to the ground floor. Joy spoke first. 'There are times when I could cheerfully kill him. I'm so sorry, Miriam, he doesn't mean half he says, he just enjoys argument.'

'Not your fault. It's a long way for him to walk.'

'Do him good. I'll go too, but not before I've helped you with this lot.' She waved an arm at the cluttered table.

'Certainly not. I don't expect my guests to work. I'll do it.' Miriam pressed her hands on the table and heaved herself up. 'Won't take long.'

Mungo sprang up. 'I'll help. Shall I see you to your car, Joy?'

'I do know the way! I'd rather you helped with all this, salve my conscience a bit. Bye-bye and many thanks. I'm sorry Duncan spoiled your birthday, Mungo. Don't invite him next year.'

Mungo kissed her cheek. 'Don't worry about it, not your fault, but he could do with keeping some of his opinions to himself.'

Joy kissed Miriam and squeezed her arm. 'Sorry! Night-night.' Joy picked up her bag, slung her jacket over her shoulders and left. Miriam sat, head down, staring at the table. 'It never leaves us, does it? Always there, dogging the footsteps.'

Mungo placed a hand each side of her head and lifted it so he could see her face. 'Expand on that. What dogs your footsteps?'

Miriam chose to say, 'The children.' Best keep Janie well pushed away so she couldn't hurt. 'Still, there we are.' She sighed.

'You must let them rest. Let go. Just let them go.'

'You've let them go, have you, then? The son the image of you. The daughter so unbelievably pretty?' A deep sob escaped before Miriam could stop it.

'Darling!' He hugged her close. 'If I could turn back the clock . . .'

'They'd still be ill, wouldn't they? Still be incurable.'

'Indeed. Good thing we found out in time before we had any more.' He was silent for a minute and then said gently, 'Lovely dinner, as always. You go to bed. I'll do this lot.'

'Why do I like Duncan so much when he's so odd?'

'Perhaps because he *is* odd.'

'He needs hugging, you know, that's what he needs, lots of hugging to convince him he's worthwhile.'

'So do I.'

Miriam laughed. 'You! You've an ego the size of a watermelon. His is the size of a grape, if he has one at all.'

'Well, don't you go hugging him or Joy might have something to say.'

Miriam watched Mungo stacking plates and then answered, 'I don't think Joy thinks about him like that; she really wouldn't mind if I did. They have the most peculiar relationship, haven't they? They've kind of stayed individuals and haven't melded.'

'Haven't noticed.'

'We've melded.'

Mungo thought about what she'd said and nodded. 'Yes, you're right, we have. I'll see to Perkins. Off you go. It's raining now. Can you hear it? Duncan will get soaked, it must be all of five miles. Serve him bloody-well right. I take a certain amount of pleasure at the idea of him getting a soaking, the thoughtless sod.'

But because of the rain Duncan hadn't taken the path over the fields as he usually did, he'd kept to the road. Consequently Joy had caught up with him and given him a lift. They drove home in stony silence. Duncan unlocked the front door, Joy put the car in the garage and stalked upstairs to bed. She was seething with tumultuous emotions, none of which she could come to terms with. When she came out of the bathroom Duncan was already lying on the bed, wearing his pyjamas. She looked down at him. 'Pleased with yourself?'

'Not at all.'

'I should think not. How could you be so crass? Have you forgotten all those agonising years of theirs? How *you* couldn't even go and see the children because you were made so desperate by their plight? Couldn't face how beautiful they'd been and how they'd descended into vegetables? Remember?'

Duncan turned over and groaned. 'Of course.'

'So?'

'I got carried away with my argument and didn't think.'

'Exactly.' Joy sat on the edge of the bed and set the alarm for morning.

Duncan rolled over and disappeared into the bathroom. When he came back he got under the duvet and lay on his back with his hands clasped beneath his head. 'I get so involved with my work I forget human beings. Do you know that? I forget feelings and things, you know. I think everyone's automatic like me and they're not.'

'Really!'

'Yes. First and foremost I should have thought of Miriam's feelings and they never occurred to me. Not once.'

'I blame computers.'

Duncan thought about this for a moment and nodded his head. 'You could be right. They've no emotion, you know, none at all, no flexibility, no give and take. They're programmed that way. Did you realise that?'

'Of course.'

'Maybe I've lived with computers for so long that I've grown like them.'

'Could be.'

'Become devoid of emotion, that's why I act so strangely. I think only of myself.'

Joy pretended surprise. 'No!'

'Tomorrow first thing I shall go down to the florist's and organise a bouquet of flowers for Miriam with a card written in my own hand.'

'What shall the card say?'

'It will come to me by morning.'

'Right.'

'Maybe it's a new disease which will shortly be discovered by science. Maybe it's at the root of all our troubles, people turning into robots through continuous association with computers. I may have hit on something here.'

'I shall be hitting you before long.'

'Maybe all the violence in the world is caused by computers because they've made people no longer feel anything at all. Consequently we're free to damage other human beings and things without any conscience whatsoever. You know, the damn things are dictating our behaviour and we've never realised. So computers *are* taking over the world like we were threatened they would and carelessly we all laughed at the idea.' Duncan sat up. 'Joy! I feel so dreadful about Miriam. To do that to such a lovely person. I'm ashamed of myself.'

Joy took hold of his hand. 'She understands.'

Duncan sighed. 'Joy?'

'Yes?'

He lay down again, still holding her hand. 'You can't stop loving him, can you? I can see it in your eyes when you're with him. It's not fair to Miriam, you know.'

Joy didn't answer but leant on her elbow and kissed his cheek.

Duncan's deep-set eyes looked up at her. The lamp cast shadows in the hollows of his eyes and she couldn't read what they were saying. She knew what she wanted to say, but she didn't say it. Instead: 'And there's you, saying you've lost all feeling to that computer of yours.'

Duncan lay silent for a while, then rolled on to his side and drew up his legs till his knees were almost touching his chin. 'I'm for sleep. Remind me in the morning. Flowers. Goodnight.'

'Goodnight.'

Before she knew it he was breathing heavily, leaving her wide awake and in turmoil.

7

'How could anyone do such a dreadful thing? Abandoning them like that? It's so cruel. Look at the dear little things! Is that one asleep or . . .'

Kate and Stephie were peering into a cardboard box a client had found at the main entrance. Inside were four kittens, two tabbies, one black and one black with white markings. The black-and-white one was lying very still. Kate lifted its little head with her finger and it flopped. 'I've a nasty feeling that one is beyond help.'

'Beyond help? You don't mean it's dead?'

'I think so. In fact, I'm sure so. How old are they, do you think?'

'I don't know but let's get that one out that's dead. Here, look, put it in this.' Stephie rooted in the waste bin and brought out an empty tissue box she'd that moment thrown away. 'You lift it out. I'm not very good with them when they're dead.'

Kate carefully lifted out the dead one and laid it in the box. 'It's so cold.' They covered it with a clean tissue and then gave their attention to the ones that were alive. Three pairs of bright little blue eyes peered up at them out of the depths of the box. The kittens looked so appealing that both Stephie and Kate said, 'Ah! Aren't they sweet?' Kate laid a gentle hand on each in turn and came to the conclusion they were all cold. 'You'd think they could have put a blanket in for them, wouldn't you? We'd better get them some help. What a lot of noise you're making! I bet you're hungry, aren't you?' She rubbed her finger under their chins, each in turn, and wished she could take one home but Mia's asthma forbade it. Responding to her touch they began clawing at the sides of the box trying to get out, their mouths opening into triangular shapes revealing tiny snow-white teeth as they mewed for help.

Stephie suggested they should get one of the vets to look at them.

The client who'd found them said, 'They look big enough to me to lap. You can't 'elp but love 'em, can you, Kate? They're so lovely. Wish

I could lay my hands on the pigs who did this to 'em. What 'arm 'ave they ever done?'

'Well, perhaps their mother has died or the person who owns them couldn't afford to keep them any more. They do get quite expensive to feed once you start weaning them. At least they brought them where they could get help. Sometimes people leave them in a bin or in a hedgerow somewhere and that really is cruel. See if Rhodri's still here, will you, Stephie?'

'He'll want us to call the RSPCA.'

'They'll have them to home, won't they? There's no one going to come forward to claim this little lot. Fancy being homeless at this age.'

'I'll get Rhodri.'

Moved by Kate's sympathy for them the client put a finger in the box and the black kitten tried to lick it. 'Ah! Look at that. D'yer know, I might ask the RSPCA to let me 'ave this one. Be a real friend for this little one 'ere.' He indicated the cat basket he'd put down on the floor. 'They'd make a right pair, both completely black and only a few weeks between 'em.' The client tickled the black kitten on his chest. 'He seems to 'ave taken to me, doesn't he?'

'He does.'

'Is it a boy or a girl?'

'I'm afraid I don't know for sure, but my granny used to say that a he always had a wider forehead even at this age than a she. What do you think?'

'If that's the case then the black's a boy, look.'

They compared the heads of the three kittens and came to the conclusion that yes, the black was a boy and the two tabbies were girls.

Stephie came back to say, 'Rhodri says take them into his consulting room and he'll run over them. A job for Lynne, this. She knows how to make up the formula for them. She'll get them to lap if anyone can, she's done it before. If they're hungry they'll probably take to it straight away.'

When Kate rang the RSPCA and explained the situation the reply was a groan. 'Oh, no! You won't believe this but we've just taken on board one hundred and forty-two cats and kittens from a place which bred cats for science. They've had to close down and we've got them all. We've sent twenty of them to another RSPCA home and even then we're packed to the doors. There is no way that we can take any more on board, there's literally no room at the inn. Could you possibly keep them till they're ready for homing?'

'Well, I'll have to ask our practice manager, see what she thinks.'

'After all, they are in good hands, aren't they? Couldn't be better, come to think of it. We'll be ages, you see, homing this lot because they're not used to being handled and we've a lot of work to do on them before they're ready. If you could manage them we'd be very grateful. They couldn't be in a better place, could they?'

'No, you're right there. Just that we're not geared for long-term care, but I'll see what I can do.'

'We'd be more than grateful, believe me. If you're in need of advice or some such, do please ring us back, won't you?'

'Will do.'

'We shall be for ever in your debt. If it really is impossible then we'll take them, if push comes to shove, you know. Keep in touch.'

By lunchtime the kittens were warm and well fed and sleeping peacefully, cuddled in a thick blanket in one of the post-operative cages. Kate took her lunch in there and ate her beef sandwiches wishing she could have one of them for herself. They'd taken to lapping wonderfully well under Lynne's supervision. Certainly, she might not be a nice person to know but she'd succeeded with the kittens in no time at all and Kate complimented her on her success.

Lynne shrugged her shoulders. 'All part of the job. They're in good nick, actually. Been looked after OK up to now. Makes you wonder, doesn't it? Why did they get thrown out?'

'The black one's spoken for, the client who found them outside wants it. That leaves the two tabbies. Just wish I could take one but Mia's allergic to fur. Brings on her asthma.'

'Is it nice having a stepmum?'

'Well, my stepmum is like a real mother to me. I've never known my own mother, you see. Dad and Mia married before I was two.'

'That's different, isn't it? Must be awful if you're fourteen, say, and your dad marries again.'

Kate sank her teeth into an apple. 'Mm.'

Lynne opened the cage door and felt the kittens. 'They're much warmer now. Right time-wasters, kittens are. So tempting to come and play with them and they need feeding all the time. Pity the RSPCA hadn't room.'

'Imagine the work, looking after all those cats.'

'They've all to be neutered too, you know, before they can home them. The mind boggles.'

Kate stood up to brush the crumbs from her uniform.

'Not on this floor please.'

'Sorry. I'll sweep them up.'

'You will. This is post-operative, got to be scrupulously clean. And don't eat in here again.'

'Sorry.'

'So I should think. You've a lot to learn.'

'I know I have.'

'A lot to learn about manners for one thing. Speaking to my brothers like you did. That Adam is a fool. A complete fool. Imagine not realising they were finding him amusingly pathetic.'

Kate, surprised by the sudden change of tack, said, 'He's a kind man, that's why. He wouldn't act like that, ever.'

'No, he's too wet.'

'Your brothers are arrogant.'

'So? Oxford and the City. They've something to be arrogant about.'

'I'm surprised that with that background they know so little about good manners.'

'They haven't got where they are relying on good manners, believe me.'

'I can imagine.'

'There's no need for your sarcasm.'

'There's no need for you attacking me like this.'

Lynne faced her, hands on hips. 'What is it about you that annoys me? Your CV for a start. What are you doing playing at being a receptionist with a CV like yours? Eh? Answer me that. Two As. You should be at university not piffling about here. Well?'

'What I do with my A levels is my choice. How do you know anyway? I've never said.'

Lynne tapped the side of her nose. 'I have ways. Just keep out of my way. I don't like people who are well in with the management, smacks of toadyism.'

'I have never tried . . .'

'Lynne!' Joy stood in the doorway. 'I am quite sure there is something better for you to be doing than gossiping in here. Kindly *move*! Sharp!'

Lynne made to leave.

Joy turned her attention to Kate. 'And you, Kate, don't eat in here again. If your lunch hour is finished please get on with your accounts. We don't want you getting behind with them, do we?'

'I'm sorry.'

'Apology accepted.'

Joy stood to one side to allow Kate to leave. The girl was flushed with embarrassment at her reprimand and Joy felt uncomfortable, for Kate hadn't deserved that but in front of Lynne it was the only thing to say to make them equal. So Lynne had been snooping around in the files, had she? Excellent worker, none better, but as a person . . . The incident made Joy recall the missing money and she wondered if this spat between the two of them was a confirmation that it was Lynne who'd removed Miss Chillingsworth's one hundred pounds. Joy went to take a peep at the kittens. With business on the increase since their move to these premises she rather felt the kittens were a burden they could well have done without. But one touch of their warm little soft furry heads and the sight of the little appreciative wiggle one of the tabbies gave as she stroked it changed her mind. Rather fun to have some healthy creatures to look after for a while.

For some unknown reason Duncan came to the forefront of her mind. Joy looked again at the one which had wiggled its appreciation and she noticed that its stripes had a ginger tinge to them which made it rather unusual. Since Duncan had sent the flowers to Miriam after his disastrous *faux pas* he'd been slightly more mellow towards mankind. Maybe this kitten, whose ears she noted were attractively larger and rather more pointed than those of the other two, might interest him. She'd drop a few hints, see how he felt. Reluctantly leaving the warmth of the three kittens, Joy took her hand out of the cage and carefully clicked it shut.

'Can I have a turn?' It was Miriam. 'Mungo said at lunchtime, so I thought I'd come for a peep. Aren't they sweet!'

Joy unlocked the cage again so Miriam could see more easily. Tears filled Miriam's eyes. 'The poor dear little things. Abandoned like that. How cruel.'

Joy watched her gentleness and felt the love flowing from her towards the three kittens. 'Miriam. I haven't said properly about Duncan. The flowers ... they were his idea, not mine. When he stopped to think he was appalled at what he'd said.'

'He's been to see me.'

'He has? He didn't say.'

'The next day with the flowers. We had a cuddle and a kiss, and we're friends still. Somehow it helped me. He is such an understanding man.'

'He is?'

'Oh, yes. There's a delicacy about his feelings which is unusual in a man and he explained how it had all come about, and, well ... it helped.'

'I see.'

'He needs hugging, you know, Joy. I expect I'm telling you something you must already know but he does, he needs hugging. At some time in his life he's missed out on it right when he needed it. Perhaps he doesn't know it, but I'm sure I'm right.'

'I see.'

Miriam stroked the kittens. 'Very therapeutic, isn't it? Touching sleeping babies, even if they are furry ones.'

Joy choked on her tears. 'Miriam!'

Miriam turned to look at her, opened her arms wide and invited Joy to hug her. They stood, arms around each other, for a while not speaking, then broke apart as Miriam said, 'I wish I could have one of them but the risk of Perkins mistaking it for a rat is far, far too great. You won't have got homes for them?'

'The black one is spoken for and I'm wondering about having one for Duncan.'

'Two down. One to go.' Miriam locked the cage. 'Must get on. If you need help with feeding at the weekends, let me know.'

'Rhodri says they need to stay together until they're six weeks; not right to separate them at this age.'

'Of course. Yes. See you, Joy.'

'And you.'

Duncan had never said he'd given Miriam the flowers in person. Miriam was right, he did need loving and, to be absolutely frank, he wasn't getting it. Weeks went by and she scarcely touched him. Made his meals, did his washing, tidied the house, but loved him? Joy shook her head. What was worse he'd known for years that she loved Mungo and to begin with she'd never intended he should realise that fact. But he had and he did and he'd been right when he'd said it wasn't fair to Miriam. Yet Miriam had put her arms round her as one did with a close friend. Like a bolt of lightning the thought entered Joy's head that if Duncan had realised without being told, then possibly Miriam had too. That idea had never occurred to her before. But if she had realised, would Miriam have wanted to be a friend to a woman who loved her own husband? Wouldn't she have wanted to keep her at a distance to lessen the chance of losing Mungo to her? Of course she would, so obviously Miriam didn't know. Joy felt a great wave of relief wash over her.

So Miriam must never know. She'd have to be very careful in future, though, because breaking Miriam's heart would be too big a responsibility for her to take. Before she left, Joy took another glance at the kittens who were just beginning to stir. The one with the pointy ears looked up at her; its muzzy blue eyes had that slightly square look which kittens' eyes always have when very young, and there and then Joy lost her heart to it.

Duncan, somehow or other, was getting a kitten.

The following week Kate had a day off and was spending it in the shopping precinct, choosing a birthday present for Mia and a wedding anniversary card for her and Dad. Well, it wasn't just for that reason. She also wanted to see about collecting some brochures for a holiday next summer and, last but not least, she had a new textbook to buy for chemistry.

For Mia some new earrings. Kate went to the ethnic shop on the first floor of the precinct and found instead of earrings a necklace, all fine silver, delicate and Indian, and she knew it would suit Mia and though it was dearer than she'd intended she bought it. For someone as generous as Mia nothing was too good. Kate wished she were wealthy so she could buy her a studio and some marvellously up-to-date equipment, and set her up for her miniatures good and proper, though it couldn't make her paint any better, for Mia was on the brink of making a name for herself and Kate was so proud for her.

At street level the precinct boasted innumerable card and gift shops and Kate went down the escalator to choose Mia's card and another for the anniversary. The precinct had been furnished with several wooden seats, planned in cosy groups to give a kind of village green effect. As she passed through a group of seats she spotted Miss Chillingsworth huddled in the corner of one, looking despondent. Kate had never noticed how old she was till now. 'Why, Miss Chillingsworth! What a nice surprise.'

Miss Chillingsworth looked up blankly at first, then recognition dawned. 'It's Kate, isn't it? How are you, my dear?'

'I'm fine. How are you?'

'I'm fine, dear, thank you.' Miss Chillingsworth looked anything but fine to Kate but she didn't comment. 'Not working today?'

'My day off. I'm working Saturday this week.'

'You sound as if you enjoy it.'

'I do. May I sit down?'

Miss Chillingsworth patted the seat beside her. 'I'd be delighted. It's nice to have someone to talk to who's congenial. How are things at the practice? I miss seeing you all.'

'We're terribly busy at the moment; one of the nurses is on holiday and we've got three kittens to look after. They're running about now and we've to be so careful because of Perkins. He reckons kittens equal rats and he's such an escape artist we have to watch him like hawks.'

'Why have you three kittens to look after?'

Kate explained and while she did so a brilliant idea sprang unbidden into her mind, an idea complete the moment it was born. 'It wouldn't be fair to separate them until they're a bit older, you see, so we have them for another two and a half weeks at least.'

Miss Chillingsworth listened with growing interest. 'How kind you all are. So very kind. I've never forgotten Mr Murgatroyd's little talk when . . . I lost Cherub. He was so good to me. I can see it must be hard work. That Perkins is a real character, isn't he?'

'He's a love, but so naughty and then, when you're cross with him, he looks up at you and you fall in love with him all over again. He's the only dog I know who laughs like a person. Miriam would love to have one of the kittens but Perkins would very likely mistake it for a rat and then . . . I can't bear to think.'

'That's what Airedales were bred for.'

'What is?'

'Clearing river banks of vermin. Water rats and things.' Miss Chillingsworth shuddered. 'I can't bear the thought of him getting at a kitten and one couldn't be angry with him if he did, could one? He would only be obeying his instincts.'

'Exactly. But it's getting more and more difficult the more active they become.' Kate left a silence while Miss Chillingsworth had a think.

'Is there no one who could take them all home?'

'Not really. My stepmother has asthma and she's about the only one who is home most of the day. All the others are out following careers and the like.'

'Of course, that's the problem nowadays. You say they have homes to go to?'

Kate nodded and counted off the homes on her fingers. 'Oh, yes. The black one is going to the client who found them on our doorstep. One tabby, the one with ginger in its stripes, is going to Joy's husband and the other tabby is going to a cousin of Mr Price's.'

'If they hadn't I couldn't do it. I can't replace Cherub just yet.'

Hardly daring to breathe Kate said, 'Couldn't do what?'

'Take them home till they're old enough. They could sleep in Cherub's basket by the Aga and I could train them to the litter tray she used at night when she got older, and they could have the run of the kitchen, couldn't they?'

'Miss Chillingsworth, what a brilliant idea. You've so much experience of cats you'd be ideal.The practice would provide all the food, of course. We wouldn't expect you to have that expense. Would you really do it for us? We'd be so grateful and it would be so much better for the kittens.'

Miss Chillingsworth nodded and beamed at her, and Kate continued, 'I could kiss you.'

So she did and Miss Chillingsworth kissed her back. 'I haven't been kissed for years. Shall we go?'

'Right now?'

'No time like the present. We could catch the bus.'

'I've got my car.'

'All the better.'

Kate left Miss Chillingsworth in reception and went to explain the whole idea to Joy in her office. Joy said, 'But they're not all spoken for, that other tabby . . .'

'I know, but she daren't take on the job if any one of them is homeless, because she's not ready to have another cat yet. So I told a white lie. Remember, it's a cousin of Mr Price who's having the other one.'

'Kate! Honestly!'

'It's in a good cause. She so needs something to throw herself into. Losing Cherub has been devastating for her, she's aged twenty years at least. We're sure to find someone willing to have one before long. Say yes. Please.'

'All right, then. It would be a great help, wouldn't it? Clever girl!' Joy stood up. 'We'll go for it.' Together they went to speak to Miss Chillingsworth.

'Miss Chillingsworth! How very kind of you to offer to have the kittens. Come in the back and take a look. They've had their dinner and they're asleep at the moment. You'll love them when you see them.'

The three of them had fallen asleep in a heap of fluffy toy mice and brightly coloured squeaky toys, and looked almost unbelievably appealing. Miss Chillingsworth gasped with delight. 'They are so sweet. Oh, my word! So sweet. Of course I'll take them. Gladly. The poor little dears, abandoned. I'll make it up to them, you'll see! How shall I get them home?'

Kate volunteered to drive her home. She loaded tinned kitten meat, milk formula and cat litter in the back, leaving Miss Chillingsworth to put the kittens in a carrier with their toys.

While Miss Chillingsworth fussed around getting Cherub's basket out and finding a piece of blanket to line it with, Kate sat on a chair in the kitchen waiting with the cat carrier beside her. Poor Miss Chillingsworth. 'Genteel poverty' were the only words to describe the circumstances in which she lived. Everywhere was tidy and extremely clean but so threadbare: the tapestry seat of the chair on which she perched had holes in it; the rug on the floor was patched to such an extent there was hardly anything of the original left; the curtains were so faded but when new had been of such quality; the almost bald doormat. It didn't take much intelligence to know that Miss Chillings-worth didn't always get enough to eat.

'There we are, Kate, my dear. I'm ready. Let's lift them out. I've put a hot-water bottle in the basket to make it feel like home.'

The kittens tumbled out of the carrier and skitter-scattered on the shiny floor, their tiny claws finding it difficult to walk on. Miss Chillingsworth picked each up in turn, pressed it to her cheek, then plopped it down in the basket. Having been thoroughly awakened by the car journey the kittens had no inclination to sleep, and they hopped out immediately and began to investigate.

'I'll bring the tins in.'

By the time Kate left, Miss Chillingsworth had shed the years which Cherub's death had heaped on her shoulders and she looked up at Kate with shining eyes. 'Thank you, Kate, my dear, I'm going to have such fun. You're a dear girl.'

Kate left her kneeling on the floor, the kittens spilling around her skirts.

'So you see, Joy, we've done her a good turn. I'll call at the end of the week and see how she's getting on, and if it's all right with you I'll take her some more tins and some more milk formula. There's no way she can be expected to pay for their food, she's so poor.'

'The dear old thing. Good idea of yours. Now all we have to do is find a home for number three.'

'We will, I'm determined.'

Joy laughed at her. 'If you've said you will, I know it'll happen. Off you go and get on with the accounts, Kate, you did a good day's work with the kittens.'

'Thanks.'

Kate took coffee out to Stephie and Joy on the dot of ten and stopped for a chat. Joy took her mug from Kate and complained it was too hot. 'Here, look, I'll leave it on there where Mungo can't see it.'

Stephie began drinking hers immediately. 'I'm ready for that. I do miss going in to play with the kittens, don't you, Kate?'

'I do, but as Lynne said they were terrible time-wasters. Do you know anyone, Stephie, who might fancy a kitten?'

'I don't. But there's sure to be someone who has to have a cat put down in the next two weeks and that's the moment to strike.'

'Sounds a bit callous but I know you're ri— My God!' Kate felt the hairs stand up on the back of her neck, her scorching hot coffee spilled over her hand but she never felt the scalding for coming in through the door was ... a man gone raving mad. A man hurling himself in through the glass doors, wearing a black balaclava and brandishing a billhook. Stephie screamed. Joy went drip-white and Kate dropped her mug. Most of the clients screamed and, far quicker than it takes to tell, Graham and Rhodri shot out of their consulting rooms to see what was amiss.

The madman screamed, 'Where is he? Where is that damned traitor? Just let me get at 'im.'

The voice sounded familiar but in the panic Kate couldn't place him.

'Just let me get my bloody hands on him, I'll bloody kill 'im.'

Not one of them could find their voice, so getting no reply the man surged around the reception area peering at each petrified client in turn, waving the billhook too close for comfort to their faces, but it was difficult for him to see for the balaclava didn't allow both his eyes to look out at the same time. The clients were close to hysteria by now and seeing their fear made Kate find her voice. 'Who is this person you want to kill?' The madman veered back towards the reception desk and leaning over it snarled, 'That bloody Aussie! That's who!'

'He's out on call.'

'I'll wait.'

'Not with that in your hand, you won't. Give it to me.' He made no move to hand it over. 'I said give it to me.'

The madman, responding to the authority in her voice, looked down at his weapon. 'I'm not giving it up.'

'You're not staying in here if you don't. That's an offensive weapon and I shall call the police if you won't hand it over.'

'Call the police! Nay.'

'Nay nothing. Try me.'

The madman looked at this slip of a girl ordering him about and some of the humour of the situation hit him and the anger in him began to evaporate. 'I'll wait, though.'

Kate took the billhook from him saying, 'You'll have a long wait, but you're welcome to sit down. Coffee?'

He nodded and Kate took Joy's mug from behind the computer and gave it to him. He sat on the chair nearest the door and though his hands were still shaking with his temper he managed to drink from Joy's mug. 'I can't forgive 'im for what he's done to me. I thought him and me was friends. Who needs enemies with friends like 'im. Stabbed in the back I've been.' He sat, shaking his head in despair.

Stephie whispered, 'Scott's coming back in any minute, with some urgent samples for the post.'

Joy, standing with her back to the madman, asked, 'Who is he?'

Kate answered, 'From something Scott said I think it's Mr Parsons.'

Stephie whispered urgently, 'He'll be back any minute. What can we do?'

Joy queried, 'What's Scott been up to, Kate? My God! It's not Blossom, is it?'

'Heaven alone knows.'

Stephie said even more urgently, 'He'll be here!'

Catching the sound of the Land Rover Kate said, 'That sounds like him now.' She rushed out to the back to catch Scott before he entered.

They each arrived at the back door at the same time. Kate opened it and pushed Scott out, slamming the door behind her. 'I think we've got a Mr Parsons waiting to see you. He's absolutely livid and swears he's going to kill you. He arrived brandishing a billhook, which mercifully I've got from him, and . . .'

Scott looked shocked. 'A billhook? Hell!'

'He's furious. What the blazes have you done?'

Scott, his hands full of samples for the laboratory, tried to demonstrate his innocence with outstretched hands and almost dropped the lot. 'Nothing. I haven't been near the place since I treated Sunny Boy's foot that time. What does he say I've done?'

'He hasn't.'

Scott dithered on the step, trying to make up his mind what he should do. Ever one for a challenge he asked, 'You've taken the billhook off him?' Kate nodded. 'Good on you, mate. Then I shall face up to him. Here, take these samples. Joy knows where they should go. Tell her they're urgent.' He happened still to be wearing the tie Mungo insisted on when he went on visits. He straightened it, pulled his collar tidy, tucked his shirt in and made sure his pullover was in order. Kate opened the door for him and tootled a trumpet call under her breath. Scott grinned, saluted her and marched inside to his fate.

In a loud, cheery voice he called out, 'Phil! How nice of you to call. What can I do for you, mate?'

Mr Parsons's fury had abated, to be replaced by a moroseness so deep it was a wonder he could speak at all.

Scott went to sit beside him. 'Do we need to go somewhere private?'

A quiet groan trickled round the waiting clients. Were they going to miss all the drama?

Mr Parsons shook his head. 'You know you said you could report me for selling milk illegal-like to the campsite and passers-by and that?'

Scott nodded and was about to deny vehemently doing any such thing but Mr Parsons didn't give him the chance. 'On reflection, I know it wouldn't be you, because we're mates, aren't we? You and me.' Scott nodded. 'Well, someone has. Some interfering, nosy-parking sod has reported me and I'm in deep water. They spied on me and set me up and caught me at it. There isn't a better drop of milk anywhere in

Britain than mine from my cows. Even the Queen's cows couldn't produce no better. Natural, wholesome milk is mine, no modern messing about with it. My Blossom and me we drink it every day of our lives and what's wrong with us?'

'Nothing. But I did say you wouldn't pass a single hygiene test, didn't I?'

Mr Parsons lifted his head and managed to look at Scott with one of his eyes. 'You did. But they're all 'ealthy, aren't they?'

'You're right there, Phil.'

'You couldn't speak up for me, could you?'

'As a friend there's nothing I would like better, but honestly I have told you before about your lack of hygiene and I'm afraid that on that basis I would have to be truthful. I couldn't support you selling milk.'

'Ah, well. I understand. It's only right. But I know it's good milk. I've got proof. There was a baby in the village not thriving, premature she was, and the doctors couldn't find a remedy for her. She was sinking, slowly I admit, but sinking. Her mother started giving her milk from my cows, in desperation I'll grant you that, and the blessed little thing began to put weight on and now she's running about like a good 'un. What better testimonial can you have than that?'

Scott shook his head. 'None.'

'It doesn't make sense. I'll be off. Where's my billhook? That sparky young lass took it off me. She's a grand girl, she is. Spirit she's got, that's what I like in a woman. Spirit. Same as my Blossom.'

Mr Parsons took the billhook from Kate and gave her a wink – well, she thought he gave her a wink; it was difficult to tell. 'Bye-bye, Mr Parsons. Nice to have met you.'

'And you. At least I've livened up your morning.'

'You have indeed.'

Mr Parsons wagged a finger at her. 'You could do worse than that Aussie. He's a grand chap.'

The big outer doors were shut this morning because of the cold and they all waited until he'd closed them behind him before they began to laugh. The laughter ripped through the reception area like a whirlwind, swirling and twirling back and forth, bubbling and frothing, clearing away the panic and the fear. Joy had to wipe her eyes and Stephie was taking great gulps of coffee to help her pull herself together. 'I have never witnessed anything like that before. Heck! Was I frightened! And you, Kate! You were so brave.'

Joy agreed. 'She most certainly was. I don't know how you dared to speak to him like that.'

Suddenly Kate had gone weak at the knees and had to grip the edge of the desk to keep herself up. 'Neither do I. I feel very odd.'

Scott moved a chair up behind her and pushed her down on to it. 'You're a heroine, that's what.'

Graham and Rhodri sheepishly retreated into their consulting rooms, feeling less than manly at having allowed a mere female to take command.

'I think I'm going to be sick.' Kate rushed out through the back. Scott suggested he follow her but Joy shook her head. 'I'll go in a minute. Leave her alone for now.' She went out from behind the desk to speak to the waiting clients. 'Sorry about that. Everyone feeling all right?' She spoke to each in turn, offering them coffee or tea if anyone needed reviving. 'It was a nasty shock for us all. I'll gladly get you something if you would like me to.'

'He needs locking up. The thumping big idiot. Scaring the living daylights out of us! He's always been a bit cracked, even at school. Poor Scott. You all right, are you, Scott? You've Kate to thank. She didn't half stand up to him.'

'She did. You should take her out tonight for a slap-up meal, to thank her.'

'All in favour?'

They all voted in favour and Scott declared he had no alternative, but dare he take her out? Was he a match for such a tough sheila?

An elderly client, clutching a cage with a sad, almost featherless canary in it, suggested he could take her instead if he liked, if Kate was too much for him.

The clients were still roaring with laughter when Graham Murgatroyd opened his door and called for his next appointment. The elderly client with the canary stood up saying, 'Another offer coming in. What it is to be in demand! Where are you taking me tonight, then, Graham?'

'I beg your pardon?'

They all laughed again.

'As I say, it's better than the theatre coming here. You should sell tickets, Joy.'

But Joy had gone to check on Kate.

8

There were words on the screen and she hadn't put them there. Kate leapt from her chair in fear. How could they possibly be there when she hadn't typed them in? She took a sideways look at the screen, too afraid to look straight at it.

TUESDAY. YOU'VE FORGOTTEN YOU'RE MY GIRL. I'LL PICK YOU UP WHEN YOU FINISH AT SEVEN. SEE YOU! DON'T BE LATE!

Kate paced up and down her tiny office. Back and forth. Back and forth. It wasn't Scott playing the fool, she knew that, because he called her his 'sweet one', never using that controlling phrase 'my girl', and he wouldn't do that kind of thing anyway, not Scott. Oh, God! How had it got there? She hadn't seen Adam for weeks now, not since they'd met by accident in the precinct. Goosebumps broke out all over her skin. Was it a coincidence that they'd met or had he been . . . ?

The door opened and the handle hit Kate in her back.

It was Joy. 'Oh, I'm so sorry! I didn't expect you to be standing behind the door. I've found the printouts from last year you wanted . . . Why, Kate, whatever's the matter? You look as if you've seen a ghost.'

Kate tucked her trembling hands into her armpits so Joy couldn't see how upset she was. 'I don't feel very well.'

'I can see that. Look, sit down. These figures can wait a while. I'll get you a glass of water; stay there.'

Joy held the glass out for Kate and she managed to stop shaking long enough to take a sip.

'Go on, take another. It always works and I don't know why.'

'Thank you.'

'Do you feel faint?'

'Not really.'

'Then how do you feel?'

Kate looked up and wondered whether or not to tell. It was stupid. She'd got this whole thing totally out of proportion. How could Adam have put that on her computer? He had no access to it unless . . .

'Would you like to go home?'

Kate answered even before Joy had finished speaking: 'No, thanks. I'd rather stay here. Dad's working and Mia's gone to an exhibition today so there's no one at home. I'll be all right in a minute. Thank you.' Kate tried half a smile but it didn't emerge properly.

Joy propped herself against the desk. 'You're as white as the proverbial sheet. If you were to ask me I'd say you were frightened. Or you've had a shock.'

Kate shook her head. 'Neither. Must be flu starting or something.'

'Come on, Kate, I'm not a fool. I'm not being nosy, I just want to help.'

'I know and I'm grateful. Please, I'm feeling better now. Thanks for the water.'

'Very well. But I'm here to help, you know. Any time.'

'Thank you.'

'Give me a shout. I'll be on the desk if you need me. I don't want to come across you in a dead faint over the keyboard, you know, so don't hesitate.'

'I'll shout if I need you.'

'Good. I'll leave the door open in case.' Joy kicked the doorstop into place, gave her a generous smile and left Kate to her fears.

Tuesday. You've forgotten you're my girl. I'll pick you up when you finish at seven. See you! Don't be late! She hadn't imagined it. It was still there. Somehow he'd got in and done this when no one was about. There was too much going on all day for him to have done it when the hospital was open. So it had happened between about eight o'clock in the evening and eight o'clock in the morning. Occasionally a vet could be doing an emergency operation during the night if there'd been a road accident or something but that was rare, very rare, so his chances of being observed during those hours were slim. Had he a key? That was unlikely too. Joy had a key, and Mungo Price and Miriam had keys, but no one else.

She had to delete it. But before she did she'd print it out. It rolled out of the printer with her figures in the top half and Adam's words below typed in capitals and bold print so there was no missing it. He'd been in here, sat in this chair, her chair, and done it. She'd left it with the screen saver on last night so he'd known exactly where she'd last worked on the accounts and that she would see it immediately, simply by touching the mouse and clearing the saver. Well, there was one thing for certain: she wouldn't leave it switched on again. Never. But this wasn't the end of it, was it? The clock wouldn't stop ticking just because she'd swiped the screen clear of his words, would it? It would be seven o'clock at seven o'clock as sure as night followed day, wouldn't it? And he'd be there, waiting.

The memory of his hand tightening on her wrist, the grasping hand on her knee, the smell of onion on his breath . . . Her heart began racing as it had that night when she'd run like hell for that string of lights in Sainsbury's car park.

Adam's physical presence loomed in her mind so vividly that he could have been in the room with her. The comforting sound of Joy sympathising with a client brought Kate to her senses. She'd been famous at school for her common sense and it asserted itself now. She was being completely ridiculous. Adam had something better to do than run about in the night gaining entrance to the office and typing threatening messages on her computer. After all, as he so frequently had said, he needed his sleep with the important job he held. She could hear him saying, 'I've a big week on this week, got to get some early nights.' Of course Adam, with his rigid timetable, his doing everything by the book attitude to life, wouldn't be tramping about in the night, would he? His mother would have something to say if he did. Kate laughed at herself. Hell's bells, she could be stupid, she could! She took the sheet of paper from the printer, folded it and put it in her bag.

She pressed the delete key and got on with her work. But somehow Adam's face kept coming between her and the screen. At one she should have gone home and then come back at four but she didn't. She should have gone out to buy lunch but instead she asked Stephie to bring her something back. Her excuse was catching up on the accounts, but it was all fabricated nonsense so she didn't have to leave the safety of the practice. Still she had not resolved the question of what to do at seven. Inexorably the clock ticked on, and even though the evening surgery was very busy the problem of Adam was ever present in her mind. Kate knew she musn't go out to the car park alone if his car was there. Then a thought occurred to her. 'Scott's late back, isn't he, Joy?'

'Yes. Up to something, I suppose. He is such a naughty boy.'

'Naughty he might be, but you like him.'

'Oh, yes! Such fun so long as you don't take him seriously.' She looked curiously at Kate. 'Feeling better?'

It was on the tip of her tongue to confide her problem to Joy when Scott burst through the back door calling, 'Hi! Here comes the golden boy.'

Joy and Kate burst out laughing. Joy spoke first. 'Honestly, Scott! What are we going to do with you? Golden boy indeed.'

'I am! I slave day in day out. I do more nights than anyone else for a start and I get all the rotten jobs, like Applegate Farm *again*.'

'It was Sunny Boy, wasn't it, this time?'

'Sunny Boy. Yes. My God, he's a bull and a half! Why he keeps a bull I'll never know. AI would be much easier and cheaper than feeding that monster. He's like putty in Phil Parson's hands, I swear, meek as a lamb, he is. One look at me, though, and his hooves are scraping the ground and his eyes are rolling. I tell you he'll be the death of me one day, he will.'

Kate asked what his problem was.

'Infected foot, *again*. But you try getting a peek at it. Oh, mate! He's dynamite.' He pulled up his trouser leg and showed them a huge, sickening bruise developing on his leg where Sunny Boy had kicked him. 'Wonder he didn't crack my shin.'

'Did you get a peek?'

'I did.' Scott bowed elegantly, hoping for applause. 'Any chance of Kate going early?' Ignoring the fact there were three clients still waiting their turn he added, 'It's a quarter to and the place is empty.'

Joy caught Kate's eye and raised an eyebrow. She nodded and Joy said, 'Just this once, and because it's you asking, she can go. She deserves to go, she's been working since eight this morning. I'll finish here.'

Kate said. 'Thanks. I do appreciate it.'

Her relief at having someone to leave with was immense but short-lived, because when they went out of the back door into the car park there was Adam, sitting waiting. But what shocked Kate more than anything was that he'd changed his car, it was no longer that nauseous purple thing but a slimy kind of diarrhoea colour, one even more decrepit than his last. So he could have been following her and she'd never realised.

'What the merry hell is he doing waiting? Have you promised to go out with him?' One glance at her face and the panic registered there and Scott had his answer. 'The sod!' He made to go across to him.

'Scott, don't aggravate him, please, for my sake.'

He picked up on her fear and stopped in his tracks. 'Get in your car and lock the doors, and set off for home and I'll follow, and for God's sake keep control of yourself. I don't fancy facing Mia if her little joy has been involved in a road accident. Take care.'

The journey home was a nightmare. There'd been an accident with a lorry carrying timber, which had caused it to shed its load across the road so the traffic had to be diverted, and the major road works close to home slowed her down so much that by the time she reached the house, only a very small part of her brain was controlling her driving and the rest was in complete terror. Scott had stayed stuck to her tail the whole time, twice going through the lights at red so as not to lose her. She'd no idea if Adam had followed them but if he had, Dad and Scott together would deal with him and she could get to Mia and safety.

Scott was parked and out of his car by the time she'd picked up her things and unlocked her door. 'Come on. He gave up following us at the diversion. When we get inside you can tell your dad all about it.' He locked her car for her, took a grip on her elbow and led her up the path.

Kate flung her things down on the chair in the hall and called out, 'I've brought someone home!'

Mia came into the hall from the kitchen. 'Oh, hello! It's Scott, isn't it? Do come through into the back.'

'If it's not an intrusion.'

'Not at all. Have you eaten?'

'Not had a bite since breakfast.'

Mia was horrified. 'That's disgraceful, you're neglecting yourself. You'll eat with us.' Having got over her surprise at seeing Scott, Mia looked properly at Kate. 'Kate! You look dreadful. What's the matter?'

'Nothing at all. Really. It's me being daft.'

Mia gave her a hug and said, 'We'll eat first, then you can tell me. It's soup and salad tonight, Scott, because I've been out most of the day. Will that do?'

'Of course; it sounds great.'

Mia called upstairs, 'Gerry! We've got company. Scott's arrived, from the practice. Come on down and open a beer for him.' They heard Gerry's muffled voice call a cheerful 'OK' from the attic and in a moment his feet pounding down the stairs.

Mia confided to Scott, 'He keeps his train set up there.'

Gerry shook hands with Scott, pumping his hand up and down with great energy. 'Good to see you, Scott. What a pleasure. Kate, love.' He offered her his cheek for a kiss and said, 'Not got 4X, Scott. Will John Smith's do or would a lager fit the bill better?'

'A John Smith's, please. Mia says you have a train set upstairs.'

Gerry's face lit up. 'I have indeed. Are you an enthusiast?'

'No. But that doesn't mean I wouldn't like to see it.'

'Have we time, Mia?'

'No.'

'Let's sit down, then, and we'll have a go afterwards. You'll have a surprise.' Mia laid an extra place and got the glasses for them for their beer, keeping an eye on Kate at the same time for she knew things weren't right, but it wasn't until Scott sat back after he'd rounded off his meal with two slices of Mia's apple pie that she spoke up. 'Well, then, Kate. You've not eaten much and you've said even less and I'd like to know, and I'm quite sure Gerry does, what the matter is.'

Both Gerry and Mia gave audible gasps of astonishment when Kate told them about the message on her computer. When she added that Adam was there waiting for her when she and Scott went out to their cars Gerry said, 'That's it. That is it. He has finally overstepped the mark. Gerry Howard can take so much and then *finito!*' He banged his clenched fist on the table and made the cups jump. 'I can't believe it of him. He's sat here and eaten meal after meal at our table, been a guest in our house and this is what he does. You were right, our Kate, to say he wasn't for you, absolutely damn right.'

Mia said in a quieter than usual voice, 'I'm not very clever where computers are concerned but how did he get a message on to yours? How did he do it? I mean, did he have to touch the keyboard to do it?'

Kate nodded.

'You mean he gained entry to the building, sat in your chair and then typed it?'

Scott answered her question with a nod, adding for good measure, 'I've always said he's a nutter.'

Gerry applauded his assessment. 'You're damned right. I never suspected that side of him, did I, Mia?'

'You did not, Gerry. Question is, what shall we do about it?'

Scott snorted his anger at Adam's behaviour and suggested, 'Beat him up?'

Gerry opened his mouth to agree with him but Mia got in first. 'I find it hard to believe that Adam is behaving like this, it is so out of character. I mean, what was he doing in the precinct on the day you bumped into him if he has got that promotion? There's no way he would step so far out of line as to be missing from work. Has he actually *said* he's got the job?'

Kate thought for a moment and recalled his words. 'It was me who said "You've got the job" and he agreed with me; he answered, "You said it."'

Scott nodded. 'That's right, I was there. He didn't actually *say* he'd got the job.'

'There you are, then. There's one thing about Adam, he never lies.'

'But that doesn't mean he didn't stay put in the job he already had, does it? I mean, he must still be working. He's certainly spoken about his job as though he is,' Kate said.

'Oh, yes, of course. Silly me. You're right, of course. Just me letting my imagination run away with me.'

Kate, keeping her eyes on the table for fear of giving away how worried she was, went on, 'What's worse, he's changed his car, hasn't he, Scott? So he could have been keeping watch on me and I haven't realised because I was on alert for his old purple one.'

Mia said quietly, 'It gets worse by the hour.'

Mia's heartfelt comment pierced Scott's habitual bravado and he stayed mute while he studied his situation. Why on earth was he, a free-thinking, free-as-a-bird chap, involving himself in this? According to his lights any self-respecting twenty-seven-year-old Aussie part-way through the ritual blooding of working his way round the world didn't stop in one place more than six months. It wasn't done, it didn't fit the picture and eight months would be up before he knew it. He looked across the table at Kate, caught her glance as she looked up and he swallowed hard. She was quality, was Kate. Real quality. Not some common-or-garden sheila to be picked up and dropped when he got bored. Kate smiled at him, a sweet, nervous smile, and he smiled back. If he wasn't careful . . .

Gerry, who'd been doing some deep thinking while they'd been speculating, burst out with, 'Nevertheless, Mr Price ought to know that Adam's got into the building. We'd be guilty of conniving if we didn't tell him what we know.'

'I'll tell him tomorrow.'

'Tomorrow, my girl, either Mia or I will take you to work and bring you home. Scott can't always be about when you need him. You're a good chap for seeing to Kate tonight, Scott, and I want to thank you man to man for looking after her.' Gerry stood up and shook Scott's hand.

'There's no need for that, Dad. I can manage.'

'Till we know the facts you'll do as I say. Tell them your car's in need of serious repair and they can't find the parts. Anything but have you travelling about on your own. You agree with me, don't you, Scott?' Gerry gave him a meaningful look and Scott took the hint.

'I most certainly do. If there's an evening like tonight Kate could ring you and I'd bring her home and save you the journey. My hours are unpredictable so I can't promise . . .'

'You're being ridiculous, Dad, Adam wouldn't hurt a fly, we all know that. I'm perfectly capable of seeing myself home. I won't be carried about like a child.'

'You will.'

'I won't.'

'You will, Kate, because I say so. It was bad enough that night you had to run away from him. Heaven alone knows what he might do next.'

Scott's ears pricked up at Gerry's words but Mia shook her head at him and he said nothing except, 'The train set?'

Gerry jumped to his feet, eager to show off the pride of his life, and they disappeared upstairs, and Kate and Mia knew that would be the last they'd see of them for at least two hours.

'I need to have a word with Mr Price, Joy, this morning. His first appointment is at ten. Do you think he might see me before then?'

'You're not wanting a reference, are you? You're not leaving?'

'No, I'm not, but I do need a word about something. Can I tell you all about it later?'

'Of course. I'll give him a buzz right now and organise him.'

'Thanks.'

Mungo came downstairs at nine o'clock to find Kate in the accounts office entering the previous day's veterinary calls in the computer. He closed the door behind him and sat down on her spare chair. 'Well, now, Kate, I understand you need a word with me.'

Kate dreaded having to tell him. In her small office his aura was striking, and she felt him to be too big for the available space, but she had to inform him clearly and concisely without any silly girlish panic. So she began at the beginning and told him about their estrangement, and how Adam had obviously got into the practice building at some stage. Out of her handbag she took the printout she'd done and handed it to him to read.

'If he hadn't trespassed I would never have told you, because obviously it's a personal matter, but he has done and my dad said I must.'

Mungo read it and commented, 'It couldn't be someone here having a joke?'

'I don't think so. He uses the expression "my girl", which is a favourite of his. I'm sure it was him and of course he was here to meet me like he said he would, but Scott followed my car home for safety's sake and Adam lost us at the road works.'

'Mm. I'm most concerned about this for your sake. It's not at all pleasant. There's also theft or destruction to be thought of. If someone is very determined to get at the drugs nothing we can do will stop them, besides which there's the operating equipment and such. We've a lot of money invested here, you know. Do you think he's likely to do it again?'

'He's behaving so out of character I really don't know what he'll do next.' Some of the horror of it overcame her and tears came into her eyes. 'It's making me feel dreadful; it's like being stalked.'

'It *is* being stalked, make no mistake. Have you tackled him about it?' Kate shook her head.

'No, perhaps that's wise. You don't happen to have a photograph of him, do you?'

'A photograph? For the police, you mean?'

'Not yet. Have you met Johnnie?'

'Johnnie? No.'

'He cleans for us. Most often he cleans at night but sometimes he takes a turn and has to come very early in the morning instead and get it all done before we open up. Johnnie King his name is. He's totally deaf and it will make it much easier to explain what we suspect if I can show him a photograph. This Adam must have come in while he's been here, you see, and he must be told not to let him in.'

'How can you explain if he's totally deaf?'

'He lip-reads and I use sign language too. Known him for years. He's a great chap. He does a good job, doesn't he?'

'He does. It's always immaculate.'

'Exactly. I admire him. He's one of those handicapped people who gets on with his own life and earns a living, and doesn't expect preferential treatment, and cares for his father into the bargain.' Mungo took her hand. 'Has your dad had a word with this Adam?'

'No.'

'I think he should. I shall tell Joy, leave it to me. Don't tell the others, best not for now.' He got up to go. 'Oh! Photograph?'

'Tomorrow, will that do? Scott knows, though, because he was with me last night when I was leaving like I said.'

'I'll tell Scott to keep mum. Take great care of yourself, Kate. These situations can escalate in no time at all.' He patted her hand, gave her one of his radiant smiles and made to go, saying before he closed the door, 'Joy will murder me if anything happens to you. She thinks very highly of you.'

At home, Mia spent the morning painting. This one was for an exhibition she'd been invited to put on in the major library in the town. Small beer, really, in the scheme of things but important to her. It was of Kate as a little girl. She'd used her facial features several times and the result had always sold well. She could put her in any century and somehow she always fitted the bill. This time the neckline of her dress was that of an early-nineteenth-century girl about seven years old. People often assumed that her paintings were of real people because they looked so full of character, so taken from life. Mia liked it best when she wasn't working to order from photographs because it meant she could use her imagination; photos were so limiting artistically.

Thinking about photos brought to mind the one Kate had chosen to take to the practice that morning. Of Adam on the harbour at West Bay with Kate. 'Cut yourself off that photo before you give it to Mr Price,' Mia had said in the car on the way. 'I don't want you on it with him. How could he be doing this to you? He must have gone mad.'

So Kate had cut herself off with some nail scissors out of Mia's bag and Mia had wished it was as easy to get rid of Adam for real. He was tenacious, certainly, and obsessive. Two characteristics Mia hadn't much of a fancy for. No one seemed to be alarmed by the fact that he appeared to have so much time for wandering about during the day. So why did he? No job, that's what. Obviously. Being so self-obsessed, he couldn't tolerate such a let-down. He hadn't got the promotion and he'd been sacked, and there was no way he would admit it, especially in front of Scott. Mia frowned. She'd find out. Yes, she would. She'd ring his office and ask to speak to him. That would give her the answer. If they said 'I'll put you through' she'd put the receiver down quick, but if he had been sacked they'd also give her the answer. Either way she would *know*.

The excitement of her little scheme made her hand jerk and a streak of the red she'd been using for Kate's lips ran across her face and made it look as though Kate had been knifed from lip to ear. Mia was horrified. What had she done? Was this a sign of what was to come? She quickly picked up one of her tiny blades and scraped the blood-red away before it began to dry. Once her portrait had been put to rights Mia put down her brush.

She poured herself a drink of water and sipped it to make sure her voice wouldn't be croaky when she spoke. Mia practised out loud what she would say. 'Could you put me through to Mr Pentecost, please? Adam Pentecost.' Or, 'I want to speak to Adam Pentecost, please.' Or, 'I'm replying to Mr Pentecost's call.' If they asked who it was she'd give a false name, call herself Betty Lomax. That was it. Right. Here we go. Before she dialled the number she questioned which answer she wanted. Did she want 'Yes, I'll put you through', or 'I'm sorry, Mr Pentecost no longer works here'? Preferably the former because then perhaps he would feel less of a danger; if it was the latter, then ... 'Could I speak to Mr Pentecost, please?'

'Mr Pentecost? I'm sorry, no one of that name works here any more.'

'But he must, he suggested I ring.'

'I'm sorry, he left last month.'

'Can you tell me where he works now, then?'

'Sorry, I'm not able to divulge any personal details.'

'It must have been sudden, it's only a matter of a few weeks since he suggested I ring him. Such a very nice man he seemed.' Mia let a kind of throwing-myself-on-your-mercy tone enter her voice, a tone inviting confidences, and it worked.

'Truth to tell he was dismissed. Instantly. A kind of "thank you but no thank you" and he left that afternoon. Worked here since leaving school. He'd fully expected to be promoted but instead ... well ... curtains. Terrible shock.'

'I'm sure it must have been. Thank you anyway for your help, you're most kind.'

'Not at all. Good morning.' And she was off, answering another call no doubt.

But Mia was left worrying. She put away her painting. It was no good trying to do such minutely delicate work when she was upset, because all she'd do was what she'd done already: make it look as though Kate had been attacked. She thought of herself as a perceptive person and sat in front of the Rayburn, considering what should be done next. He ought to be warned to leave her alone but by whom? The police? Gerry? Scott with his beat-him-up attitude? But would Adam ever *do* something serious? Maybe it was all fantasy and quite harmless. But somehow it wasn't harmless, was it? Not any more, not leaving a message on her computer. And he was guilty of deception of the highest order, giving the impression he'd been promoted. He couldn't face up to the reality of being sacked. How cruel people were nowadays. What a blow to a man, or a woman come to that. Instant dismissal. But at least Adam hadn't a wife and children, and a huge mortgage – he was footloose and fancy free. Oh, no, he wasn't! He was obsessed by Kate.

She leant back in her chair and thought about Kate; the nineteen years of caring more and more as each year went by. She'd been a handful always, on the go right from the moment she was on her feet. Into everything, talking in sentences long before most children did and so loving her dear little Kate had been. So loving. Still was. Mia picked up her bag and took out the piece of the photograph Kate had cut off that morning in the car. The wind was blowing her hair and she was laughing. Mia had a sentimental moment while she sat there admiring and loving. If anything ever happened to her to stop the laughter, to spoil that lovely face, she'd ... If she peered closely at it she could see Adam's hand, left behind on Kate's shoulder. Angrily she hunted for the scissors in her bag and snipped off the hand. There. Nothing of Adam left. If only it were proving as easy in reality.

'Hello!'

'Gerry! Is that you?'

'Who else!'

He stood in the doorway. 'Forgot my lunch.' He spotted the obvious distress on her face. 'What's up, Mia? What's happened?'

'Adam lost his job. He didn't get the promotion.'

'But he said ...'

'He didn't actually, you know; it was Kate assuming he had and he let it ride because he couldn't face up to the fact that he'd been sacked. A man like him with such an opinion of himself, and yet so scared of life he couldn't abide change or spontaneity of any kind, wouldn't be able to, would he? Such a blow to his ego, besides being a terrible shock. Now he has nothing to do but hang around after Kate.'

'How do you know all this?'

'I rang his firm. Asked to speak to him.'

'Mia!'

'I found out what we wanted to know, though, didn't I?'

Gerry picked up the photo of Kate from the table and studied it. 'What can we do?'

'I think you should go and see him. Kate mustn't, but you could.'

'Me?' Gerry didn't see himself as a diplomat or, come to think of it, as a James Bond either. 'Me? What would I say?'

'You'd think on your feet, you're good at that. I won't have something happen to Kate simply because we did nothing to help her. If he should get at her ...' Mia wept, her shoulders shaking with her fear.

Gerry put his arm round her. 'Come on, Mia, it won't come to that. Of course not. We're getting things out of proportion.'

Mia blew her nose loudly and choked out the words, 'Go, please go and see him. Tell him. Please. I mean it.'

To pacify her he agreed to go. 'But not right now. I'll go after work, tonight.'

'Thank you. I know you'll say the right thing.' Mia took his hand in hers and squeezed it. 'You know how much I love her.'

'I do. I've always been grateful for that. More than grateful.'

Mia cheered up after he said that and went into the kitchen to make Gerry his lunch. She called out, 'I forgot about your lunch with taking Kate. Ham all right?'

'Fine.' He'd call on Adam tonight.

But instead he went straight from their house to Adam's. If the fellow was out of work he'd likely be at home, wouldn't he? There'd be no point in Adam hanging about waiting for Kate at this time of day and the sooner it was faced up to the better in his opinion.

He'd never been to Adam's house, though Kate had pointed it out to him. The terrace of stone cottages stretched right from the river bank to the council park: a quiet, secluded lane with desirable cottages, some smartened up and modernised, others as they'd been for a century and more.

Here was number fifteen. He pulled up outside. It was so entirely clean it was hard to believe that Mrs Pentecost hadn't been out since dawn scrubbing down the outside walls and polishing the windows. Not a spider's web or a speck of dust anywhere; not a single patch of flaking paint. The net curtains lined up like soldiers on parade. In the window boxes were winter pansies, their faces turned to the autumn sunshine, planted with such precision he doubted they'd ever dare to die. There was something unnerving about the exactness of it all. Something almost ... Gerry couldn't find the right word but 'obssessive' crept into his mind.

He got out and went to rattle on the brass knocker. At first he thought they weren't in, but then he heard footsteps. The door opened a few inches and a face very like Adam's came into view.

'Yes?'

'Good morning. I'm Gerry Howard. I've come to see Adam.'

The door opened wider. 'Oh, you're Kate Howard's father?'

Gerry nodded.

'He's at work.'

'He is?'

The door opened wider still. 'Come in. Come in. You can leave a message.'

The chill of the house struck Gerry as soon as he walked in. Being a cottage, the front door opened straight into the living room and it seemed he'd walked into an immaculately kept shrine. On every well-polished surface stood photographs of Adam in all stages of his life: the naked baby on the sheepskin rug, the toddler playing with his brightly painted wooden engine, the schoolboy in his too-big blazer, the teenager in athletic kit holding up a trophy, and in pride of place on the mantelpiece was Adam in cap and gown. *Oh, God!* thought Gerry. *If I hadn't had Mia to keep me in check I'd have had Kate all over our sitting room too.* Mrs Pentecost went to a drawer in a table under the window. 'Here, look, write on this.' She didn't have to root about in the drawer to find a piece of paper as Mia would have had to do, because all there was in the drawer was a writing pad and a pen.

She handed them to him and waited.

'I've nothing to write, I wanted to see him.'

'But I said he isn't here. He's at work. He won't be home until half past six at the earliest. That promotion he got is keeping him so busy, but then what can you expect when a young executive is climbing the ladder of success. They have to put in all the hours, haven't they?'

Had Mia got it wrong, then? 'You must be proud of him.'

'I am. It will be lovely when Kate and he marry and we all live together in the one house.'

When what she'd said had registered Gerry cringed with disgust at the future planned out for his Kate.

'We went to look around one the other day, Adam and I. Bigger than this, of course, as suits an executive. I shall have company all day and someone to look after me then. I'm so looking forward to it. I'm not in good health, you see.'

Gerry dared a stupid question: 'Kate like it, did she?'

'She's going at the weekend with Adam. Just the two of them. You know what it's like when you're in love. You don't want a doddery old mother with you, do you?' She smiled coyly, asking him to deny her dodderiness.

Gerry got the distinct impression as he looked at her that she was no more decrepit than he himself. 'I see. Kate hasn't said.'

'I think Adam's keeping it as a surprise.'

'It will certainly be that. Look, I'll call back tonight if I may, catch Adam in then.'

'I'll tell him you're coming. Oh, he won't be in, though. It's Tuesday, so he'll be going ten-pin bowling with Kate. He'll be picking her up at your house.'

Gerry began to think he must be going insane, but swept along by her self-delusion he entered into her crazy charade. 'Of course, I'd forgotten it's Tuesday. I'll see him tonight at our house, then. I was thinking it was Kate's night for seeing her tutor.' As soon as the words were out of his mouth he knew that was the last reason he should have given, because word for word it would be relayed to Adam and he'd know what Kate had decided.

Gerry shook Mrs Pentecost's hand and levered himself out of the door. Standing on the pavement, he felt such a rush of relief to have escaped he was almost skipping. 'Bye-bye, Mrs Pentecost. Nice to have met you.'

Gerry drove away down the street a little, then pulled up and dialled

Mia on his mobile. She wasn't in, so he left a message: 'It's me. I've called at the house and he wasn't in but she was and she's crackers, I'm certain. Please, Mia, pick up Kate tonight, won't you. I'll explain when I see you. I might be late but I'll do my best. Bye, love. Keep the doors locked when you get home, just in case.'

Who was deluding whom? Was she aware Adam was out of work and, knowing what a blow it was to him, going along with his deception for his sake? Or had he deceived her completely so she truly believed he had got promotion and was working all hours? Did he, then, on Tuesdays get his ludicrous ten-pin-bowling outfit on and set out as though calling for Kate? If so, the matter was far more serious than he had ever imagined. What a tragic mess the pair of them were in.

Gerry had to swerve to miss a car pulling out at a roundabout, which forced him to put his mind to driving and work. He'd deal with it all when he got back home. Had Gerry foreseen the events that would take place that night because of his unwitting revelation that Kate was having tutoring he would not have thrown himself with such vigour into persuading a new outlet to take his superb collection of biscuits specially put together for the Christmas trade. They were so tempting that he could eat a whole box himself straight off.

9

That same afternoon Kate was scheduled to go to Miss Chillingsworth's to pick up the kittens. But having been taken to work by Mia it was Miriam who volunteered to drive her there.

'She's really quite poor, you know, Mrs Price. Genteel poverty, Mia would call it. But she's a total dear and absolutely thrilled to have been so useful to us. She's done a good job. They're all toilet-trained, which is brilliant.'

'There's no need to apologise for her, Kate.'

'I'm sorry, I didn't mean to.'

'Right turn here, is it?' They'd reached the traffic lights by the church.

'That's it and then second left. These houses are lovely, aren't they? I'd like to live in one of these. Kind of stately and Victorian.'

'Rather large for Miss Chillingsworth.'

'Much too large, but I think it's the house she grew up in and it's hard to leave.'

'I can understand that. Clinging to memories.' Miriam went silent for a moment and Kate didn't know if it was because she was concentrating on driving or if her last three words had given her food for thought. 'Here we are. What number did you say?'

'Twelve. Prospect House. That's it there.'

Miriam applied the handbrake and asked if she should come in or wait. 'Oh, come in! She loves company.'

Miss Chillingsworth was at the door almost before the bell had stopped resounding through the house. Overcome with embarrassment when she saw Miriam, she declared, 'Why, Mrs Price, what an honour! I'd no idea. Do come in.'

'Kate's car is off the road so I've brought her. I'll wait if you prefer.'

'Not at all. Come in, do.'

She led the way down the hall towards the kitchen. Their footsteps echoed on the bare wooden floorboards and Miriam wondered if the floor was bare through choice or necessity, and thought more than likely it was the latter. There were pale square and oblong patches here and there on the wallpaper and it occurred to her that pictures had been sold to make ends meet.

'Here they are!' The kittens were playing king of the castle on an old wooden apple box in the middle of the kitchen floor. They'd grown almost beyond recognition. 'Haven't they grown! The last time I saw them they were scarcely toddling and look at them now. Twice the size and twice as confident. You've worked miracles.'

Miss Chillingsworth was delighted by Miriam's praise and clapped her hands with pleasure. 'You think so? It's been a privilege to look after them and I'm so grateful to have had the chance.'

'You're grateful! It's we who are grateful, isn't it, Kate?'

'It most certainly is. We'd never have been able to give them such a lovely time. They're wonderful. I just wish I were taking that one home.'

'But they're all spoken for, you said.'

Hastily Kate agreed. 'Yes, they are. I was only wishing. Like I said, my stepmother has a tendency to asthma anyway, so anything furry is out.'

Miss Chillingsworth showed instant concern. 'Of course, you said.'

'Here, look, I've brought the carrier. Let's get them in.'

She could tell this was the moment Miss Chillingsworth was dreading, so it was best to get it over with briskly. Kate was so relieved to have got away with her slip of the tongue, because, though they hadn't anyone for the third kitten, not for the world would she tell Miss Chillingsworth, because she knew in her bones that the time was not ripe for her to be taking on a kitten of her own.

'Oh, I've got tins left. I'll get them for you.'

'I'll be putting them in the car while you do.' Kate slipped out down the hall and left Miriam to wait for the tins.

Miss Chillingsworth emerged backwards from the pantry with half a carton of tins and a bag of cat litter in her arms. 'Here we are.'

'Thank you for all your hard work. We couldn't possibly have done such a good job. Thank you for all your time and patience.'

'Not at all. I've enjoyed myself. Helped to fill a gap, you know.'

Miriam smiled at her and Miss Chillingsworth felt warmed by it. 'You're all such lovely people at the practice. I do miss seeing you all.'

Tears welled in her eyes and Miriam sensed the pain that was Miss Chillingsworth's. 'If we should have kittens in need of loving care again, could we perhaps rely on you?'

'Of course. Gladly.' She was eager to close the door and Miriam made her retreat as swiftly as she could, realising that Miss Chillings-worth would not want to break down in front of her.

Kate turned to look at her as she settled herself in the driving seat. 'I don't really know what it is to be lonely. Her loneliness makes me terribly sad.'

Miriam said, 'Clinging to old memories is what is making her life so difficult. If she sold up she'd get a tremendous price for that house, and she could buy a much smaller one and live comfortably on the residue. That's the sad bit about it all.' She started up the engine and moved off. 'We all have a lesson to learn from her predicament, haven't we?'

Kate nodded and except for the mewing of the kittens in the back there was no further sound in the car until they got back to the practice.

Waiting for them in reception was the client wanting the all-black kitten. 'You've got them, then? My word, haven't they grown.' His choice licked his finger as he poked it through the bars. 'See, he knows me already. Bless him. I'm calling him Sambo. Appropriate, don't you think?'

Joy had come out to see Duncan's Tiger. 'Here they are. Haven't they grown? I can't believe it.' She and the client enthused over the kittens together.

Kate lifted the homeless one out of the carrier and took it into the back. She was nursing it on her knee, wishing she could take it home, when Scott returned. He crashed in through the back and caught sight of Kate through the open door. 'Kate, my sweet one! How's things?'

'OK, thanks. Do you want a kitten?'

'No, but I know a man who does. Phil Parsons. Someone has poisoned his cats. Poor chap's heartbroken. Unbroken line since his grandfather's days and all gone. I just wish I could catch the sod who's done it.'

'Are you pulling my leg?'

Scott shook his head. 'Of course not. He does. I'll ring him if you like.'

'Please. I'd be so glad to find it a home. But come to think of it, will he take care of it?'

'He may be a farmer with abysmal standards of hygiene, but yes, he will and Blossom certainly will. I'll do it now, right away. We'll take it to them when I've finished and you can see for yourself.'

As Scott had no more calls and Kate finished at four that day the two of them set off with the kitten in Scott's Land Rover.

'One thing I must say is if they offer you a cup of tea or anything make up whatever excuse you can think of but do not in any circumstances drink anything at all. Their kitchen is disgusting and the risk of food poisoning is extremely high.'

'Are you certain this is a good idea? I don't want the kitten to die.'

'Believe me, it will survive. All his animals do despite the lack of cleanliness. They develop their own immunity.' Scott checked the crossroads and glanced at her. 'You're special. Know that, do you?'

'Don't be ridiculous and you're being tooted, so make a move.'

'So I am. Why do you always rebuff personal comments?'

'To be honest, I don't usually, but at the moment Adam has completely put me off making relationships with anyone at all.' Kate looked out of the window and then turned back to Scott. 'You're a lovely person and I do enjoy your company. You're such fun, but the timing's not right. I'll be all right when I've got Adam out of my hair.'

'That bloody man. Let's go out on the town tonight, shall we? Forget all about the Adams of this world.'

'Can't. Chemistry tonight, it's Tuesday.'

'Tomorrow night, then?'

'I'd love that.'

Scott braked hard, switched off the engine, put a finger under Kate's chin and gave her head a quarter-turn so she faced him. He studied her features, smiled at the apprehension he saw there and kissed her lips with none of his usual demanding eagerness. 'I don't know why it is but I kiss you quite differently from others.'

'It's not very polite to mention all the others you've kissed. It's quite spoilt it for me.'

'I'm sorry, but I have to be honest with you.'

'Not that honest, surely?'

The kitten began to struggle against being clamped so firmly between the two of them.

'Let's go. Got your boots? You'll need them.'

'Of course not. You could have told me.'

'Good excuse for me to carry you, then.'

Which he did. Through the sludge and the mud right to the farmhouse door. She refused to allow herself to be influenced by the smell of his skin or by the manly scratchy feeling of his jacket against her cheek, but it did feel comfortable and welcome, and she thought about Adam and realised he'd never appealed to her physically as Scott did. In fact, when she thought about it there had never been anything physically appealing to her about Adam at all. The kitten began to fight against being imprisoned in her jacket and out came her claws.

'Ow!'

Scott laughed. 'So the ice maiden has feelings after all.'

'I do indeed. The kitten is scratching me. Could you put me down?'

He stood her down on the doorstep, opened the door and shouted, 'Mrs Parsons! It's Scott.' They went in.

Blossom Parsons was standing at her cooker stirring something in a pan, which smelt absolutely revolting. Phil was seated in a chair where the heat from the fire drew forth his habitual body smell and distributed it around the kitchen. Kate had difficulty in resisting the impulse to put her handkerchief to her nose.

Scott took off his hat and said, 'We've brought her and this is Kate, holding her. You won't have met Kate, Mrs Parsons.'

Blossom lowered the light under the pan and came across. 'We've been a whole week without a cat. Isn't she lovely?' She took her from Kate and lifted the kitten to her cheek, burrowing her nose in its fur and luxuriating in the feel of its softness. 'Aren't you a beauty? An absolute beauty! Six weeks, you say. She's well grown for six weeks.'

'She's had a lot of care.'

'I can see that. Look, sit down, I'll make a cup of tea. Kettle's boiled already, you won't have long to wait.'

'I'm so sorry but I have evening class tonight and I'm pressed for time. Thanks all the same. But I would be glad to pop over to see the kitten from time to time.'

'Any time you like. Scott can bring you and we'll have a cuppa and a good natter. What do you think, Phil, to her?'

Phil, wearing his balaclava even indoors, said, 'I'm that pleased to have a cat again. She'll be a bit before she starts catching rats, but I reckon she'll do all right once I've taught her what's expected.'

Kate almost blanched at the thought of what Miss Chillingsworth would have to say about this state of affairs – one of her precious charges catching rats! Lying out in the sun and being fed delicious meals of cooked chicken and fresh salmon would be more what she had in mind.

'What shall you call her?'

Mrs Parsons looked coyly at Scott. 'I did think of Scott.'

'But he says it's a she.'

'Cats don't know that, do they? A name's a name to them.' Again there was this coy, inviting look and Kate remembered how Joy had said half the women in the county fancied Scott.

Kate laughed. 'You're right. I hadn't thought of it like that.'

Mrs Parsons plumped the kitten down on Phil's knee and went back to her pan. 'I'll take good care of her. Cats are my most favourite animals. They get treated like royalty here.'

Kate found it hard to believe in the circumstances but she recognised the love in Mrs Parsons's voice and had to leave it there and hope for the best.

Scott winkled them out of the situation by reminding Kate of her evening class. 'So we've got to go. I'll bring Kate to see you in a while. Goodnight, little Scott.' They left Mrs Parsons to stirring her stewpot and Mr Parsons to cuddling little Scott who had snuggled down on his lap oblivious of the smell and was preparing to go to sleep, warmed by the fire and soothed by the gentle stroking of Mr Parsons's thick, swollen fingers.

'I'll drive you home. Are you eating first?'

'I am.'

'I'll wait, then, and take you to your tutorial.'

'No, please, don't do that. I can't allow it. Mia will take me. She'll sit in the car and listen to the radio till I come out.'

'You're still not driving your car, then?'

'Dad said not. But he'll calm down in a few days and I'll be a free agent again.'

'He's right to be cautious.' He bent down, scooped her up and transported her back to the Land Rover.

'This fresh air smells good. Are you sure we've done the right thing, bringing the kitten here?'

'It won't have the pampered existence of most surburban cats but it will live an interesting life more suited to a cat and you can't ask more than that.'

'She fancies you.'

Scott sighed. 'I know, that's why I call her Mrs Parsons and never get within a yard of her if I can avoid it.'

'It's a terrible burden for you to carry, isn't it?'

His eyebrows raised, Scott asked her what she meant.

'Having all these women taking a shine to you.'

'I don't know what you're talking about.'

'You do. And you love it.'

'Have you taken a shine to me, whatever that might mean?'

'I just might.'

Scott thumped the steering wheel and caused the Land Rover to swerve.

They both laughed and he drove her home with more style than safety. They were still laughing and talking when he pulled up outside Kate's house and it wasn't until he heard her sharp intake of breath that he realised something was very wrong.

'What is it?'

'That's Adam's car parked in front of us.'

'What the hell's he playing at now?'

'It's Tuesday, ten-pin bowling night. He must think we're going bowling!'

'He can't possibly, can he?'

'Is he sitting in his car? Can you see?'

Scott peered as best he could through his windscreen but because of the shadows he couldn't make up his mind as to whether Adam was there or not, so he leapt out and went to see. He wasn't sitting in his car, so he must have gone in. Now what? Bloody hell! He got back in his Land Rover and said, 'He's not there. That's your dad's car in the drive, is it? I mean, Mia isn't in on her own, is she?'

'No, it's his office car so he'll be in.'

'What the blazes is the nutter playing at?'

Kate gripped her seat with both hands, unable to cope with what she knew inevitably would have to be faced.

'If your Dad's there . . .'

'What can he be doing?'

'Let's go find out.'

Kate clutched hold of Scott's arm. 'Please, no!'

'We can't sit here all night. You need your books for your tutorial. Anyway, perhaps your dad needs some help.'

'I can't face Adam.'

'I'm with you. I won't let any harm come to you. Believe me.'

'If I face him now, do you think we can sort him out?'

'Of course.' Scott sounded confident but in truth he couldn't begin to imagine what might be going on in that lovely friendly kitchen.

'All right, then. But I'm so frightened for Mia and Dad.'

'Well. You and I make a good team, and there'll be four of us to his one.'

'You don't think he'll have brought his mother, do you?'

Scott snorted his amusement. 'Of course not! Why should he?'

He opened the door and went round to Kate's side to help her out. 'Here, take my hand and hold on tight.'

Kate pulled her hand away from his. 'No, if he sees us holding hands he'll think we're . . . friends.'

'We are.'

'Yes, but you know what I mean. No, we won't hold hands. Let's go in as if we don't realise he's there and see what happens.'

'OK then.'

Kate opened the door and called out cheerfully, 'It's only me. Scott's here too. He gave me a lift home.'

Both of them sensed the tension in the house the moment they walked in. Panic seemed to hang in the very air, but Kate flung down her bag and coat on the hall chair as she always did and marched into the kitchen. For all the world as though time had been turned back four, five weeks, there sat Adam at the kitchen table with her dad and Mia. A strong smell of burnt vegetables came from the pans standing on the cooker. A frying pan held crisply burnt onions and liver. Adam had a mug in front of him, the tea in it untouched with the milk in a cold eddy on the top.

But this wasn't the Adam they had known. This Adam had a nerve twitching in his cheek, which contorted his face every few seconds. This Adam had beads of sweat on his top lip and clenched hands, and a patch of sweat between his shoulder blades showing through his beige tracksuit.

'Hello, Kate! It's Tuesday so I've come to go bowling.' The tightly controlled, precisely enunciated sentences were the words he invariably used each Tuesday but they sounded so different. This time they were a threat. He hadn't said 'And you'd better come with me or else', but the words hung about on the end of his matter-of-fact statement.

Kate caught Mia's eye and picked up on the very slight warning shake of her head. Gerry looked paralysed with apprehension. She had to say it. 'I can't, not tonight.' Adam took a sip of his cold tea. 'You may as well know. I'm having some tutoring sessions to help me improve my chemistry grade and there's one tonight.'

'You'd better get your meal or we shall be late. I've booked our lane, you see, for half past seven as usual.'

'Can you not hear what I say?'

'I'm feeling in good form tonight. I shall be able to give you a run for your money. I'm really looking forward to beating you.' He rubbed his hands together with apparent glee.

'Then you'd better cancel, because I'm not going.'

'Mia! Get Kate her meal. I hate having to rush.' Adam's cheek twitched rapidly.

Mia's voice sounded as though she was in the later stages of strangulation. 'She's already told you she isn't going.'

Gerry spoke up, having found his courage now he had Scott to support him. 'There's no one orders my wife about, so you can stop that straight away. Kate is not going bowling. We've told you and now so has Kate. Now clear off . . . and . . .'

Adam banged on the table with his fist. Some tea in his mug splattered out on to the tablecloth and the stain rapidly spread. 'We always go bowling on Tuesdays and that is what we are going to do.

Bowling. Right! I've booked the lane and we're going.' His cheek twitched violently.

Scott decided to enter the one-sided discussion. 'See here, mate, Gerry's asked you to leave but I notice you're still here. Now bug— clear off. Or do you prefer me to throw you out?'

There was no reaction from Adam at all. It was as though Scott weren't even in the room. 'I'm afraid I've let my tea go cold, Mia. I'd like a refill while I wait for Kate.'

Scott, enraged at being ignored, said loudly, 'Right then, mate. O-U-T spells out and out you are going.'

He grabbed Adam by the collar of his tracksuit and heaved him to his feet.

Gerry leapt up with the intention of helping Scott with Adam's departure.

Mia got to her feet shouting, 'Be careful!'

Kate opened the kitchen door, assuming that Adam would not resist. But he did. He lashed out at Scott, striking him with a frenzied thrust of his elbow on his mouth and splitting his lip. Incensed, Scott proceeded to manhandle him out of the kitchen and down the hallway, with Gerry urging them on from behind by ramming both his fists ferociously hard against Adam's back. Between them they managed to get him to the front door. It looked like they were losing the battle with Adam while Scott struggled to open the front door, but Scott hung on tightly and finally rid them of Adam by planting his safari boot on Adam's backside and shoving him so viciously that Adam sprawled full-length on the path. Gerry slammed the door shut and locked it behind him.

Mia shouted as she followed them through from the kitchen, 'His car keys! He's left his car keys!'

'Give them to me.' Scott snatched them from Mia's hand, prised open the letter box flap and flung them outside on to the path. The snap of the letter box shutting broke the spell of terror.

Between gasps Gerry, bending over with his hands resting on his thighs, said, 'My God! . . . you arrived just in time . . . the fella's mad . . . completely mad . . .'

Mia flung her arms round Kate. 'Oh, Kate! I was so scared. I thought our end had come.'

They hugged and kissed each other in breathless relief.

Scott dabbed at his cut lip and grinned at them. 'Good day's work there. You did right not to tackle him on your own, Gerry. He's dangerous.'

'What I can't understand is that he completely ignored everything we said. Before you came, Mia and I both told him you wouldn't be going bowling but it was as if we hadn't spoken. He breezed in, calling out as he always used to as though it was only last Tuesday you'd been out together. He's finally cracked, he has, and with a mother like he's got it's hardly to be wondered at.'

'Dad! When did you meet his mother?'

Gerry explained Mia's telephone call and his morning visit to their cottage, and told of his scalp prickling when he went in and the odd unlived-in feeling the cottage had, and of how mad she was. 'They deserve each other, they do.'

Mia, still clinging to Kate, said, 'He frightened me.'

'And me.' This from Scott. 'He's going to do something dangerous, he is. See that muscle twitching?'

'Could hardly miss it, could we, Mia? It was like that when he came in. We didn't cause it.'

'Let's go and sit down again, and I'll get your meal for you, Kate.'

They trailed into the kitchen after her, glad of something positive to do. Gerry peered at the crusted contents of the frying pan with a look of distaste on his face. 'I shan't ever want liver and onions again.'

'Neither shall I.' Mia, lifting the lids off her burnt vegetables, said, 'I don't think I fancy you eating it either, Kate. What shall we do?'

Scott had an idea. 'I spotted a fish and chip place down the road. Why not let me go and get some for all of us? That is, if you don't mind me eating with you.'

They welcomed the idea. Gerry prepared to get out his wallet but Scott pooh-poohed the idea. 'No, this is my treat and after we've eaten I'll take Kate to her class. Save you a job, Mia.'

Mia said, 'Well, that's very kind. Thank you for your help tonight, Scott. We shall be for ever in your debt. There must be more to your muscles than meets the eye.'

Kate agreed. 'There is! It's all those calves he castrates and the thousands of sheep he sheared back home.'

Scott took a bow and headed for the hallway. They heard the door open and as swiftly close. He reappeared in the kitchen saying, 'I'll wait a moment, if I may. He's only just stood up.'

Gerry asked, 'You mean he's been lying there this last five minutes?'

'Sure. Looks like a neighbour's helping him up.'

Kate went to the bay window of the sitting room and discreetly peeped out. The neighbour was helping him down the path and Adam was moving as though he were sleepwalking. She watched him get into his car and sit doing nothing, then his head went down on to the steering wheel with a jerk time after time, so hard he could almost be thought to be trying to fracture his skull. Her kind heart kicked in and she wished she hadn't refused to go with him, and that she could love him as he wanted, and that he were more appealing, and more confident and more . . . well anyway . . . he wasn't and he never would be. Not for her, anyway, and in a strange, cock-eyed way his desperate actions strengthened her resolve to get to college whatever huge amounts of effort it took her. Not for her a wasted life.

The others joined her and watched through the net curtain until finally he drove erratically away and they were all left feeling distressed about him but at the same time glad to see him gone.

Scott took it upon himself to cheer them up. 'Right! I'll get the fish and chips, and be back in a flash.'

Mia asked him not to bring cod. 'Anything but cod. Shall we have wine, Kate?'

'You can. I won't. I need to keep a clear head for my tutorial.'

Scott dashed away, and Gerry and Kate sat down at the table while Mia searched for an appropriate wine. 'You know, Kate, it always surprises me what a nose Mia has for wine. I don't know where she gets it from.'

'Nor her painting. Where does she get that talent from? What did her family do, you know, what were they? She never mentions them.'

'Orphan. Brought up in a council home. She loathed it, that's why she never talks about it. I can't understand how she turned out so special. Because she is, isn't she, Kate?'

'Oh, yes, and not only to you and me. Other people love her too. Except Adam never did. He thinks she's odd, which she isn't. Funny that, when you think how odd he's become.'

Gerry paused with a fork in his hand and he waved it in her direction. 'When I think about it he's always been odd at bottom. I can't imagine why I ever thought him right for you. I have to ask this, does he make you afraid?'

'Yes, he does now. You read in books about people being in denial and I think that's what he is. He's denying what's happened because it quite simply isn't acceptable to him that he's lost his job. Without the security of it, you see, he has fallen apart. I reckon his mother knows he's lost his job but she won't face up to it either.'

'God! She's a queer one and not half. I know it gets me annoyed sometimes when I can't find something I want because Mia is so untidy, but I'd rather have that than have it like his mother does.'

Mia appeared out of the cellar, holding up a bottle of wine. 'I'd forgotten we had this. It's a Miranda Estates Unoaked Chardonnay, should be good with fish. You'll like this, Gerry. I haven't enough time to chill it but we'll have to put up with that. Look at the time! You'll be late, Kate.'

'She's not to be there for half an hour, Mia. Doing well for you, is she, your tutor?'

'Dad! She couldn't be better and when it gets nearer the time I'm going to go twice a week. She's determined I shall get an A, and so am I.'

'Good girl.'

Scott came back with piping-hot fish and chips, and by the time they'd finished off their meal with cheese and biscuits and fresh fruit their good humour was more than restored. So Kate went off to her tutorial in high spirits – life couldn't be better, she thought.

But in the early hours of the morning she woke, trembling and afraid, with vivid pictures in her head of destruction and death and skeletons: a nightmare just like those she had had as a child. Her first instinct was to rush for comfort to Mia but before she could act upon it Mia was standing by her bed. 'Kate?' Their arms were round each other even as she spoke.

'I've had a nightmare like I used to. I'm so frightened.'

'I know. I know. So am I.'

They hugged each other in silence until both felt comforted.

It was Mia who spoke first: 'Your dad insists you still mustn't drive alone, so I'll take you and collect you every day. I promise. Somehow we'll sort it, love. Gerry and Scott between them, they'll sort him. You'll see.'

10

Joy put her head round the door of Kate's office and asked, 'Are you all right? I thought you looked a bit down when you came in.'

The look Joy got in response to her question persuaded her to close the door and sit down. She watched Kate fiddle with her pen, make a pretence of shuffling some papers to her satisfaction, and waited for her to reply.

Eventually Kate answered her: 'After we'd taken the kitten to Mr Parsons Scott took me home . . .'

'. . . and . . .'

'Adam was there, for all the world as though nothing had happened and it was Tuesday and we were going ten-pin bowling.'

Kate told Joy everything – each detail of what had taken place – and the relief was enormous.

'My dear, it must have been horrific.'

'It was. When Dad went to see him only his mother was there and she said that we were getting married and buying a house and she was coming to live with us.'

'Oh dear! Oh dear! I don't know what to say. They must have gone completely crackers. How does your father feel about it?'

'He's worried sick and so is Mia and so am I.'

'It's the stuff of nightmares.'

'You see, apart from trespassing here he hasn't done anything we could tell the police about. Sitting in someone's house drinking tea isn't a crime, is it?'

Joy shook her head. 'I'll talk to Duncan about it. He sees life from a different angle from most people. He may well come up with an answer. Meanwhile keep your chin up and take extreme care not to be alone anywhere.'

'I will. Is he enjoying the kitten?'

'He most certainly is. We had guidelines about not in the bedroom and mustn't this and mustn't that, but all that's gone down the pan. Tiger rules the roost.'

'You don't seem to mind.'

Joy laughed. 'Somehow I don't, no. The kitten gets through to Duncan in a way human beings can't. He said last night he couldn't understand why he'd never had a cat before. He says cats are private people and so is he, so they match beautifully.'

Kate smiled. 'I'm so glad he's pleased. I think Tiger will have a very different kind of life from poor little Scott. She's lined up for rat-catching. But Scott thinks that's a good life for a cat.'

'It is, I suppose, more natural anyway. Is Scott behaving himself? Oops! That's none of my business. I'm sorry, I shouldn't have asked.' She got up off the chair and went to open the door. Looking back at Kate she said, 'In view of Adam getting at your computer here and what happened last night at home, which shows he's getting worse, I wonder if the staff should know, then we can all be on the qui vive just in case.'

'No, definitely not. Lynne and Stephie would think the whole situation ridiculous and it wouldn't do my image any good at all.'

'You're right, it probably wouldn't. I'll press on.'

As she left Kate said, 'And for your information, yes, he is.'

'Surprise, surprise! He must be losing his touch.'

'The perfect gentleman.'

'My word. Do you sometimes wish he weren't? Sorry!' Joy's eyes lit up with fun as only hers could. 'Shouldn't have said that. But let's face it, he is a charmer, isn't he?'

'Oh, yes. And he's proud of it.'

'He is, you're right. Keep your chin up about that other, you know.'

Scott would have been highly gratified to have known he was being discussed in such terms by Joy and Kate. But at the time his name was being taken in vain he had other more important things on his mind. Phil Parsons had called him out to see Sunny Boy once more. The infected foot had decided to erupt again and, according to Blossom Parsons's muddled message on the practice phone, it was worse than ever.

An animal in pain was anathema to him, and he loathed not being successful in curing him. There was nothing more certain to destroy the vet/farmer relationship than calling time and again and coming up with one solution after another, and none of them being successful. Still worse, the farmers hated the subsequent bills. He'd done all the right things. He'd scoured his brains for reasons and solutions and each time he thought he'd succeeded within two weeks the whole problem had flared up again.

Crossing the yard to Sunny Boy's stall, he decided to call in Mungo for a second opinion that very afternoon if he wasn't operating. At least it would impress Phil, who was rapidly losing faith in him and no wonder.

Phil was waiting for him, perched on the stout four-foot-high wall of which the stall was made. 'Scott!' He nodded his head at Scott. 'He's in agony this morning. It's not fair to 'im. I need an answer.'

'I'm very sorry, Phil. I've decided we should have a second opinion. If you agree I'll ask Mungo Price to come and have a look.'

'Well, at least he has a brain. I'm beginning to doubt you have one.'

'Now, Phil, I feel badly enough about it without having a fall-out with you as well.'

'Sorry. But him and me are mates. I've had him since he was born. Born here, he was, in this byre on Christmas Day five years ago. An absolute fluke, he was. I knew the minute I saw 'im he was special.' He hopped off the wall and watched Scott putting on his protective clothing, experience of Sunny Boy having taught him that there was a high chance of being covered in filth before the exercise was over.

Scott sprang up on to the wall, not taking the risk of drawing the bolts on the stout gate and possibly having Sunny Boy charging out and running him down. He dropped slowly down into the stall so as not to startle poor Sunny Boy, who was standing with all his weight on his three healthy legs, with the fourth touching the ground tentatively.

In accordance with his strictly imposed rules Scott went to say good morning before examining Sunny Boy's foot. He stroked his huge knobbly forehead, admiring the almost mahogany colour of his head, which contrasted so strikingly with the snow-white of his nose and jaws, and spoke softly to him. 'Now, old chap, things not going so well for you today, eh? Well, never mind, your Uncle Scott's come to make things better.'

The only reply he got was the stamping of Sunny Boy's good front feet and a roll of his eyes. The snort that followed appeared more threatening but Scott delayed moving to his rear for a split second while he . . .

Sunny Boy took that as Scott's tacit agreement that he wanted to be tossed.

In less than an instant Scott was lifted from the ground and rammed hard against the outside wall of the byre. The pressure on his ribs and especially his lungs was enormous; the thrust of Sunny Boy's great head having emptied Scott's lungs of air, he hadn't even the breath left to shout to Phil to take action. All six feet two of this proud Australian son was rendered totally helpless.

Hanging there, with his spine in a vice and his feet dangling six inches above the ground, it seemed an age before Sunny Boy suddenly released him and Scott fell down against the wall, heaving great gulps of air into his starved lungs. Whereupon Sunny Boy decided that as Scott appeared to be lying there inviting further action he would oblige. His great head, with half a ton of bull behind it, butted Scott's body time and again.

Scott could hear Phil shout, 'You bloody great sod you!' There came the sound of Phil landing with a thud on the floor of the stall and instantly Sunny Boy lost interest in Scott, swung round despite the confined space and went hell for leather for Phil, snorting and pawing the ground. Phil leapt out over the wall in one swift balletic movement and Scott, while Sunny Boy's attention was absorbed by wondering how he'd missed Phil, went just as swiftly as Phil over the wall and then collapsed, painfully breathless and in agony from head to foot, on the stone floor.

'My God, Scott! I'll kill the bastard. He went for me. Me! Who's tended his every need since the day he was born. So help me, I'll kill him.'

'He didn't get you, though, did he?' Scott tried to sit up but the pain was horrific. His ribcage felt shattered and the searing agony of his stomach and thighs where Sunny Boy's head had landed so emphatically was beyond endurance.

Sunny Boy was still snorting and stamping, and Scott muttered some ugly curses he'd heard the hands on his father's sheep station using since his infancy.

Phil shouted in admiration, 'By Jove! Them sounds damn awful foul. You'll have to explain the meaning of them to me when you're feeling more like yourself. Can you get up?'

'No.'

'I'm getting Blossom.'

'I'd rather you got me to hospital.'

'Bad as that?'

'Has he ever tried to gore you?'

Phil shook his head. 'Never. I've never had a cross word with him until today. He must be in terrible pain. I'll get the ambulance.'

'You won't. This Aussie boy is not going in any poncy ambulance. Take me in your lorry, and ring the practice first and tell them what's happened. Someone'll have to do my calls. Kate will sort it.'

Phil ambled off, his balaclava even more askew than usual.

Scott lay still, wallowing for the moment in self-pity. Then he heard the shlap-shlap of Blossom's fashion boots on the cobblestone yard. He groaned.

Dressed more suitably for a brothel than a byre, Blossom paused in the doorway for a moment and then came in, overflowing with sympathy. 'Scott, you darling boy. I heard you groan, you must be in agony. Phil's phoning the practice.' She knelt down on the stones beside him and, taking hold of his head, pressed it to her chest. 'Where does it hurt the most?'

'You name it, it hurts.'

'He didn't stamp on your vital regions, did he . . . I mean you're not going to be impaired in any way? I wouldn't like to think . . .'

'Fortunately for the Spencer line, no, he didn't.'

Blossom pressed a hand to her chest. 'That's a relief. I wouldn't like to think that Sunny Boy was responsible for incapacitating you in that area, as you might say. There, now, lean against me and we'll get you up. Phil's bringing the lorry as close as he can.'

Scott, unwisely as he knew full well but in the circumstances it was unavoidable, accepted Blossom's help and slowly heaved himself to his feet. The throbbing anguish caused him almost to faint and Blossom had to take his whole weight for a moment. 'Sorry.'

'Don't apologise. I'm only too glad to be of help. I have some arnica in the house. It's excellent for relieving bruising. Could I rub some on your chest? It would help.'

Scott shook his head. He decided to pull himself together. He simply was not behaving as a real man should. Bracing himself against the excruciating pain he knew was inevitable, he straightened up and headed drunkenly for the door.

The journey to hospital passed by in a blur. He'd never realised just how many bumps and holes there were in major road surfaces. Finally he surrendered to the ministrations of the hospital staff, feeling less than himself and certainly not in charge of Scott Spencer, Australian *extraordinaire*.

He woke later that day to find Joy sitting beside his bed. 'It's you. OK?' Scott struggled to make himself more comfortable but groaned horribly and gave up trying. 'What's the damage? Do we know?'

'They've X-rayed *all* your vital parts and the news is you've cracked three ribs on your right side at the front and two on the left. Apart from that no other breakages. Heavy bruising just about everywhere, but no internal damage to vital organs so far as they can tell at the moment. Everyone sends their love and hopes you'll soon be feeling better.'

'I'll go home, then.' He made an effort to sit up and blanched with the pain it caused. 'Well, perhaps not at the moment. I'll give myself another half-hour and then see how I feel.'

Sceptically Joy said, 'That might be an idea. Do you realise how close to being killed you've been? Eh?'

'Hang that. Sunny Boy is in grave need of attention. His left hind foot is torturing him. I was going to ask Mungo to go and see him this afternoon.'

'He's been.'

'He's not in the next bed, is he?'

Joy laughed and Scott tried but failed. 'No, he isn't. He's too wise a bird to get himself trampled by a bad-tempered bull. He sent Phil in first.'

'Wise man. So . . .'

'When he got there a huge abscess had formed and he's lanced it, got rid of loads of pus and gunge, given him a massive dose of antibiotics and painkiller, and is going back tomorrow.'

'Thank heavens. I never got a chance to look, you see.'

'Might as well tell you, Phil's thinking of getting rid of him. Sending him to the abattoir. Can't believe he went for him when they are, well, were, such chums.'

'He mustn't. Tell him he mustn't. Sunny Boy was in terrible pain. No wonder he went for me, it served me right for not curing him straight away. Promise me.'

'I promise. We've sorted your work till the weekend; well, at least Kate has, so you've no worries until Monday and we'll see what you're like by then.'

'I shall be fully operational, believe me.'

'For heaven's sakes, drop the macho pose, Scott. It's the biggest wonder in the world we're not sending for the undertaker right now. Just behave yourself. The news of your accident has stunned us all. Half the county will be in here before the night's out and when you do leave hospital you're coming to our house to recuperate. Duncan's at home most days and he's an excellent nurse, despite all evidence to the contrary. He knows just when not to fuss.'

Scott eyed Joy for a moment, weighing up her offer, and thought about his bare, comfortless bachelor flat with little food in the cupboards. The idea of returning there was very unappealing, so he decided to give in. 'I shall be delighted to accept. And thank you.'

Joy stood up. 'I mean it, I'll speak to the nurse on my way out.' She leant over the bed and kissed him. 'You're a dear boy. I'm glad you've survived, it could have been so much worse. Kate is coming in later when she finishes. That'll be nice, won't it?'

'She's not driving herself, is she? She mustn't.'

'No. She's not. Mungo's bringing her. He's coming for a full briefing on the whole affair.'

'I must be ill if *el supremo* is coming to mop my fevered brow.' Scott pulled a dreadful, tortured face, sucked in his cheeks and crossed his eyes.

'You must be on the mend.' Joy blew him a kiss as she disappeared through the cubicle curtains. She returned, grinning wickedly. 'There's a queue of nurses forming at the ward door to attend to you. Make the most of it; Duncan's not nearly so appealing. For one thing he doesn't wear black tights. Au revoir.'

Duncan may not have worn the black tights but he was proving to be an excellent nurse. He had the instinct to know that Scott didn't want to be mollycoddled but that he did need caring for. The shock of the accident had to some extent at first masked the pain of the cracked ribs and the bruising, but now Scott was grateful for painkillers and even looked forward to the next dose when the relief they gave him was wearing off. Consequently he slept a lot and Duncan left him to it.

By Friday afternoon Scott was downstairs and sitting in Duncan's study in front of the fire, with Tiger snugly cuddled on his knee while Duncan worked at his computer. It was very companionable being with Duncan. His long silences were not isolating but comforting, rather, and Scott found himself relaxing more and more. He'd be back at work on Monday, though. A chap could get too used to this kind of life. No soaking-wet days, no mud, no filth, no cold, no missing meals, only warmth and solace. Yes, he could quite take to it. He stretched a little but it disturbed Tiger so he stopped halfway through the stretch. In any case it would have been definitely uncomfortable to do it properly. Scott glanced at the clock. Past lunchtime. Should he offer . . . no, he'd wait for Duncan. He dozed and only came to when he heard Duncan coming in with lunch.

'Tomato and basil soup. That sound all right?'

'Excellent.' Scott released Tiger and she jumped down and went to her little basket that Duncan had placed close to the fire. 'Thank you. This kitten will be getting soft.'

'Never mind. Bread?'

'Yes, please. Her sister will be out rat-catching before she's much older.'

'Good luck to her, that's what I say.'

'Looks cold out.'

'It is. Been out to feed the chickens. Much too cold for either man or beast. Don't you sometimes long for the sun and the heat? How long is it since you left home?'

'Eighteen months or thereabouts. I do today, funnily enough.'

Duncan fell silent and concentrated on his soup. He cut himself another slice of bread from the loaf he'd balanced on the end of the bookshelf and continued eating in silence.

Scott drank up the last of his soup, spread a little more butter on the remains of his bread and munched on it. A big log on the fire slipped and rolled over so its bright-burning red face turned towards him. The sudden increase in warmth reminded him of home, of the shimmering heat hitting him in the face the moment he stepped out of the air-conditioned house on to the veranda. The endless vista of land stretching and stretching away to the far horizon. The hot, hustling reek and clatter of the shearing sheds and the relentless day-in, day-out back pain at shearing time. The leathery aroma of his saddle and the stink of his sweat after a day's riding. Best of all he remembered the startling ice-cold shiver of the first beer when the heat had reached a hundred and you thought you'd die if you didn't get it all down in one long pull. But he'd had to get his wanderlust out of his system, otherwise he'd have been restless the whole of his life. Maybe now was the time ...

Duncan took hold of Scott's soup mug and wrested it from his fingers. He took the remains of the bread into the kitchen and left Scott and Tiger to sleep.

Defrosting on the worktop was a chicken whose neck he'd wrung, and which he'd plucked and cleaned and put in the freezer along with three of its sisters some weeks before. Duncan tested it to see if it was ready for the oven. While he prepared the casserole he thought about Scott. There'd been a very wistful tone to his reply when he'd asked him about home. He'd better warn Joy that Scott could be getting itchy feet, as they all did. Though why anyone should prefer to burn up in the intense heat of Australia he couldn't begin to imagine. Give him a hill to walk up, a summit to reach on a crisp, bright, frosty day. For enriching the soul it couldn't be improved upon. He looked out of the window at the hills. Not today, though; the air was damp, and the sky full of clouds. Even so, it would be better than scrambling his brains into oblivion working out his current computer problem.

Scott came to stand in the doorway. 'Has Joy told you about Kate's problem?'

'She has.'

'Do you have any ideas? She's being stalked, you know, and it's beginning to eat away at her.'

'At the moment no.'

'Her parents are making sure she never goes out by herself, but what more can they do?'

'Nothing. They'll have to hope his problem goes away.'

'Gerry blames his mother.'

'Mothers get the blame for most things that happen to us, especially the bad things.'

Scott laughed. 'I wish in a way he would do something we could report to the police, then at least they might put the fear of God into him and he would stop. He's obsessed.'

'Aren't we all?'

'Are we? Are you?'

'My obsession is myself, though I'm working on that at the moment.' He gestured to the chicken and the casserole dish. 'Hence all this effort.'

'Tell me, what's mine, then?'

'Scott Spencer.'

'Hold it there, mate! Is that how I seem to you?'

'To everyone. Obsessed with your sexuality, with your macho image, with the admiration of women, with your need for approval, with being an Australian male and living up to it . . .'

'Hell! Duncan!'

'You did ask.'

'You don't pull any punches, do you, mate?'

'*You did ask.*'

Scott began to get angry. 'Are you always like this? Because how the hell Joy puts up with you I do not know.'

Duncan wiped down the worktop and ignored Scott.

'Well, how does she?'

'None of your business.'

'I'm fond of Joy. She's great and she's helped me a lot. But I feel sorry for her, coping with your kind of person day in day out.'

'*She* chose *me.*'

'Not the best day's work she's done.'

'You would think like that, Scott.'

The pain Scott was suffering added malice to the tone of his voice. 'Have you absolutely no consideration for other people's feelings? Time someone shook you out of your little cocoon and you entered the real world. Joy's a treasure, though obviously you don't appreciate that.' Scott hitched himself against the door jamb to ease his pain and sensed that as a guest in the house he'd gone too far.

Duncan turned to look at him properly for the first time since their conversation had begun; his eyes bored into Scott's with an unnerving intensity. 'Being a guest in our house does not give you the right to poke about dissecting our marriage, so kindly put your scalpel away, if you please. You've no God-given right to be so judgemental.'

'Huh!' It was the cold, unemotional way that Duncan went about his attack which angered Scott. It made it more calculated, more cruel. 'Don't know what I've said to bring all that malice out of you. If you feel like that I think it better if I leave.'

Duncan shrugged his shoulders. 'Your choice.'

'You're damn right there. I'll be off, then.'

'Fine. Be seeing you.' Duncan put the chicken casserole in the oven, walked out of the kitchen and returned to his computer.

Scott slowly climbed the stairs. He hadn't intended their conversation to end with him leaving. He'd only asked for a different angle on Kate's problem and then he'd brought all that down on his head. Intellectuals irritated him; you never knew where you were with them. Give him a straightforward fella like Phil Parsons; you knew where you were with him even on one of his belligerent days.

Duncan's analysis of his personality had touched him on the raw and angered him. Who the hell did Duncan think he was? He'd damn-well order a taxi and be gone before Joy got back. He looked at his watch. One of Joy's perks was never having to work the late shift on Fridays so she'd be home in an hour. Best be gone before she arrived. His Land Rover would be back at the practice and he always carried spare keys, so he'd collect it, go and shop for food and then go home and see to himself all weekend, and stuff the lot of them.

He scribbled a thank-you note for Joy on the back of an envelope he found in one of his pockets, left it on the bedside table, flung his belongings in his bag and went downstairs to order his taxi, the weight of his bag reawakening his pain.

The taxi pulled into the practice car park and there, waiting with its doors wide open, was an ambulance. Scott gingerly heaved himself out of the back seat, paid the driver and went to put his bag in his Land Rover. He was going to drive off without making contact with anyone, but the unusual sight of an ambulance at the practice stopped him. He walked across to the back door to find Bunty being wheeled out, eyes closed, ashen-faced. He stood back so as not to get in the way. The ambulance doors shut and someone he took to be Bunty's mother came out and got into her car to follow the ambulance.

Scott stood for a moment, weighing up what to do. It most certainly was not the best week he'd had. What to do? The only right thing was to go in and find out.

Joy was standing at her desk, her hands resting on it, her head bowed.

Scott tapped lightly on the door. 'Joy?'

She looked up, her eyes unfocused and weary with anxiety. 'What are you doing here?'

'On my way home, but that's another story. I saw Bunty.'

'So you did. Close that door. Better sit down.'

'I'll stand, thanks.'

Joy pulled up her chair and sat on it. 'I've had some difficult afternoons in my life but this one has capped all.' She drew in a deep breath. 'Unfortunately or fortunately, it depends where you're coming from, Bunty is having a miscarriage. Something tells me you might be responsible.'

'God! Has she said so?'

'No.'

'Why should it be me?'

'A glance here, a laugh there. I'm not blind and I know what you're like, you love the buzz of being attractive to women, I can't doubt you get carried away with only the slightest encouragement.'

Scott wished she hadn't said that. It reminded him of the scene in her kitchen and what she would learn when she got home. Truth, he'd always stood by the truth; lies got you nowhere. Was it Walter Scott who said, '*O what a tangled web we weave, When first we practise to deceive*'? Today, it seemed, was a day for truth. 'It could be, but I asked her and she said no she wasn't pregnant.'

Joy shook her head in despair. 'Well, she is, was rather. Poor girl.'

'Indeed, poor girl. If I am responsible ... well ... it takes two. She was eager.'

'That's your vindication, is it?'

'I'll sit down.'

Joy looked at him and saw the lines of pain in his white face as he seated himself. 'Not your week, is it?'

'No, and I've fallen out with Duncan and left.'

'That's not difficult. He could pick an argument with a saint.'

'I've really upset him.'

'Let's not go into that right now.'

'If it is me ... Will you find out for me?'

'I'll try, but girls can be very funny about babies and such. There are all sorts of complicated reasons and emotions for not coming up with the truth.'

'I see.' Scott eased himself up out of the chair. 'I'll be here Monday if it kills me.'

'Sorry things have gone badly for you. I'll make things right with Duncan.'

'Thanks. See you Monday. I *did* ask her and she said no she wasn't, so what can a chap do?'

'Not do it in the first place, young man.'

Scott allowed himself a rueful smile.

The tone of Joy's voice hardened as she said, 'None of my business, but I warn you, take care of Kate or else.' She wagged her finger at him. 'I mean it.'

Scott didn't answer, but he paused for a moment, saluted her with a single finger to his head and a nod, and left.

He'd intended spending the entire weekend by himself, pottering about, sorting his washing and generally pulling himself together after his disastrous week, but at about eight o'clock on Saturday evening he heard a car pull up outside. The entry phone buzzed and when he answered to his delight he found it was Kate outside.

'It's me. I've come to cheer you up. Can I come up?'

'Kate! Of course you can.'

'Mia dropped me off. Open up. It's cold.'

He pressed the entry button. 'Third door on the left, first floor. Number eight.'

'I'll be there.'

'See you.'

He was so thrilled to see her he held his arms wide open and she went into them and they kissed. Kate hugged him as close as she dared, given his cracked ribs, and he responded by showering her face with kisses. 'You've no idea how glad I am to see you. My self-imposed isolation was beginning to drag. Sit down. Drink?'

'Yes, please. I've heard all about your walkout from Joy's. Why ever? I find Duncan so easy to get on with.'

'I trespassed on his married life and he objected. He told me a few home truths which got me annoyed and altogether we suddenly didn't hit it off.'

Kate asked what the home truths were, but he wouldn't tell her. 'Not likely. You might agree.'

'He's very perceptive.'

'In a twisted kind of way.'

'Was he right?' Kate had a grin on her face, which began to irritate Scott.

'Look, subject closed.'

'Oh, dear! He has touched you on the raw. OK. I won't ask any more.' Almost as an afterthought she added, 'I've been with Joy to see Bunty this afternoon.'

Scott looked her straight in the eye. 'How is she?'

'Home tomorrow. Rather low. None too happy. Despondent, only to be expected. Asked how you were, after your argument with Sunny Boy, you know.'

'Did she?' Scott fiddled with his glass, downed half his lager in one go and enquired, 'Anything else?'

'Oh, nothing, really. Joy seems to think . . .'

'I'm responsible.'

'Something like that.' Kate had to ask. 'Were you?'

'It was before you came and yes, I could have been, but I asked and she said no.'

Kate nodded. 'I see.'

'She's actually lost the baby now, has she?'

'Oh, yes.'

There was silence for a while and then Scott said, 'I told her I wouldn't have married her.'

He didn't like the sarcastic undertones of Kate's reply. 'Oh, great. That was a very good idea. Very comforting and so supportive.'

'I'm ashamed, really, but I don't feel anything for her. Marriage would have been disastrous.'

'Ah! Right.'

'She was as much to blame. How could she expect a red-blooded male not to respond to her kind of blatant overtures? If anyone was seduced it was me. You modern girls don't give a chap a chance to say no.'

'Oh! You poor thing.'

'Kate!'

'Time you grew up.'

'Please don't you fall out with me too; it's more than I can take this week.'

He looked so genuinely upset that Kate decided to change tack. 'You're not thinking of going in to work on Monday, are you?'

Scott nodded.

'It's far too early. Be different if you had an office job. Sunny Boy's due for another visit on Monday.'

'Well, Zoe could do that. Or Rhodri or Valentine. They could pretend he was a dog. Let them get kicked or trampled.'

'You are down, aren't you?'

'Give us a cuddle, that'll do the trick.'

Kate moved on to the sofa and sat close to him. 'Is it Duncan?'
Scott nodded.

'Well?'

'I'm not telling you.' He took hold of her hand. 'It must be the pain.
I'm not used to it.'

'It *is* Duncan, isn't it? He can be quite ruthless, I understand.'

'It's his coldness I find difficult to take. It makes what he says that
much more hurtful.'

Kate sat back to appraise Scott. 'I've never seen you so introspective.'

'Stop using long words, it's too much for a simple Aussie like me.'
He grinned at her, pulled her close to him and kissed her. Several times.
'I needed that.'

'So did I.' She pulled herself away from him and said quietly, 'I don't
know why you always put on this act of being tough.'

'Sorry. It's how I am. Kiss me again. Please.'

Which she did, gently and appreciatively, savouring the sensation,
finding it new and enthralling.

'I bet that nutter Adam has never woken anything in you, has he?'

She drew away from him again. 'Why spoil it with reminding me of
him?'

'Sorry. I can't believe he could go out with you for two years and
never manage to excite you.'

'That, Scott, was how I wanted it, with him. In any case I'm not into
relationships here, there and everywhere. It's not my scene.'

'Not even with me?'

'Not even with you.' She stood up. 'I know the other girls think I'm a
prude, and stiff-necked and such, but I don't care. It's a decision I've
made and I'm sticking with it. I'm not going to finish up like Bunty,
thanks.'

'I see. I don't want that either, not with you, you're different. I was
just feeling in need . . .'

'Of a boost.'

Scott smiled up at her. 'I admire you for standing by your principles.'

'Good. We understand each other, then.'

'How are you going to get home?'

'Mia's gone to visit a friend and she's coming back for me in about
an hour.'

'Stay here, then.' He patted the cushion beside him. 'Sit here and
we'll watch TV and I promise to behave myself. Boring though it might
be.'

She laughed. 'I do like you very much indeed, you know that, don't
you? I think I must have fallen under your spell.'

'Most women do.'

'Honestly! Your ego!'

Her comment reminded him of Duncan and he sobered down. 'I like you too, perhaps too much for my own good, but there you are.' He switched on the TV set and they sat holding hands and occasionally smiling at each other, watching an old American cowboy film until the doorbell rang and it was Mia.

She came up to sit for a few minutes. 'I'm early. My friend was just going out for the evening. My fault, I should have given her a ring first. Nice flat, Scott. I like it. Feeling better? I didn't think you'd be home so soon, perhaps Monday at the earliest.'

Scott caught Kate's eye and then answered with a non-committal, 'Thought they'd like the weekend to themselves.'

They chatted idly for a few more minutes and then Mia got up to go. 'Take care of yourself, young man, and if you're not right on Monday take a few more days off. Go back too soon and you'll only make things worse. Bye-bye.'

'Bye-bye, Mia.'

He kissed Kate gently on her lips and ran a caressing finger along her cheekbone. 'Goodnight, thanks for coming.'

'Goodnight. Take care.'

Mia drove Kate home carefully, only too well aware that Adam was following them. She didn't tell Kate that he'd been sitting outside Scott's flat all the time Kate had been visiting and that all she, Mia, had done was position her car where she could watch Adam without him knowing. When she saw him for the second time decide to open his car door as though getting out, she'd started up her engine and driven back into the road as if returning from somewhere. Adam had swiftly shut his door when he saw her and slumped down in the driving seat to avoid being noticed. But he couldn't deceive her, even though he'd changed his car for the second time.

11

No one quite knew how to treat Bunty when she returned to work. Did they sympathise or did they behave as though the miscarriage had solved a lot of problems for her? The one with the most need to clear the air was Scott and he found her at lunchtime eating her sandwiches sitting outside the back door on an old bench, which had been put there temporarily when they'd first moved in and never moved.

'Can I sit down?'

She didn't look at him. 'It's a free country.'

'Feeling better?'

'Ditto?'

'Yes, thanks, and you?'

'Well, Scott, I think they say in these circumstances as well as can be expected.' Bunty took another bite of her salad sandwich and continued looking up at Beulah Bank Top.

Scott stared at it too. 'I'm sorry it happened.'

'I'm not. Didn't fancy bringing a child up on my own. It's no picnic.'

'I don't expect so.'

'Wouldn't have had an abortion, but fortunately for me it made its own mind up.'

'I see.'

Bunty chanced a glance at his face. 'You were right. It wouldn't have worked anyway.'

'Marriage, you mean?'

'That's right.'

So the baby must have been his. Scott felt an upsurge of emotion, a sudden fierce joyousness at this proof that he could fulfil his male role to its full potential. His elation showed on his face and he almost leapt to his feet to shout 'Eureka!'

Bunty, with a quick glance, caught sight of his look of delight. Carefully folding up the the plastic bag that had held her sandwiches and gazing up at the hills again she said, 'It wouldn't have been the right basis for marriage to have saddled you with someone else's baby, now would it?' She stood up and, without giving him a chance to answer, walked to the back door, opened it and disappeared inside.

Scott's ego plummeted to new depths. Women! How could any man ever begin to understand the workings of their minds? Was she being a tease to punish him? Was she that liberal with her favours? Did she see his delight and decide to get her revenge on him? Or was she so hurt at his reaction to her pregnancy that she wouldn't allow him the pleasure of believing he'd fathered a child. *Was* he the father? Maybe he would never know. The main thing was he had no responsibility now towards her or to a child so he was still free as air. Well, not quite, there was Kate who wouldn't stay out of his mind.

He sat there for a while, thinking about her, until he grew so cold he had to go inside. As he turned to make his way in he caught sight of a car coming to a halt at the top end of the tarmac, a curious bilious yellow, it was, with a soft beige top. Some people's taste! He strode in without looking back. He'd see if Kate was free to make him some coffee and then get on with his calls. As he passed the operating theatre door Bunty rushed out of it in tears and fled into the staff toilets. Mungo, in his full operating kit, came out after her. 'Seen Bunty?'

Scott pointed to the toilet door. Mungo nodded and shouted, 'Joy! Where are you?'

Scott left him to it and went to find Kate, but she'd gone off at one, so he made his own coffee and went his solitary way to his afternoon calls. If he hadn't been so cold and had stayed out on the bench a while longer he would have seen Adam get out of the bilious yellow car, ready for a walk on the hills.

Joy had had a challenging afternoon. Bunty had gone home after her tears, leaving Mungo with no one to assist him in theatre, so Joy had to leave Lynne by herself on reception for the afternoon and get gowned up to work with Mungo. It was some time since she'd had to fill in on the operating side and she was under stress the whole time, worrying about letting Mungo down or worse, causing the animal, whose quality of life Mungo was hoping to improve, to die.

It was a very delicate operation on a cat whose leg had been shattered in a road accident and the constant reference to X-rays, handing of implements and the final framework of pins and screws to keep it all in place while the bones had a chance to heal ended in Joy feeling completely done in when Mungo finally declared he was satisfied. At the same time, though, it brought back splendid memories of how they had worked together in the early days, and the old welcome feeling of working as a team and the closeness of their relationship of those days filled her with pleasure, and for the moment both Duncan and Miriam were forgotten.

'Done! Thanks, Joy. Thanks for stepping in. Quite like old times, eh?' He patted the cat's head as Joy took it off the anaesthetic saying, 'There we are, Muffin, it's all up to you now. I can't do any more. Tea in your office for old times' sake? Yes?'

'Yes. That was brilliant. You don't lose your touch, do you?'

'Neither do you.'

'Was I nervous! But it all came flooding back.'

'What about Bunty, then?'

'Early days.'

'I'd be sorry to lose her. She's the best nurse we've got. The two Sarahs are excellent but Bunty has the edge. She's very intuitive.'

'I know. I'd hate to lose her too. The girl's all mixed up and no wonder.'

'Is it Scott?'

Joy shook her head. 'I honestly don't know, she hasn't said. He says she says it isn't him, but ...' Joy shrugged her shoulders. 'Give her time. I'll put Muffin in intensive care. Tea in my office in five minutes?'

Mungo nodded.

When they settled down to drink their tea Joy said, 'If Bunty doesn't come back, though I'm sure she will, I can help out till we find someone else. Kate is so good. She got reception and accounts under her belt in no time at all. Far too good for the work entailed. Sometimes I wonder why she's here.'

'So do I. This tea's welcome. She's never said anything, has she?'

'No. Not a word and I'm not going to ask. So long as she works well that's all that concerns me. Except ...' She put down her cup. 'Except she still has the problem of that idiot Adam stalking her. It's really preying on her mind. Her parents insist, quite rightly too, that she never goes anywhere without either Scott or them driving her. Not fair her life should be so curtailed by the man.'

'Maybe he'll cool off in a while.'

'Let's hope so.'

Mungo stood up, reached across her desk, cupped her chin in his hand and kissed her. Combined with the feelings stirred in her by working with him in theatre, the hint of fervour in the pressure of his lips served to awaken the longings she'd had for him for years.

When he straightened up he looked at her for a moment and then said, 'Got to go. Miriam's got a surprise planned for me. You've not lost the old skills, Joy. It's good to know you could still be my right-hand woman if need be. Thanks again. Keep in touch about Bunty. I'll look in on Muffin when I get back.' Mungo treated her to one of his beautiful warm smiles, which thrilled all who were privileged to receive one, and her heart jumped into her throat and she couldn't speak. She twinkled her fingers at him and let him go without a word.

Damn him! Damn him! His kiss had been a reward for helping him, nothing more, nothing less. Would she never learn that it was Miriam he loved, not her?

Having been reminded all over again of the bitter truth, Joy drove home in no mood for one of Duncan's silences. But he wasn't there. He'd gone walking and, unusually for him, he'd left a note to say he would be home in time for his evening meal. By his computer was a thick pile of printout sheets, so finally he must have solved his problem. She wished she could solve hers.

Duncan came home tired and hungry, but he'd obviously kept an eye on the clock because he was in through the door half an hour before the meal was ready. 'Quick shower and I'll be down.' He smiled at her and blew her a kiss.

Joy pulled a face. What had she done to deserve that? Maybe he really was trying to make an effort to improve things between them. She went to get a bottle of wine, because she knew she needed to make an effort too, if only to erase the guilt of what Mungo's kiss had aroused.

Duncan didn't speak until after he'd finished his first course. He sat back replete. 'That is the kind of meal a man needs when he's been walking in the hills. Was I hungry, was I!'

Joy toasted him with her glass. 'I see you've solved your problem. Loads of printouts.'

'I have. That was why I needed to walk, clear my head. Which it did. Do you fancy going out? A drink or something?'

Startled by this departure from the norm Joy hesitated and then suggested: 'Cinema?'

'OK, then. I'll check the paper when we've finished.'

'Duncan . . .'

'Mm?'

'Oh, never mind.'

'You've started so you must finish.'

'You seem happier. More relaxed.'

Duncan thought over what she had said. 'I'm trying to be more considerate. To you. After my run-in with Miriam I saw the error of my ways.'

'Ah! You did?'

'Why the hell should you care about me? Whenever do I do anything at all to deserve you? Never. So I decided to be more ... attentive.' He gave her a wry grin. 'It's hard, unaccustomed work for me, but I am giving it a whirl.'

'I'm glad. It's been an uphill struggle.'

Almost too casually Duncan asked, 'How's Mungo today?'

Joy jumped guiltily. 'Mungo? Why do you mention him?'

'I can see that look in your eyes which consigns me to the wilderness. It's very hard to bear, Joy, and hasn't helped at all. I'm so jealous of that man.'

Ashamed, Joy said, 'However *I* might feel, you can rest assured that nothing, absolutely nothing, will separate Mungo from Miriam, believe me. The battle is with myself and myself alone. Most of the time, ninety-five per cent of the time, he's just someone I work with and then something happens and the balloon goes up. It's time I packed it in.'

'Your job you mean?'

'No, not my job, I couldn't do that, I love it too much. No, letting Mungo stir me up. I'm a sentimental old idiot at bottom and I've got to put a stop to it. The trouble has been you didn't make any effort to redress the balance, if you see what I mean. Slowly but surely I've become your housekeeper and that's not what I want but it's what I've got. You gave me nothing here, so I've clung to what remained of Mungo, but if I look it squarely in the eye, nothing remains except a good working relationship built up over a lot of years.'

There was a long silence while Duncan made sense of what she'd said. He sipped his wine, finished his pudding, stared out of the window and finally said, 'I've loved you since the day we met, but my feelings have been strangled by yours for Mungo. I can understand how it came about. He is a most adorable man, but you weren't even fair to me when we married, were you?'

His question hung heavy in the air like some kind of overpowering incense that even opening a window would not disperse. Joy lifted her head and stared straight into his eyes. 'After all these years, what makes you come out with that right now?'

'My own self-searching. I'm guilty too. My cramped emotions haven't helped. You're right about me offering you nothing to keep you. Like you said, that damned computer is to blame. But you're not being fair to Miriam either. Does she know how you feel? Have you ever told her?'

Joy was appalled by his question. 'Of course not. I wouldn't dream of breaking her heart by telling her. That's dreadful. Terrible thought.'

'She's very perceptive. Maybe she's realised; picked up on that special smile you have for him?'

Joy flushed with horror at his question. 'What special smile?'

'Well, you can't see your own smile but even a congenital idiot could. I bet the staff at the practice have guessed.'

The possibility that they might have guessed was too dreadful for Joy to contemplate. Did they all know and were amused behind her back? Talking about it? Contemplating her chances? Oh, God! No! Of course not. He was saying it to upset her. She'd never given away her secret, not by so much as a touch or a look. Of course they didn't know.

'Go on, be honest, Joy. Haven't you ever wished he was me when we used to make love?'

There was that cold, analytical tone in his voice, the one which probed without emotion or thought for his victim. But his eyes told a different story: they were pleading for reassurance. If she lied would he guess? What if she told the truth?

She chose her words slowly and carefully. 'Honesty being your watchword, there were times to begin with when, yes, I wished it was Mungo. Just sometimes. Not for a long time, though. But I'm bound to you by something invisible. There's no escape. I couldn't be without you and I don't know why ... if that's any help.'

'And me to you. I'm bound by I know not what. Maybe it's a passionate love we've both of us smothered with neglect. Seeing as we are coming out in the open about ourselves, how about telling Miriam and then finally when you saw how distressed she was you might be cleansed of him and able to lay his ghost?'

'I can't do that. I couldn't! I couldn't stay at the practice if I did. For heaven's sake.'

'In that case, then, maybe the more straightforward thing to do would be to give in your notice.'

'Is this an ultimatum of some kind?'

Duncan didn't answer immediately. When he did he simply said, 'Just testing.' He got up from his chair and went to stand at her side. His mood had changed as quickly as if he'd flicked a switch. She looked up at him and scrutinised the sombre face with its deep-set eyes and sad, gentle mouth. With more desire than she had experienced in an age she wanted him to kiss her.

'Taken slowly in small doses, one step at a time, there's hope for us, isn't there?' For the second time that day her chin was cupped in a man's hand. Briefly he touched her mouth with his.

'Oh, yes!' And suddenly she felt there was. She took his hand from her face, kissed the back of it and pressed it to her cheek. 'Let's sit in front of the fire. Leave the table for now.'

They both moved to sit in the easy chairs before the fire. They were silent for a while, each running over in their own minds the conversation they'd just had. Then, out of the blue, he said, 'Met a chap today. Strange chap.'

In the silence that followed Joy said, 'That'll make two.'

'Yes, but *I'm* not weird.'

'What was he doing?'

'Walking and, like me, trying to make sense of things. He's barmy if you ask me.'

'Tell me.'

Joy put another log on the fire and settled herself to listen. Duncan, eyes half closed, remembered his meeting with the man.

There'd been at least another mile to go before he would reach the summit and he'd decided to find somewhere out of the wind to sit to eat the bread he'd brought with him. He could never be bothered with making fancy sandwiches so he'd picked out a roll from the freezer and a lump of cheese from the fridge and chosen one of those Comice pears he loved out of the fruit bowl. He knew that by the time he was ready to eat, the roll would have defrosted and be fresh and soft and rich-smelling, just how he liked them. He'd taken a couple of bites from it when a man hove into view wearing, for some curious reason, a second-rate business suit and nice shoes, with a beige-coloured anorak to keep out the cold. He hesitated, watching Duncan from where he stood on the sheep track. Duncan saw the twitch he had in his cheek and thought, *Here we go; a nutter of the first order.*

Having resolved his computer problem he had room to feel full of concern for mankind, so he shifted along the boulder he was sitting on and invited the chap to take a pew. 'You can share my roll and cheese if you wish.'

The man patted the pocket of his anorak and said, 'Got my own.' But he accepted the invitation to sit beside Duncan and the two of them sat in total silence, eating their lunches and enjoying the view.

When Duncan pulled a can of beer from his pocket the chap looked at it enviously. Duncan offered it to him. 'Have a drink; you're most welcome.'

But he rejected the offer, so Duncan, never one to make the effort to persuade people against their wishes, emptied the can himself.

'I prefer lager.'

Duncan wiped his mouth on the back of his hand. 'I'm a beer man myself.'

'I see.'

They sat a further while in silence, looking at the view, each wrapped in his own thoughts. Eventually Duncan said, 'I'm heading for the top. Coming?'

The chap shook his head. 'I've never reached the top, never had the courage.'

'What's courage to do with it? It's a simple matter of putting one foot in front of the other.'

The chap stood there, trying to make up his mind. 'I suppose it is. Do you mind?'

'I did ask you.'

'Right. I will. You lead on.' He crumpled the wrappers from his lunch and was about to stuff them into a crevice of the boulder when he saw Duncan carefully storing his empty lunch bag and beer can in his jacket pocket. So he did the same.

They strode up the rest of the way, following a sheep track, and when they reached the top Duncan went to his favourite sheltered spot to rest. It was only a small dip alongside the track, but it kept the worst of the wind off and he liked the idea that in the depths of the night sheep would be huddled here. It made him feel at one with them. The two of them found it rather a squash but Duncan, being so at peace with the world, had not minded.

'Married, are you?' the chap had asked almost immediately.

'I am.'

'I live with my mother.'

'Cramps your style, does she?'

The chap shook his head. 'Haven't got any style to cramp.'

'You should have, a chap your age.'

'Your mother. Did she cramp your style?'

'My mother scarcely noticed I existed. The occasional pat on the head for doing well at school constituted the extent of her sortie into parenthood.'

The chap thought about this and observed, 'That's better than being smothered like me. Are you out of work? I just wondered with you being about during the day.'

'I'm a computer programmer and I work at home. I've just finished a big project so I'm free for a few weeks.'

'I see. Do you come every day?'

'I shall for two or three weeks till the next project.'

'I might see you, then.' His cheek twitched furiously and his head jerked in tune with it. 'Would you mind?'

Duncan did mind but he could see the chap's need. 'Not at all. Look out for me.' Duncan watched him walk away down the hill, shoulders bent, hesitant, jerky, twitching, and thought, *Poor devil.*

'So that was all that happened and I expect I'm landed with him for the next few weeks.'

Joy asked, 'Did he tell you his name?'

'No. Didn't seem like that kind of a relationship.'

'He sounds in need of someone to talk to.'

'Aren't we all?' Duncan slid from his chair and hitched himself along the floor till he reached Joy. He rested his back against her legs and she set about putting his untidy hair to rights. 'We all need someone.'

Joy left her hand resting on his head and stared into the fire. 'We do.'

'We'll give the cinema the elbow, shall we?'

'I'd forgotten.'

'Getting too late anyway. Do you mind?'

'No. We can always go tomorrow night if there's anything decent on.'

Induced by the good food and the warmth of the fire, Joy and Duncan sat there for more than an hour enjoying each other's company. Halfway through, Tiger came in to investigate their silence and chose to climb on Duncan's legs, planning to tease him into playing with her, but she too succumbed to the warmth and the quiet between them and eventually gave up persuading him to play when she fell off his legs on to the carpet, going to sleep beside him, with his hand caressing her ears. It was the first evening for a long time that the house had been so at peace with itself.

The next day it seemed that peace had been restored at the practice too and Joy was looking forward to a busy, enjoyable day. Bunty had returned, apparently determined to ignore her upset of the previous day; Graham and Valentine were in the consulting rooms; Zoe and Scott out visiting the farms; Lynne was covering reception with help from Kate, who was doing the accounts as and when the pressure lessened on reception. Mungo had several clients coming that morning and Joy herself was going to tackle the roster for November.

She'd settled at her desk with everyone's holiday requests lined up at the side of her computer, focusing her mind on her task, when she heard the sound of argument. Her head came up and she listened hard.

Lynne's voice was strident and uncompromising. Kate's voice placatory. What was that Lynne said? '... too bossy by half ...'.

She couldn't hear Kate's reply but there again came Lynne's voice, raised even higher: 'You're not telling me what to do. You've a long way to go before you know this job as well as I do, so you can pipe down.'

Joy could hear the tone of Kate's voice but not distinguish the words.

There was Lynne again, shooting her mouth off: 'Miss Perfect, are we? Little white hen that never lays away. Huh!'

Joy shot out of her office and into reception, ready for action. Between clenched teeth and *sotto voce* she said, 'What is the matter? I can hear you in my office. Have some consideration for the clients; they can hear every word. This is disgraceful.'

Neither Lynne nor Kate answered her.

'Well, I'm waiting.' One of the phones rang but the two girls were too busy glaring at each other to answer it. Joy dealt with the problem, answering the telephone as though nothing was amiss, changed someone's appointment on the computer and then turned to them again. 'Well, I'm still waiting.'

Lynne decided to get in first with her side of the story. 'Kate has sent Zoe halfway across the county to an emergency when Scott is only four miles away and could easily have gone on his way to his next call. I told her she shouldn't have and she told me to mind my own business.' Lynne pointed to herself, continuing, 'I've been here long enough to know what I'm doing. She comes and thinks she knows it all in five minutes. Well, she doesn't. She knows damn all.'

Joy turned to Kate. 'Well?'

'Scott specially asked to be given plenty of time at his next call. The farmer's really been kicking up a stink about things and saying he's thinking of moving to another practice if they don't improve, so I thought it best, seeing as he has such a full list today, that he stuck to his schedule and Zoe, who's cutting down on her number of calls because of the baby, could fit this emergency in quite easily. That's all.'

'I see. Lynne does have a point.'

'I most certainly do. That Scott thinks he's indispensable and she' – pointing at Kate – 'favours him no end. It's ridiculous. Scott this. Scott that.'

'That's not true.'

'And if we're really getting down to the nitty-gritty, who's she anyway? With her A levels and that, she thinks herself something very special. Oh, yes! But look at the mistakes she's made ... that money for starters.'

Joy pricked up her ears at this. 'What money?'

'Miss Chillingsworth's.'

The moment she said it Lynne appeared to regret it and Joy picked up on that. 'What about that money?'

'She lost it, didn't she?'

'Well, she didn't actually lose it. It turned up.'

'Careless, though, wasn't she? Not quite part of the goody-goody image, that kind of mistake.'

'Lynne, I get the distinct feeling you know something you haven't told me. Do you know where the money disappeared to and how it came to materialise again? Because if you do, you'd better come clean right now. Kate, stay here. Lynne, my office.' Joy jerked her head towards the back. Lynne hesitated for a moment, then followed but not before she'd deliberately trodden on Kate's foot as she squeezed past.

Joy, who knew her staff and was a past master at dealing with difficult ones, had the truth out of Lynne in the sweetest, kindest way before they'd been in the office five minutes. 'So you took it, hid it, put it back when I read the riot act, all for what?'

Lynne avoided looking her in the eye. Instead, she stared out of the window. 'She really gets my back up. Too clever for her own good, she is. What's more, she was very rude to my brothers. Oxford graduates, they are, with top jobs in the City but it made no difference to her. She told them off. I mean! Who does she think she is?'

'Did they deserve it?'

'No. Well, yes, perhaps they did. So I saw what had happened, that she'd forgotten Miss Chillingsworth's money, and I thought I'd teach her a lesson. I wasn't going to keep it, you know, I wasn't stealing.'

'I never for one moment thought you were. I shall overlook the incident this time, but if ever anything of this nature occurs again and you are involved, then . . .' Joy drew her forefinger across her throat and made a strangulated sound. 'As you know, I always mean what I say and I would not hesitate to give you the sack immediately, on the spot, with no time even to collect your belongings. Kate is a good worker and with all the sickness and whatever we've had recently I don't know where we would have been without her. You're a good worker too. None better. You're quick, polite and helpful to the clients, pleasant to work with and that's how Kate is too. That's how I run this practice, with happy, hard-working people who get on well with each other and who put the clients and their pets first. As for those brothers of yours, they are only human beings after all.'

'If you were in my shoes you'd have been taught they were gods.

Public school and university for them; comprehensive for me because it wasn't worth educating me and that's how it's been all my life.'

Joy smiled at her. 'Then it shouldn't have been. Lynne Seymour is worth her weight in gold. Off you go and send Kate to me, please.'

Before she opened the door Lynne, not quite sure how she'd finished up apologising, said, 'I'm very sorry. Thanks. It won't happen again.'

'Of course not.'

Joy had made up her mind while she'd been talking to Lynne that she'd ask Kate outright why she was working there. Lynne was absolutely right: Kate was out of place as a receptionist and Joy had always known that, but hadn't faced up to it until now.

'Sit down, Kate. I've had a word with Lynne and she's apologised and said she hid the money out of spite to get back at you. Her reason being that you'd been rude to her brothers, but more so because you were too clever for your own good. Her words not mine. Which I've always known you were. So the question I have to ask is, why are you here?' Joy had no intention of letting her leave the office until she had a satisfactory answer, so she sat with arms folded, waiting.

Kate knew there was no escape; the question had to be answered and you didn't tell fibs to Joy because being the kind of person she was she'd know immediately that you were lying. She looked at Joy's lovely, kind face, at the curly blonde hair framing that face and most of all the bright-blue eyes full of honesty, and said, 'I'm a failed vet. Well, not really. Actually, I got two As at A level and the third one I only got a grade C, so I didn't get a place and I was so bitterly disappointed that I took this job as being the nearest I could get. Looking back on it, it was a stupid, stupid thing to do, but it felt right at the time.' Kate shook her head. 'No, it wasn't a stupid thing to do because I love it and enjoy every minute of my time here. But ...'

'Yes?'

'They have said that if I get this third grade A then they will have me. So I'm having tutoring in chemistry every week and taking the exam in the summer. Fingers crossed I shall get in.'

'What a wonderful surprise.' Joy got up, went round her desk and kissed Kate. 'I am delighted. So pleased to hear that, Kate. Brilliant! You'll stay with us until then?'

'If you'll have me. I know I should have been more straightforward with you at the beginning but I was so badly upset by it all and Dad would keep going on about me trying again, and I kept saying no because I'd worked so hard and couldn't face ... I could hardly bear to think about my failure, let alone talk about it.'

'What made you change your mind?'

'Scott mainly, I suppose. But also Adam, who was so resistant to me trying again because he wanted us to get married that he kind of stiffened my resolve, as you might say. I should have come clean when you offered me the job. I am sorry.'

'I'm glad you got yourself together again. It would be churlish of me not to wish you every success. If at any time you want to go out on a call in your spare time, just say so.'

'Thank you, I'd like that.'

'I think you should let the others know when the opportunity arises, just to clear the air. Meanwhile you're reception and accounts, so you'd better get back to it and please do your best to keep the atmosphere pleasant for all concerned. I value Lynne just as I value you, and Stephie and all the others. Thank you for being honest with me.'

'Thank you for letting me stay on.'

Joy sat back in her chair and pushed her fingers through her hair. Would you believe it? Kate hoping to be a vet. Well, well. She should have guessed. She'd make a lovely vet, she truly would. Such a pleasing girl. A girl she would have liked to have had as a daughter. When she married, Duncan had declared he didn't want children and she was so distraught at Mungo's marriage to Miriam that at the time she hadn't cared two hoots about anything except easing her broken heart. She'd always known Duncan had loved her deeply when they first married, but she'd been the cheat, longing for it to be Mungo when she and Duncan made love and him realising it, and finally allowing her obsession to spoil everything for them. Well, now it was too late for children but perhaps not too late for the two of them to make a real marriage of it. Duncan was making an effort and so too must she.

Joy went to the mirror in the staff loo and gave herself a frank appraisal. Not bad for fifty-three next birthday, skin still clear and unwrinkled, eyes still bright, not a single strand of white hair showing, figure slightly full but comely. She imagined Duncan standing beside her. Did people ever notice that he was nine years younger than her? Not really. He looked gaunt and older than his years with his hollow cheeks and his deep-set eyes, and that stoop from bending over his computer all these years. She'd better keep herself in trim, though, in case this was her decade for beginning to show her age. Where would she be if a few weeks striding up Beulah Bank Top every day restored Duncan's good looks and revitalised him?

That night Duncan told her the second episode of the story of the man in the beige anorak. 'He must have watched me yesterday and seen which way I'd come because as soon as I reached the stile where Beulah

Bank Top really begins he was there, leaning on it, waiting. He looked cold, as though he'd been waiting quite a while. I climbed the stile and we set off, him behind me because the path is narrow there. I know it sounds odd but we walked almost all the way to the top without speaking. I stopped in my favourite place and so did he, and we shared the boulder and ate our lunches in silence. Today he'd brought a can of lager. I looked at him and smiled, saying nothing.

' "You don't say much," he said.

' "Neither do you," I replied.

' "No." He stared into the distance.

'I said, "I'm willing to be quiet if that's what you want, or you can talk if you wish."

'He waited a while and then looked hard at me. "My problem is I have no job. I was elbowed out by someone we all nicknamed 'motormouth'. Lot to say but did very little. I was sure I'd get the promotion, I told everyone I would. Which was stupid." He eased the knees of his business suit so they wouldn't crease. "That's why I'm wearing this suit. I've not told anyone I've lost my job. I go out of the door each morning, dressed for work with my lunch in my briefcase and a wave to my mother."

' "You mean she doesn't know?"

'He nodded. "She doesn't know, and I can't tell her."

' "Can't tell her? Why ever not? What the hell!"

' "If you knew my mother." He said that so vehemently I was nonplussed. "I don't know what to do."

' "Get another job?"

' "I'd never get one that pays so well. I've so few skills."

' "There are companies crying out for loyal, hard-working, reliable staff. I bet you could get a job tomorrow."

'For a moment I saw a glimmer of hope cross his face and then it disappeared. "You're nothing without a job."

' "Right at this moment I don't know if I shall ever work again, but you can see it isn't bothering me."

'He looked me square in the face. "Is it?"

'"No. Because I've every confidence that the world is my oyster. There's work out there for everyone if you're a trier. I bet right now, somewhere, you are just the man someone is wishing they could employ."

' "Really?"

' "Oh, yes. Then you can go home to your mother and tell her that the promotion you got didn't fulfil your expectations and you decided to get another job."

' "I could?"

' "Of course. She doesn't have to know, does she? There are things mothers shouldn't be told."

' "There are?"

'I nodded. "Oh, yes."

' "I see."

'I can't say the twitching stopped but it lessened.

' "I'm ready for the top, are you coming?" I asked.

' "Yes, I am."'

Duncan fell silent, so Joy asked, 'Is that it, then? Didn't you say any more?'

'No. He left me at the top and I watched him walking away with a firmer stride, not so jerky, you know.'

'Well, send for Duncan Bastable, freelance psychiatrist. Let's hope it works.'

'I hope so for his sake.'

'And you still don't know his name?'

Duncan shook his head.

But Joy had a niggling thought that she wasn't putting two and two together.

12

'Hello, Scott here. Is Kate about?'

'Yes.'

'Get her for me, there's a darling, Lynne.'

Lynne slapped the receiver on the desk and went to find Kate. 'It's lover boy, wants a word.' She spoke abruptly with something of a sneer on her lips.

Kate went to the desk and picked up the phone. 'Hello, Scott. Got a problem?'

'I'm on my way to Applegate Farm. I wondered if you'd like to come with me? You finish early today, don't you?'

'I'd love to. I'll be ready to leave in about half an hour.'

'I'll pick you up. I've got to go past anyway. See you, sweet one.'

Lynne watched her from the corner of her eye. 'Got a date?'

'No. Just going with him on a visit.'

Lynne nodded her head, remarking sarcastically, 'Oh, of course, the budding vet.'

'OK, Lynne, OK. It is in my own time.'

'I know. Just wish it was me.'

'I wish it was too.'

'No you don't.'

'I do. I genuinely do if that's what you'd like.'

'No hope of that, I'm afraid. Science wasn't exactly my favourite subject at school.'

'What was?'

'English.'

'Ah! Well.'

'Exactly.' A client came to the desk and their conversation had to be put on hold. By the time they resumed it Kate was waiting for Scott to appear.

'In any case, I couldn't be doing with all that muck and mess. Operations would turn my stomach, believe me.'

'Good thing we don't all want to do the same things. There's always college or evening classes. Maybe you could improve your grades or something. Find a whole new career.'

'Perhaps. I'll think about it.'

They heard a banging on the back door. 'That'll be Scott. See you Monday, Lynne.' Kate picked up the boots she'd borrowed from Joy and went out.

'Fling your boots in the back. I'm running late; get in.' Scott rode hell for leather along the country roads, up hill and down dale at a furious pace.

Kate had to protest. 'Scott! Please! We're going to have an accident.'

'Sorry.' He slowed a little and took the next corner at a steadier pace. 'What's the matter?'

'Tired of the cold, that's me.'

'We all get tired of the cold and then as soon as the hot weather starts we all complain. English people are never satisfied where the weather is concerned.'

'You're right. But somehow it feels depressing. Oops! Sorry!' Scott swung the wheel over quickly to avoid them going head first into a ditch.

'Please, Scott! Your driving is going from bad to worse. Slow down!'

'OK, OK.'

'Look, here's the turning.'

The Land Rover slid to a halt just past the road to Applegate Farm. He reversed a few yards, then pulled on the steering wheel and manoeuvred into the opening to the lane.

'You'll have to pull yourself together or we're going to have an accident.'

Scott slowed right down to a crawl and then pulled into the side. Switching off the engine, he turned to face Kate and said, 'It's no use. I've got to say it.'

'What?'

'I think I might have fallen in love.'

'With whom?'

'Who do you think?'

'I don't know, do I?' Kate stared out of the window watching the wind blowing through the tattered winter grass. He wasn't going to mess up their whole relationship with some wild statement of undying love, was he?

'You.'

'Me?' She turned back to face him. 'I think not.'

'If you don't know it's you how can you say you don't think so. It's not logical.'

'No, it isn't. But you don't.'

'I think of you night and day.'

'You don't, Scott.'

'I do. You're the first girl I've ever met who occupies my thoughts all the time.' He leant forward and placed his lips on hers, kissing her with great gentleness. 'See?'

'I'll tell you why I occupy your thoughts all the time, shall I?'

Scott nodded.

Looking directly at him Kate said, 'Because you know I have no intention of falling into bed with you at the first opportunity. My resistance has to be overcome and that's a challenge for you, and that's what makes you think of me all the time, not love. Full stop.'

'Kate! That's not fair.'

'The truth isn't always fair.' Not for the world would she tell him how much she longed to make love with him.

'I've always said you were different from the others.'

'Is that what you told Bunty? That she was different?' If she wasn't careful it would show.

'No, I did not. I told you it was mostly her fault. No, that's not right. It was fifty per cent me of course. She tempted me and I was feeling . . . well, I was feeling a mite homesick, would you believe, and I was looking for comfort. But that night she was that woman in the Bible. Jezebel.'

'Oh, dear! Poor Scott.' Until she met Scott she wouldn't have known how to play a shameless woman like Jezebel, but now she would.

'Look, why won't you take me seriously?'

Kate looked at her watch. 'You're running late. Mr Parsons will have something to say and Blossom will be anxious.' Her old headmistress firmly believed that it was the female side of a relationship that dictated how far and how fast it went, so here she was, firmly applying the brake.

'Please don't mention Blossom Parsons in the same breath as you and me. I may be . . . well . . . over-friendly with certain people, but I do draw the line at Blossom.'

'Drive on.' Some instinct, deep down, warned her to keep him at a distance, because nothing but terrible hurt could result from falling in love with Scott. Maybe she was already in love, maybe not, but Kate knew she was right. Beneath his complaints about the weather she sensed a longing for home and she knew he'd be gone one day without so much as a backward glance.

'What is Mr Parsons's problem?'

'Scouring.'

'I trust you mean one of his cows?'

Scott laughed. 'Yes. It's Christabel. We can't stop it. Kidneys, you know. She's no use to him as a commercial proposition, she's far too old, but he can't bear to see her go to the knacker's yard. He's such a sentimental fool, I just hope he'll face up to it today without too much aggro.'

'I like Mr Parsons.'

'So do I. He's great. He'll never make a fortune but there you are. Right, boots. Please.' As he reached into the footwell of the passenger seat to get his own boots he made it an excuse to kiss her.

'Scott!'

'You sound like a schoolteacher.'

'Well, someone has to keep your urges in check.'

Scott grumbled as he struggled to put on his boots in the confines of the driver's seat. 'No heart, you haven't, none at all. Hard as iron.'

'I have a heart all right but it's not yours for the taking.' Tempted by the vulnerability of the nape of his neck, she kissed it before he straightened up.

'Wow! She's kissed me!' He pretended to fall out of the open door with the shock, and stood in the lane looking up at her, grinning. 'Come on, then, you temptress. Let's be having you.'

They strode across to the cow byre amicably, sidestepping as best they could the filth which, despite his constant promises, Phil had never cleared up. He appeared like a spectre through the gloom of the byre, almost colliding with them as they entered. 'She's down. Went down an hour ago, that's when I rang. That's it, isn't it? I can't get her up.'

'Let me look. I did warn you two days ago that the stuff wouldn't cure it, Phil. At her age there isn't much hope. I did say. You'll have to brace yourself, mate.'

Scott took out his stethoscope and bent over Christabel to give her a thorough examination. He shook his head. 'We could put a sling under her and get her up between us. Kate is pretty strong and if Blossom helped us ... But I really don't think ...'

Phil took out his handkerchief and pressed it to the gaps in his balaclava. Blossom appeared in the doorway. 'I heard you come. All up, is it?'

Scott nodded. 'It would be kinder. You know. Her heart's ... you know ... what with that and the kidney problem ...'

Blossom burst into noisy tears. Phil desperately tried to smother his sobs but they wouldn't be stilled. Between them he said, 'She's been my favourite all these years.' He looked at Kate. 'She knew me, yer know. Knew me, she did. Bless her. Came when I called.'

Kate weighed in on Scott's side, saying as gently as she could, 'I can understand how fond you are of her, but you'd be doing her the best of all kindnesses by letting Scott put her to rest. You can rely on him. He wouldn't put her to sleep a moment too soon. For her sake, it feels almost cruel to prolong the decision.'

Phil Parsons looked at Kate from inside his balaclava. 'You're right. I can't let her suffer, can I? That's not the way a friend would behave. I'll just have a moment with her before you . . .'

Kate and Scott went to stand in the yard. Quietly Kate said, 'This is dreadful. Are all farmers like this?'

'No, not all. No farmer likes having an animal put down, but Phil takes it all so personally. They're his friends, you see.'

'I'll be crying next.'

'Lean on me, sweet one, you can cry on my manly shoulder.'

'OK, then. Thanks for the offer.'

'Scott!' Phil shouted from inside. 'All right. Let's get it over with.' He burst out through the door and marched without looking back into the farmhouse. Blossom teetered after him, her high heels slipping and sliding on the cobbles of the yard. Over her shoulder she hissed, 'Get it done and quick, before he changes his mind.' She followed him into the house.

'Well, we'd better get on with it. You and me.'

'Right. Tell me what to do. Do you need your gun?' Kate went to Christabel's head and stroked her forehead.

'I think the situation calls for an overdose of anaesthetic.' When Scott came back with the syringe and the bottle of anaesthetic Kate unexpectedly felt ill at the thought of watching this dear old friend of Phil's take her leave. But she continued stroking her head, kneeling down in the straw to get closer. She cuddled Christabel's head with her arms while Scott prepared the syringe.

'Watch! Take note.' He plunged the needle into Christabel's vein and almost in an instant she'd gone.

They both went to the farmhouse door intending to say they were leaving. It was open and Scott put one foot inside and called out, 'It's done. All quiet and peaceful. She's out of her misery. We're going now, all right?'

But Blossom would have none of it. 'Come in, even if it's only for a moment. Phil's having a whisky. Would you have one too? In the circumstances, you know. Please.' They couldn't ignore the pleading tone in her voice.

Scott glanced at Kate and she nodded. After all, at least the whisky might be wholesome if nothing else was. She supposed that not even Blossom could do damage to whisky. So they went in and found sparkling crystal glasses awaiting them on the cluttered, dirty kitchen table.

'Only small for me, I'm driving. Same for Kate, she's not used to it.'

Blossom handed them their glasses and, picking up her own, toasted Phil. He was slumped in his favourite chair by the fire, lost in gloom, his balaclava askew, his handkerchief pressed to it. 'Twelve years I've had Christabel. Twelve years. Never a mite of trouble she's been. Eight calves she's had. Eight. Mother of Sunny Boy, yer know, and for that alone she's special. I won't tell him tonight, best not till morning. It'll only upset him, yer know.' Sorrowfully he shook his head.

Choked by the depth of Phil's sorrow, Scott muttered, 'Quite right.' He braced himself and found words of comfort. 'She's had a good life, though, Phil. There's nothing on your conscience where she's concerned, is there, Mrs Parsons?'

She shook her head in reply. 'Treated like royalty she's been.'

What she'd said reminded Kate of little Scott. 'Where's Scott? I'd like to see her.'

'Scott? Oh, the kitten. On our bed, I expect.' She went to the bottom of the stairs and shrieked, 'Scott! Scott!' In a moment little Scott came running down the stairs, a bundle of energy and well grown for her age. She wrapped herself around Kate's legs, then Scott's and then jumped up on Phil's knee. She arched her back and flirted her tail, inviting him to stroke her. Phil nuzzled her with his forehead. 'Christabel's gone, old love. Did you know?'

The three of them stood in silence, watching him. Scott broke it by suggesting it was time they were off. 'Thanks for the whisky. Sorry and all that. Take care.'

Kate swallowed the last of her whisky and said, 'Goodnight, Mr Parsons, Mrs Parsons.'

'Goodnight and thanks.' This from Blossom because Phil was too full of grief to reply.

Before Scott unlocked the Land Rover he stood Kate against the driver's door and kissed her. She put her arms round him and hugged him tightly. They kissed a few more times and then stood holding each other close. 'Scott, I was almost crying in there. It won't do for a vet, will it?'

'Why not?'

'Maybe I shouldn't be one.'

'Of course you must. You handled yourself brilliantly. Is it the first time you've put an animal down?'

Kate nodded.

'It won't be the last, you know. It's all part of the job. You never do it unless it's completely necessary, the one and only course of action. It's never pleasant, but it has to be done.'

'I know, but Mr Parsons was . . .' Inexplicably, Scott was suddenly pulled away from her, and almost hit the ground but managed to save himself.

'Who the hell!' Scott turned and found he was being gripped by . . . Oh, God! No! It was Adam, wild with temper.

'She's my girl! My girl, do you hear! I could kill you!' Adam grabbed Scott by the neck of his jacket and tried to whirl him away down the lane, but he had not bargained for Scott's superior strength.

Scott slid out of his jacket and made a stand. Taking hold of the front of Adam's anorak with both hands, he hauled him to a halt. Face to face Scott snarled, 'What the blazes do you bloody-well think you're doing? Eh? Eh?' Scott shook him viciously, making Adam drop the jacket in his desperate effort to stop his attack.

Kate shouted 'Stop it! Stop it!' trying to put an end to Scott's violent shaking. But Scott wouldn't stop. He shook Adam till his head was rocking backwards and forwards like a rag doll's, his breath pushing in and out of his lungs with great grunts.

'We've had enough of you, do you hear? Stalking Kate. It's to stop. Now. Now, I say!' Scott released him. The two of them paused for a moment, both breathing heavily.

Kate went to stand between them and summoning up some of the power she'd felt when Mr Parsons had gone to the practice with his billhook shouted, 'Please, Adam. There's to be no more of it. Just go home.'

'Home?' His Adam's apple leapt up and down in his throat with his agitation. 'Home? There's nothing for me there. Nothing at all. If you'd just agree to marry, everything would be right.'

Peering at him Kate could see the desperation in his demeanour. 'But I can't marry you. I can't love you; I said so.'

Adam jerked his head at Scott. 'There was love between us before he came. I know there was.'

'No, Adam, not really, we were mistaken.'

'I wasn't. *I loved you.*'

'I was mistaken, then.'

Scott intervened. 'It still doesn't excuse stalking Kate. Have you any idea how frightened you made her? Dogging her footsteps every day. Following her like you've done tonight.'

'I needed to know what she was doing. I couldn't allow you to . . . I wanted to watch what you were up to. I wouldn't have *harmed her.*'

'She didn't know that, did she? Have you nothing better to do?'

This silenced Adam.

Sensing his agony at the idea of speaking aloud the dreaded words, but realising he'd be all the better for admitting it, Kate quietly said, 'I'm sorry you've lost your job.'

Having the words spoken out loud in front of his adversary was the final humiliation for Adam. Just between the two of them he could have confessed his predicament but not in front of that damned Aussie. He brought back his fist and pushed it with all his meagre might into Scott's face. But Scott was too quick for him and dodged the blow. It spent itself against the Land Rover and made Adam hop with pain. He hugged his hand to his chest and achieved an appearance of such ridiculous helplessness that Kate was more upset by it than she liked to admit. He looked so defeated that she went to put her hand on his arm in sympathy, but he brushed it off.

The pain of his hand and the heaped-up despair of the last few weeks mounted up and he spat out, 'Glad, are you? Satisfied? Yes, I have to confess I have lost my job. Not only did I not get my promotion but I got the sack. Imagine. All my hours of dedication and wham!' By mistake, blinded by his suffering, he banged his injured hand on to the door of the Land Rover again and suffered even more pain. '. . . Oh, God! That hurt! I was chucked out! Not even time to say goodbye. They kindly forwarded my belongings. Huh!'

'I'm so sorry. Your mother. How has she taken it?'

Adam looked at her with burning, angry eyes. 'I haven't told her yet.'

'But . . .'

'I know! I go out every day ready for work and . . .'

'Oh, Adam. Tell her. That's what mothers are for.'

'Not this mother.'

Scott decided to put an end to all the sympathy. After all, Adam had made her life a misery and here she was, after Adam had attacked *him*, feeling sorry for him. Pugnaciously he said, 'Well, if you don't mind I'd like to get home. Do I take it there won't be any more following of Kate, then?'

Kate would have preferred a more kindly approach from Scott. 'Scott!'

'Well, Adam, do I have your word for it?'

Adam ignored Scott and looked at Kate, taking in her lovely face and the sympathy in her eyes and wished – oh, how he wished – he'd behaved better than he had. He swallowed hard, knowing she'd see that pathetic Adam's apple of his bobbing up and bobbing down. What he felt was a sense of total outrage that someone whom he considered his property was in a closer relationship than he had ever been with a man who excelled him in almost every aspect of his life. His looks, his charisma, his appeal, his qualifications, his . . . and now somehow, as he always would, Scott had gained the upper hand. Even so it had to be said. 'There'll be no more following of Kate.'

Scott was determined he wouldn't get away with it too easily and decided finally to humiliate him by treating him like a child. 'Say you're sorry, then, like a good boy.'

'I am sorry, Kate. I should never have done it. I was just so . . .'

'I know. It must have been terrible. But tell your mother. You can't keep this deception up for ever, you know.'

He shrugged off her hand from his arm and looking away from her he said, 'Mothers don't have to know everything. I'm going to get another job before I tell her. The money's running out anyway.'

'That's it. You show her. I reckon she's not nearly so frail as she makes out, you know. Stand tall. Move out.' Kate smiled up at him. 'Move on.'

Adam gave her the nicest of smiles. 'You could be right, but she'll go mad.'

'Let her. It's your life.'

He rattled about in his pocket for his car keys. 'I won't say goodbye, Kate, I'll let you know what happens.' Adam set off down the lane towards his parked car. Kate and Scott looked after him in silence.

Scott put his arm round her shoulders. 'Well, well.'

'Poor Adam. What a night! What with Christabel and him . . .'

'At least that's an end of him following you. I really do think he meant what he said. Don't you?'

'Oh, yes. Adam's always straightforward.'

'I don't think sneaking about following you around is straightforward.'

'Well, he wasn't in his right mind then, was he?'

'Where's my jacket? Ruined, I've no doubt.' He bent down to pick it up. Fortunately it hadn't rained for a few days and the jacket was dry. He dusted it off and put it back on again.

They both felt deflated by the evening's events and all Kate wanted to do was go home and eat. Without Scott. Just with Mia and Dad, and to tell them her news. 'Take me home. Please.'

'Get in.'

As it turned out, Gerry was at one of his model railway meetings so there was only Mia at home. 'Scott not coming in, then?'

'No. Only me. I'm ready to eat.'

'Two minutes.' Mia looked at Kate and, seeing the stress in her face, opened her arms wide and folded her in them. 'There! There! What's happened? You look upset.'

Kate drew away from her. 'As we were leaving Applegate Farm, Adam appeared.'

'Adam!'

'Adam. He went for Scott and they had a kind of mini-fight.'

'Oh, Kate!'

She told Mia word for word what had happened, ending her story with: 'I'm so glad it's all over.'

'So am I. Thank God for that. Here, sit down and eat, you'll feel all the better for it. I don't think I could have taken much more, never mind you. And you say his mother still doesn't know.'

Kate nodded. 'I think he's going to get another job and then tell her what happened. I felt ever so sorry for him.'

'Well, you would.' Mia patted her hand. 'That's just like you.' Mia got halfway out of her chair to reach across the table to kiss Kate. 'Too kind by half.'

They smiled at each other and Kate continued eating in silence with Mia watching every mouthful. When she'd finished Kate put down her pudding spoon, drank the last of her tea and said, 'Mia!'

'Yes.'

'I never say how much I appreciate all you do for me. You're not my mum but you are, if you know what I mean.'

'It's a pleasure. I loved you the moment I saw you.'

'When did you first see me?'

Mia drew her cup of tea out of the way and rested her forearms on the table. 'You were six months old when I moved in next door. Two years old when your dad and I married.'

'But I thought . . .'

'Do you really want to know?'

'Yes.'

'I mean really, really want to know?'

'Yes.'

'Your dad should be here.'

'Tell me all the same.'

'You're right. It would only upset him and you've a right to know at your age.'

'He's never told me, you know, not what really happened.'

'Firstly, did you know your mum and dad weren't married?'

'I didn't know that.'

Mia nodded. 'It's true. Where they met I've no idea but when I moved in next door he was on his own with you. Are you sure you're ready for this?'

'For some reason I am. I've got to know. Things are kind of moving on with Scott and I feel I need to have things straightened out before ... before I take any steps.'

'Moving on with Scott?'

'Kind of. I think.'

'Well, he's a lovely young man and if he suits you ... Here goes, then. Your mother had walked out when you were two weeks old and left your dad to get on as best he could.'

Kate gasped with surprise. 'I thought she'd died. I always thought she'd died. You mean somewhere I have a mother? A real mother?'

Mia felt stabbed through the heart by Kate's excitement and wished she'd never agreed to tell. It was too hard for her to take; she should have waited for Gerry. 'Yes. But she's never been in touch since. He told me he'd tried every avenue he could think of to find her but he never had. Before I knew where I was, I was helping him to care for you. I'd just left a savage marriage and the sight of you so beautiful and innocent, so bright and happy and kind of gurgly, gave me back my faith in the world. Just touching you helped to heal my wounds.'

Mia stopped speaking and gazed into the distance, obviously enjoying once more the happiness the baby, Kate, had brought her. She sighed briefly and went on with her story. 'I'd only been here about two months when my pig of a husband was killed outright in a car accident. I didn't think immediately, oh well that releases me from my bondage. Relief, yes, but not any thoughts of being free to get married again. I'd had enough of that. Your dad and I bumbled along for a few months looking after each other, like you do. I had you to myself when he was at work and the whole arrangement worked out very well. One thing I loved was taking you out in the pram, because people thought you were mine and I wished you were. We were bathing you ready for bed one night when Gerry said, "Why don't we?" Why don't we what? I thought. "Get married," he said.'

'Oh, Mia, not the most poetic of proposals.'

They were holding hands by now and Mia squeezed Kate's and laughed. 'No, it wasn't and I point-blank refused. Poor Gerry, he didn't know where to look or what to do. We didn't love each other, you see, we only came together because of you. He never mentioned it again but he was less forthcoming, more abrupt in his manner. Then one day, clear as light, I saw if I didn't marry him I'd lose you.'

'Did you propose to him, then?'

Mia nodded. 'I did. We acknowledged we didn't love each other but we agreed we *liked* each other and that for now we'd make do with that. He said he couldn't live with me because it wouldn't be decent for his daughter to be brought up in circumstances like that and I agreed it wouldn't. So we married.'

'All because of me?'

'It suited us both, don't forget. He needed someone and so did I and we both needed you.'

'You seem to love him now.'

'That all happened after we married. It's not the most romantic marriage in the world but we rub along very, very nicely together and I've no regrets.'

'I see.'

'It's much much better than nothing and I've got you.' Mia hesitated. 'Have I?'

'You know you have. For always. It's you who brought me up. You are my mother as far as I am concerned. But my mother, you never knew her?'

Mia's heart sank like a stone and she looked away. 'No. Your dad told me it wasn't part of your mother's life plan to be tied down to a baby and the routine it entails. How she ever came to be involved with him I don't know. I don't think she was his kind of person.'

'Has he any photographs of her?'

'I don't know, I never asked. She had a career, you see. We mustn't blame her, must we, because we don't really know her circumstances, do we?'

Kate didn't answer her question and then, out of the blue, asked, 'How do you know if you love someone enough to marry them and follow them to the ends of the earth?'

'If you're asking that then you're not in love.'

'I see.'

'You're thinking about Scott?'

Kate nodded. She poured herself another cup of tea but it tasted cold and she pushed it away. 'One day, I know for sure, he'll be going back to Australia, because sometimes he talks about it with such longing. Then the mood passes off and he's Scott again, being daft and lovely and such fun. Trouble is, I doubt if a permanent relationship is in his mind right now. But he's so lovely to be with and he claims he's fallen in love with me. Then I remember about Bunty and was her baby really his or not? He'd have left her with the baby, you know, he told her so. He was prepared to walk away and that worries me about him. But all the same ...'

'There's one thing for certain: Adam would never have done for you. Never in this world.'

'No. I told him to stand tall and move on. It's his mother who's ruining his life. She's so domineering.'

'Do you think he will?'

'I hope so.' Kate pushed her chair away from the table and stood up. 'Must go, got chemistry to do.' As she left the room she turned back to say, 'One day I'll ask Dad about my mother. It doesn't make a bit of difference to you and me, but I'd still like to know about her. Mothers aren't always the best of people to bring one up, are they?'

Mia smiled with relief. 'Not always.'

13

Scott came in as it struck eight o'clock and as not a single client had arrived he leant over the desk to kiss Kate. 'There couldn't be anything sweeter than kissing you this time in the morning. Considering how early it is, you look stunning. How's things? You must be feeling better after clearing the air yesterday.'

'Oh, I am! I drove myself here this morning. My first taste of freedom has quite gone to my head. How is my knight in shining armour feeling this morning?'

'All the better for seeing you. Give me another kiss.'

'Mm.'

'Love you. Love me?'

'Don't know.'

'Ah! There's hope.'

They became absorbed in their kissing, she one side of the desk and he the other. Their elbows leant on it so they could reach and they didn't notice that Joy had pushed open the heavy outer door and was standing watching them through the inner glass doors. So this was what they got up to. She had to smile, for she could see the attraction of Scott and of Kate, and it was a pleasure to see their delight in each other. But these were business premises and ... the phone began ringing. Immediately Scott started to pull away but Kate put both hands behind his neck and kept him kissing. When the phone had rung four times and she still hadn't answered it Joy opened the glass door and said, 'Answer that, please, Kate.'

They broke apart, startled by the sharpness of her tone, but more so because both of them were embarrassed at being discovered.

'Barleybridge Veterinary Hospital, Kate speaking, how may I help?'

Joy stalked straight past the two of them and went into her office. She put her coat in her cupboard, placed her bag beneath her desk and went to unlock the back door.

When she returned to her office Scott was waiting for her. He was holding up both hands, signifying surrender. 'All my fault, Joy. Sorry! Not in working hours and all that.'

'There's something heartening about young love.'

'There is?'

'Oh yes. Got your list?'

Scott nodded.

'Then off you go.'

She couldn't help but smile at the surprise on Scott's face. He'd expected a telling off and hadn't got one. It was none of her business, in truth. What the staff got up to in their spare time was their affair. All the same she'd have a cautionary word with Kate when the right moment presented itself. Or would she? Maybe not, the girl was no fool. Joy could hear laughter in reception and smiled to herself. He was such a rogue, was Scott. If she'd been younger she'd have fancied him too, just like Kate. She went to check if the two Sarahs had come in yet and left Scott and Kate to enjoy their romantic moment.

A draught blew through from the back right around Scott's legs. It was Rhodri opening the back door, intent on making an early start. He bustled in, rubbing his hands. 'It's cold today. Morning, Scott. Morning, Kate. How's the old love life, Scott?' 'Spect the old cracked ribs have brought a halt to it, eh?'

Scott feigned surprise. 'You're asking me about my love life? What about yours? After what I saw last night, mate, I should be asking you.'

Rhodri blushed.

Kate drew closer. 'Go on, then, what did you see?'

'Outside the Fox and Grapes. About eleven. My God, you should have seen! Talk about the old Welsh charm. These Celts!' Scott pretended to fan himself and then to swoon.

'Shut up!' Rhodri might have said shut up but at bottom he looked pleased that at long last his private life was a subject for conversation. 'Kate doesn't want to hear.'

'She does,' said Kate.

'Look! There's a simple explanation. We'd been out. I'd put Harry Ferret in the back in his cage and forgotten to close the second catch, and hey presto, while we were having a drink the little devil escaped, so before Megan and I could drive home I had the little blighter to find. Couldn't start up with him running loose. So that's what you saw.'

Scott simply didn't believe his explanation. 'Well, I've heard some cracking excuses for a rough and tumble in the back of an estate car but that's the best yet. Wait till I see Megan. I'll ask her. She'll tell me the truth.'

Kate was laughing so much at the embarrassment in Rhodri's face she couldn't answer the phone when it rang, so Scott answered it for her. When he'd finished speaking Rhodri said, 'You'll do no such thing.'

Scott feigned indignation. 'I shall. We'll see if Megan blushes any redder than you've done.'

'I've explained what we were doing. Anyway, eventually we found him curled up asleep in the spare wheel. Took us ages.'

'I bet! When are you going to make an honest woman of her?'

Rhodri sobered down. 'Don't know. I want to get married but there's her father.'

Kate's eyes opened wide with surprise. 'Get married! You've known her barely three months.'

'Get married and then tell him,' Scott advised.

Rhodri shook his head. 'No, no, that wouldn't be right.'

Kate asked whose life was it? But Rhodri didn't answer. Scott and Kate winked at each other as he walked away to see if the post had arrived.

'Poor blighter!'

'Did you really see them . . . you know . . . in the back of his car?'

'Pulling his leg, though they did look suspicious. Must go. He shouldn't let other people stop him from doing what he wants with his own life. I bet the old dad wants Megan to look after him in his old age, that's what it'll be. Selfish old basket. What time do you finish today?'

'With any luck about seven.'

'Pick you up.'

'OK. Where shall we go?'

'Don't know but we'll eat.'

'OK.'

'See you then.'

Kate spent the afternoon between one o'clock and four shopping in the precinct for something special to wear that evening. Adam being finally cleared from her mind seemed to have given shape to her feelings for Scott and she knew now for certain that he meant an awful lot more to her than she had hitherto dared to admit. And it wasn't just his looks, though they were fantastic in themselves. It was his whole attitude to life that she found exciting. His drive, his humour, his laughter, his mind and the serious side to him, the side which approached his job with such professionalism and feeling.

She studied her reflection in a shop window and remembered the gentleness of his kisses and the feel of his arms around her. Oh, Christ!

She sounded like a heroine in a cheap women's magazine. But it was true, she did like his physical presence and she did wish . . . Cold reason asserted itself. So he goes home to Australia, then what? Because he would, there was no doubt about that, and where would that leave her? Kate brushed aside her contemplative mood and went into the shop to buy something, anything that would give her a lift. As Stephie would say, a bit of retail therapy does wonders for the spirits.

She and Scott had decided to eat in a little Italian restaurant in the shopping precinct and were on the point of ordering when Scott's mobile phone rang. 'Excuse me. Who the hell is this? Hello. Scott Spencer speaking.' Kate watched him listening to his caller, and admired the way his hair grew and studied the look of frustration which crossed his face as he listened. He really was the most beautiful man. She could fall for him in a big way. In fact, if she was honest she had already done that very thing. He snapped the phone off and pushed it into his pocket.

'Look, you stay here and eat. I'm going to be some time.'

'I thought you weren't on call.'

'I'm not. Mungo is, but he's got two calls, both for difficult calvings, and he can't do them both at once. So I'm going.' He stood up to leave. 'Who'd be a vet?'

'Me for a start. I'll come. Can I?'

'If you wish. I'd be glad. But aren't you hungry?'

'We can both eat when we've finished, they'll still be open. Is it far?'

'No. Come on, then.'

The farm was only a three-mile drive away and as soon as she stepped out on to the flagged yard she saw it was the exact opposite of Phil Parsons's. The yard was floodlit and she could see that every barn and stable door, every window frame, was painted an immaculate marine blue. Each window pane shone, and huge terracotta pots holding ornamental bushes stood between the doors wherever a space could be found. If it hadn't been for the sound of a horse stamping in the stables Kate would have imagined that no animal was permitted in this hallowed place.

'Through here.' Scott led the way under an arch between the stables and immediately they were in another yard with a long cowshed running down the length of one side. Scott shouted, 'Hello! Chris!'

A short, sturdy man appeared from what looked like a small office calling out, 'Hi, Scott! Am I glad to see you. I was just ringing again to make sure you were on your way. In here. Aren't you going to introduce me?'

'Sorry. This is Kate, got a place at vet college. Wanting some experience. Kate, this is Chris, his lordship's stockman.'

'Hi, Kate. Here she is. Been straining for far too long and making no progress at all. I've had my hand in to see if I can straighten it out but she's straining that hard I thought my hand would be crushed. But for God's sake hurry her up before we lose it and her.'

The heifer was a lovely Guernsey with melting brown eyes full of distress. She was standing on lavish straw bedding and looked as though she had given up on life. Scott went to her head and had a word with her, stroking her, lifting her lips to see the colour of her gums. 'Not very impressed with her. You should have called me earlier.'

'You know his lordship's opinion of vets.'

'I do. Bucket of water and soap. Warm. Please.'

Scott stripped to the waist, put on his calving trousers and apron, washed his hands and arms, and tried inserting an arm to sort out the calf.

'No good. Straining too hard and there's not much room in there anyway. I'll give her an epidural.' Kate couldn't help but admire his approach: businesslike and yet so calm and compassionate.

'But we'll lose her if you don't hurry up. Put ropes on it and we'll pull it out.' Chris was obviously becoming seriously agitated by Scott's delay in taking positive action.

'Slowly, slowly, catchee monkey, Chris. If I give her an epidural she'll stop straining. That'll give me room to sort out the calf and then gently, gently we can pull it out. Otherwise we'll tear her and have more problems than we had to begin with. Believe me.'

Scott calmly injected the heifer at the base of her tail and then stood back to wait. 'Kate, go get the ropes for me, will you?'

Kate sped away through the arch, found the ropes and went hurrying back, desperate not to miss a thing. By the time she got back the heifer had relaxed and the fearful exhausting straining she'd been doing had ceased.

'Thanks. Now we'll see what we can do.'

'Bloody-well get a hurry on, will you? I don't want to lose this heifer.'

'Neither do I, Chris. Neither do I.' Scott inserted his arm and Chris and Kate watched in silence. 'One leg tucked back, that's the problem.' He grunted and pushed and pulled and then said, 'There, that's it sorted. Rope? I'll put it round the feet and then we'll have the other for its head and in no time . . . That's it. Look, Kate, we can see both the feet already and its nose. Rope.' He was silent for a minute, struggling to get the rope positioned correctly round the calf's head. Then very slowly and steadily his pulling began to have an effect and the calf's face appeared. 'Put a finger in its mouth, Kate. See what happens.'

To Kate's amazed delight she felt the calf make a kind of half-attempt to suck her finger. 'Why, it's trying to suck, and it's all warm and wet.'

'Good, then.' He grinned at her pleasure. 'We've got a goer.'

Chris grew agitated at what he considered to be too much delay. 'For God's sake, Scott, hurry up or we shan't have. You're being too casual. You'll be asking for afternoon tea next. Get it out.'

Calmly Scott answered, 'All in good time. Now, Kate, hold the head rope and slowly and *steadily* pull when I say.'

Kate did.

Panicking, Chris shouted, 'She's going down!'

'Push some more straw her way. Quick!'

The heifer was down and after some more steady pulling the head was out and the body followed in no time at all. With a sudden sploosh the calf was lying on the straw. All panic forgotten, Chris breathed a sigh of relief. 'Thank God. And it's a heifer! Isn't she grand?' He got a handful of the bedding and wiped the calf's face and nose with it.

Scott knelt up and gave the calf a quick check over, saying, 'Great little thing, she is. She's a real beauty. Come on, then, mother, take some interest in your calf.' Scott took off the ropes and dragged the calf around to the heifer's head to encourage her to pay it some attention.

Kate had to laugh because the mother gave the calf such a look of surprise it was almost comical. Then, very tentatively, as if instinct was overcoming her amazement at what she had produced, the mother gave the calf a lick. It made little noises and was rewarded by being licked more vigorously. Scott stood watching for a moment, and then quickly immersed his hands and arms in the bucket of water and washed himself thoroughly.

'I'll just make sure everything's OK inside.'

After he'd examined her and decided the heifer was fine, Scott moved the calf a few feet away from her.

Kate didn't understand his reasons and protested loudly. 'Oh, Scott! Don't do that. You'll upset her.'

'I want her up before I leave.' Believing that the calf was being taken away from her, the mother hastily got to her feet and moved a few steps to bring her close again, nuzzling and licking her offspring as soon as it was within reach.

Kate was totally overcome. So this was what it was all about. This moment. This birth. This lovely creature born safely because of a man's skill. She didn't think she'd seen anything more beautiful in all her life. Such a precious moment, she'd remember it always. She was privileged, that's what she was, privileged. She paused for a while to watch the delight the cow had in her young.

By the time she'd had her fill Scott was hosing down his calving trousers at the tap outside in the yard. She watched him take them off and hang them on a stable-door catch to drip. The bucket of warm water he used for swilling his arms and hands.

Chris banged him on his bare back. 'Thanks for that, Scott. Whisky to celebrate?'

Scott nodded his thanks. Kate handed him the towel Chris had provided. He grinned at her. 'Great, eh?'

'Absolutely. I'm dumbstruck. Are all Guernsey calves as beautiful as that one?'

'Mostly, yes. Brilliant vet his lordship's got, eh?'

Kate laughed. 'Is the owner really a lord?'

'Indeed. Tight-fisted as hell, he is. Except where his horses are concerned.'

'I don't remember anyone being called out to his horses.'

'Uses an equine practice. Can't trust them to people like us!'

'Huh! If he'd seen you in there with that heifer he would. It was like a miracle. So wonderful.'

'Such loyalty.' He shrugged on his jacket, put his hand on her shoulder, studied the rapt expression on her face and saluted her with a kiss. 'Come and get your whisky. Is that all right?'

'Yes.'

By the time she returned to the passenger seat and Scott was backing out prior to leaving, the whisky had hit her empty stomach with a bang. The euphoria she'd felt at witnessing the birth, rather than wearing off, was increasing: Kate felt on top of the world; there was nothing she couldn't achieve. She glanced sideways at Scott and loved everything about him. Now her admiration of his skill with the calving was as nothing compared with her absorption in his physical magnetism. Her headmistress's homily was ditched as belonging to another age, nothing to do with a new century and the new woman she had become.

He turned to smile at her while he waited to pull out on to the main road and put a hand on her knee intending to give it a squeeze, but Kate put her hand over his and held it there. When he was ready to move off he pulled his hand out from under hers reluctantly. Scott didn't speak again until they came to the crossroads where he needed to chose between the precinct and food or collecting her car first.

'Which?'

'Collect my car? Please. First.'

'First? Right. Will do.'

They drove in silence until they reached the practice. After Scott had pulled on the handbrake he turned to face her and at the same time switched on the internal light. 'There, I can see you better now. Your face! You should have seen it. A successful calving never loses its excitement even when you've done it a hundred times and more. There's nothing to compare, is there?'

Kate shook her head. 'Nothing. It was just . . . well . . . just *so* special. There's nothing like it in the whole world. One day I shall have skills like yours, I'm determined.'

'I thought as much.'

'How on earth do you sort out twin lambs, for heaven's sakes? All heads and feet and legs and things? How do you know what belongs to which?'

'Try lambing on a Welsh hill farm at dead of night with a freezing wind and icy sleet with it, believe me you learn pretty sharpish what's what.'

'Have you done that?'

'Just did locum for a few weeks before I went to Devon and then on to here. I worked for a Welsh farmer Dad met when he came over to a conference once. Never again. They deserve every penny they earn, farmers like him. I thought I'd never get warm again.' Scott put an arm round Kate's shoulders and bent to kiss her. She welcomed him more eagerly than she had ever done; wrapping her arms around his neck, caressing his tongue with hers, pressing him to her, warming to a passion she had not shown before.

Though taken by surprise, Scott still managed to match passion for passion. His hands were roving over her, undoing buttons, enjoying the feel of her smooth skin, the rise of her neck from her shoulders, the sharp angle of her collarbone, the . . . Perkins barked furiously as he raced from the back door towards the Land Rover. He clamoured to get in, leaping up, scraping his claws on the door, racing round and round, furious at finding someone in the car park when at this time of night it was his territory and his alone.

Miriam was with him and she tapped on the driver's window. 'Be quiet, Perkins, it's Scott and Kate. Be quiet, I say. Hi, you two. Sorry.'

Scott wound down the window while Kate pulled herself together.

'Hi, there, Miriam. Mungo not back yet?'

'No. It's a Caesarean, so Bunty's gone out to give a hand. Twins. Yours was easy, was it?'

'Just needed straightening out, then it popped out nice and easy. Brought Kate to collect her car, then we're going to eat.'

'Sorry to take up your free evening but there was no alternative.'

'Not at all. Someone had to go.'

Miriam peered into the cab. 'All right, Kate? Good experience?'

You couldn't be resentful with her. Not with Miriam. 'Marvellous! Thanks.'

'Good. I'm glad. Be seeing you. Goodnight.'

She went off up to the top of the car park with Perkins and disappeared into the darkness.

'I love you, Kate. Go get your car, follow me and we'll have that meal. I'm starving.'

'So am I.' She looked at him full face and laid a gentle hand on his cheek. 'I love you too.'

'If Miriam hadn't come . . .'

'I know.'

'Would you have . . . you know.'

'Oh, yes. With you.'

'I'm honoured.' Scott leaned across and opened the door for her. 'She'll be back, we'd better go. Love you.'

'I expect we had.' Reluctantly Kate got out and went to her own car. She'd come so close. So close. She did love him, then. She must do to have wanted him so much. What a night. If she were fanciful she would have classed this as a night when there'd been a turning point in her life.

She waited until he'd reversed and was facing the exit, then put her car into first gear and followed Scott to the precinct, and thought about following him across the world.

They ate back at the Italian restaurant, then each drove home, mulling over the memories of their meal; the touching of hands, of minds, of souls: Scott, overcome with concern at the way their relationship had taken off, Kate filled with joy, unable to contemplate a life without him.

She began work next morning full of energy, after a blissful night's sleep due to a long day but more so because she was in love with Scott. He was at the back of her mind all the time and filled the whole of it if there was a lull. She couldn't wait for him to come in this morning to collect his list of calls.

Stephie noticed how happy she was and asked the reason.

'I went to a calving with Scott last night. It was brilliant. Absolutely incredible.'

'And was that all?'

'Oh, yes! Well . . .'

'Yes?'

'We had a meal afterwards.'

'And . . .?'

'Nothing.'

Disbelieving the possibility of going out with a man like Scott and nothing happening between them, Stephie said, 'Oh, come on! Give us the rest.'

'There wasn't anything.'

'So what's the cause of your sparkling eyes this morning and the moments when you're in another world?'

'You're talking nonsense.'

'Can't wait for him to come in?' Stephie giggled. 'Watch out, you don't want to do another Bunty.'

Kate could have smacked her face for her. She was filled with outrage. How dare she? How dare she compare the unique beauty of what Scott and she felt for each other with what had happened to Bunty? In any case Bunty had never actually said the baby was his. How dare she?

Before Kate had managed to come up with a stinging reply Miss Chillingsworth came into reception carrying a cat basket, and Kate had to brace herself to be polite and interested, and leave the stinging reply for later. She certainly wasn't going to let her get away with a remark like that.

Kate put every ounce of enthusiasm she could muster into her greeting. 'Why, Miss Chillingsworth, what a lovely surprise! You haven't got a new kitten, have you? How exciting!'

'No, dear, I haven't. I have a cat. It's a stray. I'm very upset, actually. I've come early on purpose, because I think it's about to die.'

'Oh, dear. I am sorry. Tell me.'

'There's been a cat about for ages. Then this last week it's been looking lost and forlorn but I didn't want to start feeding it, thinking it belonged to someone. And I did suspect she was pregnant. I asked around if anyone knew whose she was but they're all too busy to bother with me and my problems. However, I didn't see her for a day or so, then I did and I noticed she was walking awkwardly, as though she was in pain.'

'Have you got kittens in there, then?'

'Oh, no! Then I heard mewing last night very late and I plucked up my courage and went to look and she was crouched in a cardboard box I'd put out for the bin men. She was in such a sorry state, and it was beginning to rain so I picked her up very carefully and took her inside. She's very poorly. It would be cruel to leave her without help, so . . .' Miss Chillingsworth took a deep breath '. . . I know I shouldn't have done it because she isn't mine, but someone had to do something so I've brought her for Mr Murgatroyd to see. It's very urgent, I'm sure.'

Kate lifted the lid a little and peeped inside. It didn't need much intelligence to see that the cat was desperately ill. 'He isn't here until eleven today.'

'Oh, dear, what shall we do? I'm so worried.'

'Rhodri's here, he'll see to her. Come with me.'

Kate took Miss Chillingsworth into Rhodri's consulting room and put the cat basket on the examination table. 'Take a seat. I'll get him.'

Rhodri lifted the cat out of the basket and had to lay her on the table, because she was too weak to stand. 'Why, there's nothing left of her, just skin and bone.' His hands gently moved over her body feeling her ribs, her stomach. He checked her gums, lifted a pinch of her skin, opened her eyelids, spoke to her and, getting no response, looked at Miss Chillingsworth and shook his head. 'She's very ill, very dehydrated, starving too. I suspect she has been in labour for far too long and now everything has stopped. I'm pretty sure she has a kitten jammed and can't push it out. Would you leave me a while, Miss Chillingsworth, and I'll see what can be done. Go and sit in reception if you wish.'

Miss Chillingsworth looked searchingly into his face. 'You're saying there's not much hope, aren't you?'

'I am.'

'If the kittens survive and she doesn't then I'm very good with tiny kittens. Ask Kate, she knows. I'd gladly help.' She saw he was eager to do what he had to do to save what he could. 'I'll wait.' Before she left she stroked the cat's head and momentarily her eyes opened and she looked at Miss Chillingsworth in mute agony. Miss Chillingsworth was choked with emotion, convinced the cat was thanking her for getting help.

She sat in the waiting room supposedly looking at magazines but in reality she was in the consulting room with the cat, hoping things were going well for her. Half an hour went by and she could hear Kate apologising about an emergency and yes, Mr Hughes would soon be starting on his client list, but it was a cruelty case, you see.

Miss Chillingsworth imagined herself feeding the tiny kittens and saving their lives. She'd get poor Cherub's basket out again, the blankets were already washed. Her fingers twitched as though feeling the soft fur, the tiny ears. In her mind she was admiring the weeny, soft pink pads of their feet and could almost hear their mewing. Such joy!

This time she might even be brave enough to keep one for herself. Or should she have the mother instead? Maybe she needed a home more than healthy kittens did. Yes, she'd ask to keep the mother. That would be the kindest thing to do; the right thing to do. It was almost as if Cherub was reincarnated for the cat was white and black in very much the same pattern as she had been. Her dear Cherub. Then she remembered the kittens she'd reared playing king of the castle on the old apple box on the kitchen floor. Maybe she'd have a kitten instead and enjoy all the pleasure all over again. No, she'd have the mother and call her Cherub in memory.

Rhodri came out from the back. 'Miss Chillingsworth, a word please.'

She followed him into the consulting room and he closed the door behind her.

'Take a seat.'

'It's bad news, isn't it?'

'I'm afraid so. I was right, there was a kitten stuck, but it was already dead. I've managed to ease it out, there are more, possibly two or three, but the mother is far too ill for me to operate today.'

'And . . . ?'

Rhodri paused and then said, 'We've put her on a drip, given her medication and now all we can do is hope she'll last through the night and be able to withstand an operation to remove the remaining kittens. I must warn you she is very ill.'

Miss Chillingsworth clasped her hands under her chin. 'I know I can rely on you. If she's going to pull through you'll do it. I desperately want her to live. You'll understand how strongly I feel because, being Welsh, you'll have a passionate soul as I do. I'll take her home with me when she's ready and I'll adopt her. It's the least I can do. Can I see her?'

Rhodri hesitated. 'I'd rather you didn't. It would upset you.'

'I see. I'll wait.'

'It could be a long wait before she turns the corner – if, in fact, she does.'

'I could ring to ask.'

'Of course.'

'Thank you. I'm sorry I've held you up.'

'I'm glad you found her.'

'So am I. I'll ring tomorrow morning.'

Miss Chillingsworth intended stopping to have a word at reception and report progress on the cat but only Stephie was on the desk and Kate was nowhere to be seen, so she wandered bleakly out to face alone, without a word of comfort from a twin soul, a whole day of worry and desperation.

In fact, Kate had departed to her accounts after telling Stephie exactly what she thought of her warning. She'd also remembered that Scott was taking a couple of days off so she wouldn't be seeing him as she had expected, which did nothing to improve her temper. How could she be so happy one moment and so unhappy the next? Now she'd upset Stephie and as they had to work together that was a stupid thing to have done. Her kind heart reasserted itself and Kate went to make coffee for Stephie and herself as a gesture of reconciliation.

Stephie accepted it gratefully. 'Thanks. I need this. I was too late for breakfast this morning and when I do that it always hits me about now. This is nice. Sorry I upset you, meant as a timely warning etc., etc.'

'I'm sorry too. But we don't know for certain it was his, do we?'

'No. But ... I reckon it was, knowing Bunty and knowing Scott.'

'But we don't *know*.'

'You're saying that because you don't *want* to believe it.'

Kate took on board what Stephie had said and quietly went away, disconcerted by how upset she was at how close to the truth Stephie had come.

Then she remembered how handsome Scott was, how attractive, how much she loved the touch of his hands, his sense of humour, the clowning he did, how dedicated he was to his work ... and knew in her heart of hearts how transparently honest he was when he said he loved her. He'd always claimed he felt differently about her than any other girl he'd met, and those clear blue eyes of his couldn't lie, could they? Of course not. He meant every word. Cheered by her own well-reasoned argument, she switched on the computer and began work, knowing that before the day was out Scott would ring to make arrangements for tonight.

But Scott didn't ring. Kate found all sorts of possible excuses for him, but pride forbade her to ring him and she spent an agonising evening.

14

The following morning it was Joy who received the first intimation of what had happened. On her doormat when she went to get the post was an envelope addressed to her. She didn't recognise the writing at first but when she did she frowned at the unexpectedness of it. A dreadful suspicion entered her mind. Surely not. Oh, no. Surely not. But she bet her bottom dollar that she was right.

'Porridge or cereal?'

That was Duncan calling out to her but she didn't answer because she was occupied reading the opening lines of Scott's letter: '*I know you will be surprised . . .*'

Joy flopped down on the kitchen chair. This was just too much. Too much . . . '*I have decided to return to Australia on the first available flight.*' She read on, seeing only the implications as far as staffing the practice was concerned and nothing more.

I know I should have given you notice of this holiday but I had a phone call from my dad to say Ma was ill and needing major surgery, so I had to make a decision quick-smart. Hopefully I shall be back once Mother has recovered. Sorry, Joy, for putting the staffing situation in jeopardy. Will keep in touch.

Joy flung the letter down on the kitchen table and put her head in her hands. 'I just don't believe what he's done.'

'Who?'

'Scott. He's had it away on his toes. Done a runner. Hopped it. He can't help it. It's his mother, she's ill. But all the same.'

'Didn't he say he was going?'

'Not a word. So far as I knew he was off yesterday and today, then on call all weekend.'

'He hasn't made his mother ill on purpose.'

'I know, but I've a nasty feeling it will turn permanent, if you know what I mean. He won't come back, I feel it in my bones. There's been no sign up until now that he was getting itchy feet. I've sensed it before and been prepared, and taken steps, and none of them has left quite so precipitately as this.'

Duncan suggested it might be woman trouble and his mother's illness had given him a valid excuse.

'Surely he hasn't got someone else pregnant.' She began spooning in cereal, not tasting it but eating out of habit. Then Joy choked and had to cough a lot to clear her throat. 'Oh, God! It can't be Kate, can it? With all her high hopes. It'll ruin things for her. The young devil! If it is I'll fly out to Australia myself and have it out with him. Ruining her chances. I'll kill him.'

'Now, Joy, you don't know that.'

'He was going to run out on Bunty if the baby had been his, but then she said it wasn't, so he didn't. I'm certain it was his, but she'd too much pride to admit it when he declared he wouldn't stand by her.'

Tears began pouring down Joy's cheeks and Duncan got up to put an arm round her. 'Now come on. This isn't like you. Go to work and see what the real picture is. Does he mention Kate at all?'

Joy pushed the letter towards him, shaking her head.

Duncan read the apologies, the thanks for all her help, about his enjoyment of working in the practice, and how he'd benefited from the experience and it would stand him in good stead, and how he hoped it wouldn't cause too much disruption, and how sorry he was for letting her down like this but he'd be back as soon as he could ... 'No, he doesn't. Maybe there's a letter at the practice for her. I suggest you ring Mungo right now and warn him. He should shoulder some of the responsibility for the practice. It can't all be laid at your door. Come on, Joy. Brace yourself.'

Before she left he said he would come to have lunch with her to cheer her up.

'That's kind. I don't suppose that during the course of your misspent youth you qualified as a vet?'

Sadly Duncan had to confess that no he hadn't, but if wishing ...

'I'll see you about twelve, then.'

At the practice the Land Rover Scott had used was in the car park and on the doormat an envelope with the keys to it and the keys to the flat and a card saying in big letters 'SORRY'.

Sorry indeed, thought Joy. *I'd give him sorry if I could lay my hands on him.* Sorry! Huh! At least Kate wasn't in until lunchtime today so she had some time in which to pull her thoughts together on how to break the news.

Mungo came down from the flat with Miriam.

'So, Joy, how did all this come about?'

'Don't look at me, I'm just as surprised as you. No hint, not even an inkling that he was off. I was saying to Duncan before I left I've usually spotted they've developed itchy feet and taken steps with the agency, but this . . .'

'But he hasn't said he's not coming back, so the big problem is him being on call this weekend.'

'Exactly! He hasn't *said* he isn't coming back but reading between the lines I'm sure as hell he won't. I'm declaring here and now that over my dead body do we employ another of our itinerant brothers or sisters from the Commonwealth. Never again.'

Miriam interrupted with, 'Oh! I don't know, they certainly add spice to life. He was definitely adding spice to Kate's life when they got back from that emergency calving at Lord Askew's. They were kissing very passionately in the Land Rover when I went out to walk Perkins.'

Joy smiled grimly at her. 'They were, were they? If he's done anything to harm Kate I'll personally do for him.'

'Look, if it's any help I'll work on reception for you.'

'Are you sure?'

'Of course I am. I've got to give a hand, haven't I? Can't let you sink. Would it help?'

'Of course it would; give me a chance to sort the staffing problem.'

Mungo said he intended doing Scott's weekend on call so that was covered.

'You two are angels. Thank you very much.'

Miriam linked her arm with Joy's and said, 'I'll pop out with Perkins first, then I'll be in. What I can't understand is why so suddenly, without speaking to anyone? Still he says he will be back, so it's only for a short while. He always seemed happy enough.'

'I don't know. I expect we shall never know.' Unless Kate has the answer, thought Joy.

Miriam kissed Joy and dashed away to collect Perkins for his walk.

The news of Scott's departure was the talk of the practice all morning and Joy had to confess to looking forward to having lunch with Duncan to get some respite from it. He appeared at ten minutes to twelve, wanting the keys to the car so he could leave his walking boots in there and change into the smart shoes he'd put in the boot as Joy was leaving for work.

'Hello, Miriam, they've had to call in the support troops, then?'

'Duncan!' She went round the desk and gave him a big hug. 'How nice to see you. All hands to the pumps this morning, but your dear wife is close to solving our problem. The agency is sending a locum round for an interview this afternoon. They've faxed his details and he seems very suitable.'

'Excellent.'

'I don't know how we would manage without her.'

'Is she ready for lunch?'

'Go and see for yourself.'

'Joy! Ready?'

Joy slammed the filing cabinet drawer shut saying, 'Get me out of here, quick.'

'You'll need your coat. It's cold.'

'Where are we going?'

'The sandwich bar down the road. We'll walk.'

'I'll put up with that if you'll take me somewhere nice tonight. I shall need a bit of cosseting after the day I've had.'

'Agreed. There wasn't a letter for Kate this morning, then?'

Joy shook her head. 'I can't be long. I've still got to talk to her. What a shambles. I'm worried sick.'

'Forget it for a while.'

The brand-new, up-to-the-minute chromium and red leather transformation of the sandwich bar took Joy's breath away. 'This is definitely not how I remember it! It was so grotty before and the name's changed. Ned's Diner, no less. You knew, did you?'

'Yes. Thought we'd give the new management a chance.'

'I do like it. Very "New York", I must say. Do they do anything so mundane as a bacon, lettuce and tomato sandwich with a *caffè latte*?'

'Let's see.' Duncan picked up the menu. 'They do. They do. Twice, I think.' Joy found a seat and Duncan went to order at the counter.

When he came to sit with her he asked, 'So, you haven't spoken to Kate yet?'

'No and I must be back before one. Whether she knows or not, I can't leave her to all the tittle-tattle that's going on. The walls are bulging with speculation.'

'Complete change of subject. I've discovered who my mystery walker is.'

'You have?'

'Yes. He was waiting for me this morning. I knew something had happened because he wasn't wearing his business suit. He starts Monday in a new job. It's transformed him.'

'Never mind about the transformation. Who is he? Someone we know?'

'You'll never guess.' Duncan deliberately paused before he told her. 'It's Adam Pentecost, Kate's old boyfriend.'

Joy's face was alight with amazement. 'No! Adam Pentecost! Of course. Of course. Why didn't I realise? Of course it was him. Well?'

'He's going to work near Weymouth for a company which all but fell on his neck with delight. He is the answer to their prayers, apparently. He's got an increase in salary and he's going to look for a flat or a room or something in Weymouth and leave home.'

'Thank heavens for that. It'll do him a power of good.'

'He hasn't told his mother he's moving out yet, though. She could be a big stumbling block.'

'It's only what she deserves by the sound of it. I'm so pleased. I wonder if Kate knows. Fancy it being Adam! Kate will be pleased. At the very least it will have restored his self-confidence, which he was badly in need of, and that is a plus for her, because it will get him off her back. Poor Kate. I feel so sorry for her about Scott leaving. I just don't know how far she felt committed to him. She'd been fending him off for weeks, but I've an idea, well, in fact I know that ...'

'Eat your BLT. Stop worrying about her, young ones have far more resilience than we credit them with. They get very badly hurt, but bounce back much more easily than older people do.'

'Yes, but she's such a fine girl, I hate to think of her being hurt.'

The subject of Joy's concern was at that moment stuck in traffic on her way to work also thinking about how hurt she felt. He'd never rung and he wasn't in today, and he was on call all weekend and she couldn't understand his silence. The phone at his flat was working, she knew, because she'd finally given in and rung him last night. But there'd been no reply to her calls and the answer machine was switched off, which was very odd indeed when he knew perfectly well she'd have gladly lost her all to him the night before last.

The queue edged a little nearer to the road works.

After an offer like that how could he now ignore her? But he had. Unless he'd been involved in an accident? Maybe he was lying in a hospital bed somewhere, unconscious. Or worse still, dead. Her mind raced through all the possibilities.

The queue moved forward another ten yards.

But he'd have to be around at the weekend because he was on call. That was it. He'd decided to go to visit a friend or something for a couple of days and he'd be back tonight to start his weekend on call. Of course! That was it.

She could see the temporary lights now, at red yet again.

Although he could have let her know. Maybe her offer to make love for the first time in her life had made this free-as-air Aussie feel the leg irons closing round his ankles and he was warning her off with his silence. That was it. She was going too fast for him. What a fool she'd been.

The temporary lights changed to green and she slid forward again.

Too fast for *him*! Whom was she kidding?

This time she got past the road works and was pulling into the car park, unfortunately ten minutes late. And there, parked for all to see, was his Land Rover. He was here! Thank heavens. Her heart leapt into her throat. Waves of vibrant joy surged through her veins. She punched the dashboard with her fist and shouted, 'Yes!' Wherever he'd been he was back. Thank God. The dear, darling man. Despite her overwhelming relief she decided to be as cool as cool in front of him. Not to punish him, no, but to let him know that she too knew how to handle a relationship. Oh, yes! The thought of him, of smelling his smell, of seeing his bright, approving eyes, hearing his footfall, pushed up her pulse rate and she walked to the back door desperately trying not to look too eager.

Kate deliberately went straight to her office, hung up her coat. Speaking to no one, she switched on the computer and began the end-of-month figures. She'd print them out too before she took one single step towards seeking him out. But she'd been working only about ten minutes when Joy put her head round the door.

'Oh! You're here.' She closed the door behind her and sat down.

'Look! I'm sorry I was late, but there were road works and it took ages. I'll set off earlier tomorrow.'

'That's all right, it happens to the best of us.' Joy studied her face and could see none of the anguish she would have expected to see if Kate had already heard the news. 'I had a letter this morning at home.'

'You did?'

'Yes. From Scott.'

Kate's heart lurched and she hoped Joy hadn't noticed. 'From Scott?'

'Yes, I'm afraid so.'

'What about?'

'Well . . .'

'He's here. Why should he need to write?'

'You haven't heard from him, have you?'

'No. Should I have?' This curiously stilted conversation felt as though it was turning into the overture to some bad news.

'I would have thought so.' Out of her pocket she took Scott's letter and handed it to Kate. 'Here, this is his letter. Read it.'

'Should I?'

Joy nodded. 'Yes, please. It explains something.'

She'd make a good poker player, thought Joy. Her face had gone drip-white but apart from that there was nothing in Kate's demeanour to indicate that she'd received a mortal blow. She remained absolutely still, read it through twice, then slowly and neatly folded it and handed it back.

She didn't speak for almost a minute and then said in a voice not at all like her own, 'You can feel underneath what he's written that he's not coming back, is he? He was supposed to be on call all weekend.'

'Mungo's covering that. I feel like you do that he won't be back. With Zoe having wound down her involvement until after the baby we are terribly short-handed. At three I've got a locum coming for an interview. Someone who's free to begin on Monday. So we've not been entirely annihilated by his departure. I can't begin to imagine what really made him go in such a tearing hurry. He doesn't say, you see, except about his mother. That seems genuine enough.'

Kate didn't answer.

'I wondered if he'd said something to you about his mother?'

'No.'

'It's come as a considerable shock.'

Kate agreed. 'Must get on, though. Going to print out the end-of-month figures.'

'Oh, right. I've put the kettle on. Cup of tea?'

'No. Thanks all the same.' *I wish she'd go! Just go and leave me alone.*

'I'll leave you to get on, then. We shan't need you on reception until Stephie goes at four. Miriam's been helping to free me to sort out a locum. She'll cover when Mungo and I interview this locum at three.'

'Right. I'll press on, then.' *Please go. Please. I can't hold on any longer.*

'I'll bring some tea in later.'

'Thanks.' *If he had to go the only good thing that's come out of this is my eternal gratitude to Miriam for taking Perkins out for his walk when she did. No. Damn Miriam for coming out when she did. At least I would have known what it was to have been loved by him. Now I'll never have the joy of it.* He would have been a tantalisingly passionate lover she was sure. The tears were just beginning to come when the door burst open and in came Lynne.

'Have you heard? Bunty's flipped her lid. It's all that Scott's fault. Mungo's operating and Sarah One's having to take over assisting him and she's shaking like a leaf because he frightens her to death. Bunty's mother's going to come to take her home. Apparently it was Scott's baby after all and she's still carrying a torch for him. We all reckon he won't be back. Sorry about his mother and all that but ... Good riddance, I'd say, wouldn't you? Catch me going to pieces over a man. I'd keep out of Mungo's way if I were you, by the way, he's furious at all the upset. Are you all right? You look quite flushed.'

'I'm fine. Got to press on.'

'Oh, all right, then. Just thought I'd keep you up to date with all the news. You should have been here this morning! Talk about rumours flying around, the air was thick. Aren't you glad you didn't get involved with him?'

'Oh, yes. Not worth it, is it?'

'Mind you, he was a gorgeous hunk. Well, everyone thought so, but I saw through him. All right for a quick fling but he's the type to run a mile if a girl began to get serious.' Had Kate been looking at her she would have seen a malicious grin on Lynne's face. 'Must press on as they say.' She shut the door behind her with a cheerful slam, which Kate felt go straight through her, so fragile did she feel.

For fully ten minutes Kate sat quite still with her hands gripped tightly together to stop them shaking, her head bowed, trying to come to terms with Scott's departure. *Not a word from him to me. Not a word. How could he do that to one he said he loved? How could he?* His last words to her were, 'Love you.' Where on earth had she gone wrong? To go without a word. If he couldn't face her he could have written to her. But he hadn't and she'd learned her first lesson about love. Never ever again would she allow herself to become so hopelessly involved. She had to get through the next few weeks somehow and she would. She wouldn't let a setback like this ruin things for ever. No. She'd do as he had done and walk away without a backward glance. Some chance.

The afternoon dragged on. Too late she found she'd printed out the September figures in error and had to begin again. The printer paper got itself into a ruck and she had almost to dismantle the machine before it ran true. Altogether, an afternoon like today she never wanted ever again.

At five past four she was on the reception desk feeling like death because all the time in her mind's eye she could see Scott: his blue eyes more blue, his tan deeper than ever, his streaked hair more blond than she could have imagined, his tender mouth on the verge of a smile. He'd been so handsome. Such fun. Like no one she'd ever met before or would again. But Kate was brought back to earth by the hurly-burly of the afternoon clinic, so the pain and the heartbreak had to be put on hold for the time being.

She drove home a different way to avoid the road works and Mia was just beginning to worry when she heard Kate opening the front door. 'Why, Kate! You are late! I was beginning to worry.'

'Hello. The clinic was so busy we overran and then we had to tidy up. Then I came home a different way to avoid the road works and all in all I'm tired out.'

'You look it, too. Sit down. I'll soon have your meal heated up. Gerry, get Kate a drink. She needs perking up.'

'Hello, love. Long day? Gin and tonic?'

'Thanks, Dad, yes I will.'

Kate slumped down on her chair at the kitchen table and patiently waited to be ministered to.

'I think I'll join you. What about it, Mia?'

'Yes, please, after all it's Friday. Why not.' Mia could see that something was wrong with Kate but couldn't for the life of her put a finger on what it was. Maybe when she'd eaten she'd be able to tell them.

Kate drank down the gin in a trice but poked her food about without appetite and made a poor show of eating it.

'Kate! That's your favourite, my chicken and vegetable pie. Are you not well?'

'You remember Scott?'

'Well, of course we do, don't we, Gerry?'

Gerry nodded. 'How could we forget. Such a nice chap. He really enjoyed working my train set. We'll have him round some time and he can have another turn.'

'He's gone back to Australia.'

Mia sat back, astounded. 'Back to Australia! But you watched him deliver that calf only, what, two nights ago. How can he have gone?'

'Well, he has.'

'Why? Did he say?'

'He sent a letter to Joy. He says his mother is seriously ill and he'll be back as soon as he can, but we all think he won't.'

Anxious to ease Kate's obvious pain Mia babbled, 'But if his mother is ill he had to go. He'll be back, surely, as soon as he can?' She saw she hadn't convinced Kate. 'Perhaps he got fed up with the English weather;

just needs a break from it. It's been diabolical recently. Perhaps all he wanted was some sun and warmth. Or maybe he wanted to see all those blessed sheep. Homesick, perhaps that was it. You can get it bad, homesickness, so bad you feel physically ill. Or perhaps he longed for all those wide-open spaces they have in Australia; here on this island in comparison we're so cramped.' Mia stopped thinking up any more reasons to make sense of Scott's departure when she saw she wasn't lifting Kate's spirits. 'Anyway, what's done's done.'

Gerry, from behind his newspaper, said, 'Not right that, leaving without giving notice.' 'Spect it's left them in a hole.'

'No. We've got a locum starting Monday and Mungo's doing his weekend for him.'

Gerry lowered his paper. 'Surprising how the waters close over your head when you leave somewhere. You think you're indispensable but in no time at all that phrase "Oh, we shall miss you!" is as hollow as a drum. Never you mind about him, Kate, there's plenty more fish in the sea for someone like you.'

Mia saw the heartache in her eyes when Kate looked at her briefly before answering her dad. 'I expect there are, but it's not much comfort at the moment.'

'Have your pudding, love. You'll feel better when you've eaten something and you always like my treacle sponge.' Mia was rewarded with a pale kind of smile. She whipped the treacle sponge into the microwave and had it in front of Kate, complete with custard, before she could change her mind. Kate plodded her way through it right to the last spoonful of custard, leaving the really treacly bit to the last as she always did.

'Thank you for that. I'll take my cup of tea upstairs with me and finish it in bed. I'm tired.'

'Of course, love, you do that. And have a lie-in. You're not in tomorrow. Goodnight.' Mia got up, gave her a kiss and sat down again, remembering how Kate had said she thought things were moving along with Scott. Obviously this very day her whole world had been turned upside down.

When she'd gone Gerry said, 'It's not like her to go to bed this early, it's only half past eight. What's the matter with her?'

Mia sighed, 'Oh, Gerry!'

Next morning there were letters for Kate and Mia, along with a parcel for Gerry. Mia tore hers open and to her surprise and delight found in it the confirmation for a commission: a miniature of a baby at the request of doting grandparents willing to pay over the odds. She handed Gerry his parcel and paused for a moment to study Kate's letter. She didn't recognise the handwriting and couldn't read the postmark because it was too smudged.

She'd take it up along with Kate's breakfast. She had the tray already laid, so all she had to do was make a pot of tea for her.

'Morning, Kate. There's a letter and I've brought your breakfast up.'

Kate's bedside table was cluttered with textbooks and papers, so Mia put the tray on the carpet while she opened the curtains a little to let the light flood in.

From under the duvet a cautious question came: 'Who's the letter from?'

'I don't know, love. I can't recognise the handwriting.'

But Kate could. She'd seen that writing on countless notes she'd typed into the computer at the practice. That was Scott's writing.

Mia noticed her reluctance to open the letter while she was there so despite her curiosity she left Kate to herself.

Dearest Kate,

I'm at the airport awaiting take-off. My mother is seriously ill with a heart problem. You will already know when you read this that I am going home to see her. I didn't intend writing to you, but at the last minute I can't help myself.

No one who saw your face when we delivered the calf that last night could fail to realise that the veterinary profession is for you. You were so alive that night. I knew if I stayed I would be tempted to want you to go home with me and that you would come, and in no time at all begin bitterly to regret not qualifying. I cannot stand in the way of you fulfilling your ambition.

I said you were different from any girl I'd kissed before and you are, so very special, to me. You will always be close to my heart. Take care, sweet one.

They're loading the plane. Must go.

All my love,

Scott

There was a splodge of a tear at the bottom of the letter and she didn't know if it was a tear of Scott's or one of hers. But it was still wet so it must be hers. Though there was another splodge near the words 'sweet one' which had dried, or maybe that was a splash of lager. Whatever it was, Scott had written that letter and she knew he meant every word. There was no address at the top. So he really did mean it to be final. Though in his letter to Joy he had said he'd be back in a couple of weeks. But like Joy, reading between the lines, she sensed he would not come. In any case if she read her own letter a thousand times it would still say she wouldn't see him again.

She lay back on the pillow, drained of emotion. Was she glad or was she not? Kate didn't really know. There seemed to be a great big hole somewhere in the middle of her, a hollowness which wouldn't go away. *Oh, Scott! Oh, Scott!*

He was right, though. If he'd asked her she would have gone wherever he went and like he said would most likely, when it was too late, have lived to regret it all the rest of her life. She thought about how she felt when she saw the calf being born and tried hard to put it foremost in her mind, but Scott would keep creeping round the edges of her resolve and obliterating her determination not to think of him. *Oh, Scott! To sacrifice yourself for me. You surely belong to the great and the good.*

Maybe one day she would travel to Australia and look up his name in the Veterinary Register and seek him out. She wrapped her arms round her waist to stem the tide of pain. This was acute physical agony she felt; a very real gnawing in her innards. Whatever, she wasn't going to let anyone at the practice know just how much she missed him. She'd brace herself to speak of him without flinching and do all her grieving at home. She hid her head under the duvet and wept for him.

Oh, Scott! Oh, Scott!

That Saturday night Mungo rang Joy and asked if he and Miriam could come round for an hour. 'Not for a meal, just for an emergency business meeting. If you're not going out, that is.'

'We're not. Of course, come round, be glad to see you.'

'That man from the agency, I wasn't keen.'

'Oh, I see. Well, come round, then. If you don't mind Duncan being here.'

'Course not. Colin's covering just for the evening so I won't get called out.'

'Right. See you then.'

'About nine. Bye.'

When they came Miriam arrived with a gift, as she always did when she visited anyone. This time it was flowers.

Mungo kissed Joy, and Miriam kissed her and Duncan, and eventually Miriam and Joy went into the kitchen to put the flowers in water while Duncan poured drinks for them.

'Whisky?'

Mungo nodded. 'You're a man of leisure at the moment, then?'

'I am. Till the next project comes up.'

'I can't understand how relaxed you are about it. I need to have daily work on a regular basis, on the go all the time. I wouldn't know what to do with leisure like you've got right now. Taking a holiday's a different matter altogether, but I find even that hard.'

They could hear Joy and Miriam laughing together in the kitchen.

Duncan sat down. 'They get on amazingly well,'those two, don't they . . . considering?'

Mungo looked at him in surprise. 'Considering? Considering what?'

There was a pause before Duncan replied, 'Both loving the same man?'

'The same man?' Mungo went deathly still.

'You.'

'Me?'

Duncan nodded. 'You. Didn't you know?'

The shock of Duncan's revelation silenced Mungo. When he did eventually answer his voice was harsh and belligerent. 'Is this you having one of your plain-speaking moments, you know, when you vent your spleen for the hell of it?'

'No, it's the truth. I'm surprised you've never realised, all these years. She loved you when she married me and still does. It's not easy for a husband to live with.'

. 'I've done nothing to . . .'

'I know you haven't.'

'I'm stunned.' Mungo's first thought was for Miriam. Slowly and deliberately, because he didn't want to know the answer but knew he must, he asked, 'Does Miriam know?'

'Of course not.'

'Joy speaks to you of it, then?'

'I've known for a long, long time, but we've never said it out loud to each other until a few nights ago.'

'I'm very fond of her, always have been, we've known each other a lot of years, worked together, you know, right from the early days. God, man, I'd no idea. You must hurt.'

Duncan agreed he did. 'Like hell. I thought you should know.'

'Why? I don't see what I can do about it.'

'Neither do I. Just thought you ought to know.' Duncan pointed a finger at Mungo. 'If ever you do anything about it . . .'

'Don't be a bloody fool. There's too much at stake, in any case . . . if you're bandying threats about, you remember to keep your mouth shut tight and don't whatever you do tell Miriam. She is so very fond of Joy and it would ruin their relationship. I won't allow it.'

'No.'

The complex emotions which had surfaced between them hung in the air. They heard sounds of footsteps and both tried to appear amicable together.

Miriam was standing in the doorway looking at them. 'What's the matter?' She looked from one to the other, awaiting their reply.

Duncan stood up. 'Here's your drink. Come and sit down.'

Mungo pulled an easy chair closer to the fire. 'Sit here, look, next to me.'

'Men's talk, then?' She squeezed Duncan's fingers as he handed her her gin. 'Joy won't be a moment, Tiger's been paddling in her water bowl so she's mopping up. She's turning into a lovely cat, isn't she?'

Duncan nodded. 'There's something you don't know.' Mungo half rose out of his chair believing that Duncan was still in his mood to shock.

Miriam asked Mungo, 'What's the matter?'

'Nothing, nothing at all.' He sat back down again but not before he'd shot a warning glare at Duncan.

Duncan continued speaking: 'I never thought I should live to see the day when I loved an animal, but I have to confess I bloody love that cat.'

Remembering his scathing attitude to Mungo over Perkins, Miriam laughed until she was almost helpless. 'Wait till I tell Joy. Oh, dear! There's a crack appearing in your armour, then?'

'Indeed.'

'Well, why not. It makes you more human.'

Mungo, sitting morosely staring into his whisky, looked up and said snappily, 'Where's Joy? Is she coming?'

Joy answered his question by appearing in the sitting room. 'I'm here at your service. Where's my drink?'

They talked business, deciding that the locum could stay till they found someone else but there was no question of him being permanent.

Mungo expressed his feelings in no uncertain terms. 'I didn't take to the chap, not one bit. He's too businesslike. It's a job not a vocation to him and I don't like that. With Valentine and Colin and Rhodri and Graham and Zoe, and for that matter Scott, they all *like* animals and put their welfare first. This chap seemed to talk too much about making money.'

'Excuse me, but we do need to make money. We've got wages to pay,' Joy said.

Mungo nodded. 'Of course, but there's a limit. We'll put up with him until we find the person we want. Right?'

Joy added, 'Colin *is* your partner. Do we know what he thinks? Shouldn't he have a say?'

'Oh, Colin! He'll go along with our decision. You know what he's like: anything for an easy life. And Zoe's too preoccupied with the imminent arrival of the baby to be bothered.'

Finally they talked of this and that, of Scott leaving, of Kate and her hopes, and it was midnight before Miriam and Mungo were saying their goodbyes.

'Goodnight! Goodnight!'

'Thank you.'

'Thanks for coming.'

Miriam called out from the car, 'The pleasure's all ours. Did you know that Duncan's confessed to loving Tiger? Isn't it a laugh? I'll speak to you Monday about lunch next week. There's something about my future I need to discuss. OK?'

Joy waited to wave to them as they turned into the road, because Miriam always gave a big wave out of the window just before they disappeared and Joy didn't want to disappoint her. She followed Duncan in, locked the front door and went to find him in the kitchen washing glasses.

'I'm so lucky to have Miriam for a friend. I don't deserve her.'

Duncan didn't answer.

'She's so kind to me, isn't she? She must never know what we talked about the other evening. I couldn't look her in the eye if she did. You won't ever tell her, will you?'

'Never.'

15

Back at work on Monday, Kate hoped she was getting away with her pretence of finding Scott's sudden disappearance no problem at all. As she'd promised herself she was keeping her grieving for home. At work she intended to be as she always was, pleasant, efficient and happy. Meeting the clients was no problem but working with Stephie and Lynne needed more will power than she had ever imagined. All weekend the pain of Scott leaving kept surfacing and real life became a nightmare, and she longed to put back the clock and pretend that she'd never let on to Scott how she felt about him; that he was still here and she could look forward to him coming in to the practice for his list, or halfway through the day with an armful of samples for the lab, or ringing up and saying he'd be another half-hour before he'd finished and should they go out somewhere? But he wouldn't, not ever.

This was the day Miss Chillingsworth was going to be able to take new Cherub home. It had been a fight to keep new Cherub alive, but with intensive nursing and Rhodri's brilliant piece of surgery she had survived. None of the kittens had been alive when Rhodri operated and Cherub had been close to death too, but the two Sarahs and Bunty had given her forty-eight hours of round-the-clock nursing and she was now fit to go home. Kate had fully expected Miss Chillingsworth to be there before the morning clinic opened but it was almost lunchtime when she came in, beaming from ear to ear, carrying her old cat basket.

'Kate, dear. Is she ready?'

'She is. Give me your basket and I'll get her for you. There's tablets to take too. Don't go without them.'

Miss Chillingsworth leant her elbows on the reception desk, wondering if she should divulge the reason for being so late collecting her dear new Cherub. She decided not. They would only think her a foolish old lady, which perhaps she was, and they wouldn't be interested. She wouldn't tell them how she'd spent the morning crying.

How it had struck her that bringing her new Cherub home to her big house, with its echoing, shabby rooms, had filled her with dread. Of how she had wept for the lost companionship of old Cherub, for her teenage boyfriend drowned at Dunkirk, for the years spent in shackles nursing her tyrannical father, for the paintings she'd had to sell to keep going, and that she'd wondered what use she had ever been to anyone at all, and where was it all going to end?

Weeping was a new experience for her, for despite all the vicissitudes of her life she'd never before weakened and found relief in crying. But the tears she'd shed today had swept away the debris of that past life and when finally she could cry no more she'd dried her eyes and decided that old memories didn't keep you warm, or put food on the table, or enrich your life, or provide companionship. Old memories were old memories and nothing more, and at this moment she'd had enough of them.

She'd recollected that an estate agent had pushed a leaflet through her door weeks before, saying that properties like hers were in great demand and why not take advantage of the boom in property prices in the area? Why not? Why shouldn't she have a slice of the good life? Sell up, buy a garden flat and provide a *real* home for new Cherub. For she deserved something better than this old, cold, comfortless house. She would. *She would.* And for once in her life she'd have spare money to spend on luxuries for herself and for new Cherub.

But she'd have to get rid of lots of things. There wouldn't be room in a flat for all this big furniture, or for all the things she'd kept in case they might be useful some time. She could begin today and collecting Cherub would be the start of her new life. Consequently she'd been delayed at the estate agents making arrangements. But now she was here and she couldn't wait to tell Cherub all about her plans.

Kate came through from the back with Cherub safely stowed in the old basket. Miss Chillingsworth poked a finger through the wire door. 'Hello, Cherub dear. We're going home. I've got some lovely chicken ready for your dinner tonight. Now, Kate, what do I owe?'

'We haven't finished doing the account yet. We'll post it.'

'I'll give you a hundred pounds on account, shall I? I have it with me.'

Memories of the last one hundred pounds she'd left in her care made Kate blush. 'No, thank you. You hang on to it until you get the account, Miss Chillingsworth.' Kate diverted her from talking about money by remembering the tablets. 'Now you see, we almost forgot the tablets. One each day. There's sufficient until Sunday and she should be fine by then. Bring her back a week today for her check-up. What she needs now is some loving care.'

'She'll get that, don't worry. Come along, then, Cherub, off we go home. Bye-bye, dear. See you next week, Kate. Take care, dear. Send me the account as soon as you can.'

Kate watched her trot away, glad that her new cat had put the spring back in her step. Poor Miss Chillingsworth with nothing to look forward to but enjoying her new cat. She thought about growing old and having achieved nothing at all. That was definitely not going to happen to Kate Howard. Definitely not. Had Miss Chillingsworth known that the sight of her had strengthened Kate's resolve to qualify and make a challenging life for herself she would have been very gratified to have been proved to be of some use after all.

Kate went to fill the fire bucket as it was the first Monday of the month and Adolf was due. Though she hated dogs to fight, she had to confess to enjoying the thrill of Perkins and Adolf squaring up to each other. They truly meant nothing by it, it was simply something they both felt a need to do.

She placed the heavy bucket under the reception desk and checked through the small-animal appointments for the afternoon clinic at four. It was so quiet today for a Monday morning. Coffee. She'd make coffee for Lynne and Joy.

Joy liked it not too hot, two sugars and plenty of milk. Lynne liked it hot, no sugar with hot milk. As she waited for the milk to heat up in the microwave she thought of Scott and how he'd grown to love her making his coffee for him. Black with two sugars. She remembered how he cupped his hands round the mug, not using the handle when he drank. She indulged herself by thinking about those long, strong fingers, the brown hair streaked with blond, the broad shoulders, the clean smell of him, and then she saw in her mind's eye how he'd looked the day he'd fallen into Phil Parsons's slurry pit and she laughed.

'What are you laughing at?'

It was Lynne.

'Life, I suppose.'

'Mm. Glad you find it a joke. I don't.'

Kate turned to look at her. 'Why?'

'Sick of everything. Time I moved on. Did something different.'

'Why don't you, then?'

Lynne shrugged her shoulders. 'Such as?'

'I don't know. What takes your fancy, I suppose.'

'You're lucky.'

'I am?'

'Yes, you've got an aim in life. What will you do if you don't get your chemistry, though?'

Kate groaned. 'Don't mention it. I honestly don't know.'

'You will, you wait and see. You'll make a good vet. It must be hard doing a day's work and then studying.'

'It is but I enjoy it.'

'Worth it?'

'Of course.'

'I might give it a go. Not veterinary but something else.'

'You should.'

'I might do that very thing. Why not.' Lynne went to sit outside on the bench by the back door and think about her options. Kate went back to the reception desk.

To stop herself from thinking about Scott, Kate worked all afternoon instead of taking her three hours off.

Joy put her head round the door halfway through the afternoon. 'You really shouldn't, you know, you should go out or go home or something.'

'I know.' She pondered whether or not to tell Joy her reasons. 'Better keeping busy at the moment.'

'I see. He shouldn't have done what he did.'

'He explained.'

'You've heard, then?'

'A letter from the airport.'

'I see. All part of life's rich tapestry, if that's any comfort.'

'It is. I suppose. A little.' Kate gave her a rueful smile.

'Brave heart, that's what's needed.'

Kate nodded.

It must have been just after six when an enormous bouquet of flowers appeared to be making its own way into the reception area. Lynne said, 'What on earth . . .!'

Finally it emerged through the glass door with a pair of very long legs below it and made its way to the desk.

To Kate there was something very familiar about those legs.

It couldn't be.

But it was.

All the fear she'd felt when he'd threatened her that time and when he'd stalked her came rushing into her heart and she instinctively stepped back from the desk, unable to stop herself from trembling. She sensed beads of sweat between her shoulder blades and her scalp prickling.

The flowers were laid down in front of her and there was Adam.
'Kate!'

'Adam.'

They both stood staring down at the bouquet, not speaking.

Stephie, embarrassed by the silence between them, tried hard to fill it. 'Aren't they lovely! You are lucky! I love the roses.'

'Thank you.' Kate made herself look at Adam. Disappointed, she saw he was still the same Adam: his cheeks were as thin as always, his Adam's apple as large, his skin as sallow, his hair as nondescript, his hands as large and bony as ever. What had she seen in him? Poor Adam.

Adam saw the lovely girl he'd loved. And lost. 'I started my new job today, it's just up my street. I've come straight from work to bring you these. To say . . .' He glanced at Stephie and disliked her avid interest. Leaning towards Kate he whispered, 'Is there anywhere we could talk, you know, all these clients listening.'

'I can't ask you in the back, it's not allowed. We'll go outside. Won't be a minute, Stephie.' She led the way out, hating herself for the fib she'd just told, but knowing she couldn't bear to be shut in a small room with him. The beads of sweat turned cold and made her shudder.

'I've brought the flowers to say sorry.'

'Right.'

'I am, really sorry. I should never have done what I did. I was so desperate, you see. I didn't mean to harm you. It was losing my job like I did. I couldn't tell Mother. How could I? She's always been so ambitious for me, driving me, you know. It was that Scott as well. He always got the better of me. Whatever I did, no matter how hard I tried.'

She opened her mouth to tell him Scott no longer posed a threat, but instinct told her not to and she closed it.

'I'm going home to tell Mother that I've got the chance to share a flat with two chaps from work.'

'Good.'

'I don't know how she'll take it, but I'm determined.'

'Good. I hope it works out OK.'

His Adam's apple bobbed up and down. 'If I gave you a ring some time . . . bowling one Tuesday, perhaps . . . oh, no, not bowling, cinema perhaps?'

'No. Best not.'

'I hoped . . .'

She got a sudden image of Adam hopping about clutching his

bruised hand after he'd missed punching Scott the night they'd had the fight. 'No, Adam, I'd rather not.'

Adam's sloping shoulders slumped. 'Good luck, then. We had some good times.'

'Good luck to you. Glad the job's turning out well. Stand tall with your mother. Thank you very much for the flowers, they're beautiful.'

As Kate closed the door behind her a terrible sadness came over her and she wished she could like him. But she couldn't. Not after Scott.

'I'll stand these in the fire bucket under here. Mr F. mustn't be coming.'

'No, don't. Mr Featherstonehough is coming. His camper thingy broke down this morning and he's been waiting to get it mended, and he rang to say he'll be in before we shut.'

But the waiting clients weren't going to let her get away with it so easily and one of them called out, 'My word, he must be keen!'

Another said, 'I've gone wrong somewhere. No one's ever come out of the gloaming and presented me with a bunch that size.'

'Nor me,' offered a client, hanging on for dear life to a particularly spiteful cat.

Stephie called out, 'Nor me. Some people have all the luck without even trying.' She gave Kate a nudge and grinned, and Kate mouthed her thanks.

On impulse Kate said, 'Dad and Mia are both out tonight so I'm supposed to be getting my own meal when I get back. I don't suppose you'd like the idea of window-shopping in the precinct and a meal?'

Stephie nodded. 'Thanks, I would. Bit short this month, though, so I can't go anywhere smart.'

'So am I. We'll go to the fish restaurant. You can get some quite cheap meals there and their chips are brill.'

'Right, you're on. Let's hope we don't run late tonight, then.'

There was a kerfuffle at the door and in came Adolf, dragging Mr Featherstonehough.

'Good evening, Mr F.' Kate leaned over the desk to welcome Adolf. 'Good evening, Adolf. Take a seat. Graham won't be long; a client's just gone in and then it's your turn. You've got the car mended, then, at last.'

'I have. Three hundred and fifty-two pounds it's cost me. It's not worth it. If I sold it I'd only get about five hundred for it. Good money after bad, but I can't manage without it, so what's the alternative?'

'Buy a new one.'

Mr Featherstonehough's bushy eyebrows shot up his forehead. 'And pigs might fly. I've had that Dormobile twelve years. I can't bear to part

with it. I know all its little idiosyncrasies, take the clutch, for instance ...'
He leant his elbow on the desk. '... You just have to let it up until ...'
He let go of Adolf's lead, dropping it on the floor and anchoring it with
his foot while he demonstrated with his hands the delicate manoeuvre
needed to let in his clutch.

Unbeknown to him, though, Perkins had achieved his freedom and
was silently racing down the stairs from the flat to get at Adolf. Mungo
was calling him, but Perkins had cast his normal obedience to the
winds as he charged through to meet the challenge. Adolf seized his
freedom with all four feet and met Perkins halfway down the corridor.
There ensued a bitter, fearful fight, the worst they had ever had. The
sight of their swirling bodies and the flashing of their fangs was terrible
to see. It was impossible for Mungo, trapped on the far side of them, to
interfere for fear of being bitten, so it was Kate who separated them
with the well-aimed fire bucket full to the brim with water. Mungo,
unprepared for this remedy, leapt back far too late and that combined
with the limited space in the corridor meant that he as well as the dogs
got drenched.

The two of them broke apart, Adolf strutted up the corridor into
reception and shook himself all over Mr Featherstonehough, and
Perkins did the same to Mungo, then grinned at him and wagged his
tail.

Mungo, dressed ready for an evening out, was steaming with temper.
'Bert!' he roared. 'Bert!'

Mr Featherstonehough peered cautiously round the door into the
back.

'If it weren't for the fact that you've been a faithful client of ours for
years I'd tell you to take that bloody Adolf home and never come back.
He's a menace. An absolute menace. If it hadn't been for Kate having
that bucket ready, heaven alone knows what damage would have been
done to Perkins. Have a care in future.'

Mr Featherstonehough began to smile. Mungo, pausing in his
attempt to brush some of the water from his suit, glanced at him and
saw the smile. 'If I'm about when they have a return match, and there'll
definitely be one because Perkins has a long memory, I'll ... I'll ...'

'Do what? They're both as much to blame. Just happens this time
Adolf got in there first. That's Graham calling my name, I'll go and
keep my appointment if you'll excuse me, for which, I might remind
you, I pay you good money.' With great dignity Mr Featherstonehough
took hold of Adolf's lead and marched to Graham's consulting room.

Mungo caught Kate's eye and when he saw her trying hard not to laugh he succumbed to amusement himself and gave her a broad grin. 'Where did you learn that trick, then?'

'The first morning I was here.'

'Well, aim more carefully next time.' Mungo took hold of Perkins's collar, gave her another grin and disappeared up the stairs. The clients still waiting gave her a round of applause and a mild cheer, so Kate bowed to them all and disappeared into the back to fetch the mop, with a beaming smile on her face.

Country Wives

List of Characters at Barleybridge Veterinary Hospital

Mungo Price	Orthopaedic Surgeon and Senior Partner
Colin Walker	Partner – large and small animal
Zoe Savage	Partner – large animal
Graham Murgatroyd	Small-animal
Valentine Dedic	Small-animal
Rhodri Hughes	Small-animal
Dan Brown	Large animal

NURSING STAFF
Sarah Cockroft (Sarah One)
Sarah MacMillan (Sarah Two)
Bunty Page

RECEPTIONISTS
Joy Bastable (Practice Manager)
Lynne Seymour
Stephie Budge
Kate Howard

Miriam Price	Mungo's wife
Duncan Bastable	Joy's husband
Letty Walker	Colin's wife
Gerry Howard	Kate's father
Mia Howard	Kate's stepmother

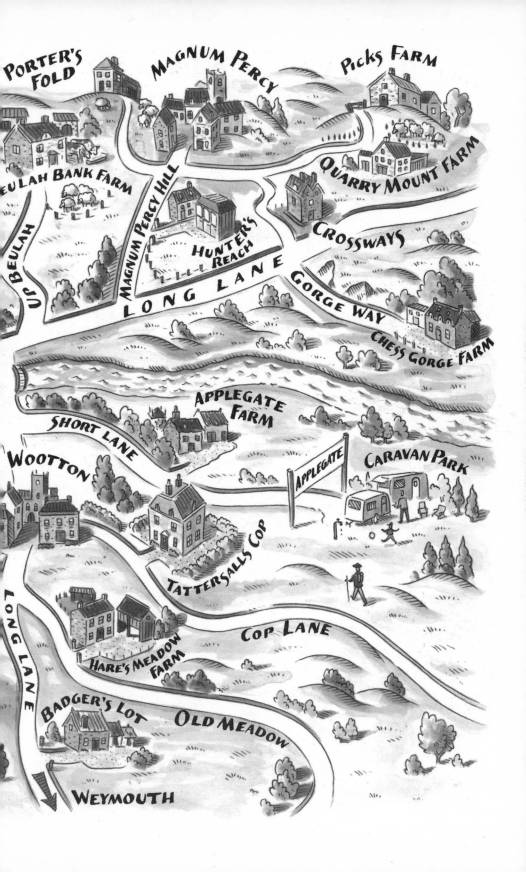

1

The locum had been working for the practice one whole week and Joy wasn't at all sure he should be there another day, never mind waiting until they had appointed someone permanently. It wasn't that he didn't work hard, nor that he didn't know his job, because he did, his experience was extensive and his meticulous punctuality and his enthusiasm were A1. No, it was none of these things, it was his *attitude* that got up her nose and not only hers but Mungo's and everyone else's too. He'd be in shortly and she was wishing like hell he wouldn't be, and that it would be the much lamented Scott who would be nonchalantly strolling in to collect his call list, his devastatingly blue eyes twinkling, his hands in his pockets, and be setting himself out to flirt with her. But it wasn't to be; all she could do was make sure that over her dead body would this particular locum become a regular member of the staff. Glancing at the reception clock she saw she had only five minutes exactly before the glass doors swung open and *he* would march in, brisk and alert, eager for whatever the day would bring, good or bad.

She checked his list of calls for the fourth time to make sure he couldn't find any fault with it and wished Kate weren't on a day off because she seemed to know instinctively how to deal with him. Kate needed a break, though, she'd been looking ghastly this last week and they all knew why, but didn't dare say a word to her because Kate was endeavouring to carry on as though Scott had never existed, but it was evident from her face that he'd worked his magic on her, as he had on others, and his sudden departure had hit her hard. Joy heard the outer door open and braced herself for the arrival of Daniel Brown.

Somehow he could have been excused some of his bluntness if he'd been good-looking but he wasn't. He was a couple of inches under six feet, well-built, very dark-haired with a kind of craggy face that even his mother couldn't call handsome, and large, challenging, alert brown eyes, which missed nothing. Also, there was a sort of 'in your face' energy about him which intimidated lesser mortals.

The inner glass door crashed open and there stood Dan, in his brown corduroy trousers, his checked sports jacket and matching cap; jaw jutting, his dark eyes wide awake, eager to begin his day's work. 'Good morning, Joy. Got my list?'

'Good morning to you. Here it is, Dan, long list today, I'm afraid.'

'Afraid? Why afraid? Isn't that what work is about? I shan't earn my keep if I'm sitting about all day twiddling my thumbs. Those results back from the laboratory?'

'The post hasn't come yet, unfortunately.'

'That isn't your fault, I'll ring in during the morning.'

Joy nodded her head. Come back, Scott, all is forgiven.

'Right, I'll be away then. There's something wrong with the Land Rover. That chap who had it before me must have driven it like a maniac. Which garage do you use for servicing the vehicles?'

'Vickers.'

'Where is it?'

Joy turned to the map pinned behind the reception desk and pointed it out to him. 'But Mungo likes to know; I'll tell him.'

'No need for that. I'll take it and see what they say. Something to do with the transmission. I can't afford for it to break down and leave me stranded with calls still to do. That's not the way to run a practice, is it?'

'Well, no, it isn't.'

'Are they not serviced regularly?'

'Of course they are but we can't repair them before they've gone wrong, can we?'

'Is it you responsible for seeing them serviced?'

'Well, yes, but . . .'

'When is the service due, then?'

'Look here . . .'

'I asked a simple question.'

'I'd have to get the records out.'

'Then do it, now, let's find out. I can't afford to be standing around here wasting time.' Dan tapped his fingers impatiently on the reception desk.

'At this time in the morning I'm busy with clients and appointments. I'll have a look later when I've a few minutes to spare.'

Dan shrugged his shoulders. 'Very well, but don't say I didn't warn you. I can't stand inefficiency and if the Land Rover breaks down today that's exactly what it will be: inefficiency, yours not mine.'

'Look here . . .'

'If it's cost you're concerned about I can assure you that if I take it to the garage myself, don't fret yourself, they won't overcharge *me*.'

Joy, seething with the injustice of his opinions, thought, *No, I bet they won't. They'll do it for free just to get you off the premises.*

He studied his list for a moment. 'This first call, Lord Askew's? Is it a stately home, then?'

Joy answered him as civilly as she could: 'A minor one, but stately all the same. We do all his farm work but his horses are looked after by a practice near Sherborne.'

'Why don't we do *all* his veterinary work?'

'Because his horses are rather special, and the Sherborne practice specialises in equine work and he prefers to use them.'

'That's enough to get my back up. However ...'

'Be seeing you.'

'Indeed.' Dan nodded his head at her and dashed out through the front door.

Livid with temper and more determined than ever that he had to go, Joy listened to the roar of the Land Rover and heard it brake suddenly, and then there was the screech of brakes other than his. But there was no sound of metal on metal so they must have missed each other. Pity.

Dan roared off, taking the sign for Askew Newton as he was leaving the town. He'd spent a whole evening in the clinic painstakingly copying on to his own large-scale map the names of the farms and their positions from the map behind the reception desk, so now with only the briefest reference to his handiwork he could head off to the various clients. It took a while to get to know all the farmers and their own particular idiosyncrasies but he was already getting the hang of the place and Dan had to admit to a liking for it. It hadn't been easy coming back to England after seven years abroad, but a clean break had been the best thing. He'd done that and found this job in less than a week of returning, and he had half a mind to stay if they would have him.

He swung into the turning for Lord Askew's place, admiring the beautifully sculptured parkland and enjoying the glimpse he caught of the large stone house through the trees.

He pulled up in an immaculate cobbled courtyard surrounded by stables. A groom was walking a horse across the yard. Dan didn't know when he'd seen a more princely looking animal. It was a wonderful roan, just the shade which appealed to him. He admired it for a moment, thoroughly enjoying its beauty.

The groom called to Dan. 'Morning, can I help?'

Dan got out and went across to him. 'My name's Dan Brown, from the Barleybridge Veterinary Hospital, come to see Chris? Has a cow with mastitis.'

'That'll be through the archway.'

'Right.' Dan paused for a moment, looked at the horse and said, 'Don't like the look of the action of his front feet.' He touched his cap to the groom, climbed back in the Land Rover and swept away through the arch. Now this really was a well-kept place. Just what he preferred to see. Attention to detail meant well cared for animals and he liked that, did Dan. Nothing he hated more than careless husbandry. In fact, if it was careless, 'husbandry' was a misnomer.

A man he took to be Chris came out to greet him. 'Where's Scott, then?'

'Gone back to Aussie land in a hurry.'

'Not surprising. Woman trouble I expect! He was a rare womaniser, was that Scott. There wasn't a female anywhere around these parts who hadn't fallen for his charm, including her ladyship. Pick of the lot of 'em he could have had. So, it's goodbye Scott and hello . . . ?'

'I'm Dan Brown, come to see a cow with mastitis.'

'I'm Chris, nice to meet you.' Chris appraised Dan with a piercing eye as he shook his hand and said, 'That Scott was a bad lad but he knew his job.'

'You'll find no fault with me. Lead the way.'

'Didn't say I would, just didn't want you to get the wrong impression of Scott.'

'How big's your herd?'

'One hundred and forty-three at the moment. All pedigree Guernseys.'

Dan was impressed but he was appalled when he saw how ill the cow was.

While he took her temperature he very, very quietly asked how long she'd been like this.

'Three or four days, not bad like, just off colour more than anything this morning . . .'

After checking the thermometer and feeling the affected quarter of the cow's udder, Dan straightened up and looked Chris in the eye. 'You're the stockman, are you?'

Chris nodded.

'Are you sure?'

Puzzled, Chris nodded again.

'No stockman worth his salt would allow a cow to suffer like this. She's been more than "off colour" as you put it for three or four days, as well you know. You ought to be ashamed of yourself. It could be almost too late to save her. Is his lordship about this morning?'

Chris took a deep breath, 'Out riding. But . . .'

'There's no buts about this. How many years' experience have you had?'

'Eleven years in charge, but look here, it's not my fault.'

'Kindly tell me whose fault it is, then? The gardener's or the housemaid's or someone?'

'No, of course not, but his lordship . . .'

'Oh! I see, now it's his lordship to blame, is it. What time is he usually back from his ride?'

'Any time now.'

'I'll deal with the cow and then I'll deal with him.'

'It's the money you see.'

Dan wagged his finger at Chris, saying, 'I don't expect owners to *lavish* care on their beasts but I do expect them to be well cared for. With veterinary work, a good motto to remember is a stitch in time saves nine and you'd do well to abide by that.'

'But that's what he doesn't . . .'

'I bet one of his eventers would have had quicker treatment than this, no matter the cost.'

'Yes, but you see . . .'

'It may surprise you to know that cows feel pain just as much as horses.'

Dan, having assessed the cow's problem, went back to his vehicle and picked out the drugs which past experience told him he would need. He returned and concentrated on treating the cow. While he waited for an injection to bring down the milk into the infected quarter to take effect, he gave the cow antibiotics into the vein. After a few minutes he was able to strip out the milk and give the cow some relief. 'I would normally suggest that I leave you some antibiotics for you to give her for the next three days, but in view of your reluctance to call us in, I'll be back in the morning myself first thing. Right?'

Angered by his attitude, Chris said, 'Right. Perhaps next time you might let me get a word in edgeways.'

Dan turned back. 'I'm so sorry, please . . . be my guest.'

'His lordship gets wild if I call in a vet too early or if he considers we could have managed without. It's the money, you see. It all goes on the horses. It's more than my job's worth; I've a wife and children, and we're living in a tied house and that. If I upset him we'll all be homeless. Scott knew that and made allowances.'

'I beg your pardon. I was angry, always affects me like that when pain could have been avoided. I'll clear it with . . .' The clatter of hooves and a loud, braying voice interrupted him.

Quietly Chris said, 'That's him back.'

'Right. See you tomorrow.' Dan, emerging from the archway, saw a splendid black horse skittering about on the cobbles and mounted on its impressive back was a giant of a man in immaculate riding kit. From under his riding hat a thick swath of snow-white hair framed a ruddy, well-fleshed face with a prominent pulpy nose dominating it.

'Mornin' to you. Who might you be? Here, Gavin, take him for me.' Lord Askew dismounted and eyed Dan up and down. He was a head taller than Dan and the word giant was very apt. His shoulders were wide, his chest built like a barrel and his arms were thick as tree trunks.

Dan held out his hand. 'I'm Dan Brown from Barleybridge.'

Lord Askew ignored his outstretched hand. 'Seeing that damned cow of mine, I've no doubt. Eh? More cost. Coming back tomorrow, are you, on some flimsy excuse? More money. Never ending it is.'

Dan deliberately kept his voice low in sharp contrast to his lordship. 'You have a herd of over a hundred cows and you can't expect them to produce milk at the rate they do without needing attention from time to time . . .'

'Eh? Speak up. Can't hear.'

Dan raised the level of his voice but kept the same quiet determination in his tone. 'I'm sorry to have to say this but I should have been called earlier. In fact, to be honest I'm annoyed your stockman has felt compelled to leave it so late.'

Lord Askew began to bluster. 'I damn well don't know who you are, but whoever you are you've too damn much to say for yourself. Too damn much, and I shall be having a word with Mungo Price about you. What's yer name, you say?'

'Dan Brown. You can have as many words as you like, but Mungo will agree with me that she shouldn't have been left for so long. As I have several other calls to make this morning, if you will excuse me, I must leave right now.'

'Damned impertinence! There's no need to come back in the morning. My stockman can see to her.'

'Either I take responsibility for her or I don't, you can't have it both ways. I shall be here tomorrow. By the way, that roan' – he nodded his head in the direction of the roan now tethered to a ring in the stable wall – 'has a problem with its front feet.'

Lord Askew's face registered shock bordering on horror. 'Eh? Eh?'

'Good morning to you.'

Dan drove away seething with temper and well aware he'd made a big mistake tackling Lord Askew in the way he had, but people like him made his blood boil. Mungo would be rather less than pleased to have that blustering idiot complaining down the phone, though. Well, if it cost him his job so what? He had his principles and that poor stockman, tied hand and fist because of his domestic circumstances, couldn't be allowed to take the blame. Dan Brown was probably heading for the biggest apology of his life.

On his way to Tattersall's Cop he called in at the practice for the results of the specimens he'd sent to the laboratory, to be faced by an indignant Joy. She beckoned him into her office with a schoolmarmish finger. 'I have had Lord Askew on the phone. What on earth have you said to him, as if I need to ask.'

'I've no doubt he explained very thoroughly, Joy, and I shall make a point of apologising to him tomorrow when I go.'

'You won't be going. He refuses to have you on his land.'

'Does he indeed.'

'Also, what on earth were you doing examining one of his horses? It's hardly veterinary etiquette, is it?'

'I didn't. It was obvious. Only a fool could have missed it.'

Joy calmed down a little and a glimmer of amusement flicked across her face. 'Only a fool!'

'Yes. I must confess his lordship looked more than a little startled. I bet their so-called equine vet will be there humming and hawing this very minute. Post come?'

'Yes. Here we are.' She handed him the letter he was waiting for and watched as he opened it.

His face lit up and he raised a clenched fist into the air. 'Eureka! I knew I was right! Ha!'

Briefly, Joy couldn't help but like him. 'This won't cancel the appointment you have with Mungo at one. He can't see you now because he has a full list of consultations this morning, but he wants you to make sure you're here. We can't afford to lose a good customer and Lord Askew has a lot of influence. It's not just him we'll lose, he'll tell half the county.'

Dan, looking at her with a dead-straight face, replied, 'You're very wrong there, very wrong, he'll tell *all* the county. Nothing I did or said was out of order, believe me. I will not tolerate neglect. Must be off. This Tattersall's Cop, is there anything I should know?'

'Beautiful, beautiful setting. Lovely people, struggling to make ends meet. We try to be economical with their bills.'

Dan raised his eyebrows. 'Tut-tut! That won't pay back the overdraft.'

There he was again, catching her on the raw. Rather tartly she answered him with, 'That's Mungo's worry not yours.'

'Indeed it is. Be seeing you at one.' As Dan went back into reception he glanced around the seating area, catching the eye of a few of the clients and giving them a brusque nod of greeting.

After the door had closed on his departure one of the long-standing clients called out to Joy, 'He looks a bit grim, Joy.'

Between tight lips she answered, 'His heart's in the right place.'

'Well, he certainly wasn't in the right place when good looks were given out.'

A general chortle broke out.

'Bring back Scott, I say,' another client contributed to the debate.

'All these bleeding hearts he's left behind, nothing short of criminal.'

'It was 'is 'ands I liked, sensitive they were.'

'Did you ever see him in his shorts?' The client rolled her eyes in appreciation.

'Oops! Steady, Bridget, you'll be spinning out of control!'

They all laughed and then resettled to discussing their animals' symptoms.

Joy silently agreed with them. Despite the broken hearts among her own staff, Scott had brought laughter and delight with him to the practice every day and that couldn't be bad; added to which, the farm clients loved him for his expertise. She'd an idea they would appreciate Dan's knowledge too but they'd never appreciate the man. And neither would she.

By a quarter to one Dan was eating his home-made sandwiches outside on the old bench by the back door. There was a powerful wind coming down from Beulah Bank Top, which seemed to slice through any clothing you chose to be wearing, but Dan preferred the peace and quiet to the banter in the staffroom where most of the staff ate their lunch. Social chit-chat had never appealed to him and still less now with so much on his mind. Though when he'd visited Tattersall's Cop, his own problems had been momentarily forgotten. What a beautiful, neat little farm it was, loving care in every inch of hedging, in every ditch, in every farm building but ... it seemed to Dan that Callum Tattersall dabbled first in this and then in that, never sticking at anything long enough to get real returns on his investment. He hadn't enough acres, not enough guts and, to be honest, not enough commitment. Bad luck had played a big part in his life too, or so Callum had said as they shared a mounting block while they drank their coffee. A sick wife needing a lot of care, one in a thousand chance of disease and his entire turkey flock had been decimated, his scheme for producing fresh farm yoghurt had fallen at the first fence, to say nothing of the race horse he bought a share in which, after falling at the first fence, was never fit for racing again. But you dratted well couldn't help but like the man. A shadow fell across his legs and he looked up to find Mungo standing beside him. Dan put the apple he was about to sink his teeth into in his pocket and shifted further along the bench to make room for him.

Mungo broke the silence with, 'Well?'

'I was polite, controlled and well-mannered, and absolutely right. Like you, I abhor animals having to suffer because their owners are too mean to get treatment for them and that's what it is, absolute, sod-awful meanness that makes that huge well-fed lord of the manor refuse to allow the stockman to call for help when the chap knows it's needed. I shall go tomorrow to attend the cow, in spite of being forbidden to do so, because my professional integrity is being challenged and neither you nor I can allow that. I shall, however, apologise.' Dan looked at Mungo and waited for his reply.

'The big mistake was examining the horse.'

'I didn't. Just watching him trot across the yard I knew his problem, without doubt.' Dan grinned. 'You should have seen old Askew's face when I commented on his limp. You'd have enjoyed it.'

'Would I? You're not wet behind the ears – I'm well aware of that – you know what you're doing, but I've spent twenty years of my life building up this practice and I don't want to lose it all because of someone ...'

'Yes?'

'... someone who thinks he's a clever beggar.'

Dan grunted and held back on an angry reply.

Mungo, sensing his anger, tried a more conciliatory approach. 'Horses. I didn't realise.'

'Worked for an Arab sheikh for a while. Learnt a lot.'

'Interesting work.'

Dan nodded. 'You'd do well to take horses on. Just that bit more money into the coffers. You see plenty hereabouts when you're driving around.'

'Never had the inclination.'

'Worth thinking about. There's money in it.'

'Got to speak frankly, Dan. To be honest, I'm not in it for the money. Yes, I have wages to pay and drugs to buy and a building to keep up, but my main reason for being a vet is the animals and their needs are paramount in my mind. Do well by them and you and I will get on famously, have money as your prime motivation and we won't and you can leave.'

'You're not questioning my integrity too, are you?'

'No, I am not. I'm just ... telling you. Putting it on the line, so we both know where we stand.' Mungo stood up and faced him. 'Watch yourself tomorrow. I dislike Lord Askew as much as you do, there's nothing gracious nor pleasing about him, but he is a client, his bills are always paid on the dot and we owe him a duty of care, and also he has a lot of influence.'

'Exactly, a duty of care and that's just what I shall be doing when I go in the morning: caring.'

'Good, then you and I understand each other. Dinner with us tomorrow night in the flat Miriam says, if you've nothing better to do.'

'Thanks. Yes.'

'Seven thirty.'

'Fine. I look forward to it.'

Dan arrived at Mungo and Miriam's at seven twenty-nine precisely after a long, arduous day. He was the last to arrive. Waiting to greet him were Joy and her husband Duncan, Colin and his wife Letty, and a heavily pregnant Zoe with no husband. Something about the tension in the air made him wonder if this was to become a third-degree interrogation because here he was, faced with all three partners.

Miriam came out of the kitchen and broke into smiles on seeing him. 'Dan! How lovely!'

She gave him a great big hug as naturally as if they'd known each other for years and he responded gladly, 'Miriam! Nice to see you again.'

When she released him she asked what he would like to drink. Briefly he studied her face, saw how genuine her greeting was and felt grateful. 'A whisky and water, please.'

'Mungo, a whisky and water for Dan. The food is almost ready.' She crossed her fingers and laughed.

Colin introduced his wife Letty. She was short and round and pale and blonde, and had the misfortune to have chosen to wear a cream wool suit and Vaseline on her lips instead of lipstick, so she appeared to have no substance at all, but her tongue belied her appearance. 'Got the practice into deep trouble and you've only been here a week.'

'Letty!' Colin protested.

'Deep trouble?'

'Hadn't you heard? Lord Askew has cancelled his account with us.'

'No, I hadn't heard. More fool him.'

'After your rudeness ...'

Colin interrupted, 'Letty! It's none of your business. Leave it.'

Looking Colin directly in the face she said, 'Our income is my business. It cost an arm and a leg to set up this place. If the practice fails, so too do we.' In profile Dan saw that Letty's nose was longer and sharper than any he'd seen in a long time. Unfulfilled, that was her trouble. Then he smiled inwardly at his assumption, or thought he had.

'It's amusing, is it?'

Insulted by Letty thinking he was not taking the matter seriously enough, Dan answered her sharply, 'No, it is not.'

'Wait till Mungo's taken in what's happened. You'll be out on your ear in no time at all.'

Dan, growing angrier by the minute, asked her, 'Shall I indeed?'

She nodded her head vigorously. 'If I have my way you will.'

Exasperated by her rudeness Colin said, 'Please! Leave it, leave it.' By his tone it was obvious he knew she would ignore his protest.

'I hadn't realised you owned the practice.'

Slightly taken aback by his directness, she paused a moment and then answered him, 'I do have a large say in the matter but then money talks, doesn't it?'

'Are you always so unpleasant to people you don't know?'

'I beg your pardon?'

'I said are you always so unpleasant to people you've never met before?'

'Unpleasant? I believe in calling a spade a spade and so do you, judging by what you said to Lord Askew yesterday morning.'

'I hadn't realised you were there?'

'I wasn't. Colin told me.'

'Ah!'

Miriam called out for help in the kitchen from Mungo and asked Joy to seat everybody.

In the general mêlée of Joy organising everyone Dan deftly separated himself from Letty and managed to find a seat next to Zoe. 'Hello, Zoe, how are you?'

'More to the point, how are you?' Lowering her voice she added, 'She really is the absolute limit. I don't know how Colin puts up with her.'

'He seems well laid back.'

'One day the worm will turn, believe me. One can put up with so much and then ...'

'Water?'

Zoe nodded. Dan poured her a glass of water and wishing not to become involved too deeply in practice politics he asked, 'Are you hoping to come back to work after the baby?'

'Of course.'

'How will you manage?'

'My mother lives with me. Between us we shall cope.'

Dan hesitated. 'I hadn't . . . I didn't know . . .'

'There's no need to tiptoe delicately around the matter, I'm unmarried and intend staying so, this' – she waved vaguely in the direction of her bump – 'is a momentary blip.'

'I see. That's a new word for a baby. Blip.'

'I hear a hint of disapproval. You can disapprove as much as you like. I don't really care.'

'I'm old-fashioned enough to believe that two are better than one where babies are concerned.'

'There will be two. My mother and I.'

They were interrupted by the soup arriving.

Miriam came to sit down and put herself out to make him feel comfortable. She was an astute and caring hostess and a thoughtful conversationalist, and after a few minutes of her company Dan dismissed his clashes with Zoe and Letty as more a misfortune on their part than his.

'Where were you working before you came here, Dan?'

'Here and there. In the the Gulf, the Caribbean, in the States. But now I'm home for good.'

'You mean in England for good.'

Dan nodded. 'That's right.'

'Good, I'm glad. There comes a time when gadding about all over the place is just not enough any more and one longs to put down one's roots. Is that how you feel?'

There was a slight hesitation, then Dan answered firmly, 'It is.'

'That's lovely. I am pleased. Is the flat all right? I paid a company to clean it and everything, they're usually very good. If there is anything you're short of let me know. The flat is my particular charge, you see, so any problems, see Miriam.'

Dan who had been about to reply got beaten to it by Letty. 'He won't be here long enough to know if anything's missing.'

Colin touched her arm and said, 'Now, Letty, now, Letty.'

Miriam flushed. Dan saw her agitation and felt concerned. She was too sweet to have to suffer this kind of unpleasantness. Visibly angry, Miriam said, 'Letty, I expect my guests to put themselves out to be *charming* while they are in my home, even if they're . . . not charming.' She stood up and began to collect the soup plates.

Dan said loudly, 'That soup was delicious, Miriam, if I might say so, some of the best I've had.'

'Thank you. I shan't be long with the main course. It's all ready.'

Joy bounced up to give her a hand and they both disappeared into the kitchen.

A long silence fell because those still sitting at the table had been surprised by the sharpness of Miriam's retort to Letty.

It was Duncan who saved the day. 'My cat, Tiger, shall I have her spayed when the time comes? Do you advise it, Mungo?'

'Question is, do you want kittens?'

'No.'

'Then have it done, it's the only way.'

'Have I the right?'

'Right to what?'

'Have I the right to have her snipped? *I* wouldn't want to have the snipping job done, so have I the right to have the cat done. It's not as if I can ask her permission, is it?'

A wave of laughter went round the table, except for Letty who pulled a disapproving face. *What else could the woman expect when sitting at a table dominated by members of the veterinary profession*, thought Dan.

Mungo stopped laughing long enough to say, 'Look here, Duncan, it isn't very long since you mocked me at this very table for loving my Perkins and here you are treating Tiger as if she were a human being. She isn't, she has no soul, no aspirations for the future, no knowledge of what she's having done, no thinking "God! Now I shall never be a mother, why is he doing this to me?", so blessed well get it done for her sake. Come on, man. There's no debate.'

'Isn't there?'

Duncan asked Zoe and she agreed with Mungo. He asked Dan and he said, 'Having litter after litter of kittens is cruelty in the extreme, and finding homes for them all even more cruel for yourself. There's no debate, like Mungo said.'

'I'm not too sure.'

Dan replied emphatically, 'Well, I am. In fact, come to think of it there are plenty of human beings who could do to be snipped, never mind the odd cat.'

'She isn't an odd cat, she's my cat,' Duncan protested.

'Your cat or not, I should have her snipped. She'll never know the difference and the world will be dozens of unwanted cats the fewer. Two-minute job. Bring her in tomorrow and I'll do it for her.'

Panicking, Duncan said quickly, 'No, no, she's too young yet.'

'Well, when she's old enough I'll do it and . . .'

Zoe forcefully interrupted him. 'Was "plenty of human beings" a reference to me?'

Dan laughed. 'About human beings having the snip? Come to think of it, there can't be that much difference between doing a cat and a human being. If you want snipping, Zoe, after your blip has arrived, just say the word. It could be a first. You wouldn't need to wait for months, we could slip you in between ops.' He pretended to look at the operations diary, using his hands as though flicking through the pages. 'Let's see. Valentine has a castration at eleven thirty, a spay at twelve, would twelve thirty suit you? How about it, Mungo? Neutering human beings could open up a whole new world for us humble vets.'

Mungo, enjoying his joke, didn't get a chance to answer because Zoe got there first. 'Did you say that to illustrate yet again your disapproval of me being a single mother?'

'The manner in which you conduct your life is none of my business, though I do have a right to my opinion.'

Zoe, losing her temper with him, demanded, 'Well, let's hear it, then.'

'I don't think it a subject for the dinner table.'

'I do.'

Dan looked at her, saying quietly, 'Very well, I'll state my case. I think it is the height of selfishness for young women to want a baby purely for their own satisfaction, and that, unfortunately, is very often the case. I understand that some single mothers don't even tell the man they have made use of about the birth. That is appalling. Babies are not a fashion accessory, nor are they there to be born simply because their mothers need someone to love. They do not ask to be born, but when they do come they deserve the very best from two parents. I do not know the circumstances of the conception of your blip, so I cannot judge, can I?'

By the end of his statement Dan was speaking loudly and the others couldn't help but hear. It seemed odd to everyone that he should have such strong views on the matter and more than one seated at the table intuitively surmised that there was more to Dan's views than just an opinion aired.

They were all embarrassed into silence by his outburst. Only Zoe was distressed by it, because he had so accurately put his finger on her own feelings about becoming pregnant.

Miriam broke the spell they were under by bringing in the main course: a huge dish of beautifully presented crown of lamb surrounded by roasted vegetables, which Mungo took from her and placed at his end of the table. Joy followed with a couple of tureens and the two of them sat down. Miriam said, I've just had a thought, you're not vegetarian, are you, Dan? I never thought to ask.'

'No, I'm not and that lamb looks delicious.' He watched the admirable almost elegant way in which Mungo carved and served the lamb, and thought how much he liked the man – he was so honest and straightforward and compassionate. It hardly seemed fair that so many enviable qualities should be concentrated in one person. Dan caught Letty watching him and he met her ice-cold gaze boldly. He smiled and raised his glass to her but her eyes slid away from him and she completely ignored his gesture. He realised he'd made more than one enemy tonight.

The dinner party never quite recovered after the argument between Zoe and Dan, and he wasn't the only one glad when people began to leave.

Mungo called him over to his side of the room as he was about to go. 'A word please, before you disappear, Dan.' He led the way back into the dining room and closed the door. 'Askew has rung me to say he is not requiring our services any more. He's going to the practice in the High Street. He claims you trespassed this morning and he is threatening you with police action. He also says that there is nothing wrong with the horse and that what you said, you said out of malice.'

Dan raised his eyebrows in surprise. 'Do you believe him?'

'I don't know what to believe. You tell me.'

'OK, in his opinion I did trespass, but like I said, the cow merited further attention and in all conscience I gave it that attention this morning, nothing more, nothing less. I wasn't able to apologise because his lordship hadn't got back from his ride when I was ready to leave, but I shall do it in writing tomorrow. As for the horse, I know I am right and his vet is wrong.' Dan shrugged his shoulders. 'But there we are. There is the possibility of doing something about it if it is treated immediately. To ignore it will cut short its career quick smart.'

'I see. Well, do not lose me any more accounts. We can't afford it.'

'I'll do my best.'

'We've advertised the job, by the way.'

'Fair enough. I quite understand.'

'Take no notice of Letty. No one else does.'

'I won't. She's a bitch.'

Mungo's head came up with a jerk. 'She's right, though, about the practice losing money when we lose clients and don't forget that.'

'Mm. Goodnight and thank you for a lovely meal. Much appreciated.'

'Thank Miriam before you go. She does all the work and it was her idea. I'm taking Perkins out. OK.'

Dan found Miriam making a start on stacking the dishwasher. 'I'm a whizz at stacking dishwashers. May I?'

'Lovely man, making an offer like that, but I have a strict rule: first-time guests may not help clear up.'

'I doubt there'll be a second time.'

'You wait and see.' She took his hand and held it between both her own. 'Welcome to the practice from me. Goodnight.'

'Goodnight, Miriam.'

2

Dan, heartened by Miriam's obvious approval of him, set off next morning to begin his calls with new heart. Before he'd gone to bed after the dinner party he'd penned a grovelling apology to Lord Askew, which it had gone against his temperament to do but he'd seen the necessity for. He'd taken it with him to the practice to post, with a copy to Mungo.

He was only halfway to the village of Wootton when the engine cut out and he came to a halt. Nothing he could do would make it start again so he rang in to Barleybridge and asked Stephie to ring the garage for him and request them to come to the rescue. He cursed himself for not having called there the previous day, but it was too late now.

Dan went to sit on the fence beside the road and enjoy the early-morning air. He'd forgotten how beautiful even a November morning in England could be; the sun wasn't shining but it was reasonably bright, and his view of the roofs and spires of Barleybridge to his right and the great sweep of woodland in front of him was very pleasing. There was something about the countryside here at home which fed the soul. Dry, arid plains, for all their feeling of space and freedom, didn't enrich him, but this did. He contemplated living here and decided once again that if it came about he'd jump at the chance.

His reverie was eventually broken by the rumble of a van approaching from his left. Even before it slurred to a halt in the middle of the road, he could see it was patently almost derelict, one headlight was missing and it was difficult to ascertain its original colour. All along the side nearest to Dan was a massive dent, which must have hindered the opening of the door. A head encased in a balaclava with slits in it poked out from the gap where the driver's window should have been. 'Recognise that Land Rover, you must be Scott's replacement?'

Dan slid off the fence and crossed the verge to speak to him. 'That's right. I'm Dan Brown.'

'I'm Phil Parsons. Applegate Farm. Nice to meet you, Dan. What's up? Enjoying the air. Nowt to do?'

'Plenty to do, but I've broken down.'

'I'll give you a lift into Barleybridge, Blossom and me's off shopping, it being market day.'

The head of the said Blossom appeared from behind Phil Parsons and gave Dan a shock. Her peroxided hair appeared to have reached the very heights of dazzle. That, combined with her lavishly applied electric-blue eyeshadow, her dark plum-coloured lipstick and her yard upon yard of cheap gilt jewellery, gave Dan the distinct impression that she was a lady ever on the lookout for 'talent'. If they were husband and wife, or partners, the two were the most incompatible pair he had ever come across: she a painted doll and he ... well, he didn't know what Phil was because you couldn't see for his headgear, but he could smell him from where he stood.

Blossom greeted him in a slightly breathless Marilyn Monroe kind of voice. 'Pleased to meet you, Dan.'

Dan touched the neb of his cap in greeting. 'And me you. I'll ring the practice again and see what the state of play is. I might be glad of your offer. If you'll excuse me.'

Stephie answered, saying they were about to ring him to tell him that the garage couldn't come out with the truck for at least another two hours as they were away on a job already and, if he could get a lift, then to come in to the practice and he could borrow Mungo's car to do his rounds, and the truck would tow the offending vehicle in, and they'd let them know the problem as and when. Dan clicked off his mobile and relayed the message to Phil.

'Jump in. Shove up, Blossom.' He threw a pile of women's magazines and farming leaflets on to the floor by his feet to make room for Dan.

'It's very kind of you. I need a few things with me. Won't be a minute.'

'Leave the keys in. Nobody'll pinch it, it's too well known.'

Dan climbed up into the van, squeezed himself in beside Blossom and struggled to shut the door. Eventually, by almost sitting on Blossom's lap, he managed it.

'Here, put your things in the back behind me.' She ducked her head away to make room for Dan to reach into the back. When he turned to look where to put his belongings he found himself staring into what appeared to be a boudoir. The inside walls of the back of the van were thickly draped in pink filmy fabric, and the floor was filled with what must be a mattress covered in shiny, lurid-pink furry stuff with frilly pink and white pillows piled on top of it. Dan, without saying a word or letting his face slip, placed his things on the nearest pink and white pillow and squeezed himself back into position. Blossom wriggled delightedly, causing waves of a rich, overpowering perfume to escape and envelop him. 'Well, set off then, Phil. We'll never get there sat here in the middle of the road like this. Turn the key.'

A vehicle behind tooted impatiently so Phil turned the key and the engine responded with the most tremendous heave. Phil shoved it into gear and off they lurched. Dan had a nightmare ride back into the town, made worse by the constant titillating movements of Blossom. His right thigh felt her flexing and reflexing her leg muscles, his right arm was subject to a series of surreptitious nudges and rubbings, and her left hand hovered constantly within reach of his knee.

'You farm then, Phil?'

'Mm. Dairy, bit o' this, bit o' that. Few sheep.'

'Perhaps I'll be round to see you one day.'

'Nothing more certain. You should try the garage at Wootton where we've just been. He charges half of that lot in the town and he doesn't use new spares either, he just ... what's that word you use, Blossom?'

'Innovates.'

'That's it, he makes his own spares; blacksmith he is, by trade. A real handy chap to have about.'

'I'm sure. But Mungo has an account with the one in town, so I've no alternative.'

Blossom asked, 'Liking it here, are you, Dan?'

He looked at Blossom and got a provocative wink from one of her wickedly cheeky eyes. 'I am.'

'Well, when Phil calls you out remember the kettle's always on and you're always welcome, isn't he, Phil?'

Phil nodded, concentrating on the traffic and taking time off to shake his fist at an innocent motorist. 'Half of 'em don't know how to drive around here. I bet none of them have passed their test.'

'Look who's talking!' Blossom giggled.

Immediately he realised Phil wasn't qualified to drive, Dan began to wish the journey at an end, but being market day the main streets in the town were packed with vehicles and they made slow progress. 'Look, if you like I'll get out and walk the rest. It might be quicker, save you hanging about.'

'Absolutely not. I said I'd give you a lift and give you a lift I shall. We're nearly there.' Phil stuck his head out of the window and called out a stream of abuse at a man on a motorbike who stuck two fingers up at him and caused Phil to abuse him even more.

Blossom giggled helplessly and lolled her head on Dan's shoulder.

'You are a card, Phil Parsons! What will Dan think?' She nudged his ribs caressingly.

'I've heard worse, not much worse, but worse.'

Blossom giggled again. 'Ooh! You've been around, then. I can tell you're a man of action! At least he hasn't used the Aussie ones Scott taught him. They're terrible.'

Phil screeched into the practice car park and banging his boot on the brake said, 'Here we are then, safe and sound. Call any time you're passing. Applegate Lane just out of town. If you've come to the turning for Wootton Causeway Farm then you've missed our turning. If you've got to Applegate Caravan Park you've gone past us. Have a care.'

Blossom squeezed his knee. 'And don't forget, the door's always open even if we haven't called you out. Come any time. We like company, don't we, Phil?'

Dan collected his belongings, jumped out, gave them his profuse thanks and went in through the back door.

Kate was working in her office and he paused in her doorway. She looked up to smile at him. 'You look white as a sheet. What's happened?'

'I broke down and got a lift from Phil Parsons.'

'Not in that dreadful van?'

Dan nodded. 'The very same. He wears the most extraordinary headgear.'

'Never takes it off.'

'Never?'

'I've never seen him without it even on a warm day.'

'How odd. Blossom. Is she his wife?'

'Apparently so. They're an odd couple.'

Dan stared into space for a moment, looking as though he was wondering how to phrase what he had to say. 'What does she do for a living?'

'She doesn't. She just helps him around the farm, if it could be called a farm.'

'I see. Have you ever ridden in his van?'

'Never.'

'I truly believed I was about to depart this life. It has no tax disc, he hasn't taken a test and he'll definitely have no insurance, so don't accept a lift from him.'

Kate laughed. 'And don't whatever you do go in their kitchen and accept a drink or anything to eat, or you most certainly might depart this life. Coffee? Before you set off?'

'It must be time, then I'll be off. Everyone will be wondering where I've got to.'

When he'd drunk the coffee she made for him he picked up Mungo's keys from Miriam and left.

Kate took coffee through for Lynne and Joy, and stopped to talk for a moment.

'I can't stand that man,' Lynne said after she'd thanked Kate for her coffee. 'I really can't. Scott was a so and so but him . . . at least Scott was fun.'

Joy snapped, 'That will do, Lynne. Enough said.'

'I disagree, I think we all have a right to have an opinion about him. After all, we do have to work with him. I say the sooner he goes the better. He never mixes, you learn nothing about him, he isn't one little teeny weeny bit of fun.'

'I have asked you once, I shan't ask again. He is actually one of your bosses and it won't do.'

Lynne put down her mug and folded her arms. 'Are you telling me you like him?'

'I don't have to like any of the staff, but we do work for him in a sense and I don't approve of you criticising him behind his back. Say no more about him, please.'

'Well, I'm sorry, but someone has to speak up. The two Sarahs don't like him and I definitely know Bunty doesn't.'

'At the moment Bunty doesn't like any man, so her opinion doesn't count and I don't particularly take to the idea of the gossiping you must have been doing to learn all this.'

Lynne turned to Kate. 'You're keeping quiet. What do you think?'

'To be honest, I like his attitude. He's paid to do a job and he's doing it very well indeed. I've an idea that underneath his bluntness is a first-class brain. Full stop. Just because he doesn't play the fool like . . . Scott did, doesn't mean he's no good.'

'Oh, yes, certainly he's doing his job well, he's already lost us one customer. Pity he didn't use his first-class brain, as you call it, when he blew it with old Askew. It's typical of you, though, you're only standing up for him because you know you're going to be a vet too. If he stays here much longer we'll all be out of a job.'

Joy was furious with Lynne. 'In my office. Now!'

With her office door firmly shut, Joy said, 'In front of clients! Have you no sense? Every word they hear in here is listened to with avid interest. It'll be all over town before we know it, that (a), staff don't like Dan and (b), he's losing us business. You haven't even the common sense to lower your voice. I won't tolerate it, Lynne. You know my thoughts on confidentiality, you've been here three years and by now you should know what to say and what not to say.'

Lynne didn't answer.

'Well?'

'It's not only me.'

'Perhaps not, but the others know when to keep their mouths shut. Kate gets on with him all right. Why can't you?'

Lynne sneered, saying, 'Oh yes, dear Kate, she would, wouldn't she? She's hoping to join the glorious profession, isn't she? High and mighty veterinary surgeon Kate Howard. Oh, yes.'

Joy didn't answer until she had forced herself to exert extreme control over her temper. 'If you are dissatisfied with your work to the extent that you find it necessary to be so unkind about a member of staff, who most certainly does not deserve it, had you better do a rethink about your whole career?'

'Are you asking me to leave?'

'I am not. I'm just asking you to have a think about your future. Jealousy will get you nowhere at all. You're young, bright, well set-up, smart, good-looking, hard-working. If you're unhappy, what's holding you back from making a change?'

'Nothing. I suppose.'

'I don't want you here if you don't want to be. But I would be sorry to lose you. Very sorry. Think about it.'

'I take nothing back. Kate's a stuck-up, too-big-for-her-boots person, too clever for her own good, she is. As for Dan ... Zoe was in here earlier. She doesn't like him either.'

Joy held up her hand. There was a strong overtone of finality in her voice when she replied, 'Enough said. I don't want to hear any more.' She glanced at her wristwatch. 'Now take an early lunch and when you come back for the evening surgery, make sure your face at least is pleasant. A Miss Vinegar face I do not want to see.'

So what with Letty taking a dislike to Dan and now Zoe – though *she* deserved all she got in Joy's opinion – and the staff, Joy felt that Dan's days were numbered. There was no way they could manage without him at the moment, though, for he did more calls in a day than any human being should be expected to do. Without him Colin would simply never go to bed.

Joy thought about Colin – thin, meek Colin with muscles of steel and a ferocious tenacity when work required it – and wondered how on earth he'd come to be married to Letty. They were exact opposites. She of the savage tongue and plump, insipid appearance and he built like a whippet, relaxed, kindly, come day go day. Maybe his temperament was brought about as a direct reaction to Letty's. But they owed her a tremendous debt, without her parents' money procuring Colin a partnership they'd never have been able to be so ambitious in buying the land and purpose-building the hospital to such a high standard. No, they owed her a debt and whatever they might think of her she'd have to be kept sweet. Which brought her back to Lynne. The girl must be eaten up with jealousy and what had Kate ever done to deserve such spite?

As she was thinking about her Kate knocked and came in. 'I'll hang on a bit longer, shall I? For lunch, I mean.'

Joy pushed her fingers through her hair and looked up. The girl was bearing up well in the circumstances. 'Leave the door open in case a client comes in. Sit down. You mustn't take what Lynne says too seriously. She's very unhappy with life at the moment I'm afraid.'

'I know. She said so a few weeks ago. Those brothers of hers have overshadowed her all her life and stopped her reaching for the stars herself, so it's left her unfulfilled.'

'Well put. Yes, that's her problem I'm sure. Very wise. We'll soon replace her if she decides to leave.'

'I'd be willing to do extra days if we're in a fix. I need the money for college. I hope.'

'Thanks. We'll wait and see.'

When Mungo came upstairs into the flat for his evening meal, he found Miriam in the kitchen making a sauce to go with the salmon she was cooking. He kissed the back of her neck and put his arms round her waist, resting his cheek against the back of her head. 'Busy day?'

'This afternoon I went to the market.'

'Yes.'

'A client came up to me and said how sorry she was to hear that we weren't doing so well in our new premises. "All that money you've spent," she said.'

'Who said that?'

'I can't remember her name, but she has five or six cats, and keeps a menagerie of hamsters and rabbits and the like.'

Mungo let go of her and leant against the worktop where he could see her face. 'That's not very helpful, is it?'

'No. Apparently she's heard about us losing Lord Askew and says they'll be leaving in droves. He has such influence, she says.'

'This is all down to Dan. Blast him.'

'Actually, when you think about it, he only did what was right. He didn't put a foot wrong and that apology of his was superb. I'd have had him back in again next day if he'd apologised to me like that. It was a masterpiece.'

Mungo had to laugh. 'Honestly, when will you stop seeing the world through rose-coloured spectacles? Whatever he did or didn't do, he lost us a client.'

'I know, but Lord Askew is the kind of client who, if there had been one single mistake, wrong diagnosis, lost calf, death of a cow, would have had us crucified. Do we really want clients like that? I reckon we're better off without him.'

'Miriam!'

'It's true. I could have slapped that client's face for her. However, what's worse is she didn't hear it from anyone connected to old Askew, she heard it from someone who'd been here at the clinic this morning. They'd overheard a conversation at the desk.'

'Did they indeed. Wait till I see Joy, I'll have a thing or two to say to her.'

'Joy wouldn't be so careless. It was more probably the girls.'

'You're right, as usual. But I can't let Dan go yet, we need him.'

'I don't see why you should.'

'Do I hear you working up to persuading me to let him stay?'

Before she answered him Miriam served the food. As she carried their plates into the dining room she said, 'As you well know, I never interfere with the running of the practice.'

'I detect ... mayonnaise?' Miriam nodded '... a hint of self-righteousness in your tone. You know full well you never say we must do this or not do that. You manage everything very competently with subtle hints here and there. I didn't realise how majestically you manipulated me until a couple of years ago.'

'I don't know the first thing about running a practice.'

Mungo almost choked. 'That must be the understatement of the year! How I love you. I really do.'

Miriam went red and fell silent.

'Darling! I didn't mean to upset you. Come on. I love you no matter what.'

She still didn't answer him.

'Come on, pick up your knife and fork and finish your food. It'll be going cold. Darling?'

Miriam shook her head. 'That's the first time you've said "I love you" and it's sounded truly, truly, truly convincing to me.'

Her voice was so low Mungo could scarcely hear what she'd said. 'I didn't hear you properly, say it again.'

She repeated it word for word without looking at him.

He was stunned. And then shattered when he heard her next words.

'When you marry someone who has lost the love of his life before you came on the scene, you're never quite sure, you see.'

It was Mungo now who was lost for words.

'You feel second best. All the time.'

'But you know I love you.'

Miriam stopped looking at her plate and looked instead at him. 'Of course you do, I know you do. You were wonderful when the children died, I don't know where you found the strength and I wouldn't have got through it if I hadn't had you like a rock beside me, but as for that powerful, overwhelming, bewildering surge that comes with first love, I've always felt I had that but that you didn't because of how you loved Janey. Somehow I feel I've missed out, there's a kind of aching void.' She placed her knife and fork together. 'I envy Janey for having been your first love. I so wish it had been me.'

Perkins ambled in. His bright brown Airedale eyes looked at each of them in turn. Then he came to sit beside Miriam and placed his chin on her knee. His head was jammed uncomfortably under the edge of the table but he didn't care; he'd sensed her need for his sympathy and had come to give it to her. Perkins's simple gesture of solidarity made her tears flow.

Mungo leapt from his chair, uncomfortable at the thought of the dog having more sensitivity than he. 'Here, look, it's clean.' He gave her his handkerchief. 'If only you knew.'

'Then tell me.'

But he couldn't for her sobbing. 'Come into the sitting room and I'll get you a stiff drink. Then I'll tell you something I've never confessed to anyone else.' He put his hand under her elbow, helped her up out of her chair and, closely followed by Perkins, they made their way out of the dining room. He sat her in her favourite chair and poured her a brandy. 'Here, sip this.'

Mungo pulled a chair close to hers and sat in it. On the other side of her Perkins watched and waited. 'Better?'

Miriam nodded.

'Then listen. Every word is the absolute truth. I've never been able to tell anyone this because . . . well . . . you'll understand when you hear.' He leant his elbows on his thighs and stared into the fire. Perkins put his chin on Miriam's knee again and prepared to listen to what Mungo had to say.

'I met Janey when I was a student. She was a high flyer in the Mathematics faculty, with everything going for her. We met at a student disco and I fell instantly in love. She was beautiful, exquisite, exciting, stimulating, amusing, highly intelligent. All the things anyone could hope for in a woman. We fell into bed together within the week. I was obsessed, totally obsessed, and I wasn't really me any more. My work, everything, fell apart, I couldn't get enough of her, either her body or her personality; she brought fire and power into my life in a way I had never experienced before. And at twenty-two that is mind-blowing. I could not believe how lucky I was.'

Mungo, so wrapped in his story, wasn't aware of the pain he was causing Miriam. The words 'exquisite', 'exciting', 'beautiful' sounded to her like the tolling of her own funeral bell.

'We were the golden couple of our year. We were asked to all the parties; no function was held without an invitation to us; socially we were the seal of success everyone yearned for. Somehow I managed to pass all my exams and the marriage we planned took place that summer. I had one friend who had uttered a word of caution when I'd first started going around with her, but I was too much in love to take note of what he said.'

Seeing a glimmer of hope, Miriam asked, 'What did he say?'

'He said, "I hope you know what you're doing. You're taking a grave risk." I was so wild with him we had a row and it was weeks before we healed the breach.'

'What did he mean?'

Mungo smiled grimly. Perkins took his head from Miriam's knee, curled up with his head on her feet and went to sleep.

'We couldn't afford a long honeymoon so we had just a week in a seaside town in Brittany, came home and I began work immediately while she played at housekeeping for a while before finding a job. We had a fantastic sex life, Miriam, believe me. It was that satisfaction and the fact that I was working all hours like assistant vets do in their first job that meant I never had any time to suspect anything was wrong for months and months. One night we went to an evening wedding reception, and I arrived there having been on call all the previous night and spending most of it up, and I was exhausted. Maybe my view of life was jaundiced because of that, but I suddenly caught sight of Janey from across the room and saw her with new eyes. She was flirting with a friend from her tennis club and there was something about her body language which alerted me; this wasn't the flirting of a happily contented wife, this was something very different. There was a kind of craving in the way she was behaving, and I looked away completely bewildered by what I'd recognised and caught the eye of a chap I'd never liked. He raised his glass to me with a mocking, knowing look on his face and I thought, my God he's been to bed with Janey. I just knew it in my bones. For certain.'

'Mungo!' She took his hand.

'To cut a long, sordid story short, I found out she'd been sleeping around quite often, with whoever took her fancy, all the time I'd known her.'

'Mungo!' Miriam kissed his hand.

His face became almost savage as he said, 'She drowned in that f-f-ferry disaster coming back from the Continent after a weekend in Amsterdam with someone unknown. I searched the list of victims to see if I could find a name I knew but I couldn't, so presumably he's still walking around somewhere.'

'Well, it could have been someone you didn't know and he could be dead, but he's of no consequence.'

'No, you're right. I spent two years pining for her, hating her, loathing her, loving her, missing her. I was in a complete daze, on auto-pilot, terrified anyone would find out what a fool I'd been, and how nastily and shamefully my passion for her had been betrayed. I sold the house and used the money to set up my first practice, with Joy as my nurse.' Mungo hesitated and wondered whether he should tell her about Joy – was this the moment? But he felt the warmth of Miriam's hand so sympathetically clasping his and knew Joy's secret was best kept to himself.

'Then one day this lovely woman walked into my surgery with a sick cat, which unfortunately I had to put to sleep, not the best of situations in which to meet your future wife, and I looked into her eyes and saw my salvation, and found new hope. And since that day I have never looked back. Her name was Miriam and I love her.' Mungo gripped her hand. 'I'm unbelievably sorry for not telling you that my silence about Janey was hiding my shame and not my love.'

'You were very badly hurt. I expect you felt so long as you didn't talk about it, it had never happened.'

Mungo nodded. 'I felt as though I would soil our love for each other if I told you and that if I did you'd think less of me. No one knows, Miriam, only you and the other men, I suppose.'

'I shan't tell a living soul.'

They sat silently for a few minutes, then Miriam said, 'You see, Dan's so like you. Firm as a rock, with tremendous integrity, professionally beyond compare and yet with such hurt in him.'

'How can you say that, you haven't known him five minutes!'

She ignored his surprise at her intuitive understanding of Dan. 'It's his dependability that makes me want him to stay. He'll do so well for us. Whatever Letty with her money or Zoe with her bigoted opinions says about him, he must stay.'

'We'll see. We're stuck with him anyhow for a few more weeks till we find someone else. Has he confided in you, then?'

'About what hurts him? No, of course not. I just sense it. Like you, the hurt lies so very deep.' She bent down to stroke Perkins. 'I'm just so deeply grateful I needn't fear Janey any more.'

'I've been a fool not to have told you before, but I'd no idea you felt second best like you do.'

'I didn't intend you should; no second wife wants to dwell on her predecessor. You see, I believed for you to have loved her so much Janey must have been perfect. But she wasn't. So I shan't feel like I did any more.'

'You've no need to at all. You're everything to me, since the day we met.'

'Thank you. Me too. I loved you that first day and have worshipped you ever since.'

Mungo tenderly placed his hands either side of her face and kissed her lips. 'I am forever in your debt.'

'And I in yours for rescuing me from such a lonely life and for loving me with a love I don't deserve.' Miriam gently released herself from his grasp and leant back in her chair. Staring into the fire she said, 'We'll get over this problem with old Askew. You'll see. I'm so pleased we made the move and got this place built. It not only gave me something to fill my mind after the children died, but businesswise it was the right thing to do. Everything works so well. Rhodri and Graham and Valentine and you and Colin and now Dan. With Zoe back we shall make a good team. Where we would be without Joy I don't know and she is such a good friend to me. We shall miss Kate when she goes, though. She'll make a good vet. Kate will be like you and Dan: dependable, strong, clever, caring.'

He thought of how it pained him when he first realised that Kate's face reminded him so much of Janey's, but having shared his anguish with Miriam it no longer seemed to matter. 'Nice girl, I hope she makes it.'

'So do I. I'm sure she will.'

3

'We've had the most horrendous day at the practice. I'm shattered but I've chemistry to do ready for tomorrow night and I've got to press on with it.' Kate leant her elbows on the kitchen table and waited for some sympathy from her father.

Gerry thumped his fist on the table. 'Think of the rewards! I'll be so proud.' He reached across and patted her arm. 'There's no father could be prouder of his daughter than me. When you go to college I shall tell everyone I meet.'

'Dad! Please, you won't say a word, will you, till we know for certain?'

'I'm not daft. I can bide my time. I never thought when you were born that you'd grow up to be a vet.'

'What did you think I'd be?'

'I never gave it a thought, I was too busy being amazed at what I had produced. A miracle you were to me. An utter miracle!'

Watching his face glowing with his memories, Kate wondered about asking him what her mother had felt on that day. The subject had been taboo all her life but there came a time . . . 'And my mother, what did she think of me when she saw me?' Kate knew she was in uncharted waters with her question but she had to ask it, she had to know. For the first time in her life she saw her father's eyes fill with tears. She watched him take out his handkerchief and blow his nose, saw when he'd finished he was too filled with emotion to answer. 'Sorry, Dad, it doesn't matter if you can't . . .'

Gerry shook his head. He got up from the table and went upstairs. Kate could hear his footsteps climbing right up to the attic and then the whirr of his train set starting up, and she knew that certainly tonight she wasn't going to hear about that elusive mother of hers. She shrugged her shoulders.

Mia came in from the supermarket loaded with shopping. 'Give me a hand, love, will you?' Mia gave her a couple of bags. 'Thanks. Where's your dad?'

Kate put the bags down and pointed to the ceiling.

Mia looked resigned. 'Train set? Do men ever grow up? Just think if I were still playing with a doll's pram. They'd be taking me away!'

'I've never thought about it like that. I wouldn't let them, though. I'd look after you.'

'Thank you, that's a relief to know. I suppose we have to be thankful he isn't a train-spotter! I couldn't be married to a train-spotter, could you?' Mia wrinkled her nose in disgust, half laughing, half serious.

'Certainly not.' Kate had to laugh. 'Do you know that's the first time I've laughed today.'

'Why's that?' Mia finished putting things away in the fridge and sat down to listen.

'It's not the same without Scott: no jokes, no pulling silly faces at the windows, no flirting.'

'I'm sorry you miss him so.' Mia laid a hand on Kate's cheek, with a loving look on her thin face, her eyes kindly and full of sympathy. 'This Dan Brown's a miserable so-and-so, is he?'

'Oh! No. He's not, but nobody but me likes him. They all think he's too blunt, too up front with his opinions, and what none of them likes is he's lost us a good client and that is bad news.'

'It must be.'

'But worst of all it seems Lynne's abandoned us. She was sent home to lunch early because of a row with Joy about Dan Brown and didn't come back, no phone call, no nothing. What makes matters even worse is that Colin's wife Letty has insisted she comes in tomorrow to help out if Lynne doesn't turn up.'

'What's happened to Stephie, then?'

'On holiday for three weeks, a family wedding in New Zealand. We are grateful for Letty's help.'

'So what's the problem?'

'You should have seen Joy's face when Colin told her. I didn't need to ask what she thought of the idea. She tried hard to sound enthusiastic but it rang very hollow. She said afterwards to me that she'd be praying like mad tonight for Lynne to come in because she couldn't stand Letty. She must be difficult, because Joy is always so loyal about people. It's not like her to talk about someone that way.'

'I like Joy, she's nice. She might do better, might this Letty, than you think. Keep an open mind.'

'I will.' Kate idly rearranged the tiny flowers Mia had put in a bowl in the middle of the table and then said, 'I've upset Dad. He said it seemed like a miracle to him when I was born, so I asked him what my mother thought of me and he couldn't answer. That's why he's upstairs with his trains.'

Mia sighed. She spotted a flower in danger of falling out of the bowl and pushed it back in. 'I'd better go see. Put the kettle on, I'm parched. He never speaks of her to me, so . . .' She got up from the table and began to climb to the attic.

She found Gerry engrossed in rearranging the figures standing on the main platform. With a cotton bud he was meticulously cleaning a porter pushing a trolley, intense concentration on his face, not noticing her arrival. It was a magnificent layout, with trees and station buildings, sidings and signal boxes, passengers and rolling stock, parcels waiting to be loaded, ticket office open, sandwich board announcing a day trip to the sea next Saturday; minute detail lovingly and painstakingly worked upon by a real enthusiast. Zooming round a wide curve at the far edge of the layout was the Flying Scotsman hurtling towards the station.

'It's me.'

Gerry looked up, startled. 'Sorry. Didn't hear you. What do you want?'

'In the best of all possible worlds your wife would like you to come clean with Kate about her mother. There. I've said it.'

Gerry didn't answer.

'I mean it, Gerry.'

He bent to replace the porter and his knuckles collided with the Flying Scotsman as it dashed by. It shot up in the air and crashed down on the signal box further down the line.

'Damn and blast! Now look what you've made me do. It's all your fault.'

'No, Gerry, it's yours. You should have told her years ago. She's reached an age when she needs to know and I can't tell her because I never met the woman, did I?'

Gerry tenderly picked up the engine and examined it. He appeared engrossed and Mia thought she'd lost the initiative but suddenly he answered her. 'How can I tell her that her mother walked out on her, a defenceless, helpless babe? What's that going to do to her?'

'Sometimes, however hard it is, it's better to face the truth. After all, it isn't as if she's been in an orphanage somewhere, is it? She's had you all her life and then me since before she can remember. She's never been without family.'

He pleaded with her, 'You tell her, Mia, for me. Please.'

'I'm sorry, I've done all that for her myself over the years, all the birds and the bees stuff and the like. But this time, Gerry, it's you who has to stand up and be counted.' She wetted the corner of her handkerchief on her tongue and rubbed at a mark on the roof of the signal box. 'Hiding in here won't make the problem go away and I can't tell her, can I? I wasn't here. Please, Gerry, explain to her.' A bush had got crushed by the accident and she plumped it straight. 'If you don't, she could well go looking for her and you wouldn't like that, now would you?'

Gerry's head came up with a jerk. 'She wouldn't, would she?'

'Why shouldn't she? You couldn't stop her if she did decide to.'

Gerry placed the Flying Scotsman gently back on the rails beside the platform, pressed the 'go' button and off it went, with his eyes following it anxiously. 'No damage done.'

Mia deliberately misunderstood him. 'There will be if you don't speak up.'

'I'll think about it.'

'You'll do more than think because if you don't do it voluntarily, one day I shall broach the subject myself in front of her and then you'll have to tell, and you won't be prepared and you'll make a mess of it. I mean it.'

Gerry looked shocked. 'You wouldn't.'

'I would. And when you tell her you tell her *everything*.'

'You wouldn't go against my wishes.'

'Try me. It will be painful for me and I know it will be very painful for you, but she has a right.'

'She hasn't. It happened to me, not Kate, she was too young to know.'

'That's nonsense and you know it. You're burying your head in the sand.' Mia put an arm round his shoulders. 'Kate's made a pot of tea. Come down.'

'In a bit.'

'I love the pair of you, you know. Not just Kate. I do understand, but it has to be faced. She's not to blame.'

Gerry finished dusting the passengers and regrouped them on the platform. Mia pointed to a dog laid on its back between the rails. 'Look! The dog's fallen on the line, the poor thing.'

'So it has.' He dusted it off and stood it beside a little girl. 'When I made this little girl I thought of her as Kate.'

'Well, unlike that girl, Kate has grown up, remember that when next you play with all this.' She waved an arm at the layout.

'*Play? Play*! I don't play, I *operate*.'

Mia laughed. Standing at the top of the attic stairs she said, 'Cup of tea ready if you want it.' From the third step she paused to add, 'I meant what I said.' She went down, looking forward to a cup of tea and watching television with Kate; but Mia drank her tea alone for Kate had gone to her room to work.

The next day began badly for Kate. The everlasting roadworks which appeared to have been disrupting Barleybridge for the last decade had caused even more chaos than usual, in consequence of which she was fifteen minutes late for work. Gratefully she saw that Letty's little Mini wasn't in the car park and heaved a sigh of relief; at least that meant she wouldn't have her wrath to face, though it also meant there'd been no one on the desk for the first fifteen minutes of the morning.

Leaping out of her car, she raced through the back door, flung off her coat and gloves, grabbed her uniform, put it on in record time and dashed into reception.

'You're late!' Letty glanced at the clock behind her. 'Fifteen minutes late. It's not good enough when we're short-handed. You'll have to work an extra fifteen before you go for lunch.'

Kate held up her hands in a conciliatory gesture. 'Fine, it's the blessed roadworks still. One day I expect they'll have all the new sewer pipes laid and then I shan't be late. It was worse than ever this morning. I thought you hadn't come, I didn't see your car.'

'Colin gave me a lift. Then you should take that into account and leave earlier.' Two phones began ringing at the same time. As Kate reached out to pick up the receiver of one of them Letty said, 'Hurry up! Answer it!'

When they'd both attended to the phones, she went on, 'You know we leave the phones ringing no longer than three rings. You'll have to smarten up. It's no way to run a practice.'

Kate put up with Letty's bullying tactics with as much patience as she could and was just reaching the end of her tolerance when Dan came in. He burst in through the door at his accustomed speed, gave a brief nod to the waiting clients and went to the reception desk. 'Good morning, girls. My list please, Kate.'

'Good morning to you, Dan. Here we are. Your first call is at Applegate Farm, I don't know what for. Sounds urgent but then Mrs Parsons always does make it sound as if their entire stock is about to expire the first chance they get, and . . .'

Letty brusquely interrupted their conversation by saying, 'Might I ask, Mr Brown, why you consider it fit to arrive to begin your day's work one and a half hours after you are expected? And unshaven, too.'

Dan glanced at Kate and she saw a spark of anger in his eyes. She knew why he was late; he'd come straight to the practice without breakfast, having been called out to the other side of town at five past six that morning. She was going to speak in Dan's defence before Letty put her foot in it any further but she was too late.

Dan answered first. 'And a very good morning to you too, Letty.' He turned his back to her and spoke to Kate. 'Yes, you were saying?'

Letty gasped with anger. 'I asked you a question. You might have the courtesy to reply.'

Patiently he faced her and said softly, 'I was called out at five past six this morning to a cow with a twisted gut. I have just finished. I have had no breakfast and I am here to start my day's work. Do you have a problem with that?'

Letty had the grace to blush. 'I see. I beg your pardon.'

'So I should think.'

Kate said, 'Look, if you've missed your breakfast Miriam will be only too delighted to find you cereal and toast. Let me go and ask her. If she finds out you've not eaten . . .'

'Colin has to manage without many times.'

Dan retorted, 'Having you to live with, I must assume he has a stronger constitution than me. I should be most grateful, Kate, if Miriam doesn't mind. I didn't get a real meal last night either because I was called out, so yes, that would be great.'

'I'll go and ask her. You can use the shower if you like.'

Dan gave a broad grin. 'Do I need to?'

It was Kate's turn to blush. 'No. I thought it might make you feel better that's all.'

'Thank you, I will. Won't be long. I want to get started on that list.' He gave Letty a mocking Nazi salute, clicked his heels and disappeared towards the shower room.

'That man is insolent.'

'That man is working his socks off, Mrs Walker. I'll leave you in charge while I get his breakfast.'

'How long have you worked here? Three months, is it?'

'About that.'

'You've far too much to say for yourself, far too much. I can see it's not a moment too soon that I've come here to work. The whole place is falling apart. Joy needs to smarten things up. Wait till she's in tomorrow. I'm making a list for her.'

'I'm going for Dan's breakfast.'

Miriam was only too delighted to make breakfast for Dan. 'Of course I will, the poor man. Toast and cereal. Right. Tea or coffee?'

'Well, I didn't ask. I imagine he's a coffee man, actually.'

Miriam got busy in the kitchen. 'I do like him.'

'So do I, but I'm afraid he's caught Mrs Walker on the wrong foot this morning.'

'Does anyone ever do any other? Sorry, shouldn't have said that. Still, I rather imagine Dan is perfectly capable of getting the better of her. No word from Lynne?'

'Joy rang her first thing and she'll be back next week. A cold, her mother said.'

'Mm. That came on rather suddenly. There, just the toast to wait for.' Miriam leant against the kitchen worktop and said, 'Don't let Letty get you down. She goes at four and then I shall be in. Just sorry I've this dental appointment, but I daren't miss it. Toothache, you know. Thanks for working all day. At least it means Joy gets her day off.'

The toast popped up and shot from the toaster with such vigour that both slices hit the window, just missing a plant on the sill. Miriam rescued them, gave them a brisk dusting off and wrapped them in a napkin to keep them warm for Dan. 'Sorry! I keep meaning to buy a new toaster, but it's such fun when it does that, I keep putting it off.' She smiled as she handed Kate the tray. 'Take care. Say to Dan he's welcome to breakfast any time.'

Kate felt she should warn Dan about the dreadful conditions at Applegate Farm. 'It's filthy. Absolutely filthy. You must put your boots on before you get out of the Land Rover.'

'Why?'

'Why? Because of the mud and filth.'

'No. Why is it so filthy?'

'Well, you've seen Phil Parsons. His farm takes after him.'

'I see.'

'Scott tried to get him to clear up but he never did.'

'Right. Well, I won't tolerate it. I shall certainly have a word. The animals must take priority. It's sheer idleness leaving a farm mucky. I'll sort him out.'

Letty heard him say this as she was going past with a message for Mungo. Putting her head round the door she said, 'You'll do no such thing. We can't afford to lose any more clients. Who is it you're referring to?'

'Phil Parsons.'

'Oh! Well, he'll be no great loss. It's like getting blood out of a stone getting him to pay.'

'I have your permission, then, to have a word?'

Letty looked uncomfortable. 'Well, no, I didn't mean that exactly.'

'Then kindly leave me to decide, Letty. I am the vet.'

Letty's face registered very real annoyance almost as though she hated the idea that Dan was the professional and she wasn't. Angrily she snapped, 'The sooner we can manage without you the better.'

Dan raised his eyes to the ceiling in despair. On her way back from seeing Mungo, Letty came in to say Mungo wanted her to remind him about attending that charity auction and had he accepted. Dan, his mouth full of toast, nodded. He emptied his cup and fled to begin his calls.

Applegate Farm proved to be as Kate had said. Dan surveyed it from his driving seat and shook his head in disbelief. The actual buildings were in quite good nick, he thought, it was the muck and mess around the whole place which shocked him. Even the farmhouse looked chronically neglected. Torn curtains at the dirty windows, doors and window frames seriously in need of a lick of paint, old farm machinery rusting in the yard and shrouds of cobwebs clinging everywhere.

He twisted round, picked up his wellingtons from the big washing-up bowl he kept them in to avoid mud inside his vehicle, put them on – which was difficult in the confines of the driver's seat – then jumped out.

Phil Parsons leapt out from a doorway on the far right of the yard. 'You're here. For God's sake, where have you been? Blossom said it was urgent. Come on!'

Dan paddled his way across the yard and went into the darkest, grimiest stall he'd ever seen, to be confronted by Phil's bull in deep distress. His head was hanging low and loud rasping noises filled the air. His flanks were heaving each time he breathed and Phil began hopping from one foot to the other shouting, 'Do something! Do something! What's up with 'im. Pneumonia, is it? Or what?'

Dan studied him for a moment and said, 'Has he been off colour?'

Phil shook his head.

Out of the gloom came Blossom. 'Right as a trivet when Phil came in to say goodnight before we went to bed. Just stop that awful noise, please, Phil can't stand it. Nearly out of his mind, he is.'

'Find him like it just this morning? No signs of it last night?'

Phil shook his head.

'I wonder. He's beginning to bloat, look, there's a lot of gas in there. He might have swallowed something and it's jammed in his throat.' With his eyes still on his patient, Dan observed the saliva pouring from the bull's mouth. Obviously his throat was completely blocked. He asked, 'His temper. What's it like?'

'Like a baby. Sweet as a nut.'

Through the gloom Dan thought he saw Blossom look a mite

sceptical, but whatever, he had to do something about it, and now. 'Has he a name you use for him?'

Filled with consternation that Dan didn't know his name Phil said, with reproach in every syllable, 'It's Sunny Boy. That's his name.'

Very calmly Dan opened the stout gate to the stall and slipped in quietly. He laid a hand on Sunny Boy's neck and said, 'Well then, Sunny Boy. You're not too good this morning, are you?' Sunny Boy shuffled from one foot to the other in apprehension: strangers weren't welcome he was saying. Over half a ton of bull not taking a liking to him made Dan excessively careful. He let his hands slide down Sunny Boy's neck and throat, feeling gently as he went.

Phil watched his every move.

Aware he was being expected to work miracles, Dan tried again, feeling with sensitive hands for an obstruction in the massive throat. 'I've an idea I'm right. Not sure, but it's worth a try. I'm going for a gag to hold his jaws open while I feel down inside. You secure his head with a rope through his nose ring and I want two ropes, not just the one, from his halter to hold him firmly.'

'He's not used to being tethered.'

'Well, if you want him cured you'd better tether him. I can't put my arm down his throat with him free to move about. Anchor him good and proper if you please.'

But the whole exercise was fraught with problems: Sunny Boy, despite his kinship with Phil, refused to respond and tossed his great head this way and that trying to avoid the ropes. In his struggles he briefly stood on Phil's foot, which brought a halt to Phil's efforts. When Dan came back he was still only tethered by one rope through a ring in the wall and his breathing was growing worse.

Dan joined Phil in the stall equipped with a gag, a powerful torch and a metre-long piece of fence wire bent into a narrow U shape. 'Give me the rope.' Phil hobbled back a few steps, leaving Dan with the rope. 'Now, see here, my lad, that will do.' He said this in a loud authoritative tone and, to his surprise and Phil's, Sunny Boy stopped tossing his head and allowed Dan to slip a rope through the ring in his nose. 'Now, Phil, tie him up. Both sides.'

With Sunny Boy's head virtually immobilised, Dan, inch by inch, got his jaws open and fixed the metal gag in place. Sunny Boy was now a model patient, though sweat was pouring off Dan. This warm, moist mouth edged with those great yellowing teeth and with half a ton of restless bull behind it was no place even for a vet to be hanging about in and, with Blossom holding the torch and Phil positioned ready to push on Sunny Boy's neck below the obstruction, Dan swift as light slipped the wire down his throat, slowly guiding the loop over and behind whatever it was jammed in Sunny Boy's throat. 'Now, Phil, start pressing upwards from behind as I pull.'

He manipulated and fiddled and twisted and lost his grip and tried again, and slowly he began to get a real grip on whatever it was and, against a background of Sunny Boy's laboured breathing, he got the wire right behind, dislodged the object and brought it out. He threw it out of the stall, removed the gag and left Phil to release his patient. 'I'll hang about to make sure all that gas which has accumulated in his rumen does come up, just in case.'

Blossom picked up the object and examined it in the light of Dan's torch. 'Why, good heavens, it's a kiddie's ball. Where did he get that from?'

But Phil wasn't listening to her. His Sunny Boy, the pride of his life, had been saved. Had Dan been able to see Phil's eyes, he would have seen tears of joy. As it was, they soaked unseen into his balaclava. He came out of the stall, bolted the gate behind him and, taking Dan's grossly slimy, dripping hand in his, shook it vigorously. 'Brilliant. You've saved his life. Brilliant! I can't thank you enough. Blossom, get that kettle on, we'll have a coffee.' Phil wiped his hand on his jumper.

Dan said, 'That sounds good. I'll wash up first. Where's the tap?'

Tremulously Blossom breathed, 'You were so masterful with him, Dan. "That will do," you said and he did just as he was told. It was like a miracle.' She clung to his arm. 'Thank you. Thank you. I don't know what Phil would have done if Sunny Boy had died. Kettle, right. Milk and sugar? No, we'll have cream today. Yes. Celebrate, that's what we'll do.'

Dan washed his arms under the outside tap using the bar of soap he always carried with him. 'You'll have to warn your children about leaving balls near your beasts, Phil.'

'Ain't got none. It's them damn kids from the caravan site. There was a load of 'em here yesterday buying milk. It'd be one of them.' He went to lean his arms on the wall of Sunny Boy's stall and wallow in admiration. Dan joined him. 'I have to say this, Phil, he's a grand beast. Beautiful creature. Where did you get him from?'

'Born right here in this stall. Absolute fluke. His mother was Christabel. I bought her as a heifer and found she was in calf and it was this great beggar. Few weeks back Scott had to put her to sleep – old age, really. Poor Sunny Boy was right upset when I told him. Off his food he was.'

Dan realised there was a deal of good, sensitive heart in Phil and that he needed careful handling. Instructing him to clean up the place could be counter-productive. While they both gazed in admiration at Sunny Boy, now cheerfully munching his hay, a cat slipped under the bars of the gate and entered the stall.

'Get out, you daft beggar, I've told you before. Come on. Puss, puss, puss.'

'Nice cat. Good-looking.'

'Come on, see what your Phil's got in his pocket for you. Come on. Puss. Puss.' The cat changed her mind and squeezed out under the gate again. Phil gave her a jelly bean. 'Them's her favourites. Blossom calls her Scott and reckons she's hers but she isn't. She belongs to me. Her and me's mates. Bit older and she'll be clearing this place of rats.'

'Problem, is it?'

Phil nodded.

'They're always a problem on any farm.' Still looking at Sunny Boy, Dan continued to pursue his point: 'Secret is to limit the number of places they have to hide in and not leave any animal feed available.' He eyed the sacks leant haphazardly against the far wall.

Phil nodded, not really listening.

'You know, clearing up rubbish, sealing up holes. While your beasts might flourish, they'd do even better with more light and air.'

Phil nodded again but this time he was listening.

'Skip. Large skip, that's what's needed.'

Phil stirred.

'Placed outside in the yard, a couple of hours' work would make a big difference.'

Blossom came with three mugs on a tray. She rested the tray on top of the wall and handed out the mugs. Dan took his first sip before he remembered Kate's warning. Too late now. Blossom joined them, squeezing in next to Dan, resting her arm on the wall. 'Isn't it lovely now he's breathing all right?'

Dan continued, 'Then the next thing would be to sweep down every wall, every window, get rid of all the muck and cobwebs, then a bag of sand and cement, and fill all the holes, replace the stones that have fallen out. Then paint.' He gave a broad sweep with his arm and his imagination full rein. 'Everywhere. Just imagine a snow-white byre, with the beams picked out in black and Sunny Boy in pride of place with the light shining in from that window above his head. A wonderful setting for a magnificent beast. What a picture! And no more than a beast of his calibre deserves.' He paused to let the picture sink into Phil's brain. 'I can see three or four wheelie bins lined up against that far wall with the feed in. Blue, I think, would look good against the white. Imagine, Blossom. Why, you could hold tea parties in here.'

He drank down the last of the coffee, put the empty mug on the tray, said, 'Thanks. Be seeing you' and left to shouts of gratitude from Blossom and Phil.

As he drove to his next call he thought about the charity auction Mungo had asked him to attend in his place. He was obliged to go but would have preferred someone to go with. High-profile animal charity event, lots of county people there, no doubt, so whom should he ask? It would have to be someone from the practice because he didn't know anyone else. If only Rose were here ... but she wasn't and wouldn't be, and he'd better close his mind to her because wishing would achieve nothing at all. Unbidden, a picture came into his mind of her striding beside him along that magnificent beach, very early one morning, almost before the sun was up ... the fine, silvery sand filtering up between his bare toes ... her slender fingers entwined in his, swimming naked in the sea, the chill water rippling against his skin ... breakfasting on the beach afterwards ... he could still smell the ripeness of the peaches she'd brought with her and even now his forearms could feel the roughness of the sun-dried towel she lay on ... pain shot through him at the thought of her. He quickly closed the door on Rose and bent his mind to solving his problem.

Whom to ask to go with him? Not Bunty, nor Sarah One nor Two, no, he'd ask Kate. Yes, Kate. He liked Kate, liked her straightforwardness and her no-nonsense manner, and he knew she liked him, which was more than could be said for any of the others.

He pulled into the yard at Tattersall's Cop with his mind made up. Definitely Kate. He was sure she'd say yes, if only for the chance to see the wealthy at play, and he guessed they'd derive the same kind of amusement from it, too.

The auction was to be held in the newly named Lord Henry Askew Hall, a splendid edifice built at the height of the Arts and Crafts movement, with wonderfully ornate decoration, richly painted walls and dramatic panelling that required none of the specially installed lighting nor the drapes with which someone had seen fit to embellish it. Vast flower displays burgeoned in every corner and the general impression was of an overdressed, very rich, stately old lady. Originally it had been the town hall and out of a kind of ingrained stubbornness the majority of the inhabitants still called it that. Lord Askew, however, was inordinately pleased to have the hall named after himself and made a point of attending every possible event ever held in it.

Dan and Kate arrived just after seven. They each left their overcoats in the cloakrooms and emerged into the hall to find a receiving line awaiting them.

Out of the corner of his mouth Dan murmured, 'I bet Mungo never thought Lord Askew might be here.'

'Oh, no! I've never met him. Where is he?'

'The last in the receiving line.'

'That's him? He doesn't look much like I imagine a lord should.'

'But he is. Here goes.'

They shook hands and introduced themselves as they went down the line, meeting the chairman of the charity and his wife and various other officials. Then finally came the moment for Dan to face Lord Askew. He took the bull by the horns saying, 'Dan Brown, my lord, Barleybridge Veterinary Hospital. May I introduce my friend Kate Howard.'

Kate shook his hand saying, 'Good evening, my lord.'

But he wasn't taking any notice of her; he was bristling with indignation at Dan. His great voice boomed out, 'Still here, then? Thought you'd have been gone long since.'

'Indeed not. Hopefully I'm here to stay.'

'Mungo Price has written to me as well as you, but it's not enough, no, not enough. I shan't come back to you, not after your behaviour. Damned insolent. Damned insolent.'

His face flushed redly but with a hint of blue about his nose and lips.

Dan played his humility card. 'It was a most unfortunate occurrence, my lord, one which I very much regret, but I cannot have my professional decisions overridden.'

'Can you not! I pay the piper so I call the tune, don't you know.'

Dan couldn't resist taunting him. 'And the roan. How is he?'

'Fine, fine . . .' He opened his mouth to add something else but changed his mind.

'If you will excuse us, my lord, we're holding up the line. Perhaps there will be an opportunity to speak later.'

'Yes, yes.'

As they moved away Dan said, 'I think he's having doubts about that horse. See his hesitation? You watch, before the night is out he'll have found a reason to speak to me about it.'

'He's not going to ask your advice, though, is he, do you think?'

'No, I expect not. His trouble is he's gone too far down the line to find it easy. Let's get a drink. What would you like?'

'Orange juice, please.'

He made no comment about Kate wanting a soft drink, took a gin and tonic for himself and found them a corner where they could stand, watching the elite of Barleybridge enjoying themselves. On a huge balcony built out over the entrance hall an orchestra was playing tunes from well-known musicals and the whole room buzzed with pleasurable excitement.

'So, Kate Howard, this is how Barleybridge enjoys itself.'

'Only from time to time and most especially because Lord Askew is footing a large part of the bill. He's terribly keen on hunting and can't abide this new legislation, you see.'

'So the profits go to the campaign, do they?'

Kate nodded.

'The sad part is having to put down all the hounds.'

'They can't be rehomed, I expect.'

Dan shook his head. 'Absolutely not. They haven't a cat in hell's chance of being domesticated. They're a savage lot underneath, having been brought up as pack animals. If you watch them for a while you see which are the leaders and which are the lowest of the low, and the consequences of stepping out of line can be terminal.'

Kate felt sad and it showed in her face. Dan glanced at her, taking in her almost classical profile and he wondered where she had got that from. 'What does your father do?'

'He's sales manager for the biscuit factory the other side of town.'

'And your mother?'

Kate corrected him. 'My stepmother, Mia, she's a miniaturist.'

'Wonderful talent.'

'It is. She's becoming quite well known. Never without work.'

'That's good. How long has she been your stepmother?'

'Since I was two months old, or thereabouts.'

'Your mother? Where is she?'

Kate looked up at him. 'I've no idea. She walked out on us.'

Dan replied, 'I'm so sorry, I didn't mean to hurt you.'

'How could I be hurt when I've never set eyes on her and don't even know her name. My dad finds it all too hard to talk about. Thinks it doesn't concern me, that only he has the right to suffer, but everyone needs to know their origins, don't they? I know I wish I did.'

Kate was appalled by the change which came over Dan. Whatever had she said to have brought such an anguished look to his face? She'd always thought of him as having emotion tightly under control, if indeed he had any at all, but here, surprisingly, there appeared to be a totally unsuspected secret, which obviously lay painfully deep.

To give him space Kate remained silent, watching people and observing the very differing fashions the women guests had chosen to wear. She looked down at her own black number, which Mia had run up for her after she'd got Dan's invitation. It was elegantly simple and just sufficiently detailed to bring it way up from downright ordinary without being ostentatious, and she knew she looked good in it. Hang not knowing her birth mother, Mia more than compensated.

Dan tossed down his G&T and abruptly said, 'Another orange? Then we'll take a look at the buffet. Eh? Should be time for the auction soon.'

'Right.'

'You buying anything?'

Kate had to laugh. She looked at the auction catalogue. 'Well, I certainly haven't enough money to buy anything at all and, what's more, I don't want corporate entertaining at Formula One in Monaco with last year's championship winner no matter who he is, nor a ghastly weekend in Scotland shooting grouse on Lord Askew's estate, nor an evening with a poxy pop star at the Café de Paris, nor a day as an extra on a film set no matter how prestigious the stars.' She paused for a moment while she thought of the worst thing possible and came up with, 'And I definitely do not want the cricket bat signed by the entire English team.'

She managed to bring a smile to Dan's face. 'What *do* you want, then?'

'That's easy to answer. To be a student at the Royal Veterinary College next October, that's all.' She checked the catalogue again. 'But I don't see that here, or have I missed something?'

'You a vet! I'd no idea. What do you need to get in?'

'They'll have me if I get a grade A in Chemistry. That's all I need now.' She clenched her fist and struck the air. 'I've got Biology and Physics, so it's only one small hurdle and I'll be there. Well, not so small, actually.'

'That's brilliant. I'm so pleased. It's five years' hard work, believe me, but you'll never regret it.'

Kate risked another look at his face. It had regained its normal inscrutability. 'It's worth it, isn't it?'

Dan nodded. 'Wouldn't be doing anything else on earth. Constant challenge, ever changing work, out in the open air in wonderful countryside. What more can a man ask? Or a woman for that matter.' He laughed and added, 'And the best of it is the patients can't argue about the treatment.'

The orchestra played a great flourish, and the chairman made his speech and the auction began. Dan found them each a chair in the back row and they prepared themselves to be entertained. Halfway through, Dan felt a touch on the back of his chair. He half glanced round and saw it was Lord Askew's great hand resting there. Tactically he knew it was good sense to ignore it. But they'd just reached the exciting part where the auctioneer announced the big prize of the evening, the weekend in Monaco at the Grand Prix. The noise mounted and the auctioneer had difficulty in getting silence.

'I say, Brown, come out. I need to talk.' Lord Askew was incapable of speaking quietly and his request boomed out just as silence had fallen. The auctioneer gathered everyone's eye yet again and began the bidding.

Dan stood up and followed his lordship, who took him to a quiet corner on the balcony where the orchestra had been playing. 'I say, where did you learn about horses?'

'In Dubai.'

Lord Askew raised his eyebrows in surprise. 'With a sheikh?'

'Yes.'

'Price has never had a proper equine vet, you know.'

'He told me.'

'Plenty of experience, then?'

'Some experience mixed with a lot of instinct.'

'Instinct. Hm.' Lord Askew pushed his hands in his pockets. The noise from the auction couldn't be ignored. He raised his voice a little. 'That roan, my daughter's, don't you know. Stickler for the horse being in tip-top condition.' He raised his voice a few more decibels. 'Don't suppose you would come to take a look? Private, don't you know. Nothing to do with the practice.'

'I am surprised, my lord, that a man of principle like yourself would make such a request.'

Lord Askew edged nearer and in a loud stage whisper said close to Dan's ear, 'Don't push *me*. I don't bargain. But I would pay twice the going rate for your opinion.'

'I'm sorry. I am going to pretend this conversation never took place. Please excuse me.' Dan walked away back to Kate and took his seat again, a grin on his face like that on the proverbial Cheshire cat.

4

Joy called out from her office, 'It's the first Monday. Have we got the fire bucket ready?' She got no answer, and wondered why. It was five minutes past eight so Kate should be on the desk. 'Hello! Anyone there?'

Getting no reply, Joy went to see why. She couldn't believe her eyes when she saw Stephie was back from New Zealand. But where had her long, lank brown hair, her sallow skin, her expressionless face gone? In their place was short, bouncy hair with blonde highlights, a tanned face and a bright, bubbly expression. 'Stephie! You're back!'

Kate said, 'I'm speechless. I didn't recognise her when she came in.'

'I can't believe this. My dear. Welcome back. So this is what New Zealand has done for you. I think I'll be on the next flight. Book me a ticket, quick.'

Kate nodded in agreement. 'Me too. God! What a change. You look fabulous.'

'You like my new look, then?'

'Like it! We're dead envious, aren't we, Kate?'

'We most certainly are.'

Stephie explained. 'It was my cousin, she persuaded me. I feel a fool, really.' She looked at Kate for reassurance.

'You don't look it. You look great.'

Joy asked her if the wedding went off all right.

'Well, apart from a massive rainstorm while we were in church, thunder, lightning, the works, it went off fine. Except the best man couldn't find the ring, and the prawn cocktails were off so we couldn't eat them, and the bride's father got the worse for drink and gave a hilarious speech, yes, it all went well.'

Kate asked her what the best man was like.

'He was superb! In fact . . .'

Joy and Kate prompted her to continue. 'Yes?'

'He'll be over here at Christmas.'

'Will he indeed!' Joy wagged her finger at Stephie. 'Coming to see you, is he?'

'Well, I might see him, might, you know. But he is writing.'

Joy gave her a hug. 'I'm so glad you had such a wonderful time. Sorry to bring you back down to earth but we must press on.' She retreated to her office, smiling to herself, thinking what an amazing effect an interesting man can have on a girl.

Stephie filled Kate in on the detail between dealing with clients and answering the phone. They had a busy morning ahead of them with a full appointment list for the general clinic and a full one for Mungo's orthopaedic clinic, too.

Stephie put down the receiver after battling to fit in yet another client for the small animal clinic and said, 'Don't you think we're busier than ever?'

'I'm certain we are. I've been working whole days while you've been away, because of Lynne.'

'What's the matter with her?'

'Virus.' A man was standing at the desk, a long-haired ginger cat in his arms. 'Good morning. How can I help?'

'I've found this cat by the side of the road, laid in the gutter. I think it's been run over.'

Kate felt Stephie give her a slight kick with her foot. 'I see. Where?'

'Near the precinct, by the multi-storey. It was crying, that was why I noticed it.'

Kate leant forward to look more closely at the cat. 'Poor thing. Lucky you found it. It looks very unkempt, as if it's a stray. Look, put it in this box and I'll get one of our vets to attend to it. I can't take it in unless I have a name and address. Really the RSPCA would be the best place.'

Quickly the man said, 'Can't get there, no car. Too far out.'

Kate nodded. 'I see.' Stephie passed her the clipboard and Kate picked up her pen. 'Right, sir. You're Mr . . . ?'

' . . . Thomas.'

'And your address?'

The man hesitated, then said, 'This cat's not mine, you know, not mine no, no.'

'But surely you'd be interested to know how it gets on?'

'Oh, yes, yes. It's . . . 43 Oakroyd . . . Gardens.'

'And your phone number?'

'Not on the phone.'

'Perhaps you have a phone number at work?'

'No, that wouldn't do. They don't encourage private calls.'

Stephie asked, 'Just a minute. Where did you say you found it?'

'Like I said, on the slope up to the multi-storey.'

Kate, intent on the cat's suffering, said, 'It's very good of you to bring it in.'

Stephie said, 'We'd really prefer a phone number, Mr Thomas. Perhaps a neighbour's? Or a friend's.'

Mr Thomas turned on his heel and left before they could stop him. Stephie dashed into the laundry room to watch the car park and was in time to see him get into a little Ford parked as close to the exit as he could get, start up, back out and drive away at speed.

She raced back into reception and wrote down his registration number. Kate, smoothing the cat's head with a gentle finger, asked, 'What are you doing?'

'I wasn't born yesterday, that chap *has* got a car and I've written down his number. I was suspicious of him right from the start.'

'What do you mean?'

'Honestly, you're too good to be true, you are. That's his own cat.'

'No, it's not. He said he found it in the gutter. Obviously it's been run over, or at least collided with a car or something.'

'Kate Howard! You're not fit to be let out. I'd bet a million dollars on it being his own cat.'

'Well, why didn't he say so, then?'

'Because he's too mean to pay for it.'

'Well, honestly! I don't believe it. Anyway, I'd better get some help. It looks in a bad way.'

'I've come back not a moment too soon. Gullible, that's what you are.'

'OK, OK. Come on, sweetheart, let's get you looked at.'

'Mungo's free for half an hour, his last client didn't get here.'

'Right.'

Kate watched Mungo's sensitive hands delicately examining the cat. She marvelled at the way they appeared to be 'reading' the cat's injuries. 'Broken left hind leg, make a note, fairly certain a crushed pelvis.' The cat yowled. 'Sorry, old chap. Fleas, look, here, several ticks. God what a state it's in. Look at this!' Mungo held the fur of its throat between his fingers exposing the flesh. He carried on parting the fur all the way round its neck and found a nasty red weal encircling it, with raw flesh and dried blood in several places. 'Goes all the way round. It's a wonder its throat hasn't been severed it's so deep in places. Like as if someone's tried to throttle it with a cord. That's not a car accident, is it?'

Kate felt sick. 'The chap, Mr Thomas, left an address.'

'Did he? Got all this down?'

'Yes.'

'Look at his pads. As if he's been dragged along the road and had the skin seared off. I've seen that before with a car accident.'

The door opened and in came Dan. 'Mungo I . . . Oh! Sorry!'

'Come and look at this, Dan. What do you think?' Together they re-examined the cat.

Dan straightened up and asked Kate who'd brought him in. She explained.

'Check his address is genuine. Please.'

Mungo asked him what he thought. 'It all appears consistent with a car accident, but the neck injury . . . We both have been vets long enough to know how cruel people can be. I wonder if this cat has been tied by the neck to a car bumper, or a bike possibly, and dragged along the road. See his claws, almost pulled from their beds, friction burns on his pads and they're bleeding in places. This isn't a normal car accident, is it. I reckon this is a cruelty case. But the cat could have been dumped and he genuinely has picked it up.'

'So why run off?'

'Frightened he might get blamed?'

'But it's unlikely he would know what we've found out about the cord round its neck. Its fur is so thick he'd never notice it without close examination. If he was innocent, what has he to be afraid of?'

Kate, feeling even more sick than she had been when listing the injuries, came back in and said, 'Must be a false address. I've looked in the street directory and there's no such road in Barleybridge.'

Mungo shrugged his shoulders. 'We shouldn't be surprised. Right. He needs a painkiller, rest and quiet, and a drip and antibiotic. We'll leave him to sleep and get some strength back, then we'll X-ray later today. He's too bloody thin as well. Get Bunty for me, Kate, please.'

When she'd left his consulting room Mungo said, 'I'm not letting this go. I'll get him for this, so help me.'

As Mungo washed his hands Dan commented, 'I thought I'd seen everything there was to see out in the Caribbean and in Dubai but this . . . in a country which prides itself on being compassionate, it takes some beating. But we've nothing to go on. False address, wrong name too, I suspect.'

'Obviously. I've another client in ten minutes. Did you want to see me?'

They were interrupted by Bunty coming in to attend to the cat. Mungo gave her instructions for its care, asking her also to photograph him, especially the neck injury, and by then his next client had arrived so Dan said he'd see him later, it wasn't important. He'd been going to tell Mungo about Lord Askew at the charity auction but in the circumstances decided it could wait.

At the reception desk Stephie was comforting Kate. 'Look, you weren't to know, the chap seemed genuine enough. It was something to do with his shifty eyes. Did you notice he never really looked us in the face?'

'That poor cat. Mungo thinks it's a cruelty case.'

'Really? Not a road accident, then?'

Kate shook her head.

Dan came out of the consulting room to have a word with them. 'Don't you go blaming yourselves, girls, just one of those things.'

Kate answered him almost before he'd finished speaking. 'I *am* blaming myself. I'm far too trusting of people.'

'Look, write down a description of him while he's fresh in your mind. It could help the police.'

'Police!'

'Yes. Mungo is livid and so am I. A disgrace. But don't you girls feel guilty, please. You weren't to know. Write down his description and as much of the conversation you had as you can remember.'

'I've got his car registration number.' Triumphantly Stephie held up the notepad she'd scribbled it on.

Dan leant across the desk and gave her a kiss on both cheeks. 'Clever girl. You should be in the police. Hang on to that, it could be our only link.'

Stephie blushed.

'Bunty's taken charge of him now.'

Stephie approved. 'He'll pull through, then. She's brill with hopeless cases, is Bunty.'

'We know now why he didn't go to the RSPCA, too afraid of prosecution. Well, bad luck. Thought we'd be a soft option. We'll get him yet. Quiet day. Finished my calls. I'll have lunch and hope something comes in meanwhile.' He gave them half a salute, but not the Nazi one he reserved especially for Letty, and disappeared into the back.

The police arrived later in the afternoon in the shape of Sergeant Bird. Only his uniform made him recognisable as a police officer, because true to his name he was a thin, bird-like little man. At some time he must have had the height qualification necessary to join the force but since then he'd shrunk. The peak of his cap almost engulfed his face and shaded a pair of piercing, almost black eyes, which viewed one with the apparent intention of taking one into custody immediately.

Placing his cap on the top of the reception desk, he said, 'Sergeant Bird. Where's his nibs, then?'

Kate asked, 'His nibs?'

'Mungo. He thinks he has a cruelty case. A cat.'

'That's right. He's operating all afternoon so he can't be interrupted I'm afraid, but . . .'

'Understandable. Mustn't disturb the great man at his work, of which I am his warmest admirer.' Sergeant Bird settled his forearms on the top of the desk. 'Five years ago my German shepherd, Duke, was within an ace of having to be put down, all hope lost. I brought him to Mungo. He operated on his hips when the practice was down the town in the old premises and he's never looked back. Since then I've had the greatest of respect for him. He said on the phone there's no evidence of identification.'

'All we have is a description of the man we wrote down as soon as he left and . . . his car registration number.' Kate brought out the notepad like a magician bringing a rabbit out of a hat.

'Ex-ce-llent. Quick thinking, that. Photographs too, I understand.'

'They're here and Bunty's done a list of his injuries for you.'

'Now that Bunty is a treasure. If she's in charge he'll pull through. I've great faith in her, too.'

'Hope so. He'll look a nice cat when he gets better and puts on some weight. He's terribly thin.'

'I'll have a look, if I may.'

Before Kate could say she thought it inadvisable as they were so busy, Sergeant Bird had disappeared into the intensive care room and hadn't come out when Stephie came back on at four.

Stephie giggled when Kate told her Sergeant Bird had come. 'I bet he's hanging about to see Bunty. Fancies her like nobody's business. Keeps asking her out and she won't go.'

'I'm not surprised. He's a lot older than her.'

'Exactly. It's been going on since I joined the practice and I've been here three years. He's round here like a shot on the flimsiest of excuses.'

'And he's smaller.'

Stephie giggled again. 'I know, I know . . . sh! He's coming back.'

Sergeant Bird came to the desk saying, 'I'll be off now. Tell Mungo I'll be on to this straight away.' He picked up his cap and disappeared out of the door, some of the spring having gone out of his step.

After the door closed Stephie said, 'She's turned him down again, you can see. Nice chap, but he's not marriage material, is he now? You wouldn't even fancy him enough to live with him, never mind marry him.'

Kate had to agree.

He was back the following day. 'It came to me after I'd left. Was your security camera switched on yesterday?'

Joy clapped a hand to her forehead. 'Of course! Of course! Aren't we fools. It's so unnatural, all this modern technology, you don't think to refer to it. He'll be on there. You're not just a pretty face, are you?'

Sergeant Bird grew a whole inch. 'No, I'm not.'

'What about the car number? Got anything from that?'

'Not registered. So that's another thing I can get him for, once I catch up with him. Where's the film, then?'

'Just a minute. I've got to think about this. Where is yesterday's film? It should be in my office safe. Hold on.'

Sergeant Bird leant his back against the desk while he waited for Joy and surveyed the waiting clients. He recognised one or two of them and said 'Good morning' to them.

'Morning, Dickie. How's things?'

Sergeant Bird hated it when people called him 'Dickie'. He always thought Aubrey was such a distinguished name but no one ever called him by it. 'Fine. Thanks.'

'I see your lot haven't solved this stolen car racket in the multi-storey we've all read about in the paper. Front page in the local paper again this morning.'

'No.' He turned to face the desk to put an end to the ribbing he knew he was going to get.

Joy returned with the video in her hand. 'All is not lost. We'll run it through, shall we?'

Eager to get away, Sergeant Bird took the video saying, 'I won't put you to any more trouble. I'll do it at the station.'

'I need a receipt for it. Sorry, but you know, must follow the rules.'

'Of course.'

Named Copperfield by Bunty, who always went in for distinguished names for any animal without one, the cat in question had been operated on that morning. It had been a long and difficult one but Mungo, when he finally stripped off his gloves, was very satisfied with the cat's condition. 'I'm handing him over to you, Bunty. Make sure the two Sarahs know what to do. He seems in good heart and he must be a fighter to have survived what he's gone through. All he needs now is careful nursing.'

'He'll get that. We'll have him up and about in no time.'

'I know you will. We shan't get paid for it, but what the hell, the poor thing deserves the best after what I suspect he's been through. I just hope Dickie Bird finds that chap before I do.'

Bunty carefully picked up the still unconscious Copperfield and took him to the recovery room, where loving care and constant monitoring had him eating and trying to get on his feet in no time at all.

They were gathered to watch him try to walk outside his cage one afternoon when the phone rang and it was Zoe's mother calling to say that Zoe had had her baby boy, six pounds ten ounces and fighting fit, and yes, Zoe was fine and would be out of hospital tomorrow, and she'd be bringing baby Oscar in for them to see in a few days.

Kate went out to buy a card for them all to sign. Dan came in at about half past six, having finished his calls, so Kate asked him if he'd like to add his name to it.

'She's had her blip then? What is it?'

'A boy. She's calling him Oscar.'

'My God! What does she think she's had, a dog? The poor child.'

'I know you always speak your mind but really . . .'

Dan sat down to sign his name. 'Oscar Savage! Has quite a ring to it, I suppose. But he still sounds like a dog to me.'

'Well, you'll be able to see for yourself when she brings him in.'

'So long as I'm not expected to do the billing and cooing.'

'You sound as though you don't approve.'

Dan stood up and handed Kate the card. 'Frankly, I don't. It occurs to me that she's having this baby as some kind of statement about making use of a man to give her the baby she wants, intending deliberately to deny him all knowledge of it just for the hell of it. One mustn't have children simply to make statements; they're not pawns in the game of life. There's five pounds towards a present for him. I expect we're clubbing together, are we? The boss, is he in?'

Kate nodded.

He smiled at her and strode off to find Mungo.

Kate stood looking at his signature. A great flourish of a signature it was: '*Congratulations!!! Daniel J.F. Brown*'. Such confidence in every stroke of his pen, big, sharply pointed letters in a stylish, authoritative hand. He must have more insight than people gave him credit for, though, because Zoe had used very similar words to her about making use of men when they'd been discussing Oscar's arrival some weeks before. She hoped he wouldn't show his disapproval of the baby in front of everyone. He'd already made enough enemies in the practice without making matters any worse; he hadn't a cat in hell's chance of staying permanently if he did. The interviews for his job began on

Monday and then it would be goodbye Dan, and she couldn't help feeling it would be a mistake to rid the practice of such a good vet.

Dan had found Mungo working at his desk. He tapped on the open door and said, 'Time for a word?'

'Of course. Sit down.' Mungo took off his glasses and prepared to listen.

'When Kate and I went to the charity auction I don't suppose you gave it a thought that Lord Askew would be there?'

'I did not! You didn't have a showdown?'

'No.' Dan had to smile. 'He took me to one side and asked me if I would see that roan privately.'

Mungo's eyebrows shot up his forehead. 'Did he?'

'I told him that I wouldn't and haven't heard from him since.'

'I see.'

'Thought I'd better tell you just in case something was said.'

'Thank you. He's obviously worried, then?'

'He is. If he should ask me again, what would you like me to say? I wouldn't go privately for obvious reasons, but would you be interested if he asked me to go as your employee?'

'I've never bothered with equine, not the slightest interest. It's not the horses themselves, it's their owners.'

'They can be the very devil, you just have to know how to get along with them. But I would do it if you gave me the go-ahead. He may never ask me again. However, I must have the position clear, in case he does. He's very influential, his approval could bring in many more equine clients and it would be another string to your bow. I know I'm not here to stay, but it might influence your choice of a permanent vet if I got Lord Askew's account.'

Mungo tapped the end of his pen on the desk while he thought. Tap. Tap. Tap. Tap. 'I'll consult with Colin and Zoe. Thanks for being so straightforward about it. Do you enjoy it?'

'Wouldn't want to be wholly equine. I like variety, you see.'

Mungo put his glasses back on and said, 'I'll let you know. Young Copperfield has been walking about today. Good news, eh?'

He rang Colin that same night and they had a long conversation about the pros and cons of the situation. The upshot of it was that Colin thought it was highly unlikely Dan would get asked again, but if he did, why not? After all, the fellow wasn't going to be there for long, was he. These new applicants seemed promising and one of them did have horse experience, so why not let Dan lead the way if it so happened?

Ten minutes after he'd spoken to Colin the telephone rang and Mungo found himself on the receiving end of Letty's bile. 'Colin's told me. You said yourself you weren't keen on him when he first came and I've seen nothing of him to endear him to *me*. Giving him this opening is nothing short of ridiculous. He'll be thinking he's here to stay and I'm not having it.'

'*You're* not having it?'

'No, I am not. The man is insolent and arrogant, and what's more it seems to me he's too keen on making the practice pay and not enough on the animals.'

'May I remind you that Colin is the decision maker and as he has gone along with the idea . . .'

'Colin is the decision maker only because I put him there and money talks.'

Mungo held a bitter retort in check. 'Anyway, I haven't spoken to Zoe yet, so if we all agree then that's final, and even if it's two out of three, namely Colin and me, it's still final. Goodnight, Letty. Thanks for ringing.'

'I haven't finished.'

'Well, I have.'

'Now look here. Colin has some rights, you know.'

'He has, and he's exercised them and he's agreed with me.'

'Just how much influence does this man have on you? He isn't in the place two minutes and he's persuading you to take on equine, something you have set your face against all the time you've been in practice. Think carefully, Mungo. The man's a devious beggar, believe me. He's carving a niche for himself.'

'If it weren't for Dan, with no Zoe available so we're a vet down, Colin would be working day and night, *every* night at the moment. So think on that, Letty. Goodnight.' He was usually too well-mannered to put the receiver down on someone but this time he did. As he lowered it to the cradle he could hear Letty still furiously expostulating. Damn and blast the woman. Was she right? Was he being manipulated? Miriam would put him straight. Mungo found her reading in the sitting room and laid his problem on her shoulders.

'No, you're not being manipulated. He's not that kind of person. Dan is as straight as a die. I know it in my bones. Since when have you taken notice of Letty's opinions, anyway? Never to my knowledge.'

'If we hadn't needed her money so desperately to enable us to move here I would never have had Colin for a partner. Letty's money put the icing on the cake so to speak, but I didn't realise we'd be taking on Mrs Moneybags too. Is Dan all bad?'

'No. But ask Joy, she has to work with him.'

'I will.' Mungo left Miriam reading her book and went to speak to Joy. When he came back he said, 'She says Dan's abrupt and speaks his mind no matter what, and gets her dander up occasionally because he expects everyone to work at the same pace as he does and won't tolerate inefficiency. But she says she's getting more used to him and she's had a couple of clients ask specifically for him, and you can't do better than that. In her weaker moments she wishes Scott were back and then remembers all the trouble he caused. Says Dan's outspoken and doesn't get on with Letty when she comes in. Bring back Lynne is all Joy will say on that score.'

He grinned and Miriam asked him why. 'Apparently Dan gives Letty a Nazi salute when he sees her . . . and clicks his heels.'

'The devil he does! Oh, dear.' Miriam closed her book. 'Just let things ride for the time being. See what the interviews on Monday bring. You can't expect Zoe to give you an answer at the moment anyway. Her answer will be no, though, seeing as she and Dan don't hit it off.'

'After our ill-fated dinner party?'

Miriam nodded. 'He struck out rather forcibly at her, didn't he? I wonder why? All very personal I thought.'

'Don't ask me. I'll leave that to your woman's intuition.'

'On his CV, does it say single or divorced or married?'

'No idea. So long as they do a good job it doesn't bother me. But all this opposition to Dan . . . it makes me wonder if inviting him to stay would be a good thing. Zoe, Letty and inevitably Colin, Joy, all against him. We have to work so closely together all day, every day, maybe we'd be inviting disaster if he stayed.'

When Zoe came in to show off the one-week-old Oscar it so happened that Dan had called in with some samples for the post. He was in Joy's office explaining to her about them when he recognised the thin wail of a newborn baby. 'That sounds like Zoe.'

Joy's face lit up. 'Really? Leave them there, I'll see to them. Got to look at the baby. Are you coming?'

'They're urgent, I want them off in today's post.'

'So they shall be.' Joy squeezed past him, then turned back and said quietly, 'You must come.'

'I am.'

Expecting a crumpled red little thing in whom only a mother could see any beauty, they were all stunned by how gorgeous he was. Oscar had a smooth pink-and-white complexion with a covering of very blond hair all over his head and the dark-blue eyes of the new infant.

His delicate starlike hands waved impatiently from inside his crocheted shawl; one of his fingers became entangled in a hole and Joy gently unhooked him. 'Why, Zoe, he's beautiful. Really beautiful.' She smoothed a fingertip across his cheek. 'Isn't he, Dan?'

'How are you, Zoe? Well?'

'Thank you, yes, I am. What do you think of my blip then, Dan?'

'He's a wonder. Very beautiful. You must be proud of him.'

'I am. Very proud. For a blip he's not too bad, is he?'

'He most certainly isn't. He didn't get his fair skin and hair from you, did he?'

Zoe's dark eyes glared at him and while she thought of a tart reply Joy intervened. 'Come and sit in my office and we'll have a cup of tea. I'll ring the flat and see if Miriam's in. I'm sure she'd love to see him.'

Stephie made the tea while Joy rang up to the flat and in a moment Miriam was down the stairs and begging to hold Oscar. 'Why, he's lovely, Zoe, really lovely.' Taking him in her arms, she gently rocked him, placed a kiss on his forehead and stood silently admiring him.

They all crowded together in Joy's office drinking tea and talking, till Joy clapped her hands and said, 'Sorry, everyone back to work.' Reluctantly Stephie and the two Sarahs left, Miriam handed back the baby to Zoe and she too left, but she didn't go back up to the flat. Instead, she went to stand outside by the back door to pull herself together. Looking up at the hills rising immediately from the edge of the car park she strove to control her longings.

She couldn't see the summit of Beulah Bank Top for the heavy looming cloud. This was the kind of day she didn't like. Sunshine and blue skies suited her personality best, but maybe the mood she was in matched up better to the dark clouds. The agonising physical pain she was feeling became unbearable. She knew she shouldn't have taken hold of the baby, that it would bring back all her dreadful memories, but she hadn't been able to help herself; so now she suffered the appalling pains all over again as bad as ever they had been. The empty arms, that was the worst. Empty arms aching to cradle . . . Gripping her hands together, Miriam put her knuckles to her mouth to stop herself from openly weeping.

The back door opened: it was Dan coming out to continue his calls. 'Why, Miriam! It's too cold to be out here without a coat.'

Miriam didn't answer. Then Dan saw her anguish and, not knowing the cause, didn't know what to say.

The shuddering, almost animal-like groan Miriam gave as she tried to gain control struck Dan's heart like a hammer blow. In his concern all he could think to say was, 'Can I help?'

She shook her head. Dan put his arm round her shoulders and gave her a comforting squeeze. 'If there's anything I can do . . .'

Miriam replied, 'There's nothing anyone can do for me. I should never have held the baby. I was a fool.'

Thinking it was because she was childless Dan said, 'I see.'

'No, Dan, you don't. It's my children, you see. We had two, Mungo and I, and they both died. A genetic disease, so we didn't dare have any more.'

'I'm so sorry. So very sorry.'

'The pain never leaves me.'

Still gripping her shoulders, Dan looked up at the hills as he said, 'There are things which happen to us on which we ourselves have to close the door. I know it's quite dreadfully hard to do, but it has to be done. We need to turn our faces to the light when we've suffered as you have and let the pain go, otherwise we're only leading half a life and life is so very short. Doing that doesn't mean we've forgotten, or that we care any less.'

Miriam blew her nose and cleared her throat. Looking at him, she found his eyes still focused on the hills. Shakily she murmured, 'You speak as if you know how I feel.'

He came back from wherever he'd been, saying, 'No, no, not at all. I just feel for you, that's all. Better now?'

She nodded. Dan took his arm from her shoulders. 'You'd best go inside. It's too cold. I'll be off. Think about turning your face to the light and enjoying all the good things life has to offer.'

She watched him rev up, reverse and swing off out of the car park at his usual breakneck speed. Miriam went to the staff washroom and splashed her face with water, found a comb someone had left behind, tidied her hair and then, hearing angry voices, went to seek them out.

Joy and Zoe were talking with Mungo in his office. Mungo sounded as though he were striving hard to keep a check on his temper. 'I had to ask what you thought, Zoe. You are a partner after all.'

'Exactly and this partner is saying no.'

Miriam stood listening in the doorway because the room wasn't big enough for four of them.

'That's all very well but we've interviewed. Two have refused the job, one wasn't suitable, one has said he'll think about it and meanwhile good locums do not grow on trees. We are short-handed and we can't expect you back just yet, can we. That wouldn't be fair to you or Oscar.'

'I still say he isn't for one minute to think he's being taken on permanently. He's a bloody pain, he is. He's an arrogant, abrupt and bloody rude male chauvinist pig.'

Mungo began to lose his temper, Miriam saw it in the way his shoulders straightened and his good looks became pinched. 'All this is becoming very personal. Your decision isn't professional at all. I shall excuse you because you've a new baby and all your hormones have got their knickers in a twist, so consequently you're not thinking straight.'

'How dare you patronise me? Just because I've had a baby it doesn't mean I've gone soft in the head.'

'It bloody sounds like it to me. Anyway, Colin and I agree so that's two out of three. So I'm afraid he'll be here for some time yet, like it or not.'

'Letty rang me last night . . .'

'Did she?' The tone of Mungo's voice left Zoe in no doubt what he thought about that.

'Yes, she doesn't want him to stay either.'

'According to my paperwork Colin is the partner not Letty. Much as she might like to think she is, she *isn't*, so her opinion damned well doesn't count.'

'She's determined to persuade Colin. They're having lunch together tomorrow to discuss it.'

'She'd damn well better not. We can't manage without Dan and that's the end of the bloody matter.' Mungo banged his fist on the edge of the desk to emphasise his determination.

Joy said, 'Mungo's absolutely right, none of us likes him but we can't manage without him.'

Zoe looked across at Joy with spiteful eyes. 'Since when was Joy Bastable made a partner? It's not for you to put your pennyworth in, either for or against.'

Joy, affronted by Zoe's savage retort, opened her mouth to shout, 'I've a right to an opinion, I have to work with him too.'

But Miriam thought things had gone quite far enough. Very quietly but firmly she said, 'Zoe! Take your baby home. It isn't right for him to be hearing all this anger.'

Zoe sneered at Miriam, finding her sentiment laughable.

Almost inaudibly Miriam continued, 'Take him home and leave the management of the practice to Mungo. He's never let you down in the past and he isn't going to let you down now. So go home, take your three months off and enjoy that baby you've been *privileged* to be given. Mungo's decision about Dan is absolutely right. The man's a gem and this practice needs him. Now, go home.' She stood away from the door to allow room for Zoe to pass her.

Zoe gave the three of them in turn a defiant stare, but when she saw the unaccustomed determination in Miriam's sweet face she stood up to go, suddenly wearied by it all.

'Drive carefully, he's precious.'

After Zoe had left, Miriam turned to Joy. 'You are my dear friend, Joy, and always will be but you must understand this. I don't want to hear any more from you about not liking Dan, because I want him to stay. You're making a serious misjudgement of his character, I'm afraid.'

She left Mungo and Joy staring at each other, nonplussed by her out-of-character interference.

5

Kate heard the entire story about the row in Mungo's office the previous afternoon from Stephie. Listening was unavoidable, Stephie said, because the door was open. The only part she'd missed was what Miriam said to settle the matter. 'Good thing the afternoon clinic hadn't started or else it would have been all over the town by last night. They really shouted at one another. I know Mungo has a temper but this was above and beyond anything I've heard before. They were swearing and you know what he thinks about that. I only got this job because he sacked the previous receptionist for using bad language to him once too often. Anyway, Mrs Price sorted them out without so much as raising her voice. For the rest of the day Joy was very subdued, so I reckon she'd had a telling off from Mrs Price too.'

'So is Dan staying, then?'

'That's what I heard Mungo say. But we can't manage without him at the moment anyway, can we?'

Graham Murgatroyd's client came to the desk to pay and from then on the morning got busier, and Stephie and Kate had no more time for discussing the events of the previous day.

Just as Mungo's morning consultations were finished and he'd gone up to the flat for his lunch, Letty pushed her way through the glass door and came striding in. 'Colin? Is he back yet, Stephie?'

'No, Mrs Walker, he's right out at Pick's Farm doing TB testing. I doubt he'll be back until the middle of the afternoon.'

'He knew I was coming in.'

'Oh, I didn't know that. He volunteered to go, actually, because Dan was down for going and . . .'

'Did he indeed. I'll have something to say about that. Mungo in?'

Stephie lied through her teeth, her fingers crossed behind her back. 'Gone out to see a client who is too ill to bring his dog in for a consultation. Right the other side of Shrewsbury.'

'There must be a conspiracy. I'll call Colin on his mobile.'

Letty marched through into Joy's empty office and commandeered the telephone.

The two of them waited for her to return, which she did in no time at all. 'His mobile must need recharging.' Her pale lips settled into a thin line. 'I'll go for lunch and make a definite appointment for tomorrow. Goodbye, Stephie.'

Stephie waited until Letty had shut the inner glass door and then said, 'Thank my lucky stars Mungo didn't come down while she was here.'

'Why did you lie?'

'Cos anyone in her bad books deserves help. Poor Colin, he won't half catch it in the neck. It's all to do with Dan staying permanently. Apparently Letty's dead against it. I'm so glad he wasn't back in time. Fancy having to lunch with her! God, it'd be like dining with a fiend.'

They both laughed, only to find when they'd sobered up that Colin was standing listening to them. Kate went bright red but Stephie, having got herself in the mood for telling lies, was unfazed by his unexpected arrival. 'Oh, Colin! You've just missed Mrs Walker. If you hurry you might catch her.'

But Colin didn't hurry out. Instead, he looked pointedly at Stephie, raised an eyebrow and said, 'If Mungo's gone to see that dog he'll be a while before he's back, won't he?' From the way he phrased his question they knew he'd been hiding in the back from Letty while they'd been talking to her. Otherwise how would he have known what lie Stephie had told?

It was Stephie's turn to feel embarrassed. 'Actually, Mungo is upstairs having lunch. He's operating all afternoon so he shouldn't be long.'

Colin nodded. 'Is that the truth or another porkie?'

Stephie had no way out but to say, 'It's the truth this time. I'm sorry.'

Colin stood with his elbow resting on the desk, apparently needing to talk. Stephie recognised a conspiratorial look in his eye and she wondered what he was about to say. 'Tonight. Dan's on call.'

Kate checked the rota. 'Yes, he is.'

'Well, he's got a bad cold, hasn't he, and the best thing for him is a good night's sleep with a couple of whiskies inside him. Isn't it? So I'd better fill in for him tonight, hadn't I?'

Kate couldn't get to grips with what Colin meant. 'He was all right this morning. I'm quite sure he hasn't . . .'

Colin looked at her with eyes full of meaning. 'Oh, no, he wasn't. He looked so bad I suspect it could be flu starting.'

'Flu? I don't think . . .'

Stephie nudged her. 'You're right, Colin, Dan was looking white as a sheet first thing.' To emphasise that she wasn't the only one being deceitful, Stephie put a lot of meaning into her next question. 'Seeing as your mobile phone isn't *working*, I'll ring Mrs Walker for you, shall I? Let her know you've swapped.'

Colin nodded. 'That's right. Thanks, Stephie. Wouldn't want her to arrange something and me not be able to go, would I?'

'Of course not.'

Colin disappeared into the back to see if anyone had left any of their lunch so he could help himself to it. He'd found before that it was best to keep out of Letty's way for a while till the wind had gone out of her sails. She'd been so adamant about Dan not staying. He'd suffered all the previous evening from her bitterness about Dan. He, Colin, was the partner after all. He knew how many hours he'd have to work if Dan left. He was the best judge of practice matters, not Letty. Now, having rearranged the rota, he'd be able to avoid her a while longer because she insisted he slept in the spare bedroom when he was on call so he wouldn't disturb her beauty sleep if he got called out. Beauty sleep! Huh! It was a bit late for that. He found Stephie's unopened packet of crisps and munched his way through it while he waited for the kettle to boil. It struck him that he, a grown man, was *hiding* and *lying* to escape the wrath of his wife. *It really shouldn't be like this*, he thought. What was worse, he'd implicated the staff in his deception and that was unworthy of him. Colin classified himself as a silly fool and he didn't like it.

Truth to tell, he'd been a fool for most of his married life. What Letty had needed most was a strong man. Someone who wanted the last word as much as she did. Someone who took the initiative, who simply would not allow her to have her own way all of the time, and now, by his being over-considerate towards her all these years, she despised him. Question was, was he enough of a man to be able to assert himself in a way that would make a better person of Letty? Always it was money, money, money, as if that were all that counted in life. Well, it did, to an extent but . . .

He put the very last half-crisp from the corner of the packet in his mouth, dropped the empty packet on the worktop and caught a glimpse of the name of the maker of the crisps. It appeared frighteningly symbolic to him that the maker's name was Walker; it could have been him lying there. The packet looked just like he felt: emptied of absolutely everything. And now it was empty there was nothing on earth more useless . . . just like he was after fifteen years of marriage to Letty. He realised it was only because he was good at his job that his sanity was saved.

Somewhere in the very far distance a bugle sounded the call to battle: it was faint, but Colin Walker definitely heard it and accordingly he laid his plans to regain the ground he'd lost with Letty. A bit of romance was called for and he'd begin with flowers. The biggest bouquet she'd ever seen and then . . .

Halfway through the afternoon Stephie declared to Kate, 'It's no good, I'll have to give in.'

'Give in?'

'Yes. I've been resisting temptation for the last ten minutes and I can't go on any longer. I'm eating those crisps.'

'Honestly, Stephie, you'll regret it. Just think how pleased you'll be with yourself if you leave them till tomorrow.'

Stephie groaned at the thought of waiting till the next day. 'I know I will, but I'm desperate. I've got terrible rumbles in my stomach and if I don't eat something soon . . .'

'Cashing up will take your mind off it. Do that and you'll forget.'

'Nothing will make me forget. Sorry.'

Leaving Kate on the desk, she went to open her crisps and enjoy five minutes of completely loathsome self-indulgence. She knew she was being weak, but she couldn't help herself.

Stephie was horrified to find the packet empty, lying where Colin had left it. Storming back into reception she said, 'He's done it again!'

'Who has?'

'Colin. In my hour of need, desperate, I am. I'll kill him for this.'

'What's he done?'

'Eaten my crisps. He helps himself to anything left lying about, it really isn't good enough. I'm sure she doesn't feed him properly.' Stephie stamped about behind the desk, flushed and angry.

'Look at it this way, he must have needed them and it's saved you from breaking your diet.'

'That has nothing to do with it. I'm starving. I saved them specially. My stomach is raw with hunger.'

'In my bag I have a Mars bar. You can have that, if you like.'

Stephie's eyes lit up and she disappeared into the back to return five minutes later complaining of feeling sick because she'd eaten it too quickly. 'I should never have had it. I feel terrible.'

'I did say.'

'I know. I know.'

As the afternoon progressed Stephie became more ill and had to go home early because she felt so terribly sick and looked as white as she had described Dan had looked that morning. There was no possibility that she would be in to work the following day. So, as Joy had a hospital appointment tomorrow, Kate rang Letty and asked her to come in. Letty agreed with surprising alacrity.

The first surprise Letty had was Dan bursting in through the door at eight in his usual hale and hearty manner. 'Good morning, Kate.' He saw Letty and treated her to his Nazi salute plus an exaggerated click of his heels. 'Good morning, Letty. Lovely isn't it?'

Through tight lips Letty managed to say 'Good morning', followed by an enquiry after his health.

Dan's eyes sparkled. 'I'm fine, thank you, yes, very fine.'

'I see. I was told you had flu.'

'Flu? I haven't got flu. Fit as a fiddle am I.'

'I see. Then why did Colin have to do your night on call last night?'

'He asked if he could. So we swapped.'

'I see.'

'As things appear to be transparently clear to you today, you must be on top of everything, so have you got my list?'

Letty whipped the list across the top of the desk in a trice with a triumphant, 'There you are. Colin's already left.'

'Hope you have a good time tonight.'

'I'm not going anywhere tonight.'

'Oh! Right. I'll be off, then.' Dan gave Kate a wink and dashed away.

'So what do you know about all this?'

Kate saw a great big hole waiting for her to fall into and decided to know nothing whatsoever about the situation. 'Stephie dealt with it.' Luckily for her, the phone rang.

The morning clinic began with Valentine and Rhodri on duty with a full list of consultations, so Letty had no more time to discuss the mysterious fact of Dan's good health. At about twelve a bouquet of flowers was delivered. Letty took them from the van driver and curiously examined the card. In neat handwriting, which she didn't recognise, it read *Mrs Letty Walker*. Flowers for her? 'Kate, do you recognise this handwriting?'

Kate looked at the envelope and shook her head. 'No, I don't. It'll be the florist's, I expect. They're beautiful. I adore roses. They smell lovely.'

Curious to know who they were from, but assuming it must surely be Colin, Kate tried hard not to look while Letty slid the card out of its tiny envelope. Letty flushed all over her face and right down her neck.

The ugly flush enhanced her appearance not one iota and Kate looked away in embarrassment. What on earth was written on the card? The phone rang but Letty didn't answer it, so it was Kate who had a protracted conversation with a drug company rep trying to engineer an appointment with Mungo. When she'd finished she saw that Letty appeared to be still in a state of shock.

'I'll fill the fire bucket so they can have a drink. Aren't they wonderful?'

But Letty didn't answer. She handed the bouquet to Kate and stood staring into the distance.

'I'll save the wrapping and the ribbon.'

Kate couldn't help but see the card. All that was written on it was '*With all my love*'. No signature. Kate stood looking at it, unable to believe that anyone would send Letty such a card. She re-examined the envelope and it clearly said Letty's name on it, so there was no mistake about that. Kate stood the bouquet in the bucket, pushing it against the wall so it wouldn't be in the way, leaving the card on the worktop above with the wrapping and the bow. Red roses. At this time of year. They must have cost a packet. Who on earth could have sent them?

Bunty came in to prepare a feed for Copperfield who was still in intensive care. 'Are those yours, Kate?'

'Would that they were.'

'They're beautiful. Who are they for?'

'Letty.'

Bunty's round, homely face registered total amazement. 'Letty! I don't believe it! Who're they from?'

Kate showed her the card.

'My God, what a laugh! Whoever sent them must be mad. "*With all my love*"! Wait till I tell the two Sarahs.'

To Letty's total embarrassment there was a positive stream of staff after that making the pilgrimage to view the flowers and come to tell her how lovely they were.

'Secret admirer, that's what,' said Sarah One.

'You're a dark horse, Letty,' said Sarah Two.

'Does Colin know?' asked Valentine.

'No, he does not.'

Rhodri suggested it might be a grateful client, which made them all laugh.

'It must be a joke.' This last from Graham who had never been noted for his tact.

Finally Letty said, 'Kate! I'm going home with that bouquet. It is my lunch hour and I can't take any more of it.'

'You should be flattered.'

'I'm not. Far from it.'

'Have you really no idea who can have sent it?'

'No. I'll be back within the hour, don't worry.'

Letty found a plastic carrier bag with which she enclosed the wet stems of the bouquet and disappeared through the back door as fast as she could.

Kate stood sucking the end of her pen, wondering who on earth it could be who would send someone like Letty such a hugely expensive bouquet. She began with Colin. No. Then Dan. No, though he might as an apology for his bad behaviour towards her but he wouldn't put 'All my love', now would he? There wasn't anyone else who would. So maybe Graham was right, it was a joke on someone's part. But it was cruel if so. Not even Letty deserved that kind of meanness, Kate thought.

That night at home, Kate was wondering why her dad had been so quiet all evening. She'd told them the story of Letty's flowers and Mia had speculated as to who might have sent them but the tale hadn't raised the slightest response from her father.

'Tired, Dad?'

'Just thinking.' He caught Mia's eye and saw from her look that he had no escape tonight. He'd have to say it. The time had come, he couldn't avoid it. He'd thought and thought, and come to the conclusion that Kate had a right to know about her mother despite his reluctance to excavate his painful past. 'Kate.'

'Mm?'

Losing confidence, he sidestepped his problem and asked feebly, 'Are you happy at work?'

'You know I am. Why do you ask?'

Gerry shrugged his shoulders. 'Just thought I would enquire, to make sure.'

Mia coughed significantly to remind him of his promise to her. It was no good, he'd have to press on. 'Kate, now you're nineteen and a young woman we . . . wouldn't mind – in fact, we'd be glad – for you to go on holiday with someone from work. Young people's holiday, you know the kind of thing. Mia and I have always been happy to have you with us but we wouldn't want you to feel obliged, would we, Mia?'

'No.' Mia stared at him meaningfully, knowing full well why he'd diverted to talking about holidays.

'The other thing is now you're older . . . well . . . I wondered if you'd like to hear something about your mother.' Quickly Gerry followed that with, 'Of course, if you don't want to that's very much all right by me.'

Immediately Kate blushed from her hairline right down to her throat. She'd never been redder in her life. Dad! Dad! Her throat constricted and her voice seemed to have gone. At last he was going to tell her. At last. Struggling, she got out, 'Yes, please, I'd like to hear.'

Gerry clenched his hands and laid them on the cloth. In a voice quite unlike his own and secretly hoping she would still say no, he told her, 'Mia said I must, so I will, if that's what you want.'

Kate nodded. 'Why now?'

'Because I should have told you years ago, but there was Mia to think of and I . . . couldn't. But I will, now. What do you want to know?'

'It would be nice if I knew her name.'

'Tessa Fenton.'

In her mind Kate rolled the name around several times to get accustomed to it. Startled to realise it wasn't Tessa Howard, Kate said, 'I had expected you'd be married.'

Gerry shook his head. 'I wanted to be but she wouldn't.'

'Oh!'

'Truth to tell, she thought herself a cut above me. Bit of rough, I think she would have described me as.'

Mia looked pained and reached out her hand to hold his.

Kate, feeling affronted that anyone, let alone her own mother, would categorise her father like that, said sharply, 'But you're not. Dad! You're not anyone's bit of rough.'

'I was to her. To her I was the artisan she fancied for a while. What she hadn't bargained for was that your old dad had more vigour than she gave me credit for and after she moved in with me she was pregnant almost immediately. But she wouldn't have an abortion, thank God.'

Mia's heart almost broke in two. She clutched hold of Kate's hand and sat like a link in a chain, connecting the pair of them.

Kate, horrified, had to ask, 'Did you want her to?'

'No, of course not. But if she had wanted one there wasn't much I could have done about it, was there?'

'No. So what did she say when she found out?'

'Not repeatable in present company. She was as sick as a dog for weeks. You had to admire her pluck – went to work every day feeling like death warmed up.'

'Work? What did she do?'

'Solicitor.'

'Solicitor!'

Gerry nodded.

'Dad, were you glad? About me?'

'Glad. The bells of heaven must have been ringing their clappers to a standstill. Glad! Was I? I was. Glad and proud and delighted and thrilled. So was she when the sickness stopped and she could feel you moving about inside her. I used to put my hand on her stomach and feel for you moving. What joy.'

Mia controlled her tears; she mustn't be seen to weep. This was Kate's night, not hers.

Kate felt peculiar. Primitive. Basic. Earthier than before. Suddenly her mother became real for her. Her dad was turned in on his memories, she could see that from the look in his eyes. He cleared his throat, saying, 'Wonderful days. You gave her a hell of a time when you were born, though. Day and a half, it took. Then you came in a rush, shot out almost. I remember the sun was shining into the delivery room and it seemed to me that you were charmed, very special, a kind of chosen one. And you were so beautiful, screaming to the heavens, but beautiful. I remember the midwife said, "She's here to stay."'

'My mother' – it felt odd saying that – 'how did she feel?'

Gerry didn't seem to want to answer.

She asked again, 'How did she feel about me?' There was an almost pathetic eagerness to know in Kate's voice, a need to hear about her mother's approval or acceptance; or, heaven forbid, rejection.

Mia heard the slight change in Gerry's voice and guessed he was saying what he knew Kate wanted to hear. 'Well, once they'd attended to her and washed you and sorted you out and given you to her to hold, she was thrilled. Very thrilled. You must understand she was exhausted. It had been a long time.'

Mia stood up. 'I'll make a cup of tea.' While she busied herself with that, Gerry went on reminiscing about Kate's first week at home. 'My, you were demanding. The midwife said she'd never seen a baby as hungry as you.'

'What did I weigh, Dad? Do you remember?'

'Engraved on my heart. Katrina Howard, seven pounds exactly. Here, look, I found this the other day, it's the identification band they put round your wrist.'

Gerry dug in the top pocket of his jacket and handed her the small plastic band. 'Oh, look, Mia! Isn't that lovely. You've kept it all this time. That's so lovely, I can't believe it. Can I keep it?'

Gerry nodded.

Mia put her hand on Kate's shoulder and loved her joy as she turned the tiny plastic band round and round with such endearing care. Mia had no idea Gerry had it hidden away. It seemed today there was a lot she didn't know about him. Tessa. Hm.

'So, Kate, that was how it all started.'

'That's not all, though, is it Dad? What happened then? Why did she leave me?'

Understandably, Gerry found this part of the story even harder to face than the beginning had been. He fidgeted with the cruet, placing it straight and smoothing the tablecloth; he found a crumb, picked it up and put it on his side plate; he looked up into Mia's sympathetic, encouraging eyes and finally gained the strength to say, 'She found motherhood wasn't all it was cracked up to be and she couldn't cope.'

'You mean she had post-natal depression.'

Gerry shifted his feet uneasily. 'Something like that.'

'Well, that is hard to cope with, isn't it. Sometimes it can drive a mother to suicide.' Immediately panicking about what she'd said, Kate asked, 'She didn't, did she? Is that why I've never known her?'

'No, she didn't.' Gerry stood up. 'There, I've said enough for one night. Can't talk about it any more.' He headed for the stairs.

Mia called out, 'Your tea! I've poured it.'

'No, thanks.' Gerry left them and went upstairs, and shortly they heard the Flying Scotsman hurtling along its tracks.

Kate sat silently, either fingering the plastic band or picking up her cup and sipping her scalding hot tea. Mia was silent too. In this situation there wasn't a great deal a stepmother could find to say except, 'More tea?'

'No, thanks. He can't leave it like this. I'm going up to find out more. He was being kind, wasn't he? Saying she might have had post-natal depression?'

Mia shook her head. 'I honestly don't know. I've learnt more tonight than ever before. It's a closed book as far as your dad is concerned. It's all so painful for him.'

Kate drew in a deep breath, so deep her shoulders heaved as she took it, 'It hurts me badly too. How could she leave me? How could she? I can't forgive that. I just cannot. Two weeks old. She can't have had much maternal feeling for me, can she?'

'We're all different, Kate. I couldn't leave you at nineteen years, never mind two weeks. But that's me. Soft old Mia.'

Kate's arms were round Mia in a second and they hugged each other tightly.

'Oh, Mia! I love you!'

'And I love you.'

They hugged a moment longer, then Kate sat down and wiped her eyes on a tissue borrowed from Mia. 'He can't leave it like this. He's got to tell me more and I know he hurts, but it might be better to bring it all out now, while he's in the mood. You know, Mia, he must have been devastated when she left. Imagine being dumped like that and with a baby too, when he loved her. I think he did love her, don't you? Otherwise it wouldn't be quite so hard for him. I wonder if they've communicated at all since?'

Mia shook her head again. 'Not to my knowledge.'

'I'm going to ask.'

Kate stood up and was at the foot of the stairs before Mia could stop her. She protested, 'No, don't, love, he's had enough.' But she was too late.

Gerry was hunched over, watching his goods train as it pulled into the station siding. He switched it off and as Kate looked on he pulled out his handkerchief and blew his nose.

'Thanks for telling me, Dad.'

'Oh! It's you.' As though he'd never broken off the conversation he continued by saying, 'She was lovely looking, was your mum. That's where you get it from; certainly not from me.'

Trying to keep it light, Kate joked, 'Oh! I don't know. You're not that bad looking. I think I've got your nose.'

'For your sake I hope you haven't. She made a big mistake, did your mum. She should never have taken up with me.'

'Don't underrate yourself.'

'I'm not. I'm speaking the truth. I don't like to say too much in front of Mia, it wouldn't be right, but your mother, though full of good intentions, should never have taken up with me. I was blessedly grateful for her, but more so because she gave me you. At least I had you to cling to when she'd gone. You to get up for, you to bath, you to feed, you to support. Without you I'd have gone under. There'd have been no point in living but for you.'

'She didn't like me, did she?'

Quickly Gerry denied this. 'It wasn't like that at all. She couldn't cope with being tied every hour of the day.'

'But she could have found someone to care for me while she went to work. She would be earning enough to do that as a solicitor. But she didn't.'

Gerry hadn't an answer to that. 'Don't let it get to you what she did. You've got Mia and she's been worth twenty of your mum to you.' Her dad took her hand in both his and muttered, 'Worth twenty, she's been. A real life saver, for you and for me. So don't you go upsetting her talking to her about your mum, wanting to see her and that.' He looked up at Kate to see how she'd taken what he'd said.

'I shan't. I'm not daft. It's just that it's important to me to *know who I am*. You haven't got a photo of her, have you?'

Gerry dropped her hand abruptly, swung back to his train layout and said emphatically, 'No. I have not. I burnt it all. Every last bit.'

Kate went to the window to look out. 'You know Zoe at the practice? Well, she's got her baby like I said and she isn't ever going to tell the father about the baby, nor the baby about his father. To me that's terribly wrong. You *need to know*. You really do. Believe me.'

'Well, now you do know. So that's that. Go downstairs and keep Mia company, because she cherishes you more than life itself and that's something for anyone, rich or poor, to be very, very grateful for.'

It was on the tip of Kate's tongue to ask if her dad loved Mia like he'd loved her own mother, but she changed her mind. Perhaps it would be best not to know the answer to that.

6

Kate was glad she wasn't working the following morning, because she was still feeling confused by all she'd learnt from her father the previous night. She lay in bed, staring at the chinks of light creeping round the edges of her curtains and thinking about her mother. It would have been so good to have seen a photograph of her. Even a faded one, just to have some idea of what one half of Kate Howard actually came from. It seemed odd that fifty per cent of herself was derived from someone she'd never seen nor really knew anything about.

She took a hand out from under the duvet and examined it in the half-light, and wondered if she'd inherited her mother's hands because they certainly weren't the square, solid hands of her dad. A solicitor. Just think, she could have wanted to be one and not realised she was being led by her genes. Or did it work that way? Whatever. Tessa. Tessa Fenton. Kate flung herself on her other side and contemplated leaving her own two-week-old baby, and knew she couldn't, not even if they'd had to go and live together in a cardboard box somewhere. A baby was part of you. How could any mother have walked away and never bothered again? But Tessa had done just that and for the callousness that illustrated Kate decided she wouldn't want to know her, ever, and she wasn't going to waste any more of her time thinking about her and what she was and what she looked like. And she'd never search for her. Never ever.

Mia shouted from downstairs 'Kate, phone for you.'

'OK.' Kate ran downstairs and took the receiver 'Hello, Kate Howard speaking.'

'Dan here, Kate. Sorry for interrupting your day off.'

'That's all right.'

'Kate, I've had a rather surprising card this morning inviting me and your good self to afternoon tea at Applegate Farm, today. At four.'

'Afternoon tea! Are you sure?'

284

'I am. As you know them, I thought you wouldn't say no. I'm going anyway. I've an idea there's a surprise in store for us.'

'I bet there is. Food poisoning.'

'Well, that too. Do you fancy going?'

'I suppose I do.'

'If you've nothing else on.'

'OK. But if I'm off work tomorrow I shall blame you. What on earth can it be about?'

'I've said I think they might have a surprise in store.'

'What kind of a surprise?'

'Wait and see. I don't want to let them down.'

'Of course not. Yes, I'll go. Curiosity is getting the better of me.'

'I'll pick you up if I may, would that be all right?'

'Yes.' Kate gave him instructions about how to find her house and saying, 'See you at half past three, then. Bye,' put down the receiver.

They were halfway to Applegate Farm when Kate burst out with, 'Do you remember me saying I wished I knew about my mother?'

Dan nodded.

'Well, my dad told me last night. About me being born and that.'

'I'm glad. Are you glad?'

'Yes, I am. He didn't tell me much, but enough. Last night I wanted to see a picture of her, but this morning I don't.'

'Why not?'

'Because I can't forgive her for abandoning me.'

'Oh.'

'You don't think I'm right.'

'It's not up to me.'

'I'd like to know if you think I'm right, Dan.'

Keeping his eyes on the road, Dan said tentatively, 'What you mustn't do is harbour resentment towards her, because it will fester. Either forget all about her and get on with your life, or forgive her. But don't have resentment hovering about in your mind, niggling away.'

'It's a very hard thing to forgive anyone for.'

'It is, I agree.'

'Mia's worth twenty of her, like Dad said, and I wouldn't do anything to hurt her.'

'We're almost there. Prepare yourself, my child.'

Kate had to laugh. 'You know what this is all about, don't you?' A suspicion gathered in her mind. 'Did you really get an invitation?'

He applied the brake and dipped his hand into his top pocket. 'See for yourself.' Dan gave her a piece of bright-pink card. On it was written:

> Blossom and Phil Parsons Cordaly invite Dan Brown and Cate
> To Afternone Tea In the Bire Tea room At four on Thursday (today).
> Pleas come.

'In the Byre tea room? Oh, God! What have we let ourselves in for? I don't know which is worse, the house or the byre.'

Dan looked across at the farm buildings and said, 'Take a look.'

There was red, white and blue bunting, dusty and crumpled, strung over the door to Sunny Boy's stall. Sitting in the doorway was little Scott with a small Union Jack tied round her neck. Then Kate saw Blossom appear in the doorway, waving.

'Here goes.' Dan waved enthusiastically through the open window. Still smiling at Blossom, he muttered to Kate that he had stomach tubing with him if need be.

He put on his boots, waited for Kate to do the same, then they both got out and marched cheerfully towards Sunny Boy's stall. The bunting appeared grubbier the nearer they got but the welcome was enthusiastic and they cheered up enormously.

Blossom had decked herself out in the skimpiest of leather skirts. Despite the winter wind blowing, her top half was clothed in a short-sleeved pink jumper the colour of the invitation card and in her hair was silver tinsel, a precursor of Christmas. 'Come in! Come in!' She placed a goose-pimpled arm through Dan's and hastened him in. Kate followed.

The transformation of the byre was breathtaking. Dan looked round with amazement.

'It was all Phil's idea. Isn't it great?' Blossom squeezed his arm and waited eagerly for his reaction. 'Phil's heard your car and he's gone to get the champagne out the dairy. It's cold in there. Well?'

'Mrs Parsons . . .'

Blossom giggled. 'Not Mrs Parsons! It's Blossom to you. You're a friend. Isn't he, Kate?'

Kate nodded. 'Such a transformation! It's splendid.'

Dan looked at the glowing black beams, the horse brasses nailed like guardsmen on parade along the length of each beam, at the burnished brass catch on the door to Sunny Boy's stall, the newly painted feeding trough, the snow-white walls and the purple wheelie bins lined up against the far wall.

'I can see you like the bins. It was my idea to paint them purple, royal purple for a royal bull, and do you like the silver stars? That was Hamish's idea. He stuck them on.'

'I am just gobsmacked. Truly gobsmacked. It is magnificent.'

'Phil's thrilled to bits.'

'It's so tidy, so smart, so different. Even the loose stones cemented in.'

Phil came in carrying a chrome tray with glasses and champagne on it, followed by a tall, gangling teenage boy with a head of the reddest hair either Kate or Dan had ever seen. He had the pale-blue eyes and the fair, heavily freckled skin which so often go with real red hair; even his eyelashes were red.

Phil put the tray down carefully on a small side table they'd brought in from the house saying, 'This is Hamish. Come to live with us. He's helped with this, haven't you, Hamish?'

Blossom beamed at Hamish and added, 'If it hadn't been for him we'd never have got finished, would we, Hamish?'

Hamish simply grinned in agreement. But it was a beautiful grin, which lit up the whole of his face and was expressive of his pleasure at their approval.

Behind his back Blossom silently mouthed, 'He can't talk.'

Dan released himself from Blossom's clutching arm and went to shake Hamish's hand. 'This is a big thank you from me to you for getting all this done. Wonderful job. No one could be more pleased.' He clapped Hamish on the shoulder and smiled at him. 'Brilliant!' Hamish grinned his appreciation.

'Now!' Phil took the champagne bottle and began the removal of the cork. 'I've left Sunny Boy out of here until we're ready to drink the toast. Thought the cork shooting out might upset him.'

The cork shot out, hitting the window with a loud ping.

Blossom dissolved into laughter. 'God, Phil! Don't break that bloody window. It took ages to get it clean and painted.'

'Right, Hamish, bring him in. He's got to be here when we drink the toast.' Phil put down the bottle and proudly opened the newly painted gate to the stall.

'Will Sunny Boy let . . .' Dan nodded his head towards the open door.

'Of course. They're buddies, they are.'

'Where's he from?'

'Tell yer later. Here he comes.'

They stood aside to make space for Hamish to lead Sunny Boy into the stall. Round the bull's neck was tied a Union Jack ten sizes larger than Scott's, he was brushed and combed, and titivated well enough to compete at the Royal Show. The restraint of the rope through his nose ring made him anxious and caused him to toss his head from side to side, and Kate shrank back against the wall, fearful of those great hooves of his. Hamish calmly secured his head rope to a ring in the wall and carefully shut the gate behind him. If Phil had declared he was a champion pedigree bull no one would have challenged him. He looked magnificent in his newly refurbished quarters.

'A toast!' called Phil. He charged all their glasses and raised his saying, 'To Sunny Boy, to his new quarters and to Hamish who did all the work!'

They all clinked glasses and drank the toast. Kate studied Hamish for a moment and wondered about him. It was obvious Phil Parsons didn't want to explain while he was there. But why couldn't he talk? Didn't he want to or couldn't he talk at all?

'Right then. Tea. Come on, Hamish, go and give Blossom a hand, if you please.'

Hamish shuffled off after Blossom, she small and dainty, he large and shambling. Phil dipped his fingers in his champagne and, leaning over into the stall, pushed them into Sunny Boy's great mouth. 'He's got to share in the celebrations, hasn't he? Come on then, have a drop more.'

Dan had to ask: 'Who is he, Phil? That Hamish.'

'He's the one who left the ball that day, the one that Sunny Boy tried to swallow. From the caravan site, he is, been staying there with a group of lads from a home. Came back to get it after you'd gone and wouldn't leave. Just hung about, not saying anything. I tried to get him to go but he wouldn't. Blossom thought he was hungry so she gave him some food and then told him to go, but he wouldn't and it's a bit difficult making a big chap like him scat. He just wouldn't. So, desperate, Blossom said go down and tell 'em. So I did. Well, he went back to the site when they came to get him. They left the next day and two days later he was back here. He'd hopped it at a motorway service station and walked till he got 'ere.'

'How could he tell you that?'

'Showed me a receipt from a place on the M4 and waved his arms about a bit. That's what Blossom says happened anyway. He won't go, I've tried, so I thought I'd put him to good use. Blossom's made a bed up for him and, well, here he is.'

'Shouldn't someone be told?' Kate asked.

'And send him back to where he doesn't want to be? He's no trouble and it does Blossom good to have someone to fuss over. She says love is all he wants; someone who cares and she's good at that. We said about his mum and dad, and he started shaking and went to bed, and wouldn't come out for a day and a night. Not till Blossom sat on his bed and told him he could stay and we wouldn't say a word to the authorities. Terrified, he was.' Phil shrugged his shoulders. 'Perhaps one day he'll speak and tell us. He eats like he's never eaten in years, straight down whatever it is, and never has an ache or a pain, even though he reg'lar has two full plates of dinner at a sitting.'

Phil's last sentence reminded Kate about food poisoning and she sent up a little prayer that she'd have as strong a stomach as Hamish apparently had. They heard Blossom's heels tapping along the yard, accompanied by the solid tread of Hamish's big feet, and through the door she came with a heavily loaded tray that she placed on the table Hamish had carried in for her.

'Hasn't she done us proud?'

Dan ate heartily, Kate sparingly, but enough not to give offence. Blossom had certainly done them proud, as Phil had said. Hamish ate as much as the four of them put together with an enthusiasm none of them could match.

They shook hands with Blossom, Phil and Hamish, and thanked them profusely for their hospitality as they left, especially Hamish for all his help with the improvements. He grinned and gave them a thumbs-up.

As Dan turned the Land Rover round in the lane Kate said, 'There appear to be a lot of people around with either no parents or only one original one. Me and Oscar and now Hamish. It's not right, is it, for no one to know where Hamish is?'

Dan thought for a moment and didn't answer until they were well down the lane close to the main road. 'He wouldn't have done a runner if he'd been happy where he was, and he is happy with Blossom and Phil, isn't he?'

Kate had to admit he was.

'So I think that adds up to you and me keeping quiet about him and leaving him in peace. He obviously knows exactly what's being said to him and understands perfectly, so perhaps the talking will come if he has a chance to feel safe.'

'Mm. You're wiser than you look. It's funny this thing about one's roots. When he told me about my mother, my dad gave me the identification band I'd had round my wrist in the hospital, you know, when I was newborn, and suddenly I felt real, as though I'd come from somewhere and hadn't simply materialised. I felt I had roots, and identity, kind of. Silly isn't it?'

'No, it isn't.'

The answer had come crisply and with a finality in the tone of his voice that brooked no further mention of the subject, leaving Kate wondering what lay at the heart of Dan: so full of wisdom and understanding one minute and then up went a blank wall and he'd gone behind it.

In truth, one half of his mind was controlling his driving and the other half was far away on the U.S eastern seaboard, and he was lying on his back on the sand, watching seabirds swirling in the breeze below a shimmering blue sky, unsuccessfully trying to come to terms with the idea of never seeing Rose again in this life. His world had splintered into myriad pieces. He'd spoken, then, to himself of his roots. His roots and his need for home. That was when he'd decided to come home to England. Rose. Rose.

He braked heavily as a red traffic light brought him back to reality. 'Sorry about that.'

Kate lurched forward, saved only by the tug of her seat belt.

'Very sorry. Won't happen again.'

'That's all right, happens to the best of us.' While they waited for the lights to change she said, 'Have you ever wondered how Phil Parsons makes a living from that farm? Because for the life of me I can't see how he can.'

'Neither can I.'

'He must have some other source of income, mustn't he?'

His lips twitched as he replied, 'One would imagine he must. You can't help but like them both, can you?'

Kate smiled to herself. 'No, you can't. The food appeared beyond reproach, didn't it?'

'I shall pass judgement on that tomorrow. Who knows what the night might bring.' Dan glanced at her and laughed. For one bright moment he appeared to her handsome. She thought of Scott when she thought of handsome and for some strange reason had difficulty remembering what he looked like. Then, like a flash, his laughing face focused in her mind and she grinned.

'What's so amusing?'

'Just thinking of Scott who was before you. You're braver than him. He refused to eat or drink there. Only whisky we had once. And he never let Blossom get anywhere near him if he could help it. She was always after his body, he said.'

'The conceit of the man! I fancy she's after any body, even half presentable, in trousers. I can't help wondering about his balaclava. It's there to hide something, isn't it?'

Kate looked out of the window. 'It's left here after the roadworks. It must be. Maybe he's an escapee from a home somewhere and he's still hiding his identity. Perhaps that's why he has so much sympathy with Hamish.'

'I've an idea it's deeper than that. Here we are. Thanks for coming, Kate. They would have been affronted if you hadn't.'

'That's OK. Thank you for taking me.'

Dan got out and went round to open her door for her.

''Bye. See you, tomorrow. Thanks again for the lift.'

'See you.'

Before she had got the front door open Dan was already charging off down the street.

Wednesday was market day in Barleybridge so not only was there a street market but a cattle market too. Dan, having a morning free because of being on call all night, decided to mingle in the cattle market for an hour, before going to the supermarket to replenish his depleted food stocks.

The sheds and pens at the market were teaming with animals of all kinds: goats and sheep, cows and pigs, chickens and geese. The hustle and bustle, the sights and sounds, were energising and he spent a happy hour wandering about looking at the condition of the animals, some good, some poor. He listened to the auctioneer to see what prices were being achieved at the moment and winced when he heard how low the selling prices were.

Here and there the odd farmer acknowledged him, and he them, with a nod or a touch of his cap and a friendly 'Good morning'. Some stayed for a chat, mostly to bemoan the low prices that day. He inspected the pigs, checked out the goats especially some pygmy goats which at one time he had rather fancied breeding, then went to view the chickens. They were a motley collection of fancy and workaday, and he paused for a while looking them over with a practised eye.

Then the rain came down. Not in a drizzle, which a stout heart could ignore, but a thundering, pelting downpour. Dan hastily retreated under the porch over the front door of the Askew Arms, the oldest and most prestigious hotel in the town. As it was twelve o'clock, he decided to take an early lunch and not bother with his supermarket shopping until the following day.

He'd ordered steak and kidney pie with a half-bottle of house wine and was awaiting its arrival when he heard the loud voice of Lord Askew in the dining-room entrance. Immediately the manager rushed forward to greet him. To Dan's eye the man would have done better to have genuflected and have done with it, for his obsequious bowing and scraping was embarrassing to watch. Lord Askew ignored him and surveyed the dining room with a haughty eye, which wavered over Dan and then came back to him. The manager pointed to a table in the window slightly withdrawn from the others, obviously intending to direct his lordship towards it.

But Lord Askew had other ideas. 'This will do!' He headed for Dan's table and asked if the other chair was free for him to use.

Thinking a bit of courtesy on his behalf would go a long way with a man like Lord Askew, Dan stood up. 'I shall be delighted to have your company, my lord. I dislike eating alone.'

Lord Askew ordered steak and kidney pie too, cancelled Dan's half-bottle of house wine and ordered a whole bottle of the most expensive red wine on the list.

They chatted about the state of the market, the need to keep a finger on the pulse, how farmers could survive in the current economic climate and the value of diversifying.

'Callum Tattersall has come up with another hare-brained scheme. Mushrooms this time. The man's a fool. Tenant farmer of mine, you know, keeps the land and buildings in good trim, better than some, but he's never going to be rich.'

'I have sympathy for him. His wife is very ill.'

'Yes, yes, that's as maybe. Drag on a man is that. My lady wife has always been a great support. You haven't met her?' Dan shook his head. 'Wonderful woman. Like you, speaks straight from the shoulder, always.' Lord Askew fell silent, a smile twitching at his lips.

Their food came and was expertly served to them by the manager himself. Lord Askew downed the wine in less time than it took to say thank you for having it poured. He'd swallowed a second glass before Dan had got halfway through his first, and Dan's plate was still half full when Lord Askew placed his knife and fork together and sat back to unfasten his waistcoat buttons. 'Excellent! Not exactly top notch, this place, bedrooms are damned ghastly, but they do know about food. You're always safe with a good old-fashioned English menu. 'Spect they've been serving steak and kidney pie for three hundred years or more.'

'You're right, it is excellent.'

'You won't mind if I smoke?'

'Well, yes, I do.'

Lord Askew stopped halfway through removing the top of his cigar case. 'You do?'

'I'm sorry, yes, and it does say no smoking in this section. That's why I'm sitting at this table.'

'Never bother about things like that. Not me. However . . .' He put away the cigar case and leant his elbows on the edge of the table, watching Dan finish his meal. 'I recommend the treacle sponge and custard to finish, and we'll have our coffee and brandy in the lounge.'

'I hadn't intended to have pudding.'

'Well, I'm footing your bill, so you will.'

'That's most kind of you.'

'One hundred and fifty-two thousand pounds we got with the charity auction. Good night, eh?'

'It certainly was.'

'Terribly keen, I am, to keep the hunt going. Shambles it all is. Complete shambles. All these job losses. Damned interfering.' When they'd eaten their excellent treacle sponge the manager appeared again to ask if everything was to their satisfaction. 'Coffee and brandy in the lounge, Firth, please. For two.'

'Certainly, my lord, whenever you're ready.'

Dan followed him to a quiet corner, though it was difficult as the hotel was rapidly filling up, but not surprisingly the quietest table was free and Lord Askew took possession of it. As soon as the coffee had been poured for them he said, 'Now, Dan Brown, will you come to see that roan. My daughter's got great hopes for him and I don't want her spending hours of time on it only to be disappointed.'

'On the understanding that I come as an employee of the practice.'

Lord Askew gave a satisfied sigh. 'I'm willing to accept that.'

'So long as you have finished with your own equine practice. I can't attend a client of theirs when they're still officially your vets.'

'Come, come, you can't expect me to . . .'

'I'm sorry. I *might* come if you tell them I'm being called in as a second opinion, though.'

Lord Askew gave another sigh of satisfaction. 'Ah! That's more like it.'

Dan sat back in his armchair, rested his elbows on the arms, placed the tips of his fingers together and said, 'But I would expect to have all your other veterinary work restored to us.'

Lord Askew spluttered into his cup, replaced it in its saucer and wiped his lips on his handkerchief. 'That's asking a damn sight too much. You're too cocky by half.'

'I'm not prepared to be made use of, to reassure you about that roan without some assurance that it's not just a one-off. Making use of my skills to save your skin isn't on.'

'Bet you didn't treat that Arab sheikh like this, else your head would've been off.'

'He knew a good vet when he saw one, my lord, so I was treated with the utmost courtesy, both professionally and personally.'

'Hmph.' Lord Askew shifted impatiently in his chair. 'Well, that's it then. Can't have your expertise, not willing even to put the horse's welfare first.'

He stood, his face flushed bright red with, again, that tinge of blue about his lips. 'Shan't ask again.'

Dan felt concern that matters between them were to be left even worse than before. 'Of course the horse's welfare is my concern, but you must understand I am not here to be picked up and put down at will. It's either all or nothing. I can assure you, you won't regret doing as I ask. In the circumstances I'll pay for my own lunch.'

'No, no. A gentleman's word's his bond. I shall pay and be damned annoyed if you persist.'

'In that case thank you again. It has been a pleasure to lunch with you, Lord Askew. Please feel free to contact me at any time, should you change your mind.'

'Hmph.'

'So I got the free lunch but unfortunately I am no nearer getting his veterinary work back.'

Mungo shook his head. 'One day you will, I'm sure. Are you certain of your diagnosis? After all, you only saw the roan briefly.'

'One hundred per cent.'

'You can be a cocky beggar, you know. Still, if he calls you in for a second opinion . . .'

'He's terribly tempted, I can see that. Let's hope he asks me before he drops down dead.'

'Heart?'

Dan nodded. 'Seems so to me. There's something very likeable about him, you know. A softness that's almost childlike.'

'I suspect you must be the first to think that. He's a hard landlord and a worse father, I understand.'

'He desperately wants to be liked, but he's not sure how to go about it.'

'Honestly, Dan, you're as bad as Miriam. She sees deep hurt where other people see arrogance. She includes you in that category.'

Dan had been getting up ready to leave, but sat down again when Mungo said that. 'Is that how you think of me? Arrogant?'

'Well, let's face it, you are. They all think you are.'

'I might be blunt but I hope never arrogant.'

Mungo laughed. 'Well, perhaps arrogant is too strong a word. But you will have your say. Look at Letty. Look at Zoe. Even Joy feels she's taken a battering. They would all cheer if you left.'

'Is that what *you* want? Because I'll leave tomorrow. Or today even.' Dan eyed Mungo with a bleak look.

'Look here, Miriam would have me strung up if I so much as mentioned the idea of you leaving and, between you and me, I want you to stay too. But for heaven's sake, man, try to be a bit more easy with us all. Right?'

'Right. Off the record, I'd like to stay if you want me. Nothing I'd like better.'

Mungo waved an impatient hand. 'Let's leave it for now. I'm still waiting for a definite answer from the chap we interviewed. See how things work out. OK?'

'OK.' He made to leave Mungo's office and then turned back. 'Thank you for your support. Perhaps it's more than I deserve, having lost you such a good client.'

Mungo retorted, 'Well, yes, it bloody well is more than you deserve, but there you are.' He grinned to soften his harsh words and Dan laughed.

'Your wife is a gem and very perceptive. I didn't know it showed. I'll be more careful in future.'

But he wasn't and he stirred up trouble the very next day.

7

Joy slammed the door of Mungo's flat behind her and flung herself down in his favourite chair. 'Miriam? Are you there?'

'That you, Joy?'

'Yes.'

Miriam entered the sitting room in her dressing gown, rubbing her wet hair with a towel. 'What's the matter? Excuse the garb, I've just got out of the bath.'

'I wouldn't notice if you were starkers.'

'Why? What's happened?'

'Happened? It's what's going to happen if a certain person doesn't mind his Ps and Qs. I'm so blazing mad. Just when I think everything's going with a swing he . . .'

'Yes?'

'He upsets everyone. Who does he think he is?'

'That doesn't sound like Mungo.'

Joy looked up at her, surprised. 'It's not Mungo, it's . . .'

'Dan?'

'Yes, Dan.' Joy's lips tightened into a thin line as she said this.

'Oh, Joy! What's it all about?' Miriam sat herself down and waited.

'It's only a little thing, really . . .'

'Well?'

'Well, no, it isn't a little thing, it's a big thing. You know we have a three-day rota worked out? Start at eight one day and finish at four. Next day work eight till seven with a three-hour break in the afternoon and the next, one till eight?'

Miriam nodded.

'Well, Dan wants us to change the times of the clinics and make it as the girls work, eight hours starting at eight in the morning and finishing at four, or start at one and finish at eight in the evening. Week about.'

'Yes?'

'Yes? What do you mean, "yes"? Why should we change our working practices just because he fancies putting his oar in?'

'It's worth consideration.'

Joy stood up. 'Worth consideration? I don't believe you. I'm the practice manager, not him, and we've worked this system for years. No one's ever complained.'

'So?'

'So? What do you mean, "so".'

Miriam placed a hand on Joy's arm, hoping to placate her. 'He may have hit on a good idea. Have you asked the girls?'

'No point in stirring up a hornet's nest unnecessarily, now is there?'

'Doing this means you'd have an afternoon clinic from, say, two until three and then four thirty till seven thirty, does it? Might be very popular. More clinic time equals more clients, doesn't it surely?'

Joy nodded reluctantly. 'Possibly. But it all depends what Rhodri and Graham and Valentine feel, doesn't it?'

'Of course. Think about it.'

'You're only saying this because you want Dan to stay. Well, Miriam, you'll be pleased to hear that the chap who came for the interview hasn't yet made up his mind. Rang him up an hour ago.'

'Ah!'

'So that's not good news, is it? Dan may be here far longer than any of us wants him to be.'

'I'm very, very sorry to hear that. I have said before, Joy, that you're making a serious error of judgement about him. Why you're getting so wild about him when you now know he'll be leaving eventually I don't really know.'

'But he won't if you have your way. It's his attitude, it riles me. Interfering busybody, he is, and he thinks everyone can work at the same pace as he does. Well, we can't.'

'Perhaps you all should.'

'Are you saying we don't work hard enough?'

'Well, no, not really but . . . '

'You don't have to work with him. Letty agrees with me. She can't wait to see the back of him.'

Miriam couldn't believe her ears. 'You agree with Letty? I thought you were sworn enemies.'

'That Nazi salute he gives her, well, it's a disgrace.'

'There was a time when you thought it appropriate and very funny.'

'On the matter of him going we are as one.'

'Name one thing he does wrong.'

'One?' Joy laughed, unaccustomed mockery in her tone. 'He lost us

Lord Askew's account his first week. Have you got the rest of the afternoon free?' She turned on her heel and stormed out.

But it wasn't the last that Miriam heard about it for when Mungo came up after an intense and exhausting afternoon operating it was the first thing he mentioned. 'You're not going to bring up the subject of Dan, are you?'

'Not if you don't want me to.'

'I don't. I've had my fill.'

'But . . .'

'I'm sick of women with nothing better to do than trump up excuses to put a spoke in the wheels.' He counted them off on his fingers. 'Letty, because she's angry at the way he treats her, but it's nothing more than she deserves. Joy, because as practice manager she feels her nose has been put out of joint. Zoe, because a mole has rung her and informed her of the argument.'

'Well, Zoe is a partner and should know what's happening.'

'And now you, because you want him to stay. I understand Joy has been up and said her piece.'

Miriam nodded. 'For what it's worth I didn't agree with her.'

'I know you didn't; she told me. Out of sheer cussedness I've a mind to ring this chap and tell him it's all off and then they'll be stuck with Dan. Serve 'em all right.'

'Well, you would be justified. He has taken much longer than need be to be accepted. It's quite a good idea, actually, what Dan says.'

'That's what I thought. They've not enough to do, that's the trouble.'

'I shouldn't say that to Joy. I got my head bitten off for mentioning that perhaps they all needed to work as hard as Dan. A longer afternoon clinic might be a good idea, but it might mean the same number of appointments, spread over a longer time with extra hours for Graham et al.'

'It's bitchiness, really personal, you know.'

'Frankly . . . here's a whisky for you . . . I don't know what's wrong with him. If he were a time waster and disappeared for hours on end keeping clients waiting I could understand it. Remember that one we had, I forget his name, we never knew where he was from one hour to the next, terrible chap. You should have heard Joy go on about *him*.'

'Thanks. I remember only too well.' Mungo took a sip of his whisky, leant back in his chair with his eyes shut and said, 'If he got old Askew's account back . . .'

'Plus the equine . . .'

Mungo smiled ruefully. 'They'd still complain.'

Miriam studied his face and thought about how much she loved him:

he could still walk into a room and set her pulse racing. She went to stand beside him and trailed her fingers across his eyebrows. 'You are a lovely man and I love you very much. Never worry, the dust will settle and they'll all calm down.'

But Miriam was wrong. Graham, Valentine and Rhodri were agreeable to changes, though they doubted if the client list would increase, but the female side of the practice were vociferous in their objections.

Squeezed into Joy's office, the lay staff had a protest meeting in their lunch hour, with Joy in the chair. The discussion grew heated almost immediately.

'I like my afternoons in the precinct,' Stephie said.

Letty agreed. 'Makes a nice break and you get things done.'

'I'd like having a morning free. No need to get up early and you could still go in the precinct before you started at one.' This from Kate who, for some reason she couldn't explain, felt she needed to support Dan's idea.

Stephie boiled over. 'Well, you would say that, wouldn't you, just to be different.'

'Not just to be different. I think you're only angry because it was Dan who suggested it. If it had been Mr Price or Rhodri you'd have given it some merit and not blown a gasket like this.'

'You're an item, then, are you, you two?'

Before Joy could put a stop to the personal turn the comments were taking Kate snapped, 'No, we are not. For a start he's years older than me.'

'That didn't stop you with Scott. You were panting after him and he was ten years older than you.'

Kate, squeezed between the filing cabinet and Letty, flushed but remained silent.

Joy rapped on the desk with her pen. 'This won't do. You'll apologise to Kate for that remark, please. Before we go any further.'

Stephie didn't reply.

'Well?'

'I only spoke the truth.'

'That particular truth is none of your business. I'm waiting.'

Stephie mumbled her apology but they knew she didn't mean a word of it. Matters went from bad to worse when Letty said her piece and implied she couldn't wait for Dan to leave. She highlighted his arrogance, his offhandedness, his insolence.

Joy, endeavouring to be fair-minded, said, 'It is not Dan who is on trial here. We're here to discuss the proposal he has about our hours. Let's keep to the subject please.'

Letty was about to speak when Kate broke in, 'With all due respect, Mrs Walker, you are only standing in. It will be us left with the new hours, not you.'

This innocent remark triggered Letty's acid tongue into action, and they were treated to a tirade about the running of the practice and the amount of effort everyone put in, and the inefficiency of . . .

Joy had to shout to get herself heard. 'Just a minute. I'm not putting up with this from anyone. This meeting is closed and we'll reconvene when we've all had time to think. Meanwhile I'll get out a draft rota and circulate it. We might all find ourselves surprised about how nicely it works out.' She stood up and looked at them each in turn, daring them to say another word and, seeing her eyes sparking with temper and her generous mouth pinched tight, they got the message and departed.

Except for Letty. 'Not putting up with this from anyone? I'm not *anyone*. I would have thought you of all people would have acknowledged that I have a right to a say about anything to do with the smooth running of the practice. After all, I did put a lot of money . . .'

'Why don't you just for once allow Colin to wear the trousers?' Joy stormed out and went to spend five minutes with young Copperfield to soothe her frayed nerves. He welcomed her attentions. He was due to have his framework of pins and screws removed the following day and as Joy sat on the floor to play with him she wondered what his future would hold. He couldn't stay with them for ever.

He purred like an old steam engine and with his huge amber eyes staring up at her in adoration she continued to scratch him gently behind his ears, a thing she knew from experience he liked. With good food and lots of attention he was growing into a beautiful cat, with apparently no resentment about the human race for all he'd been through. She examined his feet one by one and saw how well they'd healed. He got off her knee and found a table tennis ball he liked to play with. She bounced it for him and as best he could, lumbered with his ironmongery, he chased after it.

It was warm and comforting in the care room, and Joy stayed far longer than she had intended because as she played she sensed her anger melting away and she felt more like the real Joy, the Joy she preferred. Damn Letty for her acid tongue. Damn Colin for not standing up to her. Damn her money too. Root of all evil when you didn't know how to use it graciously and Letty certainly didn't. Damn them all for their animosity. She'd make the rota so attractive they'd be begging to agree to it.

Joy scrambled to her feet, gently lifted Copperfield into her arms, kissed his lovely ginger head, admired those expressive amber eyes of his and placed him in his cage, giving him a pussy treat as compensation. He badly needed a home, did Copperfield. He mewed at her through the bars and she left a small piece of her heart behind as she carefully closed the care room door behind her.

The row caused by Dan's suggestion rumbled on for days. To alleviate some of the aggravation, Joy rang Lynne to see if she would be returning soon, but her mother answered and said Lynne was still under the doctor, who declared she was far too frail mentally to be able to come back to work just yet. Joy brought up the question of keeping her job open for her and did her mother think that perhaps she wouldn't want to return. 'I'll talk to her about it. I think a complete change of lifestyle would do her more good, but I promise to have an answer for you before the end of the week.'

Joy replaced the receiver and groaned. Facing further weeks with Letty on the desk was almost more than she could bear to contemplate. How could she ever have sided with her about Dan? She must have been mad. She'd talked to Duncan about the situation and he'd agreed with Miriam. Perhaps they did have long periods when there was very little to do and the sooner she drew up a new rota and got them all sorted the better. Did they really need her and two more *all* the time?

Together she and Duncan had set about the new rota and, with his logical mind and her knowledge, they'd done a very good job on it. Today she'd be circulating it to one and all for their approval. There wasn't a single thing on it that they could quibble about, she was sure. Though come to think of it, no doubt Letty would find a few faults. She'd give it out and then depart for lunch with Duncan quick smart.

Duncan came to collect her early because the rain was coming down and he'd cut short his walk. He wandered into the care room and looked at the animals in various stages of recovery. He read their notes in turn and finally came to stand in front of Copperfield. At that moment he was asleep, stretched out full length on his cosy blanket. His notes made Duncan shudder. Copperfield must have become aware he was being watched for his huge eyes opened and stared straight at Duncan. Lazily he got up, stretched and went to the bars. They looked solemnly at each other, long and hard. They both reached out, Copperfield with his paw and Duncan with a finger through the bars and, having made contact, Duncan . . . No, he musn't. They already had

Tiger and Tiger might get very upset about an intruder, and two cats were ridiculous but . . .

Over lunch Joy and Duncan talked animatedly about a holiday they proposed taking in the spring. It suddenly occurred to Duncan. Holiday? Two cats? Impossible. What a to-do. No, he mustn't even think about it.

Then out of the blue, Joy mentioned Copperfield herself, without any prompting. 'He's a gorgeous cat. A soulmate kind of cat. Pins are out now. He'll always have a slight limp, Mungo says, but it doesn't seem to bother him.'

'I don't think there's a white hair on him.'

Joy looked up surprised. 'You've seen him?'

Duncan nodded.

'He's lovely, isn't he?' Joy's voice had a hint of longing in it when she said this.

'He is. Soulmate like you said.'

'Like Tiger.'

'Somebody will want him.' Duncan looked at her, eyes twinkling. Joy was cutting herself some cheese when he said this and she looked up at him, knife poised above the Cheddar, and tried to read his mind. 'You glorious creature you! You fancy having him too, don't you? Am I right?'

'And you?'

Joy nodded emphatically. 'I do.'

'So do I.'

'Let's.'

'Let's.'

'Oh, Duncan! I love you for it. You won't regret it. He's gorgeous, absolutely gorgeous and I love him.'

'And me too?'

'And you too,' Joy said without thinking.

'Do I have to keep on adopting cats to make you say that?' He had a strange, pleading expression on his face when she finally looked at him.

Seeing where this was leading, Joy took stock and then quietly replied, 'I'm not sure. Perhaps two might be enough.'

'I'll make do with that for now. Eat up and we'll go and declare our intentions.'

'The police haven't found out who did it to him.'

'There aren't any words to describe them, are there? And yet he still loves people. A human being would find it difficult to forgive and yet a cat . . . '

'Could be cupboard love. I'm never sure about cats.'

'I am. Done? I'll go and pay.'

'Mungo would laugh.'

'Laugh?'

'Yes. After all you've said about how could anyone love an animal.'

'Why mention *him* just now?'

'It was only about the cat, not about . . .' She looked up at him and wished she hadn't caused his anguish: she'd spoilt the moment for him without intending to. Maybe after all she did love Duncan but wouldn't allow herself to admit it, after all the years of loving Mungo. Joy kissed his cheek and took his hand. 'Copperfield, here we come!'

They walked back into a full-scale row. Letty had come in specially to see the new rota, and she and Stephie and Kate were arguing in the accounts office. Joy could hear their raised voices as soon as she opened the glass door.

'It doesn't matter what you say, Kate, if we give in to this we're done for. They'll think we'll do anything and everything they decide without a thought for how we feel. We've got to put up a protest even if it's only a token one. Alter something somewhere to show we're making a stand.' This was Letty.

Joy put a restraining hand on Duncan's arm. With a finger to her lips she stood listening a little longer and heard Kate say, 'It's for Stephie and me to agree, Mrs Walker.'

'I'm coming out on your side for your sakes.'

'Well, there's no need. Stephie and I quite like the ideas behind this. Don't we?'

Stephie must have nodded because they didn't hear a reply.

Letty declared they were both fools for accepting it so easily and 'what's more, that Dan will see it as a triumph.'

Joy called out, 'We're back!'

Stephie and Letty came out of the accounts office and took their places at the desk. Stephie embarrassed, Letty brazening it out.

'Has Mungo begun operating, Stephie?'

'Not yet, he's talking to Bunty and Sarah One in intensive care.' Stephie looked as though she wished she weren't there and no wonder, with Letty in that mood.

Duncan remembered to be polite. 'Good afternoon, girls. How's things?'

'Fine, thank you.'

'Good. We're hoping to adopt Copperfield.'

Stephie's face lit up. 'What a brilliant idea. He's a lovely cat. I shall miss him.'

'That sounds like a good CV for a cat.'

Stephie smiled, but Letty merely pursed her lips and it didn't flatter her.

Mungo agreed they could take Copperfield, Joy found a carrying cage and decided to accompany Duncan home. 'I shan't be long, but things are quiet and there's two of you, if you get in a panic give me a buzz and I'll come straight back, but I just want to be there to introduce him to Tiger.'

'Oh! We'll hold the fort, won't we, Stephie?' Letty said this with such sarcasm in her voice that Joy vowed there and then to put a stop to Letty's helping out. Either Lynne came back or they got someone new. She couldn't take much more of the woman, she really couldn't.

They placed Copperfield on the kitchen floor still in his cage. Tiger who had come to greet them when she heard their key in the door, stood in the doorway contemplating this change of events. Copperfield peered at her through the bars.

'I think we should feed the two of them right now to let Tiger know he's here to stay. Put Tiger's bowl down first because that's how it's always been for her and then put Copperfield's down a moment after. That way Tiger will feel number one.'

'Good thinking. It won't harm them to have three meals today will it?'

'Of course not. Make sure Tiger gets her own bowl, not the new one.'

As soon as Tiger realised that food was coming up she decided while she waited for it to have a look at Copperfield. Advancing across the floor in silly prancing steps, she arrived at the cage and they met nose to nose between the bars. Spitefully Tiger got her claws out and tried to scratch Copperfield's nose, but he jumped back and she missed. She spat at him and yowled her annoyance at his intrusion, lashing out with unsheathed claws, swiftly and menacingly.

Joy was horrified. 'Hell's bells! Have we done the right thing do you think?'

'She's only establishing some ground rules. They'll be OK soon enough.'

But when they cautiously released Copperfield from the cage Tiger, despite being not yet fully grown, went for him tooth and claw. It's difficult, however, to fight an opponent who won't respond and Copperfield didn't. He was submissive and evasive and non-combatant. When she let up for a moment he walked away from her with complete disdain, leaving her nonplussed. Tiger got scent of the dinner waiting, so she went to eat hers while she thought out her next move. But Copperfield took himself off as though she didn't exist and went on a tour of his new home, came back and, ignoring Tiger completely, went to eat from his bowl.

Joy went back to the practice and Duncan stayed in to act as referee. He found a cardboard box which, with a little help from a sharp kitchen knife, he converted into a temporary bed for Copperfield, lined with a blanket, he placed it on the opposite side of the fire to Tiger's and waited to see the turn of events. Tiger wasn't the only one to be ignored because Copperfield took no notice of Duncan either and the afternoon was spent with all three disregarding each other. *We'll have to call him Copper*, Duncan concluded. His full name was too much for everyday use, and anyway Copper suited him, for his particular shade of ginger was very dark and Copper described it very well indeed. Copper and Tiger. Yes. Yes. He longed for them to make friends but it was many days before there was harmony between the two.

Harmony was the last word Joy would have used about the lay staff at the practice. She wished she could put them all in a sack and give them a good shake. Letty was the problem, but the thought of the arguing that would ensue if she asked her to stop helping out before she'd found a replacement was more than Joy could bear to think of. By the end of the week she learnt that Lynne had definitely decided not to return because she had chosen to register at college and improve her qualifications, so now the way was wide open for recruiting a new member of staff. Within a few days a well-qualified girl had been found and with scarcely concealed delight Joy informed Letty that her services would no longer be required. 'Her name's Annette and she's done veterinary work before. She's newly married, and they've just moved to Barleybridge and she can start immediately, so you can heave a sigh of relief, Letty.'

'I've quite enjoyed myself, actually. I'll be sorry to go. But then Colin does take a lot of looking after. He's very demanding with the hours he has to keep.'

'Thanks for all your help, it's been much appreciated.'

'Any time you have a problem you can rely on me.'

Over my dead body, thought Joy.

So just when Joy thought Christmas was going to be a complete nightmare because of Letty, it looked to be plain sailing once more. They began the new regime when Annette started work, and Stephie and Kate agreed they liked it better. Annette proved to be a pleasant person to work with and Joy found herself with a happy team, well integrated and working with a will, though the hoped-for increase in clients had not yet materialised.

Then Dan came up with another idea. He broached it one afternoon when only Joy and Kate were on duty, and he'd finished his list and was waiting around in reception in the hope of a call. Eyeing the space between the main door and the chairs in the waiting area he said, 'That piece of wall there is a waste.'

'Is it?'

'Yes. I have an idea.'

Joy pointed the pen she was holding in his direction. 'Look! The last time you had an idea all hell broke loose in here.'

Dan smiled. 'But you have to admit it all turned out well, didn't it, in the end.'

'After a lot of suffering, I admit it did.'

'Well, I was thinking the other day, more revenue needed, more ideas. So how about . . .'

'Kate, are we ready for this?'

'Not really, but let him tell us.'

'Selling approved things for small animals.'

'Approved *things*?'

'Items we as a veterinary practice approve of. The right kind of tinned food, or dry if preferred. The right kind of collars and leads for dogs. The right kind of grooming products . . .'

'Stop right there!'

'The right kind of bedding, treats, toys for budgies, toys for hamsters, the list is endless.'

'But my patience isn't. There is no way I'm going to be involved in that kind of thing.'

'But we're supposed to be really into this business of keeping animals usefully occupied so they don't develop behavioural problems through boredom. We should be leading the way. I can just see Barleybridge Veterinary Hospital at the forefront in the field of animal behavourist knick-knacks . . .'

Joy banged her fist on the desk. '*Go away*! Go on, wait somewhere else. I mean it.'

Dan winked at Kate and made his escape into the back, deliberately pausing to study the space beside the main door before he finally disappeared.

'He could be right, you know. It could be a nice little earner. We're always getting asked if we sell things, or for advice and we've nothing to show people. It might be an idea,' said Kate.

'On the grounds that the work and the accounting for it all would far outweigh the profit, I have nothing more to say on the matter.' Joy did a final flourish on the computer and left Kate on her own.

Kate's mind raced through all manner of notions in support of Dan's idea and came to the conclusion that it was a very worthwhile scheme. She mentioned it in passing to Stephie who immediately took the idea on board and couldn't wait to get it all set up.

'Joy disapproves, though.'

Stephie's face fell. 'Aw! Does she? I just fancied having a go at selling those dinky budgie bells and mirrors and things. It's all the rage now, isn't it, activities to stop the poor things from going stir crazy? I reckon we'd be doing them a good turn. Things for hamsters and gerbils, toys for dogs and cats.'

'So do I. But . . .'

'Course, it would mean we'd be approving of Dan.' Stephie turned down the corners of her mouth to show her reluctance to give him credit for anything.

'So . . . why not, for heaven's sake? He works so hard for this practice and you have to admit you're getting to like him just a little teeny bit.' Kate measured about half a centimetre between her thumb and forefinger, and made Stephie laugh.

'OK. OK. Yes, I am. He's kind of growing on me, I admit. We'll make our plans tonight over a meal, shall we?'

'Right. We could have a look around the pet shop in the precinct and see what's on the market.' They gave each other the thumbs-up.

Deviousness wasn't in Kate's make-up really, but it occurred to her that getting Miriam on side might be a good thing and, when she broached the idea to her one afternoon while she was helping to put up the Christmas decorations in reception, she found Miriam was entirely enthusiastic. 'Is it your idea?'

'No, Dan's.'

Miriam raised an eyebrow. 'Oh, dear. We could be stirring things up again. But I'll talk to Mungo.'

'Thank you. I'm sure it would be a good move.'

'So do I. It will be storage of the stock that will be the problem and making sure people don't slip things into their bags on the way out.'

'Exactly. Well, Stephie and I think just by the door isn't quite the best place.'

'Pass me those red balloons, they'll look good in this corner.' Miriam had climbed to the top of the ladder and was balancing precariously, waiting with outstretched hand for the bundle of balloons. 'I think it's a brilliant plan and if someone is needed to take charge of ordering and checking the stock I'll take that on board. Thank you, Kate.' She took the bundle and secured it into the corner of the reception ceiling, climbed down, folded the ladder and said, 'So if I do that, no one can complain about the extra work, can they?'

'Absolutely not.'

They stood together, admiring their hard work, the heavily decorated real Christmas tree with its beautiful fairy lights, the paper bells and silver balls strung across the ceiling, the nativity scene Miriam had bought in Germany for her children and which she insisted must be on view for their sakes on the central windowsill, the silver tinsel bordering the desk and best of all the artificial snow on the window panes, which Mungo always mocked, but which Miriam loved because it made her feel all Dickensian. She squeezed Kate's arm. 'Thank you. You've been such a help.'

'It's been a pleasure.'

'I shall miss you next Christmas.'

'If I've finished college – that is, if I get there – I could come in and give you a hand.'

'You could. That would be lovely. Never fear, you'll get in if I have to throw myself on the admissions tutor's floor and offer myself to him.'

'Miriam!'

'You'll see. And about selling things, leave that with me.'

8

Joy, incensed by the manoeuvring which had been going on behind her back, complained bitterly to Duncan. 'I mean, who is in charge of the practice? Tell me that. Am I the manager or not?'

'Joy, for goodness sake, calm down.'

'They've even worked out how to alter the chairs round to make space for the shelves.' She pointed angrily to herself. 'Ask me? Consult me? Oh, no! I'm very upset.'

'When it was first mooted, what did you say?'

'I said ... all right ... I said to Mungo "over my dead body".'

'Did he try to persuade you?'

'Yes, he did. He turned on his charm as only he can and I refused to listen. He said how much he wanted to go along with Dan's suggestion; more money in the coffers, you know. Then he smiled and that did it. I thought not again, Mungo, you're not getting your own way any more with that celebrated smile of yours.' Her eyes went dreamy and Duncan sighed within himself.

'Ask yourself why?'

She came back from musing on Mungo's charm. 'Why? Why what?'

'Why you have set your mind against it.'

Joy thought for a moment. 'Because I can't stand any more controversy.'

'Who's objecting?'

'Letty for starters, despite it being none of her business now.'

'Well, you can forget her.'

'Miriam for jumping in when she shouldn't. Mungo because he thinks he only has to smile at me and he'll get his own way. Dan because he's Dan.'

'You're being petty.'

'I am?'

Duncan nodded. 'Yes. But thanks for resisting Mungo's charm ... at last.' He reached towards her with a gentle hand and stroked her cheek. 'Why don't you go in tomorrow and start straight in planning everything as if you've never objected. Give them all a shock.'

'Think so?'

Duncan's hand cupped her chin and turned her face towards him. 'With Christmas coming on we don't want trouble, do we? Spirit of goodwill and all that.' He smiled at her with such tenderness that it brought tears to her eyes.

'I don't deserve you loving me.'

'You do.'

Joy shook her head. 'No, I don't. Though by resisting Mungo's charm I could have made my first major step forward, couldn't I?'

'Indeed.'

'I wish you wouldn't get more computer work. You're so much more *here* when you're not totally absorbed in it. I don't even exist for you when you're working. Do you know that? It is hard.'

'For you I won't, then. The next project which comes in I shall send straight back by return.'

'Oh, yes, I bet!'

'I will, if it means so much to you.'

'What would we live on?'

'Love?'

They both laughed, Joy with abandon, Duncan with a sad guardedness that hurt. Joy's glance slipped past him to come to rest on the flames dancing in the hearth. She began to despise herself for so lightly dismissing Duncan's love and, instead, snatching at morsels of Mungo's, which in reality didn't belong to her and never would. How much longer would she keep chasing shadows? Joy reached out and touched his lips with her fingers. 'I'll take your advice and go in tomorrow and begin to plan.'

He kissed her fingers as they lingered on his mouth. 'I love you,' he said, but she didn't respond in kind.

Dan was delighted to find his idea had been taken up with such enthusiasm, mainly because he'd decided, yet again, if he possibly could he'd definitely stay. He liked the people, he liked the clients, he liked the countryside and Barleybridge and . . . well, for the first time in years he felt 'at home'. Before he put his things into the Land Rover he shaded his eyes and looked up at Beulah Bank Top. One day soon he'd walk up there, right to the very top, and survey his kingdom. He turned round and looked down into the town, a town unspoilt by twentieth-century buildings and looking as it must have done for centuries. The spires, the colourful roofs, the lovely mellow stone buildings, the shining band of river wending its way through and the beautiful arching trees, devoid of their summer plumage but still beautiful, made his heart sing. He'd buy a house and settle into the bustling life of Barleybridge.

Superimposed on his view of the town, without warning, came Rose, with her long fair hair hanging loose inviting him to touch it, love in her eyes and on her lips that teasing grin of hers, teasing him into making love, giving him everything there was of her . . . the thought of her wrenched at his heart so viciously he almost doubled up with the pain and his life turned to ashes in that moment.

He flung his bag and telephone on to the passenger seat, stuck his list on the dashboard and drove wildly out of the car park, missing the bench at the back door by a cat's whisker.

His first call was Porter's Fold so he took the steep road to Magnum Percy, turning left before he reached the village itself. This was scarcely more than a narrow cart track with tarmac, which had fallen away at the edges leaving great water-filled hollows on either side. The only passing places were where a field gate happened to be and Dan hoped he wouldn't meet another vehicle coming the other way. The landscape became increasingly harsh the further he drove, till he finally saw the house and the farm buildings. The land looked barely fit to support even sheep.

Hanging lopsidedly at the top of an old post was a sign saying 'Porter's Fold'. It actually said 'Poter old', the other letters having been obliterated by years of weather. The gate was open, propped back by two stones taken from the wall. He drove in, parked, put on his boots, picked up his bag and wandered towards the farm buildings, in no mood this morning to tolerate anyone at all.

Tad Porter came out to greet him. An exceptionally tall grey man, sparse of flesh, with a big hooked nose emphasised by his overhanging forehead and abnormally thick, bushy grey eyebrows shading a pair of morose grey eyes. He wore an old bowler hat on his grey hair, completely at odds with the corduroys and layers of holey jumpers on his body. All Dan got as a greeting was a jerk of his head towards an open stable door; it suited his mood so he didn't even try to make conversation. There were two heifers in the stable, one looking well, though her eyes lacked sparkle, the other looking as though death was snapping at her heels. Tad pointed with his boot toe at the sick one. 'Acting drunk.'

'You mean her movements are uncoordinated?'

Tad nodded. The heifer was tied up so Dan undid the rope and tried to get her to walk for him back and forth, but she slipped wildly about, her legs out of her control, almost going down as he turned her back towards her stall.

Dan took her temperature and, while he waited, asked, 'Scouring at all?'

Tad shook his head.

'Eating?'

Another shake.

'No temperature. Could be one of several things. Obviously some problem with its brain. Tapeworm cyst, tumour, lead poisoning . . .' Dan looked round the stable for anything at all which the heifers might have got at, but saw no tractor oil or windows where they could have reached the putty, nor old flaking paint. 'Seems unlikely in here. Whatever it is it's well advanced. I'll take blood samples. The other showing any signs?'

Yet another shake of that head.

He took the blood samples, packed his bag and said, 'I'll be back tomorrow. I don't like the look of her at all.' Dan stood looking at the two cows, his mind ranging around several possibilities, unable to put his finger exactly on the problem. 'She hasn't been out in the field these last few weeks?'

Tad shook his head.

'I see. Keep an eye on her. Ring if she gets worse later today and I'll come out. It's puzzling, very puzzling. In any case, I'll see you tomorrow, Tad. Good morning to you.' Dan touched his cap, gave a final look round the stable and left. It was the first time in his working life that he'd managed to conduct a visit with so few words being exchanged. What a strange man. What a farm. A funny mixture of farm and scrapyard, with the remains of cars and lorries and vans strewn in corners of the yard and in the adjacent fields. Not modern vehicles, but old nineteen thirties and forties ones, beaten into submission by the weather and total neglect.

After a morning filled with calls, Dan went back to the practice with a shop-bought lunch, intending to sit on the outside bench to eat it and think. Think about Rose, mainly; and however he was going to overcome his loss. Beautiful, beautiful Rose. Why had she chosen him, with nothing to recommend him compared with the men she could have had? Was he a whim? Someone to satisfy an idle summer? An amusing incident? No, that was unworthy of him. The passion she gave him was real love, that could never be in doubt. He certainly loved her or he would not have asked her to marry him. Involuntarily he reached out to take hold of her. He gazed down at his empty hand and longed for her: not only for her bodily presence beside him but for her companionship, her friendship and her humour. Dan remembered how often they'd laughed together, how ... His thoughts were interrupted by Perkins bounding out of the door on his way out for his afternoon walk.

Miriam shut the door behind her, pulled her coat collar closer and then realised someone was on the seat. 'Dan! What on earth are you doing, sitting out here on a day like this? Why don't you go inside?'

He smiled up at her, saying, 'Needed to think.'

Miriam perched on the end of the bench while Perkins did his big greeting scene, small teeth exposed in a grin, tail wagging madly, ears pricked, front feet on the bench, taking the admiration like a regular pro.

Dan rubbed his hand on Perkins's head. 'Now, Perkins, what are you doing interrupting a fella's quiet lunch? Eh?'

Perkins heaved himself up and settled upright beside Dan, shuffling along the bench until he was resting his shoulder against his. Dan removed the remains of his sandwich away from Perkins's temptation. 'They can be a great comfort, can't they, dogs?'

'They can. In times of need.'

'Very understanding.'

Perkins felt tempted to lick Dan's face in appreciation of his approval, but just in time remembered the good manners he'd been taught and snuffled in his ear instead.

'Exactly.' Miriam didn't look at Dan's face, that private look he had warranted her discretion. 'Good friends, especially Airedales.'

'Indeed.'

'I'll leave you to finish your lunch. Come, Perkins.' She stood up, facing the icy wind swirling down from the slopes. 'We'll be off.' Without looking at him she squeezed Dan's shoulder, gave it a pat and set off, with Perkins leaping around her legs in excitement. Her back to Dan, she raised both arms in the air and waved goodbye.

He called out to her. 'Thanks for taking on the ordering.'

'My pleasure!' came back to him on the wind.

What a joy, thought Dan, to come home after a hard day to someone like Miriam: warm and welcoming and sympathetic. Yet she wasn't sloppy and sentimental, honey-tongued or over-sweet, simply a loving, sensitive woman. It would be worth another try to gain that world for himself, for at the moment he was living only half a life.

The back door opened and it was Kate. 'Oh, there you are, Dan. I've looked all over for you. Tad Porter's been on the phone. Can you go out to see his cow again? She's worse.'

It was a moment before he answered her, taking a deep breath to ensure he gave nothing away with a shaky voice, to be apologised for, blaming it on a frog in his throat. Kate was no fool. 'Thanks. It's a puzzle. I'll go there first before Beulah Bank. OK.'

Tad was waiting for him in the yard, still as a statue, head hanging low like a sick animal. With a jerk of his head to Dan he turned to go into the stable. A sickening feeling of disappointment came over Dan as he followed him. The cow was convulsing. Tad spoke first. 'Third time i' two hours. She's for 't'knacker's yard. T'other's sick an' all.' Tad leant against the doorpost. 'Yer ta late.'

'I'm so sorry. This is lead poisoning or I'm a Dutchman. You said they hadn't been out for weeks.'

'Aye. Well. They're Connie's heifers, and she's 'ad 'em out. "For a change," she said.' He shook his head in despair at her fanciful ways. 'Been out in t'field and wouldn't come when she called. Taken 'em in there a lot this winter when I'm up top with the sheep. Easier, being nearer than their own. 'Appen that's it.'

'Old batteries?'

Tad looked away. 'Perhaps.'

'That's it, then. Lead poisoning. Youngsters are notoriously curious, you don't need me to tell you that. Well, either I leave her to die or we put her out of her agony.'

'Give her a jab, let's have done with it. Missus'll be upset.'

'Does she want to be here? Should she make the decision?'

'No.'

'Are you sure?'

'I said no. Get it done.'

So Dan despatched the cow out of her misery, and felt inadequate and angry with himself. 'This live one . . .'

'Going same way. Tha might as well give her a jab too, and 'ave done.'

'There's a chance here. She isn't convulsing yet. Once that starts it's all too late.'

'It's the money.' He pondered the situation for a while, during which Dan stood patiently waiting.

'It's worth a try? Isn't it?'

Tad appeared to make up his mind. 'Grand lass is this one. Let's have a go.'

Dan took blood samples, labelled them and injected the heifer with the appropriate drug for lead poisoning. 'Are these the only two young ones you have?'

Tad nodded. 'She has two house cows for her cheese making and cream for t'market and that, and these two she was hoping to bring on. We're sheep really, tha knows.'

'Right. I'll be back first thing tomorrow. I should have the results when I come so we'll know one way or the other.' He left with a cheerful good afternoon and a touch to his cap. When he glanced back before revving up, Tad was still propping up the door frame studying his remaining heifer.

He'd damn well have to save it or the whole day would have been a disastrous write-off. What hadn't helped his day was encountering Letty in the precinct when he'd shopped for his lunch. She'd emerged from the beauty salon right at his feet as he queued outside the sandwich bar. Even to his masculine eye there'd been a complete sea change in Letty's appearance and he couldn't ignore it. Gone was the pale, fading-into-the-background Letty: her cheeks had a soft, warm bloom to them and her slightly prominent eyes had been effectively made less so by skilful eye make-up; on her lips she had a rose-tinted lipstick, which softened them and filled them out. Her hair had been highlighted and cut into a smart bob, which flattered her face. He saw she had potential to look attractive. 'Why, it's you, Letty! You look wonderful! What have you been doing to yourself?'

Momentarily Letty had bridled with pleasure, then recollected herself. 'Don't I usually look wonderful?'

With anyone else but Letty that would have been a statement over which the two of them could have laughed, but not with her. 'Well, I didn't mean . . . it's just that you look extra specially wonderful today. Been treating yourself?'

'No. It was a complimentary appointment, came through the post.'

'Well, they've certainly done a fantastic job on you. You seem to be getting some surprises of late, first the flowers from an unknown admirer and now this.'

Letty, flustered by his teasing, had blurted out, 'I've also won a weekend for two from our local travel agent.'

'No-o-o-o! Some people have all the luck. Where to?'

'Our choice in Europe and we're going to Paris. We've never been, you see, Colin and me.'

She was close enough to nudge and Dan had done just that and winked. 'Romantic weekend in Paris! Eh?'

'Don't be ridiculous. Romantic! Huh!'

The queue had moved up and Dan had to go inside.

Letty said, 'I'll wait, I want a word.'

Dan had bought his sandwich and a piece of carrot cake, and came out swinging a jaunty carrier bag to find her awaiting him, arms folded, ensconced on a seat. He had stood in front of her like a small schoolboy in the headmistress's study.

He remembered the expression on Letty's face when she looked up at him. 'What on earth are you thinking of, encouraging this idea of selling things?'

'As you are so keen to maximise the earnings of the practice I would have thought it would have had your approval.'

'Well, it hasn't. It is diminishing. Selling *stuff*! As though we have to scratch about in corners looking for income. It is a professional business, not a pet shop!'

'I see your point, but we have to move with the times and, yes, it will bring in money, but also we shall be giving a service to our clients. What's more, we shan't be selling tat, Miriam will see to that.'

'Miriam! Huh!'

Affronted by Letty's disdain of Miriam, Dan sprang to her defence. 'I happen to have a high regard for Miriam.'

'Do you indeed. Not surprising considering how much she likes you. You've got her round your little finger. If you say "jump" she'll say "how high".'

Dan had struggled to control the anger he felt rising in his heart. 'I wouldn't dream of putting a lovely person like Miriam in such a position. I value her too much. However, when all is said and done, Mungo is keen, Colin approves, so does Zoe though somewhat reluctantly, Miriam has volunteered to do all the ordering et cetera, and the girls can't wait to get started. So I'm afraid you've been outmanoeuvred.' He'd leant over confidentially and, speaking softly into her ear, said, 'By the way, the angry headmistress look you've put on doesn't suit the new Letty.' Dan held up his lunch bag. 'Must go. Busy day. You look great. Colin won't recognise you.'

He'd charged off towards the car park and therefore didn't see Letty, a moment later, give herself a smile of approval at her reflection in the bookshop window.

But what had made his day even worse was having the misfortune to bump into Lord Askew coming out of the car park. Dan touched his cap and greeted him, intending to pass by without saying more than a pleasant 'Good afternoon'.

But Lord Askew would have none of it. 'How you doing, Brown? Eh?'

'Fine, my lord. And you?'

Lord Askew had looked beyond Dan's shoulder and said, 'All the better if I had you on board.'

'Roan no better?'

'Trouble is my vet can't see what you can see. Are you certain?'

'Ninety-nine point five per cent certain. Need to examine him, of course.'

Impatiently Lord Askew had replied, 'I know that. I know that. Would you come as a second opinion? For me.'

Dan had considered his request and, although it didn't comply with what he had originally said, he decided someone had to give way if he was ever going to get the equine work. 'I'll phone your vet and make arrangements.'

'Standen-Briggs. Giles. As one gentleman to another, thank you. I make no promises mind.'

'No promises.'

There were people in Barleybridge that afternoon who witnessed the handshake between the two of them and paused to wonder why on earth the new vet and that old basket Lord Askew could be doing such a thing. But they were, because they'd seen them, and Lord Askew had looked well pleased.

Dan, reviewing his day, had not been quite as pleased, but felt he'd made a significant step forward. He was picking up his things prior to leaving for home and a night on call when he heard Kate saying she must get off or she'd miss the next bus. 'I'll give you a lift if you like, Kate. Car off the road?'

'It is. I have a nasty feeling it might be terminal.'

'Well, all cars do reach that stage eventually, not worth the repair.'

'I would be grateful, but won't it be out of your way?'

'Frankly, yes, it will, but I've had such a dreadful day some pleasant company would be welcome.'

'I'm feeling flush tonight. Shall we stop for a drink on the way? My treat.' She looked at him and thought what a pity it was that he lived alone; as Mia would say, he'd make someone a good husband.

'That would be nice.'

They chatted about this and that, finished their drinks and when Dan offered to buy them another Kate accepted because she was enjoying herself so much, listening to tales of Dan's exploits in the Middle East. He dug in his wallet for a note, moaned that he'd forgotten to call at the cash point and might not actually have enough cash to pay for two drinks, and finally dragged out a crumpled note which looked as though it hadn't seen the light of day for some considerable time. Dan smoothed it out saying, 'I hope you don't think that's a sign that I'm mean with my money. I don't normally have to *prise* notes out of my wallet.'

He headed off to the bar and, as Kate watched him go, she saw he'd dropped a photograph on the floor. She picked it up and thought, 'Wowww!'

It was of a girl, a natural beauty, who positively sizzled sex appeal. Her personality came right off the picture and zonked you in the eye. She turned it over and saw the words 'Rose. At home'. She had the kind of face Kate would have given the world for. The house behind her, well! If that was 'at home' Kate could have done with being on her way there right now. It was just how she imagined the wealthy lived on the east coast of the States. Such style. She guessed there'd be a pool the size of a lake, bathrooms galore, a kitchen to die for and ... but Dan was coming back so she laid it on the table. He put down the drinks and saw the photo.

'You dropped it on the floor when you pulled out the ten-pound note. I couldn't help but look. I'm sorry.'

Dan looked at it but didn't speak. He left it lying there and it made for awkwardness between them: Kate embarrassed, Dan lost in thought. He picked up his orange juice and the ice beat a tattoo in the glass. Kate sipped her drink, outfaced by his heavy silence – so heavy it was almost palpable. She thought, *If this silence lasts another minute I shall die. Who the blazes is she to upset him like this? Mind you...*

The minute passed, and suddenly Dan picked up the picture and stored it away in his wallet. 'Someone I knew in the US of A. Ever been?'

'No. Is it nice?'

He downed his juice in one go and stood up. 'Nice isn't a big enough word to describe it. Go there some time. It's amazing, larger than life. With your sense of humour you'd have a ball. I'm ready to go. Have you finished?'

Kate gulped down her drink and stood up, glad to be leaving.

He chatted about something and nothing all the way home and she wished she could take on some of the burden of trying to keep normality between them but she couldn't. She bet that girl in the photograph would have coped wonderfully well. No crippling embarrassment for her, oh no! She'd simply have sparkled a little and the difficult moment would have slipped away. When they reached her house Kate made to get out, happy to be escaping, but Dan insisted he open her door for her and wouldn't leave until she was safely inside.

'Goodnight and thanks for the lift.'

'My pleasure, Kate.'

Kate went in to find Mia worried. 'He said he'd be back about six and it's nearly eight. Do you think your dad's all right?'

9

They waited until half past nine, growing more and more anxious as the minutes passed. Kate adopted the role of placid acceptance that Gerry could have met someone, or broken down, or gone for a drink, or got held up at the office, or was taking someone out for a meal to help push some deal through, but at bottom as the seconds ticked away she had begun to grow exceedingly anxious. 'After all, Mia, he's been late before.'

'But before he's always rung and let me know. He knows how I worry.'

'Well, don't. He'll be here.' With relief Kate remembered his meetings. 'I know, it'll be a model railway meeting and he's forgotten to say.'

Mia looked relieved. 'Of course! They're always on a Thursday and it's Thursday. Honestly, I am stupid.' She stood up and cheerfully began to fill the kettle. 'He'll be ready for this. You know how he talks himself to a standstill when he goes.' She glanced at the clock. 'He'll be in any minute now, you'll see.'

Kate occupied herself writing a letter to a school friend but she'd written four sides and her father still hadn't come home. She felt as though a cannon ball had replaced her heart. A terrible feeling of desolation came over her.

Mia asked her whom she was writing to and she couldn't answer. Looking down at the letter, she hadn't the vaguest idea to whom it was addressed. Had she a screw loose? Was this how it affected you? Unable to answer the simplest question? Kate looked up at Mia and saw reflected in her eyes the fright she herself felt. 'I . . .'

Mia took advantage of Kate's pause to say, 'You feel like I do? There really is something wrong, isn't there?'

'Of course there isn't. Honestly, Mia, if you haven't got something to worry about you find something. You know Dad, he'll be fine.'

'You don't sound very convinced.'

'Well, I am. Honestly. I am. He's probably going to come rolling home in a taxi.'

'Kate! Gerry's never the worse for drink.'

'Actually that's not quite true, is it? I can remember the time he went to that reunion . . .'

'That was different.'

'And when he won Salesman of the Year. Remember that? How you laughed.'

'Well, that was different too. He deserved to get drunk. He wouldn't drink and drive, though, would he. He's strict about that, Gerry is. Isn't he?'

'Very.' Kate looked down at her letter and hadn't the heart to write any more. She closed the writing pad and pushed it away. 'Look, we're both of us being ridiculous. Make the tea. I bet he's here before you've poured it.'

But he wasn't and Kate had eaten two chocolate biscuits and drunk two cups of tea, and still he hadn't arrived. They heard a car and looked at each other, embarrassed at having been so concerned. But it wasn't Gerry, it was Lance from next door on late turn.

'If we ring the police they'll think we're crackers. After all, it's only eleven. They'll laugh and be tempted to say he's having a night out on the tiles.'

Mia was shocked. 'Gerry! A night out on the tiles!'

'Yes, but they don't know Dad, do they, like we do. They don't know he doesn't. Plenty of men do, you see.'

Determined to be reasonable, Mia said, 'When it gets to midnight I'm ringing the police. You go to bed.'

'I shan't.'

'Did you hear me? You go to bed.'

'I shan't. It's my dad.'

'It's my husband. Go to bed.'

'You only want me to go so I won't see how worried you are. Well, we'll share it. I'm not a child.'

'No.'

That cannon ball in her chest had grown larger. Mia was quite right, her dad would have let them know if he could. He knew how Mia worried. So why couldn't he let them know? 'We are fools. I'll ring his mobile.'

'Of course. We are idiots. He's never without it.'

But the mobile rang and rang. So Dad had been separated from his phone. Why? She left a text message for him. 'He'll have left it in his car and he'll be in the meeting, or the pub. Let's stop worrying. Dad knows how to take care of himself. Always has.'

Mia thought a moment and then replied, 'Of course you're right. Well, I'm off to bed. We'll look silly if we both sit up and he rolls in, fit as a fiddle and wondering what the fuss is about. You use the bathroom first. I'll tidy up.'

But Mia didn't go to bed. She sat downstairs, desperately trying to read the novel she'd been recommended by a neighbour. It was the story of a woman who'd had more crises in her life than seemed possible, but she was rising above it all and triumphing in the end. Losing three husbands in an assortment of incidents which stretched the imagination to its limits became more than Mia could believe, so she snapped the book shut thirty pages before the end and decided to read no more. By now it was half past one. She heard a step on the stairs. 'Kate?'

'You said you were going to bed.'

'Well, I got reading. It's a load of rubbish, though, so I'm off to bed now.'

'Can't sleep for wondering.'

'You'll be cold. Go and get your dressing gown and we'll have a cup of Ovaltine or something.'

'I'm all right. I'll make it.'

They sat until two o'clock, avoiding conversation and especially avoiding looking each other in the eye.

Mia got up to wash the mugs. 'I'll ring first thing in the morning.'

'Who will you ring?'

'I don't know.'

'Hospitals?'

Mia nodded.

'Police?'

She nodded again, not trusting herself to speak.

'Shall I?'

'No. I'm his wife.' Mia took a deep breath and confessed to her fears: 'It's a nightmare I'm not brave enough to face.'

'We'll face it together. You and me.'

Mia turned from the sink and gave her half a smile. 'Let's be honest with each other, something must have happened to him.'

'Of course it hasn't. What is it they say? "No news is good news."'

'That's right. He'll be parked up somewhere because he's realised he's too tired to drive. He's fallen asleep in his car by mistake, hasn't he?'

Kate had too much common sense to have any truck with ghosts or psychic something or others but the moment Mia said that, it triggered the idea in her mind that somewhere he was doing just that, except he wasn't asleep he was dead. She shuddered.

'I said you'd be cold. Go on, go back to bed. You've work tomorrow.'

Dawn found the two of them sleeping with their heads resting on their arms on the kitchen table. Kate woke, panicking, puzzled why she was sitting in the kitchen and not in bed. Dad! She got up, stiff with cold. She stretched and felt her bones creak. Dad! How could she have *slept*? Guilt sidled through her veins. 'Mia, are you awake? We've slept in.'

'Ring up. Please.'

'I'll have a drink of water first, I'm so dry.' As she put down the empty glass on the draining board the doorbell rang.

Mia, still fully dressed, stalked like an automaton down the narrow hall. Kate stood in the kitchen thinking, *It'll be the milkman wanting his money. It must be. Please let it be the milkman wanting his money. Please. It's Friday so it must be him.* She heard Mia invite whoever it was inside. So it wasn't the milkman. She went to stand in the kitchen doorway and, looking down the hallway, saw two police officers and just before she fainted she heard one of them say, 'Mrs Howard? . . . found . . . on the hard shoulder . . . sitting in the car . . . Unfortunately he'd passed away . . . Apparently natural causes. I'm so very sorry.'

The whole ghastly shrieking nightmare put the two of them into a permanent state of shock. Mia formally identified him and once his body was released after the post-mortem, they rigidly went through the process of organising the funeral.

Every night when she went to bed Kate felt as though she were lying at least a foot above the mattress. She couldn't sleep. She couldn't rest. Couldn't eat. Couldn't smile. Couldn't anything. Every part of her was paralysed by the suddenness of his going. The whole of her life on hold. Her car was still at the garage. She wasn't going in to the practice. Not to see him ever again. She couldn't accept it, couldn't, wouldn't believe it. She couldn't talk to anyone at all. Not even Mia. And what *she* was going through Kate could only guess, for she remained stoically getting on with life as though Gerry would walk in through the door each evening and hadn't died of a heart attack after he'd pulled on to the hard shoulder apparently not feeling well.

Kate dragged herself through the funeral, and when it came to the time for his nearest and dearest to toss earth on to the coffin, that appalling, flesh-crawling act, Mia did her duty, but Kate shook her head, her mind shying away from the finality of doing that very dreadful thing.

After they'd all gone Mia said, 'I shall sell his car. I don't want that Beetle thing. And we shall move out of here. I can't stay here, not with him gone. It's always been his house, not mine. This nineteen thirties stuff he had such a passion for isn't my passion at all.'

'I've always thought you loved it. But I want to stay here. We could always sell the furniture and buy some new. Redecorate.'

'We shan't. And his train set, that'll have to go.'

'Mia, let's move slowly. We'll feel better in a while, then we can decide. Christmas isn't the time for selling up anyway. Let's wait till spring.'

'Don't think I'll change my mind because I shan't. I think we'll go away for Christmas. Can't have it here just the two of us. Disaster, that would be. We'll join a house party or something, where it's all organised. Together. No one need know we've just lost your dad. There's sure to be a cancellation somewhere and I don't care where. Then we'll sell the house when we get back and make a new start. You and me. Just you and me. By ourselves.'

They were sitting in the front room on the hard green sofa with its hard arms, drinking a bottle of wine from Mia's store in the cellar. This sofa had been part of Kate's life ever since she could remember. Could she manage without it? She doubted she could, but apparently Mia could.

Arranged on the mantelpiece were the sympathy cards. Not a single one from a blood relative. All of them were from the practice or Mia's art class or the Model Railway Society or Dad's office or the gallery where Mia occasionally had an exhibition. So now she, Kate Howard, had no living relative. Only Mia and she looked as though she was going to make life a living hell with all her unexpected ideas. What worried Kate was that Mia had never cried, not once, whereas Kate herself had wept buckets.

'Another top-up?'

Kate shook her head. 'No, thanks. I'm going to bed.'

'If you want to sleep in our room for company, that's all right with me.'

Kate shook her head. 'No, thanks. Nice of you to offer, but . . . well, we've got to get used to it, haven't we?'

'I'm afraid so.' She took a sip from her glass. 'I thought we'd live into old age together, but we shan't, not now. He's been my anchor since the day I met him. I know we were not really alike, in temperament and interests, but we complemented each other as you might say. I shall miss him.'

'Of course you will.'

'So will you.'

'Even if he was an old curmudgeon sometimes. But now you remember only the best bits, don't you?'

Mia didn't look at her. 'Oh, yes. That's human nature.' She twirled her wineglass by the stem. 'You've to get on with things, you know. If he is looking down at us, think of the pleasure he'll have when you get into college. He'll be marching all over heaven telling even the Angel Gabriel what you've achieved.'

'Now he's gone there's no one living with the same blood in their veins as I have. No one at all. Except my mother and she doesn't count. But I've got you, haven't I?'

'We'll manage, you and me, very well. A flat, a modern flat is what I want. Minimalism. That's what I shall go for.'

'Mia!'

'He wouldn't mind, wouldn't your dad.'

Kate wasn't too sure about that. She was certain he'd like the idea of them living on in his nineteen thirties world, but if it pleased Mia then . . . She wandered upstairs to bed, settling herself for sleep, feeling akin to an empty shell, utterly without life inside her, but at the last moment before she slept she remembered Dan's words as he stood beside her at the graveside gripping her arm to comfort her. 'Take heart, Kate. Stick by Mia and fulfil your dad's ambitions for you. That's the best gift you can give him now.'

Two days after the funeral Kate had her first day at work. She arrived home at half past four, exhausted by keeping up the pretence of being able to cope, no problem. Mia had made a cup of tea and they sat together in the kitchen making desultory conversation. Mia had obviously made an attempt to begin painting again, but had not got far. She noticed Kate looking at her materials laid out at the end of the table with the brushes clean of paint and the paint rag still pristine. 'I'll clear it away. I haven't the heart . . . to paint right now.'

'Never mind, it'll happen when you're ready.'

'I'm not going to answer the sympathy cards. What can you say but "thanks"? There isn't another thing to say.'

'No, there isn't, is there.'

'I've booked us away for Christmas. Two cancellations. North Devon, Ilfracombe, not too far to go. Father Christmas and all that jazz. But it'll be easier than staying here.'

'I'm not going to the staff do.'

'Why not? Your dad wouldn't mind, I'm sure. He wasn't much of a one for parties but he'd have liked you to go.' She reached across and took hold of Kate's hand. 'Go on.'

'No. I'd only be a wet blanket. They wouldn't know what to say, a week since Dad ... you know ... and a week to Christmas. It'll be kinder to keep right out of it.'

'It was nice of Dan to come to the funeral.'

'Yes.'

'He's a nice chap, a very nice chap. Knows just what to say, as if he's been through it.'

'That's it, Mia! You're not just a pretty face. She's died, that's it.'

'Who's died?'

Kate stood up. 'The girl in his photograph. He was so funny about it, withdrawn, you know. How terribly sad.'

'Explain.'

So Kate described the incident in the pub when he dropped the photograph and Mia said, 'Well, it makes sense, I suppose.'

The doorbell rang and neither of them wanted to answer it, not any more, but it rang again with such insistence that Kate, as she was on her feet, volunteered to go.

Standing on the doorstep was a very well-dressed woman, elegant almost, about her own height with hair which could only be described as coiffured. Immaculate make-up, narrow face and unfathomable eyes. A tad too thin. Conscious she wasn't looking her best, Kate said, 'Yes?'

'I've come to see Katrina Howard and I'm sure you must be she.'

'That's me.'

'I read about your father in the paper. I'm so sorry. Good thing he was chairman of the Model Railway Society, otherwise I don't suppose he would have hit the headlines and I would never have known. I would have been here earlier but I've been so busy. Work, you know. How are you?'

'I'm all right.'

'There's a Mrs Howard, isn't there?'

Kate sensed a crisis looming. 'You're asking some funny questions. Who are you exactly?'

'I'm Tessa Fenton.'

'Tessa Fenton?'

'Yes, you don't know the name, do you?'

'It seems familiar but I can't ...'

'I would have thought your father would have told you. I'm your mother, Katrina.' She smiled, exposing unbelievably even teeth.

Kate thought she might be going to faint for the second time in her life. Her mother! Her mother? Her world went black, then red, then she refocused her eyes and saw *her mother standing there in front of her.* She grasped the door frame with both hands to steady herself.

Her mother filled Kate's silence with, 'Aren't you going to ask me in? We can hardly talk on the doorstep.'

'Yes. Yes. Come in.' Then she thought about Mia. 'Wait there, I'll tell Mia. She may not ... Sit on the chair.'

Kate went into the kitchen and closed the door behind her. Mia was standing by the sink putting on her rubber gloves.

'Mia! Oh, Mia!'

Mia spun round at the sound of panic in Kate's voice. 'What's happened?'

'Are you ready for a shock?'

Mia blanched and sat down rather rapidly. 'What?'

'Well, I don't know how to tell you this, but there's a woman come to see me.' She took a deep, shuddering breath as though suffocating. 'She says she's my mother. Tessa Fenton.'

'Dear God!'

'She's in the hall. May I ask her in?'

Mia stood up, looking incredibly flustered. 'Take her into the sitting room and talk, while I rush upstairs and tidy myself. She musn't see me like this. I'm a mess.' Mia ripped off the rubber gloves and flung them in the sink.

'Right. I don't know what to say.'

'Let her do the talking then, and you listen ... I don't know why she's decided to turn up right now.' *And how I wish she hadn't,* thought Mia as she raced up the stairs. This was the one thing she had dreaded for years. Gerry had always said she'd never come but now she had and ... Mia judged her impact in the bathroom mirror. Whisked her hair into order. Flicked powder on her face. Rushed lipstick round her mouth. Too red. Mouth like a tart's. Lavatory paper. Rubbed it off. Tried a pink one. Liked it better. Despised her dress. Decided to change. Messed her hair. Combed it again. Breathed deeply. Took herself in hand. Walked down the stairs, heart hammering, mouth dry, to meet a woman she could cheerfully have murdered on sight. When she took in the expensive detail of her aubergine business suit, the confidence, the worldly look of her, Mia's fingers itched to grip a carving knife to stab her right below that big silver brooch on her lapel where she judged her heart would be if she'd had one. But there was no doubting she was genuine, for when she looked at her, Mia realised where Kate got her good looks from, except Kate's expression was sweet whereas hers was ...

Graciously the woman extended her hand towards Mia. 'How do you do? You must be Gerry's wife. Katrina and I need to thank you for all the care you've given her over the years.'

Mia's dry mouth made it difficult to answer. She ran her tongue round her front teeth but it made little difference. 'No thanks needed. It's been a privilege to care for Kate. An absolute privilege.' She shook hands and found Tessa's slight, excessively manicured hand with its aubergine painted nails bony and dry, but the grip firm. 'Won't you sit down? A drink. Tea, coffee or something stronger?'

'Whisky and water?'

'Fine.'

Made stiff with anxiety, Mia marched into the kitchen to comply with Tessa's request. Huh! Whisky! The shock of Gerry's death had affected her badly, too badly for tears, but this . . . If she lost Kate that would be the end of life. Resistance, disapproval, silence would only drive her further away. She must appear welcoming.

The glass needed a polish, the top of the whisky bottle was too tight, where was the little jug she usually chose for cream? Eventually everything was organised and she strutted, rigid with pain, back into the sitting room balancing her best melamine sandwich tray in her hand, a smile stitched on her face.

Tessa was inviting Kate to tea.

Tea! After all the years of neglect. Tea?

Mia fielded a desperate glance from Kate and smiled stiffly. 'Tea. What a lovely idea!' she said brightly.

'Look, here's my telephone number.' Tessa pulled a business card from her wallet. 'Ring me. I know I live a good distance away, but it's straight down the motorway, no problem, an hour is all it's taken me tonight, though I do drive fast I have to confess. I'm not in court with it being Christmas so you can ring me and we'll make a date. After Christmas I'm incredibly busy and it won't be so easy. You can see my house, where I live, see what you think, but I'm sure you'll love it. You can't stay here, in this . . . place.' She looked around the sitting room disdainfully. 'Not here.'

'We're not. Kate and I are moving, after Christmas.'

Nonplussed by Kate's silence, Tessa clutched eagerly at the idea. 'Christmas! What are you doing at Christmas? You could come to me, first Christmas without your father. Do say you'll come. We can really talk, get to know each other, then you can make up your mind. You'll love my home.' She said this looking only at Kate and not including Mia.

Mia had been perching on the edge of the sofa, too taut to sit properly, a great lump in her throat; she stood up and excused herself.

'Things to do ... in the kitchen. Nice to have met you, I'm sure.' Arriving at the kitchen sink she put on her rubber gloves again and started to clear up. Money. It all came down to money in the end. How it oiled the wheels, greased the cogs, smoothed the path! What a temptation for a girl who'd longed for years to meet her mother.

She heard Kate showing her mother out and couldn't resist listening at the door. The voices were muffled but she caught Tessa's commanding tones saying, 'May I kiss you au revoir? ... You have *me* now ... I want to know all about you ...'

Then Kate said something and Tessa's voice came again: 'You're lovely. I'm so proud to have a daughter like you. We'll make up for lost time, you'll see.'

Mia's hands trembled as she swished the dish mop around a cup. She braced herself for Kate's return to the kitchen, but heard her footsteps on the stairs. She spent the next half-hour cleaning and re-cleaning the kitchen worktops and anything and everything which might be in the slightest need of a wipe, then went up to find her. Kate was sitting on her bed, turning the little identification band from the hospital round and round in her fingers, head bent, deep in thought.

'Kate?'

'I can't believe I've met her at last, after all these years. Fancy her seeking me out. Doesn't she look gorgeous? So utterly splendid? *So well off!*' She looked up at Mia who saw she'd been crying. 'Fact remains, though, she did dump me.'

Mia put her arms round her and held her tightly while Kate wept again and Mia longed for the eloquence which would enable her to find the right words to comfort Kate: the emotions were there, but not the words to express them. So Mia cuddled Kate just like when she was tiny, uttering the baby words of comfort as she did so, and it helped as it had always done.

When the crying stopped, Mia leant away from her, stroked her hair back into place, wiped her cheeks for her and said, 'There, now. Feel better?'

Kate nodded. 'Shall I go for tea?'

Mia could have said no emphatically because at bottom she was panicking about Tessa, thinking of the bait her wealth would offer Kate, but instead she said generously, 'You're nineteen, old enough to decide for yourself.'

'What would you do?'

'Oh, I'd go for tea. I couldn't do any other. Just to see, you know. Curious, that's me.'

'I will, then. But not for Christmas. That's ours.'

'Thank you, I love you for that.' Mia walked on to the landing calling out, 'I can see where you get your looks from, you're just like ... her.' She'd got out of Kate's sight only just in time for, like the opening of a dam, tears began to flood down her thin cheeks and she fled to lock herself in the lavatory. Tears for Gerry but, more so, tears at the thought of losing Kate poured silently down, soaking her handkerchief, leaving her hollow and spent.

The following morning, as soon as the post office opened, Kate was dispatched to buy postage stamps for a mail shot to all their clients which Dan had initiated mainly to announce the opening of their 'shop'. His steady flow of ideas gave extra work for everyone and they all, except Kate, grumbled at him.

'I can't see why you grumble, everything he does is to improve our service to the clients and bring in more money.' She struggled into her coat and put on her gloves. 'While it's quiet we can stuff the envelopes and stick on the stamps, and as soon as Christmas is over we can stagger to the post with them all done and dusted.'

Stephie answered her tartly by reminding her that they all knew she thought the sun shone out of Dan.

'I don't. I just think he has some good ideas, that's all. I'm off. Do you want anything?'

'No, thanks.'

Joy gave her the cash for the stamps and with it carefully hidden in the deepest pocket of her winter coat Kate set off. It was quicker to walk than bother taking the car and having a problem finding a parking space, it being Christmas. She strode off down the hill into the precinct, thinking all the time about her mother's visit, hugging the event to herself, not daring to confide in anyone at work about their meeting the previous evening. She was still debating about whether or not to ring her to make an arrangement for tea. Kate felt chary of encouraging too close a contact so quickly. How could her mother be so thoughtless as to imagine that she would be welcomed with open arms and yet she should be. For years Kate had fantasised about her, imagining how she looked, how she dressed, what it would feel like to say 'Mum', yet presented with the opportunity she drew back. It seemed like taking a step forward from which there would be no retreat and Kate wasn't sure that was what she wanted. Hanging about in the back of her mind was the question. Why did her mother suddenly want her after years of total silence?

She'd ring her after Christmas, that would be soon enough, but she'd have to tell her not to call her Katrina – she couldn't stand that name –

and she wouldn't allow herself to be bought. She wished her dad had been there to advise, but she knew already what he would have said: *Don't hurt Mia, we owe her a lot.* So she'd make sure she didn't. She'd wait till after Christmas just to show her mother that she, Kate, her long-lost daughter, wasn't all that keen.

Kate turned into the precinct and headed for the post office. The queue, of course, was long and winding, and ended right at the entrance. Settling herself for a considerable wait, she let her mind wander, thinking mainly about what it would be like spending Christmas away from home and without Dad. She'd have to be lively for Mia's sake, for Mia hadn't rallied since her mother's visit and it worried her . . .

A man's voice she thought she recognised cut through her thoughts. Whose was it? She glanced discreetly down the long, winding tail of the queue, thinking she might see a client she recognised, but saw no one she knew – but there was the voice again. This time she clearly heard it ask, 'By air?' And she spotted him. It was the clerk sitting at the number six window.

But who was he? She couldn't quite see because of the reflection of the lights on the glass screen in front of him but as the queue moved she saw the face of number six quite plainly. Who on earth was he? Then she realised. It was the man who'd brought Copperfield in to the clinic. There were now only seven customers ahead of her and it would be just her luck to have number six available when it was her turn. That strange, disembodied voice called out, 'Cashier number three!' They all moved up a couple of steps and now Kate knew definitely that she was right. There he was, sitting as calm as you please, being polite and helpful, smiling and kind, when all the time he was a cruel torturer . . . And his car wasn't even licensed, when he worked where he could get one without any effort at all!

Now there were only four customers ahead of her and number six was free. He musn't see her because he might recognise her. Still, if it was true that he really had found the cat by the multi-storey then she had nothing to fear, but somehow his subsequent behaviour belied his innocence. Kate sighed with relief when her turn came, and number six was deeply occupied arguing rather nastily with his customer and she was called for cashier number one. She bought the stamps and raced back as fast as she could.

Breathlessly she burst into Joy's office. 'Joy, I've seen the man who brought Copperfield in. He's a clerk in the post office. Can Stephie go down and make sure I'm right?'

Joy shot up from her chair and said, 'Really? A clerk in the post office? I don't believe it.'

'It's him. I'm certain.'

'I'll have his guts for garters, I will. I've a good mind to go down there myself right now and give him a piece of my mind. Better still, tie him to my bumper and drag him along behind like he did Copperfield, then he'll see what it's like for himself.'

Kate advised caution. 'Wouldn't it be better to tell Sergeant Bird?'

'You're right. My poor darling Copper. Let justice be done. Stephie! Off you go. Identify the brute.'

'He's sitting at number six. Hurry up. He might go for lunch or something.'

Stephie, eager for blood, flung on her coat and rushed off.

Thirty minutes later she came charging back into reception, breathless and close to collapse. When she could speak she said, 'It's him. Definitely. I'm one hundred per cent sure. Ring old Dickie.'

The wheels of the law grind slowly and it was two days before Sergeant Bird came back to relate the news about Copperfield's torturer. He leant his forearms on the top of the desk and prepared himself for a long confidential discussion.

Joy joined Stephie and Kate, and they listened open-mouthed to his story.

'Well, him in the post office isn't the guilty party.'

'Aw! We were sure it was him.'

'But . . .'

'*Yes?*'

'But we have got the culprit.'

'Oh!'

'It was his son.'

'No-o-o-o.'

Self-importantly Sergeant Bird took off his cap and placed it on the desk. 'Took the father to the station, showed him the photos. He said he knew nothing about it at all. Didn't know what we were talking about but eventually . . .'

'Yes?'

'I got him to tell me the truth. I told him, "You've been identified by two people from the practice, we know it's you. We've got the security video to prove it, so come on, tell me what really happened."' Sergeant Bird took out his handkerchief and wiped his forehead.

'And . . . ?'

'Turned out he was covering for his fifteen-year-old son.'

'Fifteen!'

'He should have known better,' said Joy.

'He should, I suppose, but his mother's left home and he's gone to pieces, got in with a rough lot. Still doesn't excuse what he did to that poor cat. His dad is heartbroken about it.'

'Was it just the boy himself or the crowd he's got in with?'

Sergeant Bird nodded. 'The crowd he's got in with. But he won't split. Just clams up.'

'Huh! Send him round here. I'll have it out of him in a second,' Joy barked out.

Sergeant Bird took offence at Joy's lack of confidence in his ability as an officer. He removed his forearms from the desk top, drew himself up to his full height, put his cap back on and said, 'Barleybridge police are quite capable of extracting all necessary information. We may not be the Metropolitan police but we're equally well trained.'

Joy touched his arm. 'I'm sorry. It's just that we're so angry about this. So upset about what the poor thing has had to go through. It isn't as if you can *explain* to him. He's turning into a lovely cat, though. There was trouble to begin with because our Tiger took exception to him coming but now she's his slave; there's no other word to describe her behaviour. Follows him around with adoring eyes. Wherever he goes, she goes and, if she can, she creeps into his basket with him for the night. Duncan is charmed with the pair of them. More power to your elbow, Sergeant, we'll be glad to hear the next instalment. Thanks for all you've done.' Joy left the desk expecting he'd be leaving, but he didn't. He shuffled from one foot to the other, blew his nose, cleared his throat, mentioned the crisp, bright weather and were they all set for Christmas?

Kate took pity on him and, leaning across the desk, whispered confidentially, 'She's gone for lunch. The new sandwich bar. But you'll have to be quick. Mr Price starts operating at half past one and she'll be needed.'

Sergeant Bird fled reception as though the hounds of hell were after him.

'He won't have any luck. Bunty's not daft.'

'She might be desperate, though.' Kate grinned.

Stephie was scandalised. 'I know she's getting on a bit but Dickie Bird! Come on!'

'He's a good man. He'd make someone a good husband, as Mia would say.'

'A dull and boring good husband. Speaking of Mia, how is she coping since . . . your . . . Dad? Come to that, how are you?'

Kate paused while she assessed how she felt and decided she was just about coping. 'Not bad, thanks. It's Mia I'm worried about. She's very depressed and I'm dreading Christmas.'

'I was sorry you didn't come to the staff Christmas do.'

'Couldn't face it and I didn't want to spoil it for everyone else.'

'I can see what you mean. I'm dreading Christmas too. Family all turning up, you know. At least I can escape here on Boxing Day for a couple of hours for the emergency clinic.'

The main door opened and they both looked up to find Bunty, loaded with shopping, wiping her feet on the doormat.

Stephie asked her if she'd seen Dickie Bird because he'd gone to find her at the new sandwich bar.

'No. I changed my mind and went last-minute shopping instead.'

'He'll be disappointed. He shot out of here like greased lightning.'

Bunty shrugged her shoulders and walked through to the back.

Stephie nudged Kate saying 'I've just had a thought. She can't marry him.'

'Why can't she? She'd be the right size, because she's so small.'

'Because she'd be called Bunty Bird. I mean, there are limits!'

They both collapsed in giggles and had great difficulty controlling themselves when Mungo came in to begin his afternoon operating list.

'What's the joke?'

'Just laughing because Dickie Bird fancies Bunty.'

'She could do worse.' He picked up the file of case notes Stephie had ready for him and, turning his back to them both, viewed the shelves which had been put up to accommodate the 'knick-knacks', as Dan called them. 'You know, I think we . . .' He paused while he watched the person who had just opened the glass door walk across to reception.

'Katrina! Just passing. Thought I'd call to tell you all the plans I've made for the two of us for Christmas.'

10

Dan made sure he was dressed in his best on the day he was to give a second opinion on Lord Askew's daughter's roan. He wore his corduroy jacket just back from the cleaners with the matching cap, a light-brown shirt and the trousers which toned with it, a stunning countrified tie and his best brogues. He inspected his teeth and face in the mirror in the staff cloakroom, re-tightened the knot of his tie, gave himself a wink and strode out, confident that he couldn't have looked smarter.

He'd also remembered to wash down the Land Rover so when he drove into the stable yard right on the dot of ten he gave a first-rate impression. Unfortunately there was no one there to appreciate him; not a living being in sight. Through the archway into the farm part of the estate he could see activity, so he went to ask for help. 'Hello, Chris. Dan Brown. Remember me?'

'You're hard to forget.'

'Come to see that roan.'

'We've heard nothing else all week. Hope for your sake you're right.'

'I am.'

Chris put his head on one side while he contemplated Dan's confidence in his own judgement. 'There'll be the devil to pay, I can tell you, if you're wrong. His lordship's been in a foul mood all week.'

Impatient, Dan asked, 'So where are they?'

'Lady Mary likes to make an entrance. She wouldn't dream of being early.'

'Where are the others? They definitely said ten o'clock.'

'Got held up, I expect. Must press on.' Chris saluted with a single finger, casually raised, and spun away, leaving Dan alone. He wandered back into the stable yard and found Lord Askew had arrived.

'Morning, Brown.' Lord Askew shook hands and then bellowed, 'Gavin!'

Gavin appeared from the tack room. 'My lord!'

'Lady Mary's here, is she?'

'Not to my knowledge.'

'Bring Galaxy out.'

Gavin glanced at Dan and, judging by the black look he received, Dan guessed he wasn't flavour of the month in the stable yard. Simultaneously the roan was brought out, the equine vet Giles Standen-Briggs arrived and Lady Mary made her entrance.

Lord Askew introduced Dan to Lady Mary. She gave him her hand to shake and he found his gripped mercilessly. 'Good morning. So, you're the chap who knows better than the rest of us?'

Dan couldn't resist laughing and saying with a smile, 'My reputation goes before me.' He released his hand and wondered how such a beautiful fragile-looking woman could have such a deep voice and powerful grip. She reminded him of Rose: that same very slender beauty without being emaciated, the blonde hair, the athleticism, the magnetism too. One look into Lady Mary's steely blue eyes, though, and he knew exactly where she stood: four-square for her own way and her own opinions. She'd be hard to convince.

Giles Standen-Briggs he dismissed: the right manners, the right postures, the right clothes but no substance. 'Good morning, Giles. Pleasure to meet you. Let's get down to business, shall we? I'm pressed for time. Right, Gavin. Walk him back and forth, right to the end of the yard and back twice, if you please. Keep your eyes on his front feet this time. See how he's on his toes more than he should be.'

He heard Giles snort his amusement, but he ignored it. Lady Mary stood silent, watching. Lord Askew said, 'I'm damned if I can see . . .'

'Now, Gavin, at a fast trot, twice. Watch his stride . . . watch the length of his stride.' They all four watched Gavin huffing his way across the yard in front of them with Galaxy stepping out with eye-catching grace and poise. 'See there, look, as I said, just that slightly shortened stride. It's always there every time. Look. See?'

Gavin brought Galaxy to a halt in front of them. Giles Standen-Briggs, rubbing his chin, shook his head. 'You're wrong. I can't see it. Smooth, perfect action. No hint of hesitation at all. No limp.'

'If he goes on working at the pace he does, at the competitive level he does, he'll be unable to work before long. Great pity, he's a grand horse and with his spirit he'll keep going for as long as Lady Mary demands it of him.' He turned to her and said, 'You don't want him lame and unable to compete, do you? Not with his potential.'

She was looking thoughtful. 'Take him again, trotting . . . fast.' Gavin looked askance at her, but minded not to refuse. He set off once more, back and forth in front of them.

Lord Askew watched, Giles Standen-Briggs watched and so did Lady Mary. As Galaxy came to a halt she said, 'How come, Giles, you've never noticed what Dan Brown sees? You see Galaxy regularly. What's the point of my father paying you thousands to look after our horses if you can't identify the simplest problem? This man only saw him once, by chance, and picked it up.'

'I don't agree there might be a problem.'

Lady Mary's eyebrows shot up her forehead. 'If you don't, then you are a fool.' She turned to Dan. 'What do you say it is?'

Dan studied his hands for a moment to give himself time to phrase his opinions without breaking ranks with Giles Standen-Briggs. 'It's my opinion he has navicular disease. I'd have to consult with my colleague on the right course of action.'

'My God! What's that? It sounds terminal.'

'It will be if something isn't done. But I shall have to discuss the matter with Giles, as I said.'

'Closing ranks, are we? I want a decision, please. Today. Galaxy is the best horse I've ever had. He's young but he's *right* and if he can be made to reach his potential I shall be forever in your debt. He's everything any rider could ask for: spirited, tenacious, willing to learn, full of courage. Are we talking surgery?'

'That has the best chance of success, yes.'

'Have your talk, then. I shall be in the tack room when you've come to your decision.'

Dan took some time to convince Giles that he was right. Finally he persuaded him at least to X-ray the feet and that would prove the matter either way. If Dan was right, then an operation would be on the agenda. If not, Dan would retire gracefully to lick his wounds.

Lady Mary was examining a new saddle which had just been delivered, but broke off immediately the two of them came to the tack room doorway. 'Well?'

Dan could see she was anxious but endeavouring to hide it as best she could. 'We've decided on an X-ray, some time today. When the plates have been processed I'll view them back at Giles's practice and we'll decide the best thing to do.'

'Can we manage without surgery?'

'There are ways, like fixing him with circular shoes instead of the traditional shape, that would alleviate but not cure the problem. Or sometimes trimming the hoof differently to counteract his tendency to walk tiptoed, but with such a young horse, frankly, if I am proved right, surgery is the better solution. The operation is called a navicular suspensory ligament desmotomy.'

'My God, it sounds terrible! If you consider it necessary then ... hang the expense. Surely an operation on a horse as valuable as Galaxy should be done by experts in the field like the Royal Veterinary College?'

Dan had to smile. 'That's for you to decide. He'll have padded bandages for about four weeks, with gentle walking for a while and then slow progression, until after about three months he'll be fit for training again. Everything done in slow progression. Asking too much too soon would undo all our work. However, what must be clearly understood is the fact that we can give no one hundred per cent guarantee that the operation will work and none that if it does work he will be absolutely A1 for the rest of his life. It's damned bad luck this happening to a horse with his promise. Without taking the chance, though, he has no hope at all. It will quite simply get worse.'

'I see. You do appear to know what you're talking about. We'll go ahead with the X-ray, then. Can it be done here, Giles?'

Giles nodded. 'I have the equipment and I can be here this afternoon to do it.'

'Thank you. We'll make our decision when you've seen the results.' She turned to Dan, holding out her hand. 'I'll say good morning to you, Dan, is it? You're going to feel all kinds of a fool if the results prove you wrong.' She gave him a wry smile and he had to smile back at her.

'I will indeed.'

Lord Askew, who'd left all the discussion to her, took Dan to one side before he left. He was worried and showed it. 'Damn bad news, this. I don't want her let down. There'll be the devil to pay with her if this doesn't succeed. She's spent hours training Galaxy and he *is* as good as she says. Could take her to the top of the tree, don't you know.'

'I realise that and I can assure you . . .'

Lord Askew waved a dismissive hand. 'Only the best, if it comes to an operation. The best in the field. You understand me. I won't have her disappointed.' He looked across at Lady Mary and Dan saw the passionate love he held for her right there in his eyes.

By five o'clock that afternoon Dan had been proved right. He and Giles Standen-Briggs had a discussion and agreed surgery was the answer.

Giles looked shaken but didn't admit to it. He took a moment to reassemble his ego, then said calmly, 'I'll contact the College, see if they're willing. OK?'

'Of course. That's fine by me. Lord Askew says the best in the field so that's what we'll do.' He drove back to the practice, vindicated and full of satisfaction.

He sought out Mungo immediately and found him putting the finishing touches to an operation on a cat with two broken legs. 'There we are, Bunty, you know the routine. Ring the client, tell them the good news, be your sweetest, there's a love, they'll be well-nigh hysterical by now.' He peeled off his operating gown and saw Dan. 'Ah! It's you. What news on Galaxy?'

'Thankfully, I've been proved right.'

Mungo gave a great 'Ah!' of approval.

'It's the Royal Veterinary College for Galaxy, nothing less will do.'

'Of course. Beware Lady Mary: sweet as pie if things go her way, but she'll have you scrambled for breakfast if anything goes wrong. I'd like to go over the operation with you if you'd be so kind. Pure interest, you know, though I am staking a lot on the success of it, you must see that.'

Dan laughed. 'Of course. I can just disappear off into the sunset while you'll be left to carry the can. We've discussed it thoroughly with Lady Mary and Lord Askew, and they wholeheartedly agree with the decision.'

'And Giles Standen-Briggs?'

Dan paused a moment before replying, 'The X-ray has proved him wrong and he hasn't taken kindly to that, but he's bearing up.'

'Treat him with care. We don't need any antagonism between the two practices.'

Bunty left the operating room carrying the patient and as he closed the door after her Dan asked, 'Supposing it works out. Shall we take on the equine side if it's offered?'

'Let's leave it till after, shall we? The whole picture might change.'

'Fair enough. You haven't got someone else, then, to replace me?'

Mungo, scrubbing his hands at the sink, said above the noise of the running tap, 'No. I'd have told you if I had. I have advertised again, though. I'm in two minds. Miriam wants you to stay and almost everyone else is half-hearted or downright against you. That first chap kept us hanging on far too long. I reckon he only applied for our job as a lever to get more money out of the practice where he is now. But I don't have to take anyone on if I decide for you to stay.' As he dried his hands, he looked Dan in the eye and went on, 'Are you still of the same mind?'

'I'd like to stay, yes. Buy a house. Settle down.'

'A lot hangs on this operation.'

'I know.'

'I'm not sure about taking on equine. Getting his farm work back, yes, but horses...' Mungo shook his head. 'Whole new ball game. Equipment, new set-up. No, I'm not sure.'

'If you invite me to stay I have capital, and I wouldn't mind...'

'Right, right. I hear what you say. I'll think about it.' Mungo put on a clean operating gown. 'Must press on.'

Bunty and Sarah Two came in carrying a comatose black spaniel. 'You have the notes, Mungo, he's all ready for the off.'

Dan took his leave. Mungo rechecked the case file and bent to his task.

'Miriam! I'm starving.' She was in the kitchen testing a chicken casserole for flavour.

'This is the very last remains of the Christmas food. I swear, honest to God, I shan't buy as much food next Christmas as I did this. We seem to have been eating up for *years*.' She grinned at him, put her hands round the back of his neck and drew him to her for a kiss.

After he'd savoured her kiss for a few moments he asked, 'You've heard?'

'No, what? I've been out all afternoon.'

'Where've you been?'

'Walking with Perkins. That's why he's not come to greet you. He's flaked out in his basket.'

'The lazy devil. You'll be pleased to hear that Dan has come out smelling of roses.'

'No! With Galaxy, I assume?'

Mungo nodded. 'He's almost too good to be true. Not only that, Tad Porter is over the moon because Dan's saved Connie Porter's young house cow from lead poisoning and I met Phil Parsons in the town this morning and he feels Dan's the best vet we've had in years. Reckons he saved his bull, Sunny Boy, from choking to death.'

Triumphantly Miriam said, 'What did I tell you? Didn't I say?'

'I've placed the advert for Dan's job, so it's too late to withdraw but I really do think we should keep him.'

Miriam thumped her fist on his arm. 'I knew I was right, and surely to goodness old Askew will want us back and very possibly we'll get the equine work too. Dan must have an instinctive eye for horses.'

'He's volunteered money if and when...'

'Really?'

'That would mean a partnership, though.'

'Well, why not? With Lord Askew, to say nothing of Lady Mary, on our side we would do well. Oh, Mungo! Aren't you excited? A whole new chapter for us.'

'I know. Do we want it? Apart from you, all the wives in the practice have their knife into Dan. Well, women. Zoe, Letty, Joy, Stephie, the two Sarahs and, on occasion, Bunty. Perhaps it wouldn't be worth it.'

'One word from you and the whole picture would change. That smile of yours could melt an iceberg.'

'Rubbish.'

'It's true. Honestly. The casserole's ready. Go and sit down.'

'Still, we'll wait and see if the tide turns in our favour. Old Askew might have more allegiance to Standen-Briggs than we've bargained for.'

'Not if Lady Mary takes a shine to Dan. I wonder, could we persuade him to pay her some attention while she waits to see if the operation is a success?'

'Miriam! *If*? Do you doubt Dan's prognosis?' Mungo raised his eyebrows at her and she had to laugh.

'Of course not. I have every faith in him. What he needs is a good wife, though, and why not Lady Mary? She doesn't inherit, because there's a string of sons, so no one could question his pedigree, could they?'

'I've only met her once and, though I admit she has breeding and is very beautiful, having her as a wife would be hell. I don't think Dan would sit very comfortably with a wife who wants it all her own way.'

'I didn't say he *had* to *marry* her in order to get Lord Askew's account. Just flirt a little, keep her on side.'

'Are there no depths to which you will not sink?'

Miriam had to laugh. 'None.'

'Colin manages with a wife who gets all her own way. Though "manages" just about sums it up.'

'So you haven't noticed the change, then?'

'Change?'

Miriam nodded her head. 'Oh, yes! For my sins I had coffee with Letty in the precinct this morning. Her suggestion. She'd been to the beauty shop before I met her and I must say the result was excellent. Also, instead of those clothes which make her fade into the background, that dreadful cream suit, for instance, she was wearing a little raspberry-coloured number Colin had chosen for her in Paris. That weekend seems to have, well, I don't know what, but mellowed things a little. From something she said, I have an idea Colin's been putting his foot down.'

'Colin? That'll be a first.'

'What she needed, though. Finished, darling?'

'Yes, thanks. Only don't find any other leftovers. Just give them to

Perkins and let's have done with them. I don't want to see any more of this trifle.'

'I feel the same. Poor Perkins . . . New Year. What shall we do?'

'Don't know, haven't got that far yet. Let's clear up and sit down in front of the TV. I'm on call. Pray it's a quiet night.'

Miriam got up from her chair and, ignoring Perkins clamouring for their leftovers, went to put her arms round Mungo. 'Poor you. You know the knick-knacks? It's a pity Dan had the idea so close to Christmas. We'd have made a killing if we'd had more time. Most of the stock is promised for delivery by the New Year and I can't wait to get cracking. He does have good ideas, you know, does Dan. It would be rather fun if he did get himself some female company. It would fill his life up tremendously, wouldn't it? Just round things off for him, sort of? Go and sit down. I'll clear up.'

Three weekends after his opinion had been sought about Galaxy, Dan was on duty when he received a call from Lady Mary. 'Dan Brown? Mary Askew here.' He picked up on the pent-up excitement in her voice and wondered what she wanted him for.

'Yes, it's me, Lady Mary.'

'Dan, Galaxy's back from the Vet College. I thought you'd like to know that the operation has gone well. We've just unloaded him and he's in his stable, tucked up and looking fine.'

'I'm very pleased to hear that. Very pleased indeed. What a relief.'

'Amazing place.'

'You went with him?'

'Oh, yes, couldn't let him go all that way on his own. Amazing facilities there and so charming all of them. Did you train there?'

'I did.'

'Then you'll know what I'm talking about. Would you call Monday to change his bandages? Just this once. Show me and Gavin what to do?'

'Of course, I'd be delighted, but what about Standen-Briggs? Surely . . .'

He heard a sharp, impatient breath. 'I asked *you*.' Dan thought she would say something more, but for a moment she didn't. Then, 'Well? Will you come?'

'I thought Giles would be . . .'

'I asked *you*. Hang Giles. He couldn't even recognise what you could see immediately.'

'Very well, but I feel uncomfortable about it.'

'Bother that. Come. Lunchtime Monday and we'll have lunch and talk. About progress. OK? See you. The name's Mary.'

Her receiver snapped down before he could reply. He didn't really want lunch and still less did he want to upset Giles Standen-Briggs by attending Galaxy when he wasn't officially his vet. *The name's Mary.* God! He didn't want to get involved there. Those steely blue eyes didn't appeal one little bit. Lunch!

But in the event it all turned out better than he had anticipated. Galaxy co-operated wonderfully well when the bandages were changed, and Lady Mary and Gavin were excellent pupils. When it came to lunch it was laid in Lady Mary's small sitting room in the big house. The butler opened the wine and left them to it.

The day was chill even for January and Dan appreciated the huge open fire. The lunch table had been drawn close to it and what with the food and the warmth he soon relaxed. Lady Mary was an entertaining hostess and spoke knowledgeably about horseflesh and competing. The whole subject fired her up and while she was completely absorbed in talking about it her face was alight and her eyes less steely.

Then she got down to the real purpose of his visit. 'Daddy will do what I want, whatever. Being the only girl and the youngest in a family of five boys, I only have to dab my eyes and he crumbles. Mummy's not quite so amenable. Being a woman, she sees straight through my subterfuges, but Daddy! If I insist that we change vets, would you . . .'

'Would I what?'

'Don't be so damn dumb. You know what I mean. If I persuaded Daddy to drop Standen-Briggs, would you be our vet?'

Dan shook his head slowly. 'Look here. You're rather jumping the gun. We don't know how successful we've been, do we? Also, your father asked me in for a second opinion and that is the basis I came on. Fortunately I was proved right, but that doesn't mean Giles is a fool. Nor does it mean I want to be your equine vet on a permanent basis. I may not even be here permanently anyway.'

'You mean that gorgeous Mungo Price doesn't want to keep you? We'll see about that.' She layered a pile of brie on to a biscuit and snapped it in half with her beautiful snow-white teeth. When she'd eaten it she went on, 'What I want I get, and I want you. You've instinct as well as knowledge and I don't know which is the more important. So, would you?'

'I'm not sure. I'm not playing hard to get . . .'

'I know, you're not that kind of person, Dan. You and I are alike. We speak our minds, straight from the shoulder.'

'Then I'll speak mine.'

She waved the other half of her biscuit at him and popped it in her mouth. While chewing it she said, 'Speak up. I'm waiting.'

'I have experience and I have instinct. I've worked in racing stables in the Middle East and I know what I'm talking about when it comes to horses, but ... I do not want to be exclusively equine. I like variety. I actually like cows and sheep, and lambing time is upon us at the moment and I enjoy it, believe it or not. What's more, I would not want to be running back and forth at your every whim like some kind of tame errand boy. I'm not by nature a lackey; I'm not Gavin. Also, I have Giles to consider and Mungo's wishes to think of, so there's no way I am giving you an answer right away.'

'More wine?'

'A little, please. But I am honoured that you would consider me.'

'And so you should be. I'm very picky about who gets close to my horses. We've twelve altogether with my brothers' and Daddy's, and Mummy breeds donkeys, so it would be a lucrative account. Leave Giles to me. He'll do exactly as I say. You can deal with Mungo.' Leaning back in her chair, she said, 'You are arrogant at bottom, aren't you? Most men would jump at the chance to run back and forth when it was me they were running back and forth for.'

'Would they indeed.' Dan smiled sweetly as he added, 'I'm not much impressed by titles.'

Lady Mary was startled by his frankness. 'Mm. Well, that's certainly refreshing. So, shall you finish the wine?'

'I'm driving and I have calls to make.'

'Of course. I'll put the idea to Daddy and let you know.'

'I make no promises. Just glad Galaxy is doing well, but it's early days. Don't rush him, will you? He needs time. He's a wonderful animal. It must be a privilege to work with him.'

'It is. Oh, yes. He responds so well and he looks so good, doesn't he?'

'He does. There's a kind of elegance about him, powerful as he is. Wonderful find.'

'Daddy came back with him one day and I knew as soon as I saw him that he'd chosen well.'

'Lucky girl.'

'I've worked hard with him.'

'Still a lucky girl. Doesn't matter how hard you work; if the horse hasn't got that something extra you're wasting your time.'

Lady Mary shrugged her shoulders.

'Thank you for the lunch. I have thoroughly enjoyed it. Your butler took my coat?'

Lady Mary reached across to the bell pull by the fireside and tugged it. The butler shot in through the door saying, 'My lady?'

'Mr Brown's coat, Lister, please.'

She went out into the stable yard to see him leave. He wound down the window of the Land Rover and thanked her again for lunch.

'My pleasure, Dan. My pleasure. I'll give you a buzz shortly. I mean it, I'm having you, so you'd better accept the fact.'

Dan waved goodbye, thinking *heaven preserve me from ruthless women*. Out of sight of her he punched the air in triumph.

11

Mia and Kate had tried so very hard to join in with the Christmas activities at the hotel, hoping that the other guests wouldn't guess how very low they were feeling. The first Christmas Day without Gerry was almost too much for Mia and keeping back the tears an impossibility; twice Kate was up in the night trying to comfort her. At least sharing a room on the basis of cost meant she was there for Mia when she needed her. But Kate felt extremes of pain herself and try as she might to be bright and festive, she failed dismally. Deceit added to her burden, for she hadn't told Mia that her mother had been to the practice the morning after arriving at their door so unexpectedly, full of plans for Christmas.

Completely ignoring the presence of Mungo and Stephie she had addressed herself to Kate. 'I was booked in a hotel for lunch on Christmas Day and they've squeezed you in too, and I thought we'd have a cosy girls' evening together, catching up on our lives, and then for Boxing Day I've arranged . . .'

Kate had interrupted her more forcibly than she'd really intended, but somehow she'd had to put a stop to her plans. 'I never said I would come for Christmas. We said we were going away and I'm not letting Mia down.'

Her mother's face had collapsed with hurt. 'But now we've met we can be together at long last, surely. Our first Christmas. I've such plans for the two of us.' Her enthusiasm gathered pace again. 'I'm going to the States in May and I'd love it if you would come, and . . .'

'I have my exams this summer. There's no way I can go to the States, not even for a weekend.' Kate felt as though she were being mown down by a juggernaut and hysteria began to rise in her throat.

'I just don't understand you. Don't you realise I'm your own mother?'

'Of course I do. But you can't expect to come into my life at this late

345

stage and have me fall in with your plans at the snap of your fingers. It's not reasonable.'

Out had come the lace-edged handkerchief and the eyes were carefully dabbed without smearing the mascara. 'But I thought . . . I'm so disappointed.'

'That isn't my fault. I never promised anything at all.'

'When shall I see you?'

'After Christmas I'll give you a ring, I promise. I have your card, and we'll meet up and have tea or something and talk. There's a lot for us to talk about.'

'This is not at all what I expected.'

'Please. I am trying. I've sent you a Christmas card. I can't do any more at the moment. At this minute I'm working and I'm needed. I'll ring as soon as I get back. Thank you for coming.'

Mungo watched Kate and realised what a tight hold she was keeping on her feelings.

Her mother tried being hurt all over again. 'I'm so disappointed.'

'Well, I'm glad we've met at last. I've always wondered what you were like, but Dad dying like he did . . . it's all too . . . much.'

The whole emotionally charged scene was abruptly shattered by a further crisis as a client rushed in carrying a big mongrel dog in his arms with blood running from its two front paws. 'He's been wading in a pond and he's cut his feet; it's terrible. They're in ribbons. There must have been broken glass. Do something. Quick!'

Spurred into action, Mungo dashed to open a consulting room door while Kate grabbed a wad of tissues to catch at least some of the blood and fled with the client into the consulting room. By the time the crisis was over and the dog safe in Graham's hands, and she'd wiped up the trail of blood on the floor of reception, Kate's mother had gone. 'I'm going for my break. Is that all right?'

Stephie, who'd witnessed Kate's distress, nodded. 'Of course, take as long as you like. I didn't know . . .'

'Neither did I till last night.'

Kate had made herself a cup of tea and gone to take refuge in the accounts office to drink it. Rage had boiled up inside her. Now she knew that the loving, smiley person she'd always imagined her mother to be simply didn't exist. But when she reasoned it out, if her mother had been kind and motherly she would never have dumped her. In truth, she was as hard as nails, that was why she'd done what she'd done. With her clenched fist Kate wiped away the tear escaping down her cheek. It felt cold so she put her hands on the radiator to warm herself, but that did nothing to stop her trembling.

Insensitive was another word which sprang to mind. How could she imagine for one moment that she, Kate, would let Mia spend Christmas on her own? Did her mother have no understanding of feelings? Did she, in fact, have any genuine feelings? That was the question, because the dabbing of the handkerchief to her eyes was a total sham. It was simply her method of trying to get her own way. Well, if that was how the cookie crumbled then Kate Howard wasn't fool enough to fall for it.

The trembling had almost stopped so Kate picked up her cup and drank her tea. The hotness of it spread through her and gradually she began to get herself together. OK, she wanted to get to know her, see her sometimes, but *live with her*? No chance.

What really hurt was the heart-searing realisation that the mother standing at the desk this morning no way matched up to the mother of her imagination. Kate remembered how as a child she'd spent hours dreaming about her own mother, imagining eating hot buttered toast by the fire on winter evenings, seeing her proud, smiling face in the audience at school concerts, being met by her at the school gate: all those simple things which illuminated a small child's life. Instead it was Mia who'd done all those things for her. As her dad had said, it was Mia who cherished her. How right he was.

There was a knock at the door and Miriam had come in. She'd paused in the doorway for a moment and then she'd put her arms around Kate. 'Mungo said, so I've come, if it helps. What a quandary, my dear.'

'Do you know the worst thing? What must hurt Mia so much is that she's been my mother all these years and I've never, ever, called her Mum. Not once. How could I have been so thoughtless? I'm so ashamed.'

Miriam, with no answer to that, had squeezed her shoulders and remained silent.

Kate had rung her mother as soon as she'd got back from holiday with Mia but there'd been no reply to the messages she'd left on her answer machine. Now, Kate felt dumped all over again. Why had she sought her out if she was to forget her immediately?

Then, out of the blue, the phone rang at home one evening and it was Tessa, begging forgiveness. 'I was so upset, Kate, about not seeing you at Christmas, and I just couldn't . . .' There was a break in her voice and then she continued more decisively, 'I felt so low. I'm sorry, Kate, I really am. When I heard your voice on the answer machine I could have cried. But I've got over it now and I'm asking you to come to see me. Will you, please?'

Kate didn't answer immediately.

'Please, Kate.'

'Of course, I'll come to your house and see it as you suggested. When shall I come?'

'Saturday? I'll be free that day.'

'Right. About three?'

'Lovely. I'll pop a map in the post.'

The rest of the week Kate spent in a whirl of anticipation. She tried her best to hide her excitement from Mia. But Mia saw through her. 'I don't mind you being excited, you know. You don't need to be secretive about your mother. I'd like to know.'

'Dad said I wasn't to hurt you and I don't want to, but I can't help but be excited.'

'It's only natural. I shan't be able to wait until you get back to hear all about it. The house and that, you know.'

'Thanks, she's been so upset about me not going for Christmas. That's why she hasn't rung me back.'

'Understandable. Yes, understandable.'

Kate recognised from the tone of her voice that Mia was striving hard to be reasonable and finding it very difficult, so she changed the subject. 'You know the man who's bought Dad's train set? When is he coming to collect it? Because we need to clear up some of the rubbish he's got up there and make sure Mr Whatever-he's-called gets what he's bought and nothing personal of Dad's.'

'You're right. I'd better get on with it.'

'If you like I'll do it,' Kate said gently.

Relieved, Mia replied, 'Do you mind? I can't face it.'

'I'll start right now. I've done all my work for Miss Beaumont for tomorrow night so why not?'

Gratefully Mia answered, 'Wonderful. If there's anything we should keep, put it in a box all together and when I feel better . . .' She made a vague gesture with her hand. 'I'll . . . you know.'

'Right. Here goes.'

Kate switched on the light at the top of the attic stairs and for a mad, mad moment thought her dad was sitting in his chair waiting for her. It must have been the way the shadows fell as her eyes adjusted to the bright light. Her heart missed a beat and her throat tightened. It was time this train set went, because it was so strongly associated in her mind with her father that she could feel him here as though he'd left his soul behind in the attic when his heart stopped beating.

It felt intrusive handling all his boxes of train paraphernalia. Shoeboxes filled with signals, and rails, and tiny sandwich boards with old slogans half rubbed away, damaged bushes, sheets of imitation brick for the outsides of station buildings, bogies with wheels missing, rusting wheels, the odd window taken from a discarded signal box. Oh, look! She remembered him replacing his old signal box. Of course! Here it was, useless, but loved too much to be thrown away. An invoice for old carriages he'd pounced on in triumph at a sale. She'd been with him that day; clear as crystal came the memory of his excitement at finding them and of her hand in his, and being half afraid of the crowds looming above her four-year-old head.

Shoeboxes had been his favourites for storing precious things: one full of notices and handbills about exhibitions. Oh! Here was the one for the time he went to London and had upset Mia by buying an early engine which had cost the earth, when in truth they'd needed a new boiler more.

Another held a motley collection of tiny people and animals for use on platforms and the like. Some badly made, others, as he got more skilful, she supposed, admirable in their minuteness, and wasn't that tiny skirt on that tiny girl a bit cut from that favourite old summer dress of hers? And that red coat the woman was wearing? Surely she'd worn that coat to infant school? Searching the box was like seeing her life revealed year by year. How odd that she'd never noticed before.

Kate blew the dust off another box, sealed with sticky tape. She peeled away the dusty stickiness, took off the lid and there, staring at her, was a photograph of herself in the garden by the trellis in a dress she didn't recognise. Oh, God! It wasn't her, it was her mother! Startled, she swiftly put the lid back on again. When her heart had slowed its pounding she cautiously opened the box again and reverently began looking at a past she shared with her dad. But it wasn't just the past, it was her mother's too. He'd saved birthday cards and Christmas cards she'd sent him. Notes she'd left for him when she'd had to go out before he got home, even a note she'd left for the milkman one day long ago. Curiously Kate studied her mother's handwriting and saw it was very like her own.

Separately, all together in an envelope, she found photographs obviously taken by her dad because he was renowned for his lopsided photos. Some were blurred as though his hands were trembling as he held the camera but there was no doubt of their subject matter: they were of her mother first and last. Her mother, slim and dark, her mother dressed up for something special, in a swimsuit by the sea, several of her mother obviously pregnant, her mother at the door of what appeared to be a hospital holding . . . yes, holding a baby. So, that must be me. Her and me. Me with her. My mother. Kate drank in this picture in all its aspects, unable to stop looking at it, thrilled to the core. Eventually she put them all back into the envelope, her feelings totally confused. There were letters, too, in another envelope in the box, mostly ones from Dad to Mum. He'd had a way with words in those days, had Dad. They were love letters she wouldn't have minded receiving. She wondered what her mother had thought of them.

Kate put the box on one side to take downstairs and hide in her wardrobe. That box most certainly mustn't go with the rest.

Then, most painful of all, she found hidden under a shelf behind a vast pile of old model railway magazines another thick envelope of letters he'd written but never sent. All with 'Tessa' written on the envelopes and stored in date order. They were dated regularly throughout the first year of Kate's life and then they trailed off and, around her first birthday, they stopped altogether. That was when Mia had replaced her. One by one Kate opened them and read all about her dad's tender love for her mum in every line: a pining and a longing which revealed so poignantly a depth of feeling she never knew he was capable of. Poor Dad! Loving her like that. How did he survive her going?

'Kate! Are you all right up there? That serial we're watching, it's just about to start. Are you coming?'

Guiltily she shoved the letters into the shoebox along with the photos and squeezed the lid on. 'I'm on my way.' In haste, so as to prevent Mia from coming up, she got together all the boxes which could be taken with the train layout and, taking the one into which she'd crammed all her dad's own memorabilia under her arm, she switched off the attic light, went down to her bedroom, pushed aside a pile of shoes she should have thrown away months ago, put the box in the bottom of her wardrobe and heaped the shoes back inside to hide it, so Mia wouldn't find it.

Somehow she found it difficult to meet Mia's eyes when she got downstairs and sat staring at the TV, scarcely able to follow the plot because her mind was so full of what she'd just read. Her dad had suddenly, in one evening, become quite a different person from the one she thought she knew. For her father's sake Kate realised she'd have to give her mother time if nothing else. Simply because he had loved her so.

Mia patted her hand. 'Finished it all?'

Kate nodded.

'Nothing to keep?'

'No. It's all in piles. Waiting.'

'He'll be here to take it away on Saturday. The cheque's gone through the bank now, so the money's secure. There wasn't anything for me to see, then?'

'No.'

'I see.'

Kate leapt up. 'I'll make us a drink.' Before Mia could agree with her she'd disappeared into the kitchen. Now it was Mia's turn to be unable to follow the TV. Because she knew Kate so well she guessed she was hiding something. What, she didn't know, but there was something Kate didn't want her to know. If there was something up there about how much Gerry had loved that Tessa there was no need to hide it, she'd always known. A stranger pair there couldn't have been. Tessa had been a fool, because she Mia had reaped all the benefits of loving Gerry and having Kate. Nothing, *nothing* Tessa could do could take the last eighteen years from her, so she'd hug that to her heart no matter what happened. Saturday would be here before she knew it and what had been Gerry's passion would go out of the house for good with that model railway man, and perhaps, worse, she'd lose Kate that day too.

Kate, eager to see her mother, was at the house promptly at three o'clock. She parked at one side of the U-shaped drive because the road was too busy for her to park at the kerb, but there was no one there. She stood back from the front door and looked up at the house. It was very new, beautifully painted, with lavish bay windows and expensive net curtains at each of them – being so close to the road they were necessary. Two smartly clipped bay trees grew in square cast-iron tubs either side of the door and the beginnings of a wisteria, a favourite of Mia's, grew on the far side of the right-hand window.

She tried the doorbell again and smiled at the tune it played. Mia would have laughed at it had she been with her. So . . . the big meeting of mother with daughter had finished before it started. Kate went to sit in her car to wait. Just in case. She might turn up. Just might. *I'll wait until half past three; she could have been held up in traffic.* Kate wondered what car she drove and played a game of guessing while she waited. Every part of the house and front garden was as neat as a pin and shouted money. Well, stuff it. Tears welled in her eyes. Her mother seemed to be making a career out of dumping her. Then, as she prepared to pull out to drive away, she saw in her rear mirror a BMW turn into the drive and park. So instead she reversed, parked and got out.

Her mother leapt out. 'Kate! I'm so sorry! I went shopping and didn't realise the time. Can you forgive me?' From the back seat she hauled several expensive-looking carrier bags. 'This is all for you.'

Kate's heart sank and resistance to enticement grew inside her, but when she saw what her mother had bought for her she caved in and accepted. 'How did you know my size?'

'I didn't, I guessed.'

'I don't know how to thank you, it's all so lovely. This top and these trousers! I've been longing for a pair like these for weeks.' But she didn't give her a kiss of thanks as she would have given Mia.

'Tea! I'm parched. Have a look around while I get it ready. The bedroom at the back will be yours if you like it.' She wagged a teasing finger at her and disappeared into the back.

Kate wandered about the house, admiring her taste in furniture and the good eye she had for interior decoration. She loved the collection of silver snuff boxes she had, and the modern art on the walls, and the huge, inviting, cuddly goatskin rug before the ornate electric fire. When Kate saw the bedroom her mother had said would be hers if she so chose, she gasped with delight. Such an elegant quilted throw on the big single bed, the huge matching curtains looped back by tasselled cords, a long-pile carpet invited her to try the texture of it with appreciative fingers. It was a bedroom she could only dream about and with its own en suite too. Surely it wasn't real marble on the floor? It was. My God! A pink marble bathroom. What a joy!

When she got back to the drawing room the tea was laid out on a trolley, all lace doilies and delicate china, with a Georgian silver teapot; the whole works.

'Tell me Kate, what do you think?'

'You have a lovely home.'

'I've got an eye for choosing furnishings, haven't I?'

The question popped out of her mouth before Kate could stop it. 'You've never married, then?'

'No, never. Not to say I haven't had the opportunity but ... sugar?'

'No, thanks. Why?'

'Didn't see any reason why I should. I have a good job and simply didn't have any interest in any encumbrances. Do you think I should have done?'

Kate shook her head. 'Nothing to do with me, I just wondered.' She munched on a tiny sandwich, so unlike one made by Mia, which would have had the filling pouring out over the edges and be lavishly buttered and chunky. Mia always joked that it was her generous nature which made her sandwiches turn out like they did. 'You've never had any more children? I mean, I haven't got a brother or a sister somewhere?'

Her mother shook her head emphatically. 'No, you have not. Once was enough.' She looked as though, given the chance, she would have snatched back that last sentence. 'Childbirth isn't all it's cracked up to be.'

'Being a mother isn't all it's cracked up to be either, apparently. Well, not as far as you're concerned.'

Her mother looked hurt. 'Kate! How unkind.'

Kate waited for the lace handkerchief to come out but it didn't. 'You did leave me. At two weeks old. That takes some effort to understand. In fact, I can't understand and probably never will.' Kate couldn't work out why she was coming out with such unkind things; some devil seemed to be goading her. 'Didn't you give me a thought? Didn't you care about who would look after me when you were gone?'

'Of course I did. You had Gerry. I'm not entirely heartless.'

'No?'

'No. I lost my identity when you were born. I wasn't me. I was Katrina's mother and not Tessa Fenton, solicitor. And you woke in the night to be fed. Night and day demanding food. It was exhausting. I wasn't cut out for it. Believe me, I was tormented by what I did.'

Kate helped herself to another sandwich and said with a sarcastic edge to her voice, 'Well, you needn't have worried, Mia's done an excellent job.'

'She may have, but she can't give you what I can give you.' She waved her hand in the air, encompassing the elegance of her drawing room. 'A house like this to live in, a room like yours upstairs, clothes like these, and if you get to college, which I've no doubt you will being your mother's daughter, you'll have no worries about money. I'll see to that.'

Kate gasped for the second time that afternoon. 'You really mean that, don't you?'

'Of course. I wouldn't have said it if I didn't. You come to live with me and you'll want for nothing. Trips abroad, clothes, money to spend. I'll buy a flat for you near college. I'm not having you in student accommodation.'

'Oh!'

Her mother leant across and put a gentle hand on her knee. 'You see, you've turned out just as I would have wished. You need to lose a bit of weight, say, perhaps a stone, well, half a stone maybe, and then . . .' She bunched her fingers and kissed them. 'With the kind of clothes I can afford for you, you'll be stunning. More tea, Katrina?'

'Yes, please.' She held out her cup. Noticed the expensive bracelet and ring her mother wore, the long, beautifully lacquered nails, the impeccable cuff of her white shirt and thought about Mia's neatly filed short nails, and the sweetness of *her* hands and the healing they seemed to bring when they touched her. 'When I've drunk this I must be going.'

'But we haven't talked.'

'What is there to say?'

'You could tell me what Gerry was like as a father. What Mia's like. How you enjoyed Christmas.'

Kate, shocked by her use of the word 'enjoyed' in connection with her first Christmas after her dad's death, snarled, '*Enjoyed* Christmas? How could we *enjoy* it? We'd just lost Dad. It was vile. Absolutely vile. Both of us hated it, but it was better than staying at home, just the two of us without him. Don't you understand anything at all?' She sprang to her feet, angry with her mother and with herself, and bitterly disappointed. 'I'm sorry for shouting, but this, all this that you're offering me. I can't help but ask why? After all these years. Why? Why bother?'

Her mother got to her feet to emphasise her point. 'Because I thought I should when you'd lost your father. It made you an orphan and it didn't seem right. Not when I knew about you, saw in the paper you were still living in the same house. I had to do something. I didn't know how you would be placed and when I did, I knew something had to be done about it. You can't live in that dreadful house. You needed rescuing.'

'Rescuing? From what? A stepmother who loves me? A home that's mine? Where I'm comfortable and happy? Is that what I need rescuing from? Believe me, I don't.' Kate gathered her bag and coat, looked at the carrier bags holding the clothes she was expected to take with her and decided not to take them. 'I'll be in touch.'

'No, Katrina, no. Don't go like this. It's not fair.'

'Not fair?'

'To me. I've done my best.' This time the lace handkerchief did come out.

'And another thing: I'm called Kate, not Katrina, I hate it. Thank you for the tea. Do you want me to have the clothes after the way I've behaved? I expect you'll be able to take them back to the shop if you don't.'

Her mother sat down on the sofa, and looked small and beaten. In a defeated kind of voice she said, 'Take them, you may as well as they were bought for you.'

Kate hesitated and decided it would be just too churlish to refuse, and they were all that she longed for but couldn't afford. At least her mother got that right. 'Thank you, then. Thank you very much. I will. Sorry for losing my temper but I couldn't help it.'

Her mother looked up, eyes glowing, not a tear in sight, but a smile of satisfaction on her face. 'Thank you, Katrin—Kate. Thank you. I don't mean to be thoughtless. It's just that I never have anyone else's feelings to consider, so it's hard for me. But I'm a quick learner. Forgiven?'

'Forgiven.'

She went with Kate to the car and helped her put the bags on the back seat. 'I'm sorry to have upset you, Kate, I didn't mean to. Will you come again?'

'Of course. Perhaps we could go out for a meal, my shout?'

'That would be lovely. Next weekend?'

'I'm working next weekend, so we'll make it a fortnight.'

'I'll pop my diet sheet in the post in the meantime. All right?' Her mother moved as though to kiss her goodbye but Kate aborted that idea by getting into the car.

'I'll ring and we'll make arrangements. Thank you for tea and the clothes, and I'm sorry if I've been rude.'

Before her mother could reply Kate pulled away and drove home, churning with conflicting emotions which criss-crossed her mind so rapidly that each was only half formed before another took its place.

Kate threw herself into her work to avoid having to sort out her feelings about her mother. The new clothes she'd flung on hangers and left in the wardrobe, not able to bear to wear them.

It was Dan who saved her sanity one night when he got a call to a difficult lambing at Tad Porter's just as he was about to leave for home. 'How about coming with me, Kate? Fancy it? Seen a lambing before?'

'No, I haven't. Are you sure? I'd love to.'

'Of course.'

He courteously opened the passenger door for her, stored her boots along with his in his giant plastic washing-up bowl and drove off at his usual hell-for-leather pace. They'd driven right out of the town before he spoke. 'Take your mind off things.'

Kate continued looking glumly out of the window.

'Is she that bad, this mother of yours? Or isn't that the problem?'

'Between you and me?'

Dan nodded. They'd turned off the Magnum Percy road on to the lane which ended at Tad Porter's. He pulled in to allow a car to pass him on the steep narrow road and then replied, 'You don't like her, do you?'

'I didn't say I didn't like her, we're just not the same kind of people and she is trying to buy me. Like as if I'm being auctioned. Except she's the only one bidding. I'll do the gate.'

Dan negotiated the turn into Tad Porter's and after Kate had closed the gate behind him she got back in saying, 'Tries to buy me, you know, with clothes and money and things.'

'Ah!'

'But I know why she left me and ran away.'

'You do?'

'She has no feelings whatsoever. Except for herself and what she wants.'

'Ah!' Dan braked.

'I'll get my boots.'

Despite the cold Dan stripped down to a short-sleeved shirt and boxer shorts, then he put on his parturition gown, which finished just above his waist, then his waterproof trousers, tied the gown firmly to his lower ribs with a piece of twine kept specially for the purpose and tucked the legs of the trousers into his steel-capped boots.

As Kate put on her boots, Connie Porter came out of the house, wrapped in an enormous tartan blanket carrying a bucket of water and a bar of soap. 'Good evening, Dan.'

'Good evening, Mrs Porter. You know Kate, don't you?'

'No, but how do you do? I'm Connie to everyone.'

'Connie it is, then.'

'Tad won't be his usual chatty self. He's been up three nights in succession. The lambs are coming thick and fast. Best year we've had since I don't know when, that many twins you wouldn't believe. You can wash up in the outside lavvy when you've done. I've put new soap and clean towels in there and come in afterwards and I'll find something for you to eat. Tad's in the lambing shed, in the corner of the first field through the gate. Right problem he's got.'

Dan led the way across the field, guided by the lights of the lambing shed, with Kate close behind carrying the bucket, accustoming her eyes to the intense dark of the night. The air seemed filled with the sound of calling lambs and their mothers' answering bleats. Far away down the slope were the scattered twinkling lights of Magnum Percy, where people were cosy by their fires, but Kate wouldn't have swapped places for anything, even though her cheeks were already numb with cold.

Tad Porter greeted them at the opening of his lambing shed. In the scant light afforded by the lamps hanging at strategic points, Kate saw that the shed was packed full of sheep and bleating lambs: some penned off, others free to wander about knee deep in straw. Closest to her were twin lambs feeding from their patient mother, long tails waggling briskly as the warm milk gushed down their throats. Here and there lambs were curled asleep, keeping close to their mothers' warm, comforting bodies. She couldn't help but let out a long 'Aw'.

Dan grinned. 'Great, eh? Evening, Tad. Which one's the problem?'

'This ewe here.' He went to stand by a pen which contained only one ewe with no lamb with her. 'I've tried to sort her out but them's that entangled. Has twins ev'ry year, she does. They're allus right little goers.'

Dan washed his hands and arms in the bucket of icy water Kate had carried for him, then he pushed aside Tad's makeshift bed piled high with blankets, climbed over the partition and invited Kate with a jerk of his head to do the same. Despite the shelter of the huge expanse of corrugated-iron roofing and sides protecting the ewes and lambs from the chill, Kate found the icy cold almost intolerable. When she remembered how little money farmers were getting now for lambs at market she wondered at their tenacity in tolerating such inhuman working conditions.

Dan was on his knees beside the ewe, feeling inside her. 'Hold her head for me, Kate.' He concentrated on the job, muttering from time to time. 'There's another head.'

'That's two heads.'

'Another pair of back legs. Like you said, Tad, what a tangle.'

Kate felt compelled to address the ewe. 'There, there, you let Dan give you a hand. Don't worry, he'll soon get you sorted.' Then she felt embarrassed and ridiculous.

Dan gave her a smile. 'Thanks for the vote of confidence. Tad! There's two in here for sure, like you said all entangled. I think the first to come out has something wrong with it, it won't come out at all. I'm going to turn it round and bring it out back end first.'

'Do yer best. That's what yer here for.' He leant his lean length against a supporting post, pulled a thick sack more closely round his shoulders and lit up his pipe, preparing for a long wait. 'I've had fifteen born today so far. One's in t'oven cos it's a poor doer, but Connie'll bring it round.'

Dan, kneeling in the straw struggling to make sense of the lambs, with two-thirds of his powerful forearm inside the ewe, suddenly said, 'Ah! Here we go. Number one.' Out slid a tiny lamb, wet and messy and lifeless, with both its front legs seriously crippled. He broke its cord with a quick nip of his thumb and forefinger and, laying it to one side, went back to dealing with the second lamb. Kate kept her eyes from the dead lamb. She couldn't bear to look at it. What should have been a beautiful moment had turned very sour.

The second lamb came the correct way round, its little nose and forefeet arriving first, and with relief Kate saw this one was perfect, but it didn't breathe immediately.

'Clear its mouth and nose and then rub it, Kate, rub it with that old cloth. Go on. Vigorously. Go on. Do it! Hard! Harder!'

Kate was stunned to find herself with the lamb's life in her hands. In a daze she heard Dan say, 'Hard, harder than that; it won't break.' So she did as he said and rubbed its chest so vigorously that the lamb was actually moving up and down in the straw with every rub. Just as she was about to admit defeat it took a breath, gave a half-strangled bleat and began breathing regularly. Kate could have cried with relief.

'Good girl! Well done . . .'

Kate kept rubbing the lamb in case it decided to stop its fight for life. She was in such a panic that any thought of market prices and was it worth it had flown from her mind and been replaced by a desperate desire for the tiny thing to live. It just had to! Her first lamb. Her very, very first. This was brilliant.

She wished she could pick it up and hug it, mess and all. It was just so . . . so . . . wonderful. That was the word. Wonderful. Kate burst into tears.

Dan gave his attention to the health of the ewe. Feeling round inside her he said, 'That's it, everything all right in there. One good one at least. No point in trying to revive the other, Tad.'

'Ah, well, it 'appens. Yer learn to be philosophical in this game. Ewe's all right, is she?'

'All clear. I'll give her an injection to boost her a bit. She's had a hard time of it.'

Tad observed, 'She's been struggling to deliver for some time and I tried to help but it was no good.'

'Kate, my bag, please.' Dan spoke sharply because he wanted her to stop crying. When she didn't react he added loudly, 'Now.'

Kate gulped down her tears and went to get the bag for Dan, wiping her cheeks with the heel of her hand. 'Here you are.' To comfort herself she knelt down in the straw to stroke the little lamb and to her surprise found that beneath the soft wool its head was hard and almost rocklike, when she'd always imagined lambs' heads would be soft and woolly.

The ewe, having got rid of her burden, began to take an interest in her lamb and before they left the shed it was trying to get up on its wobbly legs. Kate looked back at the lamb she'd helped to revive before she left the shed and loved it. The sight of its utter sweetness, the absolute beauty of it, was just mind blowing.

She and Dan struggled across the dark field by the light of Dan's torch and eventually found the outside lavvy. 'You wash up first, Kate.' The water was ice-cold but the coal tar soap smelt good and rubbing herself with the hard, rough towel line-dried in the fresh air put life back into her.

As she watched Dan wash his arms and hands Kate said, 'I'm so sorry, Dan. I didn't know I'd cry.'

'That's life, as they say. We can't win every time, Kate. Only most of the time and it's something you never quite get used to, losing an animal. I'll get my clothes on and wash this lot off, then we'll go in.'

When he was dressed Dan called, 'Come on, then, let's see what Connie has for us.'

'They all look so sweet. The two of them. I did it, though, for the second one, didn't I. I made it breathe.'

Dan took her arm, delighted by her pleasure in her triumph. 'You did indeed, but like Tad said we've to be philosophical about the failures. Go in. Boots off first. Connie! There were twins, but the first one was a no go, I'm afraid.'

'That's life. Sit yourselves down. Lamb casserole. OK?'

Kate's stomach heaved. The very thought: lamb casserole. How could they? Lamb casserole! Those dear little lambs, the one she'd helped to revive! How could they?

Dan saw her horror and for her sake tried to cover the moment by saying, 'Smells good, Connie. Is Tad coming in for some?'

'He'll be in.'

'You're more than generous. Hadn't expected a meal, had we, Kate?' Dan nudged her sharply.

'No, we hadn't. It's very kind, very kind.' Somewhat painfully she added, 'I'm really hungry.'

The casserole was brought out of the oven as soon as they'd seated themselves at Connie's big pine table. With a clean sack for an oven cloth she carefully placed it on a big hand-woven mat in the middle of the table. On the top of the casserole was a thick layer of thinly sliced wonderfully crisped potatoes, browned and delicious-looking to anyone with even half an appetite, but to someone out in the fields all day and night earning their livelihood it would look like something from paradise. As Connie dug her huge serving spoon into the dish the rich smell of the thick, shining, brown, herby gravy as it dripped down reached Kate's nostrils and hunger overcame her squeamishness. By the time her plate was in front of her, full to the very edge with meat and gravy and glorious vegetables, Kate couldn't wait to pick up her knife and fork. There was a large glass of foaming home-made beer to accompany it and the two complemented each other superbly.

'A feast fit for a king,' Dan mumbled through his first mouthful of food.

Connie smiled, well satisfied. 'Well, when my Tad's been out there all day he needs some packing, believe me.'

After the meal Connie took the lamb from the warming oven and asked Kate if she'd like to feed it, if they had time. Dan agreed they had; the warmth of the fire and the satisfaction of the huge meal he'd consumed made him reluctant to leave and he was glad of an excuse to enjoy the warmth a while longer.

Kate knelt on the hearthrug and took the bottle from Connie. The frail lamb took a deal of encouragement to persuade it to begin feeding. When it did it worked hard, but quickly became exhausted and could only finish half the bottle.

'Never mind, that's better than he's been doing. You're a good lass. You've a way with animals.'

'How often will you have to feed him?'

'Every two hours night and day till he shapes up.' Connie hitched up the tartan blanket round her shoulders.

Dan stood up. 'We'll be off, then. Thanks for the meal, Connie, much appreciated. Ready, Kate?'

'Every two hours! How do you manage without sleep?'

'Catch up when the lambing season's done. Same every year. Goodnight and thanks.'

Dan snatched up his bag and headed for the door. He glanced round at the spartan room, the cold stone floor, the ancient oak settle by the fire, the huge old cooking range, the morbidly challenging religious picture over the mantelpiece, the old, old comfortable chairs, and brooded gratefully on the warm hospitality they'd received. 'Thanks again, Connie. You're a remarkable cook. Might be seeing you again soon.'

'More than likely.' Connie followed them out and went into the outside lavvy. They heard the catch snap shut.

Kate whispered, 'Have they no inside toilet, then?'

'I don't expect so.'

'They are so poor and yet so generous.'

'Upland farming is always difficult even in the best of times. OK?'

He put the Land Rover in gear, released the brake and set off to return to Barleybridge. 'Care for a drink, Kate?'

'Might as well, if you've time. I'd like that.'

They settled themselves in a quiet corner of the Askew Arms. The main bar and the restaurant where Dan had had that awkward lunch with Lord Askew were busy, but they chose to sit in the smaller, relatively quiet bar.

'I think I'll go to the ladies and tidy up. Coming straight from a lambing I must look a mess.'

'You don't, but OK. I'll order. What would you like?'

'A sweet cider, please.'

When she came back the drinks had been served and Dan was patiently waiting. He grinned at her as she approached. 'What did you think, then?'

'When she said lamb casserole I thought I would die. I suppose I've learnt a lesson tonight. Quite what it is I don't know. The other lesson I've learnt is that nature can be cruel. That lamb . . .'

'I know, but at least we got one good one, thanks to you.'

'And thanks to you. I wouldn't have known where to start sorting that jumble out.'

'Practice, that's what it is. Nothing but experience. I love it. I'll take you with me another time when it's convenient and you can do an examination. Would you like that?'

Kate nodded her agreement. 'Very much.'

'So satisfying and new lambs are so . . .'

'Jolly, and sweet, and lovable?'

Dan smiled.

'But was I put face to face with the reality when Connie said what she'd cooked. I thought I would be sick.' Kate shuddered at the memory.

'It's the harsh reality of farming. It's their living and sentiment mustn't come into it. Well, occasionally it does and they keep a pet one.'

'Cheers!' Kate raised her glass and toasted Dan. 'Heard any more about Lord Askew and his horses?'

'Making progress. I had dinner with Lady Mary last night.'

'No! You didn't!'

'Yes, jolly pleasant too. She can be very amusing.'

'She has a dangerous reputation. I hear she devours nice men.'

'This man's not for devouring.'

'Oh, no? Wait till she's worked her charm on you.'

'Not my type.'

'What is your type, then?' Kate looked at him over the rim of her glass, curious to know his answer.

She'd taken a long drink and put down her glass before he answered her. 'Immaterial. I'm not in the market.'

Unsure of her ground and of his reasons for saying what he did, she blurted out, 'You've forsworn women, have you?'

'No. I'm simply not free.'

'I see.' Kate could have cut out her tongue for saying what she had and quite simply didn't know how to rescue the situation. She flushed bright red and hadn't a clue what to say any more. What on earth did he mean he 'wasn't free'?

Cutting through her embarrassment, Dan asked, 'Another drink, Kate?'

'No thanks, I'd better be going. Sorry to have said what I did. I didn't mean to pry. I'll walk to the practice to get my car. Thanks for the drink and for inviting me to the lambing.'

Dan stood up. 'My pleasure.' He endeavoured to be pleasant but his effort didn't quite succeed because his eyes remained blank. 'I'll drive you, it's a long walk in the cold.' He picked up his keys from the table and, taking hold of her elbow, led her outside.

They drove the short distance to the practice in silence. Eventually, just as he pulled up in the car park, leaving the engine running so there was no question of him wanting to stay talking, he said, 'One day perhaps I'll explain, but not right now. It's all very personal. Thanks for your company, you make a good assistant.'

'Except for crying like an idiot.'

'No, it shows you have a heart and a deep concern for animals. So long as you've done everything in your power to make things come right, that's the secret. Have no regrets.' Dan waited until she'd started up her car and then with a wave drove away. Kate wasn't quite sure if his advice referred to veterinary work or his private life. Whichever, the advice made good sense. Even so, she was no nearer to finding out what made Dan so uptight about women. He must have very deep feelings for that girl in the photo for him to be so seriously affected by her. If she was dead, then why wasn't he free? If she wasn't, where was she?

12

Kate was on duty at the desk by herself the following day when Sergeant Bird arrived full of excitement. 'Just going off duty. You won't believe it, but we've caught the beggars who tortured poor Copperfield.' He clenched both fists and banged them on the desk. 'All five of 'em. Not only that, I've got them for all the car thieving in the multi-storey. They'll be drawing their pensions by the time they get out.'

'Really? Good work!'

'Oh yes, brilliant!' He thumped the desk again.

'How did you do it?'

'Well, we were looking at the security film from the multi-storey and this time they were on the film. We'd caught them red-handed doing the stealing and like a flash it came to me that I knew one of the lads. Took a day or two for it to click but then it dawned.' Sergeant Bird took time off to contemplate his delight at his inspirational moment, while Kate hung in suspense, waiting. 'One of them was the lad I'd interviewed about poor Copperfield.'

Kate stood transfixed, fingers poised over the keyboard. She couldn't help it, he was so passionate, so . . . ' "That's him!" I shouted. "I know him. It's that little sod Bobby Turner." '

'So?'

'So this time we got him to the station, showed him the video and bob's yer uncle he came clean. The game's up, I told him. Might as well do yourself a favour. So of course he agreed to co-operate and we've got the lot in the nick at the moment. They were all in it together, tying that poor cat to the back of a bike and racing him down the slopes at the car park. Terrible. Terrible. Every last one of 'em we've got. What a coup.'

'How many did you say were involved?'

'Five. Thought doing that to him was a joke, the nasty little beggars.

It's only thanks to Bunty and Mungo that Copperfield's still alive. But . . .'

'Yes?'

'But . . .' He paused for dramatic effect. 'They're only the tip of the iceberg; they were stealing the cars to order for an international gang.'

'In Barleybridge?'

Sergeant Bird nodded. 'In Barleybridge. It's not only London where they have the big gangs. Oh, no. So it could lead to a big arrest.' He winked significantly at Kate.

'Well, all thanks to you. I'm so pleased. Wait till I tell the others. If you go on like this there'll be nobody left in Barleybridge. We'll all be in the nick. I have to confess I went through a red light the other day and . . .'

Abruptly he lost interest. 'Bunty in?'

'Yes, but she's . . .'

But Sergeant Bird had gone in the back to find her. He returned in a moment, white as a sheet. In fact, almost as green as a pea. Kate had to enquire about his health. He replied in an awestruck voice, 'My God!'

'What is it?'

He looked down at his hands in horror. 'Her hands were covered in blood and you could see . . .' He fled reception with the speed of light. Kate put down her pen and rushed outside after him. Poor Sergeant Bird was being disgustingly sick in Miriam's ornamental bushes right outside the front door.

'You'd better come in and sit down a minute. I'll get you a glass of water.'

She helped him in and sat him on the nearest chair. He sat shaking, his handkerchief held to his mouth. After he'd sipped the water he wiped away the beads of sweat on his forehead and said more calmly, 'You could have warned me they were operating. It was ghastly. I'd no idea.'

'Some of Mungo's operations are a bit intrusive.'

'Intrusive! It looked like a slaughterhouse in there. Mungo shouted at me to get out. He's never spoken to me like that before.'

'He doesn't mean it. He gets tense when he's operating; his ops are very tricky, you see, very intricate. Not like a common-or-garden neutering. Don't take it to heart. We've all had to learn to ignore his outbursts when he's doing a difficult op. Must get on. Sit there till you feel better.'

As she finished speaking the alarm sounded from Mungo's operating room and Kate heard the 'thud thud' of Sarah One's clumpy shoes as she rushed in to assist. Kate maintained a calm exterior, remembering what Joy said about not alarming the clients, but inside she was turbulent with anxiety. Obviously something was going badly wrong with the operation. Then she heard the hurried tattoo of Joy's shoes as she too hastened to help. There were raised voices, controlled but anxious: the tension in the air moved in palpable waves down the corridor. Tied as she was to the reception desk, Kate could only worry.

Then Joy's unhurried footsteps came back down the corridor. Sarah's clumpy shoes returned to the other operating room where she was working with Rhodri and Kate had to know. She left the desk and put her head round Joy's office door saying quietly, 'Joy, everything all right?'

She whispered, 'Fingers crossed. Heart stopped. Got it going, though. Seems fine now. Mungo's just closing up.'

'Who was it?'

'Cadbury, that chocolate Labrador bitch. The client had been warned it was risky but they decided to go through with it. I tell you, we thought she was a goner. It was one heck of a dodgy moment back there. Tea all round, I think.'

'A cup for Sergeant Bird too.'

Joy raised an eyebrow at the prospect of making tea for him as well. When Kate had explained, she smiled rather grimly and went to put the kettle on. To Kate's surprise Bunty emerged into the reception area carrying a mug of tea, which she gave to the Sergeant and then sat down beside him saying, 'I've put sugar in for you.'

There was something about their body language that alerted Kate and while she attended to the clients she kept a wary eye on the pair of them. She heard Bunty say, 'But of course there was blood on my hands, well, on my gloves, we were *operating*, for heaven's sake.'

'I know, I know, but it was just such a shock. I've never seen . . . you . . .'

'Then you've seen the real me. All right? Got to go, another op.'

'Please apologise for me to Mungo.'

'Of course. Drink your tea.'

Sergeant Bird nodded. 'You won't have heard. I've got the scum who tortured poor Copperfield.'

'Good. Throw the book at them. See you, Aubrey.'

Kate covertly watched Sergeant Bird's face as Bunty left him. It was a strange mixture of admiration and well, let's face it . . . love. And she had called him Aubrey, which no one else ever did, and Bunty had avoided catching her eye as she passed her. Well, surprise, surprise!

Kate had a further surprise that evening when she was scheduled to take her mother out for a meal. They'd agreed to meet by the fountain in the precinct and when Kate spotted her mother walking towards her she almost died. Her outfit was more suited to a reception at 10 Downing Street than a meal at a modest Italian restaurant. Kate was thankful that Mia had turned down her invitation to join the two of them. Her mother's appearance would only have put her back up. 'It's very considerate of you,' Mia had said, 'but, no, I won't, thank you. It's something between you and her, and I shall be in the way.'

'Of course you won't. Please come. I want you to come.'

'Well, if you don't mind I won't, Kate. I feel you and she have to get to know each other and I shall just be a nuisance. Now go along and have a good time. Remember there's all the rest of your lifetime, so don't go rushing anything, will you?'

Kate gave herself a last look in the mirror. 'There's no need to worry. I shan't be going to live with her or anything. It's tempting, but no thanks.'

'I see.'

'Look, Mia, I mean it. I'm not going to live with her. I want to stay with you.' Out of the blue came the terrible idea that maybe Mia was being reasonable because she actually wanted her to go. Kate's heart shot into her throat; she spun round and looked her straight in the face, but she couldn't tell from Mia's blank expression what she was thinking. 'Do you *want* me to go, is that it?'

Mia's face crumpled and she held out her arms. 'Go? Of course not. Of course not.' They hugged each other tightly. 'I'm trying not to stand in your way, if that's what you want. I'm just trying to be sensible, not to put pressure on you, you know. Oh, Kate! If only Gerry...' Mia drew back, wiped her eyes and, putting a smile on her face, added, 'I know there'll be a time when you'll launch out on your own, that's inevitable, but right now isn't the time and I want you to stay. Till you're qualified, you know.'

'You've got such faith in me. I just hope I won't let you down.'

Mia sniffed. 'You won't. Now get off or you'll be late. Have a good time.'

So now what should she do? Change her plans to accommodate her mother's outfit? There was no way that she, Kate, could afford anywhere more expensive than the Casa Rosa and that was that.

'Kate, dear!' Her mother bent forward to kiss her cheek and gave Kate a noseful of expensive perfume. 'I'm not late, am I?'

'No, you're not.'

'Where are we going to eat? The Askew Arms?'

'No, at the Casa Rosa, just down here, round the corner.'

'The Casa Rosa? I've never heard of it. Is it Italian?'

Kate nodded. 'It is very nice, though.'

'I'm sure.' Her mother looked disconcerted. 'Look. I know money must be tight. Mia won't have much, I expect, and you certainly won't, working as an accounts clerk at that practice. So why not let it be my treat? Eh? How about it? We'll go to the Askew Arms.'

Getting no reply, her mother took hold of her arm and shook it affectionately. 'What do you say?'

'I don't know.'

'Go on. I can afford it, you can't. Let me treat you and we'll have a lovely talk. The food is astonishingly superior, considering the size of Barleybridge.'

Kate studied the smart navy suit her mother wore, the lustrous pearls at the neck, the immaculate make-up, the large pearl earrings, the gold lapel brooch studded with pearls.

'I'm dressed up to make a good impression, I'm nervous you see.'

Stubbornly Kate replied, 'It is my invitation. I've booked the table. I'm paying.'

Her mother sighed. 'Very well, so be it.'

Just as they reached the restaurant door her mother asked, 'I hope the kitchens are all right. I've asked to inspect kitchens before now.'

'Not tonight, you won't.'

The evening went downhill from there. They found no common ground. In fact, it was hard to believe that their relationship was that of mother and daughter. Her mother did her best to retrieve the situation but even her skills couldn't surmount the awkwardness between them. Finally, as Kate paid the bill, her mother whispered, 'You should have let me take you to the Askew Arms. It would have been much better.'

With her change pushed into her purse, and a zip which wouldn't close and a handbag which for no reason had become too small to hold it, Kate slammed out with a curt goodnight to the waiter and marched her way down the precinct towards the car park, her mother trotting along behind her on her high heels.

'Wait! Let me catch up.'

But Kate didn't wait. She stormed along on the verge of tears, angry and disappointed.

'Kate!' Her mother laboured up the stairs to the second floor, trying to catch her up. 'I'm parked on the first floor, Kate!'

Kate stopped and turned round. 'I think we'd better not see each other again. I'll return the clothes. I haven't worn them. It's for the best.' She looked anywhere but at her mother, breathing hard and thoroughly distressed.

'What have I done wrong? I've tried my best.'

Kate took a deep breath and let her temper rip. 'You are rude and arrogant with no thought for anyone's feelings but your own. Selfish, that's what you are. How could I possibly have afforded the Askew Arms? It's way out of my bracket at the moment and you should have realised that. If I'd suggested a fish and chip shop you should have gone without a murmur. I'm so disappointed.' Her temper spent, Kate added sadly, 'But it's no good, is it? We're not made for each other. Thanks for trying anyway.'

'I have tried. I really have. I want it to work. I want you to come and live with me and let me support you. You can't cope with five years at college without some help. That's big money. I'm certain Gerry won't have left you big money and Mia hasn't any, has she? It'll cost me nothing really to help. Let me?'

'I don't know.'

'I'll phone in another week and you come round for tea. Don't bring the clothes back, though, those are yours whatever. Smile for me? Mm? We'll try again.'

'All right, then. We'll try. Goodnight.' As Kate turned away to walk to her car, her mobile rang. She fumbled about in her bag and eventually found it and conducted her conversation with Dan with her mother listening.

'Kate? Dan here. Where are you? I'm off to a lambing at Porter's Fold. Coming?'

'Oh, Dan, yes! I'm in the precinct multi-storey. Where are you?'

'About a hundred yards away, I was going to pick you up from home on my way through. Good thing I rang first. Let's think. I know, I'll pull in at the fountain end.'

'Right. Three minutes.' To her mother she said, 'A lambing. Got to go. Give me a ring like you said.' On winged feet she fled down the stairs, heart zinging with delight. This was a world in which she knew where she was, not that slipping, sliding world her mother lived in, where you never knew what was truth and what wasn't.

Dan was just pulling up as she arrived and she leapt in with relief. 'What's the problem?'

'Don't know but Connie's worried and they need support. He must be nearly dead on his feet. Belt up.' Dan surged off into the first gap he could find and headed for Magnum Percy.

This time it was Connie who was in the lambing shed, wrapped in her tartan blanket. 'Tad's asleep like a man felled, so I've come out. We've lost two lambs today. These are the ones causing a problem at the moment.'

In the same pen where the ewe had given birth to the twins only the night before stood two ewes in dire straits. Their bulging stomachs told their own story. 'Looks like twins again, Connie. Right, let's get to work. May I ask if Kate could examine one? Just for experience. Would you mind?'

'Not at all. I'll leave you to it, go and see how Tad is.' She heaved the tartan blanket more closely about her neck before she left the shelter of the shed and disappeared into the night.

In an old set of parturition clothes belonging to Dan, Kate knelt down in the straw. Dan squeezed some lubrication cream into the ewe and left Kate to get on with her examination. She hadn't the first idea of what sensations she would experience but she was eager to have a try. It was tight getting her hand in through the ridge of the pelvic bone but once through that there was more room and inside felt warm and wettish. Kate felt a head, and a jumble of legs, bony and angular, but as for making sense of what she felt, that was beyond her.

She withdrew her hand and turned to see what progress Dan had made. He had one lamb out on the straw and was struggling with the second one. It popped out with ease. 'How do you do it. I can't make any sense of what I could feel. There could be three or four in there for all I know.'

'Let me look. Check these two for me.'

Dan had the two lambs out on the straw almost quicker than it takes to say. 'The first one needed turning round; he was coming back end first.'

When they left the barn and set off to wash up in the outside lavvy as Connie called it, there were four spanking lambs and two proud mothers in the pen. Connie gave them both a hot toddy before they left. 'Thanks for all you've done. Just couldn't manage it myself. You're blinking good at your job, Dan, there's no doubt about that. I hear his lordship will be taking you back on.'

'Really? I hadn't heard.'

'So they were all saying in the market on Wednesday. Horses and farm they were saying. I'm surprised you don't know. They all knew in the market, that's the place to be if you want to hear the latest. Here, I've just had a thought. Come in the dairy and choose some cheese for yourselves. I've had some good reports about this batch.'

Kate and Dan put down their empty glasses and followed her out. The tartan blanket hitched up round her shoulders against the biting wind, Connie led them into the dairy, which was better equipped than the house, as though all Connie's creativity were centred in there rather than her home. Well-scrubbed stone shelves, immaculate, gleaming, stainless-steel pans and bowls, huge shining spoons and ladles, and best of all, shelves holding a small selection of cheeses waiting to mature.

'These are ready, these at this end, up to there. Choose one. Go on.'

'It's very kind of you,' said Dan, 'but please let me pay you for it. I can't expect you just to give me it.'

Connie stood tall and answered sharply, 'I shall be offended if you offer me money.'

Kate, anxious not to give any more offence, said, 'Dan lives on his own and there's only two of us at home, how about if we share a cheese? Otherwise it'll take us months to eat it up.' She smiled her sweetest smile at Connie who gave in with only a slight demur.

'I see your point. I'll cut the one you choose into two halves and wrap them for you.' She busied about getting paper and a huge shining knife down from her knife rack and stood waiting.

Dan nudged Kate. 'Go on, you choose.'

They all appeared the same to Kate but she took her time choosing, knowing it would please Connie.

As they left Porter's Fold Kate said, 'I feel very embarrassed about this cheese. She can't really afford to give it away, can she?'

'No, but like she said she'd be offended if we'd insisted. Very proud the two of them.'

'I see that. A lot of veterinary work is with the people, isn't it, as much the animals. I wish I were good at that.'

'I've always thought you were.'

'No, Dan, I'm not, not where it counts. I've made such a hash of taking my mother out this evening you wouldn't believe.' She explained how angry she'd been and how disappointed. 'You see, Mia would have fallen in with my plans without a murmur because she *understands*. But my mother? Oh, no! An Italian restaurant in the precinct wasn't good enough. Even the clothes she wore were all wrong for Barleybridge. She was all set for the Askew Arms no less, you see. I can't afford to afford that, if you see what I mean. I need to keep a hold on any money I have because of college.' Kate gave a great sigh and continued looking out of the side window, deep in thought.

Dan patted her knee. 'Come on, Kate, it'll take time, you know.'

'Still, we made a good job of those lambs and that's more important. Well, to me it is.' She beamed a great smile at him and he smiled back at her, glad to see her spirits had lifted.

'So, seeing as I keep using you as my life counsellor, what do you advise me to do? Keep on seeing her?'

'Of course. You must. Forget the dreams of childhood and your disappointment at her not matching up to them, and meet her as an adult on an equal footing.'

'Mm.'

'She can't replace Mia, can she?' He got no reply. 'Can she?'

Kate snapped out. 'Of course not.'

'There you are, then. Tessa happens to have given birth to you, but Mia is your mother. You might find Tessa's very lonely and your father dying has given her a window as you might say. Here we are, then.'

'Yes.' Kate stared out at the fountain thrusting water fifteen or more feet into the air as though she hadn't seen it before. 'Oh! Yes, here we are. Right, I'll be off. Thanks Dan, for thinking of me, it's been a wonderful experience and gives me a real impetus to succeed. Thanks for the lift.' She hunted in her bag for her car keys.

'Don't forget your cheese.'

'Oh, right. You know they've caught the people who tortured poor Copperfield? Dickie Bird came in this morning to tell us, not only that but they are also the same ones who are stealing the cars from the multi-storey so he's killed two birds with one stone as you might say. He's got some daft idea about them being part of an international gang stealing cars to order. I ask you, honestly, in sleepy old Barleybridge! He's been watching too many American gangster films.'

'There are people with pots of money around here. He could be right.'

'I suppose. Good night. Thanks again. See you tomorrow.'

13

The letter asking Mungo if the practice would take on Lord Askew's equine work and also take back the farm animal work was on Mungo's desk the following morning. Joy opened it and sprang to her feet, shouting, 'Eureka!' before she'd finished reading the first paragraph.

> ... *in consequence of this a meeting next week to discuss the ... suggest Thursday at twelve noon at the practice or at Askew Hall whichever you prefer* ...

Joy raced up the stairs to the flat and burst in to find Miriam and Mungo still eating breakfast. 'He's done it!'

'Who's done what, Joy?' Miriam asked.

'Sorry! It's this.' She thrust the letter under Mungo's nose. 'See?'

Mungo, sensing the importance of the moment, slowly picked up his reading glasses, placed them on his nose, and solemnly read the letter right the way through before he spoke, his face showing no reaction whatever. Then he leapt to his feet, put his hands round Joy's waist, kissed her heartily twice and swung her round.

Miriam picked up the letter from where Mungo had dropped it on the table and read the magical words. 'What did I tell you. All due to Dan.'

'Exactly!'

With a wry grin on her face Miriam asked Mungo, 'He can stay, then?'

'Of course. What else? I never thought the beggar would do it, but he has. So we're equine too now. Champagne all round tonight before they leave?' Mungo raised a questioning eyebrow at Miriam.

'Shall we keep mum until it's all agreed? Knowing Dan, he could drive a hard bargain, or perhaps more likely, knowing Lord Askew, *he* could drive a hard bargain and *us* not agree.'

'Perhaps you're right, yes, of course. But what a climbdown on his part.'

Miriam corrected him. 'No, Mungo, what a wise man he is. He knows how clever Dan is and wants him for himself.'

Joy declared she rather thought it might be Lady Mary who'd swung things in their direction. 'I know for a fact that Dan has had dinner with her twice in the last few weeks.'

Miriam looked up from reading the letter again and asked, 'Has he? I didn't know. You don't think . . .'

'I've work to do even if you two haven't, so stop your matchmaking the pair of you and start the day.' Mungo went off to the bathroom to clean his teeth and left Joy and Miriam speculating.

Joy said, 'He'd lead a hell of a life if anything ever came of it.'

'Lord Askew as a father-in-law! God help him.'

'Apparently Dan thinks he has a soft side to him.'

'He must be the only person ever to think that. No one has a good word for his lordship.' Miriam put the letter back in its envelope and placed it by Mungo's glasses. 'And you, Joy, what about you? What if Dan wanted to be a partner. Would you agree?'

Rather primly and with tight lips Joy answered, 'As Zoe so rightly told me not long ago, I'm not a partner so I have no say in the matter.'

'For heaven's sake, of course you have. You've the rest of the staff to carry with you about this. Well?' Miriam folded her arms and looked as though she had all morning to wait for Joy's reply.

'Well, at one time I would have opposed it, but I've got used to him now and there's no doubt about it, he brings nothing but credit to the practice and that can't be bad. Now he's apparently won back Lord Askew . . . So, yes. It's fine by me.'

Miriam kissed her cheek. 'Excellent! You see I was right. I've always said he would be good for us. I may not work in the practice but I do have a nose for knowing what's going on.'

Joy looked away, wondering just how much Miriam had guessed about her own love for Mungo. God, she hoped Miriam never found out. She couldn't bear it if she did. Fast on the heels of that thought she was hit as though by a sledgehammer with the realisation that her reaction to Mungo swinging her round by her waist and kissing her had not brought the adrenalin rush it would have done at one time. As she pondered this astounding thought he came back to pick up his glasses and the letter from the kitchen table, and she found her heart scarcely stirred at the smile he gave her and there was only the slightest tingling of jealousy at the sight of him kissing Miriam au revoir. So what had happened to her? Nonplussed by the void which had apparently opened up in her life, Joy thought she'd better go before her face gave anything away. 'I'll come down with you.'

She followed Mungo down the stairs, noticing that his hair grew as vigorously as ever. For twenty years she'd fiercely resisted the temptation to lay a loving hand on his neck where his hairline began, or more tempting still, caress his temples where his dark hair sprang so strongly. Somehow the urge to do so had almost bled away. But he was still a very desirable man. As Mungo walked down the stairs he glanced back to look at her and winked. 'We're forging ahead again, aren't we, Joy? Aren't you thrilled?'

'Oh, yes! We're moving on.' But Joy wasn't sure whether she referred to the practice or to her passion for him.

When Mungo handed Dan the letter to read later that day Dan was beside himself with delight. 'This is marvellous! Just what we wanted, isn't it?' He looked up at Mungo and asked, 'Isn't it?'

'Of course. We're all thrilled. It's a whole new world opening up for us, a new chapter. We'll get him here on home ground, you and me, and have it all out in the open. Get things clear right from the start.'

'Absolutely. While I wouldn't mind building up the equine side, I don't want to be exclusively equine, remember. In any case there wouldn't be enough work to begin with until we got more clients.' Dan handed back the letter to Mungo and added, 'That business of capital and wanting to be a partner, I'd like that.'

'Let's get the meeting over with first. I'm in favour, but there's the others to consider before we can make concrete plans. Talking of plans, what's this about Lady Mary?'

'What about her?'

'Having dinner I understand. The two of you.'

'That's all. Nothing more.'

Mungo held up his hands in surrender. 'Right. Sorry. None of my business.'

'No. Would you want me at this meeting?'

'Of course. You and I, but before the meeting I'll consult Colin and Zoe.'

'Certainly. Must be off. I take it I'm staying, then?' Dan smiled. 'I'd like it more than anything. But I'd buy a house and then the flat could be available for another vet should you decide to employ an additional one.'

'Right. Thanks.' Mungo held out his hand. 'Let's shake hands on it.'

What really amazed Mungo that night was Letty's surprising response to his news. They'd agreed for Zoe and him to meet at Colin's house and when they were seated, each with a drink in their hands, Mungo outlined what his proposals were. 'I know there was a lot of opposition to Dan when he first came but I'm rather hoping that you've all had a change of heart. There's no doubt about it that he's made changes which we didn't care for, but which have proved excellent once they were up and running. His knick-knack idea has proved a winner from day one and the changes he suggested to the small animal clinic hours are making that side of the practice pick up rapidly. Now we're faced with another big change. A fourth partner joining us, with capital, and transforming us into an equine practice. We musn't stand still ... we've got to keep on going upwards.'

Zoe held out her glass for a refill and while Colin obliged she commented, 'We don't want change just for the sake of it, though.'

'Absolutely not. But our premises cost thousands to maintain and we're not out of the woods yet financially with the capital cost of the building. Dan's money would be a real boost. Plus the added income from Lord Askew, plus any more equine we might pick up ... '

Colin interrupted with, 'Don't be asking me to step in if he's away. I haven't done horses since I qualified. I wouldn't know where to begin.'

Letty patted his knee. 'Colin, don't underrate yourself.'

Zoe was struck dumb with astonishment and Mungo thought he hadn't heard correctly and had to ask her what she'd said.

'I said he musn't underrate himself.'

'Oh, no, certainly not, quite right, though I do see his point. I'd be alarmed myself, I have to confess.' Then Mungo noticed what Miriam had told him, that Letty did look different: younger, less acidic, more friendly somehow. And it wasn't just her clothes and her make-up, though they were a vast improvement. It was something about her, a kind of melting, a sort of surrender. He shook off his analytical mode, thinking he was getting as bad as Miriam, and found that Zoe was being difficult.

'He's arrogant, that's his trouble, that's what gets my back up. He's always so *right*.'

'But he is.' This from Letty, which almost made the others' jaws drop in amazement.

'He is?' Mungo asked.

'Oh, yes. Diagnostically he can't be bettered, let's face it.'

Colin smiled a secret smile. 'She's right.'

'She is?' Mungo felt there was something going on he didn't understand.

'Oh, I am. I know I didn't like him to begin with and he was very rude doing that Nazi salute when he saw me, but I deserved it. I was rude and very aggravating too.'

Mungo now felt he was swimming in thick soup. 'You were?'

'Oh, yes. When really he's a very hard-working man putting in all the hours while we've been shorthanded. And to get Lord Askew back ... and his horses to boot, is nothing short of miraculous.' She downed the remains of her whisky and held out her glass to Colin for a refill.

Colin continued to smile his secret smile and Zoe and Mungo were still nonplussed while Letty, completely unaware of the surprise the others were experiencing, sat dreamily gazing into the gas fire. Out of nowhere she said, 'We're thinking of having this fire taken out and fitting a wood-burning stove instead. Much more homely and welcoming, don't you think.'

'Good idea,' said Zoe. 'But it's not for me. I don't like the work.'

'But think of the pleasure.'

Mungo decided he'd better get the discussion back online before he finally lost the plot. 'So if I go ahead with this meeting you'd be in agreement to have Dan as a partner I take it?'

Letty nodded vigorously. 'Absolutely. Well, it's for Colin to say really, of course, he's the partner. But he does agree, don't you, Colin?'

'I most certainly do.'

'Zoe, what about you?'

'Well, all things considered I suppose I shall say yes. Let's hope he's sound financially, otherwise ...' She gave a thumbs-down to indicate it was impossible without his money to back him up. 'I've got a bit remote from practice politics since I've been at home with Oscar, but I'm back next week and I expect I'll be glad to have his support.'

Mungo agreed with her by nodding his head. 'He'll be buying a house, so the assistant's flat will be free. Shall we sell it, or keep it for an additional member of staff?'

'With the poor state of farming at the moment, to be quite blunt, I can't honestly see us wanting to take on another vet for large animals. But I think hanging on to the flat would be prudent. Perhaps a member of the lay staff could use it for a while till we see some improvement.' This from Colin who for once in his life had made a decision without first getting it approved by Letty.

'So if Lord Askew and Dan and I make music at this meeting, I shall formally ask Dan to be a partner.'

The prospective partner in question was sitting in the flat on the sofa which had once been Miriam's and Mungo's, brooding. Partly wishing he were a fly on the wall in Colin's house and thereby knew what was going on, and partly cogitating about his life outside the practice.

To be frank, he hadn't got one. It was this blessed yearning for Rose which was hampering everything he did. He wouldn't for the world not have known her, but the fallout from their relationship was colouring his life to such a degree that it was hardly worth living. Then he remembered how happy she always was, how totally wholesome and scrumptious she was in bed, giving every inch of herself to loving him, with nothing held back, and how she'd taught him to do the very same. Dan thought about how unspoilt she had remained, despite the wealth and political power of her stepfather. He'd given her everything money could offer and yet she'd remained so very sweet.

Unconsciously his hand reached out to touch her as though she were there with him on the sofa. He could almost smell her perfume, feel the swirl of her hair as she turned towards him: that long, ash-blonde hair he so loved. She wore it plaited and pleated and under control when she went out, but when they were alone she'd have it hanging loose, scented and squeaky clean.

She'd inherited her colouring from her mother. The domineering old bitch had protected her only chick with a viciousness which had to be witnessed to be believed. How Rose had ever managed to survive her dominance and become such a sweet, loving person he would never know. By all the rules Rose should have been mean-minded, devious, greedy and shallow, but she was none of those things and he'd loved her with a passion that he knew would last to the end of his days. He couldn't cast her off.

He pulled her photograph out of his wallet, remembering the day he took it, the shimmering heat outside, the chill of the air-conditioned house, the almost frozen precision of the furnishings and decoration: the untouchable, sterile chairs, the stark barrenness of the dining hall which killed one's appetite stone dead. All of it mirrored the destructive, strangling characteristics of her mother.

Whom could he find to replace his beloved Rose? He knew the answer before he formed the question: no one.

His phone rang and he snatched it up from under the cushion beside him like a drowning man grasping a lifeline. It was Phil Parsons babbling incomprehensibly something about Sunny Boy and Hamish, and could he come?

Glad of a diversion, Dan leapt to his feet and roared off in the Land Rover to Applegate Farm. Phil was standing, hopping anxiously from one foot to the other, in the farm gateway. 'He's gone mad. Completely mad! He needs a jab.'

Despite Phil's anxiety, Dan took time to put on his boots and some protective clothing. 'Come on, hurry up!' As they strode together across the pitch-black yard an ambulance chugged heavily up the lane and parked behind Dan's vehicle.

'God, Phil! What's happened? An ambulance?'

Phil shouted to the ambulance men, 'This way. This way.' He waved his arm in a wide sweeping gesture. 'This way!' Dan switched on his torch to light the way through the gloom for the crew.

'Hurry up!' shouted Phil. 'He's in a terrible mess.' He led the way into the cow byre. Being winter, the so-called dairy cows were housed inside and they were panicking. Lying to one side in the deep straw was Hamish, with Blossom kneeling beside him holding a bloodied towel to his chest. 'Here he is. Please, save him! He's only a boy.'

'Can we have more light?'

Phil hurtled about, lighting a couple of Calor gas lamps and hanging them from convenient nails in the beams. 'Hurry up! The lad's dying.'

As Dan's eyes became accustomed to the light he saw that several of the cows were gashed here and there as though they had been attacked. Streaks of blood had run down their flesh and were beginning to dry. In the ghastly silence which followed the crew started work on Hamish. Then Dan could hear savage crashing and banging coming from Sunny Boy's stall.

Before he could question Phil about it, Blossom flung herself on to Dan, weeping and wailing. He put a protective arm round her shoulders and muttered comfort to her, though he'd no idea if his words were of any use because the ambulance crew were working with a kind of desperate energy which boded ill. His veterinary training made him able to turn his attention to the cows and he was pleased to find that none of them was in urgent need. A stitch here and there would suffice. It was the sound of Sunny Boy's frantic distress which really panicked him.

'Right. Let's get him to hospital. We've done what we can here.'

Blossom screamed, 'Hamish! My baby!' She left Dan and hurled herself towards Hamish, reeling back in shock when she saw the oxygen mask and the unconscious Hamish with his deathly white face and the ambulance man padding his chest in an attempt to stem the flow of blood. As they carried him out she staggered after him into the cold night, wearing only a tiny cropped short-sleeved sweater and a skirt which just covered her bottom. 'I'm coming! I'm coming, Hamish!' Her long, black-stockinged legs seemed to vanish from beneath her as she wobbled across the dark yard, so only the Day-Glo skirt and sweater appeared to be stumbling along behind the stretcher.

Phil stood in the byre, rigid with distress. Dan couldn't think of a word to utter. What was there to say? 'They'll pull him round.' 'He's in the best place.' 'If anyone can save him they will.' Or the classic, useless, 'Try not to worry.' All this against a background of the noise coming from Sunny Boy's stall.

Dan cleared his throat. 'We'll leave the cows here to settle a bit and then I'll inspect them and stitch any that need it. First, it's Sunny Boy. What the hell happened, Phil?'

It was only when he faced him that Dan realised Phil's balaclava below his eyes was soaked with tears. Silent, painful tears he couldn't control. As usual, only one eye matched up with the slits in the balaclava and Phil, with his one-eyed stare, said, 'He went berserk.'

'I see. What set him off?'

'Don't know. It just happened. Been all right with Hamish ever since the day he came. He went to give him his titbits before he shut him up for the night while I checked the cows and wham! Sunny Boy went for him. He'd got careless, had Hamish, bit too casual yer know, not brought up with animals he wasn't ... isn't ... and he'd gone in his stall and left the gate open. First I knew, Hamish was running in here with that damn great beggar after 'im, wild with temper, and before I knew it he'd got Hamish cornered, got 'im down and stamped on 'im. The cows all took fright and he went for them, but they're more hurt by crashing into the walls and that than 'im.'

Phil paused for breath. He gave a great shuddering sob and stood head bowed. The cows had stopped milling about and all they could hear was Sunny Boy trashing his byre. 'If Hamish ... dies ... Blossom 'ull never forgive me. God 'elp me.' Phil took out his handkerchief and wiped his eyes. 'She loves him like a son. And so do I.' His shoulders heaved in sorrow.

'About Sunny Boy ...'

Phil warned him. 'Don't say it ...'

In a low voice so as not to provoke him more than he could avoid, Dan said, 'I have to say it. I'd be irresponsible if I didn't.'

'*Don't say it.*'

'*I shall.* There must be something terribly wrong with him for this to happen. Like a brain tumour or BSE, whatever, he can't be trusted ever again.'

Phil's chin was almost touching his chest.

'In fact, hard though it is for me to say this, I don't know if I want to be responsible for his health when he's so unpredictable.'

Phil shook his head despairingly.

'That boy's life is hanging by a thread because of Sunny Boy's unpredictability.'

Truculently Phil growled, 'He should have shut the gate.'

'If he had shut the gate then Hamish would more than likely have been dead. Mangled dead. I'm serious, Phil. You've a big decision to make here.'

'You wouldn't be saying that if it was someone you loved like I love Sunny Boy. You're a hard man. You don't understand pain, you don't.' He thumped his chest with his clenched fist. 'It's right here.'

'I understand the pain all right, believe me.' Privately Dan was thinking *I've got to persuade him to have Sunny Boy put down but who the hell but me is there to do it?* They both listened and each thought the crashing about seemed to be getting worse. Dan said, 'Well?'

'You asking me for a decision right now?'

Dan nodded. 'How did you get him back in his stall?'

'I didn't, he went himself. He did a couple of turns round the yard, then went in his stall and I rushed and banged the gate shut, like as if he knew where he would feel safe.'

'You were very brave. He could have turned on you.'

'On me? Naw. Not me.'

'I won't challenge you to prove that, just in case, but it seems to me he's gone totally irrational. Somehow I'm pretty sure it isn't BSE, the behaviour pattern isn't right. These cows are calming down now. Before I stitch them up I'm going to climb up on something and have a look through that nicely cleaned window in Sunny Boy's byre and see what he's up to.'

By the light of his torch Dan found an old chair out in the yard and used it to climb on to look in. The stone walls of which his stall was made had withstood Sunny Boy's panic, as was only to be expected, but the gate had two bars snapped and he was making inroads on the remaining ones. He was thrashing about uncontrollably, ramming his massive shoulders into the walls, thudding his head against his manger, rubbing it frantically against any available hard surface as though ... that was it! It was as though he had an almighty pressure in his head and he couldn't bear it.

The answer was to wait until he was exhausted and then go in and give him the lethal shot. He could hear the house phone ringing. 'Phil, your phone's ringing.'

He heard Phil clump round to the house. Dan got down off the chair and waited. Phil came out. 'Blossom. He's going into theatre as soon as.'

'That sounds as if there's hope.'

'It does. Blossom's beside herself. Well, now he's not dead there's no need to . . .'

Dan overrode this bright idea saying, 'I can't go in as he is. Let's barricade the outside door in case he gets out of the stall . . .'

'Let me look.' Phil borrowed Dan's torch and climbed up to peer through the window. 'Bloody hell.' He stood on tiptoe. 'Bloody hell! He's torn himself and no mistake. There's blood.'

'I know.'

'You can't leave him like that.'

'I can.'

'He'll need stitches.'

'Tomorrow. I'll see to the cows and then I'm going home and coming back first thing in the morning to see to Sunny Boy.'

'To stitch him, you mean?'

'No, I don't mean that.'

Between them they got Phil's tractor and drove it up against the cow byre door so he couldn't possibly escape. Dan went back to the cowshed and began examining the cows, completely ignoring Phil. It took him an hour to attend to them and then he packed his bag and got ready to leave.

Phil had gone into the house in an attempt to shut the noise of Sunny Boy's frenzy out of his head. Dan opened the door and shouted, 'Phil, I'm going. I'll be back first thing.'

'You're not putting him down. I tell yer, yer not.'

'Goodnight,' Dan answered firmly.

Colin went with him the following morning and they were at the farm by a quarter to eight. They parked their vehicles on the cart track, put on their protective clothing and, with a sharp warning from Dan about the slurry pit, they trudged across the yard to the house. To Dan's relief there was an uncanny silence about the farm. The tractor was still parked at the cow byre door and there was no sign of life.

'What the blazes! It doesn't change, does it.' Colin gazed round first at the house and then the farm buildings and the filthy yard. 'Years since I've been here. I'd forgotten.'

Dan rattled the door knocker again. He thought he heard voices inside the house, but no one came. 'I'm going to have a look.'

Colin followed him and watched while he climbed on the old chair. Dan peered in and saw Sunny Boy standing up, leaning heavily against a wall of his stall as though he wouldn't be able to stand if he didn't have its support.

'Take a look.'

Colin climbed on the chair and looked in. 'Gone quiet at least. But he looks odd. Almost comatose. Not asleep. More like he doesn't know what he's doing. Dazed, kind of. Doesn't seem like BSE to me, which it could have been, I suppose. No, the symptoms are not right.'

'Just what I thought. Perhaps my theory about it being a brain tumour is right.'

'God, he's a magnificent beast, isn't he? Such a shame to see him like this, Dan.'

'Somehow we've got to persuade Phil to have him put down. He's too dangerous.'

'I agree. He should never have kept him. What's wrong with A.I.?'

'He's proud of him.'

'That's a load of sentimental tosh and you know it. The man's a farmer not an emotional do-gooder.'

'I know that, but he loves him and you can see why.'

They heard the house door slam shut and footsteps coming across the yard. Colin got down from the chair. It was Phil, his eyes looking as though they hadn't closed for a week.

'Morning, Phil. You remember Colin? Any news of Hamish?'

'Hanging by a thread. Blossom got home an hour ago. Crushed ribs, you see, and they've penetrated . . .' He wiped his eyes with an old rag.

'Well, at least he's holding on, that's something. I'm so sorry about him. Well, Phil, I've brought Colin to give a second opinion. We both agree Sunny Boy is very, very ill, otherwise he would never have acted like he did. We both think his unpredictable behaviour is due possibly to a brain tumour. There's absolutely nothing we can do about that. At the moment he looks as though he doesn't even know what he's doing.'

Colin added, 'The decision is yours.'

'But we both feel . . .'

Colin interrupted with, 'How about it, Phil? Hamish is more important than any animal to you, isn't he? Eh? Much more important, especially to Blossom, who's such a loving woman, as you well know. Even if Hamish recovers, you can't expect her to want to live here and see that magnificent animal still about.'

Phil shook his head.

Colin continued, 'He looks to be in such pain that it's almost cruel to leave him alive.'

Dan said, 'No vet likes putting an animal down, but we do know when it needs to be done for the animal's sake, and this is one of those moments, Phil.'

'I hear what you say. I'll just have two minutes with him and then . . .'

Dan couldn't believe he was hearing right. 'Is that wise? He may not recognise you.'

'Wise or not, he's not going without his closest friend saying goodbye.'

He climbed in the tractor and backed it away from the door.

Colin and Dan stood in the doorway on red alert: quite still, watching. The gate hadn't been totally destroyed and Phil climbed over the two still intact bottom bars and approached the bull quietly. Sunny Boy, occasionally shaking his head from side to side, was still leaning against the wall dazed, his eyes clouded and lifeless. Phil spoke gently, holding out his hand with a few titbits in it, but Sunny Boy never even recognised that his dearest friend was standing by him.

'Watch him, Phil. Watch him,' Dan warned quietly.

By now Dan was almost in tears. It seemed so incredibly sad that at the last Phil couldn't have the gratification of saying a proper goodbye to the pride of his life. Dan recalled his last goodbye to Rose, how he'd wondered that his brain could still send signals to his body when his heart had burst with such deep sorrow.

Ignoring the danger, Phil reached out to stroke Sunny Boy's dark-red flank, then he grew brave and stroked his huge forehead. Only the sound of Phil's quiet murmurs and the blowing of the breath of half a ton of bull broke the silence.

Phil backed away from him, stepped over the broken gate, and as he passed Colin and Dan said painfully, 'I 'ave to say he's been getting unreliable for a while. Like that time he trampled on Scott. We thought it was the pain of his leg but I think perhaps it was more than that. I've warned Hamish once or twice to be careful. It's come to something when I have to back away from 'im. Never had cause to do that in all his life. Get it done. It isn't 'im, not any more.' He stalked into the house and left Dan and Colin to do their job.

When Dan got back to the practice, Miriam asked him up to the flat for breakfast. 'I know you've a list of calls but come, I've put the kettle on. It's the least I can do.'

She settled him at the kitchen table with a pot of coffee, cereals and croissants, a block of golden butter, and a dish of home-made marmalade and another of raspberry jam.

As he sat at the table Dan rubbed his hands. 'This looks wonderful. Thank you.'

His thanks were so gloriously genuine that Miram placed a heartfelt kiss on his cheek. 'You deserve it. It must have been harrowing at Phil Parsons's. How is he?'

'He went straight off to the hospital with Blossom. He's shattered.

The hunt agreed to come for poor old Sunny Boy and I didn't want him to see that. Neither did Blossom so she persuaded him she was too tired to drive safely. They're an odd couple, on the surface so totally unsuited, yet . . .'

'Look at Bunty and Sergeant Bird . . .'

'What do you mean?'

'Oh, I shouldn't have said that. Don't tell anyone but they're getting married on Saturday. She doesn't want anyone to know.'

Dan's eyebrows shot up with surprise. 'Now there is a very odd couple. I'd no idea.'

'Poor Sergeant Bird. His mother died three or four years ago and he's been desolate ever since. Needed a good woman, you know. Well, now he's got one.'

Dan put aside his empty cereal bowl and began on the croissants.

Miriam clasped her hands round the mug of coffee she'd poured herself from Dan's pot, noticed how gratefully he was devouring his breakfast and said daringly, 'You need someone to look after you, too.'

This was greeted by total silence. Dan put down his knife and picked up his cup, but didn't drink from it. 'Do you have a twin?'

'No.'

'Then I am destined to walk the path of life alone.' He had sombre vibrations in his voice when he said this and Miriam had to laugh.

'Honestly, Dan, you are a flirt.'

'I'm nothing of the kind. I'm speaking the truth. Mungo is a very lucky man.'

'I'm lucky too.'

'Yes. I can see that. There's much to be admired in Mungo.'

'I'm so glad you're joining us. Oh! Perhaps I've jumped the gun there too. Sorry. My big mouth.'

'If I didn't know you better I'd think your gaffes today were deliberate.'

'I'm so sorry. I seem to be off my guard this morning.' Miriam felt extremely uncomfortable. She didn't really know what was the matter with her; she was usually the soul of discretion and here she was with all her barriers down.

Dan finished his second croissant, drained his cup but didn't offer to leave.

'More coffee?'

'No, thanks. What was worse for Phil was Sunny Boy not recognising him when he went in to say his goodbyes.'

'I can imagine.'

'That was the most awful bit.' Dan stared at the plants on the windowsill. 'Final goodbyes are never easy, are they.'

'No.'

'Damn stupid for a vet to be talking like this, but that great beast was like his own flesh and blood. I just hope to God Hamish survives.'

'So do I.' Tears brimmed in Miriam's eyes.

'I'm so sorry. I didn't think.'

'That's all right. Just me being a bit soft in the head.'

'Must go before I get maudlin.'

They sat a while in companionable silence.

Head down so as not to catch his eye, Miriam dared to say, 'One day, Dan, perhaps you'll be able to talk to me about her.' When she finished speaking she looked him full in the face.

Dan's eyes registered shock momentarily, then he smiled. 'Thanks for the breakfast. Much appreciated. Work to do.' He paused for a moment with his hand on the kitchen doorknob, indecisive, lost in thought, then said, 'Rose, her name was . . . is.'

14

Of course Kate could have told her that but the matter had never come up. Kate was far too absorbed anyway in her work and in sorting out the problem of her mother. She'd rung Kate exactly a week to the day from the appalling evening they'd had together in the Italian restaurant. Kate hadn't expected her to be so prompt but she was, so maybe she did mean it when she said she wanted things to work out between them. They made arrangements for Kate to go for tea the following Saturday. Kate asked rather hesitantly if Mia could go with her if she wanted and after a moment her mother had agreed.

But persuading Mia to go was altogether another matter.

'But I want you to go, I want you to see what it's like there. Please, for me.'

'What good will it do? I don't want a relationship with her. You do. I don't. She's nothing to me. Because of her, your father could never love anyone again. She'd stolen him from me before your dad and I even met each other.'

Kate was appalled about the thinking behind Mia's declaration, but she still wanted her there on Saturday. 'But I want you to come.'

'Why?'

Kate didn't really know why but she said, 'Because I want you to help me decide.'

'Decide what?'

'I don't know.'

'In that case I won't go. Perhaps later when you know her better.'

'I don't know if I want to know her better, that's the trouble.'

'Only you can decide that.'

'Please, Mia.'

'No. I can't offer you what she can offer you. I can't provide you with pots of money, which she can, nor the clothes and a better style of living and the holidays, none of that. All I've got to give is love and a roof over your head. Right? So off you go by yourself and make your own decisions. I won't stand in your way and I don't want to hear any more about it.' Mia got up and left the kitchen, came back in an instant, put her head round the door and added, 'What's more, I don't fit in with her kind, not at all.'

Kate had never known Mia be so adamant, so irate, it made matters even worse and reaching a decision even more remote. Mia had changed towards her since her dad had died. But truth to tell it wasn't so much since then, it was since her mother had turned up so unexpectedly.

Putting herself in Mia's position, it dawned on Kate that Mia felt threatened. Of course, that was it. Tessa had such tempting options to offer: money, a lovely home, position. And what had Mia to offer? Nothing except love, as she'd said, and a roof over her head. As if she, Kate, could leave Mia! She couldn't. That was what Mia needed to know.

Kate leapt to her feet and went to look for her. She found her in her bedroom, sitting on the bed. 'Mia!'

Mia looked up at her, miserable and tearful. 'I shouldn't have snapped, sorry.'

'Yes, you should, because I've never made myself clear. You're my real mother, not Tessa. I'm not going to leave unless you prefer me to.'

Mia shook her head disbelievingly.

Kate pressed on, 'It's all terribly tempting, her money and such, the holidays, the support while I'm at college, but she doesn't love *me*, she loves the idea of a grown-up daughter who is old enough not to make babysitting a problem, someone she can mould into a likeness of herself. She wants me to be slim. I ask you, as if I shall ever be slim. Some chance! She fancies me well-dressed. Smart. Up to the minute. A daughter to show off. Well, she's not getting that from me.'

'Is that what you think? That she wants a model daughter?'

'Oh, yes. The actual caring years are behind me, you see. I'm sure she'd much prefer me to be a doctor or a barrister or something. Being a vet is messy and cold and dirty and smelly, not nearly high-profile enough. But being a vet is what I want to be. I've seen Scott . . .'

'. . . of blessed memory . . .'

Kate had to smile. 'Yes, of blessed memory, at work, and I've seen Dan, such completely different people but so dedicated. No matter how tired they are, how much they dislike the client, how unhappy they are about their own lives, the animals always come first. It's all so fascinating working out what's wrong. You can't ask a sheep or a cat where the pain is, or does it hurt when they cough, you have to work it out for yourself. That's the magic. That's what I *want to be*. A vet. When I see her next Saturday you can bet she'll do her very best to persuade me otherwise. Well, she won't.'

Mia took hold of Kate's hand and drew her down to sit beside her on the bed. 'Your dad would have been so proud. So proud. I'm just sorry he didn't live to see you qualified.'

'Talking about Dad, I didn't tell you everything about the attic.'

'No, I know you didn't. I guessed there was something.'

'There was a shoebox full of stuff about Tessa. Photographs and letters. I've half a mind to destroy it all, but for Dad's sake I feel I can't, not yet. If you want to see it, it's in the bottom of my wardrobe. But perhaps you don't, after what you've said.'

Kate felt Mia's hand tremble slightly. 'No, thank you. I don't want to know how much he loved her. He was fond of me in his own way, but not like he loved Tessa. I was useful and amenable and I loved you, and that had to suffice. For him and for me. But I do miss him. More than I ever thought. He was a good man was your dad, and you were the light of his life. Do him proud, won't you?'

'I'll try. But I want you to know I'm not going to live with Tessa, because you're my mum and always will be.'

Mia put her arms round Kate and they hugged each other. Hard.

'Love you, Kate. I've seen a flat you might like. Will you come with me on Saturday to look round it, before you go to Tessa's? It's new and modern and bright, and there's a lovely window I could paint by, such wonderful light.'

'Try and stop me.' Kate stood up. 'I'm not saying I shan't visit her or go shopping with her, or even on holiday with her, but . . . that's as far as it will go. Promise.' She bent to kiss Mia and went downstairs.

A few minutes later she called up, 'I've made a cup of tea.'

'I'll be down.' But Mia sat a while longer, feeling grateful for what Kate had said. Losing Gerry was bad enough but to lose Kate . . . Perhaps she could housekeep for her when she qualified . . . or something. Mia thought of all the years she still had to live without the two of them. At forty-six she possibly was only a bit more than halfway through her life. Well, she'd throw herself into living it to the full and most important of all she'd find a job, and at forty-six that was not impossible nowadays. A job where she met people and had a bit of excitement. Take hold of life and give it a good shake by the scruff, that's what she'd do. She straightened her shoulders, wiped away all trace of tears and went downstairs to drink tea with her Kate. Damn Tessa, she'd been stealing Gerry all these years, but it looked as if she wasn't going to steal Kate too: Kate, it would appear, was still *hers*.

In the event, Tessa phoned to say she had to be away for the weekend and could Kate come one evening during the week, say Thursday? So Kate did but she found the long drive exhausting and arrived tired and certainly not in a diplomatic mood.

Thursday had been the day when Lord Askew came to agree to the practice taking over his equine work. Though it was Joy's day off, she came in and had been scurrying about right from the start, making sure everything was in apple pie order for the big moment. Hands on hips she said, 'Nothing, but nothing must go wrong today. Files at the ready, reception area spruce, chairs lined up, knick-knacks in spanking order, and a goodly smell of disinfectant about the place, if you please.'

Behind her back Stephie sniffed her disgust. 'As if we don't do that every day. Anyone would think the Queen was coming.'

'Well, he is royalty around here, isn't he? And his account is important to us.'

'I suppose. I'll get the spray ready to freshen things up.'

The morning sped along at its usual pace and before they knew it Dan was back from his calls, and Mungo and he were conferring on their strategy in Mungo's office. Kate was dispatched to carry down a tray Miriam had prepared with coffee pot and china cups so they could offer Lord Askew some refreshment in respectable cups instead of their collection of mugs given as gifts by the drug companies: it hardly appeared seemly to be offering him coffee in a mug advertising worming tablets. She'd intended going back to close the door at the bottom of the stairs to the flat but a client had come in needing advice, and as Stephie was taking money and trying to answer the phone at the same time Kate had to help, and all thoughts of the door slipped her mind.

At five minutes to twelve, just as Joy was beginning to come to the boil, there was the scuttle of dog claws on the reception floor and Adolf the Rottweiler with Mr Featherstonehough in tow appeared in reception. He omitted his usual pleasant greeting and in a state of high tension he stuttered out, 'He's got a lump come up on his groin. Can someone see him? It's inflamed and he won't let me touch it.' Adolf, too, was in a highly excitable state, on the verge of uncontrollable, and his front paws came up on the counter and his great frothing mouth dripped pools of saliva on to the surface.

'Could you quieten him down, Mr Featherstonehough, or it'll be impossible to examine him. Valentine's had a cancellation so he'll be able to see you in about ten, fifteen minutes. Take a seat.'

Mr Featherstonehough dragged Adolf off the counter and went to find a seat. But just as Lord Askew opened the inner door Adolf pulled free and went skidding across the polished floor towards the corridor leading to the back. Perkins appeared and the wholesale fight to which they had all become accustomed began. Adolf coming in unexpectedly meant that they hadn't got the old fire bucket at the ready and the fight progressed with almost terrifying ferocity. Total confusion reigned as clients lifted their feet, or grabbed their pets to avoid their flashing fangs: the air filled with vicious snarling and growling.

Kate picked up a bucket filled with soapy water concealed in the accounts office, which had not been emptied from their cleaning frenzy earlier, and threw it, cloth and all, over the two dogs. Experience had improved her aim no end and the two drew apart with the shock and shook themselves all over everyone. Perkins, his tail wagging furiously, eyes sparkling, grinned his delight at his own prowess and Adolf, as he always did, went to lean his wet body against Mr Featherstonehough who'd also taken the brunt of the fallout from the bucket.

'Lively morning you're having.' Lord Askew's great voice boomed through reception. 'Feisty pair of dogs you've got. Like to see a bit of spirit, what the nation's short of. Now, young lady, kindly inform Mungo Price I'm here.' Stephie disappeared to get Mungo.

The clients waiting their turns were glued to their chairs. More than one relied directly on him for their livelihood or their home and knew exactly how to mind their Ps and Qs. There came a chorus of 'Good morning, my lord'.

'Good morning to you all.' He stood, this giant of a man, dominating them with his size and his bearing, a smile of approval on his lips. Kate began mopping up. Perkins went to have a word with Lord Askew. He showed his small front teeth in a grin and wagged his tail, looking up at him appealingly. For his pains he got his head, about the only dry part of him, well patted by Lord Askew's big beefy hand.

Mungo appeared, took the decision to ignore the whole fiasco and greeted his visitor with great style, leading him through the back to his office and asking Stephie to make the coffee as though nothing untoward had taken place. Kate had to admire him; she'd have been apologising all over the place if she'd been Mungo. They could hear Lord Askew laughing loudly as they went out of sight.

The clients broke into quiet out-of-the-corner-of-their-mouths speech.

'Old bastard! Still, he took that well.'

'Thieving old bastard yer mean.'

'He's given 'em notice to quit next door to us.'

'No!'

'Hard as nails he is.' Several heads nodded at this.

The most vocal of the clients called out, 'It's all over town he was coming back on your books, Stephie. Must be true, then.'

Joy answered non-committally on her behalf, and shot Kate and Stephie a warning glance. Kate, having mopped up the water, went to empty the bucket. Joy put their 'slippery floor' warning sandwich board out on the wet patch and peace was restored.

But the day had carried on in much the same chaotic fashion so, when Kate arrived at Tessa's, she was not her usual common-sense self. What she needed was Mia's kind of comfort. What she got was, 'Are you keeping to that diet I gave you?'

'No, I'm not. I work hard, I'm studying and I've started playing badminton but apart from that . . . no.'

'I'm disappointed, just half a stone would make all the difference. Still, sit down. I thought you'd have been here earlier. I thought you finished at four.'

'I should have done, but we were busy and I had the end of month accounts to finish.'

'Go into the drawing room, I've got it all ready.'

Kate plumped herself down on the sofa and tried to concentrate on what she had planned to say. But her mind drifted away to the day she'd just got through and to how thrilled she was that Dan had at last justified his existence and how she'd watched a jovial Lord Askew wend his way out, laughing and joking with Dan. What a coup for him! The rattle of the tea trolley brought her back to earth.

'Here we are. This must be just what you need.' Tessa placed a delicate china plate in her hand and invited her to help herself.

'You know, I'm going to Norfolk for the weekend, why don't you come with me? Staying with friends who are clients of mine. They have a huge house, plenty of room and I'm sure they'd love to meet you.'

'These sandwiches are lovely.'

'Only the very best for my daughter. Which brings me to an idea I've had. I don't feel that being a vet is something I want my daughter to be. It's cold and dirty and . . . well primeval almost, and you'll never be rich. But . . .' Tessa smoothed her skirt over her bony knees. 'Why not try for the law? With me behind you . . .'

Head down so as to betray none of her feelings, Kate answered, 'I hardly think so . . .'

'Why not?'

'Because' – Kate raised her head and looked full at her – 'I don't want to.'

'I see. That's not very helpful, is it?'

'No, it isn't, but it's the truth.'

Tessa put down her plate rather sharply. 'I'm doing my best here to make things come good between us. Why can't you be more co-operative?'

'Why should I? For the last nineteen years you have deliberately ignored my existence and now, because it suits, you're all over me like a rash, even offering to change my career for me. I want to be a vet and a vet I shall be. I love it.'

Tessa looked at Kate long and hard. 'It's Mia, isn't it? She's poisoning your mind against me. Well, I can tell you she was welcome to Gerry, more than welcome. A more boring man, with his damned train sets and his biscuit factory, I couldn't hope to meet. It was no wonder I left.'

'So why did you hop into bed with him? If he was so boring?'

Tessa shrugged her shoulders. 'Bit of fun really. Seeing how the other half lived, I expect.'

Kate didn't reply for a moment, reminded how her dad had said he'd been a bit of rough for her. When she did, it stunned Tessa. 'Never as long as I live will I either understand or forgive you for abandoning me. A more callous, mean, nasty, cruel thing to do to your own flesh and blood I cannot conceive. In fact, it makes me not even want to get to know you, because of the kind of person you must be to do such a thing.'

'How dare you! You don't even begin to understand how I felt. I couldn't help myself.' Out came the lace-edged handkerchief. 'I really couldn't bear it.'

'What's more, I will not hear one word against Mia. She is being so good to me about you, standing back and trying hard not to influence me. Nor do I want to hear one more bad word about Dad. I found all his letters to you. The photos he took, the letters he wrote to you after you left and never posted . . .'

'Letters to me, after I left that he never posted? What was the point of that for God's sake?'

'To ease his broken heart I expect. He adored you.'

Tessa had the grace to look ashamed for a moment but then that element of amazement at Gerry having been so devoted to her came back into her face. 'Fancy, him with such passions. I'd no idea. Though I wouldn't have stayed even if I had realised. He was a bore. With his Beetle car and his obsession with keeping his house like some nineteen thirties mausoleum. Hell!'

Kate felt as though her tea was choking her. She put her cup on the trolley, her plate beside it and stood up. 'If you imagine this is going to endear you to me you are very wrong. The more I hear the more I realise you and I have nothing in common. I've fantasised all my life

about this wonderful mother I had, who one day would come and . . .'
To her absolute fury Kate burst into tears.

She blundered out of the room and headed down the hall, but the front door was locked and she hammered against it in despair with clenched fists.

She smelt Tessa's perfume close at hand, felt Tessa's arm round her shoulders and furiously shook it off. 'Unlock this door. I want to go home. Please.'

'My dear, I'm so sorry.'

Kate snorted her disbelief. 'For what?' She turned her tear-streaked, crumpled face towards Tessa and demanded, 'Well? For what?'

'For letting you down so badly. For leaving you with Gerry. I know I shouldn't have done, but please forgive me. It's a long time ago now and . . . I realised before you were born that I'd made the most terrible mistake going to live with Gerry. He wanted me to marry him so you wouldn't be illegitimate. Well, he used the word bastard, which only served to emphasise the enormous gap there was between us. Frankly, I'd just lost my father and I think I must have been looking for security, a base, someone to be a substitute for him and at the time Gerry seemed to fit the bill. Then, when I found myself pregnant, I could have died. A baby to him! Oh, God! I didn't want one in the first place . . . but his! Heaven forbid. A girl like you, your mother's daughter, must have felt embarrassed sometimes at his coarseness, his lack of . . . well . . . refinement? I'm just so glad you've inherited my refinement. It makes me so proud. So do you understand my side of it a little better now?'

'Well, thanks for shedding so much light on the matter.'

'I knew you'd understand.' Tessa smiled and patted Kate's hand. 'It's better to have cleared the air, isn't it?'

'You've certainly done that. You've made it all clear as crystal. You've made me feel a whole lot better, made me understand, you know.'

'I have? Oh, that's good. I am glad.'

'So much better, in fact, that I never want to see you again. I've tried to like you but I just don't want to try any more. It's finished. For good. Don't try to contact me ever. Never ever. I mean that. Goodbye.' Kate found the latch for herself and left, closing her ears to the anguished howl her mother gave, possibly the only honest thing Tessa had done since that first fateful night they'd met.

Kate stormed down the steps on to the drive, couldn't unlock her car, managed it, got in, shut her coat in the door, released it, started the engine twice before it fired and drove out into the road in exactly the state of mind her father had always warned her against. Within two hundred yards she nudged the car in front as she stopped for the lights and was faced with a furious pernickety owner who physically threatened her, even though no damage had been done.

After they'd exchanged addresses she pulled into a service road, switched off the engine and began to calm herself down. Five deep breaths later she knew she needed to get home. To Mia and the familiarity of that much despised nineteen thirties house her dad had so lovingly preserved. Stuff Tessa, just stuff her! Mother? Huh! Kate drove home, knowing that Tessa had killed dead the whole idea of being restored to that caring mother she'd so mistakenly conjured up all these years.

15

Joy went up to see Miriam as soon as she got to work to make sure she was all prepared for the lunchtime celebrations. 'I know I'm early, Miriam, but we're very busy today and I thought I'd just confirm the arrangements.'

'It's all in hand, don't worry. I've got everything out of the freezer, I've found a cloth to cover the desk, I've got the champagne in the fridge, and the paper plates and the glasses are all to hand. Don't fuss!'

'Sorry. But I want to make a good start for Dan. It's a big day and not just for him. I can't quite believe that Mungo has agreed; he's always been so set against equine.'

'With the state of farming at the moment and no prospect of it improving, I rather think he's been forced into coming round to it. Have you time for breakfast?'

'I'll have a cup of tea. I don't need feeding. Duncan brought my breakfast to bed this morning.'

'Did he? I didn't know he was that kind of person.'

Joy smiled. 'He isn't, but he's agreed to a new contract for a computer firm he's worked for before. Consequently he'll be in another world for the next few months so he's trying to appease me.'

Hearing footsteps in the hall Miriam said, 'Here's Mungo. Sit down, Joy. Here's a cup.' She handed Joy a cup and saucer and Joy sat at the table. Mungo came into the kitchen and smiled at them both. 'My two favourite women both breakfasting with me. What a pleasure.' He gave Joy a kiss on her cheek, blew one to Miriam and sat down.

Joy kept her eyes on him, finding she could relish his freshly showered presence like a lovelorn teenager but without the old passionate longings. 'You are a flirt, Mungo. A real flirt. No wonder we all adore you.'

'You're being ridiculous.'

Joy tapped his wrist with her forefinger. 'No, I am not. All the girls

395

think you're the absolute tops in men. Good-looking, handsome, athletic, charming. That smile of yours is worth millions.'

'Nonsense.'

'You'd have made a wonderful film star, romantic lead, you know, wouldn't he, Miriam?'

The phone rang and Mungo went to answer it.

Joy, enjoying being free from her anguish about Mungo, pressed her case with Miriam. 'He would, you know. Don't you think so?'

'I'm biased.' Miriam went to rescue a slice of toast which had sprung out of the toaster and landed in an African violet on the windowsill. 'It doesn't hurt like it did, does it?' She gave Joy a smile as she spoke, but Joy didn't respond to it, because she realised with a shock that it sounded as though Miriam must know her secret.

Miriam gave Joy the slice of toast and absent-mindedly Joy accepted it and reached for the butter. By mistake she spread raspberry jam on it too, which she didn't really care for at breakfast but it served to cover her confusion. After all she'd said about never letting Miriam know and here she was on the brink of it all being out in the open. What could she say to avoid a major revelation?

Before Joy had collected her thoughts, Miriam said in a small voice and almost reluctantly, 'I've always known, you know.'

Joy's head shot up in horror.

'Right from the first day I met you. It was the pain in your face when Mungo said I was his wife. It wasn't surprise I saw, it was terrible, terrible pain. I knew all right.'

'Oh, God!' Joy was frozen with shock.

Miriam sat down and calmly began to eat her cereal. 'Don't worry, Joy. But you did give yourself away, you know. It was the look in your eyes when I caught you watching him. The way you lit up when he spoke to you. Mungo doesn't realise, I'm sure, and I shan't say a word.'

It was the sweetness of the way Miriam spoke, the gentleness, the obvious effort not to hurt which devastated Joy: there was no anger or jealousy, only sadness and understanding.

With her head in her hands, Joy tried to explain. 'I've never wanted you to know ... I'm more sorry than you'll ever know. I'd no idea you knew, you've always been so ... Never let him know, please ... I wouldn't want him to and I'm so sorry, Miriam, so sorry but he's just so ...'

'But what about Duncan? Does he know?'

Joy nodded.

'He must be so hurt. Why ever did you marry him feeling like you do? The poor, dear man.'

Mungo came back. 'My first client won't be in till later this morning. Car broken down on the way, so I can have a nice comfortable breakfast and read the paper before I go down.' He looked closely at Miriam as she handed him his cup of tea. 'All right, darling?'

'Fine.'

Joy stood up, her toast left half eaten on her plate, her tea not touched. 'I'll switch the phones through, then you can eat in peace. See you later, Miriam. We decided on twelve thirty for Dan's celebration. He knows and he'll make sure to be back.' She shot out of the kitchen with the speed of light.

'What's got into her?'

Smoothly Miriam said, 'Getting worked up about the celebration. There's going to be quite a crowd. I've planned champagne and orange juice for those who don't drink. I'm not bothering with wine as there won't be enough time.'

'Where? In here?'

'No. There's not enough time like I said. We're holding it in reception. If clients come they can join in. I've done plenty of food.'

'You're a marvel, darling, you really are.'

'I love doing it and after all, I've got my own way, haven't I?'

Mungo grinned at her. 'You have, haven't you. We're all putty in your hands.'

'Do I come across as manipulative? I do hope not.'

'Of course you don't. Not at all. Just persuasive. Yes, that's right, persuasive.'

Miriam had to laugh at his attempt at discretion. 'All right. All right.'

'I'll have more tea, please.'

'Certainly. What does it feel like to be a film star?'

'She's talking rubbish and you know it. It's all nonsense. She's just pulling my leg. I'll get the paper.'

Miriam smiled to herself as he left the kitchen, certain he hadn't realised about Joy's feelings for him. In her mind's eye she could see Joy's face the day Mungo had introduced her as his wife at the old surgery. The terrible shock she saw registered there and the pain. It had been disconcerting and because she was so nervous she hadn't been able to deal with it at the time. Afterwards, from the security of her own deep love for Mungo, she'd taken it in her stride. Joy, she had realised, presented no threat to her and Mungo. The one most hurt must be Duncan.

When Mungo came back in, Miriam put an arm round his shoulders and hugged him. 'Love you, darling.'

'I love you. Seen this headline. What will they come up with next?'

Miriam organised the two Sarahs and Stephie to carry the food and drink down to reception. 'This all looks gorgeous, Miriam, absolutely lovely. Better than a packed lunch any day. I don't suppose . . .' Sarah One raised her eyebrows, quizzing Miriam with a hopeful look.

'Get on with you, I've better things to be doing than making lunch for everyone every day. Take care down the stairs. I've laid out the cloth already.'

By twelve twenty-five they'd had a phone call from Dan to say he was running ten minutes late, but he'd be there.

'Typical!' said Stephie who'd taken his call. 'Why can vets never be on time? Ten minutes. I guess that means twenty minutes really, but we can't start without him, can we?'

They'd all gathered: Bunty, the two Sarahs, Stephie, Annette, Kate, Letty, Colin, Zoe, Zoe's mother with little Oscar, Graham, Rhodri, Valentine and his wife Nina, Mungo, Miriam, Duncan and Joy. All they needed was the man himself.

'Got a speech prepared, Mungo, have you?'

Mungo smiled at Letty. 'Indeed I have. Not often we welcome a new partner, is it?'

'No. Sorry to be mentioning money, but it is all watertight, is it?'

'Of course. Naturally. All legal.'

'Good. He'll be a great asset.'

Hunger and pleasurable excitement were just beginning to get the better of them when the glass door opened and they all prepared to applaud, expecting it to be Dan at last. But it wasn't. On the mat stood a stunning young woman. From the top of her beautiful head all the way down to her feet she shouted wealth and style.

'Hi, there!' She looked at them all staring at her and added, smiling, 'Thanks for the welcoming committee.'

Her slight American accent took them by surprise and they fell silent. She said, 'I'm looking for Danny Brown?'

Miriam answered, 'So are we. He'll be here any moment. And you are?'

'I'm his wife. Rose Franklin Brown.'

If a bomb had dropped they couldn't have been more stunned. En masse they stood open-mouthed with bewilderment. Kate recognised that this was the girl in the photograph, but she had become so convinced that she had died that the sight of her, apparently coming back from the dead, silenced her completely.

Rose surveyed them each in turn and eventually, getting no response from anyone, she asked, 'I guess it must be a shock?'

'A surprise rather,' said Miriam. 'Yes. A real surprise. We're about to have a celebration lunch you see, because he's officially a partner from today. He's never said ... though he did mention the name Rose to me once. You're from ... ?'

'The States. Flown in, hired a car and driven here.' She looked down at herself and said, 'I must look a mess. I'd like to freshen up before I see him. Is that possible?'

Miriam stepped towards her. 'Of course. Come upstairs to the flat and use our bathroom.'

'Thank you. I appreciate that.'

They all waited until they were sure Miriam had closed the door at the bottom of the stairs to the flat and then a hubbub broke out.

'Did you see those gorgeous clothes?'

'That fur coat will have to go.'

'That fur coat must have cost a fortune.'

'To say nothing of the handbag. Beautiful leather.'

'And that wonderful blonde hair. That's not come out of a bottle.'

'I bet when she's done up she'll look fabulous.'

'I'd never dare to drive just like that.' Stephie snapped her fingers. 'Straight off the plane and here. What a woman!'

'But, Dan, *married*.'

Letty commented, 'Dan's a sly puss, isn't he? I wonder what the story is behind her sudden appearance, and pregnant too.'

'Letty!'

'She is, I'm certain.'

'There'll be hell to pay if it isn't his,' Zoe said *sotto voce*, with an odd look in her eyes.

The comments stopped when they heard the door being opened and Miriam's footsteps.

They all looked expectantly at her as she came into reception.

'She's coming down when she's freshened up. She's lovely, isn't she? Such a sweetie! But she's totally exhausted. She needs to sleep and sleep and sleep.'

Zoe commented, 'Someone's going to get a surprise.'

Letty proclaimed, 'I think "shock" would be more appropriate. I don't think he knows she's coming otherwise you would think he would have said ...' She broke off when they heard the back door open and Dan's quick step coming down the corridor.

Miriam swiftly stood in front of them all and put her finger to her lips. 'Not a word.'

The air of suppressed excitement bubbled about as Mungo said his speech of welcome to the practice, seconded by Colin who, unusually for him, spoke with verve and enthusiasm, and was gazed upon approvingly by Letty. Graham, by practice tradition, opened the bottles of champagne, the two Sarahs poured out, and Valentine and Nina served it to everyone on two silver trays purloined from Miriam's kitchen.

Dan called for silence after the toast and made a speech. 'Firstly I should like to say thank you to you all for making me so welcome to the practice. I know I made a bad start' – cries of agreement from everyone – 'but I hope perhaps I may have made up for it by now. I have every intention of making a great success of the equine side of the practice which, thanks to Mungo, I have been given the opportunity to do. I know some of my initiatives have not been welcome but I think you have to admit that my knick-knacks have proved a huge success and that the new staffing rotas are a boon.' He raised his glass. 'To everyone, your very good health and a very prosperous future for us all. I give you a toast: Barleybridge Veterinary Hospital and its great future!'

When they'd all drunk the toast Miriam called out, 'Food, glorious food! Please eat it all. I don't want any left for Mungo and me to finish up.'

Zoe nudged Miriam and whispered, 'She's a long time. Where's she got to?'

'I don't know.'

'If she doesn't come down soon, you'll have to go and see. Do you think she really is pregnant or is it Letty fantasising. I can't think *she's* much of a judge, can you?'

'It was difficult to tell with her coat on. If she is, wow!'

Two clients appeared early for the afternoon clinic and found themselves being fêted with a champagne lunch.

Dan went round to each of the staff in turn to have a word of thanks and say how much he was looking forward to working with them on a permanent basis. Eventually Miriam, after he'd completed his rounds, could wait no longer. She took him on one side and said, 'Dan, there's someone up in our flat who's come to see you. Take a plate of food and a glass of champagne with you.'

'Someone wanting to see me? Who is it?'

Miriam spread her hands and shrugged her shoulders. She selected food, arranged it on a plate, gave him a glass of champagne and pushed him gently towards the corridor. 'Go on. Off you go.'

'Why won't you tell me who it is?'

'Just go, Dan. Do as I say.' She watched his progress towards the flat with tears in her eyes. Miriam had no idea what Rose's sudden arrival was all about, but she fervently hoped Dan was about to get everything he had ever wanted.

Dan put the glass of champagne down on the carpet while he opened the door to the flat. He picked it up and went into the hall. It was a moment before he smelt her perfume. In a daze he went to the kitchen but found it empty; he tried the dining room second, knowing full well he was putting off the dreadfully scary disappointment of finding it was someone else wearing the same scent as her, for he hardly dared to hope. It was such an impossibility. Finally he went where he should have gone in the first place: into the sitting room. Her fur coat lay on the arm of a chair. The smell of her perfume was stronger in here. Then he saw her, his beautiful Rose. Asleep, lying on the sofa. The powder compact he'd bought her in New York lay open ready for use in her hand. Obviously she'd been too exhausted to stay awake. She'd undone her hair and it lay spread out over the arm of the sofa. Dan put down the food and the glass on a side table and went to kneel by her.

In total silence he studied every inch of her, savouring his remembrances of her: her jokes, her laughter, her love of her work, her enthusiasm for life, her exuberance. His hand tentatively reached out to touch her as he'd done dozens of times since they'd parted, but this time was different, for she was here, breathing, sleeping. He put his ear close to her face and felt her breath on his cheek. Very gently he touched her hand, grasped her fingers, those delicate, expressive fingers he so loved. He knelt there, wallowing in his joy. Then he couldn't resist giving her cheek a light kiss.

Rose's eyes flicked open. 'Danny, it's you! Forgive me! Forgive me for driving you away.'

Dan was so choked by his emotions that his voice stopped in his throat.

'I've caused you such anguish. I had to come. I've come just as I am. I've left everything behind. Will you have me?'

Dan nodded, hardly daring to believe.

'I had to come, you see, to bring you him.' She sat up so he could see for himself she was pregnant.

Dan simply couldn't take it in. One minute he was pining for her, the next she'd materialised in front of him and pregnant too.

He laid a reverent hand on her stomach and the barely distinguishable word 'Rose' came from his mouth. She kissed his lips so sweetly, so gently, begging his forgiveness. 'Am I forgiven, my darling? Am I? I'm here to stay, if you'll have me.'

Gruffly Dan replied, 'There's no need to ask. I let my temper get the better of me, but your mother had to be told. She'd driven me right to the edge. So, does she know you've left for good?'

Rose laughed. 'She might by now. I walked out of the house, leaving her thinking I was having lunch for old times' sake with friends from the office, but instead went to the airport and boarded a flight. I couldn't deny you your son. We both need you. I'm so terribly tired, I just fell asleep. That drive. I'd forgotten English roads and round-abouts.'

'And I'd forgotten how courageous you are. So you were pregnant then, as you half suspected?'

Rose nodded. 'With a boy. My mother can't reconcile herself. She simply won't acknowledge I'm carrying a baby of yours. I'm glad to have made the decision to leave. If all this has proved nothing else, it has proved I cannot live without you.'

'Nor me, you. I wrote but you didn't reply so I sent e-mails. You read them?'

'I didn't get the letters, I guess my mother saw to that. But when your e-mails began coming I lived for them. But I was so angry deep inside I didn't reply. I'm a fool, an absolute fool.' She took hold of his hand and, raising it to her lips, kissed it.

Dan shook his head. 'Never that. Never a fool.'

'And you're a partner they tell me?'

Dan grinned. 'I am indeed. I'm buying a house. When you've slept I'll take you to see it. You'll love it. It will appeal to your Englishness. We can furnish it together. You and I.'

Rose smoothed back his hair from his face, placed her hands either side of it and looked deeply into his eyes, studying every facet of the face of this man she adored more than life. How could she ever have allowed him to leave? How could she ever have listened to untruths and, worse, believed them? 'Never again as long as I live shall I allow anyone to come between us. That's my solemn promise. Jonathan Daniel Franklin Brown shall be the first of many. Believe me. The first of June is B-day.'

'It's going to take some getting used to, being a father.'

'And being a mother.'

'Will you need yours when it comes to the time?'

Rose shuddered. 'God help me, but I never want to set eyes on her again.'

'Will she guess where you've gone?'

'I hope not.'

'Rose!'

'She'd only follow me. I'm exhausted, Danny. Can I go and sleep in your flat?'

'I'll take you home this minute. We'll leave introductions to another day. I know they'll all understand.'

Rose stood up. 'That sounds like the best offer I've had in months.'

Country Lovers

List of Characters at Barleybridge Veterinary Hospital

Mungo Price, senior partner, his wife *Miriam*, and his dog, *Perkins*
Colin Walker, partner, and his wife *Letty*
Zoe Savage, partner
Dan Franklin-Brown, partner, his wife *Rose* and son *Jonathan*
Rhodri Hughes, Practice vet
Graham Murgatroyd and *Valentine Dedic*, Practice vets
Joy Bastable, Practice Manager, and her husband *Duncan*
Senior nurse *Bunty Bird* (née Page) and nurses *Sarah One (Cockcroft)* and
  Sarah Two (MacMillan)
Receptionists *Kate Howard*, *Stephie Budge* and *Annette Smith*

CLIENTS AND OTHER VILLAGERS
Lloyd Kominsky, Rose Franklin-Brown's stepfather
Idris Jones, farmer of Beulah Bank Top, and his daughter *Megan*
Callum and *Nuala Tattersall* of Tattersall's Cop
Miranda Costello, an eccentric animal lover
Bryan Buckland, manager of Chesham Chicken Farm
Mike Allport and *Graham Hookham*, officers of the State Veterinary Service
Phil and *Blossom Parsons*, of Applegate Farm, and their foster boy *Hamish*
Billy and *Adele Bridges* of Bridge Farm, and sons *Gabriel* (Gab), *Gideon*, *Ben*,
  Simeon, *Joe* and *Joshua*
Inspector Richie Jamieson, uniformed police
Declan Tattersall, Callum's cousin, and his seven children
Bert Featherstonehough, ex-army dog handler
Lord Askew, the local squire and stud-owner
Bernard Wilson, puppy breeder at Badger's Lot and his sister *Hannah*
Tad Porter, farmer at Porter's Fold

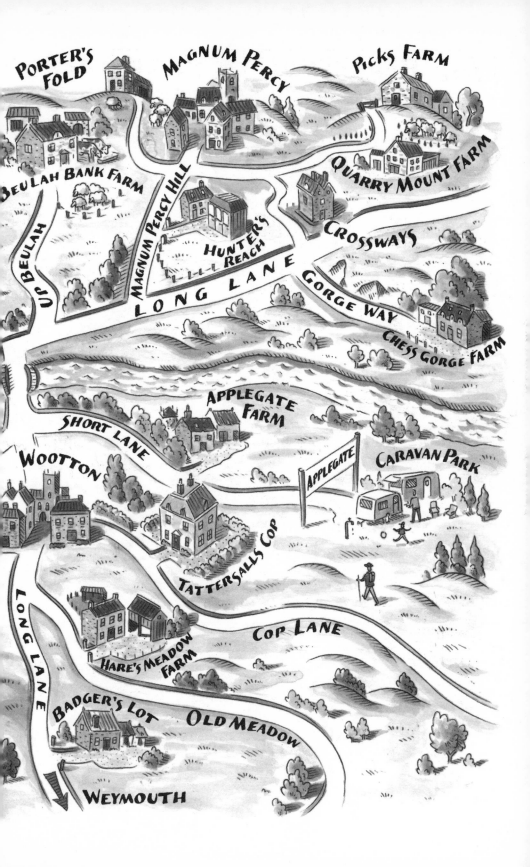

1

It was Joy, as Practice Manager, who struggled with the staff rota every month and with Graham Murgatroyd off with flu, and Dan hovering distractedly waiting for the birth of his son and likely to be off for at least a week, and Rhodri behaving like the lovelorn chap he most decidedly was, it was proving more than usually difficult to plan June's staffing. She sat in her office in the last week in May, planning and replanning until her head spun. It was no good, she'd have to get Duncan to take a look. Joy rested her head against the back of her chair and closed her eyes. Briefly she dropped off, drained by a long, busy day. Moments later, someone clearing their throat disturbed her.

'Sorry, Joy, to disturb you but . . .'

'My fault. I've developed a splitting headache trying to plan the rota for June, it should have been done days ago.' She rubbed her eyes to refresh them and saw Mungo looking down at her with sympathy. Her heart raced, though not quite as wildly as it had at times during the last twenty years. She sat upright. 'What can I do for you?'

'Just to say I've finished operating for today and I'm going up to the flat. I know you're shorthanded, so Miriam and I are not taking this weekend away we promised ourselves, just in case.'

'That's wonderful. Thanks. If things get any worse I shall be doing the operating myself!'

'You've had plenty of experience assisting me in the past. I've no doubt you'd do an excellent job.'

Joy laughed. 'I don't think so, things have moved on since I first helped you. New techniques, new equipment. No, no, our reputation would go straight down the pan! As they say, you're only as good as your last operation.'

Mungo leaned across the desk and placed a kiss on her cheek. 'Thanks for all you do and thanks for being such a good friend to Miriam. She does value your friendship.'

Joy's eyes slid away from his face. 'And I hers. Must press on. I'm taking this rota home to Duncan. He'll sort it for me. There's a solution somewhere but I can't see it.'

'Don't hesitate to ring if you need me. Any time, and I mean it. It's just a difficult patch and we have to gut it out.'

'I'll ring, you can bet on that.' Joy allowed herself to watch him leave, to smile at him when he turned to say, 'Be seeing you,' to enjoy his handsome bearing, his restless energy, those splendid eyes and the gentleness of his mouth. She swallowed hard. There I go again, she thought, just when I'd begun to think he didn't matter any more. When he'd closed the door behind him she clenched her fist and banged it on the desk in anger. Would she never learn he loved elsewhere? That his kiss was that of a comrade and not a lover and never would be.

Duncan. Duncan. She focused on Duncan's face as she'd seen it that morning when the alarm had gone, making no impression on him at all. He lay snugly tucked in right against her back, one arm laid carelessly across her waist. When she'd tried to get up, he'd held her down and grunted his contentment. But she'd managed to turn over so she could look at him. She was always surprised how young he looked first thing. Which he was, all of nine years younger.

Joy said, 'Got to get up. Let me go.'

'Five more minutes.'

'No.'

'Please.' It was more of a command than a request. The arm across her waist had tightened and kept her there.

Joy tolerated the five minutes and then pushed off his arm and sat up on the edge of the bed. But he followed her and was kissing the back of her neck and his arm was round her waist again, gripping her.

'Duncan. Please. I'm going to be late.'

Duncan turned away from her without a word.

She'd stood up and headed for the bathroom and a shower and for an assessment of her allure in the bathroom mirror. It hadn't made good viewing. That mood had stayed with her all day and was still with her as she parked her car and went into reception the following morning and found she was five minutes late.

Ordinarily she would have apologised for being slightly late, but this morning, instead, she could find fault with absolutely everything. In reception, Stephie and Annette came in for a few broadsides, Sarah Cockroft for leaving dirty, blood-streaked operating sheets out on the laundry worktop instead of putting them immediately in the washing machine, and finally Mungo for arriving late for his first appointment. 'You should know better than to leave your first client waiting.'

'Sorry.'

Mungo saw the way the wind blew and escaped Joy's office as soon as he could, salving his conscience by being as charming as he possibly could to his client. 'Please, forgive me. Do come this way.'

'Don't worry yourself, Mr Price, we know how busy you are.'

Joy saw the owners of the dog shake his hand and smile and she thought he could charm the devil himself, he could.

He ruffled the head of his patient and asked, 'This is Teddy, is it? Hello, old chap.' To the owners he said, 'Now, tell me in your own words what the problem is.'

Joy watched him lead them into his consulting room, and smiled grimly to herself. It really wasn't fair for one man to have so much charm and such good looks. She saw Annette putting her empty coffee mug down on the reception desk. 'You know how much Mr Price dislikes empty mugs standing about in public view. Take it away. Please.'

Duncan had organised the rota to her satisfaction and after she'd pinned it up on the staff notice board and made sure everyone of the veterinary staff had a copy in their pigeon hole she put her own copy on the noticeboard in her room and sat down to think.

But not for long. Dan Brown came in to see her.

Dan had lost weight these last few weeks and was not looking quite as stocky or well-built as he used to. But the craggy face and the penetrating brown eyes were still there and so too was his in-your-face-energy, which sometimes caught one on the raw, but not now, not since he'd won her over. She greeted him with warmth and affection. 'Dan! You're soon back, is everything all right with Rose, you know?'

'She's fine, we got there early and they're delighted with her and we've to go back next week same time if the baby hasn't happened in the meantime. She's furious that she can't drive herself any more.'

'Have they said she shouldn't?'

Dan gave the happiest laugh he'd given since she'd known him. 'No. The truth is she can't get behind the wheel and reach the pedals.'

'Oh, well! Go have a coffee or something and take a rest. You've no calls for the moment.'

'None?'

'None whatsoever.'

'Right. I will.'

'You do that, it may be your last quiet day for some time!'

'We can't wait for the baby, you know. Just can't wait. Rose's stepdad has arrived and is out buying every item of baby equipment he can find. We wanted to wait ... not tempt fate, you know.'

As Dan went off to take his break, Joy said quietly to herself, 'I can understand that.' She had just finished speaking when she heard the most terrifying sounds coming from reception. The papers on her desk flew in all directions as she squeezed out of her chair and raced to see what was happening.

Joy was appalled at the scene that met her eyes. A very large, heavily built dog of uncertain ancestry had a cat in his mouth. The cat was hanging upside down, yowling and trying to swing itself round to scratch at the dog's face, its claws unsheathed, its mouth wide open, but the dog was hanging on tightly, his fangs exposed below his drawn back dewlaps.

The waiting clients were panic stricken, clutching their pets to them, lifting their feet to avoid the whirling dog. Mrs Parr, the owner of the cat, was screaming with terror. 'Get him off! Quick! Somebody! Get him off. Oh! Oh! Oh!'

But the dog was intent on his trophy and had no intention of giving it up.

The clients were behaving like a coop full of chickens with a fox at their throats and Annette and Stephie were hysterical and no more use than a pair of mice.

Above the clamour Joy shouted, 'Who owns this dog?'

A small, agitated man spoke up. 'Bingo! Let go! Bingo! Let go!' He was sweating so much his glasses were steaming up. 'He hates cats.'

Mrs Parr shouted. 'Get 'im off! Oh hell!' and promptly fainted. Another client began to beat at the dog with a magazine, which only served to infuriate Bingo even further. He altered his grip on the cat, was now holding it even more firmly, and the cat had stopped struggling. Joy grabbed his collar, and instantly, Dan, appearing apparently from nowhere, took over from her, stood astride Bingo and deftly manhandled the dog's head to the ground, keeping a firm grip with both hands on its head and neck and his knee on its flanks. Taken by surprise the dog released its hold on the cat and it crawled away, trembling, its fur bristling and its mouth open wide, spitting hoarsely.

Joy took charge.

'Right. Stephie! Ring for an ambulance for Mrs Parr. Annette! Capture the cat and put it in a cage in intensive care. Dan! Get that dog in the back and tie it up. Tight! I'll get a blanket for this lady.'

She came back into reception with a blanket and a pillow. A client with her own cat safe from harm in its basket, got up to give her a hand.

Mungo came out with his clients to find uproar. If Joy hadn't been so preoccupied she would have laughed at the astonished expression on his face. 'What on earth . . . ?'

Dan finally managed to drag Bingo out. Annette caught the petrified cat and carried it away to make it safe, and Stephie called out, 'The ambulance is on its way.'

'Thanks, Stephie!'

Dan came back and faced Bingo's shivering owner. 'He's yours?'

The man nodded.

'Why have you brought him in?'

'For his injections, it's time.'

'Yes?'

Realising that he was holding a very public discussion, Dan broke off and invited Bingo's owner into an empty consulting room.

The man shuffled after him, still sweating, still shivering.

'Sit down. Please.' Dan pulled the desk chair forward and waited for the man to sit, then leaned against the examination table and asked, 'Yes? Mr . . . ?'

'Tucker. Alan Tucker.' He pulled out a handkerchief and mopped his top lip. 'She should have had the cat in a basket or something. It wasn't Bingo's fault. Not at all, no. The cat spat at him and tried to scratch him. What else is a self-respecting dog supposed to do? I ask you.'

'Apparently you haven't got him under control or you could have stopped him.'

'Under control in circumstances like that? He's an angel at home. We've two children, little ones,' he gauged their height with his hand, 'this big and he's like putty in their hands. They can ride on him, sit on him, cover him up with a blanket as if he's baby, anything they like and he never murmurs. It's only cats he can't stand.'

Dan looked a little sceptical at this. 'So you say.'

Alan Tucker mopped his face with his handkerchief again. 'She should never have brought her cat in without a cage . . . it was her fault.'

'You have got a point there. But I can tell you this. Never once in all the years I've worked as a vet have I known of such an attack. All the animals are so overcome by the smells and the strangeness or have memories of having been here before for injections or treatment that they are usually very subdued. He was alarming.'

'I still say it was the cat's fault . . .'

'Well, Mr Tucker, quite what the owner of the cat will be thinking

415

when she's come round I don't know. It has all been very distressing. You are a client of ours, are you?'

'First time. We've only just moved here, changed my job, you know. Dog's all upset, you know, children too. New vet, new house, new garden, different walks, it's all been too much for Bingo, and then, on top of all that, that bloody cat.'

'That's understandable. Now, I must see to the cat. But be aware, Mr Tucker, that he's nervous. Keep an eye on him when he's with the children. He's big, and could do a lot of damage. I'm serious, a special eye till he's calmed down. OK?'

Mr Tucker stood up. 'Thanks for getting him under control. I was too shocked to do anything. Never seen him like that.'

Dan opened the door. 'Take care, Mr Tucker. Bring him back when he's feeling happier. I'll get him for you and then I'll see to the cat.'

When Mr Tucker came back into reception holding Bingo tightly, the ambulance had just arrived and Mrs Parr was being taken out in a wheelchair. Mr Tucker said to her, 'I'm so sorry.'

Ashen-faced she replied, 'My cat. Where's my Muffin?'

Joy said, 'We'll take care of her, she'll have the best of attention. The vet's examining her now.'

'Thanks. I really don't need to go to hospital. I only fainted. I think I'll just go home.' She made to get out of the chair.

Joy gently pressed her back. 'Believe me, it's best to have a check-up just in case. And it will make me feel easier in my mind that you've been looked at. I'll ring tomorrow and let you know about Muffin, or if you feel up to it, you ring later today. I'm so sorry this has happened.'

After Mrs Parr had gone Stephie said, 'Why were you so insistent that she went to hospital? There was really nothing wrong with her.'

'You're a doctor, are you?'

'You know I'm not.'

'And neither am I. Best to make sure in case of legal proceedings.'

'But she's nice, we've known her for years.'

'She's never had her cat attacked before though, has she? She might feel she should be safe to bring her cat here, which is quite right, but today she wasn't . . . so . . . you never know.' Joy wagged her finger at Stephie and disappeared into the back to find Dan.

He had carried the cat into a consulting room and was gently examining her. She wasn't in the best of moods for a close examination and Dan was having to be very careful not to stress her more than necessary.

Dan glanced up at Joy as she watched his sensitive hands moving so sympathetically over the cat as he assessed her injuries. 'She's been punctured here, look, one of his fangs. She's in deep shock. We'll have to set up a drip, can't do anything until she stabilises. Nothing broken I think.'

'I'll set up the drip. The girls are all busy.'

'Are you sure?'

'Absolutely. If Mrs Parr had brought her in a cat carrier none of this would have happened.'

'Exactly. Mr Tucker says the dog's as soft as butter usually. Just cats he can't stand.'

With a wry smile Joy said, 'That's plainly obvious.'

'Even so, I've warned him to keep an eye on him. It really was a nasty attack.'

Mungo took a couple of minutes between clients to find out what was happening. 'No farm calls this morning?' he asked.

'None so far. Colin's out, but he only has three calls.'

'So what about the cat? How is she?'

'Shocked, Joy's setting up a drip. I've found a hole where his fang caught her, but she's too shocked for me to do anything about it.'

'New client, was he? Didn't recognise the owner.'

'Yes. Claims the dog can't abide cats. Otherwise no problem.'

Mungo shook his head. 'Rose not pupped yet then?'

Dan laughed. 'Not yet. You'd better not say that to her, she wouldn't find it funny at the moment.'

'Exciting times we live in, eh?' Mungo clapped Dan on the shoulder, added, 'Thanks for that just now. Got a client. Must go.'

Muffin the cat was an exceptionally beautiful Siamese, and one after another the staff came to see her. 'Isn't she gorgeous? Just gorgeous,' Stephie said, and Annette thought she was utterly beautiful too and very take-homeable. 'Hope she's going to be all right. The poor thing. I hate big dogs.'

'Muffin. It's a poor choice of name for such an elegant cat. Sounds like a name for an ordinary moggy, not an aristocrat.'

Rhodri came in at this point.

Stephie turned to greet him. 'Good morning, Rhodri, come to see our new patient?'

'Who organised this?'

'Dan did. You had a client and we had to do something quicko.'

'I see. Did no one think to consult me? I am the only small-animal vet on duty this morning.'

This outburst silenced the two girls because they honestly didn't know how to answer him.

Rhodri turned on his heel and went back to his consulting room.

Stephie looked at Annette and they both pulled a face.

'Honestly! He gets worse. It's always poor Dan he has his knife in.'

Halfway through the morning, Dan went home to Rose, promising Joy that if a farm call came in he would go. Rose was seated in her favourite chair by the French windows looking out on to the garden. Beside her on a small table was the book she'd put down the moment she heard him coming. 'Darling! What are you doing home at this time? How lovely.'

'It's one of those strange mornings when there are no calls for me. It can't last, I'm quite sure. You all right?'

'I'm fine. Absolutely fine. So you've had an idle morning then?'

'No, not really, just a bit of an upset at the morning clinic.'

'Dresden china I am not. Please tell me.'

'Sorry. Huge great dog attacked a cat in the waiting room. Total uproar.'

'Poor thing.'

'I had to tackle it to the floor and then drag it out and tie it up.'

'You didn't have to put it down?'

'It did occur to me that perhaps it would be for the best, but one can't just rush about putting dogs down; it's not on and it would give the Practice a bad name.'

Rose grinned up at him. 'It most certainly would. I shall have a dog or a cat sometime. I always wanted a pet but mother would never let me. Too messy, she said.'

'Then you shall. You can choose, so long as it's not a huge one like a St Bernard. This cottage isn't big enough.'

'Could you get me a glass of water, Danny, please? Save me having to heave myself out of this chair.'

'Of course. Nothing stronger?'

'Like orange juice?' Rose smiled at him. It was a smile he had missed those months while they'd been apart. He should never have walked out on her. But the blazing row he'd had with her mother over an entirely mythical 'woman' she swore he had hidden away, had hurt him beyond belief. There had never been anyone but Rose. He found a glass, turned on the cold tap and let it run to make sure it was cold. As he watched the torrent of water gushing out he remembered looking for Rose at that time and finding her climbing out of the pool after her daily dozen lengths. She had stood in front of him, water streaming from her, and said, 'You're still here, then? Just go away. I can't bear it. Go away.'

Dan hadn't been able to come to terms with the fact that she sided with her mother. 'You know there isn't anyone else. No one. On this earth. No one but you,' he'd told her.

He'd seen her hesitate, but a lifetime of agreeing with her mother had overcome her natural inclination to believe him. Thankfully, she'd soon discovered the truth.

He turned off the tap, took the glass to her, and as he handed it over he bent to kiss the top of her head. 'Love you.'

Rose drank the glass right to the bottom before she said, 'I don't deserve you, my darling. I simply don't.'

'Clean slate, we said. You stay right there, and watch me mow the lawn. Got to do something. Can't sit about. I'll open the window. If you need anything, give me a shout.'

He glanced at her once or twice and saw she'd picked up her book again. Then the next time he checked, the book had slipped off her knee and she was asleep. Do her good. She didn't get much sleep at night now. It was just what she needed. He paused for a moment to admire her. Everywhere she went people stared. And no wonder. She really was beautiful. Halfway through cutting the lawn his mobile rang. It was a call to Tattersall's Cop. One of Callum's goats was ill, and he was worried. He didn't want to bring it in because his wife, Nuala, who was very ill, couldn't be left. Dan left the mower where it was, wrote a note and put it on the table beside Rose and left.

To get to Tattersall's Cop Dan had to cross the river in the centre of Barleybridge by the Weymouth Bridge and then take the left fork, called Cop Lane, in Wootton. He was struck once again as he approached Callum's farm by how smart it looked. Dan sometimes thought that Callum spent too much time keeping the premises in order. While that was commendable and something other farmers could do well to think about, keeping the farm immaculate didn't fill the coffers.

'Good morning, Callum. What's the problem?'

'It's little Sybil.'

Callum had bought the complete stock of a goat farmer who'd died, and amongst them were seven pygmy goats; perky, bright versions of full-sized goats, born with more than their fair share of curiosity. They'd been brought into a pen close to the house, and leaning on the gate alongside Callum, Dan paused to study them for a moment before going in. 'They all look fit. Which is Sybil, then?'

'The all-black one.' All seven of them were springing around the pen on a familiarisation tour. They were a mixture of black, white and fawn, and looked as though they'd all been in the washing machine that morning so fresh and smart did they look. What with their appealing looks and their cheeky antics, Dan couldn't help but smile at them.

'Settling down nicely, are they?'

'All of them are. Think they'd been getting a bit neglected towards the end. Nothing serious mind, but neglected.'

'What did you want them for, Callum?'

'Fancied a change and Nuala was keen.'

'How is she?'

Callum didn't reply for a moment and then he said, 'You'll see for yourself in a minute, she's coming out to see you. Wants to know about your wife.'

'I see. So why am I here? There doesn't seem much wrong with Sybil.'

'I reckon it's worms. Appetite like you wouldn't believe.'

Dan climbed over the gate and was immediately mobbed by all seven of the goats. Dan crouched to examine Sybil and found himself with pygmy goats endeavouring to raid his pockets, steal his mobile, climb on his back, and generally get in on the act by making their own diagnosis.

'How long have you been farming, Callum?'

'Fifteen years or thereabouts. Why?'

'Don't you know what happens when you put a billy in with nanny goats?'

Callum's eyebrows shot up when he'd absorbed what Dan had said. 'Oh God! You don't mean ...'

'I do. Sybil's in kid.'

Callum rubbed his hands with glee. 'No! Never thought it might be that. Nuala'll be delighted. Delighted. Well, I never. That's great. Sure it is.' His tanned face almost split in two with delight.

'Not long to go, I shouldn't think.' He stood up, trying to escape the goats' attentions without knocking any of them down. 'In fact, this one looks as if ...'

'That's Cassandra, she's Nuala's favourite.'

'... she might be too.'

Callum's Nuala came out of the house and walked slowly towards them, every delicate step an effort. Dan hoped his face didn't register the shock he felt when he saw her. She was emaciated beyond belief. It didn't seem possible that she was still able to stand upright.

Dan touched his cap. 'Good morning, Mrs Tattersall. I've just been giving Callum some good news.'

Callum interrupted. 'Let me tell her. Sybil's expecting!'

'Really!' Nuala's face burst into life and the small spark of what was left of her lit up her beautiful blue eyes. 'Well now, isn't that good news, for sure. When?'

'Within the week, I would have thought.'

'Within the week!'

Dan watched Callum hug her as though she were made of the finest glass. So tenderly.

'I might just see that. Yes, I might. They must look so sweet.'

'They do, Mrs Tattersall, nothing sweeter.' Dan noticed a grimace cross her face. Immediately Callum said, 'I'll take you in.' He picked her up as easily as he would a baby, and set off for the house, calling over his shoulder, 'I'll call you when she's in labour. Can't afford to take any risks.'

'Right. 'Bye, Mrs Tattersall.'

' 'Bye, Dan. My love to your Rose.' Her feeble voice just reached Dan and he was glad she couldn't see his face, because he felt so distressed. He looked at Sybil and said quietly, 'You'd better hurry up or she won't see that kid of yours. Do you hear me?' Sybil, however, had other things to think about as Callum had left the goats some titbits in the feed trough and she was concentrating on getting the major share.

Dan was almost home when he decided to ring the practice to see if there were any more calls for him, but found he must have left his mobile in the goat pen. One nil to the goats. He just hoped Rose hadn't been trying to ring him. He drove all the way back to Tattersall's Cop, parked his Land Rover, intending to knock at the farmhouse door, but saw a doctor from the medical practice in Barleybridge just going in. So he went quietly to the goat pen to find his mobile laid abandoned and unharmed in the long grass by the fencing.

It had a text message on it from Rose. 'Baby started.'

2

It was eleven o'clock that night before things really got going with Rose, and it was half past one in the morning when the consultant decided a Caesarean section was advisable.

Dan was almost beside himself with anxiety, and even considered offering his services, after all he'd done plenty in his time, but arrived at the conclusion he'd probably pass out if he witnessed Rose having surgery and that he'd be better keeping her stepfather, Lloyd, company.

He was worse than Dan himself; taking sips from his hip flask, marching round the waiting room, tap tap tapping his fingernails on the table, asking questions to which Dan couldn't possibly have the answers, and generally behaving like someone on the brink of a breakdown.

'Have a cup of tea, Lloyd. I'll get one from the machine.'

'Tea? What good will that do. A glass of whisky, yes. Tea? No. I've nearly run out of whisky. Do they sell it here? No, of course not. Narrow pelvis they said. Big baby. God! If I'd known I'd've had you castrated.'

'Thank God you didn't. Rose wouldn't have wanted that.'

Lloyd gave Dan half a smile, which he smothered instantly by reminding himself that he should be ringing Rose's mother. 'I should you know, she ought to know. She should be told. I'll ring her.'

Dan clamped his hand on Lloyd's mobile phone. 'Not here, it might interfere with the equipment. And ... what's more, it's Rose's decision. She'll tell her if she wishes. Not you and not me.'

'You're damn right. Of course. God! I'm tired. What the hell are they doing all this time?' Lloyd stood up and began prowling again. 'I love that girl. Like she was my very own. She's a gem. Gutsy, you know. I've tried to shield her from her mother's more crass ideas, but ... God! That woman's something. She's a hell of a woman to keep in check.'

Wryly Dan said, 'I know.'

Lloyd looked at him. 'Huh! You don't need me to tell you that. I could have killed her when I found out she'd driven you away.'

The door opened and the consultant came in smiling. Dan's heart felt fit to burst. 'All's fine! A wonderful baby boy, four kilos exactly. Mother's doing fine. Wonderful patient.'

He shook Dan's hand and offered his congratulations, and then Lloyd's. 'Mustn't leave out Grandad!' He pumped Lloyd's hand up and down vigorously.

Lloyd asked, 'What the hell's four kilos? What does it mean in America?'

Dan said, 'About eight and a half pounds. Wait here and you can see her after me.'

'But I ...'

'After me.'

Dan and Lloyd were completely enraptured by the baby. Lloyd was convinced he looked exactly like himself, though how he worked that out Dan couldn't think. But everyone else said he was the spitting image of his father and he was. The same nose, and the same shaped face, but hair the colour of Rose's. He'd always imagined that all babies looked alike but this one was his and no doubt about it. Rose was bone weary but immensely happy, and kept saying, 'Isn't he wonderful? Aren't we clever? You and me?'

She came home three days later to find that Lloyd had been to the supermarket and bought up what appeared to be half its stock. He'd also bought another freezer to put in the garage and filled that too. 'Can't have you running out of anything at all. There's not a thing I haven't thought of. There won't be any need to shop for weeks. Now, let me have a hold of young Jonathan Daniel Franklin-Brown.'

Dan got out his wallet. 'Look! I must pay you for all that.'

'Nonsense. *He* is my reward and anyway money can't buy him.' He sat in a chair where the sun couldn't reach, holding Rose's son, in a world of his own.

Dan made coffee for the three of them, settled Rose in her favourite chair by the window, and gave her some post to open. She flung the junk mail on the floor, then voiced her anger when she recognised her mother's handwriting. 'She's written to me! She knows where I am.' Angry disappointment showed in her face. 'I know it won't be you, Danny. Is it you, Pa?'

Lloyd, absorbed in delicately smoothing his fingers over the baby's face and his tiny starlike fingers, time and time again, had to be asked twice before he answered. 'Mmm. I felt it only right. She is your mother.'

'She lost all her rights as a mother when she persuaded me that Dan was a no-good son-in-law. I shall regret right to my last breath being so influenced by her. You'd no right, Pa.' Tears poured down her face in rivers, unheeded. 'I feel awful. So miserable.'

Lloyd stood up and went to put Jonathan in Rose's arms. 'It's your hormones, I read about it in a book. Here, hold him, your mother can't take him away from you, he's yours and Dan's. I won't let her come between you and him, if I have to throttle her to do it.'

The phone rang. Dan went to answer it. 'Dan Brown here.'

It was Kate from the Practice. 'Sorry to disturb you when you're off limits so to speak,' she said, 'but you know Callum Tattersall, well, he's rung in to say Sybil is in labour and it's not going right. He wonders if you'd come out to see her. I told him you were off but he says he can't bring her in and you'll know why. Who's Sybil?'

'A pygmy goat. Yes, I do know why. I'll go. OK.'

'Thanks ever so much, Dan.'

Dan picked up his car keys from the hall table, and went back into the sitting room. 'Lloyd, you're not planning going somewhere, are you? Can I leave you to make lunch for Rose and yourself and be generally useful?'

'What the hell, you're not going out on a call?'

Rose interrupted. 'Pa! Don't interfere. What is it, darling?'

'Callum's goat having problems delivering. You know who I mean. I'll be two hours at most.'

'Of course. You go. I shall be fine. I guess Pa and me will cope. There's one thing for certain – we shan't starve to death. My love to Nuala.' She pursed her lips ready for him to kiss, so he bent to do as she asked and whispered his thanks.

When he arrived at Tattersall's Cop he found Sybil ensconced on a makeshift bed in the kitchen with Callum seated on a chair keeping an eye on her, a glass of neat whisky in his hand.

'She's in a poor way.' There was a very slight slur in his speech, and it occurred to Dan that the bottle on the table had reached its present level that very day.

'Now, Sybil, what are you making such a fuss about?' After he'd examined her he asked how long she'd been in labour.

'I got up at half five to see to Nuala and decided to go check on Sybil while I was up. She was very restless then. Jesus! Don't let her die, it'll kill Nuala.' Once he'd said that Callum looked as though he wished he hadn't.

Dan ignored his mistake and continued to check Sybil. 'It's my opinion she can't deliver. Her pelvis is too narrow for such a big kid to get through. I'm going to have to operate.'

Callum shot upright, his face drip white and beads of sweat breaking out on his forehead. 'Operate! Oh God! No! I can't stand it. Not Sybil.' The remains of his whisky went down his gullet in a trice.

'If I don't, she and the kid will die a slow death. Pull yourself together, Callum. My Rose had a Caesarean only three days ago and she's home and doing well. So stop the blather and give me a hand.'

'I can't. I can't stand the sight of blood. Not Sybil's.' Tremblingly he refilled his glass, but Dan took it from him before he could drink it.

'When we've done you can celebrate with that.'

'But . . .'

'No buts.'

Dan did a businesslike job of the operation, aided and abetted by Callum who continually threatened to pass out.

When the tiny kid was pulled from his mother Callum was massively impressed. He ran excitedly into the hall shouting, 'It's a girl! All safe and sound!' Then rushed back in to eulogise over the kid all over again.

'Isn't it fantastic? Have you ever seen anything as wonderful as that? Why, it's astounding. Honest to God. A marvel!'

'Clean her up while . . .'

'It's a girl. That's what Nuala's always wanted, a little girl.'

'. . . I stitch up and finish off.'

Callum said decisively, 'Right. When we've done, we'll take her to Nuala to see. Her being so near the end I can do nothing but exactly as she asks. She just wants to hold her. To have a share in all this loveliness.' Callum concentrated on making the little kid as pretty as a picture for Nuala. 'Her hooves, look! Aren't they beautiful? So tiny, why, you can't believe she's real!'

'She is though and she won't be the last, by the looks of Cassandra.'

'Black with these white patches, you have to agree she's well marked.'

Dan finished closing up Sybil, and then suggested Callum took the kid for Nuala to see. He intended staying in the kitchen and getting washed before he left, but Callum insisted that Nuala would like to see him. 'She doesn't get much company, you know. People don't know what to say.'

So he followed Callum into the dining room now converted into a bedroom for Nuala. She lay in a big double bed, propped on snow-white pillows the colour of her face. If it were possible Nuala looked even more frail than the last time he'd seen her. There was no flesh on her face, it was quite simply skin stretched over bones. Once she had been pretty, he could see that. She was wearing a bedjacket so only her hands were visible on the counterpane and they too, like her face, were skin and bone. Nothing more. There was such a terrible stillness about her you could have thought she was already dead.

Callum, carrying the kid in a baby's blanket, laid it reverently on the bed beside Nuala just where she could reach to touch it. Her eyes glowed with delight. She whispered to Callum to put the kid in her arms, so he did, protesting that it was too heavy for her. She shook her head. Taking a big breath, which ran out before she'd finished speaking, Nuala said, 'I always wanted a little girl. Remember that time when . . .'

Callum nodded. 'What shall we call her?'

Breathing deeply she gasped, 'Carmel.'

'Sure, that's a great choice. Carmel it shall be. I'm going to take her back to Sybil now, she'll be missing her.'

The tiny kid made a sweet attempt at an anxious bleat, so Callum scooped her up in his arms and left. Dan said, 'Good morning, Mrs Tattersall. I'll be seeing you. Rose sends her love.'

Nuala looked at him and whispered, 'Thank you. God bless. Look after Callum for me. You know, when I'm . . .'

'Certainly, I most definitely will. 'Bye Nuala.' He smiled at her and raised his hand in a half salute, at a loss to know what else to say. Dan found Callum seated in the kitchen watching Sybil and Carmel getting to know each other.

'That's what we were going to call our baby that we never got to hold. Losing her broke Nuala's heart.'

Dan's answer to that was to squeeze Callum's shoulder in sympathy. 'Best be off.'

'There'll be no point in it all without her.'

'I'll call tomorrow perhaps, or better still, ring me if you need me. Right?'

'Right.'

Dan left Callum downing another whisky while he supervised Carmel having her first feed. He paused for a moment at the back door, thought about the cards life had dealt Callum, and remembered Jonathan Franklin-Brown and Rose and how happy he was by comparison.

'You say Dan's gone to Tattersall's Cop? That's good of him.' Joy looked over the top of her glasses at Kate but had to wait for her reply while Kate counted the money a client had given her for some budgie seed.

'That's right, exactly and there's your receipt. Thank you. 'Bye. Well,

Callum rang to say his goat was in dire straits and he wanted Dan and Dan would understand, and so I rang him and Dan went.'

'Well, try not to ring him again, he needs this holiday, and with Rose . . .'

'I know but you see Callum's wife is . . . well she's dying and he can't leave her.'

'Ah! Right! I see. And your exams, Kate? How are they going?'

'Third paper on Tuesday.'

'Yes, I know but what about the two you've already done? Are you feeling happy about them?'

'Well, yes, I am, I seem to have aimed my revision in all the right areas so far, so fingers crossed. Thank you for giving me time off.'

'My pleasure. I don't know why I'm wanting you to do well though, because it means you won't be here after September.' Joy laughed at her and all Kate could say was, 'Sorry,' with a smile on her face.

'You've done so well learning this job. Hardly a foot wrong all the time you've been here.'

'Well, not quite, I have had my moments.'

'Well, yes. There was that time when . . . and the other when . . .' They both collapsed with laughter.

'Seriously though, I shall be thrilled when you've passed and delighted for you to go. You've got just the right strain of common sense to make a good vet.' Joy picked up a stack of files from the counter and disappeared into the back to get on with some administration, leaving Kate on her own, as Stephie had had to go to the dentist for an urgent appointment. She wasn't by herself for long though because the afternoon clinic was beginning and the first booking was for a budgie to have its claws and beak trimmed.

The client came in carrying a cardboard box punched with dozens of holes to give the bird air. She was a strange person, this client, she believed quite adamantly that animals were far superior to human beings, yet could allow her rabbits' teeth to overgrow so much they couldn't eat, neglect her ponies' hooves so they could hardly walk, and her cats to have fleas to the extent they were completely overrun with them. Nevertheless, all of them at the Practice had a great affection for her and her eccentricities. Her appearance was out of the ordinary, to say the least. It appeared she'd used a builder's trowel to apply her make-up and her hair was blacker than black, if that were possible. Today she wore a full-length black skirt, which looked as though it had done the rounds of the Nearly New Sales for far too long, topped by a mustard yellow twinset covered in beaded embroidery, over which she wore a scarlet sequinned waistcoat. Miranda Costello was nothing if not colourful.

'Hello, Mrs Costello. Take a seat. Rhodri's almost ready for you.'

Mrs Costello wagged a finger at her. 'How many times have I told you, it's Miranda to all my friends.'

'Sorry. Habit, you know.'

'That's all right, dear. I do hope Rhodri won't be long, Beauty hates being shut in. Listen to him making such a fuss, he's usually so quiet when he can't see me.'

Mrs Costello sat herself down on a chair close to the counter and Kate made the foolish mistake of asking her how all her other animals were. The moment the words were out of her mouth she could have kicked herself. There followed a long monologue of how wonderfully intelligent her animals were and of the tricks they got up to and ... with an indulgent smile, Miranda added, 'Listen to him talking to me. He's such a talker he is, aren't you, Beauty?' By then she had inched open the lid of her cardboad box to ensure that Beauty was in full working order and he'd swept out before she could stop him and perched in the top of the giant cheese plant in the far corner of reception.

'Oh! Beauty! Well, bless him, isn't he clever? Knowing just where to perch. Doesn't he look lovely all amongst the leaves? Come to Mummy, Beauty.' She held out her finger and made tweeting noises to Beauty, but he was listening to none of her enticements. Eventually she climbed on a chair and made a grab for him, and got him squawking and struggling in her hand. He nipped her hard on her fingers and made her squeal. She kissed him before she put him in the box, protesting and squawking, and fastened the lid back on. 'I told you he was clever and he is. Better company than people he is, and certainly more obedient.' Then Beauty went completely quiet. 'There you are, you see, he does know how to behave really.' She preened herself like a budgie might, and sat back to continue her monologue.

Kate listened with half an ear to her stories for a few minutes more, wishing all the time that Rhodri would hurry up with his lunch. Eventually he did open his consulting room door and call out, 'Beauty Costello, please. Good afternoon, Miranda, and how are you this afternoon?'

'Oh! I'm fine, Rhodri, and you?'

'Fine thanks. Claws again, is it? And beak I see.'

'That's right. Yes. His claws and his beak.'

While he looked for the right piece of equipment to do the job, Rhodri asked her how her menagerie was getting along. 'Oh! Fine, you know. Every one a treasure, the delight of my heart. Wouldn't know what to do if I didn't have animals to get up for in the morning. Dogs to walk, cats to feed, Beauty to clean out, stables to muck out, you know. Life's full of promise for me.'

'Good.' Rhodri slid the lid off the cardboard box cautiously; he wasn't in the mood for a bird flying round his consulting room resisting arrest. Without taking the lid off completely he slipped his hand in and felt about for Beauty. All he could find was an inert budgie. Laid on its back! Feet in the air! A sure sign of having gone to glory. Oh no! Not dead. He put a finger on Beauty's chest, but could feel nothing. In his very bones he knew it was all hopeless. He quickly replaced the lid, and said, 'I think maybe, Miranda, you'd better take a seat.' Rhodri, in a state of total panic, cleared his throat. This had happened to him once before and the client had threatened legal action. He came over all cold and the stutter he'd thought he'd got rid of for ever came back. 'I-I think all is not w-w-well with B-B-Beauty.'

'What do you mean, "All is not well?"'

'He appears to have had a h-h-heart attack.'

'A heart attack! Well, get him out and do what they do.'

'I'm afraid it's t-t-too late for that.'

'Too late? Let me look.' She wrenched the lid off the box and saw Beauty feet up, laid motionless. 'You've killed him! You've killed him! My Beauty!' She picked him up and tried prising his beak open and breathing into his mouth but to no avail. Beauty was dead and gone.

'I'm so sorry, Miranda, so sorry. It must be the shock, you know, of being fastened up in the box when he's used to his freedom. A free-as-air budgie like B-B-Beauty, well . . .'

'Give him an injection, go on, something to bring him round.'

'Unfortunately there isn't anything I c-c-can . . .'

Mrs Costello clutched hold of the front of his white coat and begged and begged for Rhodri to resuscitate Beauty. 'Please. Please.' When she saw him shake his head she screamed and fell back onto the chair holding her handkerchief to her face, howling like a banshee. 'Beauty! Beauty! Beauty!'

At this point Kate, hearing the sounds of distress coming from Rhodri's consulting room, and noting that the level of conversation in the waiting room had been reduced to nil as the clients pricked up their ears, decided to go to his assistance. She gingerly opened the door in case Beauty was free again, but saw him laid on the examination table and recognised instantly what the problem was. 'Oh dear! It must have been the shock of it all.'

Grasping at straws Rhodri repeated, 'Shock of it all?'

'Well, he escaped in reception and Miranda had to recapture him from the top of the cheese plant. He was very upset, wasn't he, Miranda?'

The howling stopped while Miranda shrieked, 'Did I kill him then?'

'Not at all, it was no one's fault, was it, Rhodri?'

Rhodri shook his head. 'No one's. Budgies do this sometimes, stress and strain, different environment, travelling here, escaping, you know. It's all been too much for him.'

'Oh! My poor Beauty! What will his wife say? Oh! Beauty! I shall take him home and they can all come to his funeral. My poor Beauty. My little darling. My dearest Beauty.' She kissed him before she put him in the box. 'You are sure he's dead? Quite sure? I'd hate to bury him and then find ...' Miranda looked hopefully at Rhodri.

Rhodri said reassuringly, 'Quite sure. Quite sure.'

Kate took her elbow and led her out into reception, still weeping. Between sobs she said, 'I owe you, for the consultation.'

'There'll be no charge, Miranda.'

'Oh! Thanks.'

'You'll be all right getting home?'

'Oh yes, I've got the van.' She braced her shoulders.

'Are you sure?'

She nodded. Kate opened the door for her and saw her out to the car park.

'I shall miss him.'

'Of course you will, it's only natural. Drive carefully.'

Kate returned to have a private word with Rhodri. Closing the door behind her she said in a loud whisper, 'That was a close shave.'

'Too right. He was dead even before I put my hand in to get him out. I can't believe it, that's twice it's happened to me.' He completed his report of the consultation on his computer and said, 'You're a star, Kate. An absolute star.'

'Any time!'

'Don't tempt fate, I don't want that happening again. Who's next?'

Rhodri carried on with his afternoon clinic, with the niggling thought of Beauty's demise at the back of his mind all the time.

But he did have dinner at Megan's to look forward to, and tonight he would do his utmost to be polite to Megan's dad, Mr Idris Jones. About the only thing they had in common was home rule for Wales, after that their conversation was barely civil. The old man was the last of four generations of farmers and now he was crippled with arthritis and chronic asthma he had to rely on a daughter to carry on the farming tradition and with all that to bear he was bitter. Words could scarcely describe the extent of his bitterness. Made worse by the fact that his only son, Howard, had left home to become a barrister in London, unmarried and with no prospects of marriage, which meant there would be little chance of a successor to the family heritage.

But Rhodri was determined he wouldn't rise to the bait tonight, for Megan's sake, because she took the brunt of Mr Jones's unpleasantness every day of her life. When he thought of Megan his face broke into smiles. She was the loveliest, most beautiful, most delightful woman he'd ever met in his life, and he was determined, resolute even, that one day he and she would be married. He blessed the day there'd been all that confusion in reception, which had resolved itself by Megan coming to the Practice, pet sheep on a lead, to get veterinary help. To fall in love, on a bleak winter day with the wind blowing down from Beulah Bank Top fit to slice a man in two, was the last thing he'd ever expected, but it had happened. Gloriously, magically it had happened for her too.

At home, as he shaved for the second time that day, Rhodri promised himself that tonight he would broach the subject of marriage to Mr Jones, firmly and considerately. Though why he should have to ask his permission to marry Megan was beyond him; she was thirty-five and didn't need anyone's permission.

Showered, shaved and changed, Rhodri scooped up his pet ferret, Harry, from under a sofa cushion, shut him safely in his outdoor cage, and set off for Beulah Bank Farm singing his heart out with his favourite tenor solos from the *Messiah* as he drove, his spirits soaring the closer he got to Megan.

The climb up to the farm was spectacular. Mile after mile of wonderful hills piling one on the other with amazing views at every turn of the road. The farm itself stood tightly nestled into a hill, looking as though it had grown there rather than been built over two hundred years ago, and one didn't come upon it until the turn into the farm gateway. There it was, grey-stoned, solid, secretive almost, but inviting at the same time.

And there she was, Megan Angharad Jones, waiting in the kitchen doorway for him to arrive, arms outstretched, her whole face filled with a smile. Half the house was in shadow but the sun still shone on the back door, highlighting the glints of red in Megan's hair, the sparkle in her dark eyes, and he thought, not for the first time, of the wonders of the world and that surely it must be the eighth wonder that she loved him.

Rhodri went straight into her arms and kissed her hard and long. He stood back from her at arm's length and asked, 'How is it you always know when I'm about to arrive?'

'I'll let you into a secret. I look out of the kitchen window and as you drive over the humpbacked bridge I can just catch sight of you before you disappear into the trees and then I need to count to thirty-five and I know you'll be here.'

'And there was I thinking we were telepathic.'

'And a bit of that too!' They laughed at each other and, arms entwined, went to find her father. He was seated as usual in his winged chair, a rug over his knees, a pipe in his mouth, the *Daily Telegraph*, which he read from cover to cover every day, discarded in the wastepaper bin at his side.

'Good evening, Mr Jones.'

'It's you, is it? I'd forgotten.'

'Hasn't it been beautiful weather this last week? It's the sort of weather that makes you wish you were somewhere exotic under the palm trees with a soft breeze just beginning to take the heat out of the day. Isn't it now?'

'You wouldn't if you were me. This heat is stifling.'

'It must help the arthritis though.'

'Well, summer, I can't stand because the asthma always seems worse to me and, winter, I can't stand because of the arthritis. Gets me every which way.'

Rhodri didn't stop to think. 'You can't win, can you?'

Mr Jones rounded on him. 'Are you being impertinent on purpose?'

'I was trying to sympathise.'

'The only thing that saves your bacon is the fact that you're Welsh.'

'It's not the only thing that's good about me, Mr Jones. I love your Megan as you know. All we want to do is marry. Why can't you see your way to it?'

Mr Jones banged his fist surprisingly hard on the table beside him, making all the invalid paraphernalia on it jump and rattle and he shouted as best he could, 'I've said it and I'll say it again, she isn't marrying anyone. I need her. When I die, then she can marry.'

'But you've years of life in you yet, you know that. Years *we* could spend enjoying our life *together*.'

'Not while I'm alive. That sounds like Megan dishing up. Tell her I want wine tonight. Go on, tell her. Quick man, before it's too late.'

Rhodri moved his special table to one side so Mr Jones could lever himself up without any hindrance and said, 'I'll go *ask* her about the wine.'

'When I need my vocabulary correcting I'll let you know.'

They ate their meal at the dining table, Mr Jones at the head with Megan to his right, and Rhodri to his left. Rhodri wasn't well versed in the appreciation of furniture, but he could tell that the Jones family had dined off this very table for many, many years. The wood had a patina that only years of use and care could have produced. The chairs were the same, they invited you to sweep your hand across them for the sheer pleasure of touching the wood. In some ways it was a delight to dine in such splendour, in others an irritant because with the table came Mr Jones.

'Not enjoying your food? Young man like you, you should be wolfing it down.'

'I am enjoying it. Having to cook for myself makes me very appreciative of Megan's cooking. You're lucky, Mr Jones. Just wish I—'

'Rhodri!' Megan stopped him short of annoying her father again with one of his innocent remarks. 'It's Myfanwy. Her feet, she's limping. Can you take a look?'

Rhodri shook his head. 'I really shouldn't, I'm not a farm vet. They won't like it.'

Mr Jones snorted his disdain. 'Oh God! Professional etiquette rearing its ugly head, is it? You're a vet, aren't you? So get on with it.'

Rhodri addressed his reply to Megan. 'It puts me in a very awkward position. Can I get Dan to come? Is it urgent?'

'No. It's not urgent. Is he back at work then, after the baby?'

'Yes, he's back and full of being a father, though he says he hasn't had a full night's sleep since Rose got home.'

Megan smiled. 'Yes, of course. I imagine the baby will be just as beautiful as Rose.'

'God help it if it looks like Dan.'

Rather wistfully, Megan suggested that if the baby was half as beautiful as Rose he'd do all right. 'She's not just beautiful, there's a vibrancy about her ... I wish ...'

Her hand lay on the table while she spoke and Rhodri covered it with his. 'I agree Rose is beautiful and Dan's a lucky man, but you're just as beautiful and I'm just as lucky as Dan.'

'Hmm,' Mr Jones sneered, looking pointedly at Rhodri's hand holding Megan's. But Rhodri didn't remove it until he was good and ready and not before he'd taken her hand to his lips and kissed it reverently. The thought crossed Mr Jones's mind that Rhodri needed taking down a peg or two and that he was just the chap to do it. Matters were getting dangerously close to being taken out of his control and he wasn't having that.

3

Rhodri was spending ten minutes he really couldn't afford at this time in the morning searching for Harry Ferret. He'd let him out for his early morning run around while he got ready and the little devil had disappeared. It was partly his own fault because he'd left the kitchen door open by mistake. Experience had taught him not to leave the house without getting Harry back inside his outdoor cage: left all day with the freedom of the house spelt total disaster, so he had to find him before he went to work and time was running out. Rhodri muttered to himself while he crept about in an attempt to sneak up on him unawares, but those bright brown ferret eyes and wickedly twitching whiskers were nowhere to be seen.

Ah! The bathroom! Yes! Got yer! Harry loved nothing better than a tussle with the loo paper and Rhodri found yards of it spilling all over the floor. 'You little devil, you!' Harry gleefully nibbled on Rhodri's ear and babbled his own brand of ferret talk to show his appreciation of Rhodri's tolerance.

With Harry safely fastened in his run in the garden, Rhodri checked his appearance in the mirror in the hall, made sure the house was secure and ambled out to his car. He sniffed the air and found it gentle and summery as it should be at this time of year. A hint of damp though, which might presage rain later in the day. Before putting on his shades he adjusted his rear-view mirror, winked at himself, and agreed with no one in particular that he was handsome in his dark Welsh way with his thick, jet-black hair, dark brown eyes and a sensuous mouth second to none. He shoved the car into reverse and backed out onto the road, jerked into first and set off to the Practice, arriving with only minutes to spare.

The car park was already filling up with clients' cars, so he was definitely much later than he liked to be. He raced in through the back door and into his consulting room, slapped his shades down on a high

434

shelf along with his keys, took his freshly laundered white coat from the back of the consulting room door, buttoned it up, picked up the top file from the pile on his desk and saw his first client was Venus Costello, a cat. His heart sank. Not Miranda *again*.

When he put his head round the door into reception he saw it was filling up nicely with clients and Rhodri took on board the pleasurable buzz and excitement of a morning doing what he liked best. 'Good morning, everyone. Venus Costello, please!'

Mrs Costello stood up and bounced into his consulting room with a bright, 'Good morning, Rhodri. I was expecting it to be Graham ...'

'Very heavy cold, poor chap, can't make it today.'

'Oh dear, I am sorry. I do hope it isn't anything serious, there's so much flu about.'

'Don't worry your head about him, he's tough. I've no doubt he'll be back tomorrow hale and hearty. Now, it's time for Venus's booster, is it?' He peered into the basket and saw Venus sitting with her back to him.

'Yes, it is. She's used to Graham, really. He's always seen to her. By the way, I've bought another budgie to replace Beauty, well, no, not replace, but you know what I mean. I've called him Toots. Beauty's wife, the shameless hussy, has taken to him immediately. Had I better come back when Graham's better, they have such a rapport with each other?'

'Don't fret yourself, Miranda, I've done this thousands of times, there's nothing to it. She's used to coming here, isn't she? Now, I'll get myself organised and you get her out when I'm ready.' Rhodri checked Venus's card and prepared the syringe.

Though the door to her carrying basket was open, Venus didn't move, so Miranda put in her hands to lift her out. Venus gave an angry howl as she was placed on the examination table, shot Rhodri a belligerent glare as he approached with the syringe and took to her heels. She leapt from the table to the desk and hid behind the computer. 'Ah! Right. Miranda, you get her, I'll only panic her.' But Venus saw straight through his subterfuge and as Miranda, speaking in her softest, most caring voice, put her hand in behind the computer, Venus leapt out on to the top and began racing round the consulting room as if the Hound of the Baskervilles was on her tail. She hurtled about over every level surface she could find, from desk to chair, from chair to table, from table to shelf, to computer, to printer, to fridge, at such a speed she was almost a blur.

'Oh! Oh! Oh!' whispered Miranda, her earrings tinkling vigorously and her hands covering her mouth in horror and helplessness. 'What are we to do?'

Rhodri was at a loss for words. He couldn't face another crisis with Miranda, not so soon after the episode with Beauty. He dodged past Venus, as she shot from table to desk, to lock the door into reception, but as he did so Venus sent his shades flying from the top shelf and he trod on them. Biting back an angry response, he raced to lock the door into the Staff Only section of the building. 'We mustn't panic! Stand quite still and so will I and she'll get tired. I've locked the doors so no one can come in by mistake; if she gets out of here we'll never catch her.' He put down the syringe and, dodging the flying figure of Venus, went to stand with his back to the wall and advised Miranda to do the same. 'Keep quite calm and don't speak. It's the only way.'

After a few minutes, with great relief, they noticed a definite slowing of Venus's mad race to avoid the needle and, when Rhodri saw her pause for a moment on top of the waste bin, he quickly stepped forward with an old towel he kept for securing cats who took pleasure in clawing a vet's hands to shreds, and flung it over her. 'There we are!' he whispered in triumph. Rapidly, he expertly wrapped Venus so that only her head was visible. She struggled but couldn't make her escape. Rhodri tucked her under his arm and gently stroked her head, speaking softly to her, so that gradually the fight in her dissipated, leaving her yowling in protest but not struggling.

Very, very quietly Rhodri said, 'Now, hold her like I'm doing, firm but not tight, no, no, don't take the towel off, that's it, firm but not tight. All I need to get at is her scruff. Gently does it, gently. Slowly.' Venus eyed him viciously, made to struggle free, admitted defeat, and allowed him to inject her. 'Well done, Miranda, well done. Put her in the basket.'

Mrs Costello was a shattered wreck by this time. 'Oh! Rhodri! Oh! What an experience. She's usually so amenable.' She tried to still her beating heart by fluttering her heavily ringed hands on her chest. 'I feel quite faint.'

Rhodri tossed the used syringe into the waste bin. 'I think next time you come we'd better make sure it's Graham who sees her. She obviously feels more relaxed with him.'

'I'm so sorry. So sorry to have caused such an upset. I'd no idea she would react like this.'

Rhodri patted her shoulder. 'Don't worry! No problem.'

'You're so kind. Has she scratched you?'

Rhodri shook his cuff down over his wrist to cover a nasty claw mark. 'She has not, no.' He turned to put the information into his computer. 'Are you all right, now?'

'I'm a little shaken, but I'll sit down in the waiting room for a while before I leave. Thank you, Mr Hughes, for being so kind.'

'All in a day's work. Good morning, Miranda.' He lifted Venus's basket from the examination table and handed it over.

In a caressingly sweet voice Miranda said, 'Come along, Venus, you naughty girl. What are you? A naughty girl. Yes, you are.'

With the door unlocked, Miranda left, Rhodri picked up the next file and got on with his morning's work.

Mrs Costello went to the reception desk to pay her account, and to her delight saw it was Kate on duty. 'Oh Kate, my dear . . .'

'Mrs Costello! You look quite flushed. Is everything all right?'

'Well, my dear, this naughty Venus of mine took a dislike to Mr Hughes and has been flying round the consulting room like a cat possessed.'

'Oh dear!'

'Exactly! Mr Hughes was so clever, he knew exactly what to do.'

'Has he managed to give her a booster?'

'Oh yes, eventually. We had to lock the doors to make sure no one opened them or else we'd never have caught her. He really is a wonderful vet, I feel so embarrassed that Venus was so ungrateful.' Miranda looked at Kate and thought yet again what a lovely looking girl she was, with her hair so nicely arranged, her fine dark eyes, and her lovely expression, so thoughtful and kindly. Just the kind of daughter she would have liked if only . . . 'Now, dear, tell me how much I owe.'

With her account settled Miranda asked if Kate minded if she sat in reception for a while till her heart stopped racing.

'Please, feel free.'

Once her heart had stopped beating so fast Miranda got into conversation with a client who had driven fifty miles for a consultation with Mungo Price. 'We never noticed there was anything wrong with him when we got him at eight weeks old, but as he's grown we can see there's a definite deformity in his hind legs. We've been recommended to come here, apparently he's very well-known in the veterinary world for his orthopaedic work.'

'I can assure you that if Mungo Price can't fix him, no one can.'

'Is that right?'

'Oh yes, they're all quite marvellous here. Quite marvellous. Rest assured, I'm certain Mr Price will be able to help. I must be off now. 'Bye, Kate!'

Kate waved her goodbye without speaking as she was on the phone taking a message from a client. 'Of course, of course. I'll check who's the nearest and let them know. Absolutely, yes, before lunch.'

Kate put down the receiver and groaned. They were already very shorthanded and could well do without any emergency calls this morning. She checked all the farm calls for the morning, then the map on the wall behind her. That, thought Kate, means ringing Dan, definitely not Colin, he's too far away to ask him to divert to the Chesham Chicken Farm. The manager had been well-nigh hysterical when she'd spoken to him, heaven alone knew what the matter was.

Dan protested. 'Can't Colin go? I'm not very *au fait* with chickens.'

'No, he's too far away.'

'Oh! Well. Never been there, could be interesting. I'll be half an hour though. If Bridge Farm ring, tell them I'll be there to do the TB testing in about an hour and a half.'

'That's fine, Dan, so long as you get to Crispy Chicken before lunch.'

'Right!'

When the manager opened the door to the second of the huge chicken sheds, Dan was stunned by the sheer number of birds inside. Hundreds upon hundreds of white-feathered birds scurrying about almost shoulder to shoulder, the ones nearest began scrabbling to escape him by climbing over the heads and shoulders of their compatriots. And the noise! He was deafened by it. They might claim they were free to roam, but ... he guessed there was barely a square foot of space for each bird. They appeared to move collectively in great surges, as though they were all of the same mind. They looked perky enough though, from where he was standing. The shed was well ventilated, he had to admit to that. Huge extractors were stirring the air so that the smell, which would normally have been overpowering from so many birds, was just tolerable. The floor on which they stood was inches thick in wood shavings. Dan asked himself how on earth they managed to keep it so fresh looking. Good management, he supposed.

The manager said, 'What do you think?'

'About what?'

'About the way they're kept.'

'They're clean, they look healthy enough, bright, active, but at the same time I can't help but feel sorry for them.'

The manager studied Dan's face. He saw the strength in his features, the no-nonsense eyes, and the power of his personality. He'd be no easy pushover, this one. 'Haven't seen you before. Are you new?'

'Fairly new, we're very shorthanded, sickness, holidays et cetera today, so I've come instead of Colin. Name's Dan Brown.'

'I'm Bryan Buckland. I remember now, you're the one who upset Lord Askew! It was all round town.'

They shook hands.

'Quite right, but it's all been resolved.'

'So I heard. You've made quite a coup there I understand. Difficult beggar to get on with though.'

'Can be. But we've reached an agreement.' Dan laughed and Bryan Buckland laughed too, thinking Dan must be the first ever to know how to handle his lordship.

With no time for social niceties Dan got down to business. 'So, how many a day do you lose on average?'

'Ah! Well, that's the point. In a shed this size we usually find perhaps five a day absolute max. I can live with that, profit-wise, but these last few days it's gone from five to ten then fifteen then between twenty or thirty, and this morning it was forty-two. That's bad news.'

'Show me them.'

The poor pathetic remains were piled into a trailer standing outside the door, ready for taking away to an incinerator. 'Obviously it's in our best interests to destroy dead birds quickly. I've held these back for you to see.'

Dan didn't want to touch them with his bare hands, in case of passing any disease on elsewhere. With his ears still clamouring from the noise in the shed he poked them around with a stick. 'Can't tell from looking. They need equipment and expertise I haven't got. Post-mortem and such. You should seek advice from the state veterinary service. They're equipped to deal with situations like these.'

'If they start poking their noses in—'

'If they don't, you might find yourself losing the whole lot. In such close quarters, whatever they've got will pass round like wildfire, then where will your profit be?'

Bryan Buckland was obviously nervous. He bit his lip, looked at Dan, looked at the dead birds and asked, 'No idea what it is, then?'

'I'm not a poultry man and certainly not qualified to make decisions about such a large-scale operation like yours. You need an expert. But it's my opinion it could be Newcastle disease; it certainly can't be ruled out. However, you're probably more able to assess the problem than I am. You do realise it's a notifiable disease? If I'm proved right it would mean every bird slaughtered in this shed and the other two. Are they following the same pattern?'

Dan thought the manager looked sly. 'No, no, no. They're all right.'

'They soon won't be, if you're not careful. When will these be ready for dispatching?'

'Another six days.'

'Exactly?'

The manager nodded. 'It's all fine-tuned, this business. One day's feed too many and the profit margin starts on the slippery slope.' His right forefinger made a downward plunge. 'So you can't help me?'

'I'm afraid not. Wish I could.' Dan dug in his pocket and brought out a card with names and telephone numbers on it written in his flamboyant handwriting. 'This chap here, look, ask for him, I'll write the number down for you.'

'No need to bother, I have Mike Allport's number.'

'In that case then why have you called us?'

The manager gave Dan an apologetic stare. 'Didn't want to get officialdom involved if I could help it.'

'You must, absolutely must. I have to notify the authorities of my suspected diagnosis. I could be wrong, but I don't think I am. I'll call Mike Allport now. I can't leave until he's been to confirm.'

'There's no need.'

'There is. By tomorrow you could be in dead trouble. As chicken farms go you're doing a damn good job here. Don't ruin it for yourself, nor for these poor birds. I have to act *today*.'

Dan went back into the second chicken shed for another look. He walked up and down the passageway examining the mechanical feeders, looking for any chickens beginning to droop and lose interest in life, but found none. 'I'm ringing Mike Allport straight away.'

'Don't. Thanks all the same.'

Dan went to stand outside the shed to make his call. Bryan Buckland followed him. 'I said, don't call him.'

'I am not willing to sacrifice my professional integrity for some scheme of yours to avoid an informed diagnosis. It's more than my job's worth.' Dan dialled the number.

Bryan Buckland made to snatch the phone from him but Dan pushed him away.

'This is my livelihood. Don't do it to me.'

'I'm sorry. Am I speaking to Mike Allport?'

Bryan Buckland strode away, bitter resignation in every step. Shoulders bowed he headed for the office. Dan went to sit in his Land Rover to brood at the injustice of it all. But if he shut his eyes to it and took Bryan Buckland's attitude, his professional integrity would indeed be nil. He had to do it. Dan waited an hour and a half for the veterinary officer to arrive. An hour and a half he could have made good use of.

Those poor damn birds. Free to roam? It must be a nightmare living like that. Like being trapped in a concentration camp. Dan shuddered at the thought. But if they'd never known freedom in their short lives and they'd always been well fed ... He rang Bridge Farm, his next call, to let them know he would be much later than he'd thought.

As soon as the veterinary officer arrived Dan leapt out and went to shake hands. 'Dan Brown, Barleybridge Farm Veterinary Practice.'

'Gerard Hookham. Newcastle disease you say?'

'I'm almost one hundred per cent sure. Check for yourself. Second shed. He's kept the dead ones for you to see.'

Dan stood aside and watched Buckland and Hookham greet each other. He felt there was a camaraderie between the two, which didn't sit well with someone who had impartial decisions to make. He could be wrong though.

When the two of them came outside again Gerard Hookham was shaking his head. 'I'm not convinced. In fact I'm sure it isn't.'

'Are you certain?'

'I have probably got more experience than you with poultry and I'm telling you it isn't Newcastle disease.'

'I see. And that's your considered opinion, is it?'

Gerard nodded and stepped back a little, suddenly aware Dan was someone to be reckoned with. 'Yes. It is.'

'Well, I'm certain I'm right. What are you going to say if next week they're dying like flies?'

'They won't be. Forty-two today is a fluke.'

'What is it then?'

'Just one of the hazards of having so many birds together.'

'If I'm proved to be right ...'

Gerard smiled.

Dan grew angry. 'What about spreading the disease? You go onto dozens of farms, you could spread it. Have you no conscience, man?'

'I've told you it isn't what you think.'

'On your head be it.'

Dan turned on his heel and went to leave. Before he did so he poured some powerful disinfectant into his wellington boot bowl and washed down his boots and his car tyres. He made a rather ostentatious performance of it for Gerard's benefit and left for Bridge Farm.

On his way he tried to remember if they kept poultry. He had a suspicion they did, and so instead of driving into the farmyard, which he normally would have done, he left his Land Rover out in the lane as a precaution. He put on his disinfected boots and walked into the yard where there was some furious clucking and squawking going on from some Welsummer chickens. Fine, upstanding pedigree birds they were, and Dan was glad he'd taken precautions.

By two o'clock he was back at the Practice ready for lunch. The staff had always known right from the day Dan began working there that, for some reason, he and Rhodri Hughes didn't hit it off. Nothing specific, but there was always that sense of touchiness between them and for why no one could make out. They were both first-rate vets, versatile, agreeable, pleasant with clients, skilful, but somehow they . . . and this lunchtime was no exception.

'Hey boyo! That's my mug.'

Dan examined the mug he was drinking from. 'I thought this was mine.'

'Yours is like that but the printing's red on yours. That's green so it's mine.'

'Does it matter? Here, you have this – I've only taken a sip.' He handed the mug across the table.

Rhodri shook his head. 'No, thanks, not when you've been drinking from it. But remember in future.'

Dan looked up at Rhodri, his face humourless. 'Trouble is with bachelors, they get set in their ways.'

Rhodri's swarthy skin flushed and he remained silent. Dan wasn't to know that last night he'd proposed another wedding date to Megan and been refused. To save himself from being taunted, Rhodri walked out of the staff room taking his lunch with him and left Dan to eat alone.

He decided to eat his lunch outside on the old bench by the back door. Damn that blasted man. Why did he let him get under his skin? Why couldn't he just ignore him? Rhodri sank his teeth into a smoked salmon sandwich Kate had been out to buy for him, and brooded on his bachelor state, beginning by damning the domineering old man who kept such a tight rein on his unmarried daughter and ruined her life. Twice they'd named the day and twice her father had had a bad asthmatic attack, been rushed to hospital and hovered at death's door for days. Rhodri had convinced himself that the old man brought on the attacks himself. Could you do that with asthma? In his mind he trawled through friends and relatives for a doctor in the know, but realised he knew none.

Rhodri had suggested that they married secretly and told her father afterwards when the deed was done, but Megan, being a straightforward, honest character, refused. She wanted her father to give her away. When she'd said this Rhodri had replied, 'But that's archaic. You've been your own person for years, you don't need anyone to give you away.' But Megan had stuck to her guns. 'I want him to do just that, please, I know it's only right. I'm sorry.'

Maybe she didn't want to marry him. Could it be her way of

escaping life's challenges? Rhodri kicked some loose gravel away from under his feet, opened the plastic casing of his slice of apple pie and began to eat it, but couldn't taste it. He looked up at the hills beyond the Practice car park and deep in his heart longed for the bleakness of the Welsh mountains. It was all too mild hereabouts, even the air he breathed wasn't bracing enough, nor the landscape, nor the people.

The back door opened and out came Kate. 'Your extraction's arrived, Rhodri. Sorry.'

'OK. Just finishing my coffee. Ask Sarah One to get him ready.' Teeth extraction. Diseased teeth, all because the owner didn't take enough care. Six out. No wonder the poor dog's breath smelt. He crumpled up the sandwich wrapping, placed it neatly in the plastic casing that had held his apple pie, gulped down the last drop of coffee, examined his mug and questioned why he had made such a fuss of Dan using it. He'd have to apologise, no, he damn well wouldn't. He wouldn't give it another thought. Instead he'd think about Megan and going out with her for a meal tonight.

Six extractions, four spays and a castration later Rhodri left for home. He'd take Harry Ferret out for a walk first, then have his shower, then call early for Megan.

The moment he heard Rhodri's voice, Harry unrolled himself from a deep sleep, and came to the front of his cage, stretching luxuriously. 'Oh yes! Here I am slaving away earning money to support you and what are you doing? Sleeping the day away. What a life! Time you went out to work and earned your keep.' Harry appreciated the nuzzling he got from Rhodri when he lifted him out of his cage. He slipped inside Rhodri's jacket and snuggled down while his red harness was found and the front doormat was checked for post. Then, holding the lead, Rhodri set off for a walk, out of the garden down the footpath that ran alongside their fence and out into the field behind the house.

Harry scurried along, keeping pace. No time for dawdling until Rhodri had worked the tensions of the day from his stocky frame and was able to wander carefree. Well, almost carefree, apart from the long, nagging loneliness of not being able to be with Megan all the time. Rhodri shaded his eyes and watched a kestrel hovering, but it didn't dive and he lost interest. He'd known for certain that Megan was his kind of person when she'd taken so readily to Harry. Seemed a daft criterion for a life partner but it mattered and she knew it did. She also loved Welsh male voice choirs, and adored hearing his wonderful tenor voice singing the old Welsh songs. Megan swore he could have been a soloist on the concert stage had he not wanted to be a vet. He'd give her six more months and then ... and then? What? Her da couldn't be left to live on his own. Megan wouldn't do that anyway. No, whichever way he looked at it, he'd have to live with them on the farm, but the thought of eating every meal with the old man made his spirits drop even lower.

Without warning a huge cloud covered the sun and a chill wind began to blow. Rhodri decided to head for home. Lengthening his stride Rhodri turned back, still with no solution to his lovelife. He just wished Dan had no reason to say that he was set in his bachelor ways. Dan had everything Rhodri wanted, a home with a beautiful wife in it and a newborn son.

4

Rose took Jonathan to see everyone at the Practice when he was just two weeks old. She went in their lunch hour and immediately found herself surrounded by admiring faces.

'Why, he's beautiful, Rose, absolutely beautiful. Can I hold him?' This was Joy, eager to join Jonathan's admiration society. 'Well, there's no doubting who his father is. He's just like Dan, isn't he? So like him it's almost comical.'

'I guess he is. There's no mistaking, is there? Danny's as proud as punch.'

'Of course he is. He's a changed man since you came back, you know.'

'Is he?'

'Oh yes. He was very difficult to get on with, but he's soft as butter now.'

Everyone wanted a turn at holding the baby, including Letty, Colin's wife, who had come in especially to see him. 'Here, give him to me.' She sat herself down on Joy's chair and held out her arms. Joy handed him over and Letty rather awkwardly took him from her. 'Am I getting it right?'

Rose laughed. 'Yes, of course you are. Actually, you're not looking quite well, Letty.'

'No, just some bug I've picked up.'

'Are you actually sick?'

'Not really, no. You're very lucky. Maybe I'd better give him back to you or I'll be tempted to take him home.'

Before they knew it Sarah One and Sarah Two with Bunty came in to join Jonathan's admiration society followed by Stephie and Kate.

'He's gorgeous. Absolutely gorgeous.' Kate gave Jonathan her finger to clutch and he did with a surprising strength. 'He's so strong and he's got his father's looks.'

Rose had to laugh. 'Everyone says that. I feel quite jealous.'

'Don't worry. Have a girl next and she'll be like you.' This from Letty who was still captivated by him.

'Have a heart, Letty.'

'No, it's best. Close together and then they all grow up at the same time. No good having too big an age gap.'

Stephie muttered to Kate, 'Little she knows about it, anyone would think she'd had a whole tribe of children.'

'Sssh! She'll hear you.'

'Can't quite see Colin ...' Stephie nudged Kate and winked. 'You know.'

'Are you going to have some more children?' Letty asked Rose.

'Hopefully, but not yet awhile.'

'You should. People like you should have babies.' Without warning, Letty burst into tears and left Joy's office.

She left behind an embarrassed silence. To fill it, Rose said, 'I'll just go show him to the clients.'

'You do that.' Joy stood to one side to let Rose out. 'They'll love him – they've been asking when they'd see him. Back to work all of you. I'll just go find Letty, see she's all right.'

Joy found Letty sitting in her car crying as if her heart was breaking. She opened the driver's door and said, 'Letty! Please don't cry.'

But Letty couldn't stop.

She fumbled in her handbag for a tissue and dabbed her cheeks, but still the tears rolled down. 'It's this blessed sickness, I never feel quite right. What a fool you must think me.'

'Not at all, babies get you like that. Well, they get me like that.' She went round to the front passenger door, opened it and got in beside Letty. 'Shall I get Colin?'

'No, no. He has enough on. I'm just being a fool.'

'No, you're not. It just goes to demonstrate that you're human. Come back in, have a cup of tea or something.'

Letty stopped crying and turned her blotchy wet face to Joy. 'No, I won't. I don't want to see the baby again.' She stared straight ahead and after a moment commented, 'I've not been very kind, have I? In the past?'

'Well ...'

'No, be honest. No beating about the bush.'

'It's not for me to say.'

'Please, Joy, be honest with me, even if it's going to hurt. We've known each other long enough for you to be totally frank.'

Joy was completely thrown by this touchy-feely Letty. It was a Letty she had never known. 'If you want the truth, I'll give it to you, but it won't be nice. So I've warned you, right?' She thought for a moment. 'You've been a miserable, unkind, edgy, frosty, nit-picking person and very difficult to like. Thought yourself right about everything, you know, and you weren't always. And as for the way you've treated Colin in the past! Though you have changed for the better of late, I must admit.'

Letty flinched as though she'd been hit. 'I see.' She stared through the windscreen. 'I see. Not just Colin though. What about Dan?'

'Especially about Dan. He's a thoroughly decent chap, you know. He speaks his mind, I'll give you that. But ... he is rock-strong, fair-minded, and straightforward, and he's done this Practice a lot of good, hasn't he? And I've grown to like him.' Joy half turned to smile at Letty. But Letty ignored her. Instead she started up the car and put it into gear. 'Hold on, Letty, let me get out.' Joy struggled to open the door and Letty reached across to open it for her. Joy got out, but before she closed the door, she said, 'Letty! I don't like the idea of you driving when you're like this. Come in, just to talk, eh?'

Letty shrugged her shoulders and the car began to move, so Joy had no alternative but to shut the door and let her drive away. She watched Letty disappear into the main road thinking that she'd never seen her so emotional since she'd known her. Actually asking for people's impressions of her! Unheard of. Perhaps she shouldn't have been so blunt. All that emotion right there at the surface. There was something definitely wrong with Letty.

As Joy passed the accounts office Kate called out, 'Oh, there you are. We've been looking for you. Rose is just going.'

'Oh, right.'

Rose asked Joy if she'd done something wrong. 'Did I say something I shouldn't? It's not like Letty, is it? Is she still here?'

'She's gone. For some reason she's very upset and she won't tell me what it is. So don't worry. I'm going to catch up with Colin and have a quiet word. Lovely to see you, Rose, pop in any time. You'll be most welcome.'

'Should I go see her? Would she mind? Apologise or something?'

'Well, I expect she'd prefer to be alone right now, because she asked me what people thought about her, and I told her. I wish I hadn't, but she insisted.' Not for the world would she tell Rose it was the baby who had upset Letty.

'Perhaps I'll send her a card, yes, I'll send her a card.' At this point Jonathan began to cry, a pitiful, heartfelt cry that couldn't be ignored.

'That's his I-Am-Hungry cry so I'd better go.' Rose left in a flurry of goodbyes and good wishes.

Joy saw her to the car. 'You've got a lovely baby there, Rose, you must be very happy.'

'Oh, we are, Danny and I, very happy.'

'I'm glad, so glad. Be seeing you.'

After Rose had left, Joy rang Colin and told him of the afternoon's episode and how worried she was. Colin didn't reply for a moment and then said, 'I'm worried too. She's not a bit like herself. I've only one more call, I'll go straight home from there.'

'Good, she might need a large dose of TLC.'

'Of what?'

'TLC. Tender Loving Care.'

'Ah! Right. I'll see she gets it.'

So Joy went home that afternoon feeling uneasy about Letty. Duncan had started another contract and with him being withdrawn, his mind on solving his computer problems, she guessed she wouldn't be on the receiving end of some TLC. In fact she'd be lucky to get a word from him all evening.

But the moment she opened the front door she could smell . . . what was it? Beef casserole? Chicken? So she was to get some loving care after all.

She found him in the kitchen putting a dessert in the fridge. 'Duncan! How wonderful you've started the meal. What's in the oven?'

'That rooster who kept waking you up and driving you mad.'

'Not the Duke of Wellington?'

Duncan laughed. 'The very same. The dish is called Joy's Revenge.'

Joy put down her bag on the table and pulled out a chair. 'I don't know if I can eat him. I got very fond of him latterly.'

'Well, you'd better, there's nothing else. We need to stock up.' Duncan kissed her and asked, 'How's it been?'

'Rose brought the baby in. He is gorgeous, very fair skin like Rose, but dark-haired and so like Dan it's laughable. And Rose of course, as slender as ever, looking perfectly lovely. I do envy her. She's one of those people who, if you called at the house on the off chance, and she was wearing torn jeans and an old sweater and her hair was all over the place and she was painting the ceiling, would still look beautiful. It simply isn't fair.' She smiled ruefully at Duncan.

'You look beautiful always. No matter what you wear. You never give yourself enough credit.' Duncan had his back to her so she couldn't see if he was sincere or simply teasing.

'Duncan?'

Duncan turned to face her. 'I've put a bottle of your favourite wine in the fridge so all we need to do now is sit down with a drink and wait. I've done the dessert too.'

'Duncan?'

But he'd gone into the sitting room and was at the drinks cupboard getting her a vodka and tonic.

'Duncan? Look at me.'

When Joy saw his face she almost choked. He was looking at her as though he couldn't get enough of her, as though his immense love for her was almost too much for him to bear. His eyes were shining with love for her, for *her*.

'Darling! Oh darling! I'm never fair to you, am I? I don't know why you keep on loving me as you do.' She held her arms wide, but he shook his head. 'Please.'

'No. Mungo's still there between us. You will not let him go, will you?'

'I do try, but then it all comes back again as bad as ever.'

'I could kill him, if I didn't like him as much as I do.'

'Duncan. Don't.'

'Both of us, with unrequited love. Ironic, isn't it? You know at bottom that he'll never leave Miriam. Doesn't that hurt?'

'He doesn't know how I feel. I never give him a clue. Never.' There was something in Duncan's face she couldn't interpret. 'Why are you looking at me like that? What are you thinking?'

'He knows, my love, and has done for a while.'

Joy shot to her feet, horrified by the thought. 'I've never told him how I feel. It must be Miriam who told him. I can't believe it of her.'

It was Duncan's turn to be shocked. '*Miriam* knows?'

Joy sat down again, her legs having gone weak with shock. 'She's known right from the first day she met me. She told me the other week.'

Duncan stared at her trying to take in what she'd said, then he threw his whisky down his throat and poured himself another before he answered her. 'Well, it wasn't Miriam who told her husband you loved him.'

'No one else knows.'

'Are you sure about that?'

Did they all know then? Joy felt . . . Well, she didn't know what she felt . . . Did they all whisper behind her back? She'd never noticed if they did. Never. If Miriam didn't tell Mungo, who did? An awful suspicion dawned on her.

Ice cold with anger, Joy looked Duncan full in the face. 'Was it you?'

Despite her anger she noticed Duncan didn't even have the grace to look ashamed. 'Yes.'

'Yes? How could you? How could you?' This time she leapt to her feet and faced him, her fists hammering on his chest, to emphasise her anger. 'How could you? My deepest secret and you've told him. Why? Why?'

Duncan gripped her wrists tightly and forced them away from him. 'Can you believe I'm capable of jealousy? Me? Laid-back Duncan? Self-absorbed Duncan? That Duncan who lets his life slide by year after year, patiently waiting? Doing his computer programmes, salting money away for that wonderful day when his *wife* finally gets round to loving him and they can travel the world on a gargantuan honeymoon? Imagine that! Funny, isn't it?' He released his grip, drank his whisky and walked away from her into the kitchen.

But Joy couldn't let what he'd said go without knowing exactly how long Mungo had known. She followed Duncan into the kitchen and asked him point-blank. 'When did you tell him?'

He was lifting Joy's Revenge from the oven. When he'd placed the dish on the worktop he said, 'That night they came for a drink and we'd just got Tiger and she paddled in her water bowl. Don't ask me why I did but the demon jealousy was sitting on my shoulder that night, and that good-looking-I-own-the-world sod walked in and I couldn't resist. It gets to sound more like a Whitehall farce every day. You didn't know he knew, I didn't know Miriam knew, but you knew she knew because she told you, but you didn't tell me she knew. He didn't know you loved him, he told me never ever to tell Miriam you loved him, now I've found out she's always known, so I needn't have bothered to keep my lip buttoned.' Duncan spooned the sauce over the chicken, tasted it and added another spoonful of wine. 'Ten minutes more, and Joy's Revenge will be ready.'

Unexpectedly the thought exploded in her head that the whole situation really had become a farce, like Duncan had said. Joy felt ridiculous. Completely ridiculous. She had become a laughing stock, particularly if everyone at the Practice had guessed how she felt about Mungo. She only had to think his name and the feelings she had for him surfaced, but had they become like beloved old shoes that fitted beautifully, comfortingly, but now it was time to bin them? Well, she'd brace herself to eat Joy's Revenge and then see how she felt on a full stomach. Good food always helped to gear up her thought processes and that night was no exception.

But the happy atmosphere usually engendered by fine wine and good food didn't happen. Duncan rapidly became morose and abrupt. No amount of telling him the news of the day from the Practice could cheer him.

'I'm sorry. Duncan?'

He raised his face from looking at his dinner plate and she saw the pain there. The skein of his hair, which always fell across his forehead despite his efforts, was brushed impatiently back from his face and he said, 'One day, you know, all hope will be gone for us.'

'Hope?'

'All hope that one day it will be me you love.'

'But I do.'

'No, Joy, you don't. You cling helplessly to your feelings for Mungo, uselessly really, as well you know. Why can't you see that?'

'I can. But I can't help it. And I do love you.'

'Not like I want it. Rather more like you'd love a devoted spaniel. Not with fire.' Duncan clenched his fist and held it up and shook it to demonstrate the strength of his feelings. 'Not with deep desire. Not with overwhelming desire for *me*.' He thumped his clenched fist against his chest. 'Your love isn't even a comforting, all-embracing, cuddling kind of love. That might be tolerable. What we have isn't even that.'

Joy remained silent, well aware of the truth of what he said. If only she could love him like he wanted. But she couldn't. 'I do try.'

Duncan's face registered such disappointment at the word 'try' that Joy felt as though she'd been whipped. 'Joy! I was fool enough to believe when we married that your love for me would grow, and all it would need was patience on my part. But I've worked to fan the flames. Recently I've come to realise there isn't even one small jet of flame to fan. And still the years roll on. I believe you when you say you try, but you shouldn't have to *try*! Now . . . now, I'm reaching a point where I don't care a damn whether you do or not.'

'You've given up on me? Is that it?'

Duncan nodded. 'You could say that. I've waited and I've just run out of time and patience.'

'But what shall I do? What can I do?'

'Abandon Mungo. Love me instead.'

'But look at the times you've ignored me for weeks on end. When it's been like living with the walking dead? Work! Work! Work! That's all it's been for weeks on end. What about those times? Eh?'

'It's never been as bad as that.'

'But it has. It has, from where I'm standing.'

'I can't help it if my work drives me and drives me till I hardly know I exist as a person. It's the only way I have of earning a living, even though I know I get right to the wire with it, time after time. But then it gets better when I've resolved the problems.'

'Oh yes. It gets better, but not better enough. You're still withdrawn, still an odd bod. At the Practice they know what you're like – don't want to go anywhere, don't want to socialise. They've asked you times without number to go out for a drink to celebrate something or another, but Duncan go? Oh no! You're so arrogant, so self-obssessed, you don't care what people think of you. Not one jot. And for you to tell Mungo I love him, that . . . that, I cannot forgive. I bet you enjoyed the telling, didn't you? Mmm? Relished it. I bet you did. Not caring how much you upset him. Not thinking about how he'd cope, how *he'd* feel. Oh no!'

'Why *ever* should *I* give Mungo's feelings even a moment of consideration, when he's stolen my marriage from me? Tell me one reason why I should? Come to think of it though, there wasn't anything to steal, it wasn't a real marriage in the first place, was it? You loved him even then. It's all been a complete lie. It leaves a very bitter taste. Why should I have to feel *grateful* if I rouse the smallest response from you when we make love? Make love? Huh! That's a misnomer if ever there was one. *Love*. Huh!'

Joy couldn't find an answer and wondered how on earth she had arrived at this desolate bleakness of soul. Duncan stood for a moment, looking down at her, then he left the table and went to stand outside in the garden, looking at the lights of Barleybridge far below, hunched up, feeling crucified.

Joy cleared the meal away, Joy found washing that needed putting in the machine, Joy needed to take a bath to relax her, and Joy was asleep in bed before he came up. When she awoke next morning Duncan had gone. A note said: '*Gone walkabout. Yours for always, Duncan.*' It sounded so final. She was used to him leaving to walk alone to clear his thinking processes, but he'd never written '*Yours for always.*' Never, ever. When he said 'walkabout' he meant walking for the day, and sometimes he rang her and asked her to pick him up from somewhere and he'd be refreshed and more like himself. It always did him good, to walk alone for mile upon mile. So perhaps he'd ring her tonight.

Occasionally he would mean longer than a day, but he had his present contract to fulfil so he'd have to be back. She sighed with relief. Obviously he did mean just for the day. Of course, just for the day. All the same Joy checked his sock drawer and found he'd taken several pairs of his walking socks, changes of underwear, sweaters. So he was going for a while. Something akin to a pain filled her chest.

A phone call as soon as she arrived at the Practice that morning put all thoughts of Mungo and Duncan out of her head. She raced out of her office calling, 'Anyone seen Dan? Has he gone?'

Colin answered her. 'He's here, sorting his post in the staff room.'

Joy found him reading a letter from the laboratory, punching the air with delight.

'I knew I was right! I knew it! This letter proves it.' Dan looked up and raised an eyebrow at Joy. 'Yes?'

'Crispy Chickens?'

'Yes. Why?'

'Bridge Farm are protesting because the State Veterinary Service intend culling all their flock.'

'Why?'

'Because I've just had a call to say that as Crispy Chickens have now got Newcastle disease and all their flock are about to be slaughtered, there's a strong chance you might have carried the disease to Bridge Farm.'

'I knew I was right. The idiots. Anyway, I disinfected myself before I went to Bridge Farm.'

'They say it's because of you going straight there, you could have carried it.'

'I'll ring Bridge Farm straight away. There's absolutely no need for that flock to be slaughtered. I'll tell them I'm standing up for them. It's wholesale murder it is.'

Before Joy could stop him, Dan had phoned Bridge Farm and told them his position. He followed that with a call to Bryan Buckland and another to the Veterinary Service. By the time he came off the phone he was boiling with temper. 'It is sheer blind stupidity. Sheer stupidity. I don't know when I've been more angry. Think of all the people who've visited, all the lorries that have delivered to Crispy Chickens in the week since I was there. They've all to be traced. It's criminal. Absolutely criminal. There could be an epidemic. What's the point of reporting a notifiable disease if they can't recognise it when they see it?'

Joy tried to calm him down. 'Dan! Dan!' By now he was pacing the staff room like a caged lion, planning terrible revenge.

'There's one thing for certain – they're not culling all those chickens at Bridge Farm on my account. I'm not having it. Definitely not.'

'I don't see how you can stop it.'

'Neither do I at the moment, but something must be done.' Muttering threats of drawing and quartering Mike Allport and hanging Bryan Buckland from his extractor fans Dan stormed out to start his calls.

'Dan! Don't do anything stupid, will you? Speak to Mungo first. Right?'

She heard him call out, 'I will.' And hoped to heaven he wouldn't do anything too damaging. Joy followed him out into the car park. 'Look here. Mungo will decide on the right course of action when he's had a chance to talk things through with you. Don't whatever you do go to Crispy Chickens, will you?'

'No, because I might murder Buckland. A whole week! God!'

'Exactly. So . . . leave it with me. Right? I mean it!' She began to return indoors but turned back to say, 'And whatever you do, don't go to Bridge Farm either. Do you hear me? Mungo will know what action to take. OK?'

'Of course, you're right. But it's dammed urgent if we're going to stop them. First, I'm going to see Phil Parsons's new bull.'

Dan went off with his list of calls, in no mood to suffer fools gladly. As he turned onto the track that led to the Parsons' Applegate Farm he determinedly pushed his anger to the back of his mind. He parked in his usual place, on the track and not in the yard, and changed into his boots before he got out. The farm was just as muddy and chaotic as it had always been but there was Phil leaning on the gate waiting for him, grinning cheerfully. 'Wait till you see this one, Dan! He's a beauty.'

Phil's cat came running to greet him, and Dan bent down to stroke her. 'Morning, Scott. Morning, Phil. Well, lead me to this magnificent beast.' Phil led him across the filthy yard into the byre he'd renovated with such loving care for his old bull, Sunny Boy. The byre was still immaculate, a fitting setting for a prize bull. The new bull graced it every bit as well as its previous occupant. He was young but already showing the signs of a perfectly splendid adult. There was a sheen to his black coat, which only good breeding and good food could have brought about. He was restless, moving about and stamping his feet with a kind of pent-up vigour that was a pleasure to witness.

Dan leant on the wall and admired him in silence.

Anxious for an opinion to corroborate his own, Phil asked, 'Well, what do you think?'

'I think he's a prime specimen. Indeed. Yes. A prime specimen. Where the devil did you pick him up, Phil?'

'At an auction. Farmer packing up, selling everything, including the farmhouse, fed up to the back teeth not making money at the job, and I went along.' He tapped the side of his nose, well, more accurately tapped his balaclava in the area of where his nose would be if one could see it. 'Heard a rumour, you know how it is, glad to be shut of the lot and everything might be going cheap. So Blossom and me went along and there he was, one of the last lots. Blossom nudged me and I nudged her and told her not to look too enthusiastic but you know Blossom, anyways, things went according to plan, and I got him for a song. What do you reckon?'

'I reckon you've got a gem. An absolute gem. What have you called him?'

'Blossom's named him Star. What do you think?'

'Spot on. Oh yes. Spot on. Star! I like that.'

'Well, he is, isn't he? A star.'

'He certainly is. Is he friendly?'

'Hamish is training him.'

'How is Hamish?'

Phil looked at Dan as though pondering what to say. 'He's OK. Got over Sunny Boy goring him, but the youth still isn't up to scratch in here.' Phil banged his chest.

'Not talking yet, then?'

Phil shook his head. 'Not yet, but Blossom keeps hoping. The youth's been through something terrible that's for sure, what, we don't know, and we can't ask the authorities for any help else they'll be for taking him away and that wouldn't do. He's happy and that's what matters after all. One day it'll come when he's been loved enough.' Phil fell silent after his final perceptive statement and the two of them leant companionably on the wall watching Star.

Dan heard the rapid tap tap tap of Blossom's high-heeled shoes and she appeared carrying a tray with three glasses on it. She and Phil were so totally mismatched. Dan found it hard to believe that this peroxided, heavily made-up, dazzlingly dressed, twiglike person could possibly be the wife of stout, rotund, good-natured, shambling old Phil. She held out the tray. 'Here we are, take one. A whisky to toast our new bull. Isn't he brilliant, Dan?'

'He most certainly is, Mrs Parsons. I reckon Phil's got an eye for a good bull. He doesn't get taken in by a lot of show, but recognises stamina and good breeding when he sees it, and that counts.' Dan raised his glass. 'To Star. Long may he reign!'

'To a perfect physical specimen!' Blossom clinked Dan's glass with hers and by the twinkle in her eyes when she winked at him, it wasn't only the bull she was toasting. Time he went, Dan thought.

'How's your son and heir, Dan? Doing well? And Rose? We'd love to meet them both.'

'Well, perhaps sometime when I'm calling I'll pick them up and bring them along. I'm sure Rose would like to meet you, too. Must go.

Other calls.' His visit with Star had cheered him considerably but at the back of his mind was the problem at Bridge Farm.

After Dan had left, Joy sat pondering the situation with Newcastle disease and what it would mean at Bridge Farm. It would be a terrible shame if their chickens had to be slaughtered, after all they weren't any old chickens but a pedigree flock. It would have to be dealt with very delicately. Thinking of delicate problems reminded her of Duncan. She wondered how he was. Striding out over the hills in his steady, relentless pace.

Joy took the photographs she had picked up in her lunch hour out of her bag. There was a particularly striking one of Duncan leaning on a fence looking ahead, apparently oblivious to the camera. She'd caught him in profile and focused on him so that the camera was looking slightly upwards at him. Anyone else would have admired the drama of that shot, and briefly so too did she. He really was eyecatching. Almost handsome, with his high cheekbones and ... Help! She wouldn't tell anyone he'd gone. They'd never notice. They all knew how withdrawn he was. She hastily put away the photographs and went to see if Mungo was free for five minutes to talk about Bridge Farm and its problems, not knowing that Dan was already on his way there.

He deliberately pulled up in the lane and didn't drive into the farmyard, which he would normally have done. The farmhouse was on the roadside with a short path between lawns and flowerbeds leading to the house. There wasn't a single sound of chickens. His heart sank. Surely they hadn't already been to slaughter them? He got out of his car and stood listening. A voice shouted from the farmhouse window. 'Dan!'

He raised an arm in salute. 'I've come to see how things are progressing.'

'Thought you were them coming. Come in.'

It was only when he moved nearer that he saw Mr Bridges had a gun pointing at him. Dan walked towards the house door, realising as he did so that there was another gun trained on him from an upstairs window.

He went in the house without knocking because the door had mysteriously been opened for him as he approached. In the kitchen with Mr Bridges were three of his sons, all armed with shotguns. 'Mrs Bridges has made a big pot of coffee. Want one?'

'Yes, please. I'm not too late, am I? They haven't already been?'

Dan felt like a dwarf. Mr Bridges himself and all three of his sons were well over six feet tall and big with it. Mrs Bridges was a tiny person shaped like a cottage loaf and looking incapable of producing boys of their great size. He heard big boots coming clattering down the stairs and yet another of the Bridges boys appeared, shotgun in hand. 'Did I hear coffee's on the go?' His voice was so like his father's it was uncanny.

'No, you're not too late. We've shut 'em all away 'cos they're bloody well not killing 'em. They'll get killed first. Get yer coffee, Gab, and up the stairs quicko.'

'I am on your side, but I didn't think things would get this far. Thank you, Mrs Bridges.' Dan's coffee was in a pint mug and he wondered how on earth he'd manage to down that lot and not give offence by leaving half of it. All of them had pint mugs, except Mrs Bridges who was sipping her coffee from a delicate china cup and saucer. She might have been a tiny woman but there was authority in her voice when she spoke. 'Sit down, Dan. Gab's watching out. That lovely wife of yours keeping well? And your little son?'

'She is, thank you, I didn't know you knew her.'

'Not much goes on in Barleybridge that we don't know about. It may be a sleepy old place but it doesn't mean we're deaf, dumb *and* blind. Lovely girl, she is. You haven't got any more where she came from, have you? These great lummoxes of mine won't get from under my feet. Gab's the eldest, so you can find someone for him a.s.a.p. They all need women like your Rose.' There were groans of heartfelt approval of Rose from them all and the red-haired one said with a good-natured grin, 'Shut up, Mum.'

'You're too good to them all, Mrs Bridges.' Dan raised his pint pot to her and sipped his coffee. It was steaming hot, rich with cream and a distinct hint of rum. 'This is excellent.'

Things became convivial, shotguns were laid aside and lots of leg-pulling and camaraderie ensued. The atmosphere became quite party-like until the laughter was abruptly halted by Gab shouting from upstairs, 'They're here!'

Instantly the boys left the kitchen, went to other downstairs rooms with windows facing the garden and when their father shouted, 'Fire!' they all let off their shotguns into the air. This brought the Veterinary Service's vehicles to a grinding halt. A great roar of delight went up from the Bridges family. In the midst of it all Mrs Bridges quietly and calmly began kneading a great mound of dough on her kitchen table, her small, floured hands working it with furious energy.

Dan said hesitantly. 'I say, you wouldn't actually . . . you know, fire at them? Properly, would you?'

'Try me,' came the grim reply from Mr Bridges.

Matters intensified when Mike Allport gingerly got out of his car, stepped onto the garden path and shouted, 'Now, Mr Bridges, you know it has to be done. Put the guns away and let us get on with it.'

'One step nearer . . .' Everyone heard the cocking of his trigger.

Mike Allport shouted, 'Don't let me have to get the police in.'

'Get who the hell you like, you're not slaughtering my flock. Get off my premises, you're trespassing. Fire!' Mr Bridges fired another shot into the air, which prompted the other four guns to go off, and Mike Allport to get back into his car. The noise was stunning and served its purpose in warning Mike they meant business.

Give him his due, thought Dan, Mike Allport isn't backing off. But he was phoning someone on his mobile. He was getting the police no doubt. It occurred to Dan that this put him in an awkward position. Aiding and abetting? Or innocent bystander held at gunpoint? 'Shall I go out and have a word? See what I can do?'

Mr Bridges turned the gun on him. 'Don't move, unless you want a barrel load from this in your backside. You're here and here you stay.'

The kneading stopped and a quiet voice said, 'Steady, Billy, Dan's not the enemy.'

Mrs Bridges's moderate tones cooled the hot atmosphere a little but Mr Bridges kept the gun trained on Dan. 'I mean it. They are not ruining years of careful breeding all because they think they have a right. Not one of my birds has died, and, if they were going to, they would have done so by now. So you keep right out of it.'

'Can I phone the Practice? They'll be wondering where I am. I've calls to make.'

'Very well.'

Dan went by the window to get a better signal and dialled in. It was Kate who answered his call. 'Hello, Kate. Dan here. I can't do my calls for the forseeable future today. Can Colin or Zoe do them for me?'

'Are you ill?'

'No, I'm at Bridges Farm and we're under siege.' As casually as he could, he whispered, 'Guns, you know.'

'Oh! my God! Guns! You mean you're being held hostage?'

'Well, not quite, but I can't get out and I think Mike Allport has sent for the police.'

'I thought your voice sounded funny. Right. We'll reorganise things. Let us know as soon as the situation frees up. Take care, Dan. Shall I tell Rose?'

'Under no circumstances. She mustn't be worried. Do you hear?'

'Right. We won't phone her. Take care, Dan. 'Bye.'

The situation didn't free up as Kate put it, in fact it became worse because the police arrived and Dan pointed out to Mr Bridges the penalty of threatening a police officer with a firearm.

'To hell with that. This is bureaucracy gone mad, and someone has to take a stand.'

'Where are the chickens?'

'Shut in the big barn at the back with Ben and Gideon on guard. Crack shots they are, like all my boys. Fire!' The salvo of five guns firing at once was deafening.

Mrs Bridges placing baking trays and loaf tins in the Aga said, 'Heed what he says. Don't lose your head, Billy.'

'Better that than dying of shame.' He opened the window further and shouted out to a uniformed inspector, 'These guns will be put away when those so-and-so's leave my farm. Tell them to leave.'

'They have a duty to do.'

'The murdering beggars have no duty to do here. My chickens are not infected. Full stop. I'm a reasonable man as you know, but I defend my right as an Englishman to guard my property as I see fit.'

'Now, now, Billy. Let's have some sense here.'

'Say that to that Mike Allport. He's the one who needs to see sense. One step out of that car of his and he'll get both barrels.'

'That's threatening language, that is.'

'I know it is. Don't think I don't mean it. I'm a man of my word.'

Tugging at Mr Bridges's jacket sleeve, Mrs Bridges said softly, 'Don't back yourself into a corner, Billy.'

Dan tried again to ask for a chance to negotiate, but found himself on the business end of Mr Bridges's gun. 'No negotiation until he's left the premises.'

'Tell them that.'

Mr Bridges shouted through the window. 'I'll talk to a police officer, but not to one of *them*. Tell them to leave.'

They all watched while a conference took place out in the lane. Mike Allport backed up and disappeared round the bend in the road. Mr Bridges put down his gun and told his boys to do the same. Josh came clattering down the stairs again and, leaning his gun against the table, slouched onto a chair. 'You're not giving in, Dad. Understand?'

'I know, I know.'

The police inspector came in. 'Good morning, Mrs Bridges. Nice smell of baking bread.'

'There'll be a loaf for your Tina, if you behave like a gentleman.'

'Now, now, no bribes.' He laughed, took off his cap and placed it upside down on the table, smoothed his hair where his cap had ruffled it, and said, 'I've to remain impartial, I have. Yes, indeed, impartial.

Hard for me though, my dad being a farmer, my sympathies are all with you, Billy.'

Dan spoke up. 'May I speak in support of Billy's actions?'

'You're ...?'

'Dan Brown, vet at Barleybridge Veterinary Hospital. I informed the Veterinary Service that I considered that Crispy Chicken had Newcastle disease, which as you are aware is notifiable. They came out, examined the birds and in front of me and Bryan Buckland said no way was I right. Over a week later they declared I was right after all, so his birds were slaughtered. Then they began tracing to find out where the disease could have been carried to in the interim. I'd come straight from Crispy Chicken to here, having disinfected my boots and my car before I left, which they watched me doing.' Dan tapped the table to emphasise his point. 'There is no sign of the disease in this flock, I have Mr Bridges's assurance on that. So if after two or three more days there is still no sign I would say he is completely free. If he can have some days' grace it is my opinion that slaughtering the birds on this farm is entirely and completely unnecessary. In fact it would amount to a crime.'

'Coffee, Richie?' Mrs Bridges handed the inspector a mug of her special brew of steaming coffee. 'I've put extra sugar in just how you like.' She turned her back to the policeman and winked at Dan.

Richie forgot about being impartial when he tasted the coffee. 'Just how I like it, Mrs Bridges.'

She smiled and went to get some bread rolls out from the Aga as calmly as if shot guns and police in her kitchen were an everyday occurrence. The rolls were placed to cool on a wire rack at Richie's end of the table and they noticed him sniff appreciatively. The atmosphere in the kitchen had become relaxed and homely and the inspector stretched out his legs and sipped his coffee, seemingly enjoying the hospitality.

They all chatted about farming news, and the latest gossip in Barleybridge and the inspector got teased about his Tina, who appeared to be well-known amongst the Bridges sons, and just as they were thinking they were getting their own way without any serious threat to life and limb, Mike Allport drove back and parked in the lane outside the house. Mr Bridges stood up, dashed to the open window and prepared to fire a broadside, but Mrs Bridges knocked his elbow purposely, he missed his target and the shot spattered viciously against the front door of Dan's Land Rover.

When Joy heard that Dan had disobeyed her orders and, as a result, his Land Rover was peppered with shot, she went ballistic. 'Wait till Mungo hears about this.'

But all Mungo could do was laugh, and he made her furious. She could have hit him she was so angry.

5

It was impossible to resist going out to take a look at the Land Rover. Joy point-blank refused, so she and Rhodri were the only members of the staff who hadn't seen the holes by teatime that same day.

Dan said, 'I can't think why Joy is so wild with me. We got the result we wanted. They're giving Mr Bridges three more days' grace so long as no one leaves the farm or visits it.'

Mungo, still amused by the whole incident, laughed some more. 'Joy's angry with me too, because when she told me what had happened I roared with laughter and she can't forgive me for it.'

'She did say I shouldn't go until we'd got some advice from you, but it was urgent, desperately urgent. However, I suppose there's a first for everything, I've never had a loaded gun pointed at me before.'

Mungo clapped a firm hand on Dan's shoulder. 'Well, it's certainly made you the hero of the day; just glad you weren't sitting in it when he fired. However, I'm not paying to have the door replaced, it's not worth it. The blessed thing's almost ready for the scrap heap, anyway. Do you mind?'

'Not at all. I don't care what I drive, so long as it gets me from A to B.'

Neither had realised that Rhodri was standing behind them listening to their conversation.

'I've come to see the hero, I have.'

Mungo moved aside so Rhodri could see the holes in the door and, with a broad grin on his face, said, 'He'll never live it down, will he?'

Rhodri instantly realised the kudos Dan would have driving to the farms. Every owner would have heard the story of the siege and no doubt embellished it with excessively heroic deeds by Dan.

'Bit childish, if you ask me.'

Dan, deflated, said angrily, 'What, exactly, do you mean by that?'

'Always wanting to be the centre of attention, you are. If it isn't wrestling mad dogs to the ground and dealing with the injured cat, when you're farm animal and not small, you're seeking media attention with all your heroics. At gun point, my eye. Old Bridges wouldn't hurt a fly.'

'You were there, were you?'

'No, but I've heard the story a dozen times this afternoon. The whole of Barleybridge will have heard by now and any minute the press will be sniffing around. Everyone in Barleybridge knows you were instrumental in getting Lord Askew back on our books. "Magic he is with horses," they all say. Magic! Huh!' Rhodri stared at the holes, ignoring Mungo, who looked angry and as though he was about to intervene. ''Spect you'll have Rose hanging on every word, typical American making a sensation of the smallest thing.'

'For your information Rose is English with an English passport, and has her feet firmly on the ground. I don't know what I've done to deserve this backlash from you, Rhodri, but I wish you'd stop it. It's turning into a bloody vendetta, and none of it is my fault.' Dan spun on his heel and went back inside. He stormed into the staff room, boiled the kettle, made himself a mug of tea and too late realised he'd picked up Rhodri's mug. So what? he thought.

Joy was leaving to go home when she paused at the back door and saw Mungo having a go at Rhodri. She only heard the gist of the conversation, but it sounded as though Rhodri was being told not to be so childish, to pull himself together and get his life sorted out. Rhodri stumped over to his car and drove away. Mungo came back in, his face ugly with temper and in no mood for Joy to say, 'He didn't deserve that. It should be Dan getting told off for disobeying *me*, and I bet you haven't said a word about that.'

'And you, Joy, need to remind yourself who is in charge here. You may be Practice Manager but you're not managing *me*. Dan's done nothing to cause Rhodri to be so unpleasant and if there isn't an improvement in his attitude I shall be having something serious to say about it. Right?'

'Oh! That's how things are, is it?'

'Yes.' Mungo raised an eyebrow at her. 'Do you have a problem with that?'

Joy looked away. She was so furious with him she knew she'd say something she'd regret, so she reined in her temper and answered, 'No problem at all. See you tomorrow.'

Joy rushed home, hoping Duncan would have returned but he hadn't and her bad mood sat badly on her all evening and kept her awake till the early hours.

Rhodri, however, couldn't rein in his temper. He drove home like a madman, rushing red lights, mounting the kerb on corners, going over zebra crossings when he shouldn't and in general behaving like a driver from hell. He screeched to a halt outside his house, dropped his door key onto the gravel and unwittingly kicked it under the car as he got out. He went in the shed to get a garden hoe to reach under the car and hook it out, trapped his fingers in the shed door and eventually arrived on his doorstep in despair.

Not even Harry could disperse Rhodri's gloomy mood. Still, Megan would be here for dinner tonight. He was doing soup followed by a gutsy salad, some toffee ice-cream, which they both adored, and then coffee, though no, it would be tea because Megan preferred it.

Having a shower, changing his clothes and organising the meal went a long way towards assuaging his distress. By the time he was setting the table he was singing 'Bread of Heaven' and feeling more like himself. How he longed to have Megan for his own. To have Megan to come home to, Megan to go shopping with, Megan to sit watching TV with, to love and to cherish. This terrible need he had was what had driven him to say what he'd said this afternoon. Dan seemed to have just about everything. A star of the Practice and a star at home, because it was obvious that Rose adored him. You only had to see her face when she looked at him; there was passionate hunger there, and a look on her beautiful face that came close to reverence. And a son, Dan had a son. He, Rhodri, didn't mind what he got, boy or girl, so long as it was his and Megan's.

No, he wouldn't wander down that path, no, not today. It was ridiculous that in this day and age he and Megan had never slept together. If Dan knew that, he'd be so scornful.

He heard her car pulling up outside and because of his thoughts he was suddenly shy of meeting her. He wiped his sweating palms on his trouser legs and listened for her voice. 'Hi Rhodri! It's me.'

Rhodri stood beside the dining table, awkward, speechless almost, all his problems about her foremost in his mind.

The door from the little hall flew open and there she stood, glowing with health and vitality. What a lucky man he was! She swept into his arms and kissed him heartily.

'Darling!'

Rhodri showered her with kisses instead of speaking, gripping hold of her.

'Darling! Let me go!'

'Sorry.'

'That's all right.'

'Food's almost ready, come in the kitchen with me while I serve.'

'Right, Rhodri bach.' Megan teased him by tidying his hair. She knew he didn't like her to do that, but something had to happen to break his dour mood. He relaxed against her, making strange moaning noises as though his feelings were getting the better of him.

'Rhodri! I smell burning.'

They both rushed into the kitchen to find the soup just beginning to catch on the bottom of the pan.

'Hell!'

Megan found a fresh saucepan and tipped the soup into it. She took a clean spoon and dipped it in the soup and tasted it. 'Salt! It needs a speck of salt and it'll be fine.'

Rhodri watched her at his cooker, in his kitchen, looking as though she lived there. Watched her hands, those hands she kept looking so fineboned and almost poetic in their movements despite the hard farm work she did; Megan should have been an artist or a musician with those hands. He stopped her switching on the gas under the soup by taking her hand to his mouth and kissing it. He turned it over and examined each of her slim fingers in turn, feeling their softness, luxuriating in the pressure of her hand on his as he caressed the scoop of her flesh at the base of her thumb.

He cleared his throat. 'Think we'd better eat.'

'It's that strict nonconformist upbringing you had that holds you back, isn't it?'

'Holds me back?'

'From doing what we both want. I'm almost panting here, waiting for you to make the first move!'

'My da would kill me if he knew I was in danger of being seduced by someone I wasn't married to.' His voice trembled a little.

'Your da wouldn't understand the pressures we're under. We're both quite old enough to do exactly what we want.'

'But should we? And there's your da too. And he's not two hundred miles away.'

'Rhodri, my darling . . .'

'I need you tonight more than ever.' They stood looking out of the window across the valley, side by side, arms around each other's waists, squeezed tight.

To break the deadlock Megan turned on the cold tap and flicked water at him. 'Better cool you down, then.'

'And you!' Rhodri splashed water at her. Megan released him and, cupping both hands to collect the water, threw it at him. Rhodri picked up a glass from the draining board, filled it and made to throw it at her,

Megan twisted out of the way too late, and the water caught her full on her face.

'Right! This is full-scale war!' She took a plastic jug, began filling it with water, while Rhodri desperately tried to force her away from the tap. But he hadn't bargained for how tough she was. She half filled the jug and as he set off out of the kitchen bent on escape, she aimed and caught him on the neck and shoulders.

'You've wet my best jumper!' Rhodri turned back, pinioned her arms behind her, leant her against the edge of the sink and kissed her. 'You're right, Megan, we are old enough.'

'This making love business has made me disgustingly hungry.' Megan spooned her soup in as fast as she could. 'It was your first time?'

Rhodri flushed bright red. 'No. But my first real time and it meant more to me than I could ever find the words to say.' He was managing to look at her by the time he added, 'Thank you.'

'Less of the thank you, Rhodri bach. We're equal partners in this enterprise.' Her dark eyes viewed him from above the rim of her spoon. 'In fact, after I've eaten, I could be prevailed on for an encore.'

Rhodri emptied his soup bowl. 'It's the risk.'

His word of caution stopped her in her tracks.

'I know.'

'It is a risk. What would your da say if . . .'

'Damn and blast him! He ruins my life at every turn. I should have been born a boy.' Megan burst into tears. Even hugging his arms around her did no good.

'Stop it! Stop it! You'll have me crying next. Please, Megan. Stop crying. I'm very glad you're not a boy. I really wouldn't fancy you if you were.'

Megan had to laugh. 'I've a good mind to make love again just to spite him.'

Rhodri let go of her, saying, 'Can you go on the pill? Or something. Or I'll do something, shall I?'

'I shall, from tomorrow. See the doctor, then we can do what we like. Yes. Definitely. Yes. I will. But tonight, I'm finishing my meal, that salad looks too good to forgo, and after that I shall make love to you like there's no tomorrow.'

'Toffee ice-cream to finish?'

'We'll eat that in bed.' Though slightly shocked by her unsuspected decadence, Rhodri agreed and decided this newly released Megan was a revelation in his sheltered life.

'It looks to me as if the cat has been at the cream, Rhodri. You're looking in fine fettle, this morning.' Dan took a closer look. 'I even think you might have . . .'

'Dan! Here's your list.' Kate handed it to him with a slight shake of her head. She knew exactly what he meant. Rhodri had got a spring in his step and half a smile on his lips this morning, but she didn't want him upset because she had to work with him all day. 'First call Tattersall's. If you could remind him he owes us, three months now.'

'Do my best. What does he want me for?'

'He rang last night and left a message on the answerphone asking you to call this morning. Didn't say why.'

'Oh, I see. That's odd of him. Not got your results yet? No? Right, I'll be off, then.' Dan gave a thumbs up and a wink to Rhodri but got no response. Tattersall's. Poor Nuala. He hadn't thought about her since he'd delivered Sybil's little kid that day. He checked his list while he waited at the traffic lights, but it didn't say what he was called out for.

Tattersall's Cop was as smart as ever. Grass well clipped. Bedding plants flourishing, buildings as trim as usual, nothing to warn him of what he would have to face when he did find Callum. He wasn't around the farm buildings, which were oddly silent. Almost unnervingly silent. Not even Callum's two dogs there to give him their rapturous greetings. So Dan went to the farmhouse door, knocked and opened it. 'Hello, it's Dan here. Where are you, Callum?'

Tentatively he opened the kitchen door but Callum wasn't there. Whistling loudly to make sure people knew someone was in the house, he began to wander about the downstairs of the house calling upstairs, 'Callum! It's Dan. You asked me to come.' Finally he braced himself to knock and then open the door of the room where Callum had laid Sybil's kid on the bed beside Nuala and she'd named her Carmel. He pushed it open slowly saying, 'It's me. Dan. Callum! Are you there?'

His heart juddered.

Then raced.

Throat tightened.

Breathing stopped.

He swiftly closed the door behind him and stood against it, his heart pounding as though he'd climbed a mountain at reckless speed.

He drew breath with a sound like a shriek.

She couldn't be, could she? And him laid there?

Holding her.

When his pounding heart had slowed and he'd calmed his spinning mind, he slowly opened the door again.

There was the smell of sickness in the air. Such stillness too. Surely she was dead. Very cautiously he walked towards the bed.

'Callum? Callum?'

Nuala's eyes were wide open, but she was dead to this world.

And Callum? He was laid on his side, facing Nuala, an arm under her shoulders holding her close.

Dan touched his shoulder and shook it slightly. 'Callum?' No response. 'Callum?' He pressed his fingers to just below Callum's jawline and felt for a pulse. And there was none. Vomit began rising in his throat and Dan fled, overwhelmed with horror.

When he'd finished heaving up his breakfast in the drain outside the back door, Dan wiped his mouth and stood, ashen-faced, deciding what to do. Doctor? Police? Doctor. He'd know what to do. He had the Health Centre's number on his mobile because of Rose and Jonathan so he rang and explained and they promised a doctor immediately. To still his bursting heart Dan decided to do something positive and went to feed the animals. He found the two rescue ponies had gone, as well as the lame donkey they'd taken in from the sanctuary, the three cows, two dogs, and the half a dozen chickens Nuala had kept for the house. So he'd planned it all, except she had died before he'd found a home for the pygmy goats. He could hear them tap tapping about in their stable.

He opened up the top half of the door to see how they all were. There was an instant clamour and all except one were on their hind legs, pawing at the door. The one that wasn't was laid at the back of the stable, quite still. In the gloom he thought it might be Cassandra, Nuala's favourite. When Dan had finally prised the door open without letting any of them escape he found that Cassandra had died while attempting to give birth.

He lifted her dead body out onto the cobbles, put feed in the trough to keep the others going, filled their water bucket and then firmly shut the lower half of the door behind him, clipping back the top half to let in air and light.

When the doctor came Dan explained the circumstances and left him to go in by himself. Dan stood in the kitchen looking out of the window, waiting ... knowing what he was waiting for.

The doctor came in and went to the sink to wash his hands. 'Both dead. A blessing for Nuala, there was nothing left of her but a beating heart. As for Callum ... He's left a note for Dan. That's you, isn't it?'

From his pocket he took an envelope and then busied himself at the kitchen table filling in forms. Dan had assumed it would be a few brief words but no, Callum had written a letter, and with it a long list of who to get in touch with, who to inform, where the furniture had to go and the addresses and telephone numbers of relatives who needed to know. Directions, also, about their joint funeral, which church, which hymns.

The letter was almost his undoing. It read:

Dear Dan,

We shall both be together in heaven when you read this. My darling Nuala fell asleep for ever in my arms at teatime today. That strong dear heart of hers could fight no longer and she had already lost the will to suffer any more. I'm writing this at the kitchen table where she and I planned our useless money-making schemes. Without her, I have no fight left in me.

We may not have had success in business but where it really matters we did. She and I were childhood sweethearts, married at seventeen and never had a bad day ever after. Nuala could see the funny side of anything at all and we spent more time laughing, even when she was so ill, than any other couple in Christendom.

If you want to tell anyone what happiness is, think of us. We had it in spades.

Thanks for all you've done for us, and your kindness in not flinching when you talked to Nuala, she valued that. Thank Rose, too, for bringing the baby. He gave Nuala such joy.

Yours sincerely,

Callum and Nuala Tattersall

Dan folded the letter. Before he read his instructions he asked the doctor how Callum had died.

'Overdose of Nuala's painkillers, I suspect. There's hardly any left in the bottle. He certainly meant business. I gave him a prescription only yesterday. I'll have to inform the police, you understand.'

The phone rang so Dan went to answer it. 'Tattersall's.'

'Phil Parsons here. That isn't Callum, is it?'

'No. It's Dan Brown.'

'Something wrong?'

'Yes, well ... bad news I'm afraid. I've just found both Nuala and Callum. They're both ... dead.'

There was a long silence from the other end of the phone. 'But I spoke to him only yesterday, afternoon, it was. What the blazes has happened?'

'Can I tell you some other time?'

'What a sad business. Nuala, yes, but Callum ... I was ringing to say I'm coming to collect his pygmy goats. He's sold the others to a goat farm but they didn't want the pygmy ones 'cos commercially they're not much good, so I said I'd have them for Blossom and Hamish. I paid him a few days ago, but we've been getting the shelter ready for 'em. Hamish and me, shall we come?'

'Right now, you mean?'

'Yes. Straight away.'

'Yes, I've got to wait for the police, so come, yes.'

'If you'd rather I didn't . . .'

'Well, Phil, someone has them to feed, so why not and if you've paid for them . . .'

'Right. We're on our way.'

Phil must have disconnected because Dan was left standing looking at his receiver. Still severely distressed by the morning's events, thoughts tumbled through his head with frantic rapidity. Rose, here with Jonathan? Phil taking on the goats. Callum killing himself for love. Rose had never said she'd been. Suicide. He'd miss Callum. Poor Nuala. I wonder why Rose came?

She told him at lunchtime. It was his half day and he'd gone home, glad his ghastly working day was at an end.

'Here, hold your son and heir and get up his wind while I make lunch. I can see you're upset. Tell me.' Rose carefully handed Jonathan to him, and waited.

'You didn't tell me you'd been to see Nuala.'

'Ah! Yes. I met Callum in the supermarket and we talked, so I went. Is it Nuala?'

'Yes. Rose, she's died. But so too has Callum.'

Rose drew in a long breath. 'But how? He wasn't ill. He didn't . . . kill himself?'

'I'm afraid he did and I found them when I went in response to a message he'd left on the answerphone last night.'

Rose flung her arms about Dan and he drew such comfort from her sympathy. 'Oh darling, how dreadful.'

'Once I'd got over the shock, they looked so peaceful, together. The ultimate in happiness. You'd never met Callum, how did he know it was you?'

'Took a look at Jonathan and realised he must be yours, and then he asked me if I was your wife, just to make sure.'

Dan peered at the baby's face in amazement. 'My God!'

'So I went.'

'He thanked you for that in his suicide note. Said it gave Nuala great joy to see the baby. I'll have to spend the afternoon ringing all the people on Callum's list. Not exactly a pleasant occupation. But it's the least I can do. He never got on well with the other farmers round here. They all thought him feckless. One scheme after another, but a great chap.' Dan sighed, adjusted his hold of Jonathan while he wiped his mouth of milk. 'Part of life's rich pattern. Must put it all behind us.'

Rose gripped his shoulder and smiled to herself. Knowing he couldn't put it all behind him as easily as that and understanding he was taking this attitude because of his concern for her, she answered, 'Of course. Yes. Life goes on. Actually, tomorrow I'm having tea with Letty.'

'Letty? Colin's Letty?'

'Who else? She's not at all well. I think I'm going to persuade her to go to the doctor, she can't go on like she is. And I upset her the last time I saw her and she cried, so I feel guilty.'

'She's difficult to get on with.'

'I know. That's the challenge.'

6

Rose arrived at exactly two forty-five, the time Letty had specified. Jonathan wasn't exactly full of joy, and she had hoped the drive in the car would put him to sleep. Which it did, but the moment she tried to lift him out he woke, miserable and weepy.

Letty and Colin lived in a dream cottage. Roses around the door, thatch on the roof, lovely old red-brick walls with timbers exposed here and there. To Rose, with her American heritage, it seemed utterly, utterly splendid. Before she could knock on the door it had been opened by Letty and she was standing beaming from ear to ear welcoming the two of them in.

'Oh Letty! What a wonderful house! It's like a picture book. I've always longed for a house with roses around the door. You are so lucky.'

'Come in, Rose! It was derelict when we bought it and it took hours of work with damp proof courses and septic tanks and new floorboards and things. It must have been two years before it was really habitable.'

'Well, it was well worth it. If it's not asking too much, can I look round before I leave? You know what we Americans are like about old houses.'

Letty visibly gathered herself before she agreed wholeheartedly that Rose could look round. It almost seemed to Rose that Letty found her request intrusive, so she thought to leave it for the moment.

'Can I put Jonathan down here? You haven't got a dog or a cat, have you?'

'No. We haven't and yes, of course you can. Isn't he beautiful?' Letty bent to stroke Jonathan's head. 'So like Dan. I didn't like Dan when he first came you know, in fact I insisted he was dismissed.'

'I'm sorry. I didn't know. Do you like him now?'

'Oh yes. He's been a real asset to the Practice. He's like me you see, speaks straight from the shoulder, no messing, and like doesn't always get on with like, does it?'

'No, I suppose not. When you know Danny like I do, you know he's pure gold.'

Letty looked Rose up and down. 'I like your dress. You've an instinct for what suits, haven't you?'

'I guess I could lose some more weight though, I can only just get into this dress. Specially round the top.'

'Sit down. You still look lovely. You always do. I'm envious of that.'

'Hey! This isn't a Rose Franklin-Brown admiration day. I want to know how *you* are. Last time we met I thought you weren't looking too well.'

'Kettle's boiled, I won't be a minute.'

Letty rushed to the kitchen and Rose could hear her organising cups and opening the fridge and pouring milk. In a moment she was back carrying a tray and placing it exactly in the middle of the coffee table. Jonathan began to grizzle again. 'Sorry, this isn't one of his best days. Here, darling, have your comforter.' Rose popped his dummy into his mouth and Jonathan sucked loudly on it.

'You approve of dummies, then?'

'Oh yes. If he's unhappy, why not?'

'Lots of people don't.'

'Well, that's up to them. I've read all the books and then some and I'm determined to do as I think fit. No milk for me, thanks.' Rose accepted her cup and sipped it gratefully. 'This is lovely tea.' She stretched out her long elegant legs under the coffee table, wriggled her shoulders to get more comfortable and asked again how Letty was.

'Well, I'm no better. Can I confide in you?'

Rose nodded. 'Confide away.' She gave Letty an encouraging smile.

'I mean really confide, I'm not really into confiding in women friends, but then I haven't got any. I'm not very good at women's chat, you know, all girls together.'

'Neither am I, but I'm a good listener.' She gave Letty a beautiful smile, the sort of smile that made Dan's heart do head over heels, and Letty began to relax. She drained her cup of tea in one go, dabbed her lips, laid down her napkin, placed her teacup and saucer on the coffee table exactly lined up with the tiles on the top, cleared her throat, fidgeted for her handkerchief, straightened her skirt and then said so softly Rose could hardly hear, 'I'm so afraid.'

Cautiously, fearing what she might be told, Rose asked, 'You are? What of?'

'Either I've got something wrong with me or I'm going quietly crackers.'

'You are?'

'I think I might be pregnant. I haven't told Colin, he won't like the idea, you know.'

'Won't like the idea! Of course he will. How can he not like it, a lovely man like Colin? He'll be thrilled.'

'But I can't be pregnant though, can I? I mean, after all these years. So I must be ill. *Cancer* or something.'

'Have you seen the doctor?'

'No. I daren't.'

'But you must.' Rose hesitated, thinking about how to phrase her next question. 'Why do you think you're not pregnant and that it must be cancer?'

Letty flushed with embarrassment. 'I've missed ... you know ... four times now and I'm always so sick. Sometimes actually sick, but mostly feeling sick. Sometimes I retch and retch and nothing happens. It leaves me exhausted. I can't keep food down, and I could swear my stomach has swollen.'

'That sounds remarkably like being pregnant. But it's no good not knowing. What makes you say Colin will be angry? You've got to find out one way or the other. If you're not pregnant and it is something serious ... they work wonders nowadays. It's no longer the death sentence it was, you know.' Then Rose remembered Nuala and could have bitten her tongue out. 'I'll go with you, to the doctor; either way you need a friend.'

Letty got out her handkerchief and blew her nose. 'You see, Colin doesn't want children.'

'How do you know that?'

'He told me once. He said, "I do not want children. Our lives are perfectly satisfactory without children all over the place." So he means it. How do you bring up a child when its father doesn't want it?' Letty looked up at Rose and almost pleaded for understanding.

'With difficulty I should imagine. Dan and I ... well, I know it sounds intensely coy and mushy, but we want to make babies together. Our babies, you know. Men are immensely proud when they've proved themselves to be male in every aspect. I honestly don't think you need worry about Colin. He may need time to become accustomed to the idea, but believe me, when he holds in his arms a child born of his flesh, the whole picture will change. He's such a caring man. Well, that's how he always seems to me.'

Letty didn't answer.

Rose tried to catch her eye. 'Yes?'

'But if it's cancer ... I've still got to tell him.'

'I guess that he'd rather hear about a baby than cancer. Which do you think would be the worst?'

Letty began to smile.

'I'd come with you to see the doctor.'

'Would you? Would you really? I could be brave if you were with me.'

'Make an appointment, let me know and I'll come. Honest to God. I'll come.'

'I feel better already. It could be a week at least, you know what it's like getting a doctor's appointment these days. Unless you're actually dying ...' Letty gave a single, painful sob, got things under control, then said, 'I do appreciate you offering to come. I don't deserve it, really.'

'Of course you do, what the heck. I'll gladly go with you. In fact, ring right now.'

'No. I won't do that. I'll ring when you've gone.'

'No time like the present. Here.' Rose got her mobile out of her bag and pressing the appropriate keys had the phone ringing out sooner than it takes to tell.

'I can't. I can't.'

'Then shall I?'

Letty nodded.

'Hi! This is Rose Franklin-Brown speaking on behalf of Mrs Letty Walker who is a patient of ... ?'

'Dr Mason.'

'Dr Mason. She urgently needs an appointment, but a proper one, none of this emergency business, two minutes and you're out with a scrip in your paw. This is a serious matter and needs instant medical appraisal. Next Friday? You mean Friday of this week? Oh! Friday of next week? It won't do.' Rose felt Letty pulling at her sleeve. 'Just a moment.'

'Don't worry. Next Friday will do.'

Rose ignored Letty's plea. 'If she were a dog I'm sure a vet would see her tomorrow, most likely today. I wonder if it would be better if she went to the vet instead? She'd at least get immediate attention.' There was a pause while Rose listened. 'I'm not surprised, I don't find it funny either, believe me. *And I'm still waiting.*'

Rose sat listening to the muffled altercation going on at the other end of the line.

'Yes, it is urgent.' Rose listened and then said, 'Her symptoms?'

Rose's voice was full of apology. 'I'm so sorry, I'd no idea I was speaking to a doctor. I do beg your pardon. Oh! You're not a doctor, then to whom am I speaking?' Rose winked at Letty. There was a pause while Rose listened and then Letty heard her say, 'As you're not a qualified medical practioner I fail to see what telling you her symptoms will achieve. So *we're still waiting for an appointment*. Absolutely. Yes. Twenty minutes. Yes. Thank you.'

Full of dread, Letty looked at Rose.

'If we go now you can be seen straight away and I guess that's what we should do. I'll drive. No, Letty, I know what you're going to say, but it's better to get it over with.' She scooped up Jonathan, now fast asleep, gave Letty's arm a squeeze and said, 'I know I'm inclined to hassle, but it's for the best, isn't it?'

Reluctantly Letty nodded. She would never have allowed Colin to take over like she'd just allowed Rose.

'Purse, Letty.'

'Oh! Yes. I should have a bath or a shower or something before I go.'

'No time. I'm quite sure you're the cleanest possible person, so don't fret.' Rose gave Letty a reassuring grin and gently pushed her out of the door. 'Keys?'

'Oh. Yes.'

Five minutes from the surgery Letty said, 'I'm sure I'm troubling them for nothing. Let's go home. It's the menopause come early or something.'

'If it is, then at least you'll know for sure. But being sick all the time doesn't sound like it to me.' She stopped speaking while she negotiated a notoriously difficult roundabout and then swung with practised ease into a parking space right outside the surgery. 'Right. Here we are. Wait while I get Jonathan out, it takes a minute.'

Letty, glad of any excuse to delay facing the truth, stood by the car twisting her hands in agitation, trying to think up good reasons why she shouldn't go in. Rose, sensing how very distressed she was and thinking she'd be just the same if it was her, heaved the baby carrier onto her arm and putting on her encouraging face despite her dread, took hold of Letty's free arm and led her into the surgery. She whispered, 'Sit down, make yourself look even more ghastly than you feel.'

At reception Rose said, 'I've brought Mrs Letty Walker for her appointment with Dr Mason.' The receptionist referred to the screen on the desk and with a condescending look on her face said, 'I'm afraid you must have got the wrong day, there's no appointment down for her. I've just come on and no message was left for me to that effect.'

'She has an appointment, because I have just made one over the phone. We were told to come straight in and we have done.'

'Well, I'm sorry, but he hasn't any free appointments until next Friday. Can I make one for then?'

'No, you may not, because we already have one. So, get checking.'

Luckily at that moment Dr Mason came out of his consulting room, couldn't miss seeing Rose and almost rushed to greet her. 'Mrs Franklin-Brown! How wonderful to see you! How are you and the little babe?'

'Absolutely fine, thank you, Dr Mason.'

He held out his hand to shake Rose's as though she were a long lost friend. 'And what can I do for you?'

Pointing at Letty, Rose answered. 'My friend here, Letty Walker, is your next appointment.'

The receptionist sprang to life. 'I beg your pardon, she is not . . .' Then she shrank back in her chair, intimidated by the threatening look Rose had given her.

The welcoming smile slid from Dr Mason's face. 'Ah! Right. I don't think I have a free . . .'

Rose smiled sweetly at him, one of those dazzling smiles of hers that no one could resist, and he succumbed to her charms. 'But perhaps I can fit her in. This way, Mrs Walker.'

Patiently Rose waited for Letty to emerge from the consulting room. She occupied herself looking round the room at the motley collection of people waiting their turns, categorising them and wondering what their complaints were. They all looked remarkably fit and she came to the conclusion that half of them at least had minor ailments they could have treated at home. No wonder they said Letty couldn't have an appointment until the end of next week, the place was cluttered with malingerers.

Letty came into the waiting room, eyes red from weeping and grim-faced. It wasn't until they were back in the car that she spoke. 'Rose.'

Head down in the back of the car busy securing Jonathan's safety seat, Rose replied, 'Mmm?'

'Rose. I've a card here to go for a scan . . . right now.'

The alarm bells began ringing in Rose's brain. For a moment she went quite still and then carefully closed the back door and swallowed hard. 'You have?' Hoping it sounded much more casual than she felt.

'I'm supposed to go right now. But I think I'll leave it till tomorrow. There isn't time.'

That urgent? Hell! Rose thought. 'Well, then we shall. If he's arranged it for you for today we'd better go. Scan appointments are as rare as hen's teeth. They must have had a cancellation. You direct me.' She patted Letty's knee and then leaned across to give her a reassuring kiss.

'Turn right out of here, then first left turn and then the left fork, no, no, right fork and we're there.'

'So, we did right then, getting a quick appointment.'

Letty was obviously preoccupied and didn't answer, so Rose paid attention to her driving instead. She pulled up in the first available space in the hospital car park, switched off the ignition and took hold of Letty's hand. 'Best get it over with. Eh?'

'Oh Rose! I never thought for one minute I'd have to go for a scan. I'm absolutely bowled over with it.'

'Well, the only way to tackle it is head on. Straight in for the big punch, no messing.'

'Oh yes. I may be a while though. What about Jonathan?'

'Don't worry about him. If he needs feeding I shall feed him, I've no fine sensitivities about the matter. Come on.'

So Rose did feed Jonathan because he began his I-Am-Starving routine the moment she sat down to wait for Letty. It seemed an age, worrying about what Letty was to learn. At least they hadn't let the grass grow under their feet. Full marks for that. No, siree. But that meant it was urgent, didn't it? Poor Letty. Poor Colin. They'd both need all the support possible.

Eventually just as Jonathan had fallen fast asleep with his stomach so full he was fit to burst, Letty returned. A transformed Letty. A buoyant, bouncing Letty. A shining Letty who bent to kiss her cheek and kiss the baby too.

'Oh Rose! Oh Rose! Come on, let's go.'

She picked up Rose's bag and hastened her out of the hospital. 'Oh Rose!'

Scurrying along behind her Rose said breathlessly, 'You've got the all clear then. It isn't cancer?'

Letty nodded her head.

'Oh!' With the baby firmly strapped in, Rose got into the driving seat. 'Thank heavens for that. What is it then?'

Letty said. 'I must be the biggest fool under the sun.'

'Oh, I don't know about that, you'd have to go a long way to beat me.'

Looking out of the side window to avoid Rose's eyes Letty said, 'I can't believe it but, they say, they say,' Letty took a deep breath, 'I'm about four months pregnant. I feel such a fool. At forty-seven, it's not a joke, is it?'

Shocked, Rose took in a great gulp of breath, then huge relief made her blurt out, 'It is not funny!' But Rose began to laugh, in fact she roared with laughter, until she complained of a stitch in her side. 'Oh Letty! All this worry. All these weeks. A baby! Oh my God! No wonder you thought you had a lump. Some lump!' She went off into peals of laughter again, leaving no pause for Letty to speak. In the end it was catching and Letty began to laugh too. Then relief and thankfulness became two emotions too many for Letty and streams of tears began running down her cheeks and yet she was laughing at the same time.

Rose got out a tissue from Jonathan's bag of necessities and gave it to her. 'I can't believe you didn't think it could be a baby.'

'I'd given up all hope years ago and ... at forty-seven I didn't dare think it, for one moment. I knew I felt differently, more sentimental and such, and I caught myself drooling over some kittens at the Practice one day, and there was that day when I cried when you brought Jonathan in and I couldn't bear the sight of him. I was so desperate thinking that it was all much too late for me and Colin. Life didn't seem very fair that day. But I never thought ... would you have done?'

'If I'd never been pregnant then I suppose perhaps I wouldn't. Jeez! Colin's going to get a shock. Catch your breath and then ring him. Go on, use my phone.'

'No, no, I'll wait till I get home. Thanks.'

'I insist. Think how pleased he'll be. What's his mobile number? Here, it's ringing.'

Colin had just come in from a full day of calls and was standing by the reception desk talking to Kate. They were discussing her options if her chemistry grade wasn't an A. 'But it will be!' said Colin. 'It's bound to be.'

'It isn't bound to be. I got a D last time and it's a big jump up to an A. Sometimes I think I've done all right, others I'm totally convinced I've done really badly, like last time.'

'It is not the end of your life if you don't get in. It might feel like it, but it isn't. There are other avenues for you.'

Colin's mobile began ringing and he hadn't appeared to notice. Kate said, 'That's your phone, Colin.'

'So it is.' Colin took it from the clip at his waist and switched it on. 'Oh hello! It's you. Something wrong?'

Kate watched him as he listened, saw his face go pale. 'The hospital. For a what? The line's breaking up. Say it again. A scan? Whatever for? Are you ill? I didn't know you had an appointment. Yes. Yes. What? I thought you said ... You did. Hell's bells! How did that happen? Yes,

yes, OK. I'll be home as soon as I can. Jeepers creepers!' Colin switched off his phone and stood gazing at it.

Kate asked, 'Everything all right, is it, Colin?'

Colin looked at Kate. 'She's getting a lift home from the hospital.'

'Letty?'

Colin nodded, eyes fixed again on his mobile, preoccupied and silent.

'Are you all right? I mean, is it bad news?'

Dazed might have been the best word to describe Colin's appearance, he moved like a man in a trance. Finally as he reached the main door and opened it he said, 'Kate! You won't believe this, but I think Letty said she was pregnant. She can't be, can she?'

Kate grinned. 'No good asking me, how could I know?'

'Mmm. No. Of course you don't. I can't understand it,' Colin said and left, shaking his head in disbelief.

But when he got home Colin was finally convinced because Letty showed him the printout of the scan and there for all to see was a baby. A baby he'd fathered, a child Letty had conceived, a child, which, after nearly sixteen years of marriage, was nothing short of a miracle. A total, definite, absolute, downright, without any doubt at all, *miracle*.

'I thought I had cancer.'

'Why didn't you say?'

'I was too frightened.'

'Letty!'

'Rose made me go. You know what she's like for being so sweet and kind, somehow I just came out with it and said how terrified I was, so she made an appointment for me at the doctor's and took me. She was dreadfully rude to them, but it meant I got an appointment straight away. I've been such a fool! I daren't believe that I might be pregnant.'

Colin studied the printout again. 'It is true, isn't it?'

'Oh yes! But they don't tell you if they can see it's a boy or a girl, unless you ask.'

'Did you ask?'

Letty shook her head. 'I was in shock. It never occurred to me. I couldn't believe what was happening. I told Dr Mason he was wrong. I refused to believe him, in fact. I said I'd got cancer. I told him I couldn't possibly be pregnant, not after years of giving up all hope. But it's true. Isn't it? I mean, look.' She showed him the printout again.

'When we wake up in the morning and it's still true then I shall really believe it. I can't take it in right now.'

'I thought you ... you said ... you said ages ago you didn't want children. I was so disappointed when you said that, it took me weeks to get over it. You see, I thought I was a disappointment to you, I know they said we were both OK, keep trying, but I honestly felt it must be me.'

Colin put an arm around Letty's shoulders and kissed her temple. 'I remember saying that, I only said it so you wouldn't feel too badly about not having children. Thought it would help.'

'So you are pleased then?'

'Of course I am.' He squeezed her shoulder again, his eyes on the scan. 'I can't believe it.'

'Neither can I. It feels like a dream. I've been so disappointed so many times. All that yearning and longing. Maybe that was why I bullied you so much.'

Colin opened his mouth to protest that she hadn't.

Letty laid a gentle finger on his mouth. 'Hush! *I know I did.* Don't try to be kind. I did, Colin, and I'm ashamed of myself. Rose says Dan is pure gold, and I could say the same about you. Pure gold. And I'm sorry I've been so unpleasant all these years.' She stretched out her hand to straighten his tie for him. 'It was you sent me those flowers and the complimentary card from that beauty shop and the weekend in Paris. You organised that, didn't you?'

Colin nodded.

'I never guessed, you know, not till just now. Pure gold, I said, and pure gold you are. Thank you for that. It was just what I needed. It made such a difference to me. It made me a new person, lighter hearted, kind of. But it did the trick, didn't it?' Letty laughed up at him and was rewarded with another kiss. 'We'll light the stove, I've laid it, it just needs a match, and to celebrate we'll have a pre-dinner sherry before we eat and talk about babies and what we'll need. Dinner won't take five minutes to put together.'

Colin looked at her with a solemn expression on his face. 'Mothers-to-be shouldn't drink alcohol.'

Letty's hand flew to her mouth. 'Ohhhh! Of course not. I never thought! That's the loveliest thing anyone has said to me, ever.' A younger, fresher, more vibrant Letty kissed him on his mouth and then said, 'I've always loved you, Colin, but it kind of got lost under layer upon layer of resentment and anger. But that's sloughed away like a snake shedding its skin and it happened all in a moment.'

The news was all round the Practice by first thing the next morning. The reaction to the news went from sheer hysteria at the amazingly unexpected announcement, to wholehearted delight. Colin had to take huge amounts of leg-pulling from the male members of the staff, someone suggested with a wink that it must have been the trip to Paris which had done the trick, others said how pleased they were for Letty and for him, and Dan mentioned the sleepless nights and the upheaval a small baby can make in a household, but shook his hand with vigour as he congratulated him.

Colin took it all in good part but found Rhodri's response difficult to understand. He didn't say the right words and the expression in his voice was all wrong. 'Lucky man, you are, Colin, bach. Very lucky. Bit of a surprise for us all, let alone you and Letty. Still, congratulations are in order.' And he'd shaken Colin's hand with less enthusiasm than if he'd been congratulating him on winning the father's race at a school sports day.

But Colin wasn't to know how despairing Rhodri was. He'd had as much as he could take from Megan's father the previous night. Megan had asked him to go for a meal and take a look at their farm cats while he was there. She'd managed to capture them all in the tack room close to the house when she fed them that afternoon.

'They're mostly feral cats who appear and disappear at will. These two black ones are ours, we brought them with us when we moved, the rest we kind of inherited. I don't know much about it but I wondered if they had cat flu. Some of them are very low in spirits and three of them have sticky eyes. What do you think, Rhodri?'

Rhodri counted ten cats altogether. 'You feed all these every day?'

'Well, our own two come in the house and are fed morning and night, but the others I feed out here every afternoon, and our two turn up in the hope of stealing food but they never do, they're too soft to put up a fight.'

'I suppose you never handle these others.'

'They won't let me.'

'See the grey and white, I'm pretty sure that has flu. Its eyes are all bunged up and I saw it sneeze just then. Appears listless too, disinterested kind of. Those two ginger ones might be going the same way. Are yours vaccinated? I expect they are.'

'Yes, definitely. They won't catch it, will they?'

'They shouldn't. The only way is for me to prescribe antibiotics and you put it in their food every day, and hope for the best.'

'Is that all we can do?'

In the dim light in the tack room, Rhodri looked at her, the wholesomeness of her refreshing his spirits after his hard day. 'Give me a kiss.' She did with her familiar gusto, arms wrapped round his neck, hair tickling his face, and in his nostrils the lovely fresh smell of her he so loved.

'Must go in, Rhodri, the vegetables will be boiling dry. You always smell so nice, of tweed and disinfectant.'

'Oh! Thanks. I did shower before I came out.'

'Doesn't matter, it's always there, but it's the nicest possible disinfectant. My favourite, but that's only because it's you. Come on, see Da.'

Rhodri's heart sank. The price he had to pay for Megan's company felt too high tonight. Old Man Jones was sitting scrunched up in his favourite chair, all the trappings of an invalid scattered on the usual table. Tonight, despite the warmth of the August evening, he had a rug over his knees.

'Good evening, Mr Jones. How's things?'

'Much the same. Grateful for the slightest easing of the pain. What about the cats? Megan says she's asked you to take a look.'

'That's right. I'm fairly certain they've got flu. Well, some of them have, but the thought of taking blood samples from that wild lot! So I've decided a general intake of antibiotics will possibly do the trick, and we'll have to keep our fingers crossed.'

Mr Jones almost snarled, 'I've told her not to bother with the wild ones. They're a waste of her time. As if she doesn't have enough to do. Damned idiotic of her.'

Rhodri sat himself down on the sofa. 'It's her kind heart, she can't help but adopt them.'

'You should know.'

Rhodri looked at him and raised a questioning eyebrow. Mr Jones said with a sarcastic lilt to his voice, 'Well, she's adopted you.'

'Are you putting me on the same level as a feral cat? Am I no more than that?'

Mr Jones shrugged his shoulders. 'Take it how you like. That's how I see you. You're also a waste of her time.'

Rhodri, angry because he'd used the same words about him as he had about the cats, answered angrily, 'That's insulting to me and to Megan. We love each other, a fact you appear well able to ignore. Do you know what she said to me the other night?'

'How could I?'

'She said she wished she'd been born a boy.'

'She's right, I wish she had.'

'Don't you feel that's terribly sad?'

'Not at all.'

'Well, you should, you should be ashamed to have made her feel like that. Ashamed.'

Mr Jones painfully levered himself out of his chair, and standing as upright as he could he shouted, 'You are a guest in my house, how dare you speak to me in that way.'

Rhodri rose to his feet expecting Mr Jones would topple over any minute but he didn't, he didn't even search for his stick.

Rhodri shouted equally loudly, 'Because what I've said is true. She sticks by you, managing your farm, taking orders like a lackey when she'd prefer to be taking part in real life instead of being locked up here with you. You're a tyrant. A bully. A selfish, mean-minded bully. But you're her da so she takes it, but watch out because one day the worm might turn.' He sat down again, more angry than he could remember.

'She'd *never* leave *me*. And if you think for one minute that she'd leave me to marry you, I can tell you now she *never* will. So you might as well stop sniffing after her like a randy dog. Just disappear and get a job somewhere else. You're not welcome here. Now, help me into the dining room, she must have got the meal ready by now. Come on, where's my stick? Jump to it.'

Rhodri was so full of anger that he decided to leave Mr Jones to find his own stick and stagger into the dining room alone, but Megan came in and asked him to help her father. 'I've put the food out. Would you like wine tonight, Da?'

Mr Jones shook his head. 'No. Ale will do instead.'

'Oh! I thought we'd have wine with Rhodri being here. I'll get a bottle.'

'Did you hear me? I said no wine.'

Megan blushed with embarrassment. 'Would you like wine, Rhodri?'

'As it would appear we are going against your father's wishes, then I suppose we both have to say no, him being the grown-up.' He put such an edge of sarcasm in the tone of his voice that Megan quaked.

Mr Jones's colourless eyes focused on Rhodri. 'Insolence will get you nowhere. You're a boy, a fresh-faced youth, you are. I don't know why Megan bothers with you.'

Megan leapt to Rhodri's defence. 'Da! Rhodri is my guest. Please! Make an effort to be polite.'

'In my own house I shall behave as I wish. Seeing as we all feel able to speak our minds tonight, we may as well have it out here and now. I shall not under any circumstances permit you to marry. Not under any circumstances. Let that be an end to it.'

Rhodri, normally intimidated by Mr Jones, answered with firm determination. 'Has it occurred to you that we could be married by the weekend? All completely lawfully because both Megan and I are above the age of consent. It's only her affection for you which prevents us.'

For the second time that night, Mr Jones got to his feet without assistance. 'If you dare do such a thing I shall disinherit her. Mark my words I shall.' He wagged a finger at them both. 'Do you hear me?'

'I hear all right. I might remind you that I earn a perfectly adequate salary, ample to support the two of us, and I own my house so we'd have a roof over our heads. We don't care where your money would go. We don't need it. We shall marry, whether you give your consent or not. I will not give up that happiness for anyone. Not even you. We'll find a way, believe me.' He said it in such a matter-of-fact way that it was a moment before Mr Jones fully comprehended what he'd said. Rhodri started to eat his dinner though the fish tasted like chalk and the potatoes like cotton wool. As for the peas and carrots, they resembled the Plasticine ones he used to make in his childhood in the Manse.

Megan sat with her hands on her lap, head down, suffering.

Mr Jones abruptly sat down again. White-faced and breathing heavily. Lost for words. He reached for his stick and raising it high he whipped it down, aiming to hit Rhodri with it, but Rhodri dodged and the stick crashed onto the table, breaking his plate, scattering the food and smashing his glass of water. A deep silence fell. For a moment no one moved.

Appalled, Megan broke the spell by shouting, 'Da!'

Rhodri hastily pushed back in his chair to prevent the water running onto his trousers.

Mr Jones sounded as though he was being strangled. Every breath he took scored its way into his lungs as though each would be his last. He fumbled to loosen his collar and began gesticulating with his hand. Megan rushed for his inhaler, when she gave it to him he inhaled deeply several times and gradually his breathing relaxed and became more normal. Even so it was loud and rusty. Much to Rhodri's relief, as he didn't fancy having to do mouth to mouth with Mr Jones. In fact he doubted if he would bother to, anyway. The nasty, conniving old man that he was.

'Now Da! What a to-do! Let me help you back to your chair. I'll keep your dinner warm, no problem.' She helped him up and holding him by the arm she guided him away from the dining table, but Rhodri couldn't help notice the vicious glance Mr Jones gave him as he passed his chair. No, it wasn't vicious; it was triumphant. So that's how the cookie crumbles, thought Rhodri. He *is* a conniving old man. All he wants is to make sure that Megan stays with him to make his meals and do his washing and look after him when he's ill. Without her he'd have to go into a home. Uncharitably Rhodri decided that would be the best place for him too.

The remains of Rhodri's dinner had spread from his plate onto the tablecloth, soaked to a sloshy mess by the water from his glass. With Megan distraught and Mr Jones's rasping breath dominating the house, the evening was in ruins and Rhodri decided it was time to leave.

Heavy with disappointment he declared, 'I'll go, Megan.'

'Come in the kitchen.'

He followed her in and closed the door behind him.

'Rhodri, you should never have answered him back. He'll be ill all day tomorrow now.'

He took her hand to his lips and kissed it. 'Megan, you are a slave to that man. No father has the right to keep you tied like this. Hand and foot, you are. Hand and foot. It simply isn't fair.' He brushed away her hair from her face. 'When are you going to claim back your life?'

'What can I do? What can I do about it?'

'Stand up to him. That's what. Get help to look after him, let him see he can exist without you at his beck and call.'

'He won't have anyone but me.'

Rhodri gave a great sigh of despair. 'Exactly. Exactly. I love you so.'

'I love you.'

'Then we've got to plan.'

'What though?'

'Don't know yet. Goodnight, love.'

'Here, take your pudding, it's sticky toffee.' Megan placed a portion in a lidded bowl and handed it to him. 'It's best you go, give me a chance to calm him down. I'm so sorry about what he did, so sorry. Got to get back to him. Goodnight.'

Rhodri went out into the night, desolate.

So when he heard Colin and Letty's wonderful news, he found it genuinely hard to be happy for them. They were getting all he dreamed about and the events of last night seemed to have pushed the dream even further away. What had possessed him to stand up to the fellow? He must have been out of his mind. Getting Mr Jones to like him had been his aim from the start but all that patient work had gone in a single flash of temper. Daring to attempt to hit me though! Rhodri wished he'd snapped his stick in half, though he'd have looked a fool trying to do that, it was an almighty thick stick. He went to bed, thoroughly depressed and full of anguish, and seeing no way out of his situation.

7

Kate went to bed that same night also full of anguish and dreading the morning. Fortunately for her the post always came early and she hoped that tomorrow would be no exception. Exam results! Oh God! What a fool she'd been to think she could get a good grade just doing tutorials with Miss Beaumont, a chemistry teacher from school. She should have had more sense. She flung off the duvet and lay under the sheet, hot and uncomfortable.

She and Mia, her stepmother, had been in their new flat three months now, and though she liked it Kate still hankered for the old house where she'd grown up. For the familiar sounds, the friendly smell of the place, the garden; though she'd hated working in it, she'd always been able to leave it to Mia because she loved gardening. Here they had communal gardens kept strictly regimented with none of the casual charm that a garden of Mia's was capable of. Park benches to sit on and architectural features rather than the mad medley of Mia's country-type garden. Still, moving had triggered Mia into going back to her painting, which was a blessing for her, and at least the frantic activity that her dad's death had set off in Mia had abated and the relaxed, sweet-natured person Kate had always known had returned.

Would she get an A, or would she get a B, or worse still a D, like she'd got first time round? Kate decided that if that were the case then she'd do Zoology or something instead, because although she loved working at the Practice, doing reception work did not tax her brain nearly enough.

I'll let you know, Dad, what I get. I know you'll be pleased whatever it is. Just wish you were here to crack the bottle of champagne you'd been keeping for the Big Day, as you called it. Tears slid quietly down her face and she wiped them away with a corner of the sheet.

Kate tossed and turned and eventually fell asleep but kept waking because of the heat and her own agitated state of mind. About three o'clock she was fully awake and went to make herself a drink of tea. A terrible sickening feeling had come over her. *Failure*. It was staring her in the face. But as Mia would say, she could only do her very best. As she sipped her tea from a mug she'd had since she first went to secondary school and only used when she needed mountains of emotional support, Kate realised that it was all too late anyway. The die had been cast. Whatever would be would be, no matter how much soul-searching she did, no matter how many times she went over her answers, no matter how many times she saw the question paper in her mind's eye, it was all over and done with. Finished. Decided.

Well, she had done her best and if she wasn't good enough to get in to veterinary college then so be it. It wasn't for her. But she remembered the time she'd helped Scott of blessed memory deliver the calf, and when she and Dan had been chilled to the bone during lambing at Tad Porter's, and the warmth of Connie's kitchen and the frail young lamb she'd fed. All the wonderful kindness so peculiar to a farming community. Then she started laughing about when she hosed Scott down after he'd fallen in Phil Parson's slurry pit, and a large tear came in her eye which she angrily brushed away. Scott couldn't stand commitment, which was why he ran away from her, back home to Australia. But it was for the best. She'd never have qualified if anything had come of their affair.

The kitchen clock, once holding pride of place in a schoolroom and rescued by her dad when the school was being pulled down, chimed out four o'clock. Kate went to bed and her last thought as she slipped into a dreamless sleep was, whatever happened tomorrow she'd still be Kate Howard, and the sun would still shine and the clock still chime. She comforted herself with 'Time and the hour run through the roughest day.'

The first she knew about the morning was the sound of Mia placing a breakfast tray on her bedside table and pulling back the curtains. 'Post's come.'

'Oh no!'

'It's here. The letter. Can I stay while you open it?'

Kate shot upright, eyes wide open. 'Yes, of course. Give me it.'

She tore the envelope open, pulled the sheet of paper out, and in one swift movement sprang up to stand on the bed shouting, 'Yes! Yes! Yes!' with a clenched fist punching the air. 'I've done it! Mia! I've done it. I have! I have! Look!'

Mia studied the paper and read the magic 'Grade A'. 'Oh Kate! Oh

Kate! That's wonderful! You clever girl, you! I'm so proud. Vet college, here she comes!'

Kate leapt off the bed and flung her arms around Mia, so tightly she could hardly breathe, but Mia didn't mind. This was the day of days. 'What a pity you have to go into work.'

'Oh! It isn't a pity at all. I'm so looking forward to telling everyone! Can you believe it? I'm so excited. I'll ring Miss Beaumont and tell her. She'll be so pleased for me. Last night I convinced myself I'd failed and was thinking up some alternatives, but I haven't failed, have I? Oh Mia! I feel quite sick. Help! I do really.'

'Calm down. Here, have a cup of tea, it might settle your stomach. You can't be ill on a day such as this. You can't.' Mia poured a cup of tea for her, and made her sit in bed with her pillow to rest against. 'Steady, steady, sip it.'

Kate looked up at her. 'Mia! Wouldn't Dad have been delighted?'

'Delighted! There isn't a word in the English language big enough to describe his pride. He'd have been like a dog with two tails. Maybe he knows. Somehow, in that great big yonder wherever he is. I like to think he does.'

'So do I. Oh Mia! It's like a great weight has lifted from my shoulders. They'll all be so pleased for me at the Practice. I'll ring the minute I've eaten my breakfast. Have you eaten?'

Mia shook her head. 'Too excited.'

'Well, go get something and share my teapot. You can sit here while we let it sink in.' Kate patted the bed, and moved her legs to make more room. 'Look, just here. Please.'

When Mia came back Kate was looking concerned. 'What's the matter, Kate?'

'I've just realised I'm so excited I haven't given a thought to you.'

'Why should you? I'm excited too.'

'I know but—'

'But nothing. Now's the time for me to get a job. I shall only have myself to look after and getting a job after all these years will be the best thing for me.'

'Are you sure?'

'Absolutely.'

'They'll be needing someone to replace me. The money isn't much but it would be a start.'

'Oh! I don't know about that. They wouldn't want me.'

'Why not?'

'No. No.'

'Nonsense, you'd be lovely with the clients and you love animals.'

'No, Kate. It won't do at all. Think of my asthma. I'd spend all my time with watering eyes and striving to breathe.'

'Of course, I never thought. But what are you going to do?'

'Paint. And possibly work in the art shop in the High Street.'

'Have they a vacancy?'

'I don't know but I can always ask. Mrs Boulder is thinking of retiring, and not before time. They've given her the nudge a few times but she won't take the hint. She's immovable.'

'Boulder by name and Boulder by nature!' The two of them collapsed in a fit of giggling, which lightened the atmosphere and made them both feel light-hearted.

'Oh Mia! Isn't it wonderful? I know I'm not in till one but I'm going to phone and tell Joy. She'll be so pleased.' Kate flung back the sheet, got out of bed and charged into the hall, leaving Mia in the bedroom alone.

Mia looked up at the ceiling deep in thought. After a while she said, 'Well, Gerry, you've got what you wanted. Your darling daughter at vet college. Aren't you pleased? She's done it, exactly what she wanted. I can't begin to tell you how pleased I am.'

Kate was back in the bedroom before Mia realised. 'Mia, who were you talking to?'

'Your dad. I often do, especially when it's something about you.'

Kate swallowed hard. 'I never realised.'

Mia patted her arm. 'What did Joy say?'

'She's thrilled and they're cracking a bottle of champagne at lunchtime specially for me.'

'Good. You enjoy yourself, you deserve to, all the work you've put in this year. Don't worry about me, when you go to college I shall be busy making a life for myself. And there'll always be you home in the vacations. Won't there?'

'Of course.'

Mia looked around the bedroom and said, 'I'm glad we've moved to this flat. I'd never have coped in that house. Too many memories, you know.' She got out her handkerchief and blew her nose. 'What am I doing crying on a day like this? Get up, you lazy girl, and get some ringing round done! Miss Beaumont for a start.' Mia busied herself collecting together their breakfast things. 'Go on, into the bathroom, quick smart.'

On the stroke of one o'clock Graham opened the bottle of champagne they'd been keeping for Kate's Big Day. Valentine filled the glasses standing on Miriam's silver tray and Zoe served them all where they stood in reception. When everyone had a charged glass in their hand they raised them to Kate and wished her all the best. She came in for a lot of kissing and masses of good wishes.

Joy hugged and kissed her, putting both their glasses in jeopardy. 'What a wonderful day. Absolutely wonderful.'

Mungo pecked her cheek and clapped a hand on her shoulder. 'Brilliant. You'll have a whale of a time. Don't forget us, will you?'

Dan, Valentine, Stephie and Annette all wished her well. Clients began to arrive for early afternoon appointments and a second bottle of champagne was opened so they could join in the celebrations. By the time the two bottles had been emptied the atmosphere was convivial to say the least.

Joy clapped her hands. 'Sorry! Everyone back to work. I'll clear the glasses. Let's make a start.'

Dan called out, 'Speech! Speech! Silence for Kate's speech.'

Kate's face was flushed from the champagne and she was in no mood for thinking clearly. 'I can't. Sorry.'

But a chant begun by Dan and supported by everyone else started up. 'Speech! Speech! Speech!'

Kate said, 'All right then. I'm no good at speeches, but thank you for all your good wishes and for this.' She held up her glass. 'Thank you for being so kind to me, and making me one of the team and I'll do my best to bring you credit when I'm at college.'

Mungo shouted, 'Three cheers for Kate. Our clever Kate!'

The cheers bounced off the walls, making Kate want to hide in her accounts office. Eventually things got back to normal, Stephie behind the reception desk, Kate to accounts, Joy to sorting her paperwork, Bunty and Sarah Two to assist Mungo with a tricky operation, and the clients to discussing their pets' symptoms.

Stephie brought Kate a mug of tea during the afternoon. She put down the mug on Kate's desk and said, 'I shall miss you when you've gone.'

'I'll miss you. I'll miss everyone. Everyone's been so kind.' Kate invited Stephie to sit in what she called her consultation chair. It was a rackety old thing, which Joy kept saying she would take to the tip, but somehow never remembered to do so.

Stephie sat down in it, adjusting her position to avoid slipping off it onto the floor. 'Do you miss Scott?'

'Not any more.'

'What about Adam?'

'Certainly not Adam, though I do wonder what he gets up to nowadays since he struck out on his own.'

Stephie looked uncomfortable.

When she didn't reply Kate asked her if she had something to tell her.

'Yes. I have.'

'Well then?'

'You know Adam?'

Kate nodded.

'Well, we ... we've ... been going out a bit.'

Kate's eyes were large with surprise. 'You and *Adam*?'

Stephie nodded. 'Yes. Not till after the day he arrived with the bouquet to say sorry to you. But, yes, we have. He's altogether different now. In a few short months he's changed completely. He even does things spontaneously.'

'Wow! And his mother?'

Stephie had to laugh. 'I told her off good and proper. She's eating out of my hand now.'

'I don't believe this, she was always so ... clinging with Adam.'

'She isn't any more. I told her if she didn't lighten up I'd make sure she never saw Adam again.'

Kate was appalled and at the same time full of admiration for Stephie. 'You didn't!'

'I did. That soon sorted her out. Told her to get a life of her own, and leave Adam to live his.'

'Well!'

'So ... we're thinking of getting engaged. Is it all right, I mean with you, you haven't still got the hots for him, have you?'

'No. Why didn't you tell me sooner?'

'Because, Kate, I felt embarrassed about it. I saw him at a club, soon after he brought you the bouquet. He was there with his new flatmates and I knew one of them and it went from there.'

'But, his mother wanted to live with Adam and me, is she ... ?'

'No, she isn't. I straightened her out on that score too. She can be quite pleasant ... that is if you stand no nonsense from her.'

'Well, good luck to you, Steph.'

'So it's OK, then?'

'Fine. Absolutely fine.' Kate handed Stephie her empty mug. 'I hope you'll be very happy. I'm just so amazed. I never thought.'

After Stephie had gone Kate shuddered. Adam and Stephie? She shuddered again; remembered the night he went wild with temper and she'd escaped into Sainsbury's and rung her dad for help. And his ridiculous bowling outfit, which he thought so groovy. His obsession with doing the same thing week after week. Tuesday, bowling. Friday, cinema. Sunday, lunch at the usual pub. Nothing could be allowed to disrupt his routine. She shuddered again when she thought about him kissing her. Stephie was welcome to him. But maybe he had changed. She hoped he had for Stephie's sake.

Kate's next visitor was Rhodri. He just about managed to put a small degree of enthusiasm in his voice when he congratulated her but she knew his heart wasn't in it.

'Just sorry, Kate, that I wasn't here for the champagne. Called out to a whelping. Sorry, then.'

'That's fine, Rhodri. Successful, were you?'

'Successful?'

'With the whelping.'

'Oh yes. But they shouldn't breed from her. Bulldog. Very narrow pelvis. Saved three. Wanted to bring her in for a Caesarean but they wouldn't have it. "Using a knife on her? We can't allow it. Oh no!" They didn't give a thought to the agony she was going through. I've told them, this is the last time.' He slumped down on the chair Stephie had just vacated and sipped his tea.

Kate waited for him to say something but he didn't, so she made a pretence of getting on with the accounts. Eventually she asked, 'Are you all right?'

Rhodri looked up at her, preoccupied and distant. 'Right as I shall ever be.' He stood up, leaving his mug on her desk and went off, meeting Dan going out through the back door to the car park.

'Good news about Kate, isn't it, Rhodri?'

'Of course. I'm glad for her. Though why anyone should want to be a vet I can't imagine at this moment.'

'There's worse jobs. Like working in a call centre. I'd go mad, completely mad, working in one of those.'

Being the same height their eyes were on a level and Rhodri looked straight into Dan's and said, 'You're mad already.'

Dan, startled by Rhodri's obvious enmity, drew in a deep breath and said, 'Me? Mad? What do you mean by that?'

'You just are.'

'I most certainly am not.'

'Mad for money, mad for forging ahead, mad to succeed at any price.'

'I don't take kindly to remarks like that. I think you should have a good think about what you've said.'

'I've never liked you since the first day. Arrogant. That's what you are. A big dose of humility would not go amiss.'

'Just a minute . . .' Dan stood back and looked at Rhodri, seeing not an angry man but a sad misfit. 'Look, I don't want to pick a quarrel with anyone, least of all a colleague.'

But Rhodri was apparently determined to pick a fight and squared up to Dan. 'Is that so?'

Kate couldn't help overhearing the quarrel and went out into the corridor hoping to calm things down. Rhodri saw her and said, 'Here comes another one full of herself.'

'There's no need to speak about Kate in that way. She's a right to be full of herself today. She's succeeded, which apparently you've not or you wouldn't be like this. None of us want an argument with you . . .'

'Well, you're getting one. You haven't been in the place five minutes and you've got a partnership.'

Dan opened his mouth to justify himself but decided against it. 'Hmm. I've work to do, even if you haven't.' He endeavoured to get past him to get on with his calls but Rhodri wasn't having it.

'I haven't finished yet.'

'Well, I have.'

Kate intervened. 'Please, Rhodri, let him leave. He's got calls to make, and you've got clients waiting, I know for a fact.'

The fight went out of Rhodri when he heard Kate's calming voice. Neither Dan nor Kate missed the bitter tones in his voice though when he answered, 'Mustn't have them all waiting for me, must I?' He turned and headed towards his consulting room.

Dan raised his eyebrows at Kate. 'What the devil was all that about?'

'Don't know, but something's not right.'

'It'll be that Welsh maiden of his that he's so keen on. Turned him down . . . again.' Dan began to laugh.

'It's not funny, Dan. He loves her to bits and she has a father she can't leave.'

'Sorry. Sorry! Got to go. But I didn't start it, remember, it was him.'

Rhodri greeted his first client as warmly as he was able in the circumstances. It was Miranda Costello, dressed head to toe in dark brown shaded velvet, with a strange brown velvet turban inexpertly wound round her head and not quite covering her dyed hair. She pointed to her cat basket. 'Rhodri, it's this young man.'

'A new cat?'

'Oh, you don't know. No, he's my new dog. I took him on from a friend who isn't able to walk him any more and I said I'd take him but I'm beginning to regret it.'

'Why is that?'

Miranda looked round the consulting room to make sure there was only her and Rhodri present and said softly, 'I don't like to say it in front of him because I don't want to embarrass him, but he's,' she mouthed the word, 'incontinent'. All over the place. Both, you know. I don't want the others to begin copying him. I thought it was because he's upset at being moved but he's been with me three weeks and it doesn't get any better. I know I've a lot of animals and it takes me all my time, walking them and attending them and I know I'm a bit happy-go-lucky about fleas and things, but I won't allow that. Absolutely not.'

'What breed is he? He must be small to get him in your cat basket.'

'Oh he is! Look!'

Rhodri peered into the wire front of the basket and saw the smallest, fully grown Yorkshire Terrier he'd ever come across. 'Never have I seen such a tiny dog! Why, he's minute.'

'You wouldn't think so if you were cleaning up after him.'

'Is he friendly?'

'Oh yes. No trouble.'

'Did the previous owner say why she couldn't cope with him?'

'Just that she couldn't take him out any more. Rheumatism, she said. I fell for him straight away. He's a little beauty, isn't he?'

'He is. Get him out. What's his name?'

Miranda began to laugh uproariously, but controlled herself for just long enough to blurt out, 'Goliath.'

For the first time for a while Rhodri laughed too. 'Goliath! Are you pulling my leg?'

'As if I would. It's true, that's what she called him, and I can't change it, can I?'

'Of course not.'

Goliath, out on the examination table, looked as though butter wouldn't melt in his mouth. He was neat and smart, and a tough looking little chap with bright, alert eyes under a mop of unruly black and tan fur, and an engaging personality which made you smile when you looked at him. He wagged his stump of a tail and looked up at Rhodri, panting, with his tiny pink tongue lolling from the corner of his mouth. A little gem, thought Rhodri as he examined him.

'Have the other animals accepted him?'

'Without a murmur. In fact he's boss dog.'

Surprised, Rhodri said, 'He is?'

'Oh yes. It took him three days but he made it. One growl from him and the cats, and the dogs, were putty in his paws. He sleeps in whichever one of their beds he chooses, and it's a different one every night. When I feed them he chooses whose dinner he eats. He's a rascal.'

'I think you have a dominant dog problem here. Before you know where you are he'll be dictating to you. But . . . to be a successful dog owner, you, Miranda, have to be the leader of the pack, like it is in the wild, where the leader stands no nonsense.'

'But I am.'

'Not according to this little chap. He's mastered the animals and you'll be the next. That's what this messing all over the place is, a way of dominating you. Next he'll be biting you if you don't please him, just as the leader of a pack of dogs would do, and you don't want that.'

'You think so? But look at him, he's so sweet.'

'And he knows it. He might be a toy dog on the outside, but in his head he thinks he's Hitler.'

'What shall I do?' Miranda looked at Rhodri as though he were the high priest of dog psychology.

'You've a battle on your hands. A long one too. But in everything, you must have the upper hand. What you say he must do, he must, whether or not he likes it. If you say "Come", don't let him off if he defies you, even though he looks so sweet. Which he does.' Rhodri was scratching him behind his ears and Goliath was loving it. 'Try doing dog training with him, at a class if you're not sure what to do. You've got to get the upper hand. I've examined him and short of taking an X-ray, I can't find anything the matter with him. Try my plan. If you're not succeeding in the least little bit, bring him in and we'll have another look. But I'm almost certain, from what you've told me, it's a psychological and not a physical problem.'

'Thank you. Well, I'll have to work at it, won't I?'

Rhodri invitingly opened the wire front of the basket and patted the blanket inside. He tried out his command voice. 'Come along, Goliath, in your basket.'

Goliath eyed Rhodri eyeball to eyeball as though weighing him up, made the decision that it suited him to allow Rhodri the upper hand and meekly trotted into the basket and sat down.

'Oh! Look at that. He knows you've rumbled him. Bless. Isn't he sweet?'

'He won't be if you don't master him. It's all for his own good in the end. He'll be a much nicer dog for you to live with.'

Miranda gazed at Rhodri, full of admiration. 'You're so wonderfully wise. What I would do without you I don't know. Thank you.'

Her appreciation of his skills went some way to salve Rhodri's wounds, but not entirely, for the wounds were deep. He really rather felt as though everyone in the world was successful in anything they attemped. Look at Kate. Missed out on Vet college and here she was with a place ready and waiting. Dan, *Dan*, damn and blast him, gets his wife back, plus a baby, and not only that but Colin, stick-in-the-mud-wife-battered Colin finds himself about to become a father. What had he got? A house and a ferret. Much as he loved Harry Ferret he had gone lower down in his priorities than Rhodri had ever imagined possible. As for Old Man Jones ... if he died tomorrow, he Rhodri Hughes, would be more than capable of dancing on his grave. As he finished completing Goliath Costello's record, Rhodri decided that action had to be taken. He'd work out a plan and ring first thing tomorrow. She wouldn't be able to refuse.

8

Rhodri rang Megan when he knew she'd be having breakfast in that vast farmhouse kitchen of hers. She answered after the second ring, her voice weary and resigned.

'Beulah Bank Farm.'

Eager to tell her his plans and full of love for her he said brightly, 'It's me, my darling. Good morning.'

'It's you. I'm so tired. I've had a terrible time with Da. Up and down all night.'

'I'm so sorry, sweetheart, so sorry.'

'It does no good to answer him back, you know. I've learned that over the years.'

'I'm sorry.'

'I think it best if we don't see each other, for a week or two, till it all blows over.'

Rhodri met this reply with complete silence, unable to believe what he'd heard.

'Are you still there, Rhodri?'

'Yes.'

'It's for the best.' He heard a break in her voice as she spoke. 'I'm sorry, Rhodri, but I can't take any more.'

'But I was just going to say that—'

'No, my love ... we'll just play it cool for a while. OK?'

'Cool? For how long?'

'As long as it takes.'

'Please, Megan, you need—'

'I need time for Da. That's all. Just for a while.'

But there was a finality in her voice that angered Rhodri. 'You're not meaning to throw away everything we have, are you?'

Megan hesitated. 'No.'

'I love you. You love me.'

'We can't have everything in this life. I'm going to put down the phone, that's Da calling.'

'He can wait a moment. Look! I've got a plan—'

''Bye, Rhodri.'

He knew from the tone of her voice that she was starting to cry. Damn that bloody old man. How dare he ruin Megan's life because he wanted to be looked after. How dare he? What human being had the right? Mr Jones apparently. Rhodri was burning up inside with love for Megan. He wanted so desperately to give her a life but after all his resolutions of the night before about taking action, *fait accompli* and all that, he was exactly where he was, and always would be, for the rest of his life.

Rhodri recalled Mr Jones trying to strike him. He'd only missed because his own reactions had been sharpened by learning to move quick sharp when he was treating animals who didn't take kindly to even the slightest degree of interference. A bitterness formed in Rhodri's soul, a hard core of bitterness and what was worse, anger at Megan. How could she reject him? He thought about that night they'd made love. The supreme joy he'd felt bounding through him as they'd laid in each other's arms afterwards. She'd reached his innermost soul that night. Didn't it mean anything to her now? Who was it who had made loving a sin?

That triumphant old man.

Rhodri arrived at the Practice that morning nothing like the person who, only a few short days ago, had been so full of happiness and with a spring in his step. He felt desolate and even considered giving in his notice. Small animal practices were always looking for staff. He'd have no problem getting another job. No, he would not. He opened his consulting room door and called out the name of his first client.

Kate called out, 'They've not arrived yet, Rhodri. You can relax.'

Rhodri nodded and went back into his room thinking he'd open his post while he waited. But Kate came in. 'In fact the first two of your appointments are going to be late.'

On the spur of the moment Rhodri said, 'Doing anything imperative at lunchtime?'

'Not specially.'

'Come out for lunch with me?'

'OK. That will be nice. Thanks. Where shall we go?'

'Not much time, can't get as far as the precinct, so shall we say the new snack bar down the road? Food's good I'm told.'

'That's lovely. See you at one in reception. Fingers crossed I don't get held up.'

Kate told Joy about her lunch invitation and Joy said, 'Good idea. That's nice of you. He does seem down in the dumps, it'll do him good.'

'I think it's Megan. Her father still won't agree to them getting married.'

'Frightened I expect.'

Kate looked at Joy and asked her what he had to be frightened about.

'See it from his point of view. Megan marries, they want a home of their own, children perhaps, who looks after him I ask?'

'Ah! Yes, of course. I see what you mean.'

But Kate got a different view of Mr Jones when she talked to Rhodri over lunch.

Kate sat back in amazement. 'Hit you? Whatever for?'

'Because I stood up to him and told him there was nothing on earth to stop Megan and me getting married except him. I told him good and proper how selfish he was.' Rhodri peered glumly into his vegetable broth as though searching for something reprehensible in it. He tore another lump of bread from his roll, smeared a small splodge of butter on it and devoured it as though it were his last bite.

He briefly related the events of that terrible evening and Kate, realising his desperation, said as kindly as she could, 'My advice is to let it cool off for a few days like she said. It must be exhausting getting up time and again during the night, she's bound to feel defeated this morning. See it from her point of view. She can't walk out on him, can she? Be honest.'

Rhodri envisaged those gnarled hands of his, with their stiff knobbly joints and twisted fingers, struggling to prepare a meal and in that gentle, sentimental, Welsh heart of his he had to admit, Kate was right.

'Well, then. You've to win him over, haven't you? Megan you've already got in the palm of your hand, but him ... you've really gone and done it as far as he's concerned.'

Rhodri looked up to find himself staring straight at Dan's back. 'Oh blast! Not him. Don't look round.'

'Who is it?'

'Wonder boy Dan.'

Kate whispered, 'Rhodri! We can't pretend we don't know he's here, in a place this size.'

She glanced over her shoulder, caught Dan's eye and beckoned to him, patting the table invitingly and smiling at him. He came across with his tray and noticed they'd all chosen the same thing from the menu. 'Great minds think alike! Is it good, then?'

Kate nodded. 'It is. Very nice. Best thing on the menu.'

'That's what I thought. Do you mind if I join you, Rhodri?'

Rhodri looked up, 'There's nowhere else at this time of day. Sit down.' He felt cheated; Kate was a good listener and he'd just got into his stride, and now the opportunity was lost.

Dan began on his soup. Kate continued with hers. Rhodri watched Dan spooning in the soup as fast as he could. 'Hungry then, are you?'

'Been up at Tad Porter's, it might be summer but by heck was it cold. And windy. Rain spitting in the wind, you know. They'd even had a slight frost last night. It puts an edge on one's appetite, believe me. ''Spect it must be the same at Beulah Bank Farm, isn't it, Rhodri?'

Rhodri didn't reply. So Kate said, 'In more ways than one!' Meaning the atmosphere *in* the house as well as out. Rhodri gave her a warning glance, which Dan intercepted. 'You're not flavour of the month then with Old Man Jones?'

Still Rhodri didn't reply. Kate said, 'You could say so.'

'I was up there the other day, he's a sick man.'

Rhodri grunted. 'Less sick than he makes out.'

'Come on, Rhod, he *is* a sick man, only a fool would say he wasn't.'

Rhodri rose to his feet, his face like thunder, 'I know what I'm talking about. He puts it on to keep Megan chained to his side. When he chooses he can get out of his chair just like that,' Rhodri snapped his fingers, 'but he insists that Megan or I, when I'm there, help him up. He's a malevolent, embittered old fraud.' Rhodri picked up his mug of coffee, downed the whole lot and stormed out.

Dan half rose from his chair but changed his mind. 'I've stepped on his toes and not half. Sorry. Didn't know things were so bad.'

'He stood up to him the other night and they had a frightful row.'

'That's not the way to go about it.'

'It's difficult when you're in love like he is. What riles Rhodri is that her father orders Megan about as though she were his slave. I feel sorry for her.'

'Mmm. I'm up there on Thursday for routine TB testing. Perhaps I'll see what I can do.'

'For heaven's sake, don't make things any worse. He worships Megan.'

Dan thought for a while. 'It is a problem, isn't it? Three people locked in without a solution. But I don't like to see people, especially thoroughly good people, letting the years pass by when they could be so much happier than they are.'

'You do rub him up the wrong way.'

Dan turned to look at her. 'What have I said just now that could possibly have annoyed him?' He raised his eyebrows to emphasise his point.

'Pointing out how sick Mr Jones is. Crikey! Look at the time. Joy will be giving me the sack.' She began putting on her cardigan.

'I doubt it. Finish your coffee and we'll saunter in together. I'll make your excuses.'

'What makes you think you can win Joy over about anything? She's really annoyed with you about going to Bridge Farm, when she said you shouldn't.'

They did, however, saunter back to the Practice and wandered in without any trouble because Joy was in Mungo's office talking about Rhodri.

'Joy! I heard him being quite abrupt with a client yesterday. It won't do. They don't come here to be chastised.'

'Sometimes they blinking well need it.'

'They may do. Heaven alone knows I've had a few of those myself over the years, but from their point of view they are willing to pay for advice and treatment, but not, and I repeat, *not*, to be told off.'

'What do we do then? Bop Old Man Jones over the head and get an immediate solution?'

Mungo grinned. 'Well, if it has to be done I'll gladly—'

'Seriously, Mungo.'

'I don't know. We've all had ups and downs in our private lives, but it shouldn't be allowed to interfere with one's professional life.'

Joy got to her feet. 'I agree. I'll have a word.' As she came out of Mungo's office she caught sight of Dan talking to Kate. She pointedly looked at her watch and said, 'Could you be gracious enough, Dan, to get back to work or is that asking too much?'

'On my way, Joy, on my way.' Dan gave her a cheerful wave and headed for the car park.

To Kate she said, 'You set off with Rhodri and came back with Dan?'

'Rhodri lost his temper with us and walked out.'

'I see. Right. That's it.' Joy marched off towards Rhodri's consulting room, the light of battle in her eye. But he wasn't there. Eventually she found him sitting in his car. She opened the front passenger door and got in. She seemed to be doing a lot of counselling just recently sitting in cars.

'This won't do.'

Rhodri glanced at her and gave her such a fright; he looked as though he was in hell. Joy cleared her throat while she decided what to say next.

After a moment's pause she said softly, 'No problem is unsolvable, you know. There must be an answer somewhere.'

'Tell me. If I stand up to him, he has an attack and makes Megan ill with worry and attending to him. If, in his eyes I behave myself, then he claims a victory. He'd treat a dog better than he treats me.'

'He's frightened.'

Wryly Rhodri answered, 'Is he? I don't think so.'

'Oh he is! Frightened of losing his place in the world and sinking into a kind of wheelchair mentality. Are you not going up there at the moment?'

Rhodri shook his head. 'No. Megan asked me not to.'

'I think, despite your better judgement, you'd better grovel. Really grovel to him, just to get yourself back in his good books, so you can at least see Megan.'

'Mmm.'

'You see, Mungo heard you being a bit brutal with a client the other day and as he rightly says they don't pay to get told off. It's not like you, Rhodri. What were his exact words? Oh yes. You mustn't let your private life interfere with your professional one.'

'Right.'

'Which you are doing now. Sitting here brooding, when you should be in your consulting room ready for the off.' Joy patted his leg. 'Now come on. Inside. Please. With a smile on your face. You love your job really, you know.'

Rhodri made to get out, changed his mind and then changed it again, and finally stood out on the tarmac. He waited until Joy had got out, then locked up the car and marched towards the back door. Joy caught up with him and as she drew level he said, 'Have you ever been hopelessly . . . in love with someone and can't see a way out?'

'Oh yes. It's very painful.'

Rhodri looked at her and said, 'Of course, I'd forgotten. Sorry.' He pushed open the back door and let her through first. Her cheeks burned with embarrassment because it was the first time ever she'd had confirmation that the staff knew about her love for Mungo. How humiliating! It was enough to destroy her love for him instantly. The pain in her chest that had come when she'd realised Duncan had gone serious walkabout grew worse by the day. Mungo had never spoken a truer word than when he'd mentioned the ups and downs of one's private life. Well, so far so good, she hadn't let it slip that Duncan was missing, so she wasn't letting it affect *her* professional life. She went to her office, leaving the door open so she could hear Rhodri calling the name of his first patient. Ah! There it was. 'Paddy Tattersall.' New client, thought Joy. Thumping great dog, thought Rhodri.

Paddy was a gigantic Irish wolfhound. A vast, grizzled, grey creature with the softest, kindest, most appealing eyes any dog could hope to have. Rhodri didn't think he'd ever seen such a huge dog. In fact he would be better described as a pony. He was so tall he could rest his chin on the examination table and when he wagged his tail the papers on the desk were swept to the floor. His diminutive owner said firmly, 'Paddy! Sit!' So Paddy sat. 'Open your mouth!' So Paddy did. 'Bad tooth, I think. Look, down there. At the back, this side.' Mr Tattersall poked a finger down inside the cavern which was Paddy's mouth. 'Broke a piece off chewing on a stone a while back and sure there he is with a bad tooth.'

Rhodri peered inside and saw how bad the tooth was. He even put his own finger down inside. The centre of the very back tooth was rotting away and the outer edges were beginning to crumble. 'He seems very relaxed.'

'Oh he is! Not a bad thought in him. No indeed. Not a bad thought.'

'How old is he?'

'About four. I think.'

'Beautiful dog. Nice nature.'

'Can you pull it out?'

'Well, not this minute, he'll need an anaesthetic.'

'No. Just give him something in his gum to numb it as if he were a person, like at the dentist, and he'll let you do it.'

Appalled by the prospect, Rhodri considered for a moment and then shook his head. 'No way. Unnecessary suffering and all that. It's too big a risk. What if the tooth breaks up when I start pulling, which it well might seeing the condition it's in. I might hurt him. No, I'm sorry, he'll have to be put out. There's no way I can tackle it without ...'

'And I'm telling you he'll be OK. Soft as butter he is. Soft as butter.'

Rhodri pretended to be assessing the pros and cons of doing as suggested, but had already made up his mind. 'No, it's too big a risk. Can you bring him in tomorrow afternoon, one thirty?'

The diminutive owner looked disappointed. 'Very well, then. One thirty it is.'

'You're not any relation of Callum Tattersall, are you?'

'I'm a cousin. Declan Tattersall. That's me. I've inherited the farm. They've let me live in it till the papers are all sorted. Then it's legally mine. Wonderful for all the children, living there. So much space.'

'How many have you got, then?'

'Six, ah! No. Seven. That's right, seven. We've certainly livened up the old place.'

'I can imagine. I saw Callum a time or two with his dogs, great chap, so sad about him and his wife, lovely lady. She'd have been thrilled to bits to have your children running about the farm.' Both Declan and Rhodri were silent for a moment while they both thought of Nuala's joy, and then Rhodri said, 'Right then, one thirty tomorrow. He'll be ready to take home by about half past four.'

Paddy rose to his feet and filled all the available space between the door and the examination table. His tail wagged cheerfully and whisked Rhodri's pen and calculator from his desk, then he ambled out with Declan who, Rhodri swore, could have ridden on his back, and his feet would have been dangling.

When Paddy came back the following afternoon Sarah One and Sarah Two had prepared an operating room by moving the table over to one side and leaving a wide floor space for Paddy to lie down on, and laying the operation cloths on the floor instead of the operating table. Declan insisted on coming into the operating room with him and instructed Paddy to lie down. 'Roll over, Paddy.' So Paddy rolled over onto his side. He lifted his head for a moment to give Declan a baleful glance as though saying to him, 'Now what have you let me in for?' and then laid it down again and closed his eyes. 'There we are! Ready and waiting. I swear he could speak if he could.'

'I'm sure you're right,' Sarah One said, trying to get her mind round how they would move him to get on with the next operation, after the tooth had been pulled out.

Declan surreptitiously drew a handkerchief from his pocket and wiped his eyes. 'I'll be back. Four you said.'

'About four, half past might be better.' Sarah One opened the door for him and Declan crept from the operating room mopping his tears as he went. 'He's a close friend you understand.'

'Of course. He's a lovely dog. So gentle.'

But Declan, overcome with emotion, was unable to agree and simply nodded his head.

Later that afternoon those waiting in reception for their appointments thought they'd been invaded by an entire children's home. The main door flew open and a hoard of children ran in followed by a man no bigger than the oldest boy. Bubbling with excitement they went to the desk and proclaimed in varying degrees of lucidity that they'd come to collect Paddy and was he all right and could they take the tooth home like they did when they went to the dentist?

Declan was carrying the smallest girl, who was shrieking, 'Paddy' at the top of her voice. So when they stayed still long enough to be counted, the clients found there were five girls and two boys. All clean as new pins and well dressed.

'My God!' said one client. 'Thank heavens they're not all mine.'

The man sitting next to her said, 'Same 'ere. Who'd want that lot?'

Joy said, 'I'll go make sure Paddy's ready. We've taken the tooth out and—'

'Have you saved it? We want to take it home.' This from a tiny girl who didn't look old enough to speak.

Joy peeped over the desk at her and said, 'We've saved it in a special box.'

'Ohhhhh! Lovely. Can I go to get Paddy?'

Before Joy could reply the whole tribe of children followed by Declan had invaded the rear premises. Joy hurried after them but was too late as they were opening each door as they came to it calling, 'Paddy! Paddy!' as they went.

Rhodri came into the corridor and shouted, as though addressing a ship's crew in a hurricane, 'Quiet!' They stopped instantly, much to Rhodri's surprise. 'Paddy hasn't come round properly from the anaesthetic, so you need to be quiet and gentle. Can you do that?' He put his finger to his lips and said, 'Shhh. On tiptoe.'

They squeezed into the operating room and gathered round Paddy. He struggled to his feet and tried to wag his tail, but it would only wag in fits and starts and his legs clearly weren't his own. Declan's elder son took hold of his leash and, very softly, they all tiptoed out and then crept down the corridor with Paddy, who was trying desperately to keep on his feet on the slippery floor.

Declan took a fistful of notes from his back pocket, laid them on the reception counter and said, 'Take what you need.'

Kate counted out what was needed to pay the bill and handed the rest back to him. They all left one after the other with Declan leaving last. 'Your receipt. I haven't given you your . . .' But Kate was too late, they'd all flooded out into the car park. 'I'll post it,' she shouted.

'I'll say this for them, they're well behaved,' said a client holding a glass tank with a particularly evil-looking snake in it, which was writhing about.

'There's some could learn a lesson from them,' said another client, looking daggers at a small boy who would keep poking his fingers into the hamster cage she was holding.

Rhodri relived his moment of triumph when he'd asked the children to be quiet for Paddy's sake. Such moments added satisfaction to his job. Yes, he had to admit he loved it, and tonight he was going to grovel to Mr Jones like he'd never done before to anyone. A performance to rank with Richard Burton, or possibly Anthony Hopkins. He would rehearse his speech on the way there.

Rhodri drove to Beulah Bank Farm that same evening as he'd promised himself he would. He didn't ring first, because that would have given Megan the opportunity to tell him not to come, but he had popped into the precinct and bought a big box of Mr Jones's favourite chocolates. They were handmade Belgian, totally gorgeous, and utterly too expensive for words. For Megan he had a bottle of perfume, which after much sniffing and discussion he'd bought because he thought it suited her personality and in any case he loved the smell of it and fancied Megan smelling of it.

As he crossed the humpbacked bridge, he remembered Megan telling him that, when she knew he was coming, she watched from the kitchen window to see him crossing it and then counted to thirty-five. He felt sad she wouldn't be doing that tonight.

He arrived in the farmyard as quietly as possible, wishing to keep his presence secret. There was no Megan to greet him, and suddenly, though he knew she didn't know he was coming so there was no reason to feel disappointed, an ominous feeling spread over him and he decided it was one of the worst ideas he'd ever had. But he was there and he was going through with it.

He decided to knock and open the door, and called out, 'Megan! It's me, Rhodri!' His joyful greeting was met with complete silence. He laid his gifts on the kitchen table and went into the hall. He opened the sitting room door and put his head round. Mr Jones was sitting in his usual chair, reading. 'Hello, Mr Jones. Hope you don't mind me coming in like this. I called out but there was no answer.'

Mr Jones looked over the top of his reading glasses at him and said, 'Surprised you've the gall to come again after what you said the last time you were here.' He closed his book and took his glasses off, placing them on his table amongst his sick man's clutter.

Rhodri went further into the room and stood before Mr Jones, hands behind his back, contrite. 'That's what I've come about. To apologise. I had no right, no right whatsoever to speak to you as I did. Under no circumstances should I have allowed myself to behave in that manner and I would be grateful if you would accept my apologies for behaving in such an unseemly and totally disgraceful way. Quite inexcusable.'

Too late he remembered the chocolates but immediately decided that maybe to hand them over straight away would be too gushing for words. Rhodri waited for a reply.

Old Man Jones studied him from under his eyebrows, his eyes unfathomable. 'Apology accepted, but it makes no difference to the marriage question. Megan is not marrying you. Not while I'm alive.'

'I can understand that. You being in need of care. I can see why.' He took a deep breath. 'But we must be allowed to go on seeing each other.'

'I don't think so. There's no point.'

It was on the tip of Rhodri's tongue to question that last statement but just in time he changed it to: 'Is Megan out this evening?'

'She's asleep in bed. Tired out.'

'I see. I've been into the precinct and bought you a box of those chocolates you like. I'll go get them. Part of my apology, you know.'

He returned to the kitchen and picked up the chocolates and crossed the hall to give them to Mr Jones. 'Thank you, Rhodri. I'll open them now and you can have one with me.' But the intricate ribbon bows, tied time and again to seal the box, defeated his gnarled hands and he had to humiliate himself by handing the box back to Rhodri and asking him to open it.

'You choose first.'

Rhodri chose a liqueur, and held the box while Mr Jones picked one for himself. 'Marzipan, I'll have that one.'

They were silent for a moment while they each enjoyed the delicious flavours of their chocolates. Then Mr Jones beckoned him to hand back the box, pushed the lid back on and said, 'Makes no difference you know, these.' He pointed to the box. 'No difference at all. Megan's needed here, for the farm and for me. I'm her da and she owes me.'

Rhodri agreed. 'You need her, I know.'

'You've got the message then?'

'I've got the message all right.'

'Good. Well, you might as well go, there's no point in wasting my time with useless chit-chat.' He put his reading glasses back on and picked up his book. Removing his bookmark he began to read.

Rhodri stood fidgeting like a small schoolboy in the headmaster's room. The self-centred, miserable, mean old codger. Then he saw the twisted fingers clumsily trying to turn a page, and he wondered how he would feel if he were as handicapped as this old man.

'Goodnight, Mr Jones. I've a present for Megan. I've left it on the kitchen table.'

'Very well. Goodnight.'

Rhodri got into his car and started up the engine. He didn't move off, but sat full of gloom at the disappointing outcome of his evening. Then he thought he heard Megan's voice. He looked out and there she was waving to him from an upstairs window.

He got out and went to stand below her window. 'Megan!' All the passion he felt for her welled up inside him. She might have just woken up, but she looked so beautiful. Almost ethereal.

'Rhodri! I'm coming down.'

The house door opened and there she was crumpled, but comely. She ran into his arms and held him tight to her. 'I'm so sorry I said don't see me, but I was so tired, and so worried. I'm so glad you didn't take any notice of me. Kiss. Kiss.'

After he'd complied with her command he said, 'I've told your da I realise we can't marry. Just to put his mind at rest, you know.'

Megan almost fell from his arms with horror. 'But . . . don't you want to?'

'Of course, but we've got to be subtle about it. Careful, come up with a plan.'

'But you said you had a plan?'

'It was a stupid one. I was thinking of us pretending to go for a walk and coming back married, not much good as a basis for a happy marriage. We'd never forgive ourselves.'

Her eyes began to fill with tears.

'Not tears, Megan, please. I'll come up with something. For the moment he thinks he's won, so at least his mind is at rest. I've left you a present on the kitchen table. Goodnight, love.'

Rhodri held her face between his hands and kissed her lips, not with his usual hungry passion, but gently and with respect. 'Goodnight. Sorry you're so tired.'

When he got home the phone was ringing. It was Megan, to thank him for the perfume and to say she'd be round for a meal tomorrow night wearing bucketfuls of it.

9

Dan climbed the steep hills to Beulah Bank Farm later that same week. Over the stone humpbacked bridge, then through the trees and finally out into the farmyard. Megan was waiting for him at the kitchen door. 'Hello, Dan! Come in the house first, we've got delayed this morning and Gab has just gone to sort the cows out for you.'

'OK.' As he walked into the kitchen he said, 'I didn't realise Gab Bridges worked for you.'

'Just this last week or two. The other man did a moonlight flit, no warning no nothing, so Gab came to give us a hand for a while but I think it might be permanent. There's not enough work or money for six sons on one farm.'

'I see. How many head have you?'

'Twenty, that's all, not enough pasture for more, you understand.'

'That's a lot of work for you.'

'Not really, we manage. Go in, see Da for a while, he misses company.'

Dan thought about what Rhodri had said about Mr Jones being a malevolent, embittered, old fraud. Better approach with caution, he thought.

As he half-expected, Dan was greeted with a terse question. 'You up to this TB testing job?'

'And good morning to you, Mr Jones. To answer your question, yes I am. All in a day's work to me, and at least the rain's held off. How are you this morning?'

Mr Jones paused while he contemplated whether or not Dan's brisk manner constituted impertinence but he didn't get a chance to retort because Dan went on.

'It's a long climb up here but well worth it when you get here. Wonderful spot to live.' Dan crossed the room to look out of the window. He could see right down into the valley and just, but only just, see the nearest roofs of houses in Barleybridge.

'Not if you can't get out.'

Dan turned back from the window and asked, 'What stops you?'

Mr Jones snorted his anger. 'Are you blind? Can't you see I'm handicapped?'

'Of course, but why should it stop you going out? Megan drives.'

'And make an exhibition of myself? I'm not one to like putting on a spectacle for everyone's amusement.'

'I doubt if they'd even notice you.' He went to sit down. 'I remember once going to the amusement parks in Florida with my wife and seeing "the handicapped" as you call yourself, going on the rides. They didn't care two hoots about being manhandled on, they were too busy having a wonderful time. Some of them in far worse nick than you. Just needs a bit of courage, and I'm sure you're not short of that.'

Megan came in to sit with them. 'Dan, I've been meaning to say, we'd love your Rose to come to see us one day. Would she, do you think, and bring the baby? Come for tea?'

'I'm sure she would. She'd love it. If it's not too much for you, Mr Jones . . . you being handicapped.'

Mr Jones, used to more deferential treatment, snorted with anger for a second time that day. 'So long as the baby doesn't grizzle all the time. What is it?'

Megan answered. 'A boy, Da.'

'Lucky man. You need two or three more the same.' He looked at Megan and she flushed.

They heard the back door open and a voice bellow, 'OK Meggie, my love, we're all set.' It was Gab.

Dan got to his feet. 'I'll get my boots and then we'll start. Lovely day for it, out of the wind.' He winked at Megan and went outside.

Gab had organised the run and the crush, set the farm lad to getting the first cow into it, and was marking off the list. 'Number!'

'One two five.'

Dan had his syringes ready and took the blood. He heard something of a commotion, but he was concentrating hard and ignored it. When he took a breather for a second he saw that Megan had brought her da out to watch and he was seated booted, behatted and blanketed on a chair, out of the wind. Dan smiled to himself. There was more than one way of skinning a cat, he thought.

When they'd finished, Megan wanted him to stay for coffee but Dan declined. 'No thanks, Megan. I've got a busy day ahead. Must press on.

I'll tell Rose about the tea invite. Thanks for it, she loves getting out to meet people.'

'Good. We'll look forward to that, won't we, Da?' But her da was getting ready for the journey back to his own chair and he ignored her.

Dan asked Mr Jones if he'd done it right?

Mr Jones proffered a grudging compliment. 'For a young strip of a lad you didn't do badly. I'll give you that. Come along, Megan, get a move on.' He flung off the blanket and grasped Megan's arm to help him rise to his feet. Dan took his other arm and between them they got him into the house. Mr Jones thanked him for his help.

'A pleasure. Any time. Good morning, Mr Jones.'

Seated back in his chair, Megan's father said, 'Arrogant beggar, he is. But he does a good job, I'll say that for him.'

'He's well respected in Barleybridge is Dan. He's an excellent vet. Even your arch enemy Lord Askew approves of him.'

'Does he? Wouldn't call that a recommendation coming from him. The fat, thieving, manipulative ... Where's the blanket for my legs?'

'I'm just putting it on, see?' She draped the blanket over his knees in the way, from long experience, she knew he liked the best.

'I need a hot drink, Megan.'

'I'll put the kettle on, but first I need a word with Gab.'

'You're a good girl to me. Don't think I don't appreciate you because I do. I've a fancy for ... Never mind, it'll all be too much for me.'

'What will, Da?'

'Nothing.'

'You know how I hate half sentences. Just tell me.'

He pressed his lips into a straight determined line and then relented. 'That wheelchair you got and I refused to use.'

'Yes.'

He shook his head. 'No, never mind.'

'Are you wanting me to get it out?'

Belligerently he replied, 'No. No. Even if you do, I shan't sit in it.'

'I see. Won't be long.' Nevertheless, later that morning, she got the wheelchair out from under the stairs and gave it a dust and left it out in the passage to the back door. When she was in the kitchen preparing lunch for Gab and her father she heard him closing the downstairs bathroom door and knew by the noise his slippers were making that he hadn't gone straight back into the sitting room. Putting her eye to the crack of the door she saw him inspecting the wheelchair. She heard him tut-tutting and complaining. 'Pretty pass things have come to. Huh!' Megan realised he was coming into the kitchen, so she went back to washing the lettuce for the sandwiches.

Her da stood propped against the door frame catching his breath. 'I'll eat in here with Gab. Make a change.'

'Right.'

Gab came in at the stroke of twelve, washed his hands at the sink and took his place at the table. A huge hulk of a man, the twin by twenty minutes of Gideon and the oldest of the Bridges's brood, he had his mother's light blue eyes, and the sandy hair and the long, thin, hook nose of his father.

'Thank you, Meggie, my love.'

Her da grunted disapproval of 'Meggie' but had the sense to say nothing, for without this man to help on the farm they'd be in deep trouble. Good farm hands were rare nowadays, so he made an effort to begin a conversation, but Gab would have none of it. He ate every sandwich on his plate and then began eyeing Mr Jones's plate so ravenously that he felt compelled to offer him one of his. 'Here we are Gabriel, *Megan*'s made too many for me.'

Gab devoured that and then began on the fruit cake. When he'd eaten two big slices of that he moved on to the bowl of fresh fruit. He then poured himself two successive half pints of cider from the big jug Megan had put out, drinking them without a pause, then he stood up, said, 'Thanks, Meggie, my love.'

As he left the kitchen, he turned back to look at Megan and Mr Jones caught the look Gab gave her; an alarming mixture of love overlaid with deeply felt lust, which shocked him. Megan, busy peeling a peach, didn't notice, but when she realised Gab hadn't gone she looked up to see if he needed a word about something and blushed to the roots of her hair when she read what was in his face. He'd undressed her, in his mind, but not like Rhodri did with love and tenderness. This was something quite different. He'd *stripped* her. Mentally she re-dressed herself, prayed her father hadn't noticed, and concentrated hard on removing the stone from her peach. Gab abruptly turned towards the door, opened it and was gone. Megan's da said, 'I'm . . . going . . . for a lie . . . down.' Placing both hands on the table he heaved himself to his feet.

Megan said, 'I'll get your inhaler, you sound as though you need it.'

Mr Jones nodded. Damn the man for looking at Megan like that. How dare he? As she came towards him carrying his inhaler he looked at her with new eyes, and saw for the first time in his life just how attractive she really was, the red hair, those large tender eyes, the proud carriage of her head, the slender, expressive hands: she was attractive, so very attractive, no wonder Gab had looked at her like that. He could see why now. His daughter! The subject of such . . . lewdness. He'd have to watch him. Better still he'd advertise for a man, and get rid of him that way.

But it was easier said than done. The current downturn in farming had meant that young men were seeking work in the towns and leaving farming far behind them. So they were stuck with Gab, until times changed. Megan's da had seen the other Bridges boys when they'd all been going in to Weymouth together one Saturday night and had called to pick up Gab. They'd filled the kitchen and, to a man, they'd plainly showed their appreciation of Megan. There wasn't one of them who could be trusted one iota more than Gab, so he couldn't even swap one of them for him.

Rose called for tea one afternoon as Dan had promised. 'Are you sure, Megan, that Jonathan won't be too much for your father?' she'd enquired on the phone one day that week.

'Absolutely certain. Please come, Rose, we do want you to. Winter's coming on and we feel the need for company. That sounds as if I'm being rude to you, but it's true we do. I've got a present for the baby and I'd love to give it to him myself. So, yes, we'll see you Tuesday.'

Rose instinctively knew how desperate Megan must be feeling, with an invalid father and a lover she longed to be with. Not much of a recipe for happiness. No, sir!

When she got there she found Mr Jones ensconced in his chair looking grumpy and outfaced by her coming. But she was determined he wasn't going to find her lacking in respect and affection.

Rose shook his hand and keeping hold of it, impulsively bent forward to kiss his cheek. Despite himself, he enjoyed her vital femininity and her open friendliness. 'Hi, Mr Jones! What a pleasure, I've heard all about you from Danny.'

'Have you indeed? Not much to the good, I expect.'

'Indeed, it was. He said you'd been out to watch him TB testing and that you'd approved of him.'

'I did, but he's an arrogant beggar. I can see it won't bother you though, you're tough enough and shrewd enough to be able to cope with him, aren't you? So where's this baby of yours?'

'I've left him in the kitchen, I didn't know if . . .'

'Bring him in. I want to see him. We never get babies visiting us. Go on, girl, bring him in.'

So Rose went back to the kitchen, picked up Jonathan's travelling seat and carried him in. He was looking particularly like Danny today and she loved him for it. She held the seat so that Mr Jones could see him without having to get up. As he looked at him Jonathan opened his eyes and stared straight at Mr Jones. Two little hands waved haphazardly about, he yawned and then pulled a face as though he was concentrating very hard on something that was worrying him.

'Why, there's no mistaking who he belongs to. My word I've never seen a little chap looking so much like his father. Just look at that expression, see? Just like Dan, that is. Isn't he a grand baby? Megan! Where's the present?'

'Coming!' Megan came in from the kitchen carrying a teapot in one hand and a parcel in the other. 'Here it is! It's more fun for adults at the moment but he'll grow into it.'

With Jonathan on her knee, Rose opened the parcel and out came a fluffy white toy sheep. 'Oh look, my darling, look what Megan's bought you!'

'Turn her over and look at her tum,' Megan said.

There was a long slit down the length of the sheep's stomach and, when Rose put her fingers inside, she could feel something in there. When she pulled at it out came a small fluffy black lamb. Then another one all white this time and then another white with a black face. She gave a delighted cry of surprise each time one appeared. 'Oh, Megan! Where did you find this?'

'In the posh toy shop in Barleybridge. I couldn't resist. I almost bought one for myself.'

Rose pushed the three lambs back in again and pulled them out one after the other. 'I could do this all afternoon! It's absolutely splendid and thank you very much indeed. Very appropriate for a vet's son.' Clutching the sheep and Jonathan, Rose stood up and kissed Megan and then kissed Mr Jones again. 'Thank you very much. Isn't it lovely? I'm so pleased with it. He'll love it when he's bigger, and can do it by himself.'

Unexpectedly Mr Jones said, 'If I'm careful I could hold the baby, couldn't I?'

Without hesitation Rose placed Jonathan in his arms. Megan went to the kitchen to bring in the rest of the tea things. Rose sat back in her chair and watched in silence. Mr Jones, in a world of his own, didn't speak a word. He simply sat looking at the baby in his arms as though he'd never seen a baby before. His crippled hands clumsily stroked Jonathan's cheeks, cuddled his little feet, which were fidgeting about, and tried to get him to hold tight to a finger. Then he cleared his throat and said huskily without looking up, 'You are lucky, my dear. He's perfect. Here, take him, before I drop him.'

Rose got up, took the baby from him, and looking down at him she said, 'Have you no grandchildren?'

'No. Nor likely to have. That fool of a son of mine hasn't the slightest interest in having a family at all. It's all glitz and glitter with him and he gets plenty of that in London. As for Megan, she can't marry when she has me to look after.'

Before Rose could answer Megan came back with a loaded tea tray. The business of pouring tea, handing out plates, cutting cake and consuming it took time, and Rose still hadn't found the right moment to put in a word for Megan and Rhodri to Mr Jones by the time Megan was clearing their tea things.

But she did notice that Mr Jones was beginning to tire.

'I think I'd better be making tracks. Any minute now this son of ours is going to be shrieking for his food. I wonder ... Mr Jones ... could you find the time to come to our house for a cup of tea one afternoon? Just for an hour, if Megan can spare a few hours?'

Megan stopped what she was doing and waited, fully expecting that her da would say no. But to her surprise he said the opposite. 'If you can be bothered with an old man, yes, I'd like to. Thank you.'

'Good! I'll ring next week and we'll plan a day. Lunch perhaps, too? Will that be all right with you, Megan?'

Before Megan answered Rose, they heard Gab calling. When he didn't get an immediate answer he came on into the sitting room in his stockinged feet. He loomed in the doorway. 'Sorry, didn't realise you had company, I just need some help with ordering some more feed, please, Meggie, my love. Don't know your supplier and we're nearing the end of what we've got. Must do it today. Afternoon, Mrs Brown. Nice to see you.'

Rose smiled at him. 'Hi! Gab. It's nice to meet you. Dan said you were helping out.'

Megan picked up the tray. 'Yes, you're right. I meant to order it last week and never got round to it.' She headed for the kitchen carrying the tray, and as she went to pass Gab, still standing in the doorway, he took the tray from her and gave her a long, hot, lustful look, which wasn't lost on Rose. Without moving her head she turned her eyes to see if Mr Jones had noticed and he had; he looked livid.

'I'll be off, then.' Rose gathered her things together, picked up Jonathan and said, 'I'll give you a ring, promise. I'm so glad you said you could come. Be seeing you, Mr Jones.' Rose went into the kitchen to thank Megan.

Gab was seated at the table with Megan beside him studying a file. 'I've come to say my goodbyes. I'll ring next week when I know what Dan's doing, and we'll make a date for lunch. Perhaps Saturday. Is it all right me asking? I didn't know how your father would feel.'

Megan looked up from studying the file. 'It's fine, no one's more surprised than me that he wants to go out. Thank you very much.' She gave Rose a smile of thanks, and it was still on her face as she pointed something out to Gab who wasn't looking but was occupied with admiring Megan's hair. Again Rose caught sight of the desire in Gab's eyes and wondered if Megan recognised it for what it was.

''Bye, Rose, thank you for coming. 'Bye, Jonathan.'

''Bye, Megan. Thank you for asking me. The tea was lovely. 'Bye, Gab.' She left the kitchen, went down the short passage and out into the farmyard to get into her car. A frisson of apprehension shot through Rose, which she tried hard to shake off, but couldn't. She'd seen desire in men's eyes herself many times, but never with the hint of threat which she recognised in Gab's look. Megan was a stunner. Who would have guessed there was such sweet beauty hidden away in that remote farmhouse? No wonder Rhodri had fallen for her. No wonder at all. But Gab!

From the depths of his chair, after Rose had gone, Mr Jones watched Megan dusting crumbs from the table she'd used for serving the tea. 'Isn't that Rose a lovely girl? So kind to want to be bothered with a crippled old man. It will make a change. Yes, a very pleasant change. Fresh she is, New World fresh. That Dan's a lucky man. Don't know how he's managed to get her. He wasn't exactly at the front of the queue when good looks were given out.'

'Not many people are.'

Megan's da didn't tell her how he'd realised what a beauty she was, didn't want to rock the boat. He was damned if she upped and left. Damned to a procession of 'helpers' or else a nursing home and he wasn't having that. No, she'd just have to wait.

Dan shifted Jonathan round so he could see his face. 'Darling, I certainly won't tell Rhodri. He's far too wound up about the situation. If he finds out, he'll probably murder Gab. What a mess! What with Megan's biological clock ticking away and Rhodri fit to die for her and Gab obviously fancying her like crazy, things could be hotting up.'

'Mr Jones knows it too. He was livid.'

Dan looked up at her and asked if Mr Jones was willing to come for lunch or had he to be coerced?

'Willing. Very willing. I was amazed.'

'So am I.'

'He's an old sweetie really, just in so much pain and so resentful of not being able to do what he wants, which is farming, he can't help but let it spill out into every corner. He treats Megan like a servant, but what alternative has either of them?'

'Not much. I bet you're the first person to say he's such a sweetie.'

'You should have seen him with your son. Watch out, he's being sick!' By the time they'd cleaned him up and Dan had changed his trousers and Rose had given the baby her favourite recipe for wind, and then they'd got him to sleep, the evening was almost over and they gave no further thought to Old Man Jones, except for Rose to say that she was going to solve their problems.

'Rose! You're not to interfere! Promise!'

Eyes wide with innocence, she agreed she wouldn't interfere, just help things along a little. Sitting up in bed during the night, feeding Jonathan while his father slept the sleep of the righteous, Rose thought how to bring it about. She could make a beginning by inviting Rhodri for lunch at the same time as Mr Jones and Megan. No, that would be too obvious. Or she could ask other people she knew and then the larger group would make it not quite as obvious. No, that would be too much for Mr Jones. All those people. No. What she'd do was encourage him to go out more and then he would have less time to brood and more time to see how the other half of the world lived. He needed cheering up. The whole balance of his life wanted rejigging. Brightening. Freshening up. Revitalising. And she was the person to see to it. Yes. Coming here for lunch would be a start. But as she put Jonathan back into his cradle, sated with milk and almost asleep, Rose remembered the glittering of Gab's eyes and the lust in them, and hoped Rhodri's and Gab's paths would not cross.

10

It was, however, Rhodri's afternoon off the following day and he and Megan were taking the chance to shop in Barleybridge. He couldn't find her when he first arrived at the farm, but he did find Gab in the nearest field, mending a fence.

He was lifting a huge hammer with the greatest of ease and raining blows on a new fence post. Rhodri watched the rhythmic strokes of his powerful arms with admiration. Strength like his was amazing. 'Gab! Hi!' He guessed Gab would answer without the slightest shortness of breath.

The post as secure as he could make it, Gab rested the mighty hammer on the ground and turned to see who'd called his name.

'It's you. If it's Meggie you're wanting she's inside getting ready.' The light eyes appraised Rhodri. 'Business brisk?'

'Yes, thanks. And you?'

'Busy, you know, always something to do on a farm. Nice autumn though. Easy to get jobs done when the weather's good.' Gab eyed him again with a speculative look. 'Lucky for you Old Man Jones is having a good day. He cramps your style, doesn't he?'

'What do you mean?'

'Having that old git ordering you and her about. She never has a minute.'

'I know. He doesn't order me about.'

Gab leant on the post he'd just put in, his chin resting on his hands. 'He does. He tells you marriage isn't on the agenda.'

'Who told you that?'

'Obvious, isn't it? All he needs is a ... *man* with a firm hand to tell him where to get off.'

Rhodri felt at an immediate disadvantage. 'Does he indeed? Well, thanks for the advice.'

Gab nodded his head towards the house. 'She's coming.'

Both men watched her walk across to them. Rhodri saw his beautiful lover walking towards him. Gab saw the swing of her hips, her slender ankles and her red hair blowing in the wind. To avoid getting her shoes dirty Megan didn't walk through the gate into the field but stood on top of a small stone wall alongside the gate and waved. Rhodri looked at Gab intending to say he'd be seeing him sometime, but the words stopped in his throat when he saw the lecherous look on Gab's face. A furious rage welled up in his chest. How dare Gab harbour thoughts like that about his Megan? She was his. Absolutely his and his alone.

He snapped out, 'You'd better get back to your fence mending, Gab,' and looked at the darkening sky, at the heavy grey clouds lumbering across from Beulah Bank Top. 'Looks like rain. Get on with it, man.' He waved cheerfully to Megan, his heart like a stone in his chest.

Gab's answer was, 'Get stuffed.' He waved to Megan himself and shouted, 'Meggie! Where's that lad? I need another pair of hands or I'll not get done before milking.'

On the wind came Megan's reply. 'OK.' She got down from the wall and went into one of the outbuildings from which the lad emerged in a second and hurried across the field to Gab.

Rhodri grimly strode towards Megan, focusing his eyes on her lovely welcoming smile knowing it was for him, and him alone. Childishly he made a show of kissing her so Gab could see she belonged to Rhodri Hughes. When they were in the car fastening their safety belts Rhodri said, 'You know Gab?'

'Of course.' She knew what he was going to say.

'Does he ever try it on?'

He noticed her slight hesitation but she said, 'No. Of course not.'

'He looks as if he might, but he'd better not.'

Megan turned to look at him full face. 'He won't. I shan't let him.'

'You've noticed his face then when he looks at you with those greedy eyes of his.'

'I have, but he won't.'

'Does your da know?'

'Of course not. He's not that perceptive.' She turned to look out of the car window. 'If we don't get off the afternoon will be gone and I shall be needed back for Da. Start her up, Rhodri, and don't fret. Trouble with the Bridges boys is there's too many of them and too few suitable girls. They fancy anyone in a skirt.'

'You're a stunner you see, that's why I worry.'

'And I'm his boss and pay his wages, better wages than he's had since he left school, I bet. Thanks for the compliment, though. Are we going or are we staying?'

'Going.' Rhodri revved up and charged out of the farmyard. They were over the humpbacked bridge in no time at all and speeding into Barleybridge. While Megan was choosing some lingerie, Rhodri excused himself and slipped away to buy a gift for her. He chose a manicure set in a leather case crafted into the shape of an old-fashioned cigarette case. He knew how she loved to keep her hands as immaculate as she could.

On the way back in the car he handed it to her. 'Present for my lovely.'

Out of the corner of his eye he watched her face as she opened up the box it was in.

'Why, Rhodri, that's lovely. I've never had one of these. It's just beautiful. Thank you.' Megan kissed his cheek, twice. 'Thank you.'

'When you use it think of me.'

'I think of you every day, my darling. All day.'

They'd almost reached the humpbacked bridge and Rhodri decided to stop there for a short while. 'I won't come in when we get back. You'll have enough to do. Let's pull in here and talk.'

'OK.'

When he'd parked the car Megan said, 'I like sitting on the slope down to the stream, there's a big flat boulder in just the right place . . .'

'Do you come here often then?'

'When I'm sick of the house and Da, I come here to get away. Escape it all . . . for a while.'

Rhodri felt immeasurably sad. 'Well, let's then.'

So they sat huddled tightly together on the stone watching the busy stream attending to its own affairs. 'This stone's only just big enough for the two of us.'

Megan grinned. 'Cosy though.'

'Oh! Yes. It is.' His arm tightened around her shoulders. 'Could stay here for ever.'

'Too cold.'

'We're sheltered from the wind.'

'Nice place to make love, though.' Megan chuckled. 'Slope's a bit steep. It'd be something of a challenge, wouldn't it?'

'Have to mind you didn't finish up sliding down into the water.'

Megan laughed. 'You're right there.'

He loved to hear her laugh, there wasn't enough of it in her life. There would be if she married him.

Megan shuddered.

'Cold?'

'No, just a weird feeling. Premonition or something.'

Abruptly Rhodri got to his feet. 'Time to go.'

Megan looked up at him. 'You sound as though you felt it too.'

'No. Not me.' He hauled Megan to her feet and made an effort to kiss away their strange feeling of something about to happen. 'What was it you felt?' He gripped her hand to help her up the slope to the road.

'Just nothing, really. I'm being silly.'

He opened the car door for her, made sure she was comfortable and then went round to get in his own seat. As they drove up between the trees, he could feel her discomfort settling on him too. He tried to force it out of his mind but couldn't. Not her da? Not something happened while they were out? He checked the car clock. They'd been exactly two and a quarter hours.

As he put on the hand brake he said, 'I won't come in. I'll wait till you wave to say your da's all right.'

Standing with his back against the car, he watched her unlock the door and disappear inside. Then she came to the door again and waved. So it wasn't that, then. The old sod was still alive. So what was it? He blew her a kiss and she returned it and then closed the door. He didn't know when he'd ever felt more alone than when the door closed behind her. Loneliness, like great waves of shocking pain, rolled over him leaving him desolate. It would be tomorrow morning before he spoke to another living soul. What kind of a life was that? He started up the engine, and was about to drive away when Gab came out of a stable door and went to open the back door of the house. He called, 'Meggie, my love. I'm off.' He'd better not go in or . . .

Rhodri heard her say from somewhere inside the house, 'OK. See you in the morning, Gab.'

There was something dashing about Gab, something lean and handsome and . . . what was the word? Virile. Earthy. Like that gamekeeper in that book . . . what was it? He'd recall it when he wasn't thinking about it. But he was just like him.

Politely Rhodri waited for Gab to get in his scruffy little car, more fitted for the knacker's yard than the road, and drive away. When he'd gone Rhodri thought, Gab sees more of her than I do, and remembered the peculiar feeling they'd both had sitting by the stream that ran under the humpbacked bridge. No, he really was being stupid. He bet Dan didn't have such daft thoughts. No, not Dan. Dan would have found a solution. But he was damned if he could. Dan would have compromised on something or other, and had Old Man Jones eating out of his hand. That gamekeeper. Yes, that was it. D.H. Lawrence. *Lady Chatterley's Lover*. That was who Gab reminded him of.

His worries were still with him the next morning. Everyone else seemed focused, busy, enthusiastic; he was preoccupied with thoughts of Megan which were gnawing his innards, rendering him useless. But the arrival of his third client rapidly emptied the forefront of his mind. It was Adolf, Mr Featherstonehough's Rottweiler. A soaking wet Adolf.

'Good morning, Adolf, good morning, Bert. You've been fighting Perkins again, haven't you, old chap? I can tell. Kate's been throwing water over the pair of you, hasn't she? You're not looking too perky, Adolf. What's your problem?'

Mr Featherstonehough answered on Adolf's behalf. 'It's the old problem. That lump in his groin. Only this time it's worse and well . . . see what you think.'

'Ah! I'll have a look.'

Rhodri felt around Adolf's groin with trepidation. He knew what Adolf meant to his owner: the whole world. But the news wasn't good.

'Let's see, how old is Adolf now?' Rhodri flicked the records through on the computer and found Adolf's name. 'He's almost twelve?'

'That's right. And as good as ever till these last few weeks. But he's lost heart. If it hadn't been for Kate's bucket of water Perkins would have had him for breakfast this time.'

'Do you get the feeling he's in pain?'

Mr Featherstonehough couldn't bring himself to answer. 'No. No. Not pain exactly. Well, to be honest . . . yes . . . I think so. Yes, it's in his eyes, it's as if he's asking me to help him. And the way he behaves. Laid with his eyes shut but not really asleep, and I hear him prowling about in the night.' He bent to ruffle Adolf's ears and did it with deep affection.

Rhodri said to Adolf, 'Excuse me,' bending to feel the lump in his groin again. It appeared to be much more extensive than the last time. 'I think I'm going to keep him in and do some X-rays.' He looked up at Mr Featherstonehough and very slightly shook his head. 'It may not be as bad as I think but . . .'

'Be honest with me, Rhodri, no beating about the bush. I need it straight from the shoulder.'

'I have an idea the lump has spread. We said when we operated a year ago that we didn't know if we'd got absolutely everything cut out. I'm afraid it looks as though we haven't.'

'I see. Well, he's almost twelve. If he was younger would you operate again?'

'Can't say anything until I've seen the X-rays.'

'Bad as that, is it?'

Rhodri nodded.

Mr Featherstonehough ruffled Adolf's ears again. 'I shall need to see the X-rays to convince myself.'

'Of course.'

'Adolf's been a grand dog all his life. I shall miss coming here. We'll miss Perkins and his damned fighting. Miss my wet trousers.'

'You could always get another.'

Mr Featherstonehough slowly shook his head. 'Not fair to get a dog when you're not sure you'll see it through its life. No. Might get a rescue cat though. My wife always wanted a cat, but we couldn't have one, not with this old codger, nor with old Fang either. They both hated cats. I'll leave him with you. I'll come back for him. Tomorrow, eh?'

'That's right. Tomorrow, first thing.'

'I shall want to be with him when . . . you know . . . at the end. If it turns out that . . .'

'Of course.'

The X-rays confirmed Rhodri's worst suspicions. He got Mungo to take a look and the two of them stood together shaking their heads. Dan came in and joined them. 'Who's is this?'

Without looking at him Rhodri replied, 'Adolf's.'

'Mmm. Looks like very bad news. How old is he?'

'Almost twelve, he is.'

Dan said, pointing to the huge mass of the cancer, 'Curtains for Adolf then.'

Rhodri turned to him. 'You're a hard-hearted beggar, you are. Colder than ice, that's what.'

Mungo added, 'Practical might be a better word. He is right. It's all too late for Adolf.'

'I know that! I have got eyes, but is there any need to say it quite so bluntly?'

Dan apologised. 'Sorry, very sorry. Didn't mean to be unfeeling.'

'Unfeeling! You haven't got a thoughtful bone in your body, see.'

Mungo interrupted. 'Steady, Rhod, Dan doesn't know Adolf like we do.'

As though Mungo had never spoken Rhodri continued. 'This dog is well loved both at home and at this Practice, we shall miss him, all of us. But you, having no heart, don't have an inkling what we mean.'

Mungo's lips went into that thin line, which anyone who'd crossed him could have recognised, but Rhodri was too eager to put Dan in his place to notice. 'You're a damned nuisance you are, always right, sticking your nose in where it's not wanted and putting everyone's back

up. This is none of your business. I know what I have to do, just needed
Mungo to confirm it for me.'

'Dan, I wonder if you'd care to leave us now? Did you have
something to say to me?'

Dan hesitated. 'I did. But it can wait. I apologise, Rhodri, I wasn't
trying to tell you your job. Sorry.' He closed the door quietly behind
him and left to start his calls.

Mungo waited for the sound of his brisk footsteps to die away and
then turned to Rhodri. 'I've a full morning of appointments, so I can't
see you till about one. In my office. I've a few words to say to you.'

He also left, going first to collect his list of appointments and the
client files along with them. In reception he saw Bert Featherstonehough waiting patiently. Without warning Perkins hurtled down the
passage from Mungo's flat door, straight as an arrow into reception and
to where Adolf always preferred to sit. He put on his brakes when he
realised Adolf wasn't there, stood for a moment studying Mr
Featherstonehough and then placed a paw on his knee. Mr Featherstonehough bent forward to stroke his head and Perkins forgot his
manners and licked his face.

'Well, now then, Perkins, young fellow m'lad, he's not here, is he?
No, he isn't, you're right. And I think you know what's the matter.
You've been a good mate to my Adolf, haven't you?' Perkins snuffled in
his ear. 'Well, old lad, you won't be getting Kate's bucket of water over
you again, I think, perhaps. Unless there's been a miracle. My Adolf's
going to that doggy heaven where the rabbits all run slowly and the sun
always shines. Yes, indeed.'

How Mr Featherstonehough kept himself from breaking down no
one knew, for they were all close to tears. It felt as though a chapter in
the life of the Practice was ending. Perkins accompanied him into
Rhodri's consulting room, which he well knew was not allowed, and
was briskly removed by Rhodri, but no one had the heart to stop him
sitting outside Rhodri's consulting-room door.

Stephie whispered to Joy, 'Do you think Perkins knows?'

'It looks like it. Dogs are very perceptive, some sixth sense, you
know.'

'Poor Perkins, no more fights with Adolf. I shall miss him.'

'So shall I.'

Mr Featherstonehough came out of the consulting room, ramrod
straight, and marched to the main door, like the old soldier he was,
looking neither to right nor left. One of the waiting clients half rose
from their seat intending to say something consoling to him, but sank
back down again when they saw how close to breaking down he was. As

for Perkins he watched his friend disappear through the main door and then stood up and walked slowly into the back and up the stairs to Miriam for comfort.

When Stephie went to get a clean uniform from the laundry room she happened to glance out of the window and saw that Mr Featherstonehough's Volkswagen Camper was still parked outside. He was sitting in it staring out of the front window like a man made of stone.

'Should we go out to him do you think, Joy?'

'No. He's tough, regular in the military police, worked with army dogs till he was forty. He'll come to terms with it in his own way.'

'He'll be lonely when he goes back in the house and there's no dog there.'

'Of course, but knowing him he'll do something about that before too long.'

Stephie thought about that and then said, 'I expect you're right. Can't have been easy for Rhodri.'

'No. It's all he needs at the moment. Putting Adolf down. Poor Rhodri.'

Mungo knew the value of Rhodri's experience in the Practice and had no intention of asking him to leave but he did know he had to be firm. There must be no more being tough with clients and no more of this unpleasantness to Dan. He took off his reading glasses when Rhodri came into his office and leant back in his chair. 'Sit down. I've had a long morning and so too have you, and we both need our lunch hour, so let's not beat about the bush. How did Bert take it?'

'Very well. Said his goodbyes and marched out like the good soldier he is. Everything well held in, no tears, no breaking down. But underneath ...'

'I expect he'll be a while getting used to the idea. If it were Perkins ...'

'Exactly. You wanted to see me.'

'Rhodri, you know how much we value your experience? I don't want to lose you, either by you giving notice or me suggesting you find another post, but I really do have to say that I can't tolerate this business of you being at loggerheads with Dan. He's an excellent asset to the Practice and you must agree about that. He's bringing in more equine work than I'd ever hoped possible so not only his expertise but the money he's earning through equine is improving our finances no end. We can't expect that everyone will get on with everyone else just because they work together, but this vendetta with Dan is becoming childish.'

Rhodri strove to interrupt but Mungo held up his hand to silence him. 'I won't have it. Do you understand? It's all over nothing.'

'It isn't all over nothing. He dealt with that crazy dog Bingo and then examined the cat and more or less told me what I needed to do to save it, when it should have been either me or Graham or Valentine who should have done it. He's arrogant, he's always right and ...'

'Yes?'

'And he seems to have everything I want.'

'What's that?'

Rhodri shrugged his shoulders, he'd look a fool if he said he wanted a wife and a child like Dan. That he wanted some of Dan's 'get up and go'. Some of his bluntness. That it was sheer jealousy motivating the vendetta.

'Is there nothing to be done about Megan? Can't you marry her and go live there and sort it that way?'

'And have to tolerate that dreadful old beggar every day of my life?'

'God, man, the house is big enough, you could make him rooms of his own. Surely?'

'He wouldn't have that.'

'Wouldn't he just. Well, if he wants taking care of all the rest of his life the compromise can't be all one-sided. Megan's a great girl and very attractive, I can see why you want to marry her, but ...'

'Yes?'

'I do think that all this business is what is really at the root of your attitude recently. Something has to get sorted. I won't tolerate it much longer.' Mungo placed his fingertips together and looked at him very directly. 'You may be envious of Dan but with some effort you can be in the same position as him, with a lovely wife and a family. However, in the meantime, no more being abrupt with clients and no more fuelling this vendetta with Dan. I know he's outspoken, but at heart he's a very fair-minded, kindly man doing a good job, and well liked. Just like you.'

Rhodri looked at his hands as they lay on the desk. Well liked? Kindly? Fair-minded? Well, yes, he, Rhodri, was all of those. And in his better moments he knew Dan was all of that too. 'You're right. I'm starting to become a bit cracked over it all. Yes, you're right.'

'I know I'm right. Get your personal life sorted then and we'll all feel the benefit. Thank you for dealing so well with old Bert. I need my lunch.' Mungo got to his feet and Rhodri did too. 'No hard feelings?'

Rhodri shook his head. 'No hard feelings. You'll have no need to speak about it again.' But in his heart he knew he was defeated before he'd even begun. There wouldn't be a solution for him and Megan so long as that selfish old man lived.

That selfish old man as Rhodri had called him was being just that. Demanding and irritable and making Megan feel shredded. She kept her patience as long as she could, hoping that the bad mood would pass but eventually she snapped.

'Da! That's the tenth time you've called me in all over nothing. I've work to do even if you haven't, please let me get on with it.'

'I think that's the cruellest thing you've ever said to me. How can I work? I want to but I can't. And don't get in the habit of answering me back. I don't deserve it.'

'You do. This morning, you do. It's only nine o'clock and I'm worn out and I've a day's work to face. You're not being fair to me.'

'Fair? What's fair about the state I'm in, eh?'

Megan simply looked at him intensely.

'And you can take that sullen look off your face, I don't need that this morning.'

'I'm thinking of getting some help in.'

'I'm not having strangers wandering about this house pretending to flick a duster and costing a fortune. We're all right as we are.'

'We're not. And I wasn't thinking of someone to dust.'

Mr Jones's face went almost purple with rage. 'To do what, then?'

'To put you to bed at night and get you up in the morning and do your ablutions and stuff. A nurse, kind of.'

'A nurse? Absolutely not. That would be the end of me trying hard to be a person instead of an invalid. I try, damned hard too.'

'Don't try to appeal to my better nature, I'm reaching the end of my tether, but I don't suppose that's occurred to you. There's only Mr Jones in the whole wide world who's allowed to do that. Well, I'm telling you, Da, it's me who's done for, me who's exhausted, me who's—'

'What's got into you, girl? That Rhodri been at you again, trying to get you to marry him? Believe me, marriage isn't all it's cracked up to be, and I should know.'

Megan knew just where this was leading: into a tirade about her mother. But Megan had witnessed her mother weeping in the kitchen when her father was out in the fields. Knew about the physical revulsion her mother felt, the hatred when he'd raised his hand to her, never striking her but leaving her with the threat of it. The compassion Megan felt for his predicament flew out of the window on days like this.

'Da, for heaven's sake, don't start down that line. I'm sick of it. Now, I'm getting on with my work, you'll have to read the paper while I do.' She turned to leave the room, knowing he'd think of one more thing as she left.

'Don't forget my morning coffee, I—'

'When I'm good and ready, Da.' As she crossed the passage into the kitchen she heard him shuffling about on his table for his glasses and the rustle of the paper as he picked it up. For two pins she'd escape this very day. Leave him to rot. She looked round the kitchen and thought, there's nothing here that can't wait until tomorrow. She'd do it, just for the day. She put out on the worktop all the things for lunch, put the kettle on to boil for the coffee and then raced upstairs to get changed.

'Here we are then, Da, coffee with a piece of your favourite shortbread. I've left everything out for lunch, I'll have a word with Gab before I go.'

'Where are you going?'

'I don't know yet, but somewhere, because if I don't I shall go mad.'

'But what about me?'

'I've told you, I'll ask Gab to keep an eye.'

'But I don't want Gab to keep an eye I—'

'Just for today. Be seeing you.'

As she opened the door to go find Gab before she left, she heard him say, 'When will you be back?' but she didn't answer.

Gab was taking a break in the old tack room and his eyes lit up when he saw her in the doorway. 'Hello, Meggie my love, what can I do for you? Dressed up and off somewhere to see that feeble Welsh lover of yours, I've no doubt.'

'Right first time, but he's not feeble, not feeble at all. I'm leaving Da. Everything's out for lunch, could you see to him for me, Gab?'

Gab stood up and moved closer. 'Of course.' He put a hand on the door frame, just above her head, which placed him only a foot away from her. Looking into her eyes he said, 'Wish I was coming with you. Need a chauffeur? Eh? Though we'd have to go in your car, couldn't ask a lovely girl like you to ride in my old ramshackle thing. My, but you're beautiful. This morning there's a light of rebellion in your eyes and well do I like it.'

Megan pushed his hand off the door frame. 'Much more from you and I shall tell your mother about you and your fast ways.'

A slight blush had come on her cheeks and Gab revelled in it. 'Ooh! You wouldn't! She's fiercesome, she is.'

'So am I. Now make sure the lad does some work today. I caught him in the hay loft yesterday, in the middle of the morning, reading an obscene publication.'

'It's what boys do at his age.'

'Well, not in my time, not when I'm paying him to work. See!' She prodded his chest to emphasise her point and found her hand being taken to his mouth and kissed. 'Stop that, Gab! You need the money and I need you for the work and that's it. Full stop.'

Megan turned on her heel and marched to her car. The drive into Barleybridge cooled her temper. It was a wonderful morning and here and there shades of autumn were on all the trees, just enough to let you know winter wasn't far away. First she went to find Rhodri, an unprecedented move on her part. In the car park she met a neighbour. 'Hi there, Megan, come to see Rhodri, have you? He's busy, but I expect he'll find time for you!'

She met a receptionist from the medical practice just coming out of the main door, who put down her dog and said, 'Hello, Megan. How's your da at the moment? Keeping well?'

'Very well, thanks.'

'He's a lovely vet that Rhodri of yours, treated my Duke something lovely he has.' She twinkled her fingers teasingly at Megan and went round to the car park.

Honestly, thought Megan, your life isn't your own. They know everything. After a talk with Joy, who didn't seem to be her usual happy self, and a natter with Mungo, she began to feel like a person again and seeing Rhodri lifted her heart to such an extent that she kissed him in full view of the waiting clients and embarrassed him to death. But she didn't care and neither did he when he thought about it. They lunched at the Askew Arms, and thought about going away for a weekend together so they collected brochures from the travel agents. They were standing outside discussing where to go when Rhodri looked at his watch and said with horror, 'My God! I should have been back a quarter of an hour ago!' They fled hand in hand for the car park, zoomed down the slope to the exit with more speed than sense, and then raced off down the road to the Practice.

They were greeted with a round of applause by the clients in reception which embarrassed them both.

'He's getting as bad as that Scott, he is.'

'Where've you two been then?'

'I don't know, what it is to be in love.'

An old man, with a grin on his face, asked Megan, 'Does your father know you're out?'

Rhodri beat a hasty retreat to his consulting room, slipped on his white coat and when he saw who was the first on his list he almost groaned. 'Goliath Costello.'

Megan apologised for their late arrival to Joy, but she simply laughed and said, 'Don't worry, I'm glad you've put a smile on his face, he's badly in need of it.'

'I know. Something has to be done.' But she didn't enlighten Joy about what it should be.

Megan's last words echoed around Joy's head long after she had left. Had the time come to do something positive about Duncan being missing, but was he actually *missing*? Or had he kind of mislaid himself for a while because he needed time alone? He'd been dreadfully distraught and exceedingly frank the night she'd admitted she *tried* to love him. What a stupid, hurtful thing that was to have said.

When Joy got home that night she searched frantically for his passport, first in the place they always kept them, namely the secret drawer in his desk, but it wasn't there. They'd both renewed their passports at the same time so she checked her own and saw it was another two years before they needed renewing again, so it wasn't because he'd sent his off for renewal. But he wouldn't anyway without hers. So the truth dawned on her: he'd decided before he left that he might go abroad. A grown man in his right mind was free to go where he wished. It didn't mean he was in danger, did it?

Money! Did he have access to money? She checked the small amount of post, which had accumulated since he left. They'd always been scrupulous about not opening each other's post, but she overrode her feelings on the matter and stuck her thumb in the flap of the envelope from his bank and took out the statement. He'd withdrawn all the money and closed the account. This was when she began to think she should contact the police.

The next morning she went straight up to the flat to find Miriam. Mungo, she knew, had already gone downstairs to begin work so this was her chance. She found Miriam still at the breakfast table reading the morning paper.

'Hello! What can I do for you, Joy?'

'Just need a word.' Perkins hurtled in to have a word before she could say anything. 'Hello, my best dog. And how are you this morning?'

She found comfort in his greeting but it did nothing to lighten the pain in her heart.

Miriam put down the paper. 'Tea?'

Joy shook her head. 'Tea, no. Sympathy, yes.'

'What's the matter?'

'It's Duncan.'

'Yes?' Miriam realised Joy didn't look her usual self this morning and dreaded what she might hear.

'He's gone.'

Relieved, Miriam said, 'Oh! Is that all? He often does. How many times have you told me that? In the middle of a project, can't sort it, goes out for long walk, comes back. Resolved! Hey presto!'

'He's been gone for days and days. Taken his passport, clothes, and never got in contact once.'

'Why?'

'We had a row.' She told the whole story in detail and then, surprisingly, broke down in tears.

Miriam pulled a tissue from the box on the window sill, and handed it to her. 'He is a grown man, well used to surviving on his own. Accustomed to solitude. Just because he's taken his passport doesn't mean he's gone abroad. He's taken it just in case he decides to, I expect.'

Joy looked up at her and said sharply, 'Don't take it so calmly. He's a missing person, don't you understand?'

'But, Joy—'

'Never mind "But, Joy". That's what he is: a missing person. I just want to know where he is. If he's all right. You'd think the least he could do is ring me.'

'Joy! Joy! You should never have asked him to have sympathy for Mungo, of all people. No wonder he disappeared. He's probably sitting in some mountain hut somewhere in Switzerland, enjoying the sun, eating his breakfast, wishing you were with him.'

'Ever the optimist.' Joy wiped her tears away. 'I'm going to the police. Just to say he's kind of missing.'

'If it makes you feel better, you do just that. Take photographs in case.'

'Do you think he's laid on a mortuary slab somewhere and no one knows who he is?'

'You've watched too many TV hospital dramas, you have, Joy Bastable. He's got his passport, you said so yourself. Of course he's not, but if it puts your mind at rest then go to the police and inform them.'

'I will. At lunchtime.'

'Go now. I'll keep an eye downstairs. Look, I'm fully dressed, I'll fling the breakfast things in the dishwasher and be down there in two ticks.'

'Don't tell them where I've gone. Say it's a doctor's appointment. OK?'

'OK.' Miriam stood up, hugged Joy and said, 'Why shouldn't they know, though? You've a right to be anxious about your husband, surely? Go in our bathroom and adjust your make-up. I feel quietly confident he'll be all right. There's no need to worry.'

The police took it calmly too. Her husband was adult, in his right mind, and free to come and go as he chose. But yes, they'd keep an eye. Let them know if he came back. Description? Ah! A photo. Good. Well, it was on the records now, madam. With a lovely lady like you to come back to, he'll soon be home. Don't worry.

What else could she do but worry? The fool. In her heart she knew she'd have a long wait. Why on earth should Duncan *want* to come back to her? She looked in her rear-view mirror at herself. She didn't look like a lovely lady this morning . . . more like an old hag. To have said she *tried* to love him! She was such a fool. As she swung into the Practice car park, Joy braced herself to face everyone.

11

Dan was on veterinary duty at the weekly cattle market, so Rose had arranged to collect Mr Jones and take him to see it. He couldn't remember the last time he'd been to one and was up and about early to make sure he didn't delay Rose. Megan was flustered, hoping against hope that he didn't turn vicious on Rose as he did on her; some mornings the slightest thing could set him off. But he appeared too enthusiastic about his trip to bother being aggravating.

'You'll be all right on your own today? I'll be back before lunch though.'

'I shall be fine. Absolutely fine. You go and enjoy yourself. More toast?'

'I think I will. Now you're sure Rose will have room in her car for me? And the chair?'

Megan nodded. 'Of course. I've told you, they have a huge Mercedes estate. They've room for two wheelchairs.'

'Is the baby going, did she say?'

'No, the cleaner's taking care of him.'

'Pity, I'd have liked to see him. Rose is a lovely girl. Full of zest about everything.'

'She's very beautiful too. Such poise. Yet she doesn't rub your face in it like some people would do when they know they're lovely to look at.'

'Can't think why she fell for that ugly beggar. She could have had anyone she liked.'

'Da! He isn't ugly. Not at all. Just a bit craggy. He's lovely when he smiles.' Megan paused with her teacup almost at her lips and looked far away into the distance. Her da looked up and saw what he called her 'Rhodri look' on her face. He was about to say something cruel that would hurt her, but he changed his mind. He'd realised she was just as beautiful as Rose but she hadn't been given the opportunity to glow with love like Rose had. And that would make the difference. And why didn't she glow with love? He didn't get time to answer his own question because Rose was at the door calling, 'I'm here. Are you ready?'

They left for the market in a flurry of fitting in the wheelchair. Had he got his blanket for his knees? Would he need a hat? Should he . . .? Impatient of Megan's concern he said abruptly, 'Let's be off, Rose, or it will all be over.'

Rose kissed Megan goodbye and whispered, 'Have a quiet morning to yourself.'

Megan waved them off and went indoors, glad to be alone.

Rose parked her car in a space reserved for the disabled and got Mr Jones out and ensconced in his chair. He was so eager to see what was going on he didn't complain once about her ineptitude with the wheelchair nor the fact that she hadn't Megan's strength when it came to helping him out of the car. Mr Jones could taste the sounds and sights of the market before he could even see it, and he was looking forward to a reminder of life as it used to be.

He relished the goat pens, admired the cows, studied the chickens, ducks and geese, saw some pigs he rather fancied, and thoroughly enjoyed listening to the farmers and the farming community exchanging news and views.

They spotted Dan after a while near the sheep. He was arguing with a farmer about a dozen or so sheep in a pen in front of them. 'I'm sorry, I'm saying this for the last time, these ewes are not fit. I have to insist you withdraw them from the sale.'

The farmer, Bernard Wilson, a big burly man, unshaven and unkempt with a noticeably prominent broad nose, folded his arms across his chest and said belligerently, 'I'm damn well not listening to a load of soft in the head do-gooding tripe. There's nothing wrong wi' 'em that some good food won't cure.'

'I shall need to examine each one and if I find that any of them are unfit to travel then I'm afraid I shall have to put them down.'

'Put them down! You damn well will not.' He squared up to Dan, prepared to fight for his rights.

Tad Porter materialised beside Dan. 'I might have known that lot were thine. They're rubbish and tha knows it.'

'Since when 'as Tad Porter known better than me. I've been in't sheep business for forty years and I say there's nowt wrong wi' 'em.'

'I'd shame to own sheep in that condition.'

Phil Parsons erupted from nowhere shouting, 'You're at it again then, Bernard. I knew them were yours the minute I clapped eyes on 'em. Rubbish, they are. It's neglect that caused that lameness and there isn't a peck of flesh on 'em.' Phil leant over and reached into the pen, digging his fingers into thick fleece and feeling the spine of one of the sheep. 'Skeletons they are. Skeletons.'

Bernard put up his fists. 'And you can mind your own damn business. Yer can't even see 'em wi' that balaclava over yer eyes.'

Phil shouted, 'I may not make a fortune from farming, but I do know neglect when I see it. He's right, is Dan, they're not fit for sale. Cruel neglect, that's what.'

Tad Porter, puffing on his pipe, drew a powerful pull of smoke into his lungs, released it in a pungent cloud then said, 'Trouble is, Bernard, tha's idle. Phil's right, it's nowt but sheer neglect.'

Dan hadn't heard Tad speak in such long sentences ever before and sensed he was deeply stirred by the condition of the sheep, though there seemed to be another bone of contention mixed with his anger. Dan said firmly, 'You know as well as I do they are not in good condition and I've half a mind to get the RSPCA involved.'

By now a small crowd had gathered, hoping for some excitement to add an extra thrill to their day. There were murmurs of agreement from the crowd and someone who looked as though he might be an animal rights activist waded in with, 'Criminal! That's what. He shouldn't be allowed to keep animals if he can't care for them better than this. It's my opinion he should be prosecuted. Are you willing to put the wheels in motion?' He addressed his question to Dan, but before Dan could answer, Bernard had planted an almighty fist on the man's nose, knocking him back into Tad and Phil and scattering them into the crowd. Blood poured from the man's nose, splattering on anyone close to him. Bernard roared, 'And you can keep your nose out of it, too. I know you from before, you're another of them do-gooding activists.'

Dan intervened. 'Now, now this can all be settled quite amicably. Let's not get too excited.' Bernard advanced on Dan, who nimbly skipped out of his way, hands palm upwards. 'That's enough. We can't have a brawl in the middle of the market. I'm doing my job to the best of my ability and in all conscience I cannot allow these animals to be put up for sale. They are in such poor condition it amounts to neglect, like Phil said.'

Tad Porter stepped forward. 'It's not the first time he's brought sheep unfit for sale. He's done it before, but no one does anything about it. Even the RSPCA can't pin 'im down. You go for 'im, Dan. And while you're at it, look at 'is dogs.' In a quiet aside, Tad volunteered to take care of Bernard's sheep for a couple of months, get them up to scratch, sell them and give Bernard the money. 'Can't abide to see animals neglected like this, I may not like the chap, but his animals aren't to blame for that. It's a genuine offer. I feel real sorry for the poor old sods. You tell him.'

When Dan put Tad's proposal to him, Bernard exploded. 'Definitely not. I'm not a charity case. Far from it.' He took up his belligerent position again, arms folded, chest stuck out, bottom jaw jutting. 'Do your worst.'

The activist, having stemmed the flow of blood from his nose, said thickly through the clots of blood still blocking his nostrils, 'There's Richie! Come over here, you're needed. We'll see what the police think to this. I'll have him for assault.' He vigorously beckoned the inspector over.

Dan had had no intention of involving the police but it was now too late. Richie, whom he'd met at Bridge Farm, was coming across.

Mr Jones rubbed his hands with glee. 'I haven't had such fun in years.'

Rose wasn't quite so sure. She didn't count it as fun to see her beloved under threat from a bully like Bernard Wilson, and was, truth to tell, relieved to have the inspector on the scene. The activist wanted Bernard prosecuted for grievous bodily harm, and insisted on his right to have him charged, but Dan declined to get involved in charges about neglect, preferring to approach the whole matter on a long-term basis of ensuring Bernard was supervised much more closely and, dare he use the word, educated into a positive attitude rather than being under threat of prosecution.

It all fizzled out after a while because the inspector had to make notes and Bernard, seeing he was about to be arrested if he didn't calm down, lost his belligerent edge and was positively meek and mild. Only Phil Parsons and Tad Porter remained to see it through.

Phil said quietly, 'His dogs, he breeds beagles, are a disgrace. Disgusting conditions. Broke my Blossom's heart once when she fancied one and went to have a look. Filthy they were. The RSPCA had a go at him a year or so back, he improved for a while but they're as bad as ever I bet. Honest. He advertises pedigree puppies for sale in the newspaper, but I bet there isn't one that's in good nick. I'm off to the trailer for a coffee, want one?'

Dan nodded. Phil asked Mr Jones and Rose if they wanted one too and they both agreed. He came back with a tray laden with paper cups steaming with coffee, wooden spatulas instead of spoons, and a mountain of packets of sugar. Very pointedly he'd brought one for Richie too but not for Bernard Wilson. Tad Porter insisted he paid for his own. Phil refused his money. 'Don't be daft, there's no need.'

'I won't be beholden to anyone. We're all of us doing badly, you can't afford to be generous.' He pushed the money into Phil's jacket pocket. Phil said gruffly, 'There's no need for that.'

Mr Jones and Rose took their coffees to a quiet corner and Rose sat down on a wall to drink hers. 'I guess I'd no idea being a vet could be so ... well ... lively.'

Mr Jones gratefully took a sip of his coffee and then said, 'You've no idea how much I've enjoyed myself this morning. I haven't been to a market for ... well, I can't remember when, and I want to thank you for taking the time. You've made an old man very happy.'

Rose patted his arm. 'I've an idea you're not much older than my stepfather, so less of the old.'

'Where is he?'

'Coming to England next week on business. Privately, I think it's an excuse to see Jonathan. He's so proud of him, you'd think he was his own grandson. Which he is in a way, but not really.'

Mr Jones stared ahead at the auctioneer working his way down the pens. 'I miss out on life, you know. Megan can't marry, because she has me to look after and as for my son, well, he won't marry in a thousand years. He's ... you know.'

Rose thought she knew what he meant and simply answered, 'I see.' The tension between them was relieved by her mobile ringing.

'Rose, here.' She listened then said, 'Right, I'm on my way.' She snapped her phone off and said, 'Sorry, got to go. Jonathan needs feeding and won't be pacified with a bottle. I'll tell Dan. He'll look after you and see you home. I should have expected this.' She stood up from her seat on the wall, and Mr Jones thought yet again what a lovely girl she was. So elegant. And so ... well, beautiful.

'That's all right, my dear. I'm sure Dan will take care of me. Hurry home. And thank you.'

'I'll find Dan for you—'

'No. No. That's all right, I'll find him myself.'

'Are you sure, I don't like leaving—'

'Of course I'm sure, I *can* manage this thing you know. Megan can always come for me if needs be.'

Had Megan witnessed her father's surprising spurt of independence she would have been astounded. But at that moment she was more than occupied with the situation she was facing. Her dogs were not allowed to sleep in the house, but had warm, snug beds in one of the unoccupied stables. From time to time she cleared out the stable, washed their bedding and today, while her father was out, she was painting the inside walls to keep them fresh. She was wearing an old scarf around her head, because she always managed to splash paint everywhere and most especially on herself, an old pair of black wellingtons kept specially for the purpose, old cotton trousers and a shirt that had seen better days. This job she could do without his continual interruptions and she was busy singing while thinking about the coming evening when she and Rhodri were going to a classical concert in the old town hall.

She'd promised herself to make plans that would free her from her daily obligations to her da, but so far had not come up with any ideas. Bending down, Megan painted the last corner on the third wall and then turned the ladder round to paint the wall with the window and the door in it. She was adjusting the ladder to enable her to reach the topmost part of the wall when Gab appeared in the doorway.

'Here, let me do that.'

'No, thanks, Gab. I'm fine. I'm enjoying doing a job without a single interruption from Da. It's a pleasure, believe me.' Megan smiled at him so he would know she wasn't being uncooperative out of unfriend- liness. The dogs eddied around Gab's legs in greeting, he bent to acknowledge them and ruffled their ears, and chucked them under their chins. 'Great dogs, these. They know who is and who isn't welcome, don't they?'

'They do.' Megan placed the bucket of paint on the top step of the ladder and climbed up to begin painting. 'They're old and they're wise you know. Gyp is nine and Holly ten, you wouldn't think so, would you?'

'They still work the sheep like young 'uns, though. You'd never think . . .' A splash of Megan's paint landed on his sweater.

'Oh sorry! Here, use this old cloth to wipe it off.'

But as Gab took the cloth from her hand he gripped her wrist. She looked down in surprise and saw that look on his face, which he kept specially for her when her da wasn't looking. A blazing look, a daring, passionate look that unnerved her. There was something crude about it, and a boldness of which nothing good could come.

'That's enough, Gab.'

'No, it's not enough, it isn't even the beginnings of enough.' His grip tightened.

'Gab! Let go.'

'Come down.'

'I said, let go.'

'I said, *come down.*'

'I won't, Gab. Please. Don't make a scene. Please let go.' He didn't so she tried to twist her arm free, but it made him grip her even tighter.

Balancing on top of the ladder she couldn't put all her strength behind pulling her wrist away so she climbed down, but he mistook her reasons, thinking she was doing it in response to his demand. As her feet touched the ground he wrapped an arm around her waist and bent his head to kiss her. It was a ruthless kiss, which numbed her lips and stifled her breathing. Megan pressed both hands against his chest and pushed hard.

'Ahhh! I like reluctance, it enhances the chase.' He bent his head to kiss her again but this time she twisted her head away so he couldn't. 'It makes me all the more determined.'

'Damn you, Gab. Let me go. If you don't I'll—'

'Yes?'

She realised she had nothing to threaten him with. 'Just leave me alone. Please.'

Gab released her. 'You've no idea how I feel about you, have you? It hurts like a great pain in here.' He banged his fist on his chest as he spoke. 'Day in, day out. Unbearable. I need you, like a plant needs sun for its very life. I ache for you.'

'However much you feel, it won't get you anywhere.'

'Why not?'

'You're not my type.'

'Not your type? I'm the eldest son of a farmer who owns acres of land, and even you have to agree I'm attractive to women. I'm a good catch. Do you not feel even the tiniest little bit of something for me? I can have any girl I choose, you know, but it's you I want. Come on, Meggie my love, it's the lad's day off, your da's out, so why not? Let me show you what loving can be like. You won't be able to get enough of me, if you give me a chance. Believe me, I know.'

Gab pressed her hand to his lips and then he kissed her wrist, then the softness at the curve of her elbow and then the hollow of her throat, and Megan, briefly yielding to his persuasive lips, could sense the the truth of him saying he could have any girl he chose.

'Ha! The ice maiden begins to melt.' He kissed the hollow of her throat again and nuzzled his face into her neck while his lips pressed kisses on her warm skin. He lifted his head and looked intensely into her eyes. His hand strayed to the buttons at the neck of her shirt and began fumbling to undo them. That was when she came to her senses. Her hand holding the paint brush full of paint jerked into life and she smashed it as hard as she could into his face. Gab, blinded by the wet paint, was so startled he let go of her.

Megan, in charge of herself once more, followed up her attack on him with a vicious punch to his throat. He backed off coughing and complaining. Wiping off the paint as best he could without a mirror, he began to laugh, a roaring bellow of a laugh till his face grew red and he had to stop. Propped against the door frame he gasped. 'By heck. You're a harridan, you are. But it excites you, resisting me, doesn't it?'

'No. You disgust me.'

'You mean you're disgusted with yourself for fancying me, just then, just a tiny little bit. I felt a small surrender, I did.' He grinned a lopsided grin, which confirmed for her his attraction to women. He was going to add something but they both heard the sounds of a lorry turning into the yard so Gab stuck his head out of the door to see who it was. It was the feed.

Megan climbed the ladder again, dipped the brush in the can of paint and continued working on the rough stone surface of the stable wall. She trembled inside herself, shocked at finding just how vulnerable she had been for that moment. Her mobile rang, so she rubbed her hand on her trouser leg and fished it out of her pocket. 'Hello?'

'It's Da here. I'm ringing to say I'm lunching with Dan at the Askew Arms so don't worry about me.'

'You are?'

'Yes. He's bringing me home afterwards, Rose has had to go home to feed the baby, you see. Are you all right?'

'I'm fine, thanks. Have a good time.'

'You sound funny, odd like.'

'Bit breathless, I'm at the top of the ladder painting the dogs' stable. Enjoy, as Rose would say.'

'I can come home.'

'No. No. There's nothing the matter at all. Be seeing you. Enjoy. 'Bye, Da.'

Megan stuffed the phone back into her pocket, picked up the paintbrush again and carried on with her painting. By the time the lorry driver and Gab had unloaded the bags of feed, she'd put the last brush stroke on the wall and was ready for lunch. She stood for a moment admiring her handiwork thinking there was something enormously satisfying about completing a job like this. Washing out the brush under the outside tap Megan thought about her da having lunch with Dan.

But her father wasn't thinking about her at all as he sliced through a very tender piece of steak. 'I must say, Dan, I do appreciate you taking time to have lunch with me. Most considerate. What's happened about the chap with the sheep in such poor condition?'

'I've put three of them down. The rest are just about well enough to travel back. I've officially reported him.'

'So you should too. They were a disgrace to the farming community.'

'Tad Porter's taking them on, and he'll sell them and give Bernard what he gets. More wine? There's no love lost between them, but being a farmer Tad puts the animals' welfare first, even though he finds profit a thing of the past.'

Mr Jones proffered his glass to Dan with a nod. 'Thank you.' He took a sip. 'Remarkably good wine cellar they must have.'

'It was Lord Askew who introduced me to this wine. It's a good choice, isn't it?'

'You've dined with Lord Askew?'

Dan agreed he had, but only the once. 'He paid for it too, even though I was rude to him.'

'Can't stand the chap, myself.'

'You have to know how to handle him. Believe it or not I think he desperately wants to get on with people but doesn't know how.' Dan saw Lord Askew approaching their table.

'The man's a damn fool.'

Dan tried to catch Mr Jones's eye to warn him Lord Askew was coming up right behind him.

'A damn fool he is, that Lord Askew. A big, fat, blustering, self-opinionated fool. I've no sympathy for him.'

Dan cleared his throat, looked behind Mr Jones and said, 'Good afternoon, my lord.'

Mr Jones paused and then slowly put down his fork and painfully turned his head to look behind him, thinking Dan was joking. But, by God he wasn't. For once in his life Idris Jones was dumbfounded.

'Afternoon, Brown. Saw you in the market, thought I'd lunch with you, but you have a guest.'

'You'd be most welcome ...' Dan moved his chair to make room.

'No, no. Be so kind ... to introduce us.' He nodded at Mr Jones.

'This is Idris Jones, Beulah Bank Farm.'

'Never seen you here before.'

Lord Askew received a brusque reply. 'You're right, you haven't.'

Lord Askew moved forwards and offered his hand to Mr Jones and pumped it with comradely vigour. 'Good afternoon to you. You do right to get out and about despite your infirmities. Stunts the mind, makes one inward looking, selfish even, and one's view of life becomes ... distorted ... don't you know, if one doesn't make the effort. You'd better mind this chap,' he pointed at Dan, 'he's dynamite once he gets on your case. He'll have you climbing mountains before long. Enjoy your lunch.'

The restaurant manager, appalled by what he knew Lord Askew must have overheard, had been hovering nervously during this conversation and was relieved to be free to lead Lord Askew to the table he'd reserved for him.

Mr Jones commented, 'Hmm. He must have heard me.'

'He did.'

'Hmm. More of a gentleman than I gave him credit for.'

'Shall you climb mountains?'

'All depends what mountains you have in mind.'

Dan hesitated knowing he must choose his words carefully. 'I was thinking of . . . no, no. It doesn't matter.'

'Speak up, man.'

'I was thinking of a colleague of mine, lovely chap, sincere, who deserves a wife, and he's found a lovely girl he'd like to marry. But she can't marry him.'

Mr Jones put down his knife and fork, dabbed his mouth with his napkin and leaning back in his chair asked, 'Might I know this girl?' He raised his eyebrows at Dan.

'She's a stunner, an absolutely lovely woman, and deserves a happy life. You know, love and children and such. I can heartily recommend it. Believe me I can. Heartily.'

The waiter came to clear their plates. 'His lordship recommends the almond torte, sir. He said to say.'

Dan agreed. 'Then the almond torte it shall be and for you, Mr Jones?'

'The same.' When the waiter went away to get their pudding Mr Jones said, 'Has Rhodri put you up to this?'

'If he knew what I was saying he'd more than likely choke me to death. We don't get on. Neither professionally nor socially.' Dan smiled half an apologetic smile and waited.

The pudding had arrived before Mr Jones answered him. 'It's none of your damned business this. It's between Megan and me. Look at me, go on, really look at me.' He waited while Dan looked at him. 'I need her at home with me, I can't manage on my own, so that's an end to it.'

'That's selfish and what's more you know it.'

'How dare you speak in that tone to me?'

'Someone has to and today I'm your man. The days when elderly parents kept one of their girls at home to care for them in their old age are long gone and good riddance I say. Megan has as much right to a

543

life of her own as your son has. He's disappeared off into the night leaving the farm and you, without, I suspect, so much as a backward glance. So why shouldn't Megan disappear too?'

'Because she knows which side her bread's buttered, that's why.'

'There are other ways of going about it. What Megan needs is more help with her workload.'

'Like?'

'Help with the house, help to look after you. It's all possible with a bit of thought on your part. You could organise it for her, you haven't lost your faculties, your mind is razor sharp.'

'Hmmph.'

'Lovely pudding.' Dan raised his glass in the direction of Lord Askew and thanked him with a nod of his head. Lord Askew looked enormously pleased.

'I won't have coffee.'

'Right. I'll get the bill, time I was back at the Practice anyway.'

'I'll get a taxi then, can't stand much more of your sermonising.'

'I'll get shot down in flames if Rose finds out I didn't take you home. So please, allow me.'

Dan swung the wheelchair out from the table and went out of the restaurant paying the bill as he went. 'I promise not to sermonise all the way home, but think about what I've suggested.'

'Hmm.' And that was all that was said all the way back to Beulah Bank Farm.

That afternoon, Megan's da spotted some small flecks of dried white paint on Gab's eyebrows when Gab called in for his cup of tea in the kitchen, and he wondered if there was a reason for Megan sounding out of breath when he'd spoken to her on the phone. Purposely he invited Gab into the sitting room for a word when he was about to leave for the day. 'You're a good worker, there's no mistake about that. You've put more hours in than I expected and it's much appreciated, I shall give recognition to the fact in your wage packet.'

'Thank you, Idris. Thank you. It's a pleasure working for Megan and for you. I'll say goodnight.' He came back to ask if Megan was around. 'I've a message for her.'

'Upstairs, getting ready to go out, and she's running late.' Before Megan's father could say no, he couldn't go upstairs, Gab had gone, pounding up the stairs two at a time. Gab found her on the landing, in her dressing-gown, searching for something in a cupboard.

Megan looked up startled. 'What do you think you're doing coming upstairs?'

Gab ignored her indignation and came straight to the point. 'Not fallen out with me about this morning, have you?'

'Actually, I'm very angry about it. There's to be no repetition, you understand?'

'There won't be. I promise.' But the insolent grin on his face belied his words. 'See you in the morning. Half past five. I'll come and give you a knock if you like.' Again those lustful eyes slid from head to toe of her. Again that disarming grin, the joy of so many girls.

Megan gave Gab a disdainful look, found the shoes she was looking for, slammed the cupboard door shut and went into her bedroom, closing the door behind her.

Gab laughed to himself, ran back down the stairs to find Mr Jones in a fury waiting for him at the bottom. 'I did not give you permission to go upstairs. Under no circumstances do you go up there ever again. Your place is the farm. That's where you belong. Right?'

Gab sprang to attention, saluted and said, with an insolent grin on his face, 'Yes, sir! Three bags full, sir!' He bounded out of the house obviously unscathed by Mr Jones's anger.

12

Going home in the early hours from a night call Dan's headlights lit up someone weaving about in the road ahead of him when it was almost too late to take evasive action, and at the last minute he had to swerve to miss. A gateway came conveniently into view and he drove into it, thankful he hadn't hit whoever it was. Switching off the engine, Dan grabbed his torch and got out. His torch picked out a person now scrabbling helplessly in the road, trying to get up.

At the same moment, Dan heard a car coming from the opposite direction and waved his torch back and forth on the road to prevent the man being run over. As the vehicle drew near he saw it was Phil Parson's old van. By the light of his torch he realised Blossom was in the driver's seat. She jumped out leaving the engine running and the van in the middle of the road and shouted, 'Why Dan! It's you! Who's this?' Dan shone his torch on the person in the road and both he and Blossom said at the same time, 'Bernard Wilson!'

He was stoned out of his mind and reeking of alcohol.

Dan shouted, 'Bernard! It's Dan Brown from the veterinary practice. Can I give you a lift home?'

Bernard sat up, clutched Dan round his knees and mumbled, 'Taken a wrong turning. Where am I?'

Blossom answered him. 'On your way to Applegate Farm and the Caravan Park.' To Dan she said, 'This isn't the first time. Since his wife did a runner he's been on the bottle more often than not. He came to us one night and Phil made him sleep it off in a stable, wouldn't have him in the house. Phil has a drink but I've never seen him the worse for wear.' She gave Bernard a light kick with her foot. 'Get up, you daft ha'p'orth.'

But Bernard didn't get up. He said, 'Eh! I can't be. Applegate P-p-park Caravan, you say?'

'You are. Shall I give you a lift? Come on. Get up.' Dan put his hands under Bernard's substantial armpits and tried to heave him up but couldn't quite manage it, so Blossom volunteered her help.

'I'll take him home. I can lie him down in the van. I've done it before.'

They each put their hands under Bernard's armpits and together they staggered across to the van with him, his feet trailing on the road. Bernard protested. Blossom opened the back doors of the van and with an almighty effort they got Bernard in, lying him flat on his back on the mattress amongst the pink and white fluffy pillows. Blossom said, 'Couldn't be comfier, now could he?'

'Well, no. But I'm coming with you, you'll need someone to get him out at the other end.' Dan stood looking at Bernard laid in Blossom's boudoir of a van and wondered.

Blossom said, 'She left him destitute, you know, she took a load of money with her, he's never picked up since. In his own way he loved her. Poor chap.' She shut the van doors with a shattering, grinding clang, closing them on Bernard shouting loudly, 'Badger's Lot! First stop Badger's Lot. Hurry up. Badger's Lot. Home, Jameth and don't thpare the hortheth!'

Blossom giggled. 'Wait till I've turned round.' Blossom gave a masterful demonstration of how to turn a sluggish, out of condition van round in a narrow road, sprung it into second gear and moved off with Dan following, hoping Bernard would not retch his entire night's drink up on Blossom's fluffy pillows. He daren't begin to imagine what she'd been up to that night, returning home to Phil in the small hours.

When they opened up the van on arriving at Bernard's farm he was still singing his heart out, rolling about on the pillows, merry and exceedingly happy. Dan grabbed his ankles and pulled him to the edge of the van floor and then he and Blossom reached in to grab his arms and get him upright. As he straightened up he said, 'Go on, then, Blossom, my love, give us a kiss. Ten pounds for a kiss. Go on then. Ten pounds for a kiss.'

Blossom roughly pushed his head away from her face as his pursed lips drunkenly searched for her mouth. 'Not when you stink of beer. You know the rules. Ready, Dan?'

'We need the door open first. Let's see if he has a key.'

'He never locks up. It'll be open.' Together they headed for Bernard's house door, staggering under his weight as he was now almost unconscious with sleep and drink.

The door was not only unlocked but wide open. They squeezed in through the doorway and Blossom directed Dan to Bernard's bedroom.

'Thank God he sleeps on the ground floor, we'd never have got him up the stairs in this state.'

With the light switched on and coming in from the fresh night air Dan not only saw but smelt the state of the house. He'd seen some sights in his travels around the world but he didn't think he'd seen anywhere that matched the downright neglect and degradation of Bernard's kitchen. He'd thought Blossom's own kitchen was ghastly but this ... They had problems getting through it because the three of them kept tripping over things left abandoned on the floor, slipping on old food spilt carelessly and left to rot, and Dan was sure he'd spied a fat rat sneaking behind the cooker as they passed. Oh God! he thought, not rats too. Inside the house! They emerged into the hall where Dan unintentionally kicked a score of empty beer bottles, which dribbled their dregs onto the filthy threadbare carpet as they rolled about, adding to the general stink of the place.

He and Blossom finally heaved Bernard onto what passed for a bed; a greasy mound of sheets and blankets reeking of Bernard's unwashed body. Blossom pulled off his boots and heaped the blankets on top of him. 'There you are, Bernard, sleep it off. Goodnight, old man. Goodnight.' She patted his shoulder, shook her head in despair and made to leave.

The two of them, Blossom and Dan, stood outside Bernard's back door looking up at the night sky. Blossom said, 'Magnificent, isn't it? Puts everything into perspective, doesn't it, looking up at a night sky. All those millions of miles out there that you can't get your head round. Anyway, must get back.'

'Phil all right?'

'Oh yes! My night out tonight. He's used to me being late.'

Dan opened his mouth to say he didn't know Barleybridge had the kind of nightlife that kept one out on the tiles till this hour, but shut his mouth before the words were out.

'Something should be done about Bernard.' Blossom hooked her hand in the crook of his elbow. 'Every bit of him's in a mess. Especially his dogs. He's a great chap if only he didn't drink so much. He'll be all day getting over that skinful. Goodnight, Dan. Thanks for being a good Samaritan.' She reached towards his cheek and planted a kiss on it with her ruby red lips. 'Goodnight! You're a great chap. One in a million. My Phil thinks the world of you and so do I.'

She swung up into the van, her slender legs and her very neat bottom a temptation for any full-blooded male. Dan thought what a strange mixture she was. At once a tart, a good wife, and by the looks of the back of her van a ... no, she couldn't be could she? ... But where had she been till this time of night? Still, he'd never have got Bernard home without her. He remembered the rat and shuddered. Thought about his home and his own lovely bed and Rose snuggled beside him, warm and comforting and sweet smelling. As he turned for home, he looked forward to spending what remained of the night in bed with Rose and hoped to tempt her to stay there for at least part of the morning.

But the next day when Dan went in to the Practice at lunchtime he was a man of action again. First he had a word with Mungo concerning what steps he should take about Bernard.

'Want to keep the officials out of it, if we can. He's a desperate man, needs a good woman, but no self-respecting woman would take him on in the state he's in.'

Mungo retorted, 'We'll be running a marriage bureau for farmers next. Just watch your step, Dan. There is a limit.'

Dan eyed Mungo and thought, What's got him out of his pram this morning? But he ignored the sarcasm. 'Can I take Rhodri with me to look at the dogs? He puppy farms you know. Beagles.'

'I think that would be a good idea. But not too much of the social work, Dan. We're not a charity.'

'I appreciate that, it's the animals' welfare I'm most interested in. We can't stand by and just let it happen. That would be irresponsible on our part.'

Mungo sighed. 'It would. Yes. Not too many hours though. Like I said ...'

Together they both added, 'We're not a charity,' and laughed.

Dan went to find Rhodri. 'Have you time to spare today for going with me to see Bernard Wilson's kennels?'

'You mean you're actually asking me to go with you, actually asking me for help?' The sarcastic tone of his voice couldn't be missed.

'Yes. You've told me more than once to keep to my side of the Practice so I am. In any case, you're much more au fait with dogs than I am. After all, it is your field of expertise. I understand they're being kept in appalling conditions. Could all be hearsay, but I've an idea it isn't.'

'Someone brought a puppy of Bernard Wilson's in a few months ago. I didn't reckon much to him – too thin, flea ridden, riddled with worms, you know the kind of thing. I'd be glad to come. Very glad indeed.'

'Excellent. Bring something with you, whatever you think might be needed. I'm more interested in his sheep after an altercation in the market about the condition of some he brought in for sale.'

'Right. I've no operations this afternoon, if you're free?'

Dan nodded his agreement, and within the hour they were on their way to Badger's Lot and Bernard Wilson.

Rhodri had refused to go in Dan's Land Rover so they were travelling in Rhodri's own Citroën. To break the ice Dan commented on how much he liked it.

'It suffices.'

'More than suffices, it's great. Comfortable ride too.'

'Yes.'

Badger's Lot was a turning off the main Weymouth Road. The lane was narrow and in places the tarmac had worn away, but with Barleybridge having had a dry summer the ruts weren't too bad, though Rhodri's suspension took a bashing as they passed the open gate to the farm.

'Good grief! Those ruts.'

'I'm afraid that's symptomatic of what we shall find when we get there. Though to my knowledge he's never called us out all the time I've been at the Practice, so I don't actually know. He was blind drunk when Blossom Parsons and I took him back home last night. I've no idea what state he'll be in this afternoon.'

Rhodri didn't answer, giving the whole of his attention to the preservation of his adored car. But as they reached the farm buildings he said, 'Oh my word! What a mess.'

Corrugated iron sheds were in a state of imminent collapse. There were stables with gaping holes in the roofs where the tiles had fallen away. The surface of the farmyard had sprouts of weeds growing between the cobbles, a stable door swung bleakly on its broken hinges. Bernard's old lorry stood lopsidedly, one tyre completely flat. But the silence was the weirdest thing. A deep, deep silence in which only the gentle purr of the engine of Rhodri's car could be heard.

Dan hoped he wasn't going to find anyone dead. He'd been there, done that, and he didn't want to face it again.

But he didn't have to. Bernard was in the kitchen, sitting at the table drinking tea from a mug. A gigantic teapot, once brown and shining and welcoming, now streaked with old tea stains and even older dust, stood on the table and Bernard was refilling his cup from it as they went in.

'Visitors! By hell! Visitors! Busybodies more like. Come to see if I'm drunk, have you? Well, I'm not.'

Dan spoke up. 'Dropped you off last night. Found you in the road. Come round?'

Bernard eyed him up and down. Slurped some more tea into his mouth and having swallowed it said, 'It was you? Thought it was Blossom Parsons.'

'Her too, we happened to arrive at the same spot at the same time and took you in hand. Feeling better?'

Bernard nodded. 'Grand woman that Blossom. Grand loving woman.' He slurped at his tea again and asked Rhodri what he wanted.

'Well, boyo, I've come to see your dogs.'

Sensing interference, Bernard, slowly and with great control, asked, 'Why?'

Rhodri stepped back a pace. 'To check if they're all right, see.'

'Joined the do-gooders, 'ave yer?'

'No. But I'm a vet and I can't bear to see neglect.'

'Who said anything about neglect? Not me. I suppose I've no option seeing as there's two of you. They're in the sheds. Not fed 'em yet, only just woken up. That was my next job.' Bernard stood erect by levering himself up via the kitchen table. He was a mountain of a man, bulging in all the wrong places with his pugnacious, heavily jowled face set just how it had been over the sheep in the market. He lurched out of the back door into the farmyard.

To their horror Dan and Rhodri realised Bernard was leading them to the sheds. They exchanged glances but said nothing. Once inside the sheds they could distinguish through the gloom several runs carelessly constructed from chicken wire. In them were dogs of all ages wading in their own filth. The stench was appalling. It was difficult to see through the gloom if any of them needed attention. Above one run the roofing had fallen in allowing the rain to penetrate. It was mud-filled and young puppies were listlessly paddling about in it. There were wretchedly dirty feeding bowls standing about, bereft of food, and worse, no drinking water anywhere.

Dan stood silent, hurt beyond belief. Rhodri's heart was pounding with distress. Dan flashed him a warning glance, which Rhodri minded to heed. Taking a deep breath he said, 'It seems to me you've not been well, Bernard. Otherwise you wouldn't have let it be like it is.'

'Tha's polite if nothing else. Yes, I've been ill, you could say that.'

'Managing on your own?' Dan enquired.

Bernard nodded.

Rhodri shouldered the responsibility for action. 'I see there's one stable that's still got the whole roof left on it. How about if we clear it out and I'll sort out which dogs are OK and we'll put them in there. Dan, you can wash out the bowls and Bernard you get the food ready for the bowls when Dan's finished. Also water, if you please.'

'That stable has nowt in it at all, 'cept a load of old sacks from years back,' Bernard volunteered.

Dan raised an eyebrow at Rhodri but he didn't notice, so to inspire Bernard, Dan began his job by collecting the bowls. The worst job was Rhodri's. He carefully removed any dogs who appeared reasonably healthy and carried them across to the stable he'd decided upon. Bernard was right, it was full of old sacks. Rhodri kicked them aside, thinking he'd keep them clean to use as bedding. Ten dogs, of all ages and in varying degrees of neglect were put in the stable. The rest Rhodri carefully examined; two breeding bitches, old and in such poor condition he would be doing them a kindness by putting them to sleep. This left eight young dogs all about five or six months old, which Bernard had bred but obviously had not been able to sell, and no wonder.

Dan appeared with a stack of feeding bowls and a plastic washing-up bowl he'd spotted amongst the rubbish in the corrugated iron shed. He'd cleaned them all, and filled the plastic bowl with fresh water. 'Where's Bernard?'

Desperately distressed by what he'd found Rhodri said, 'I can't believe this. There's two I want to put down, because they're worn-out breeding bitches, too many litters, too little food, and looking at this motley lot, three have dicky hearts, three are so thin because of starvation and worms I don't know whether to put them to sleep or let Bernard give them a second chance.' Rhodri pointed to one. 'That pup's got deformed legs, due, I've no doubt, to too much inbreeding and too little calcium over the years. So he'll have to go. I think Bernard should be prosecuted.'

'He's coming. Put that one to sleep that's deformed, he can't be helped, he's leading a miserable life and can only get worse. Let's give the others a chance.'

Bernard arrived with an enormous bucket of feed for the remaining dogs. Rhodri gave himself no time to think. 'These two bitches, I want your permission to put them down.'

'Nay! Them's my two best bitches.'

'*Were* your two best bitches, Bernard. They've worn themselves out breeding for you. Two litters a year, was it? The first before they were a year old? Eh? For what, seven years? Eh?'

Bernard put down the bucket he was carrying. 'Sometimes.'

Rhodri raised his voice in anger. 'It's criminal, Bernard. This one I'm putting to sleep because he'll never find a home crippled as he is. You should never have let him live, it was cruel. These I'm hoping, with your help, to build up into handsome little dogs. They're well marked, someone will want them. They all need worming absolutely without doubt. I'm deeply grieved.' He shot such a woeful look at Bernard that he looked embarrassed.

'I don't want 'em like this. It's that I haven't been well, and things have gone from bad t'worse. Just needed some help. You know.'

Rhodri nodded. Silently he got on with worming the dogs he wanted to save, organising Bernard to dig a hole to bury the ones he'd put down, and then between them they emptied another stable that only required plastic sheeting to cover the place where the tiles had slid off the roof and it made a safe, warm, clean place for the younger dogs to be kept.

Finally, the dogs got fed and watered and the hessian sacks, stored for years, were shaken out and used to make reasonably satisfactory bedding for them.

Dan looked at his watch. 'Time we went. We've made a start for you. Tad's got your sheep, and we've done what we can today for the dogs. Either Rhodri or I will be back tomorrow afternoon to see the progress you've made in erecting an outside run for these dogs so they can move out of the stables and into the fresh air and be able to get some exercise.' He glanced at Rhodri hoping he had his approval and said, 'We don't want to get the authorities involved, but by God, Bernard, Rhodri will have your guts if you don't improve your standard of care of these dogs. Won't you, Rhod?'

'Absolutely.'

They were both silent for a while after they left Badger's Lot and then Rhodri broke it by saying, 'I don't think I've seen such systematic cruelty in all my life. Downright appalling, it was. And the strange thing about dogs is they don't bear grudges.'

'I thought they were all very quiet, very subdued. I think if we hadn't gone there today some would have died in the next few days. They might still die if we don't give him support. The chap's completely lost heart. You should have seen his sheep! Thanks for coming with me. Thanks for your expertise, too. I've nothing but admiration for the way you kept your temper when you were so angry.'

'He's a mental case really.'

'What good will it do anyone if he ends up in hospital?' Dan cleared his throat and looked out of the window for a moment and then said, 'I reckon his stud dog has already died. Otherwise where is he?'

'Hadn't thought about that, but I bet you're right. He must have had his own stud dog, no self-respecting breeder would want him taking his bitches for mating when they were in such bad condition. He must have had his own.'

Dan decided on a change of subject. 'Old Man Jones enjoyed the market the other day.'

'Yes, he did. Full of it when I went to see Megan. What he needs, really.' He fell silent while he negotiated the dreaded roundabout just outside Barleybridge. 'Can anyone tell me why they have to make a roundabout where you can go either way round it? I think the transport planners should be lined up and shot.'

Dan chuckled. 'Too right. Will you go tomorrow?'

'I will. My half day today so I'll drop you off now, and then I'm going to see Megan.'

'She's worth fighting for. Old Man Jones might be coming round to getting Megan some help. I put the ball in his court at lunch.'

'You did?'

'Told him he was no fool. I said his mind was razor sharp . . .'

'Too right, it is. In more ways than one where Megan's concerned.'

'Rose is taking him to a game fair at the weekend. She's determined to get him out and about.'

'That's wonderful.' By now they were parked in the Practice car park. Rhodri turned to look at him and spoke without any of the resentment his voice frequently held when speaking to Dan. 'We do appreciate Rose taking him out. By the time Megan's done the farm work and the cooking and things and attended to her father she hasn't any spirit left for taking him anywhere at all. Anyway he wouldn't go even if she could find the time, but he will with Rose.'

Dan thanked him and added, 'Tell you what, Rhod, you'd better watch that big beggar Gab, he's got "stud" written in large letters on his forehead.'

Rhodri's mind absorbed the shock of hearing his own fears voiced and then he replied, 'Well, I wouldn't have put it quite like that, but I do know what you mean.'

'If he decided to act upon his feelings Megan wouldn't have a chance, and Old Man Jones couldn't do anything about it if he did.'

'Get out. I'm off.' Rhodri revved the engine up with spirited determination and Dan leapt out, thinking if he didn't he'd be at Beulah Bank Farm before he could draw another breath. As he shut the car door he said, 'I'll leave Bernard to you, tomorrow.'

Rhodri nodded and the wheels were turning before Dan had shut the door.

Rhodri reached the humpbacked bridge and as he passed over it he thought he'd caught sight of Megan's jade cardigan out of the corner of his eye. He braked, reversed, parked and jumped out. He went to lean his arms on the wall of the bridge and look over. He was right, it was

Megan, lost in thought, gazing at the stream, as it bubbled and dashed along over the stones. She hadn't realised he was there and for a moment he enjoyed watching her. She'd fastened her hair back with combs so it hung down her back but off her face, so he could see her profile unhindered. There was a loveliness about her that almost made his heart stop beating. The sun wasn't shining but it seemed to him that she glowed without its help. His heart flipped into action again, but he still didn't let her know he was there. What Dan had said about Gab sprang into his mind. God! If ever he . . . He'd better let her know he'd seen her. Rhodri found a small loose shard of stone on top of the wall, picked it up and threw it into the water, looking forward to her brilliant smile as she looked up and recognised him.

But he didn't get what he expected.

Instead, the face he saw when she looked up was filled with a kind of bitter determination as though she was steeling herself to keep a grip on fear. Then when she saw it was him, relief flooded it and he was rewarded with a wan smile and a wave of her hand.

He was down the slope and beside her in a moment, his arm around her waist, hoping to dispel her mood. 'My afternoon off. Would have been here earlier but I went with Dan to a cruelty case. Kiss?' Rhodri squeezed her tightly to him and kissed her temple, because she still hadn't looked at him properly.

Megan's arm crept round his waist and they stood silently staring at the water. She couldn't tell him. Couldn't find the words, not the right ones that would explain why she was here in her private paradise, trying to come to terms with the dreadful afternoon.

It had all begun when her father had had an altercation with Gab about some minor neglect of the farm work, so minor that in fact the reason for the upset had become quite lost in the subsequent turmoil. The three of them were in the kitchen eating lunch, her father having taken to eating with her and Gab at lunchtime to make sure, as her father had put it, there couldn't be any nonsense from Gab.

They'd both ranted and raved about it to begin with but then more pressing matters emerged and Gab became exceedingly angry.

'Look here, Idris, I'm not a common or garden farm hand for you to take to task, I'm the eldest son of a well-to-do farmer, helping you out. That's all. Helping you out. I could walk out of here this minute and leave you to it. Up to milking, are you, up to going up the hill to the sheep, checking they're OK? Rounding them up. Marshalling the dogs? Eh? I don't think so, bit of hedging and ditching, unloading the feed bags? Up all hours in the lambing season? Eh?'

Mr Jones didn't have an answer to all that.

'Getting the cows in the crush for TB testing? Are you up to that? I don't think so.' He paused expecting an answer, and when he didn't get one, continued his tirade. 'In that case, if you've nothing to say, don't come criticising me from the comfort of that armchair of yours. Meggie and me manage very well, don't we, Meggie?' He took her hand and held it and she couldn't pull it away.

'Please, Gab, let go of my hand.' She said it so quietly, so gently, that anyone else would have done as she asked immediately. But not Gab. No, not Gab. He held it even more tightly and said to her da, 'Mr Jones, this daughter of yours, I want to marry her. I'll live here and when you get as you can't even walk about, I'll carry you wherever you want to go. I'll look after you, in a way that that Welsh lover of hers isn't willing to do. How's that for a promise? I'd be a fine asset for this place. Very useful to have about, and I'd care for Meggie here, like no one else could. So, I'm telling you I'm marrying her and she wouldn't be unwilling.' He looked round the kitchen as though he already owned it.

'Marriage! To an ape like you? I don't think so. Ha! Certainly not! She's here and here she stays.'

'Exactly! Here she stays with me, the three of us together.' The tone of his voice was eager. 'You'd have some fine healthy grandchildren, I'd see to that.'

Megan had shuddered and he'd felt it because he was still holding her hand. 'She won't admit to it but she can't wait. That poofter of a Welshman couldn't stir a rice pudding never mind Meggie. She's mine is Meggie. So what do you say? Come to think of it, you haven't much choice.'

Megan's da replied, 'I'd sell the farm first.'

'Oh! Brave words, those. Brave words. But only words. In the present climate you'd get nothing like its value.'

Megan's da got to his feet. 'Megan, help me back to my chair in the sitting room. I've had enough of this.'

Gab released her hand and she took her da back to his chair. As he sat down he whispered fiercely, 'I would, you know, I'd sell it first.'

'Don't worry, I'm not marrying him whatever he says.'

She'd waited to hear Gab leaving the kitchen and when he'd gone she'd tidied up the lunch things and made the dinner for the feral cats. They were waiting for her, stood about at various vantage points, eyes glinting. Only six today. Briefly she wondered where the other two were, but she opened up the stable door and put down two bowls of food. They always waited outside, fearful of being trapped, but it was Megan who was trapped because in the gloom of the stable she hadn't noticed that Gab was standing in there waiting for her. Her heart leapt into her throat and she thought, he knows my movements as well as I know them myself. As she turned to go out he took her arm and pulled her to him. 'I meant it. I really do. You and me. This farm. We'd make a go of it.'

He reached out and snatched at the stable door to close it.

Megan struggled to free her arm.

'Gab, please don't. You can't make me marry you. You really can't.'

'Then I'll leave. This minute. Right now.' He folded his arms across his chest and waited. By now the cats had gathered their courage and were standing by the door, the bravest daring to squeeze their way in.

Her heart sank at the prospect if he left. 'Forcing my hand is no way to make me want to marry you.'

'I could always tempt you instead.' He'd looked at her with that passionate look she'd grown to dread.

'Well, you won't. Sorry, Gab, but you won't. You'll find someone one day. Believe me.' Out of the corner of her eye she saw the cats trying to get in. Matter-of-factly she'd said, 'Now, the cats are getting desperate. Come on. Let them in.'

Some of the determination went out of him and he looked less the passionate suitor and rather more the determined supplicant. 'I won't give up wanting to marry you. And I'm not leaving. I think enough of you to know what it would mean if I weren't here. I love you, Meggie, like I've never loved anyone before. I've said it plenty of times to girls, but only because I knew that was what they wanted me to say, never because I really *loved* 'em. But with you it's different. I haven't even looked at another woman since I came to work here, if that's any recommendation. Faithful. That's what I would be. Staunch and faithful. I'd do what was right by you, and I'd work this farm, till they'd all be jealous of our success. You and me together.'

He took her into his arms, despite her resistance, and kissed her with such passionate ferocity that she knew instantly that his kind of loving couldn't ever be right for her. When he'd stopped long enough for her to draw breath she said, 'It's no use, Gab, it's no use.' Gab looked down at her with a kind of raging disappointment in his eyes that frightened her. He strode out of the stable across the yard and into the milking parlour, leaving her exhausted and emotionally spent. That was when she'd abandoned everything she'd meant to do and come here to her private paradise to recover.

Eventually Rhodri said, 'What is it, love? Needing five minutes to yourself?'

'Yes.'

'Shall I leave you here then? Or can I give you a lift up to the farm?'

'Don't leave me here. I'll come.'

'Before we go, tell me what the matter is. Please.'

No reply.

'Is it your da playing up again?'

No reply came, but her arm tightened round his waist.

Rhodri held on to her and waited.

'I'm being ridiculous. It's time I pulled myself together.'

'You're never ridiculous, and you don't need to pull yourself together, you're the most pulled together person I know, see.'

He turned her to him and hugged her, but after a moment she drew away from him. 'It's Gab.'

Oh God! thought Rhodri, recollecting what Dan had said. He asked as gently as he could, 'Is it, love? What's he been doing that's upset you?'

'He comes closer every day. You could say, and this sounds stupid, he's getting a hold on my mind. I know he's wanting to . . . oust you.'

'But what's he *doing* to make you feel like that?'

'Nothing. Not really.'

'Well then, perhaps you're overtired, things always seem worse when. . .'

Megan stood away from him, her eyes blazing with indignation. 'I'm not in my teens, Rhodri. I do know what I'm talking about. Don't belittle me by saying I'm tired, I'm always tired. I've a massive sleep debt, but it doesn't mean I've lost my senses. Far from it. I'm acutely aware of him and his need of me and I don't like it. If I sack him then I've everything on the farm to do myself and I can't, simply can't, take on any more work. I need him like a drowning man needs a lifebelt. So don't suggest it, unless you have a viable alternative.' Megan flaring up as she did only made Rhodri think she must have good cause.

'Are you sure he's done nothing?'

Her temper cooled instantly but all Megan could say was that he came too close to her, all the time and had in fact kissed her, the more angry she got with him the more daring he became, mistaking her anger for passion.

'Passion!'

'He thinks every woman he meets finds him irresistible. And I can see why. He is irresistible. That's the trouble.'

'Irresistible? My God! I'll kill him.' Rhodri clutched Megan to him and held on to her till she protested. He released her saying, 'Megan, get in the car. Your da in?'

'Of course, what else?'

'We'll make him a cup of tea and then you leave me to talk to him.'

He gripped her hand as they climbed the slope up to the lane, stowed her in his front passenger seat and, still breathing heavily, climbed in on the driver's side and revved up the engine. Beating in his brain was the word 'stud' till there was nothing else in his head but that.

They roared up to the farm. Rhodri parked beside Gab's crumbling heap of a car and in his fevered imagination he thought, That sod will be like his own car by the time I've finished with him. Gab was nowhere to be seen, so they went into the kitchen and prepared a tea tray together. Rhodri carried it into the sitting room to find Mr Jones waking up from his afternoon sleep, stretching as best he could and yawning too.

'Good afternoon, Mr Jones. Nice bright day for September.'

'But there's a chill in the air, we can't forget it's autumn.'

'You're right there. Now here's your tea. We've timed it nicely. Who's this mug for, Megan?'

'Gab. Pour it and I'll take it into the kitchen for him.'

Rhodri, grateful Gab didn't drink his tea in the sitting room, said generously. 'Cake too?'

Mr Jones answered him. 'Of course. Cake. He needs to be kept sweet, does Gab, we can't manage without him.'

'I wish you could.'

Megan went out with Gab's tea and cake and didn't come back.

Rhodri took his opportunity. 'Look, Mr Jones, I'm feeling very concerned about Gab. I feel, no, I *know* he's a threat to Megan, and I want something doing about it.'

'I've tried to find someone else but I can't.'

'Do *you* find him a threat to her?'

Mr Jones hesitated and then said, 'Has she said so?'

'This afternoon.'

Mr Jones put down his cup of tea. 'He's getting too familiar with her. I can see that, and far too cocky.'

'Will you agree to us marrying? That would put a stop to it, I'm sure.'

'Absolutely not, Rhodri Hughes. I need Megan here with me and that's that. Good try, Rhodri, good try.'

'And you're willing to put her in jeopardy for your own selfish ends?'

'He won't dare make a move on her, not with me here. Believe me. I have his measure.'

'What I fail to understand is that you bought this farm in the full knowledge that you wouldn't be able to do the work yourself. I can't help but ask why.'

'I'll tell you why. Howard, that's my son, Megan's brother, is one of those who lost his job in the city overnight. There was an ugly fraud case and it meant they had a complete clear out of anyone even remotely connected with it. Howard was one of them. He claims he had nothing to do with it, but I have my doubts, he's easily led. He'd a massive mortgage on his flat, and no money coming in. So he rented the flat out and came home. Came home! To Wales, and did nothing but moan about how isolated we were. Can't imagine why he thought it was any different from when he'd grown up there. He was at a loose end, not knowing what to do so I suggested he took up farming. I said, it's a thriving business, hard work but the returns are there, so why not? He leapt at the chance but said he had to be nearer London, so he could be up there in a couple of hours at the most. I was so delighted he'd come home and was willing to farm I agreed to move. We sold up and came here. We'd been here three months and I was beginning to think it was working out well, after all he'd been brought up with farming and as a boy he'd loved it. Then, out of the blue, he got a call from one of his so-called friends with the promise of a job and immediately he went back to the city and the life he preferred, leaving me and Megan to carry on as best we could. That's why we're here, and as Gab so rightly said only this afternoon, to sell up now would be sheer idiocy.'

'I didn't realise. Megan never mentions him.'

'No wonder. Such a betrayal. She can't bear to say his name out loud. She was distraught when he left. So was I.' For the first time since Rhodri had known him Mr Jones's eyes filled up with tears.

Rhodri stood up and made the feeblest of excuses. 'I'll get some more hot water, I expect you'd like another cup?' Not waiting for an answer he went to the kitchen primarily to make sure Megan was all right. She was. Gab was sitting at the table with her, concentrating on his tea and cake.

'Here comes the Welsh lover. Hot-foot, ardent and up for it.'

Rhodri objected to his familiarity. 'For a start, you can shut up, nobody asked your opinion. More tea, Megan?'

'Oh! The worm has turned.' Gab laughed and, imitating Rhodri's Welsh accent, he said, 'More tea, Megan?'

'That will do, Gab. If you've finished, you'd best get back to work.' Megan glared at him as she spoke, but it only invited Gab to be even more confrontational towards Rhodri. He stood up, bent over towards Megan and said, 'Right, Meggie, my love, I'll be off then. Milking calls.' Then he darted towards her and kissed her on the lips and with a jeering glance at Rhodri he went out. But he hadn't bargained for Rhodri leaping into action at this affront to his male pride. Before he knew it he and Rhodri were wrestling out in the passage. The noise they made brought Mr Jones to the door of the sitting room.

Unfortunately for Rhodri, his anger had made him reckless; he'd disregarded how big and how fit Gab was. The fight was unequal in every way. Gab was a head taller, and much stronger than Rhodri and if it hadn't been for Megan picking up a tin tray in the kitchen and hitting Gab on the side of his head with it so he was momentarily stunned, there would have been an ignominious ending to the fight for Rhodri.

Breathing deeply Rhodri stood back and Mr Jones shouted, 'Get out! Get out the pair of you. Fighting in my house. I won't have it. Gab, pull yourself together. It was a mere tap she gave you. Get on with the milking, that's what you're paid for.' He was gripping the door frame by this time and his breath was rasping in his throat, his chest visibly heaving with every breath he took.

'Da! Da!' Megan rushed to his side, all thoughts of the threat of Gab gone from her mind.

Rhodri opened the back door and almost kicked Gab out. 'Get back to doing what you know best.' There was a very satisfactory feeling for Rhodri as he said that. He slammed the door shut so hard the house echoed with the noise.

Mr Jones could no longer castigate him, for he was incapable of speech. Megan got him back in his chair and gave him his inhaler. Rhodri took the tea tray out, put the cups and plates in the dishwasher, lined the tea canister up with the other kitchen jars, put the sugar in the cupboard, and sat down to wait. There would be no point in going to see if he could help Megan with her father, his presence would only make matters worse.

What he didn't like was the realisation that had hit him when he saw Gab kissing Megan. Out of the blue he could understand what it was Megan was talking about when she said that Gab was irresistible to women. He was. He had a kind of sexy charm to him, a sinewy, physical, powerful sort of attraction, and Rhodri hated him for it. His own part in the drama appeared useless if not downright pathetic. He admitted to himself that Gab was more of a man than he.

He heard Megan's footsteps coming towards the kitchen. Rhodri stayed silent, trying to pick up on her state of mind so he wouldn't say the wrong thing.

As soon as she shut the kitchen door she burst out, 'What made you do it? Honestly, Rhodri, I thought you would have had more sense. You'd better go home, while I see to Da.'

'He's got to go.'

Horrified, Megan said in a loud whisper. 'I'm not putting Da in a home. What are you thinking of?'

'No, no. I meant Gab.'

'Oh! I see, of course. Find me someone else to do his work and he'll go, till then I've got to stick with him.'

'Right.' Rhodri didn't dare offer to kiss her before he went. 'I'll be off. I'll go to Kate's drinks party by myself, then?'

Megan nodded. 'She'll understand I can't come. Give her my good wishes. 'Bye, Rhodri.'

She went out of the kitchen leaving the door wide open for him. So that was it. He was dismissed and he couldn't even have the pleasure of her company at Kate's leaving party. All he had to look forward to tomorrow was visiting Bernard Wilson to check on the dogs. Big excitement that would be. He was so angry about the whole situation at Badger's Lot he knew he'd have to keep his temper in check or else Dan would have something to say if he lost it and made the whole situation even worse than it was. He paused by the back door, debating whether or not to say goodbye to Mr Jones, but decided not to. He went out into the yard hoping against hope he wouldn't bump into Gab before he left. He'd been such a fool to pick a fight with him. Thank heavens Megan had saved his skin. A little smile escaped and lit up his face at the thought. She was resourceful if nothing else, but how much better it would have been if he'd won the fight though. That would have put that damned Gab in his place. As it was . . .

13

As it was, Megan spent a large part of the night awake worrying about her da and about Rhodri and wondering if she and he would ever be safely married to each other. That likelihood appeared even more remote than ever, if that were possible. There wasn't any sense in alienating her father by getting married without telling him; in any case she wanted to have friends and family about her to enjoy their day. Not some hole in the corner event as unmemorable as going to the supermarket or visiting the doctor.

Megan felt mean and shallow sometimes when she thought about her da. Much as she loved him, much as she wanted him to be happy there were times she pondered on his selfishness and wished . . . no, she wouldn't indulge herself. If only Howard would help, would come home even if only for a weekend, just to relieve the pressures on her. A phone call once a week did nothing either for her or her da. You'd think a brother would show more interest, if only for her sake. She turned over in bed, thumped her pillow to make it more comfortable, and closed her eyes again.

But opened her eyes immediately and sat up, thinking she'd heard someone trying the front door. Her clock said twenty past five. Twenty past five? The fleeting thought that she'd forgotten to lock up last night passed through her mind, then she heard a foot on the stairs. Then another. It wouldn't be Da, he never came upstairs. Megan reached for her dressing-gown, put it on while still in bed, got out and stood behind the door listening. As she tied the belt there came a tap at the door right by her ear. Megan was so twitchy she actually jumped and clamped a hand to her mouth to stop herself from calling out in fright. But the stealthy movements of the person the other side of the door now centred on the door knob which she saw was being turned, slowly but surely. She stepped back to allow the door to open and a head appeared. It was Gab. In a loud whisper he said. 'Meggie, my love, like I promised, I'm giving you your early morning call.'

Gab didn't actually step into the bedroom but he did wait for an answer. 'Meggie? Are you up already? Meggie!'

Seething with a mixture of temper and fright, Megan answered, 'I'm up. Thanks.'

She heard him chuckle, then say, 'Cup of tea ready for you in the kitchen in five minutes. OK?' The door shut and she was left with a pounding heart and fury boiling up inside her. How dare he? How dare he? What was worse, how had he got in?

She found out when she finally got down into the kitchen. He was standing there, bold as brass, his sandy hair spiky and tousled, his light blue eyes boldly hypnotising her with his direct glance, his shirt neck wide open exposing his bare muscular chest, and their large back door key tauntingly displayed on a chain around his neck.

'I said I would. And I did. I'm a man of my word, you see.'

'Give me that key. Please.'

Gab dodged to the other side of the table. 'Come and get it!'

The singsong tone of his voice incensed her. 'Don't play your stupid games with me. Give me that key. Now.' She held out her hand and waited.

'If you want it, come and get it.' He grinned that attractive grin of his and for a split second she ... his eyes sparkled as he recognised her hesitation for what it was. 'Come on. Come on.' Gab beckoned with both hands. Softly he whispered, 'You want the key. You come and get it. I'll exchange the key for a kiss. That's fair, isn't it?' Again those inviting, beckoning hands.

'Stop playing the fool. You'd no right to take that key. Give it to me.' But she daren't get close to him.

His eyes roved over her, drinking in the essence of her, draining her will power from her in a way Rhodri never did. 'Even at this early hour you're beautiful. There can't be another woman in the whole world so beautiful at this time in the morning as you. You're a sight for sore eyes.' Gab removed the chain from round his neck and held it out to her. 'Here you are, Meggie my love.'

'Lay it on the table. Go on. On the table.'

With a show of reluctance he did as she asked. He placed it carefully down, arranging it delicately as though it were a great treasure. 'I didn't take your key, I had another one made, at the key cutters in the precinct when I went to get my hair cut yesterday afternoon.'

Megan slipped the key from the chain. 'Here, this is yours. So where is our key, now?' She laid the chain on the table again, the key itself held tightly in her hand behind her back.

'Hanging where it always hangs, on the wall in the passage.'

The tension between them was so strong it was almost visible.

He drank his tea down, his eyes never leaving her face. 'That's better.' He nodded his head towards the door. 'Milking. OK?' He paused for a moment, his hand on the knob of the kitchen door and looked again at her with eyes full of passion. She sensed the intensity of his feelings beating at her. 'I shan't be satisfied till you and me's married. I don't mind your da. It won't bother me it being a threesome, but he won't cower me like he does that Rhodri. If I say, then I say and that's that. Must go.' Before he closed the door, he looked at her with triumph in his eyes.

The lad rapped on the window as he went by with the cows to the milking parlour and it broke the spell. Megan went to the window and watched him and Gab fooling about on their way to begin the milking. God! If she could find someone else, even half as energetic as Gab, she'd take him on this minute. What worried Megan was his magnetism. She knew full well if she hadn't met Rhodri first . . . she would have been in his arms in an instant. That was the danger. Pull yourself together, Megan, she thought. He's a farmhand, that's *all he is.*

Megan sipped her tea. Nevertheless, she thought, he's an attractive devil. She allowed herself to think about him for a moment. Life would be exciting, that's for certain. Her da would have the asthmatic attack of all asthmatic attacks, though, if she said she was marrying Gab. Or would he? There was no gainsaying the fact that Gab's father had a huge acreage, an enormous farmhouse in an enviable position, with amazingly rich pasture land so in actual fact he wasn't just a farmhand . . . the lights flickered as they always did when the milking machine was switched on. The flicker snapped Megan out of her mood. Tea for Da. He'd be waiting, waking early, like farmers always do. As she poured his tea she wondered if this was all it was to be for the rest of his life? She would so have enjoyed the party last night, and Rhodri would have enjoyed it more if she'd been there. They would have left early and gone to Rhodri's and made love. She looked around her kitchen and felt it enclose her like prison walls.

'Good party last night, Kate! Thoroughly enjoyed myself!' Dan dashed past reception and into the staff office at the back. 'Rhodri in?'

Kate, trying desperately to rally her resources after her late night and the excitement of the party, called out, 'No, not yet.'

Dan called over his shoulder 'OK. If he doesn't come before I go, remind me to leave a message for him.'

Kate busied herself organising the appointments for the small animal clinic and printing out the call lists for the farm vets.

Dan came back in. 'My list? Please.'

'You've an emergency at Applegate Farm. Came in five minutes ago. Sounds urgent, but then when Blossom calls it always is. Go there first. The rest is more or less routine.'

Dan picked up his list and said, 'Tell Rhodri I want to know how Bernard Wilson and his dogs are doing, and does he need me to call?'

'Right.' Kate added a note to Rhodri's list, at the same time answered the phone and hoped Annette wouldn't be too long before she got there. Surely she couldn't be blaming the road-works again.

Dan hurtled off to Applegate Farm decidedly pleased with life. Phil Parsons was leaning over his farm gate awaiting his arrival. He'd obviously purchased a new balaclava, for this one was tweedy and brown, but with the two self same slits for his eyes and a bigger one for his mouth. 'About time.'

'Sorry, came as quickly as I could.'

'Come on, then. Come on. It's Star. Right off colour, he is. I'm worried sick.'

As Dan pulled on his boots he asked how the pygmy goats were doing.

'Grand. When you've seen to Star you can 'ave a look at 'em. Hamish is doing a grand job with 'em, and Blossom's right taken with 'em too. Come on, before it's too late.'

'What are the symptoms?'

'You tell me, that's what I pay you for.'

Dan held up a placatory hand, went through the farm gate and headed for the byre where Sunny Boy the bull had always been. He felt quite a pang that it wouldn't be him he'd be attending.

Star, the new occupant of the first-class byre at Applegate Farm, was looking uncomfortable. Dan approached with caution, gently making Star aware of his presence and noticing with approval that his head was tethered firmly, both sides, to the two-foot thick wall.

Phil muttered, 'He's tethered, not taking any more chances. It breaks my heart to see him like that but after Sunny Boy gored Hamish . . . well, I can't take the risk.'

'How is Hamish?'

Mystifyingly Phil replied, 'You'll see after.'

By this time, Dan was in Star's stall using his hands to feel him all over. 'When did this start?'

'He looked a bit uncomfortable last night, Hamish said, not himself you know, but nothing specific. This morning he's worse and hasn't eaten a bite. Not even his favourite snack.'

'What's that?'

'A bag of crisps.'

Dan had to laugh. 'A bag of crisps! Honestly, Phil, I can't believe it.'

Phil chuckled. 'It's his favourite, honest. Loves 'em. Do nearly anything for a bag. Has t'be plain, doesn't like them artificial flavours.'

Dan shook his head in disbelief. 'You've not been giving him anything else strange, have you?'

'Absolutely not.'

'Well, I've taken his temperature and he has got a slight one, which shows things are not quite right. I'll stand here for a bit and watch him. There, look, did you see him look down his flank? There's something causing him pain.' Dan placed his fist on Star's left flank and stayed silent.

Phil whispered, 'Are you doing a bit of faith healing or something? Laying on of hands, like?'

Dan didn't answer, but concentrated hard. Then he said, 'Watch!' and Star glanced down his flank again as though anxious. 'I think he might have something lodged in his rumen because every time it contracts it's making him wince. Got a piece of planking? About five or six feet long?'

Phil, thinking Dan must have taken leave of his senses, disappeared and came back a few minutes later with the required piece of wood. 'Will this do?'

'Excellent! Now you stand the other side of him and pass the wood through and you hold your end and I'll hold mine and when I say lift, lift as hard as you can up against his body.'

'Here! Just a minute, what are we doing?'

'We'll put pressure on his body right where it counts and if it causes him pain, which we'll know by his reaction, then I shall know my diagnosis is correct.'

'Oh! Right!' Still convinced Dan had entirely lost the plot, Phil waited for the signal.

Dan bellowed, 'Lift!' and the two of them heaved the plank of wood up against his body and Star grunted, loudly.

'Just what I thought. Once more to make sure.'

'Well, I'd grunt if someone was heaving a plank up against my insides.'

'Now!' Poor Star grunted again, and lifted a back leg.

'We're right. He's got a piece of wire or some other solid object jammed at the point of his rumen, and he feels it when the rumen begins to contract from that end, and we make him feel it when we push the plank up against him.'

Full of hope Phil asked, 'Maybe it would pass through him with a pint of castor oil? Do you think?'

'No, absolutely not. We've got to get it out.'

In a feeble voice Phil asked, 'You mean, putting your arm up his arse?'

'No, cutting him and pulling it out through his side. It's the only way.'

Phil clung to the top of the stall gate. 'Hell's bells. No, you can't mean it.'

'I do. If I'm going to save him.'

'Think of the risk.'

'Think of the risk if I don't.'

'Knock him out for a few minutes, you mean?'

'No, an injection to numb the whole area and do it while he's standing here.'

'Oh God! Will you need 'elp?'

'An extra pair of hands would be helpful, yes.'

'I'll get Blossom, she's better at this kind of thing than me.' A distraught Phil shuffled off to the house, feet dragging as though taking his last steps on his way to hell.

Blossom appeared in the doorway of the byre wearing a spanking blue-and-white striped butcher's apron over her skimpy clothes, vivid pink rubber gloves on her hands, and her peroxided hair wrapped tightly in a tea towel that had seen better days.

'I've come. Phil's sitting by the fire, stroking the cat and praying.' Her glossy ruby lips broke into a conspiratorial smile. 'No nerve for this kind of thing. Where do we start?'

'Are you sure? It's not pleasant and I've no idea what I shall find when I get in there. He's certainly got a temperature, which will mean a lot of infection and possibly a smell when we get inside.'

'Women are tougher than we look. The main thing is to get Star better. He can't go on as he is. So ...' She held out her pink rubber hands and they were as steady as a rock. 'See ...'

'Right then, we'll begin. I shan't say please or thank you or will you, I shall give commands and you'll have to act on them. First, I need a bucket of hot water and some soap to clean myself off now, and again halfway through the operation.'

'Right. I'll get that straightaway.'

Blossom survived the initial opening up of Star's flank, and really admired Dan's stitching technique when he sewed a pocket of Star's rumen to his skin to keep the sack in place and enjoyed watching as Dan made an incision into the rumen, but it was when he put his arm deep down inside, right up to his armpit and was obviously searching about for the foreign body that Blossom came over faint. She clutched hold of the sty wall, swallowed hard, took some deep breaths and was sufficiently in charge of herself to be able to appreciate Dan's shout of triumph as he brought out a huge, crooked, rusty nail, which he examined and then placed carefully on the windowsill of the byre.

'Oh my God! Was that what it was? This nail?'

'In a very painful place. Don't pick it up, I need you to stay clean. I'm stitching next.'

'No wonder he had stomach-ache.'

Blossom pulled herself together and helped Dan disinfect himself, passed him the appropriate needles for stitching up, and didn't really relax until Dan was giving Star a pat of approval.

Dan couldn't have had better help if he'd sent for Bunty to assist him. 'Thank you, Mrs Parsons. You've done very well. Quite remarkable. I wonder, have you trained as a nurse?'

Blossom gave him a wry smile. 'I know it's hard to believe but I have. However, I got caught in a patient's bed one night, Sister found me and went berserk, and I was dismissed. Served me right, it wasn't the first time. But there we are.' She shrugged her shoulders. 'I loved it while I was there, but . . . you can't have everything, can you? I'll go tell Phil, if he hasn't passed out by now. Thank you, Dan, for what you've done. Marvellous.' Her ruby red lips broke into a wicked smile, she twinkled her fingers at him and left.

Before he left, Dan went to find Phil to ask for a look at Callum Tattersall's pygmy goats. He found him leaning on the gate of a small field. A brand new shed had been put in to act as a night shelter, and there busily supervising Hamish tidying it up were the goats, Sybil with her kid at her side.

Phil nodded towards Hamish and shouted, 'Put your shoulder to it, it'll be dark before you've done.'

Hamish looked up, grinned and shouted back, 'Come and give us a hand, then!'

Dan's eyebrows shot up with delighted surprise.

Phil nudged Dan and said quietly, 'Surprised? I bet you are. I told you he'd speak before long, didn't I? Well, it was these here goats that did it, believe it or not.' Phil kept his voice low and told Dan the whole story. 'We came to collect 'em that day, you know, when poor old Callum snuffed it . . . anyway, we knew, Blossom and me, that Hamish was getting close to talking, but he couldn't quite make it. We could see, you know, he was on the brink. Well, he was delighted with the goats and especially the little kid; she was only about two weeks old, wasn't she? Well, that night he went out to make sure they was asleep and comfortable like, it being their first night and he was ages. Blossom said I should go out and check up on him. So I did.'

Phil paused for a moment, unable to carry on speaking. He dug in his pocket and brought out some titbits for the goats, clicked his tongue at them and they came running across to him.

'There you are. That's it. All gone. So, there he was, sitting in the night shelter on the floor in the straw, rocking back and forth with the little kid fast asleep on his lap, holding her like you would a baby, talking away like I don't know what. All like baby talk, you know. I was amazed. Couldn't believe it. All of a sudden he realised I was there and he looked up and smiled and said, "Isn't she beautiful, Phil?" Just as if he'd never been dumb. I just said, "She is that." Then we locked up and went in. I don't mind telling you I was gobsmacked. Soon as we got in Blossom asked him if he wanted hot chocolate or Horlicks before he went to bed, thinking he'd point to the jar like he always did, but he *said*, "Horlicks." Well, she was that overcome she burst into tears. Since then he's talked, almost nonstop. So, you see it was something about that little kid that must have gone right to the very heart of him and kind of healed him up inside.'

'Has he been able to tell you why he couldn't talk, what it was that clammed him up?'

'No. But we were talking the very next day about another kid being due soon, you know, and how we were looking forward to it and Hamish said out of the blue, "He killed the baby, right there, in front of me." And he wept, such terrible grief, like I've never heard before. Broke Blossom's heart it did, and mine, I can tell you. So what that means I can't bear to think, but I reckon it'll all come out in the wash one day. Some kids have rotten lives, don't they? Rotten.'

'Poor chap. But he's happy here, Phil, you must be doing a good job.'

'It's Blossom mainly.' Phil straightened himself up and said, 'Thanks for Star, sorry I couldn't help. By the way, I've given Bernard Wilson a hand to make new runs for his dogs, and I've more or less promised I'll buy one of the young ones off him for Blossom, it'll be one less for him to feed. But don't tell her, it's a surprise for her birthday.'

Rhodri phoned Dan on his mobile later that day and asked him if he had time to go see Bernard Wilson and his dogs. 'I'd promised to call today but I've a road accident come in and I can't leave till I've finished operating and it's a major op, so I don't know how long I shall be.'

'So long as it's all right with you?'

There was a short hesitation and then Rhodri answered, 'Yes, of course it is.'

'Right I'll go, leave it with me. Good luck with the op.'

'Thanks, it's tricky. Crushed ribs. Do or die job.'

'Good luck, then.'

Dan called at Badger's Lot and as he pulled into the farmyard he was greeted by the sound of barking, and an ancient vacuum cleaner grinding away in the farmhouse. He couldn't see Bernard outside so he rattled on the back door of the farmhouse.

The noise of the vacuum stopped and the door was opened by a large woman who looked like a female version of Bernard, except she hadn't got a three-day growth of beard. Instead she had a smooth, fat, rosy country face, with frank, no-nonsense eyes and unfortunately for her, Bernard's bruiser of a nose. 'Yes?'

Dan took off his cap. 'Good afternoon, I'm Dan Brown, Veterinary Surgeon, called to see Bernard's dogs.'

'I'm Hannah, Bernard's sister. He's gone to the feed place, back soon. Feel free to go look, I've shut them all in the stables, 'cos Bernard's cleaning the runs when he gets back. I'll get on if you don't mind.'

Dan thanked her and went to see the dogs. As he turned to cross the yard he noticed a rat trap standing under the kitchen window with two vast rats in it. Hannah's voice boomed out from the door, 'And he's those two to kill when he gets back. The mucky devils that they are.'

'Right!'

The runs had been well constructed, they were large and afforded the dogs plenty of room for exercise. He opened the double doors of one run, closed them safely behind him and opened the top half of the stable door for a view of the dogs. There was a light switch by the door post and Dan switched it on. Today he was greeted by noisy young dogs, not quite as healthy as he would have liked, but a vast improvement on how they'd looked a week ago.

They were rolling and tumbling about, wrestling energetically with each other. One came to the door scrabbling to reach him, Dan bent down to stroke his head. 'Now then, young man, you look better than you did. Bernard been taking care of you, has he?'

Before he got an answer to his question Bernard's old lorry rumbled into the yard loaded with feed bags. Bernard climbed out and came across to speak to him. 'Afternoon, Dan.'

'Afternoon, Bernard. Just happened to be going past.' He nodded his head towards the open stable door. 'You've done a good job. They're looking better.'

Bernard came into the run and hitched his bulk onto the stable door in the space left by Dan. 'By hell! That Blossom Parsons has got something to answer for. She rang my sister, she did, they knew each other when they were nurses together. Told her I needed 'elp.' He jerked his head in the direction of the house. 'The blasted woman's come and she's turned my house upside down. Says she intends living here. "*We're both lonely*" she says.'

Dan studied what Bernard had said and then replied, 'She looks to me as if she'll take care of you all right. Meals and such and you have to admit the house was ... worse than a pigsty.'

Bernard looked at him. 'Yer nothing if not outspoken, you. Upset all my arrangements, she has.'

'But I bet you've nice clean sheets on the bed and the kitchen's spotless. You've a lot to be thankful for, Bernard.'

'Ummph. Depends how you look at life. Says she wants to put a shower in, so I says if you pay for it you can, thinking she'd back off, but did she? Did she hell as like. Right, she says, I will, when I've got this place cleaned up to my satisfaction, I'll get a plumber in.' Bernard shook his head in disbelief.

Dan decided to change the subject. 'These dogs are beginning to look better. I'll just have a look at the others and then I'll be off.'

'I even have to take my boots off before I go in the kitchen. Says she wants a porch building over the back door so there's room for my boots and farm clothes undercover.' He grunted and groaned at the prospect but Dan could tell, though Bernard wouldn't ever admit to it, that he was quite liking being looked after.

Hannah's foghorn voice boomed out from the back door. 'There's these two to see to.' She was pointing at the rat trap. 'Hurry up. And then there's the dogs' runs to clear up. When you've done that there'll be a nice bite of fruit cake and a cup of tea ready. I'm gasping. How about you, Dan?'

Dan shook his head and refused on the grounds of pressure of time.

Hannah had to have the last word. 'And there'll just be time for you to walk the young dogs before dark, Bernard. I've got some lengths of rope ready, so be sharp about it.'

'Wouldn't mind but she's poured all my beer down the sink. Not a drop, she says, till I've done all the jobs that need doing. Poured it down the sink! How can a man function without his beer, I ask you?'

Dan surveyed Bernard's well-rounded stomach and said, 'Before long you'll be as thin as a whippet!'

Bernard snorted his disapproval, let himself out of the dog run and headed for the rat trap. Dan beat a hasty retreat. If there was one thing he loathed, it was rats. He shuddered, put the Land Rover in first and headed off towards Porter's Fold, the last of his calls for that day, chuckling to himself about Hannah's clean sweep of Bernard's house. She was just what the man needed, was Hannah. He had a good farm with acres of good land, all it required was diligent application and it could become quite a goldmine.

When Dan had finished his last call he went back to the Practice to check in. The waiting room was half full and Kate was behind the desk talking to a client. They both broke off when he approached.

'Hi, Dan! Finished? There're no more calls. Joy says go home if you like. Zoe and Colin have already finished. Slack day today.'

'OK. Will do.'

The client took her credit card from the counter, saying, 'See you Monday, Kate, half past nine. 'Bye.'

'I shan't be here Monday. This is my last day. I'm off to college next week.'

'No! Really. You got in then?'

Kate gave the client one of her winning smiles. 'I did.'

'Will you come back here when you've qualified?'

'I honestly don't know. We'll have to wait and see. They might not want me.' She gave a bubbly laugh and the client laughed too.

'It would be lovely if you could. Good luck, then.'

'Thanks! Be seeing you.'

Dan said good afternoon to the client and then asked Kate if Rhodri was still about.

'He is, but he's not in the best of moods. The dog, you know the road traffic accident? Well, it died. He's awfully upset about it.'

'Oh! Sorry about that. I'll go find him.'

Dan caught up with Rhodri in the staff room and found him in the depths of despair, slouched on a chair, staring into space.

'Sorry, Rhod, about the dog. You did say it was do or die. We can't win every time.'

Rhodri stirred himself. 'No, we can't, but it would have been nice to have made it with this one. Mungo gave a hand but it was no good.'

'Ribs, you say.'

Rhodri nodded. 'Caved in, they were. The owners were distraught.'

'I've been to Bernard's for you. His sister has turned up and is making Bernard's life a living hell. She's cleaning up, trapping rats, and generally organising him with every intention of staying put.'

Rhodri sat up. 'That's a plus then. Just what he needs. And the dogs?'

'Doing much better. The young ones were rolling and tumbling about and beginning to enjoy life.'

Rhodri nodded. 'Good. Good.'

'He could make a go of it, you know, breeding dogs. Nice little earner if it's done properly. And with that sister of his behind him . . .'

'He could. But he'd have to do a sight better than he is now if he's to attract enthusiastic buyers.' Rhodri gave a heavy sigh. 'I wouldn't buy one off him at the moment.'

'What's up, Rhod? It's not just the dog dying, is it?'

Rhodri stood up. 'You don't want to know my troubles.'

'That's for me to decide.' Dan deliberately planted himself on a chair and made himself comfortable.

Rhodri sat down again but stayed silent. Then opened his mouth as though he was going to speak, closed it and then changed his mind again. 'My ferret, you know, Harry, I found him dead this morning. Old age, you know. And this dog dying on me hasn't helped. I've had Harry since he was a few weeks old. We knew each other so well, and he could still surprise me.'

'In the scheme of things Harry going is really quite a small thing . . . You—'

'Small thing? It might be to you but it isn't to me. That's your trouble, always seeing things in black and white. I wonder sometimes if you have a heart at all.'

'Oh I have, indeed I have, but you need to get your priorities right. I think Megan is far more important. I saw Gab in a shop in the town the other day. The assistants were round him like bees round a honeypot. You can see why, where women are concerned us lesser mortals can't hold a candle to him.'

Rhodri was standing up looking out of the window by now and ignoring Dan's remarks. He was thinking of Harry. Of how, that morning, Harry had not come to the bars of his cage when he'd gone out to bring him in the house for a run before he left for work. Of how he'd dreaded opening up Harry's sleeping quarters, guessing what he'd find. But there he was, his eyes wide open, his mouth open, his lips drawn back in a grimace, and dead. He'd picked him up and held him to his cheek to remind himself of the feel of him and for a last goodbye, but it simply wasn't Harry any more, he'd left already for wherever it was ferrets went at the end of their lives. There'd never be another Harry, he couldn't bear another parting like this.

'Rhod?'

'Sorry. We were talking about Megan, weren't we? I don't need you to tell me that. Megan herself admits how attractive he is. Not that *she* finds him attractive, but she knows he is, which he is and I wish he wasn't. You don't know of a farm hand in need of a job, do you? Because that's what she wants, someone to replace Gabriel Bridges.'

'I don't, no, but I do wonder if you should persuade Megan to marry you and you say that you'll live at the house with Old Man Jones.'

Dan thought Rhodri would explode, the expression on his face was so outraged as he turned from the window. '*Live* with that conniving, nasty old beggar? Not likely.'

'But when he sees he's not threatened with being left on his own or having to go into a nursing home, he'll come round to it. Heavens above, the house is big enough. I bet it would be possible to make quite separate living quarters. You and Megan in one part and him the other. He's scared he'll be no longer in command of himself, no longer in charge of his life and all that. You've got to try to see it from his point of view.'

'You haven't had him raise his stick to you and miss hitting you by a hair's breadth. That is humiliating, see.'

'I can believe that, but that's what I'm saying: he's not given up on himself and isn't likely to, so you do some compromising and I think he is enough of a man to do the same. He'll want to match up with you because you're treating him as though he's a man and not an embittered invalid. It's not giving in, Rhodri, on your part, it's using your brain. He's a tough chap, as well you know, so it's the two of you at loggerheads.' Dan clenched his fists and banged his knuckles together imitating the two opposing forces. 'You're just as stubborn as he is in your own way, Rhod, but it's for you to make the first move.'

'It's just the thought of living under the same roof. I have this picture in my mind of us getting married and living in my house, see. On our own. That's what I wanted above everything, to *rescue* Megan.'

'But he wouldn't be in *bed* with the two of you, would he? It would be you and Megan at the other end of the house. Just think of that. Every night in bed together.'

Rhodri blushed bright red. He looked away out of the window again and quietly asked, 'Would you compromise like that for Rose?'

Dan nodded his head. 'I'd find it very difficult, if not impossible, but for Rose's sake, yes, I would. And believe me, her mother would be twenty times more difficult to live with than that old man, because she's chosen to be a bitch for absolutely no reason at all. And think, you'd be better placed for keeping an eye on Gab too, there is some merit in that.'

'Do you know, you're right there.' Rhodri became seized by the idea. 'I could rent out my house to someone, live at Beulah Bank Farm married to Megan, and see how it all pans out. It's not the solution I would have preferred, but you've made me see it's better than nothing at all.' Rhodri pounded his right fist into the palm of his other hand and looked triumphantly at Dan. 'You've persuaded me, I don't know how, but you have.'

'I'm sure it would take the edge off Gab's obsession too, her being married.'

'Oh yes. I think it would. Why have I never thought like this before? I can't believe I've been so blinkered. Of course old Jones is frightened and quite rightly so. The poor beggar.' Rhodri paused and then said, with a wry smile on his face, 'It crosses my mind he won't live to an old age, will he? Not in his state.'

'Now Rhod, now Rhod, I didn't put that in my equation.' Dan wagged a warning finger at him. 'But it is a thought.' Then he burst into laughter.

Rhodri caught the infectiousness of it and laughed too. 'By God! I'll do it. Yes, I will.'

'You're a wise man and kind with it.'

Rhodri smiled and said, his voice full of excitement and energy, 'I'm off to propose.'

14

He did just that with flowers, a bottle of champagne and the engagement ring he'd bought months before. Halfway there he rang her on his mobile and suggested she walked down to the bridge to meet him because he had something special to say.

She hadn't got there by the time he arrived so he sat in the car admiring the emerald and diamond ring he'd bought her. It sat so beautifully in its box, contrasted so well with the black velvet lining, it almost seemed a pity to take it out, but he knew how much better it would look on her finger. The oblong emerald caught the rays of the sun and dazzled him, to say nothing of the wonderful sparkle of the diamonds surrounding it. Apart from his house and his car, it was the most expensive thing he'd ever bought.

Rhodri looked up when he heard her quick step on the tarmac of the road. His heart leapt. Having her da under the same roof seemed a small price to pay for such a prize. He closed his fingers over the box.

They held hands as they walked down the slope to the edge of the stream. Silently Megan drew his attention to a kingfisher poised alertly on a stone just above the water's edge. His bright eyes shone in the sunlight as he made to fly off, changed his mind and then in a flash he was gone. Rhodri tried to follow his darting flight down the stream and thought what a good omen it was to have seen such a rare sight. It gave him courage.

'Megan. I've decided. I want us to be married and I'm willing to live at the farm with you and your da. I've always imagined that you would come to live with me in my house, always thought it was the only way, because I wanted to rescue you from slaving for your da, Sir Galahad to the rescue, you know, but I realise that's not possible, so I thought if he saw I was willing to compromise then he might compromise as well, if that's possible.'

She said nothing, but he felt her fingers tighten on his.

'So, I've bought you an engagement ring. I love it and I hope you do, but if you don't I'll gladly exchange it for another one. It's an emerald with diamonds round it and it will suit I'm sure but, as I say, if it doesn't then that's all right by me and we'll go back to the jewellers. Of course, it may not be to your taste so if it isn't . . . well we'll change it. I don't mind in the slightest.'

'Rhodri! Hush! Show me.' His hands were shaking so much he couldn't open the box. Megan placed a gentle hand on his and said, 'Darling! Why the nerves?'

Rhodri, filled with hope, calmed his racing heart and opened the box. Megan gasped with pleasure when she saw it, a gasp so genuine he knew instantly that she loved it. It slid on her finger as if it had been designed especially for her. She held up her hand and admired the fire in the diamonds and the wonderful, deep, flashing green of the emerald. In a hoarse, reverent whisper she said, 'I love this. Absolutely love it. If I'd been with you I'd have chosen this very ring myself. And I want to say how much I appreciate you offering to live at the farm. It's a big sacrifice and I realise how much you must love me to make it. I'm proud to wear a ring given to me by such a loving man, such a dear, kind man like you. It's an honour, it truly is.'

Megan flung her arms around Rhodri and she kissed him like she'd never kissed him: gone was the sweet tenderness of her kisses, replaced by a wild, fierce loving, the depths of which he had not seen before. This was a Megan full of a deep, rousing passion. When she gave him time to draw breath he said, 'Put me down! Put me down!' Then clutched her tighter than ever and kissed her frantically. When they stopped kissing from shortage of breath Rhodri burst out with, 'Harry Ferret died today.'

Megan released herself from his arms and said, 'Well, honestly! That's nice! Harry dies, so suddenly you're willing to come to live at the farm. Would you prefer to stay where you are and get another ferret instead of me?'

Rhodri took her seriously and shook his head sorrowfully from side to side. 'It's been an awful blow losing Harry, but no I shan't get another.'

'I suppose that's some consolation even if I, obviously, come second best.'

'Now, Megan, you know I don't mean that, what I really meant to say was . . .' Rhodri saw she was laughing and knew he'd dropped himself right in it. 'Sorry, I didn't mean it to sound like that. I'd have proposed even if he hadn't died this morning.'

Megan's eyes filled with tears. 'I know. I shall miss him. I'm so sorry, love. It must have been dreadful.'

'I knew it was coming, he hadn't been himself for a few days. Not interested in anything and not a pest when he was out, so I knew.' He turned away from her and bent to retie his shoelace so his voice was muffled. 'It won't be easy for me coming to live at the farm, but I'll do my best. Perhaps if I'm willing to compromise on what I would have preferred, your da might too.'

'Don't spoil a lovely moment talking about how stubborn Da is. Let's go tell him. Better still, ask his permission.'

'His permission?'

'His permission to marry his daughter, see.'

'Ahhh! Right.'

He stood outside the sitting-room door, nervous beyond measure, knowing he musn't make a mess of asking permission this time, knowing he must do it thoroughly and properly and most of all humbly but firmly. He felt Megan's hand push him right in the middle of his back as she whispered, 'Go on, he can't bite.' Oh no? Rhodri pushed open the door.

He put the ring in its box on the table beside his chair. 'Good evening, Mr Jones.'

A bent twisted index finger pointed at the box. 'What's this?'

Courage came to him when it was most needed, and he spoke without a stammer, plainly and forthrightly. 'An engagement ring. I've asked Megan to marry me and before you say anything, I've asked her on the understanding that we live here, in this house after we're married. I know there might be difficulties, but I realise you can't live on your own and I wouldn't want to deprive you of your daughter and maybe if we both try to be civilised we would manage quite nicely. It's what I want. It's what Megan wants and we both hope it's what you will want. So, I'm asking for your daughter's hand in marriage, and I hope you'll give us your blessing.'

Mr Jones didn't reply.

Rhodri, running out of steam, sat down abruptly and waited patiently, and when he still didn't speak he suggested he should open the box and have a look at the ring.

'You open it.'

So Rhodri did and Mr Jones for once in his life was quite taken aback. 'Has Megan seen it?'

Rhodri nodded. 'Just now.'

'She likes it?'

'Loves it.'

'I see.'

He seemed very calm and Rhodri became anxious that it might be the calm before the storm. He closed the box and put it in his pocket. 'Well?'

'She's very precious to me. Never realised how much till a week or two ago. Always felt boys were more important in a family, see. Then I saw that Gab, of the lustful eyes, admiring her and I thought, no, you're not getting this precious daughter of mine.' He paused, looked up at Rhodri, with what passed for a smile for Mr Jones, and said, 'I wish we had champagne in the house, we need to crack a bottle open.'

'Great minds think alike. I've just put one in your fridge.'

'What are you waiting for then? Open it. Never mind waiting for it to chill. Go on, boy.'

Rhodri stood up. 'It's all right with you, then?'

'I wouldn't be opening champagne just for fun, now would I?'

'Thank you.' Rhodri put out his hand. 'Let's shake on it.' Mr Jones extended his arm and they shook hands.

His heart bursting with love and complete delight that he'd finally got Old Man Jones on his side, though he'd never actually said he could marry Megan, not in so many words, Rhodri charged at the kitchen door, flung it open and shouted, 'Crack open the champagne! Your da says . . .'

Seated at the table drinking tea was Gab with a face like thunder.

Looking back on the whole episode that night before she slipped into what proved to be a fitful sleep Megan cringed at the horror of it. Immediately before Rhodri had flung the door open with such heartfelt delight, Gab, in a wild burst of silent anger, had broken every stem of the flowers Rhodri had given her and flung them in the waste bin. When he'd returned to sit down his hands shook so violently they were almost beating a tattoo on the table, and the tea was jumping out of his mug at every beat. She wished she'd never told him.

Megan had leapt out of her skin when the door had bounced open and revealed Rhodri standing there, his face glowing with his overwhelming happiness. There must have been much less than thirty seconds of silence but it felt an age and then Gab, with a snarl on his face like that of a cornered fox, said, 'You'll never have a moment's joy, Meggie. Never! I'm the man for you. I've told you before and I'm telling you now, you're mine. *Mine*, do you hear!' Gab had got to his feet and in one surprising fluid movement had skirted the end of the table, grabbed her by the arms and kissed her full on the lips. Taken so completely by surprise it was a moment before Rhodri took action.

He'd run round the end of the kitchen table to prise Gab's arms from Megan, but Gab held her in a vice-like grip. She struggled to escape, fearful for Rhodri's safety, but neither he nor she could get her away from him. Gab threw his head back and gave a tortured roar, 'Leave her be! She's mine!'

Megan's da came in. 'Let her go! Do you hear me? Let her go!'

Gab shook her like a terrier with a rat, till her brains felt as though they were thudding against her skull. 'Listen to me! Listen to me! You're mine! Mine! Do you hear?'

Megan cried out, 'Please, Gab! Please stop.' Gab's fury fell away from him just as quickly as it had come. What all three of them were fearful of was the anguish of his eyes and the violence of his shaking body. For a moment he stood there looking at them standing in a tight cluster by the table. He spun on his heel and headed for the kitchen door in a wild zig-zag as though his legs didn't belong to him, muttering to himself. Megan knew he was in love with her, that he was passionate about her, but she had never realised just how deeply he felt. She was terribly shocked by his reaction to her engagement, shocked to the core.

They listened for his next move. His car ground and whined as it always did as he strived to start it up, then it fired and he roared away out of the yard.

No one spoke.

No one moved.

Till Megan pulled her frock straight.

Her da picked up his walking stick from the table.

Rhodri tried to pull himself together.

In a strange, high voice Megan said, 'I think we'll have tea and leave the champagne till later.'

Her da said, 'Thank God he's done the milking before he left.'

Rhodri said, 'You're not having him back after that, are you?'

'No! Put a drop of whisky in mine, Megan.'

Megan put a drop in each of their cups and carried them through into the sitting room.

For two hours they'd debated how they'd manage the farm without Gab, and whether or not they should tell Mr Bridges exactly why he wouldn't be allowed back.

In the end Megan's da had said firmly, 'I shall tell him. In fact I'll tell him right away. Pass me the phone, Rhodri. Please.'

Before Rhodri had found the number in the telephone book there was a loud knocking at the door.

They'd looked at each other in turn, uncertain what to do. 'Who's that?' they said. 'Who's that?' 'Is it Gab?'

The hammering began again, so Mr Jones said, 'Rhodri, would you be so kind as to answer the door?'

Megan recalled the fear she'd felt in her bones when she heard Richie Jamieson's voice in the hallway. What did he want with them? Questions had raced through her head, one after the other.

The inspector had removed his hat before he spoke and they all watched him intently as he smoothed his ruffled hair. 'I might as well come straight out with it. I'm sorry to have to tell you that Gabriel Bridges has been shot. As you apparently were the last people to see him we wondered if you wouldn't mind making a statement?'

Rhodri flinched at the word 'shot', feeling this was one shock too many. He licked his dry lips before he spoke. 'When you say shot, do you mean he's *dead*?'

'No, but it would appear he's very close.'

The inspector had taken statements from all three of them. They'd each described the events of the evening as they saw them, trying desperately to be accurate. Finally the question came. 'Rhodri. Did you leave the house at all? For any reason.'

'No, I met Megan at the bridge and then came on here and I have never left the house at all. I've not even gone into the yard, since I got here.'

He asked both Mr Jones and Megan if they could verify that.

Mr Jones tapped his stick on the floor. 'Richie, I don't quite know what you're getting at with that question, but I can tell you that Rhodri has never left the house, not for a second. If he had he would have said so, when you asked him.'

The inspector smoothed his hands over his hair. 'Do you own a gun, Rhodri?'

'No, never.'

'Mr Jones?'

Megan's da shook his head. 'I do not. I will not allow them in the house.'

'Megan?'

'Never, ever. I know nothing about guns.' The awful suspicion the inspector was implying made her ask, 'Tell us exactly what you mean when you ask us if we have guns and have we left the house?'

When the inspector answered he emphasised each word very deliberately. 'Mr Bridges says that if Gab had shot *himself* he would not have missed. He's very adamant about that. He would have done the job properly he says, him being a crack shot.'

Mr Jones was horrified. 'It isn't an attempt at suicide, then? You're sure about that?'

'Not had time for forensics to come up with any firm evidence. Just making inquiries.'

'Where was he found?'

'Well, Mr Jones, he was found in one of the Bridges's barns with the gun beside him. None of them had any idea he'd been in the house, that he'd got his gun out of their special reinforced gun cupboard, gone out to the barn and used it. The first they knew was when they heard the shot. They went out and found him. Stunned, they are.'

Megan broke down in tears. She kept repeating, 'All because of me.' Time and again.

Then her da spoke with more vigour and conviction than he had for a long time. 'Get Megan a brandy, Rhodri, please. Megan, you're not to blame. He knew full well that you and Rhodri were . . . well, together and wanting to marry. It most certainly wasn't your fault, because you never gave him any encouragement. Now, pull yourself together and drink that brandy. Go on. I want to hear no more of you being to blame. You're not. Now inspector, we've told you all we can, may we be left to ourselves?'

It was a polite way of putting it and the inspector could find no more reasons for staying so he'd agreed he would leave. 'It may turn out that the evidence proves he tried to commit suicide in which case I shall trouble you no more. Mr Bridges was so certain, you see, that he wouldn't do any such thing. Not Gab. Don't fret yourself, Megan. All may turn out better than we think. I'll be in touch.' Then the inspector had left the house.

Later, Megan flung herself over in bed, and tried to sleep but all the time, racing through her head, were the events of the evening and they wouldn't go away. She'd had no idea that Gab was so intense about his feelings for her. No idea at all, well perhaps that was not strictly true, because she'd felt a response to his advances more than once, which she'd hurriedly squashed knowing he wasn't right for her, but for this to happen . . . She went downstairs to make herself a drink only to find the kitchen light on and her da boiling a kettle.

'Da! Why didn't you shout for me? I would have come down and made you a drink. You know that.'

Mr Jones put an arm around her shoulders. 'I'm not entirely useless, my dear, not quite anyway. You've been through enough tonight, I can't ask any more of you. I'm making the tea, is that all right?'

'Yes, but I can do it.' She tried to intervene but he would have none of it, so they sat in the kitchen drinking the first cup of tea he'd made in years. 'I shan't make a nuisance of myself when Rhodri comes to live here. I'm making plans.'

Megan reached across the table and touched his hand. 'There's no need to make any plans. We'll be all right. Believe me.'

'But I am. You and Rhodri deserve me making plans. You don't need an old chap like me on the scene all the time. We all need privacy and I shall see the two of you, and I, have it.'

'Thank you, Da, I do love him, really, really love him, you know and he loves me. So very much. We're going to be very happy. Living here was his idea, not mine. He's always fancied us being together at his house you see, but ... anyway ...'

'I appreciate him thinking of me, and in return I've to do my best for both of you, because I want you to be happy.'

Megan had stood up, put an arm around his shoulders and squeezed him tight. 'Gab saying we'd never be happy, he's wrong, isn't he?'

'The man was out of his mind when he said that. Take no notice of him. I'm determined you'll be happy. Somehow I just needed Rhodri to take that one step forward to make me see daylight. I'm sorry I've been so unthoughtful, cruel almost—'

'No, Da, never cruel.'

Rather sharply Mr Jones replied, 'Don't tell me what I am. I know I've been cruel. Now drink up and then bed and we'll see about Gab in the morning. You and I, we'll go together and sort things out.'

The following morning Rhodri had a long string of appointments and he couldn't let his clients down, so he arrived at the Practice early and was waiting to start his day. After the night he'd had he was in no mood for tender loving care for anyone but Megan.

He'd buried poor Harry when he'd got home from Megan's: in his garden, in the dark, with his sitting-room window open and his CD player blaring out Jeremiah Clarke's *Trumpet Voluntary*. It seemed appropriate for such a time. He'd stood for a moment, silent and introspective, brooding on the day he'd had, a day of unbelievable contrasts. The road-accident dog he couldn't save, Dan turning his mind round so completely about living at the farm, proposing to Megan and her absolute joy when she saw the ring he'd bought her. Then the pleasure of Mr Jones's acceptance of him, though it was his due after all, and then the horror of Gab and the possibility in Richie Jamieson's mind that he, Rhodri Hughes, the epitome of stern moral values, might have tried to *kill Gab*. It made him shudder when he thought about Gab's desperation. He felt he kind of owed Gab something, he'd be creative about that tomorrow, because Gab wouldn't actually die if it wasn't as serious as first thought. No, Gab was tough, he'd survive.

Rhodri looked down at the fresh mound of earth covering Harry. Poor Harry Ferret, no more walks, no more unravelling of the loo roll, no more finding him hidden fast asleep under a cushion. No more Harry burying his busy nose and whiskers in his jumper. Poor Harry. He'd miss him. The final flourish of the trumpet ended. Rhodri had cleaned off his spade, shaken his Wellingtons off on the back door mat, propped the spade against the wall and gone in to bed and sleep.

So, here he was about to begin another day, his first as a betrothed man, engaged to be married to the light of his life. For a moment he indulged himself by thinking about breakfast in the kitchen with Megan each morning before he left for work and how that would set him up for the day, and smiled to himself.

Goliath Costello was the first client on his list. He opened his consulting room door and called out, 'Good morning, everyone, Goliath Costello, please.'

Miranda leapt from her chair and dashed in with Goliath. 'Have you heard about the eldest of the Bridges? Been shot he has, according to the police, in one of their own barns. Honestly, who'd do a thing like that? A lovely young chap like him?'

'I did hear. Booster for Goliath, is that right?'

'Yes. Can never remember which one is which of those boys, they're all so alike. Ben, Gab, Gideon, Simeon, Joe and ... what's the other one, all out of the Bible, I know! Elijah, no, that's not right, I know: Joshua. Poor chap. Never done no harm to anyone, Gab hasn't, but to shoot him in his own barn! I ask you.'

'There, that's Goliath sorted for another year. How's his behaviour, is he still messing all over the place?'

Miranda looked up at him, eyebrows raised. 'What?'

'I said has he stopped messing all over the place?'

'Goliath? Oh yes. I realised you were quite right when you said he was top dog, so after that, when he did it, I started picking him up by his scruff and growling at him and shaking him, like his mother would have done and chucking him out the door and completely ignoring him and it worked. So, they say the police are hot on the trail. I mean why would one of the Bridges boys want to kill *himself*. I've just had a thought. Was it over that Jones girl? You know her, don't you? From Beulah Bank Farm? Lovely looking girl. Have you heard any more news, is he still holding his own?'

'I don't know.' Rhodri, completing the data on the computer for Goliath, wished she wouldn't go on about it. 'That's it, then. Be seeing you, Miranda.'

'I reckon it's a *crime passionnel*. That's what. I reckon some boy got jealous of him, followed him home and shot him. With his own gun though, that's a bit much, isn't it? They could at least have used their own.' Miranda looked at Rhodri for some response and realising she wasn't going to get any, finally decided to go. 'I'm off then. 'Bye!'

His next client, surprisingly, was Mr Featherstonehough and in his hand a brand new cat basket. 'Spect you're surprised to see me?'

'I am. But it's very pleasant. Who's this?'

'This is Cleo. About six months old she is, I think, and I've come to have her checked over and to see about having her spayed, that's if she needs it. I don't know, you see.' He lifted her out of the basket and placed her on the table. 'Now, isn't she beautiful? My late wife's name was Cleo, so I've called her after her, seeing as she'd always wanted a cat and couldn't have one.'

Rhodri admired Cleo. She had the most unusual deep amber, slightly slanted eyes set in a pointy, elegant face and her fur was the colour of milky coffee. She pranced about the examination table in a most delightfully giddy manner. 'My word, but she's a very pretty cat. A bit of the oriental about her in her face. Where did she come from?'

'Found her under a bush in my garden, sheltering from the rain, lost and alone, fed her a couple of days, advertised I'd found her but no one came forward so I took her in. She's a bundle of love she is.' He kissed the top of her head and looked at Rhodri slightly shamefaced and embarrassed.

'Can't see any sign that she's been spayed, but she does seem very young to me. I shouldn't guess her to be more than eight months.'

'I don't want no toms after her and all that business.' Mr Featherstonehough placed Cleo back in her basket. 'I miss him you know, Adolf, I mean, the great beast of a dog that he was. I can't quite forget him, you know. Still listen for his claws on the kitchen floor, or I think I can hear him scratching the door to come in. It's hard, but she's beginning to fill the gap.' He patted the basket.

'It's bound to be hard. I mean, you had him for almost twelve years, that's a long time in anyone's life.'

Mr Featherstonehough rapidly changed the subject. 'Talking of life, have you heard about Gab Bridges? Terrible, isn't it? They say he's blown half his face away. Have you heard that?'

'I understand things are not quite as bad as first thought. They say he's been very lucky, and they've every hope—'

'Can't understand why he did it.'

Rhodri answered as non-commitedly as he could. 'Love life gone to pieces, I understand.'

'Ah! Well, poor chap. See you Tuesday.'

And so it went on, client after client, all with their own theories as to what might have happened, the stories increasing in intensity and wild supposition as the day progressed. Even Alan Tucker, newcomer though he was, had theories to air when he came in for Bingo to have his foot looked at.

'Thought we'd come to the country for a quiet life and what do we find? A near murder within weeks. Are they clients of yours? I expect they must be, them being farmers. 'Course that's the trouble, isn't it, farmers with guns all too easily available. It's his front left foot, it's swelling up and he's limping. They say the Bridges boy's close to death. Poor chap, at his age. What an ending. I did hear they thought he'd interrupted some poachers and they'd shot him. They say he shot at them first but missed. Blood! Never seen the like, you could have taken a bath in it, they say. It's a what?'

'A thorn or a needle gone right into his foot between the pads, here look, it's gone in slanting and very deep. He's very sensitive about it. Must be painful.' Rhodri crouched on the floor and held Bingo's foot so Mr Tucker could see. 'See, I think I can get it out with tweezers. Will he be all right, do you think?'

Mr Tucker, uncomfortably reminded of the incident in the waiting room with the cat Muffin, agreed he would. 'He's settled down now in the new house. No problem. That cat! God that was embarrassing.'

'Hold him tight with his head well away from me. That's it.' Rhodri gripped hold of the end of whatever it was and pulled. Bingo stood for him as though carved from stone.

It was a sewing machine needle Rhodri finally extracted from his pad. 'There we are. You're a good patient, Bingo. Very good. Don't walk him on muddy ground for a day or two, help prevent infection, see. If he's still limping badly two days from now, bring him in and I'll take another look. It should be OK, though, but you never know.'

'Thank you, Mr Hughes. Thank you. You don't know anything about this Bridges boy then?'

'I know he isn't going to die, that's a fact, and you can tell anyone you meet the bullet didn't go into his brain. Skimmed it by a millimetre. Good morning, Mr Tucker.' Rhodri patted Bingo on the head. 'You're a good dog, Bingo, nice to know.' Bingo looked up at him, his fine dark eyes viewing Rhodri benignly. 'I'll give him an antibiotic to fight any infection. Right? Bit of Rhodesian Ridgeback in him, is there?'

Mr Tucker smiled. 'Bit of everything, I think.' He turned to leave and then turned back. 'The cat, was it all right?'

'Couple of stitches and some frayed nerves but otherwise absolutely fine.'

'Good. I'm glad. Good morning and thank you, Mr Hughes.'

The waiting area had buzzed with rumour all morning and if a client hadn't known about it when they came in they did before they left. When he took his break Rhodri rang Megan but there was no reply so all he could do was leave his love to her on the answer machine.

That was because Megan had driven Mr Jones to Bridge Farm and they were sitting in the kitchen around the big old pine table with the five boys and Mrs Bridges.

'My Billy's at the hospital, he hasn't left since they took him there.'

'What's the situation today?' Mr Jones asked.

'It is not nearly as serious as they first thought. The bullet has skimmed his brain down the left-hand side and come out again. He had a scan last night and they're very hopeful he'll make a full recovery. Half an inch the other way and he'd have been . . .' Mrs Bridges took a deep breath and gained control of her trembling voice.

'So, Mrs Bridges, I'm sorry to talk about such painful things but we do need to know the truth. We are involved. Have you any more news about who shot him, if indeed that was the case?'

All five of the boys went on red alert at the thought that Gab had fired the gun himself but Josh, ever the peacemaker, said quickly, 'Later today they'll be able to tell us.'

'I can tell you it certainly wasn't Rhodri, he was with Megan and me in the house and never left it after Gab had gone. We're truly very distressed about it all. Please believe me.'

At the mention of Megan's name the Bridges boys all looked at her and she flushed at their scrutiny.

Mrs Bridges said, 'You've no call to be upset, girl. I knew he was in a bad way over you. I told him you were promised, but he wouldn't listen. Gab's tough, he'll pull through.' Her bravery was all the more commendable when you saw that her normally bonny face was drained and aged with her anxiety.

Megan said, 'I'm so sorry about it all, Gab was terribly upset when he left, I'd just told him Rhodri and I had got engaged. He took it very badly. He couldn't stop shaking. That would be why . . . he missed. Him shaking . . .' Her voice trailed off.

Josh asked how they'd managed the milking this morning.

'I did it with the lad.'

Mrs Bridges tut-tutted. 'Well, then you shouldn't have, my dear. One of our boys will be there this afternoon and take over Gab's work till we see how things go. So don't you fret . . .'

The back door burst open and in came Mr Bridges, haggard, unshaven, tousled. He gasped when he saw eight faces looking at him. 'What about work? Done everything, have you? And what are you two doing here?'

Before anyone could answer him, Mrs Bridges stood up and went to him. Looking up into his face she asked so softly they could barely hear. 'Come now, Billy, tell his mother how he is.'

Billy looked down at her, the belligerence set aside for the moment. 'Well, he's coming round, Adele. Like they said, it's not nearly as bad as we thought at all. The bullet missed his brain by only a hair's breadth, and they emphasise it's early days, but things are looking very good. That's why I've come home for a shower and some food and a change of clothes. So he'll be back before we know it. He'll have scars and that, but they say plastic surgery can do miracles.'

Mrs Bridges put her hand to her heart and sat down again before her legs gave way. 'Thank God for that. I shall go in a while to see him, while you get some sleep. One of you boys will drive me.' They all five nodded their agreement.

'Dad! I'm volunteering to take over from Gab at Beulah Bank till we get sorted.'

'I see, Josh. That's if I agree. Now what have you two to say for yourselves?' Billy Bridges turned to look at Megan. 'You, young filly, been enticing my boy, have you? Driving him out of his mind with your temptations?'

Indignantly Megan got to her feet. 'Indeed I have not. No.' She sat down as abruptly as she'd got to her feet. What else was there she could say? Talk about his obsession? His deliberate goading of Rhodri? Certainly not.

Mrs Bridges took hold of her hand and said sympathetically, 'I know what my Gab is like, once he's made up his mind, nothing will alter it. But you must be someone very special for him to have tried to . . . kill himself.'

Billy Bridges was beside himself. Fists clenched, face livid with anger he roared, 'He did not try to kill himself, it was someone else who shot him. I reckon there was a struggle and the gun went off, unexpectedly like. If Gab had fired it, he would have made a proper job of it. Him being trained to firearms.'

Mrs Bridges sprang to her feet with such speed she knocked over her chair and it bounced with a tremendous clatter onto the tiled floor, and small though she was, she battered his chest with her fists shouting, 'Do you want him dead? Is that it? *Dead*, to satisfy your pride? Eh? To want him dead rather than admit he didn't shoot straight? And to break my heart. Is that what you want?' She moaned in her anguish. 'He's so very precious to me. Oh! *Billy!* What are you thinking of? Shame on you.'

A shocked silence followed her outburst. No one knew what to say. The boys had never seen her like this. Then Mrs Bridges threw herself on Billy's chest and sobbed so painfully not one of them could bear it. Mr Bridges stood there helpless, as though this accusation was the last straw for his muddled exhausted mind. He was in such shock that he didn't even put an arm around her as she lay against him. Josh got up and went to take hold of her. He hugged her tightly and then sat her down on a chair and fished a tissue from a box on the kitchen worktop and handed it to her. He stood behind her and bent to rub his cheek on the top of her head. His father stood, head down, grieving.

Mr Jones, uncomfortable at witnessing such an intimate moment, cautiously got to his feet and said, 'We shall be more than glad of your help, Joshua, if your father approves. The lad's quite useful, just needs a kick up the behind sometimes, lazy, you know. We'll go. Billy, I'm sorry for all this and about Gab, but nothing Megan or I have done caused it. We are deeply grieved and we're grateful it isn't as bad as everyone first thought.'

Megan gave him her arm to hold on the way out. It was Josh who opened the door for them. Mr Jones said quietly to him, 'We're so sorry, believe me. You'll let us know about Gab?'

Josh nodded and closed the door behind them.

15

Josh settled down to work at Beulah Bank as though he'd been there for years. He was the gentle one of the Bridges boys, at nineteen the baby of them all by five years, with the same height and colouring as them but an entirely different temperament from Gab. He worked hard, with none of the swagger and gutsy energy of Gab; he got through the work, and got the best out of the lad without even so much as raising his voice. Within a couple of days it was as if it had been him helping them out all these weeks and not Gab. What he refused to do was drink his tea or have his lunch in the kitchen. He and the lad had decided to eat together in the old tack room. They found a couple of old chairs in a barn and an old blanket box dumped in there years ago to use as a table and set themselves up very comfortably.

'No, thank you, Megan. I'll have mine with the lad. Keep an eye on him, you know.'

'I really don't mind, we'd be glad . . .'

Firmly Josh repeated his refusal. 'Thanks all the same.'

Megan hadn't realised until the pressure was lifted just how much Gab had upset her with his constant closeness. She'd never noticed that she was adjusting her behaviour all day to accommodate the vagaries of his moods and his working patterns, and to avoid at all costs being left alone with him, either in a barn or the cow byres or any of the stables. In fact her whole life had been governed by him and that didn't include trying to avoid those hot greedy eyes of his, nor the constant fear of his temper erupting. But she was grateful he hadn't succeeded in killing himself. That would have been one responsibility too far. She thought of Mrs Bridges and how she would have been slaughtered by his death. No, she had to be glad for that. It seemed as if a great load had lifted from her shoulders and as Josh's first week progressed and Gab too made progress, life suddenly took on a whole new aspect. She put her engagement ring on and wore it constantly, frequently pausing to admire it, much to her father's amusement.

They were sitting in the kitchen a week to the day of Gab's accident when her father said, 'I've got these plans.' He brought out a folded piece of paper. 'Writing's a bit shaky, but I think you can see what I mean.' He opened up the paper and showed her a rough map of the downstairs rooms. 'You see, I already have this room as a bedroom and the downstairs bathroom, and I thought if we broke through into the old dairy from the bedroom we could make the dairy into a bedroom and have my current bedroom as a sitting room. Then you could have the sitting room for yourselves and we'd still have a dining room too.'

Megan studied his plans and deep down inside her she was exceedingly grateful for his ideas and could see instantly that it had a great deal of merit, but she was afraid to show too much enthusiasm in case it looked as though she was glad to be done with him and have him shut away. This new considerate parent she'd unexpectedly acquired was taking some getting used to.

'It's very thoughtful of you, Da. It would obviously work and we've never had any use for the old dairy, have we? Yes, that is a good idea, if you're happy with it.'

'Of course I am. We've loads of furniture so furnishing it would be no problem and if you and Rhodri wanted to buy new . . .'

'Well, there's not much of his we'd want to keep. He set up house when he first started earning so it's all a bit shambolic, nothing matches.'

'I'll find a builder. Rose has been having some changes made to their cottage, and she liked the chap who did it, so we could try him. There's another thing. I want him to change his name to Hughes hyphen Jones.'

'Da!'

'I mean it. Yours are going to be the only grandchildren I shall get and I want them to inherit not just the farm but the name too. I'm sure Rhodri won't mind.'

'And if he does?'

'We'll cross that bridge when we come to it.'

'But his parents might object. When we go down to see them next weekend I'll try to introduce the idea. It's a bit of a tall order, though, don't you think?'

'Why? When it means his children will be inheriting this place. When we bought it two years ago we got it for a song, it's worth twice what we paid for it. He'll be a wealthy man, and you'll be wealthy too.'

'No, Da, his children will be wealthy. Not Rhodri. He could take umbrage.'

'I don't see why he should, after all—'

'Have you had this planned all along? Let us get engaged and then catch us off our guard with this name scheme?'

'Now, now—'

'Well, you can tell Rhodri, because I'm not and you can tell him soon because I'm not doing a thing about the wedding until it's been sorted. Honestly, Da! I can't forgive you for this.'

'But it's not much I'm asking. Just to add a name to his own. That's all.' Patiently Megan's Da protested it hadn't been in his mind all along, it was something that had occurred to him only the previous day.

'Just when I thought you'd had a complete change of heart. It's not fair, it simply isn't fair. You've got your own way about me being here to look after you, is there anything else you'd like to dictate to us about? Because if there is, let's have it out in the open right away.' Megan glared at him across the table and waited.

'It's just an old man's fancy, you know. I wouldn't like to die with no one carrying on my name.'

'They'd be of your blood line though, wouldn't they, any children we have?'

'It's not quite the same. I think it has quite a ring to it – Hughes-Jones. Yes, I rather like it. Hughes-Jones. Sounds quite distinguished. Or should it be Jones-Hughes. I can't decide.'

'It's not for you to decide – it's for Rhodri and me. I'm so disappointed.' Megan burst into tears.

'Megan. Megan.'

But Megan fled the kitchen and disappeared upstairs to her bedroom, broken-hearted by this new scheme to upset her and Rhodri. How many more hurdles did he intend putting in their way? She'd marry Rhodri and be damned. She would. She'd leave him here to rot and rot he would because he didn't lift a finger for himself. She did it all. He couldn't help that, she knew, because he was so twisted and crippled with arthritis, but just sometimes she had a suspicion that he could if he wanted. Only last week after Gab, he'd gone into the kitchen and was making a cup of tea all by himself in the night. So he could do things if he wanted to enough.

There was a knock at the bedroom door. For one stupid startled moment she thought it must be Gab, because no one else had come upstairs since they'd lived there. 'Yes.'

'It's your da. Cup of tea ready for you in the kitchen in five minutes. OK?'

His words were the exact echo of what Gab had said that morning when he'd got into the house before milking. Da had got upstairs! He hadn't been up there since the week they'd moved in. Megan dried her tears, looked in the mirror, brushed her hair, tied it back with a length of ribbon and went downstairs, almost afraid to acknowledge that her da had kept her running about after him all these weeks and months when all the time he was capable of doing small things for himself. She saw him with new eyes when she entered the kitchen. He was just lifting the kettle to pour the boiling water into the teapot. Slightly shaky but not dangerously so. Just as he sat down at the table she said, 'I fancy a biscuit. Do you?'

'Yes, all right,' he said and got up to get the tin. He had to take his time but he did it, and when he sat down again, by dint of holding the tin to his chest he got the lid off and offered it to her.

'You said you'd been cruel to me and I denied it, but you have, haven't you? You've made me wait on you day in day out, every little thing, but look at you now. The times I've had to come in from the fields in the middle of doing something, taken my boots off, washed my hands just to get you your morning coffee, then gone straight back out again. You could have done it yourself, couldn't you?'

He didn't reply.

'Couldn't you?'

He still didn't reply.

'Well, I'm sorry, Da, but you're not pulling the wool over my eyes any more. I'm going out tonight, I've already put the dinner in the oven and I don't know when I shall be back.'

'There's no need to use that tone to me. I'm your father.'

'Really. The mood I'm in, I don't know when I shall be back, if ever. You've climbed the stairs, you've boiled the kettle, you've got the biscuit tin, and opened it. The milk from the fridge and not spilt a drop, the cups and saucers from the dishwasher. You've hurt me beyond anything you've ever done before.' Megan left the kitchen and didn't speak to or see her father again before she left.

Rhodri was surprised to see her at the Practice. He was just about to leave, regretting as he always did at this moment of the day that Harry Ferret wouldn't be there to greet him when he got home.

'Why! Megan, what a lovely surprise!'

'Footloose and fancy free I am, Rhodri bach. Shall we go out for a meal?'

'Of course, that would be lovely. Where shall we go?'

'We'll ask Dan for ideas. I expect Rose will have sorted somewhere good.'

Dan was about to leave and was standing talking to Mungo. They broke off their conversation and both said how pleased they were about the wedding and when was it to be?

'Soon. In fact very soon.'

Mungo kissed her on both cheeks and stood back to admire her. 'Good! You'll make a lovely bride. Lovely.'

Megan blushed, she couldn't help it, because he so obviously really meant what he said. 'Rhodri and I are going out for a meal tonight, do you have any bright ideas for where to go?'

Dan suggested the Italian restaurant in the precinct. 'Lovely food, and the staff are so welcoming. They'll be fighting to serve you. They love a good-looking woman.'

'The Casa Rosa?'

'That's right, it doesn't look much from the outside but the food is fresh, none of that microwave nonsense.'

'Right, we'll go there then. It seems funny here without Kate, doesn't it?'

Mungo nodded his agreement. 'It does, we miss her. Her stepmother rang yesterday to say that she's got settled at college and loving every minute.'

Dan said, 'She'll make a good vet, she has a large dose of common sense, no sickly sentimentality and a good brain. And she's hard-working.'

'I'll be off then.'

'How's your father, Megan? Keeping well?'

She didn't answer immediately. When she did all she said was, 'He's fine.' She knew if she said any more she'd burst into tears and look a fool.

Mungo said, 'Good, I'm glad. Be seeing you, Megan.'

Rhodri parked his car in the multi-storey and they walked to the restaurant hand in hand.

'The ring looks lovely.'

Megan held up her hand and admired it. Rhodri kissed it and said how proud he was that she was wearing it.

'Rhodri, I'm not ready to eat yet. Can we just sit somewhere and talk first?'

'Of course. I'll pop in and make sure of a table for, what? Half an hour or an hour?'

'An hour.'

When he came out of the Casa Rosa he said, 'The food smells marvellous. Let's sit by the fountain.'

This time he gripped her round her waist, sensing something was wrong. They found a seat by the fountain, and quite by chance there was no one else sitting around it so they were almost in a world of their own. 'There we are. Now what's the matter?' Rhodri put his arm along the back of the seat and held on to her shoulder, giving her a loving shake. 'There's something, isn't there? I know, so out with it.'

Megan told him about her father, how suddenly he found himself able to climb the stairs, to make a cup of tea and manage the biscuit tin. How he'd come up with the plan for making himself a set of rooms so they would have the sitting room to themselves. And ... how he'd brought up the idea of Rhodri adding her surname to his.

It was such a startling idea that Rhodri couldn't reply immediately. He gazed instead at the fountain throwing the water about twenty feet into the air. He'd always liked fountains where the water shot straight up into the air before it came down. He didn't like those new-fangled ones that simply dribbled water over stones so the right sound wasn't there. 'Well, Megan, I don't want to make a mess of things, because it all appears to be going in the right direction. I feel like this fountain, as though my spirits are flying up into the sky, and nothing, nothing can stop them, but this ...' He shook his head. 'This, I'm not sure.'

'I think he's gone a tad too far. I'm so angry with him, when I think of the times I've come in from the fields, boots off, coat off, gloves off, hands to wash, coffee to make, all because I thought he couldn't do it for himself, when all the time he *could have* if he'd wanted to.'

Rhodri went back to studying the fountain. It wasn't adding her surname to his, in truth it was adding *Mr Jones*'s surname to his. That was what he meant. The old sod. Did it matter in the great scheme of things? Yes, it did. Why? Because it meant Jones was dictating to him again. Getting the upper hand. Dominating him. And he wasn't having it. 'We'll have to think about that. I'm glad he's making an effort though. Won't do him any harm and I like his idea about the dairy. Good thinking, that.'

They sat a while longer, until Megan's stomach rumbled loudly and made them both laugh. 'Time to eat I think.' Rhodri took her hand and pulled her up off the seat, drew her close to him, and said, 'I love you. I can't wait for my parents to meet you. They'll both love you to bits. Anyway, lead me to the food, I'm starving.'

'So am I.' Megan smiled hesitantly and he knew why. She was so nervous about her da. Well, he was going to see to that for her. Tonight, in the old man's own house, he'd tell him where he stood.

They hadn't realised a sudden strong wind had got up while they'd been eating in the precinct, but as soon as they came out of the car park onto the main road the wind caught the car and Rhodri had to grip the steering wheel tightly to prevent it being pushed against the kerb.

'My word! Would you believe this? Some gale this is, Megan love.'

'Let's get home. I'm worried about Da.'

'No need. He'll be all right.' But perhaps he won't be when I've said my piece to him, Rhodri thought.

They battled their way to Beulah Bank, expecting any moment that a tree would be down across the road. Up Beulah was a difficult road at the best of times, with all its steepness and twists and turns but now it was a nightmare.

Rhodri had to hold on to the door so Megan could get out of the car. They struggled across the yard and into the house. Megan's first words were 'Da! We're back! Are you all right?'

She'd no need to have worried. He was as cool as a cucumber, reading a book. 'I'm fine. Hello, Rhodri. Bad night.'

'It is. I was expecting a tree across Up Beulah, but there isn't, not yet.'

'Can I get you a drink, Da?'

'No, thank you. I haven't finished the wine I had for dinner.' Mr Jones picked up a wine glass from the table beside his chair and drank from it. 'Nice wine, this.'

'Would you like a drink, Rhodri?'

'I'd like tea, please. Don't want any more alcohol when I'm driving.'

'OK.'

Rhodri sat down on the chair nearest to Mr Jones. 'Megan has been telling me about your plans for opening up the old dairy as a bedroom for you. It sounds an absolutely splendid idea and very astute of you to have thought of it. It will be great for you to have a room where you can go when you're fed up with the two of us and great for us to have space to ourselves, and I reckon it's a very civilised way of going about it.'

'But ...?'

'You're right, there is a but. I shall come straight to the point because you're a man who prefers to look things squarely in the face and I admire that. You know where you are with a man like that. So ... at the moment, I cannot see my way to changing my name. So that will have to be put aside for the time being. You're not, please, not, to make things difficult for Megan. She's had quite enough worry over Gab and your health without adding to it with this suggestion of yours.' Rhodri looked Old Man Jones straight in the eyes and didn't lower his gaze for a second.

But he didn't get a reply, so Rhodri continued the conversation as though he'd never mentioned the Hughes-Jones question. 'I hear you're going to stay with Dan and Rose while Megan and I are in Wales. You'll enjoy having the baby to watch, he's getting to look quite human. Smiling and such.'

Still there was no reply to his statement so Rhodri fell silent and watched the logs burning in the grate instead of talking. Megan came in with a tray and he got up and pulled a small table in front of the fire so she had somewhere to place it.

'You two are very quiet. What's the matter, Da? Cat got your tongue?'

'No, definitely not. Rhodri here has been telling me how pleased he is with the building work I've suggested, you know, breaking through into the dairy, and that he knows me as a man who likes to look things squarely in the face, and one who values honesty. So that's how he likes things too, and he's agreed to add Jones to his name, like I suggested. Jones-Hughes. Sounds imposing, don't you think?'

Rhodri's mouth dropped open in disbelief. Once or twice he'd used the word 'conniving' when he'd spoken of Old Man Jones, and he'd never been more right.

Megan looked amazed. 'Have you?'

Rhodri shook his head at her. 'No, I have not. I said, at the moment, I can't see my way to changing my name. Not at all. At the moment.' He turned to face Mr Jones. 'You know full well that's what I said, and what I say I mean. If it is a prerequisite for marriage then I'm afraid it's just not on. We shall marry anyway and damn the consequences. You once said to me that there wouldn't be a penny of your money for Megan if we married, and I said we didn't care. We still don't care. We shall still marry whether you like it or not. We shan't starve, believe me.'

Rhodri got to his feet and put a cup of tea on his future father-in-law's table. Mr Jones dashed it aside and the tea spilt all over his table and on his bottles of tablets. Rhodri saw his hand stray towards his stick as he shouted, 'I said I didn't want tea.' His fingers closed as best they could over the handle of his stick, his intention only too obvious.

His voice fierce with anger and more Welsh than ever, Rhodri shouted, 'Pick up that stick and threaten me with it, and I shall walk out of this house with Megan and we shan't return. I will not be dominated by your temper and your wishes to the exclusion of everyone else's feelings. Megan comes first now and not before time.'

'I see. You can shout at me now, can you, now you think you've got your feet under my table?'

'I don't want to shout. What I do want is Megan's happiness. She's had little of that lately, at your beck and call seven days a week. I hear you've actually made a cup of tea, got upstairs without any help, served your own meal tonight while we've been out. That doesn't sound like the helpless man I've always thought you were. If ever it got out that you'd been *acting* helpless all this time, it wouldn't reflect very well on you, now would it?'

'Hmmph.'

Megan was silently crying, but, intent on their quarrel, neither of them noticed.

'Wanting me to change my name is your way of dominating me. Well, those days are done. Believe me. It is the most enormous sacrifice on my part to live here in this house. I so wanted Megan to live in my house, with me, away from all this, free from this slavery.'

Rhodri waved a hand at the invalid paraphernalia on Mr Jones's side table. 'I can just hear Rose tut-tutting if she heard about your behaviour.'

That stung Mr Jones. A picture of a smiling Rose came uppermost into his mind and he knew he didn't want her to know. Not Rose. No. Not all weekend knowing that in her eyes he'd behaved less than honourably. But, he asked himself, why did he feel able to behave dishonourably to Megan, then?

Ah! But if he was honest he knew the answer to that; it was because she was so like her mother in looks that he harboured a passionate desire, buried very deep, to get his own back on her. Her mother. His wife. Who'd despised him. Hated him even. He remembered how his behaviour had driven her to weeping bitter tears and he hadn't thought about those tears for a long time. Mr Jones looked about him. Saw Rhodri standing quite still, looking down at him waiting, waiting for an answer. Megan quietly crying so despairingly. There was an awful lot to lose at this moment. She wasn't to blame for what was happening now, simply because she reminded him of his failures. The bitter tears of her mother had to be laid at his door. And this Rhodri fellow was stout in his defence of her, a rock he was, a loving, devoted rock that's what – and a Welsh Nationalist too.

Old Man Jones took another drink of his wine, hoping it would steady his nerves. The glass almost slipped from his twisted fingers as he put it down, but he mustn't let it, he mustn't show his weakness. 'The matter of changing your name can be left in abeyance. We'll have the reception at the George and I shall foot the bill like all brides' fathers do, and, if I can, I'll give the bride away but not from that damned wheelchair. I shall be upright on my own two legs.'

'Thank you. Thank you.'

The wind hammered at every window and door of the house, and howled down the chimneys. 'You must stay the night. It's too risky driving back in this gale. There's only Megan's bedroom aired so you'd better sleep in there.' He picked up his book, placed his reading glasses on his nose, and didn't look up to see their reaction. There was nothing like a magnificent gesture to impress everyone. He couldn't read a word, he was too confused. The lines wavered and waltzed over the page, so he had to pretend he was reading, till his head cleared.

He glanced up at the two of them. His daughter was sitting on a stool at Rhodri's feet and they were holding hands. He had an idea that Rhodri'd make sure Megan wouldn't be crying bitter tears, ever.

Megan must have forgotten he was still in the room. He watched her look up at Rhodri crouched on the edge of his chair, his arm around her shoulders, staring into the fire, and the look on her face caused her father's heart to lurch. He hoped Rhodri knew how blessed he was to have a wife who loved him like Megan did. But then he caught sight of Rhodri's face as he turned to her with a look full of love and adoration, and the dried-up, wizened core of him warmed to them both.